VOOG'S OCEAN

BY THE SAME AUTHOR

FICTION
Clay
Dreaming in Cornish
Proper Job, Charlie Curnow!
Electric Pastyland
The Cult of Relics
Voodoo Pilchard

DRAMA
Ordinalia: The Cornish Mystery Play Cycle
Nativitas Christi
Oogly es Sin
The Tin Violin
Surfing Tommies
A Mere Interlude

POETRY
Grunge
Out of the Ordinalia
The Hensbarrow Homilies
Love and Seaweed
Assassin of Grammar
Stannary Parliament
Druid Offsetting
The Hope of Place: Selected Poems in English 1990-2010

NON-FICTION
Wives, Mothers and Sisters: Feminism, Literature and Women Writers of Cornwall
The Literature of Cornwall: Continuity, Identity, Difference 1000-2000
Pulp Methodism: The Lives and Literature of Silas, Joseph and Salome Hocking
Cousin Jack's Mouth-organ: Travels in Cornish America
The Theatre of Cornwall: Space, Place, Performance
Celtic Cornwall: Nation, Tradition, Invention

AS EDITOR AND CO-EDITOR
Voices from West Barbary: An Anthology of Anglo-Cornish Poetry 1549-1928
Looking at the Mermaid: A Reader in Cornish Literature 900-1900
Inside Merlin's Cave: A Cornish Arthurian Reader 1000-2000
The Dreamt Sea: An Anthology of Anglo-Cornish Poetry 1926-2004
The Busy Earth: A Reader in Global Cornish Literature 1700-2000
Four Modern Cornish Plays
The Francis Boutle Book of Cornish Short Stories

VOOG'S OCEAN

ALAN M. KENT

ryelands

First published in Great Britain by Halsgrove 2012
Copyright © Alan M. Kent 2012

A CIP catalogue for this book is available from the British Library

ISBN 978 1 906551 35 3

RYELANDS
An imprint of Halsgrove
Halsgrove House, Ryelands Business Park,
Bagley Road, Wellington, Somerset TA21 9PZ
Tel: 01823 653777   Fax: 01823 216796
email: sales@halsgrove.com

Part of the Halsgrove group of companies.
Information on all Halsgrove titles is available at: www.halsgrove.com

Printed and bound by CPI Group (UK) Ltd, Croydon, CR0 4YY

FOR TIM

ATLANTIC PEOPLES: COMMUNITIES & CONNECTIONS
500 – 1000 CE

This major new exhibition provides a unique insight into the importance of the peoples around the Atlantic Ocean seen through the innovative perspective of objects, finds, literature and antiquities gathered from the British Museum and partner institutions across the globe.

Free, open daily 10.00–17.30
Fridays until 20.30

Until 2 September

Supported by American Express

Includes a gallery talk by Professor Barry Radford, Department of Prehistory and Europe.

Handling session for the blind and partially sighted.

Free family activities during the summer holidays:
Come to the Museum for a range of free workshops, activities and performances during the summer holidays.

E-newsletter sign up.

Follow the British Museum on Facebook, Twitter, You Tube, Flickr and Blog.

8

Onen

"The hermit withdrawn to himself, avoiding the settlements, sings himself a song."

From 'When Lilacs Last in the Dooryard Bloom'd' by
Walt Whitman, 1865

"History needs to be rewritten. The North American continent is awash with evidence of pre-Columbian settlers who left their impact on the landscape."

From *Foreword* by Niven Sinclair to *Ancient Stone Sites in New England and the Debate over Early European Exploration* by David Goudsward, 2006

VOOG'S OCEAN

1

Male Skeleton, State Forest, Massachusetts, 7th Century CE
This male skeleton was discovered in 1954 by the Massachusetts State Field Society, and measures five feet, ten inches tall. Its burial was part of a ritualised death ceremony. Unusually, the body was buried with a number of Wampanoag objects, as well as tools containing wood with an isotope which has been traced to Penwith, West Cornwall. This individual had some skeletal disorders. Among these are Madelung deformity of the wrist. This is characterized by a growth disturbance in the volar-ulnar distal radial physis that results in a volar and ulnar tilted distal radial articular surface, volar translation of the hand and wrist, and a dorsally prominent distal ulna. The left hand also shows polydactylism – an extra digit. Courtesy of the Massachusetts State Field Society.

MY PROFESSION IN LIFE BEING an architect, builder and repairer of what my people call a *fogou* (pronounced 'foo-goo'), like the smith, the thatcher and the weaver, I soon came to be called by my trade, and became known as Fogou. But my people are complacent and lazy, and because their mess and mishap of a tongue is unable to differentiate between *F* and *V*, this became shortened first to Vug, and by degree, became transformed through use and custom into Voog. My name then, is crammed with delicious vowels – they make a sound good enough to eat.

Say it – Voooog.

Vooog.

Voog.

It is a name tasty as mackerel, sweeter than scalded cream.

Voog then, sole son of Donyerth.

When I was a tiny child I had another name (the one my mother Athwenna and father gave me), but I have been Voog for so long now, that past nomenclature has long left me. So Voog I became and Voog I now am – and this is my story. Like all stories ever told, I can chip, carve, knap and sculpt it to fit you, the listener, any way you like. I can turn and place it in exactly the right spot for you. I can make it corbelled to support other stories or stand alone: an entry marker into a different time, a pointer into my past doings and dabbles. Stories have the same power as stones. They have alignments, particularities and functions. They may have different surfaces, grains and densities but all contribute to the whole. You see, I come from a line of itinerant stone-workers, earth-movers, and let me be honest here – word-spinners, fable-tellers and down-right liars, who have all shaped the world in this mizzle-drenched, granitic peninsula. My wise and patient father Donyerth taught me, and his bow-legged and revered father taught him, and so through time immemorial the hidden art and craft of the fogou has been passed down. Our work is sacred and protected. We are, in effect, a guild. As you will soon learn, we build life and death. With stone and soil, and with light and dark, we build the places between this world and what comes before, as well as this world and the next.

We live however, as you will see, in a time of change, when a new belief sweeps through the land (the fad that is called a Christian god), and perhaps I will be the last of my trade. Like the great mammoths of whom the elders still talk, maybe one day soon I, too, will become extinct. There are fewer and fewer of us, and as the world alters, the old ways are not so easily passed on to the young. In this way, knowledge, skill and story are lost. They fall into the deepest dark of oceans, the unknown fathoms of tin workings. But for now, let me hold your hand and lead you through my life.

I was seemingly apprenticed into the fogou-builders' guild ever since I could hold a chisel and mallet. Indeed, no sooner had I stopped suckling my mother's sweet milk, than my father said I was piling pebbles upon pebbles on the beaches at Porth Ledden, already testing the weight and particularity of stone. Aged six, I began to construct my first fogou on my grandfather's ancestral lands at Nanquidno. At best the earth-work was a boggy tunnel; at worst, a watery death-trap. Now in my twenty-sixth year I can look back at my seven years of learning the craft as I have travelled around this jutting horn of land into the ocean. I can laugh at my mistakes and celebrate my successes which dot this windswept landscape of cliff and cove, moor and menhir, madness and mayhem.

You will come to feel the strength of my hands. You will come to note them because they are different: different to other people and different to each other. The right hand is like a spade, born of my progeny and mason's lineage. It can scoop and pull, chisel and carve with ease. As each successive generation came to handle rock, boulder and pebble, gradually we became more adept at doing so. We mutated and evolved. I can carry in this one skilled hand alone the stone it would take two men to carry normally.

But my left hand... is a different matter.

My lineage seemed to want to mark me out. Looking at it now, it resembles the gnarled root of an old oak tree. See, my arm here is slightly shorter, the wrist bends backwards (somewhere inside me, the gods determined that my skeletal frame would be distorted), and then instead of four digits, I have five. Yes – the anomaly of an extra finger. It is not much use – more vestigial than anything else – and smaller in form and shape than most men's little finger. Still, it is there though, a subnormal fork reaching, feeling and pressing upon stone. I am thus deformed, and inferior in some way to most men. Whatever made me and formed me inside my mother's womb got it slightly wrong. I am misshapen with a supernumerary finger.

I am sure that when my father first saw my hand, wrist and fingers, he cursed and believed it would be impossible for me to follow his trade – and yet, I have persevered. He blamed himself for it – some past misdeed that resulted in a mutated son. Paradoxically this twist in the wrist sometimes allows me to reach angles and spaces that no other mason could possibly achieve. I held my chisels, tools and levers in ways no other man could. Once my father saw this, he became happier and believed I might continue the line. So I have come to value it and know its power. It still hurts the soul, though, when children avert their eyes from it, and when new clients stare and ask questions. Because of such anguish I used to hide it as a child, afraid of what others might say. Now, I don't bother. Now I know all humans are, to some extent, deformed and disfigured – sometimes in ways we can see, and sometimes in ways we cannot. It is all the same, I tell myself. So, I have come to value my gammy hand, wrist and finger, and celebrate their uniqueness. Their twist helps me remember.

Now you must feel my skin. On both hands – both regular and misshapen – it is hard and leathery, the pads of my fingers calloused and tough. These digits are now built for handling and spinning the unyielding surface of heavy granite, as other men use the plough and ox, or pony and wagon. My strong thighs too, are shanks made to work stone upon. On them, on an apron of thick leather, I turn, cut and shape the stone, before levering it into position. The work has given me shoulders wide as Carn Kenedjack and a backbone of iron. Sometimes it is hard to tell with me what is human and what is stone. I am the stone and it is me.

You may not know what a fogou is. I will explain. A fogou is a souterrain, or an underground dry-stone structure. Just like my story here, I will show how it is both entry and departure point, beginning and end. Fogous have been built here for centuries. In my limited knowledge of the world (in my early years at least) and from the conversations I have had with travellers (those from Gaul, Iberia and Phoenicia), they are quite unique to us. They define my people. In some cases they were there before settlements gathered around them (human moths to sacred flames, so to speak), but often too, there are new commissions, repairs or adaptations asked for by their communities. The initial construction of a fogou takes time. They cannot be rushed. Speed would violate our path. First, you must select your location. This must be sacred and significant. It has always been so. Second, check your alignments. The sun and stars dictate much in my work (indeed, they will be essential in my story). The summer and winter solstices mark our ritual year. Thirdly, gain approval and blessing from those who commission the work (always a bit of a pain, but necessary). Then, and only then, may excavation begin. Dig a sloping trench in the earth as wide and as tall as a man. Make it as long as you can; seven men head to feet at the minimum. The slope is important, for this is the run in and out of the Annown, what my people call the 'Otherworld'. When the trench is completed, then line it with a corbelled stone wall, which tapers to the top. Then cap the whole structure with slabs. Depending on the specifications, the whole is then covered in earth. My work will then be done. Ceremony and initiation may begin. Sometimes, we are called back to insert new creep passages, to extend into beehive huts, to insert new altars or reconfigure the slope. Much depends on those who then enter as babies and those who leave as the dead. We know our work will be judged and evaluated. So far, I have been lucky. My skills are known and valued in the community. But as any fogou-builder will tell you: you are only as good as the last one you built. Past reputation holds little with the successful birthing and death of the present.

Just as my name changed and altered then, so too did the way my people named their world of underground chambers. In the north, they call them *Vau*; the second syllable somehow slipping away into the ocean's foam. In the south, they are *Vug Holes* only; the emphasis on their cave-like nature. In the west, say *Fuggo*, or *Vuggo*, depending on dialect and intonation. The east uses none of these, though believes in tales of the *pobel vean* (the 'little people') inhabiting them – such is the mystery and arcane nature of my profession. We are not magicians though. Our work is rooted in manual skill and labour. Yes, we have our rituals in the profession but these have only built up and survived because of the important nature of our work. The fogou-builder will use local labour to help in the construction, but all is directed by him. It is he who makes the important decisions, and eventually, it is he who sets and positions the stone. Each stone you see, has bearing, belief and beatification.

Fortunately, my work as a builder has become easier. We now live an Age of Iron. This was not always so. Centuries ago, we laboured with little more than rope and pulleys to position stone. This land is crammed with constructions made this way: barrows and cairns and henges. Men and women gathered flint and bone to use to help carve, scratch, dig and hone. Bronze (that born of what is streamed and mined in this land: tin and copper) altered construction methods for the better, but decorative bronze is still no match for the durability of iron. Thus we constructors of stone now work hand-in-hand with the sweating smithies who make many of our tools. Thus always with me are my mallets and chisels, my levers and crowbars, my hammers and my pointers. I carry these in a sack upon my back. Many are adapted for the shape of my left limb. In my trade, a man also has to have an idea of mathematics. One needs to understand proportions, angles, ratios, leverage and velocity. When stone moves on rollers or is levered into place with crowbars, one needs to understand its physics. Stone can be static but it can also be visceral and fast – so fast that it can maim or kill.

The mathematics of stone were to have their due influence on events which were to transpire, but perhaps now the moment is right, the stone dressed enough for me to begin to outline what my fate was to be. For certain, had I known that soon I would be swapping (temporarily at least) stone for the ocean, and company for loneliness then perhaps I would have done things differently. Yet such are the ways of young men. How I came to be upon an ocean began in the last flurries of the winter of that year. I was working at Halliggye putting the finishing touches to some new cap stones on the fogou there which had been damaged during the winter months. Halliggye is located in the south, on what is known as Lys Arth, the 'high court'. They think a lot of themselves (all bustling bravado and belief in their superiority over other tribes) – but no matter. A job's a job. Frost and ice had penetrated the surface of the old capstones and they'd badly needed replacing. The elders had moaned to me about water leakage during the winter solstice ceremonies and so had commissioned me to make the replacements. It was a month's work that I'd badly needed. I'd had to quarry the stone myself and lug it on a sledge back to the site, but down there, the granite was of good quality – hard as nails, and tougher than the cheaper and pocked first lot they'd used.

Before then, I'd been forced to complete regular building work for a wind-blown hole of a village above Kynance. The working conditions there were poor for the whole of January – sleet and snow for much of the time and barely a welcome from any of the grumpy, root-munching villagers. I'd had to tent-up down there, given that the majority of houses were being remodelled. As well as that, you'd have to put up with the stinking chough-shit everywhere, and those buggers cawking 'chee-aw' every hour of the day. Kynance lies just above Predannack – 'the headland of Britain' that the Romans were always so fond of mentioning, and was always a significant sight on the horizon for the tin traders from the far south. The cove below the village was beautiful – tall pyramids of rock rising from azure waters – but in these conditions you were lucky if you could see heather on the moor stretching out in front of you, rather than the incessant sleet or snow.

I was inside the fogou that morning. Outside it was pissing down and I was testing the dryness inside. Of course, there was a bit of the usual leakage coming in the doorway, but that was to be expected. You could easily stop that with placer stones. It was deeper inside where it needed to be dry. I'd had trouble with the far end the previous day where a fair trickle of water could be seen coming in off one of the top slabs, but I'd shored that up earlier and was hoping that would counteract any problems. My methods (as you will see) are not always conventional. My father would probably turn in his funereal urn. He'd probably have reset the lot. That seemed to me to be a waste of time and energy when it was clearly the packing earth that needed redoing. I wiped my hand across the stone back there and found no dampness. For a completing job, I'd spread the floor with fresh ferns and flowers gathered earlier that morning from the moor. One of the village women was nine months pregnant and the elders had been pressing me to complete in order for the birth to take place. This lot still affirmed the old ways of doing things. Annown would deliver her a fine and healthy new son or daughter if she was deep in the earth during her labour.

All of this was on my mind when I saw him. He'd obviously scrambled inside for the dryness overnight. A big bugger too – that scared me rigid. See, I don't like them. I've never liked them ever since I came across a pack of them as a boy on a job over Carn Galver. What I am talking about? I was face to face with the curse of we fogou-builders – a brown rat. Of course, you might say that such rodents are an occupational hazard for the likes of me, committed to working underground and often dealing with left offerings of fruit. You'd have thought I'd have got used to them, but I haven't. That morning, he was snuffling around in the far recesses of the fogou when I encountered him. I put my left hand on his tail in the darkness. I knew instantly what I was touching – the ribbed skinny form of twisting bone. The flinch backwards was instant. In my experience, bucks such as this one were fearless. Penned in like this, he might go for my leg. They'd try it if they felt threatened enough. I could do without a bite from him.

My eyesight gradually adjusted to the blackness and I could see his nose twitching, sensing the air for my smell and movement. Always opportunistic, fogous were their ideal lairs in some ways. The *pobel vean* or 'little people' of the vugs were probably not magical beings at all. Instead, what people heard and saw were probably rats. The worry was that if the pack was tucked in there somewhere, it might compromise the safety of those about to use it. Rats brought disease to humans. You didn't need to be a herbal druid to work that out. Even if he was a single occupant, I'd have to clean up his shit – not a job I liked. They liked to mark their territory – even if it was human sacred space.

Rats and I were uneasy bedfellows. We coexisted, but avoided each other as much as possible.

Killing the creature was not a good option within the souterrain. Annown did not look favourably upon such actions. Having said that, my father impaled many a rat underground using his crowbar – without seemingly dire consequences, although that said, perhaps the deformity of his son's hand was Annown's revenge for his previous insensitivity. The golden rule was that blood should not be spilt in the realm of the fogou. This was on my mind, and from what I could see of him, the rat's too. The creature seemed even to sense I could do no harm to him. This was the other thing about rats I disliked. They were cocky with it – proper know it-alls who seemingly had human humiliation at the top of their priorities. I wanted to wash myself, cleanse myself of their filth but at present that was no option. I had to act quickly or the rat would squeeze himself further into the stonework, and disappear. That was also them see – unlike me and my gnarled bones, they had flexible skeletons that transformed the narrowest gap into the widest space on the moor.

This bastard wasn't going to elude me though. I initially kept him in his place at the rear of the fogou by throwing some crusts of bread down to him. I carried these morsels of food in one of the side pockets of my sack. That kept him there, happily attacking the bread with gusto and relish. Carefully, I emptied the tools from my sack onto the floor, and then eased the open bag towards the pest. He tried to dart into a crevice but misjudged the width between the stones. I knew them better than he did, having fixed them there the previous week. The rat had no choice but to be enveloped by the material and he was soon squeaking wildly inside the sack.

At this, most rats became frantic and frenzied. Because of the angle, I had been able to use my left hand, but it being a little less strong, and because of the rat's haphazard movement, for one moment I dropped the sack. The beast was within inches of escaping before I scooped him up with my stronger right hand and bore the wriggling body out into the light. I released him beneath a spread of dripping ferns and hoped that he wouldn't re-enter. As a polite gift to me, he had shat in the bag, and I used a frond from the ferns to scrape it away. Off he went into the rainy wilds of Lys Arth gabbling his anger at me. I returned to the recesses of the fogou, and by candlelight checked for any further defecation. Fortunately, there was only a little which I removed, and then gathered up my tools. My hasty breathing returned to normal.

The job was complete. Despite the rat, thank fuck I was no longer down Kynance completing walls for people who couldn't care less and knew even less about the significance of ships passing Predannack than I did. Good riddance too to other pests – those pesky choughs who drove me mad. From the opulent darkness of the chamber I made my way back to the entrance. On one of the stones there, as is our way, I took a small chisel and mallet from my sack, and made my builder's mark. This would be Voog's work now. The original builder's mark had long-since faded. Mine needed to be incised. The elders would not consider it complete if my mark was missing. In the late morning light, I gradually chiselled my symbol – the upper torso of a figure holding a staff and a snake. I took care over it. The hair of the head of the figure now displayed my two long braids, while the staff was actually modelled on the fogou-builder's crowbar, essential for just the kind of work I had been completing with the cap-stones. The snake was a joke derived from my days as an apprentice. A deep fogou in the north, at Pendeen, which my father and I had been lengthening, held in it a surprise one morning – just like the rat. I had gone stumbling into its far recesses, only to discover an adult adder nestled into the warm leaf-litter. Innocently I had picked it up and carried it outside, much to my father and his workmate's amusement. Seemingly, I'd calmed the snake as it had not tried to bite me. Since then, I had always scribed a crowbar in my shrivelled left hand, a snake in the right.

"Whoa. It's Cernunnos that idn't it?" remarked one short-sighted elder in a job I'd done at Trewardreva.

He had got close up to my mark, peering at is significance.

"Who's that?" I asked.

"God of all healing... he is master of the serpent," he answered. "You choose a mighty symbol there mason..."

I chose not to tell him its history but let him instead contemplate the wonder of Cernunnos' power at Trewardreva. Such moments as these have enlightened me to the power of stories, and how one thing can so easily be mistaken for another in our modern world.

Once the carving was finished, I blew dust away from it and stood back to admire my work. Not much could cause this structure to collapse or buckle now. Rat or no rat it would be ready for another century of use – and for the specific birth just ahead. I smiled at the thought of the new life emerging in the recesses of the tunnel and tapped the stone one last time for luck.

"A completing job," came a voice. "We heard you were working over here..."

"Who's *we*?" I questioned.

Outside the fogou's mouth was a figure on horseback. I recognised him right away. He was a hunched man of around forty – by the name of Kenal. Prematurely grey, his beard and hair were saturated from the westerly that was blowing in that day. A sword was strapped to his waist.

"I speak for Howel of Carn Euny. Word says that the great fogou-builder Voog may be found at Lys Arth. You remember me?"

After the darkness inside the vug, and with the light behind the rider, I could only see Kenal in silhouette, and yet I knew him well enough.

"Kenal isn't it?"

"Yes. Master Voog. We fought alongside each other at Heyl..."

I remembered that time. It was one I wanted to forget. A Viking horde from the north had decided to make a raid on the long beaches there – a common enough instance these days. Until the tribes here had united in resistance against what they all called the *Ancredhor Mor* or 'sea pirates', several villages as far in as Gwinear had been torched. I nodded, affirming our past brotherhood in arms.

"We have work for you at Carn Euny," Kenal continued.

"Euny eh?" I asked. "The last time my father Donyerth worked there he wasn't paid. He walked away with nothing."

"Things were different then."

"And are different now?" I ventured.

"They are. Howel has assumed chiefdom now. He is a man of honour."

I heaved myself from out of the fogou's mouth and plucked a fistful of wet grass for Kenal's mount. The horse's tongue rasped over my left hand, grabbing the tasty greenness. Kenal observed the twist of bone and skin.

"And he assumes I will work for him?"

"He thinks you may be tempted," waged Kenal.

"What's the job?"

"Reconstruction... One of the elders is nearing his end... and so..."

"... you need it looking shipshape to send him to Annown."

I finished his sentence for him.

"Precisely."

"The old story then..."

I stepped back into the fogou to pack my tools into my sack.

"What's the pay?" I asked, as I wiped my chisel.

"The standard rate for your guild. No more, no less. Do you accept?"

This was quite typical of bastards like this Howel. They tended to call all the shots whenever they wanted. However, given that fact that I had no other opportunities presenting themselves to me, and knowing that I didn't want to spend any more time at guano-coated Kynance or a rat-infested Halliggye, a grudging acceptance came out of my mouth.

"I'll be over," I said. "Tell Howel. Give me a couple of days."

In life, you are never quite sure on the timeline when things alter, when they change, when they get better, or when they get worse. I didn't know it then, but this was one of those seemingly innocuous moments when the earthquake or tempest actually happened. When Kenal arrived with Howel's request, this was the day when I became *me*, the Voog you will come to know – when all that I had known was left behind, and that all that I was to know suddenly arrived. Had I known my fate, I might have taken better notice of the ships that passed by Predannack; their crews battling waves and surf to offer our tin and copper to some distant part of the earth.

As Kenal left, in celebration, the ebullient villagers at Haliggye were escorting their waddling pregnant woman down into the fogou.

"Her waters have broken," an old crone noted to me. "Is all ready inside?"

"All's ready. Just as you requested."

"They say you'm the best you know. The best builder. I'll be double-checking in there..." she laughed.

Their chief followed the procession and noted Voog's work.

"I see you've finished. Perfect timing eh?"

He nodded at the wise women and the pregnant young woman preparing for the entry ritual.

"You've marked it?"

"All done," I replied.

"The elders have agreed to your fee. Do you want it now?"

"No," I said. "Forget the fee. Give me a pony if you can afford it."

"A pony?"

"Yes. I've another job – in the west..."

By now, the women were singing their birthing songs and their procession entered the souterrain. It would not be long before a baby's crying would be heard. The men stood outside, nodding and admiring my work.

"Nice bit of stonework..." I heard one of them say.

"They say he's the best goin' now," another added. This was music to my ears.

"If it's a pony you want, then yes... Go up to the village with this man. He will sort you out."

I shook the chief's hand. As I left, I could hear the entry of a new soul into this world of ours. Somewhere, as my land preaches, an old soul would be leaving it. This was my fogou working, staff and snake having done their duty, and the rat exiled.

In the late afternoon, I could still hear the baby crying some half a mile away as I rode into the west, towards distant Carn Euny. The journey would take two days. Compared to what epic voyaging was to follow, it was completed in the mere blink of an eye. Thus my destiny stops and begins. I was unprepared, even though the real and surreal were about to reveal themselves to me.

NOW, IS IT DEAR ANNOWN, or dear Father, or dear God, or dear Somebody Else?

Come now. Try to decide.

Come, close your gawping, great vug-hole of a mouth before the flies sneak in – and listen.

You must know by now that when they spoke to me in the way they did – softly and warmly, yet so tentatively and timidly, I could barely believe it. I was astonished. They were as skittish as deer; their dark eyes flicking from side to side, scanning for understanding and kindness – like I had just caught them in a snare, instead of them catching me. After all those lonely miles and all that arduous journeying, to meet somebody who knows your language so deliciously satisfies your soul that there is the strange sensation of coming home again, even though you are distant from your origins. Home is suddenly in the here and now, and not all that long way away. It was as if, in those tumbling, frantic seconds, there was never any distance to begin with, and that the interstice between leaving and arriving snapped tightly shut, never needing to open again. I knew this sensation permeated every part of my body – a body that I was told was conceived out of sin and shame. I wanted this to last.

First, "Re rollo Diu dith da dit. Fetel iu genet?"

These words growing here? What Paradise had I entered?

And then, "Pleth edos trigit?"

In those spluttering sounds and mutated initial letters, momentarily, the world stopped suffering from the confusion of tongues. It shifted its axis and gave new utterance. Responding to only a couple of my initial, tiny and hesitant words, the enormous edifice that was the Tower of Babel collapsed right there and then, in front of me. Clay, brick and stone toppled down. Dust and debris coated the floor. A single language returned. In seconds, the very top of the tower burned, the bottom became swallowed, and only the middle was left standing to slowly erode over time.

It would not have its day again.

I would not let it. Not ever.

Although their intonation was not perfect, the vowels pitched slightly oddly, and the accent very 'different', still the clarity of dialogue rang out, echoing around the landscape and hammering into both of my ears.

In stuttering, malformed gobbets of sound, I greeted them. I told them my name. I explained where I was from.

It was instantaneous – we both understood the other, and so gently smiled. I remember the look of complete surprise on their faces, as if I had stepped out of one of their myths, as if I had been placed there as some new portent or prophecy. It was the first full sentence I nervously got out: I told them I definitely wasn't – that I was human and just like them, and they listened and appeared to understand that. They exchanged glances, trying to read each other's minds. Sometimes they didn't need to speak to me. I could read their thoughts: how on earth had I walked in on them now, at this point in time, at this particular moment? How do all of us alter our fate?

When they spoke again, in confederation, in union, in complicity, it was like the very mosses and lichens had nestled close, and created for me alone a soft bed of linguistic wonder. Nouns, verbs and adjectives were poured upon me as if a creamy milk, and as well as this opulence, a luxurious grammar returned that I had thought, in my roving, I may well come to lose (perhaps you can tell that, from the alien language I now use here). Maybe in that short moment, the very best features of all languages came together – in pauses, clauses, questions and answers. In my mind, there was no confounding, no variation, and no fragmentation – only homogeneity. We correlated imperfect tenses, pressed the conditional, and gave breath to inversions and idioms. All my learning and knowledge fell out of me like an open sack. The vocative forms of my world transcended this one, making, for once, the imperfect perfect. Lenition conjoined and the disjunctive coalesced.

In short, we let our tongues loose: what different worlds were described; what wonders were explained. Instead of being caught and at the mercy of each other, eyes widened. Universes collapsed in upon themselves. Stars fell to earth. Stories unfolded.

I can't remember now exactly how long we first gabbled and babbled. I explained where I had come from and how long it had taken me to find this place. None of this surprised them. I tell you – it was as if they knew it already. Probably, it was that which made me certain; it was that which made me realise, after so many false dawns, improbable coordinates and wrong turns, that at last, I was following the right path. One man (who for some reason carried himself differently) even seemed to recognise me – he knew my features, or sensed something in me that, despite his fluency, he couldn't fully articulate. I could feel his stutter. Despite his skill, vocalising his intrigue was too much for him. I could tell. His eyes gave away an understanding though. He knew

I knew as well. Maybe – although you may not believe it – we stared at each other as brother and sister.

Although they were all armed, I never felt threatened at all. In essence, I was at their mercy – I was the intruder, the stranger, the violator, stepping into this sacred place of theirs. Yet, there was no danger. The words we used negated that. I noted they carried iron-tipped arrows and I knew, from home, the crunching punch these could pack. Bone could be ripped to shreds; flesh parted like a wave. That had become the way of things of late; a way I despised. It was one of the reasons why I left. I suppose in my coming here I had taken my life into my hands. I had been warned. The result could have been very different indeed. But by this stage, nothing could stop me. I had come so very far, and was not about to be defeated.

I knew I was close to the quarry.

It was waiting somewhere ahead.

Would I have tried still, if they couldn't converse with me? Of course, I would have. Somehow, by gesture and drawing, tone and intrigue I would have made myself understood. I have had to do this before, and would do so again. I believe that even when there is no common tongue, I can communicate well. It is something I have inherited. Or perhaps, knowing my history, something I have had to do.

They weren't about to let me proceed without precaution though. Courteously, they checked me for weapons. There was a sense too, I garnered from some of their words, that I might be a witch about to inflict harm without the use of weapons. But I earnestly explained to them my purpose. I opened my palms to them to display I had no enchantment. It was my skin that intrigued them the most though. I let them touch me to show I wasn't magical or odd – but just white. Just me.

The colour of the moon, one of them said.

Another asked what I was looking for and why I was so far from my family and friends, especially since I was a young woman and young women usually didn't do such things. At this, I couldn't help but smile.

And when they asked me that, because of who I am and what I have endured, that's when I told them. That's when I became even more lucid and precise.

That's when, politely, I asked for him.

That's when they asked me to go with them.

2

Iron Slag, Noëpe Hill, Massachusetts, 6th to 8th Centuries CE
This rare piece of Iron Slag (or waste) is from a well-preserved metalworking furnace uncovered by the Department of Archaeology, Harvard University. Aerial photography and geo-physical prospection have found much evidence of metalwork conducted amongst the former territory of the Wampanoag people, a federally recognised tribe, based on the coast of southwestern Massachusetts. Slag is a partially vitreous by-product of the process of smelting ore to separate the metal fraction from the unwanted fraction. The slag here is a mixture of metal oxides and silicon dioxide. The metal fraction would have been used to create weapons and tools. Courtesy of Department of Archaeology, Harvard University.

AND SO MY STORY SWIRLS in foam and spume, and breaks its waves upon the shore. I must tell you, though, that we were always a people hemmed in by an ocean. The bouncing and bottomless sea was our key-clinking gaoler and we its solemn, foot-gazing prisoner. Although my people spent productive hours at the coast – looking for food, for building materials or whatever else the ocean gave up as a gift – for the most part, they utterly feared it. It didn't matter that the ocean gave them delicious crab, dog-whelks, limpets or seaweed; the sea – with its incessant crash and boom, its tides and turns – was a presence that restricted and chained them in. Some were brave enough to venture on the ocean in order to fish for cod, pilchards and lobster, but these were few in comparison. If they could have just seen it, then the ocean was a rich larder – a resource perhaps more important than the hard stone and dry land I work, put together. I knew it. That's why I stowed a boat in a cave (my own natural 'fug hole') down at the coast, and when times were hard, why I put to sea. You will learn more of my boat soon, but let us not launch that thread yet. You will see why soon enough.

Yet as I have explained, for my people, the ocean was a dangerous place. It held the *Ancredhor Mor*, the Vikings, who it was believed conducted their raids on land from temporary military bases on the southern coast of Ireland. No-one really knew whether they did come from there – it was just folklore and superstition, and what was said. Stories again, see. The truth was that, unlike us, the Norse 'sea pirates' had absolutely no fear of the ocean. They had obviously come from a long way away – from somewhere in the North – mythical places about which we had no knowledge; these were places off our maps of which we had no conception. Someone (an elder who reckoned he knew the whole of the world) once mentioned they came from the land of Yggdrasil – which sounded right – but this was as alien to us as what lay in the distant western horizon, past the rocks, past Lethowsow (do not worry – you will come to know this land or sea soon enough). What leviathans, monsters and evil lay out there, we could not contemplate. We had only heard stories of places. These Vikings spoke strangely, using odd sounds and noises that I did not believe human tongues could ever make. The threat of them set a powerful cloud of unease over all of us. This unease was to prompt, as you will see, a change in my working conditions: a new view of the function of each fogou.

The Vikings were not our only deep fear in this Age. If you were born in our land, then always the threat came from the east. Word, chatter, conversation, talk, gossip in all the communities I worked in, always there was the undercurrent of apprehension in what terror would come over the great river in the east. We had not met any of these new peoples who had pushed into the land from the east, but we knew that they were spreading. They seemed to reproduce like keen rabbits do up on the moor. What we did know was that people who spoke and dressed like us had been sent into the west as refugees. Most had stayed near the great river itself, as close to their traditional homelands as they could, but the common view was that they'd never make it back there. So there were refugee camps of our own dispossessed people, starting their lives again. For the settled people of the far west, this was the worst thought. Given the *Pedn an Wlas* – our very land's ending – there was nowhere else to go. The dread was simple enough: that we'd simply be pushed over the cliffs, impaled on the rocks below and left to the mercy of the ocean's force.

The odd detail came from traders or merchants about these so-called Saxons. Like the Vikings, they spoke oddly in a tongue that was sharp and un-poetic to various observers' ears. They ate strange foods, built odd homes, worshipped gods no-one had even heard of. There were, of course the usual rumours: that they had multiple wives; that they sacrificed their children on bloodied altars; that they fucked sheep sideways, upside-down and back-to-front. The only redeeming factor about them seemed to be that their push to the west had slowed down of late. Perhaps we, as a people, had retreated enough down through the peninsula, and some of us had already travelled across the choppy Channel to new lands in Gaul, replicating our peninsula life. Our hope was that we were too distant, too peripheral to be counted or invaded. Nonetheless, the word Saxon was a homonym for 'bogeyman' wherever I went. Mothers used it to threaten badly-behaved children. Fathers spoke of them when cursing. Anyone telling a story who wanted hush, just said that word. Its two syllables spoke a terror.

I was contemplating this as I rode west from Halliggye to Carn Euny. Today though, there was no threat of the Norsemen, nor the bogeymen named Saxons. Instead, the evening light was crossing the bay of the Mount, glaring into my eyes. The Chief at Halliggye had given me a fine creature to complete my journey. The chestnut pony had powerful shoulders and withers; his loins and flank strong enough to carry my tools and me. He was so gentle I carried the reins in my left hand, wrist bound to leather. In our land, there were few tracks that did not require ponies with strong cannon and pastern. So far, the track had been muddy and so my ride's fetlocks were soon filthy and the black clay spread up his legs as far as each gaskin. As the night eased in, a slight chill came over the bay, so I wrapped my cape around me a little more, checking that my tools were safely stowed.

Despite the lateness of the day, many people were still at work. This was a tin-streaming region that I was passing through. Here the countryside was covered in ant-like humans, blackened from the base dirt and grime of their work. It was hard labour this, and not for the faint-hearted. The people who did it usually had no other option. It was either stream for tin or go hungry. Now that the evenings were pulling out, this made their working days longer, but more profitable. Gang-masters ruled these groups, providing accommodation and sustenance for their workers, but then collecting a hefty commission on what was streamed daily. Not only men worked there – women and children too had their part to play in the process.

The tin streamers found themselves wedged between the dry stone walls of the lower fields where cattle sometimes grazed and the unenclosed wilderness of the moor. Here, alluvial deposits could be found where they had accumulated after being eroded from the tin-bearing grounds. Such alluvial tin was said be highly pure and was much sought after by the traders from the far south. The tin was easily sorted by its specific gravity, it being heavier than most of the minerals. The workers passed a stream of water over the gravels so that the lighter gangue (carrying quartz, mica and feldspar) would be washed away faster than the tin. Of late, technology had improved and now there was a complex system of launders and leats across the landscape, which tumbled down the valley into the trenches the children dug (known locally as the *tye*) in which the tin would sink. Further up the valley, the men and women worked at the ground itself, digging out rock debris for the waters to pass over. As the work progressed across the landscape, ridges of gangue were left in long lines through the valleys. They were sometimes as beautiful as the barrows we built a few generations ago.

I had to admire the ingenuity of it all. At the very top of the valley, they had constructed small reservoir ponds to maintain the water supply for the streaming. The one problem was if there came a dry summer. Without water, no work could be done. The streamers would go hungry and be forced to forage in the woods and along the shoreline until the rains came again. Most of the tin streamed here would be exported to other lands and to assist this exportation, along from the ridges of gangue were the temporary smelting huts, where inside the ore was roasted and its impurities reduced. These huts stank and were best avoided. The men who worked them were a breed on their own – semi-naked hairy giants who turned a metal sludge into blocks of tin with fire and iron. The smelting huts were moved every couple of weeks or so, built over the *guag* – the term these people used for places that had already been worked. This kept them close to the current streaming.

My presence riding past the tin-streaming works caused a cessation in the work. Launders were dropped, water splashed in the wrong direction and ground stayed unbroken. The gang-masters barked orders, but the workers knew it was almost the end of the day. What could the masters do now? The effect was eerie. The whites of the women's and children's eyes peered at me out of the gloom. They said nothing, but it was as if they wanted me to save them; to pluck them out of this mess of sludge and slime. It was something I could not do. For one thing, there were too many of them. For another, my lifestyle would be too fragmentary for them. Women and children require stability and security – not the craziness of some fool who busily told stories and moved stone. What woman would want a contorted hand of oak touching her body anyway? Besides, their moving of stone was really no different than mine. We just worked on different scales. They worked with particles while I worked with slabs. We both used and abused the earth. What difference could I make? Perhaps that is why I have not settled down with a woman and 'streamed' and searched – so to speak – for children of my own.

What saddened me as I passed these blackened forms was that hope seemed lost in them. Never mind sea pirates or Saxons, their own fears had already come to pass in the launder-edged nightmare of gangue and guag. If they had followed due custom, one time, these women would have given birth to their children in a fogou: baby and warm afterbirth slipping out onto flowers and ferns, the midwives chanting welcoming songs to the new soul arrived from the Otherworld. The cord would have been cut and the baby held aloft for all to see. He or she would have been cleansed and readied for this world. There would have been such hope, such joy, and such wonderment in what the future would bring. Now that was distant. The fresh smell of lilacs and ferns long gone; the earth-womb welcome of the fogou disappeared. Instead, there was the unending wetness of barefoot work in the streams, the rings of tin dust around their child's eyes and then the unrelenting stench of the smelting. Even rats stayed away from such workings.

The ocean had made it so. It was it that brought the traders from the far south. It was it that made them seek the tin islands. It was it that now held the ships waiting in the bay below this stretch of gangue and guag. The only thing that perhaps kept their imagination working was what became of the tin they streamed. Rumours and stories always said that it decorated the mighty temples and palaces of distant lands; that all this muck and mess might actually lead to the creation of unequalled beauty, shimmering in some remote desert, reflected in some far off lake. For this purpose, the last job of the day was now being completed. The blocks of tin were taken from the smelting huts and loaded onto carts. These laden carts would then trudge down to the bay where they would cross over the causeway to the island. The island's harbour had waters deep enough for the ships from the far south, whose hulls pressed far into the blue when loaded with the tin. These working people never met the traders: that was left to the gang-masters alone. The latter seemed afraid that if the olive-skinned crews from the south ever met their blackened streamers they may not come back again – for fear that they were real bogeymen and women.

In my contemplation of this, I hadn't noticed that my pony had been standing still for a while, resting and feeding on the long grass that lined the track. There was something in me, I knew, that the women and children recognised – some glint of humanity maybe, some light of empathy even – which they saw in my eyes. Perhaps it was the weakness of my left hand. It mattered not that I built fogous (their way in and out of this illusion of happiness) but that I simply understood. As you will learn, I have a way of doing this which means I barely need to use any words at all. These thoughts needed shutting down. After all, I had work on. I needed to continue on the track towards Marghas Vyan. Despite my antagonism to the masters who ruled this empire of tin, it was one of their metal-laden carts that I followed down off the moor. As night fell, I saw candles and lights emerge on the side of the streaming works where the workers eased aching joints, ate and slept. How they must long for escape and freedom.

On the wide shoreline of the bay, I watched the carts gather from many other streaming works all along the south coast and wait for the waters to recede so that they could trundle out along the causeway and transfer their loads to the ships. It being night, the ships were also lit now; the reflective ocean waiting to receive these blocked and shiny pieces of our world. I elected to stay on the beach this night in the lea of some rocks that dotted the shore near the village of Marghas Vyan. I left the pony tied where the grass grew in the dunes and in the lea I built and lit a fire of driftwood; eating some seaweed bread that remained from my time at Halliggye, and peeled mussels off the underside of still rock pools. I added threads of garlic grass and cooked them in a pot that I always carried. This hearty meal allowed me to sleep and dreamily contemplate the day's events. In my semi-conscious state I wondered how could I, as leading fogou-builder, architect and repairer, do more to make my people great? Where were our ships that should strike out and encounter foreign lands? What could free those people from the grim labour of the streams? When I finally decided that such tasks were unanswerable and unachievable, eventually I fell asleep.

When light came, it was coupled with a stinging shower of rain. The drops fell on the still warm ash of the fire and immediately sharpened my senses. I looked to where the waiting carts had stood. They were now gone, as were the ships of the far south. The tide had turned again, and now covered the causeway's stones. Already up on the moor, the tin-streamers would be back on their work, their masters counting their payments. A chill wind came in from the Bay; the same strong wind that allowed the ships to depart. When our weather turned like this, I imagined – just like that rat – being in the warmth of one of my creations, feeling the heat of the earth comfort and nourish me. But such fancies would not get me there. I needed to crack on.

The sun was still low in the east when I rose. A fit of coughing turned into a more hushed sore throat – no doubt caused by the recent wet weather. I resolved to make tracks to Howel's lands. Breakfast was not altogether awful. I always carried a supply of grain with me and gulped a couple of handfuls. Then pulling down my shelter on the beach, I climbed up the dunes to where I'd left my pony. Clearly we were both thirsty and found a clear stream (unpolluted by tin-streaming) just to the west of the settlement of Marghas Vyan. That morning, the view out to *Carrack Looz en Cooz* was unobstructed, and the island looked magnificent in the morning light. I had to laugh. Aside from the traders who docked their ships there, the island was said to house many a hermit, but when I had chatted to fellow builders about this, we'd wondered how could they be hermits if there was a community of them? Surely this was a contradiction in terms?

According to tradition it had not been that long in the past that the waters had risen and engulfed what we called the 'Grey Rock in the Wood' but it was long enough in the past for my grandfather never to have witnessed it. Stories came to me that it had been the melting of the last great Ice Age that had raised the waters and submerged this and the land of Lethowsow. I'd never thought much about lands being made and taken away, and did not then as I passed the great stone that was the Mount, and yet very soon (within a matter of weeks, in fact) my thoughts would return to this moment.

And so this is how my story grows you see. Once it was a tiny fish (just like the kind we all are when we are growing inside a woman's belly), but it is becoming bigger, stronger and smarter and soon it will be able to swim not just in the rock-pools or shallows, but in the ocean itself. Who knows? Maybe in time it will become as huge as a whale. Now wouldn't that be a thing? By the end of the morning I had thought over my stories and my experiences, and wondered what would befall me at the court of Howel. The end of the morning had also witnessed me reaching the western end of the bay's beach and climbing toward the higher land. Again I was glad of the pony's legs but even then I could sense his dismay at the length of the climb. Breathless, he finally carried me over the brow of the hill, the bay opening into a spread of blue, green and yellow behind us.

Once past Bologgas I knew I had entered the realm of Howel. A standing stone on the side of the road reminded visitors (or invaders) that a new territory had been breached. In reality, I knew little about Howel. He'd been a child when my father had worked for his father, but there was a connection there. He knew of me by my reputation of course. A little further along this road and I would have been able to head southwards towards where I kept my boat, but for now I turned right and headed north in the direction of old Ennestreven. Howel's realm covered much sacred space in our land. Wells were venerated for their spirits, power and healing qualities and the world here was littered with standing stones and stone circles from an earlier time. Carn Euny lay beneath the black ridge of Bartinney Downs but to access it from the east one had to cross the boggy reaches of Caer Bran. It was at this point that I was glad I had asked for the pony as payment. Nothing makes a man more miserable than when he is plodding through tufted wetland, with no end of the bog in sight.

I knew a little about Carn Euny. My father had talked of it many times. His memories were mainly fond, but as you know, there was the issue of him not being paid and that had soured his happier recollections of it. I knew much about the fogou there already, so vividly had my father described it to me. From his tales, I knew the layout of the houses as they'd been in his day, and I imagined not much had changed. There would hardly have been the whole-scale rebuild as I had witnessed at Kynance. Once past Caer Bran, and out of its wa-

32

tery, pellucid slopes, things started to take shape. Up on Bartinney I could see the stretch of an enclosure, connected to Howel's dwellings here, and from the village settlement stretched out lines of field systems, bursting with newly-planted crops. Some cairns and cists littered the northerly horizon too – obviously where the community had buried their burnt dead. The construction of some further courtyard houses to the east was also taking place, with the masons already busily at work. A few of them recognised me and put up their hands in acknowledgement. Howel's world was obviously a well-organised one, in which he clearly had money to burn on improvements and building projects for his community. This was interesting. In this I saw that Howel was an ambitious man, with hopes of sustainability here in this location for a long time to come.

A turn to the northeast brought the village itself into view. Smoke wisped gently from the tops of the houses, blowing to the east from their conical timber roofs. A stranger arriving at Carn Euny riding a pony brought a variety of reactions. Young men herding tiny piglet boars stopped their work and let the small razorbacks run crazily before realising the error of their ways. Two middle-aged women, who sat sewing before the most southerly of the houses, stopped their needles' courses and nodded knowingly. Children playing with sticks and hoops eyed me – fascinated by my presence, and by my deformed wrist. These younglings did not have the haunted eyes of the tin streamers though. Oh no. Instead, all was bright with life and energy, the very Awen beams of the sun's light seemed to shine down upon this interlocked community.

The union of the houses here was highly distinctive. Each turned into the other, by way of courtyard and wall; the stone of one house gossiping with the stone of the next. I knew the inside of them and what they would be like. Their round rooms were sub-divided into smaller units – bedrooms, cupboards and storage areas; these were of stone like the outer walls, then wattled walls dividing them still further. Just as the structures seemed to interlock, so did the conversations it would seem. Within minutes, it was clearly known that I had arrived at the top of Bartinney Downs. The masons at work on the eastern huts by Caer Bran had downed tools and come to see the spectacle of my arrival. Howel's house was easy to spot. It was oval, grander and with an open roof at the head of the village, closest to the enclosures and field systems of Bartinney. There, he could survey all.

"Let me take your pony Voog," offered Kenal appearing from the second courtyard house. "He can be stabled in my quarters for now..."

"Thank you," I offered, stepping down to the kaolin-laid white floor of one of the neatly-kept yards.

"You made a wise choice in coming here," added Kenal. "I told Chief Howel that you might arrive this afternoon. As you can see, we are all honoured that you have come."

Kenal led away my pony, his mouth lusting for water and hay after the long ride.

"Do you want to leave your tools and possessions here as well?" Kenal asked.

"No. They stay with me. Always."

Kenal nodded a look that meant he understood their importance. Meanwhile, the villagers gazed upon me, with no-one saying a word, but perhaps wondering if some enchantment might be pulled out of my sack – preferably by my left hand.

"My name is Voog," I shouted heartily. "Good to meet you all."

No-one answered except an elderly lady.

"We've heard tell of you."

"Good..."

"You'm fur the fogou en't ee?"

"Yes," I answered nervously. "Yes..."

"I'm glad to hear that," came a new voice from behind my shoulder.

I turned to face the direction of those words.

"Voog. Welcome to Carn Euny. I am Howel."

The chieftain shook my hand and embraced me. He managed to find the right one, and glanced over at the left's additional digit.

Howel was not as I had imagined him. He was a slight man, with blond hair and blue eyes; slightly child-like in appearance, as if youth and innocence had never been quite chased out of him. I had expected a powerful leader, physically strong, dark and sullen at the need and expense of redesign and reworking. Howel was not this at all.

"Walk with me..."

The villagers nodded for me to leave their presence. Gradually however, they followed us, longing to know what would be requested of me.

"I have spent several years building my realm here Voog. The druids and I have worked hand-in-hand to ensure prosperity and success. We believe in what we do. We think that one day, all the communities in this horn of the land might live as we do – in peace, in harmony, in understanding."

"You've done a fine job," I noted.

"Good. I am glad you think so. Now, come with me up to the fogou... I want you to take a look at it."

Howel put his arm around my shoulder. This was unexpected, and as the chieftain was somewhat shorter than me, our movement was clumsy as we wove in and out of the courtyards and up the gentle slope to where the sleeping fogou lay. Eventually we reached the roof-top, with me bending down to examine the cap-stones.

"She's the finest one, they tell me... one of the oldest..." Howel began.

"I heard that. It's always the one referred to – the one most modelled elsewhere..."

"Your father Donyerth may not have begun her, but he certainly made her what she is today."

"He loved this souterrain," I explained.

"It's unusual," said Howel. "Not many have the beehive cell leading off it... It's very sacred obviously."

"Absolutely," I offered.

"And in good condition?" questioned Howel, obviously hoping for my approval.

"By the look of it... though I haven't seen the inside yet..." I argued.

"Jump down then. By all means, take a look..."

Howel gestured me to do so at the western end of the fogou. I crouched and entered. Howel followed me in. From my father's tales, it seemed I already knew every stone of this structure, each placing, each decision he had made. A couple of the cap-stones were clearly his work. They were exactly as I would have laid them now.

"We had a birth here just a few days ago. The chamber was cleaned this morning. The Otherworld delivered us a fine, healthy boy. No birthmarks or deformities..."

He paused, correcting his line of argument for me.

"It still works well."

"That's pleasing..." I said, "although I'm not sure why you want me here. The corbelling's in good shape, the roof's dry..."

We proceeded to the beehive cell.

"The cell looks perfect."

After a quick peer into the cell we emerged at the eastern end, close to the chieftain's house.

"So what do you want me for?" I asked, my face conveying my complete puzzlement.

"Voog, the world is changing. The old way will not always be the right way. Honestly, I respect the tradition, the sheer wonder of this, its portal status – back and forth from the Otherworld – but I've happened upon another use for this fogou."

"You say another use? What use?"

"You may wonder how I can possibly even contemplate this – but I am, Voog, I am... Kenal told me of your bravery at Heyl. He says you singularly took out twenty of the Norsemen's party."

"What of it?" I couldn't help but say. Anyone who knew me well enough knew that I detested such action. I did it so our way of life could continue. I knew instantly that Howel didn't really rate me as a true warrior. How could I be – with *that*.

"We live in a world that is unsafe. I want my family and people to be safe. This fogou could work not only as a gateway – but imagine, Voog, imagine it as a refuge."

"Refuge, you say?"

"Yes – I have seen something similar in Armorica. Travellers tell me of it in Hibernia also. Say if we were attacked, there'd be enough warning to get all the women and children into the fug. Then we'd roll massive stones across the entrance, so big that many men could not remove them in a short space of time..."

"Entomb them you mean?"

"Not so. We'd keep enough water and food in there for them to survive for some time, and then when the danger had passed the stones could be removed by rope and leverage and so on."

"I see. Do you fear the *Ancredhor Mor* then?" I asked.

Howel shifted on his feet.

"All leaders do," he responded solemnly. "I have to."

"And raiding Saxons?"

"Those bogeymen? Less so, but still, Voog... I feel the winds of change."

"From the vessel of life and death into a refuge you say?"

"It's what we need."

"Can you make the adaptations for me, Voog? Perhaps seal up one end. Load it with stone and fill in with earth. Create larders inside. Maybe some hidden creep passages. Make runs for the sealant stones?" Howel said excitedly.

I was about to ask him what the guardians of the fogou thought about this notion, when our conversation was interrupted. A red-faced boy of around eight years old came running towards us, through the doors of the chieftain's house, clearly holding some news. Once reaching Howel, he went down upon one knee, his breathing erratic and strained.

"My Lord Howel... you must come..." he said breathlessly.

"What is wrong?"

"It is Eleder. He has stopped breathing. I think death has finally come to him. He does not move. Casvellyn told me to tell you."

At this news, Howel looked pained. Other villagers standing around watching the arrival of the famous fogou-builder lowered their eyes in grief. Everyone except me knew who Eleder was. My expression must have conveyed this to Howel, for he led me aside and then explained.

"Eleder was our most ancient and most respected druid. His passing had been long expected, but nonetheless you can see the final shock of it on the faces about us."

The village was silent in its grief. Partners comforted each other. Adults gave children the news in the best way they could.

I gestured towards the fogou.

"You want it prepared for him?" I ventured. "I will do it."

"Eleder was fond of your father Voog. It is fitting, is it not, that you will prepare his way back to Annown? Looks like you arrived just in time."

"And the changes, the adaptations...?"

"Leave them for now – until after the ceremonies," Howel said hurriedly. "Eleder's spirit will protect us from any attack in the meantime."

I bowed and re-entered the fogou.

FOR THE TIME BEING, I will still settle for this place and 'thing' called Annown, but perhaps that will change. You perhaps see how I am unconvinced, and as you know, change is always the way of things. I have spoken already of homogeneity. Now, in turning back time, I speak of change.

But, for now – dear Annown, I address you.

When placed next to the struggle I had in coming to know my mother, finding him was comparatively easy. You see, with him, there was just the small matter of an ocean to cross (though more on this later), and then reacquainting, or perhaps just acquainting ourselves with our probable pasts. With her, things were much more difficult. There was every obstacle you might imagine put in my way. I faced stone walls everywhere. I had doors shut in my face. No-one spoke her name – or even wanted to hear it when I shouted it from the cairn.

Even in the aftermath, even now, I am not sure if I truly knew her. I have 'reconstructed' her. That is how it has been. But, I ask you, how could it be any different? When you know fully the events that have shaped my life, you will understand. These events were beyond my control. They were chosen for me long ago, when I was a tiny fish in my mother's womb, not knowing the ferocity of the world outside her belly: sharks and predators I never wanted to meet. When I was born, things started to alter. They were chosen while I slept in a warm cradle. Decisions were made while I dreamt, gurgled and puked; and when I cried, laughed and sucked at my rattle. While I nuzzled into breast, and dozed to lullabies, whole futures were being decided. My innocence then, is therefore my excuse.

They say that all children who have their parents taken from them at a young age still have some physical sense of who their parents are: a phantom idea of what they look like and how they might behave now. Even though surgery has removed the limb of them, there is still a sense of them being in the here and now. Nerves still tingle. Synapses connect. It is like that for me. You see, she was taken from me when I was just four years old. Imagine. She was everything to me, and then suddenly, she was no longer there. How I cried. Oceans of tears fell.

After that, everything I gleaned about her was hearsay, gossip and speculation. They were words (so unlike that encounter I have previously relayed) that I did not want to hear, but couldn't help but listen to. It is a pain you know you don't need, but still must seek. I hoped that somewhere in them would be nuggets of gold, the shimmering ore that would reveal the truth about her (the bitch!). She went before I could question her, before I could articulate my curiosity. Over time, I tried to listen less, and as the developing child, I filtered out what I didn't like. I admit – I embellished all that I heard that was good about her. In truth, though, there sometimes didn't seem that much that was positive. Any thread which carried hope, I nurtured and extrapolated, teasing it between my thumbs.

As time has crept on, those memories have become hazy and more mythic. Everyone in Chysauster says I look like her, so each day, when I look into a mirror, I see something of her in myself. I do recall her devotion to me though. Just like all young children, I put endless demands on her time and energy, but she was always patient, always willing to give me more. The love she showed me was complete and pure. I sensed that was because, despite what is said, I had been conceived in that way as well. I was a product of that purity – though no-one ever told me that. With her, there was not a single ounce of emotion that was either held back or falsely given. When we are that young, events can become distorted. What was fantasy can become real, and yet my overriding memory of her during this time was her willingness to walk upon the moorland with me every day – whatever the weather. It was there she could escape. There she could be free. Then she would place me on top of the granite rock piles and tors and have me gaze out over it all. In particular, she loved me to see the ocean. I think I understand why now. He became it.

As I tottered on some precipice, she held my hand tightly and then led me down. Below the stone, she'd show me flowers. We'd sit in the ferns making daisy chains. She'd show me how to collect herbs (always a passion of hers). She'd make me a whole household of dolls from wood and wool. We'd play in the courtyard of the roundhouse, having imaginary adventures, playing imaginary families. When the sun went down, she'd sit with me as we listened to the tales of the bard – tickling me in the funny sections, and holding me tight when terrible monsters were mentioned. I'd go to bed excited with a head filled with the marvels of the adventurer Bryok, and be unable to sleep. That's when she'd sing to me. Her voice charmed me to slumber:

Shining white is the moon and sweet is my song,
quiet is the sleeping by the fire;
A song in my mouth, wind in the corn,
the coat of my little girl is warm, warm.

I often wonder what she saw in my face as she looked down upon me. I like to believe she saw her true love. She saw everything that was good in the world. All this time, of course, I knew nothing of the prejudice, the hatred, the im-pounding, the prison that she endured. When she eventually disappeared, at the time, it came to me as a great shock. Looking back on it now, maybe I should have seen it coming. But as youngsters we never read the signs. We be-lieve all will always be well. Eventually, I came to discover that her fate had been written a long time ago. I was a stump of that delirium, an unwanted bas-tard who, under different circumstances (perhaps if I were male), would have been conveniently cleansed out of history too. Yet although they took my mother, taking me, a child, was a decision that even their heart was not hard enough for. I have always imagined me being yanked between two people pulling – one at my arms; another at my feet. Although others tugged fero-ciously, my grandmother tugged harder, and so it was with her I landed.

It was she who saw me through the years that changed me from a child to a girl, and then from a girl into a woman. She it was who fed and clothed me when others walked by. She taught me to read and write. She it was who com-forted me when I first bled. She it was who told me of the ways of men and women. It was she who, in time, I got to speak to about my mother, and it was she who, in the end, felt I should seek him. I say him, because that was what she called him. She could not bring herself to say anything else.

Melwyn was the name of my grandmother, though I never called her that. To me she was Grandma. She had status, my grandmother – the chieftain's wife. He was a man named Cadreth. Because of the way things were, Cadreth cared little for me. You see, I learnt that my arrival had wrecked a far wider union, and that my birth broke an alliance that had been a long time in the forging. He knew of me, acknowledged me, but I could tell he didn't love me. With Melwyn, it was different. Her love was unconditional. Whatever fate had spawned me, whatever configuration of hatred and confusion had made me, didn't matter. It didn't matter because I was *her* granddaughter. Any grandmother will tell you the same: that love is unbreakable. In your granddaughter is your future. It is the way you will go – when you are dust deep in a cist.

I knew I caused arguments between Melwyn and Cadreth. I knew I was a bone of contention, though both denied it. I was spoken of always in hushed tones, as if I were different, as if I were subhuman.

When I realised my mother had finally gone, I had many questions for my grandmother. I interrogated her each day. I can't imagine the hurt and grieving she must have endured. My mother was her daughter.

"*Henvam*, Grandma – where's she gone?"

"Don't trouble yourself with that child."

"No. I need to know where she's gone."

"She's gone somewhere she can't come back from."

"Where's that then?"

"A long way from here. After I've finished baking, shall we go feed the boars?"

"No. I want to know where she is."

After this I would sulk and cry, and wonder why I had no other parent. But I was bright, and I started to put two and two together. I started getting awkward. Now you can see why I loved the questions and answers with those people who spoke my tongue in the 'Land of Bliss'.

"Did Cadreth get rid of her?"

"No."

"Did he kill her?"

"No."

"Why doesn't he like me then?"

"He does like you."

"It doesn't feel that way. He never smiles at me."

"Child, men never smile. They have to think of stone, war and death."

That got me thinking – of stone, war, and death.

I was still playing with dolls then, you will understand. Still, I asked it though.

"Has Annown taken her away?"

My grandmother carried on with kneading some bread dough. I could see tears drip into the mixture.

"Was she placed in the fogou?"

She bent down to me.

"No. Not in the fogou. Not now. Not any more... I mean not now. Listen... when you are old enough, I will tell you, I promise. Now, go outside and play."

I went outside to play, hoping I would become old overnight.

3

Bellshrine, State Forest, Massachusetts, 6th Century CE
This intricately embellished bronze cover protects an ancient iron bell associated with a probable Brittonic saint – from perhaps Wales, Cornwall or
Brittany – who must have crossed the Atlantic to the western coast of North
America. There is some salt damage to the niello and enamel work suggesting
that at some point the bell shrine was used on board a sea-going vessel. The
shrine probably once had a jeweled cross on the front, lost during the bell's
chequered history before it came to the Massachusetts Historical Society
Museum in the mid-nineteenth century. It was recovered in the State Forest,
near Leominster, Massachusetts, suggesting early pre-Columbian contact with
the indigenous people there. Courtesy of the Massachusetts Historical Society
Museum, Boston.

INSIDE THE CHAMBER THAT AFTERNOON, there was a beautiful and
benign stillness, the kind that I still treasure and desire to this day – this far
away from that time and place. It is a stillness that only comes briefly in our
lives and when it comes, it is to be consumed and inhaled so fully as to nurture
both body and soul for months, or even years to come. There is something
about stone and its energy that creates this stillness – a sense of communion
between the human and the natural world. Here, mosses, algae and liverworts
had blended themselves in and around the stone of the walls, seemingly knowing their proximity to the Otherworld, and revelling in it. The union of plant
and stone in this way was something the druids celebrated, so it was fitting
that Eleder would lie here; his spirit conjured away past the green and grey interior of the sententious chamber. It was tradition to whiten the floor, to cleanse
the space in order for the transition to take place. I had asked for a sack of
kaolin powder for this and when a dilatory boy eventually arrived with some,
I ritually scattered it across the packed earth.

You can see how I find myself becoming both onerous shaman and obfus-
cating storyteller here. Somehow, I had drifted into it that day. These duties
were – how shall I put it? – over and above the normal duties of my guild, but
given that I had a direct family connection to this fogou's construction and that
I needed to impress the community at Carn Euny I went the extra mile. Outside,
above me and around the altruistic cocoon of the fogou I sensed the wider ur-
gency in readying all for the ceremony. Everyone knew the process. Even the

42

young children, who had not encountered the grim reality of death before, knew what should be done. This was because our ideology, our belief, our understanding of the afterlife permeated our lives. From the earliest times in their lives, the young were educated about their idiosyncratic entry into this world, and how they would leave it. They knew that the death of Eleder, as a respected druid, would require a further level of gravitas and respect above and beyond that given normally to the elders of the community who passed away. When a death occurred to one of us, it became a communal act, one that in doctrine demanded everyone be involved in its ritual and ceremony. To be detached, to be outside of the process, was to display reproachable disrespect to Annown.

The objective of the ceremony was to allow Eleder's spirit to depart to Annown. There, he would be safe and in good company of those already in its realm. To allow this to happen, it was important to place his body into the chamber of the fogou as soon as possible; the lacuna between life and afterlife best kept short. The placement was to be conducted initially with a procession of his body through this world; then he would lie in the fogou for twenty-four hours – enough time for his spirit to be fetched. Once this was deemed complete, the necessary burning of his physical body would take place, his ashes then placed in an urn and stowed inside a cist in one of the cairns. Song, poetry and story would mark his life and celebrate his achievement.

"Fine flooring I see, Master Voog," came an auspicious voice at the eastern end of the chamber.

I brushed a slight dusting of kaolin off my moustache and turned to see a tall, long-bearded figure clad in white. His jutting chin began to speak again.

"Howel told me of your arrival. Such sad circumstances today though... with good Eleder's passing. He was my teacher you know, all these years."

"Sorry," I ventured. "Have we met before?"

"We have," said the figure. "I knew your father very well. I met you once when you were still a baby. He took you to see me – regarding your hand. You will not remember, of course! I am Casvellyn – this day, now chief druid for our community."

Casvellyn was a name I had heard of. He was undoubtedly one of the most respected spiritual leaders in our land. He came closer so I could see his face more clearly. His hair long, plaited and grey, he must have only been in his late fifties but looked older. Standing at over six feet tall, his white robes glowed in the semi-darkness of the chamber. This then, was the venerable Casvellyn – one of the last of a dying breed, I sensed.

"Your reputation is great, Master Voog. But I would expect nothing less. You were taught, as I was, by a master of your trade.

He paused suddenly, then slowly, almost as a whisper, questioned, "You know of the changes Howel wants?"

As Casvellyn spoke, he looked up and around at the fogou's interior, and added, "What do you think?"

"It is not for me to say," I said. "We simple builders do what we are asked. We work by commission alone."

"Nonetheless, you must have a view. You are no simple builder, Voog. You are an architect, an artist in stone no less. What the world has given you never impeded you."

"I know Howel is thinking of the future."

"Yes – a future in which we do not exist perhaps. He seems to think the land will be overrun with Saxons, does he not?"

"I don't know."

The last thing I wanted was to get into this kind of conversation with a druid.

"The Romans thought they could wipe out our kind, Voog, but they failed. They forgot about our little corner of the earth didn't they? Eleder's generation may have gone, but we continue. We thrive still..."

"You have apprentices here, ovates even?"

"Indeed. Two boys have been selected to be trained, to join the order. They have potential. Aptitude is all."

"That's good," I heard myself say.

In many ways, it was good, for as I have outlined already we fogou-builders and druids have an interdependency – a sometimes awkward and tricky symbiosis, but a relationship nonetheless. Mitigation between dreamy druids and practical builders was not always easy.

"When the next twenty-four hours are over, we must talk further, Master Voog. I wish to pick your brains about many things. You bring an intellect that is sometimes missing here."

"I look forward to that," I said, actually wishing that I wouldn't have to endure any more questioning from a pompous druid such as Casvellyn. Always questions with them; never answers.

"In your travels, Voog, tell me, this Christian god... do you hear much about him? I am intrigued..."

"I don't travel far Casvellyn... not really – I'm no gadabout these days, so I don't know. You probably know more than I do anyway. If this new god comes, he won't replace..."

Our conversation was interrupted by a group of grieving villagers at this point.

"Druid Casvellyn," one of them said tentatively, "May we dress the chamber? Please give our work due blessing."

I could predict what was coming. It was tradition for the chamber to be filled with the leaves and, if possible, the buds or flowers and fruit of twelve trees. In the time that had passed since the boy announced Eleder's death, clearly they had gone out roaming into the countryside to seek out such material. However, given the fact that not all trees could be found in the immediate vicinity, sometimes a community like this one would store these items for a ceremony such as this. These had thus been picked beforehand, in woods not in the immediate vicinity of the village. Fresh leaves and flowers were however considered more desirable and appropriate, so these still formed the bulk of their offerings.

I stepped back to allow the villagers to enter the space. As was custom, each stopped to touch the entrance stone, offering prayer and dedication. Then they moved into the tunnel. Casvellyn moved down into the space as well, giving blessings in our tongue. In order to do so, he had to bend double, then, selecting a suitable spot for the offerings, he crouched and pointed his staff to the appropriate space.

"Here are birch, rowan, ash and alder," a woman said respectfully. "All these for Eleder."

These were placed down and spread into a sacred pattern by Casvellyn. I didn't look too closely at what he did. It was, in my experience, best to keep one's distance from druids and their arcane work.

A man moved forward with another bundle.

"I place willow, hawthorn, holly and oak. These I give for Eleder."

Casvellyn nodded and accepted the offering. An enchantment was spoken and these trees placed in the space made sacred by the druid. The man left, nodding at me, knowing the power of what he'd brought.

Finally, a shy girl of around thirteen nervously stepped towards Casvellyn. Casvellyn stopped his incantation and looked up at her. He smiled.

"Eleder was always fond of you, you know..."

"I know," she said. "For him, I bring hazel, ivy, reed and elder..."

The girl turned and left the fogou, her eyes not making contact with anyone.

Further villagers entered the fogou bringing both dried and fresh flowers, the fronds of ferns, as well as their own individual gifts for Eleder's spirit. Among these were polished and painted pebbles, corn-twisted figures and effigies of his spirit and small pots of herbs. Casvellyn blessed each offering and gave thanks for the bed of nature building up on the floor of the fogou. In the beehive hut, as was custom, Eleder's possessions were brought and placed. In our minds, these would somehow end up with him in Annown, even though in a physical sense they remained, and would no doubt be passed on to the druid apprentices: the ovates.

"Are you happy with the way the fogou is?" I asked the druid.

He looked at me, with a satisfied smile.

"We are ready for his departure," announced Casvellyn.

As always, the landscape was very still before the ceremony began. The birds were already roosted for the night and even the normally noisy domesticated animals kept their snufflings and yelps low. Eleder's hut, like Casvellyn's was set a little distance away from the courtyard community. It was how things were done. Druids were always to keep some degree of distance. It was in their code. As full darkness drew down and the long shafts of light in the west ceased, that is when torches were lit, and the men of the village brought the fragile body of Eleder outside. He had been placed on a wicker frame, the lengths of willow tied with bindings of leather. He wore his usual white robe. I examined his face. It was not pained at all, and looked as if death, when it finally came, was a welcome relief. Howel had informed me that Eleder had been fading these past six months, barely able to speak and eat. Once outside his hut, the drumming began. The hides of cattle stretched across a frame of wood and beaten with oak sticks made for effective percussion as the procession wound its way down off the moor. Customary wailing was delivered by the women; their voices knowing how to play upon the heart's strings. This was their duty. The route followed took Eleder into the west, for this was where we believed the Otherworld to be. The two small ovates, heading the ceremonial group, looked at me sheepishly as the procession touched the outskirts of the courtyard village. Rumour of my presence had already reached them. Next followed Casvellyn, in full druidic regalia, wearing a bright bronze torc and collar. On his belt was his sickle and he carried a tall oaken staff, with a quartz stone set at the top of it. He was walking before Howel, who looked pleased to be completing this civic duty, proud of what his people had achieved. Yes, he had collided often with the prophecies and predictions of Eleder (that much I had noticed), and yet he had respected the elderly druid for his views. His eighty-five years in this life had taught him much – this Eleder often said. Behind Howel was Eleder's body, held high in the air by six men. Behind the body came the children; those who held the future of the community – most of them not quite sure about being in the procession, but nonetheless walking behind the body, as they knew they should. As the procession passed further roundhouses more people joined onto the tail end of the cortège. Kenal and his group came from the south of the courtyard community and joined in. He acknowledged me.

To enter the fogou, the procession had to pass through Howel's oval hut – in effect, the parliament of the village. Here, a paved entrance showed the significance of the route they were about to take. The body was lowered slightly to fit beneath the lintel and then turned ninety degrees to begin the descent down the stone steps into the fogou. As observer, I stepped onto the higher ground and watched proceedings. There was no need for me to see what would transpire inside the fogou. I could guess what would happen, and besides, I had seen such ceremony – with both commoner and druid – a thousand times. The body would be laid upon the offerings. For a druid's transferral to Annown, the presence of the twelve trees was essential. These would be spoken of by Casvellyn. Once the body was down – his head facing the west – then all would leave except the druid. Here the final incantations would be spoken, and water from a local well given to his lips – refreshment so it was ritually thought – for the journey ahead. Inside the fogou, the tallow lights that I had set would be glowing beautifully, casting dancing shadows across the corbelled stone. Finally, when Casvellyn left the chamber he gave a swift movement of his staff, which signalled the start of a chant. I had heard many such songs before, which celebrated a life, and asked for the spirit of the dead to be safely transported to Annown, but here at Carn Euny, their words and melody had a special quality that I would not forget.

Casvellyn and Howel eyed me. I could not make up my mind about them and the motives of each of them. They were indecisive about me as well, I sensed. Whether they thought I had too much power, or too much lip, they did not show it that day. The days ahead would reveal just how our relationship would go, and just how far it would unravel. I knew nothing of that then though, and so joined in, as best I could, with the singing of the chant. That day though, there was a sense of passing, in not just me, but the rest of the village; a sense that this Age was ending and Eleder had somehow represented its former safety and comfort. I hoped that whatever magical mechanisms which conveyed the spirits of the dead to the Otherworld were taking place in the fogou. I looked to the west, and hoped that good Eleder's spirit had made it there. In order to celebrate this, a bard named Remfra recited a poem about the druid's life:

This is the incantation of a boar that is for me
I pray for a quiet journey across a shore
a prayer for you Eleder, poet of the people
for you, your people created a sacred space

This is the incantation of a bird that is for me
I pray for the voice of low waves
a prayer for you Eleder, seer of the land
for you, your people created a sacred space

This is the incantation of a fish that is for me
I pray for a smooth journey to Annown
a prayer for you Eleder, chief poet of the world
for you, your people created a sacred space

As was customary, a day of mourning was planned. This meant that after the chanting ceased, all the people of the community returned to their homes, and stayed inside for the next twenty-four hours. Such a cessation of any other activity allowed all to meditate on the fragility of their own lives. This I followed, gaining valuable rest and recuperation from the past few days' events. It had seemed an Age ago in itself, since I watched the ghoulish men, women and children of the tin stream. I had been given quarters in part of Kenal's complex of dwellings, and was shown to a comfortable ante-room. It was a veritable palace compared to what I had experienced at Kynance. There I received a wicker bed, laden with soft straw and cloth, as well as enough tasty boar meat and vegetable stew as I could eat. Were there any, rats would have had good pickings here.

For some while I slept and contemplated all that had transpired. The next day it rained heavily anyway – which suited the mood of the village in mourning for one of its own. Kenal and I spoke little; he seemed content to leave me to my thoughts. Dialogue with him only opened out when we discussed Howel's leadership and his plans for the fogou. Kenal was, like Casvellyn, keen to know my thoughts. I gave him the same response as I did the druid. I sensed in Kenal more mixed feelings. Clearly, he was aware of the ceremonial tradition attached to my profession, but he was also a man who had glared into the wild eyes of a ravaging Norseman. Like me, he seemed to sense the change.

The rain did not relent for the remainder of the day. I had wondered how the floor of the fogou might be – whether it was dry still, or now running with water. My answer would not come then. Instead, again, just as the day was descending into night, we were called by the sound of a thrice-blown horn to the top of Bartinney Down. Here, Eleder's now spiritless body had been brought, and here, upon a flattened bed of granite, he would be set alight. The whole village, dampened by the rainfall (only now just starting to cease), watched, as slick tallow was poured upon his white robes and smeared upon his face, legs and arms. The offerings were taken from the fogou and placed upon his body, these too covered with flammable oil. Casvellyn himself made a flame from two flints, and with a wooden taper set the pyre alight, steadily working around the body. With a whoosh, the pile ignited; flames swiftly engulfing Eleder's physical form. For the first time, I could clearly see Casvellyn's grief and sorrow at the death of his master. Howel's face was harder to read.

Although it was to be hoped Eleder's soul was in Annown, we watched the fire eat flesh and bone. It crackled and hissed, the red and orange flames occasionally transforming into mesmerising flickering purples and deep blues. It was, as all cremations are, quite beautiful to observe. Flakes of black ash drifted to the northeast of us, scattering Eleder's form upon the vibrant yellow and green gorse bushes of Roskennals and the stunning violet of the heathers at Tregerest. Later, when the cooling wind subtly changed direction, it took him over the wide form of Tredinney common and the basking hill at Carn Brea. From there he would be spun out over the iridescent ocean and, like his soul, be carried into the sunset of the west. Ashes would fall into wave and crest, melting the man into salt and seaweed. When Casvellyn was satisfied all was well, he took the back edge of his bronze sickle and scraped the dust and heavier ash into a cordon-decorated pot. Before the dawn came, this would be ritually placed in a cist and left there for nature to claim, just as Eleder would have wanted.

In such ways, this was how our dead became the earth again. From here, one day would grow a strong oak.

DEAR ANNOWN,

I WRITE NOW, tentatively, in the tongue of another, all these long years after. Back then, in the light of what I knew, I had questions for you, shaped and composed in my then innocent mind. Is the Otherworld really bad? If I do some evil in this life, will I come back deformed and damaged? Is it dark there all the time? You never answered them for me though. In fact, you said not a word. On reflection, though, maybe that was for the best. Sometimes saying nothing is the best thing to do.

Despite my wishes, growing up overnight was much harder than I thought. Revelation was to come very slowly, step by step; one word after another. I wanted enlightenment and epiphany. What I got were thin chinks of light that sometimes illuminated the past. These bright shafts of knowledge ignited my curiosity more than ever. But there were still shadows, darkened patches which revealed nothing. They followed me wherever I went; they dominated all I did.

They still do, even now that I have found my way here.

They say children always pick up on an atmosphere. They are sensitive to it – maybe more so than adults. Let's get to the heart of this time and why things were the way they were. There was always a fear present in my grandmother, but it was not only her – it was the entire community. They all spoke of raids and treaties, of dowries and pacts. I remember the words used. They fell as often upon my ears as the westerly rain did during February. It seemed to me (even in my naïvety) a house of cards that might fall down at any point. But if 'they' could be placated, perhaps there was hope; perhaps Chysauster might endure. I will reveal more of this soon, but you must understand, this was all I knew at that point.

In realising all of this, I gradually came to learn more of my community. On Fridays, we visited Lulyn to buy fish, oil and hides. But we were always accompanied by warriors, as if some bogeyman might emerge from behind the mill or out of the bushes. I came to know well the lands to the north and east. Often, Cadreth and Melwyn were invited as honoured guests to feasts and rituals. I tagged along. There is no doubt that we lived well. From the east, rumour came of starvation, and famine, but ceremony here made for a fat belly. I thus became bonny and thrived.

I heard tell of a nearby village named Carn Euny. Its name conjured much for me. The sound of its second syllable seemed to express a singularity: the 'U' sound seemed to equate with it being 'u'-nique. It was a uniqueness I could not access. The other 'non-royal' children went there – they told me about it. They travelled there sometimes with their relatives, to see family, to trade and to play. I was never invited though. It was a place out of bounds to me. It was off the map: literally, at the edge of the world – and so was forbidden. It seemed that if anyone went into the west, Melwyn purposely took me to the east. I was kept close, and never put into exile. You will know though, that what is kept from us is what we most want to discover. It then becomes what we lust after. They should have known that, the fools.

Things changed when Cadreth passed on. That's when I learnt more. That's when I really started to grow up. Cadreth's death came not long after my mother went, so it came as a double blow to Grandma Melwyn. Cadreth suffered from many old war wounds (mainly against the *Ancredhor Mor*), and in one of them, infection set in. When this would not go, he caught pneumonia alongside it. He died shivering in Melwyn's pink arms. I felt nothing. I never knew the man. He'd decided who I was and because of that, I made a decision about him. The village went into mourning, but I was as uncaring as stone. We cannot mourn what has hurt us. I felt for my grandmother. She didn't deserve this. There was talk of Cadreth's line ending, of the requirement of a new Age of leadership. Though of his blood, I did not count, for I was a girl – and something unwanted too. Questions were asked. Who would negotiate now? Who would placate the incomers? Who would allow us to keep our ways? In the hours after he died, I stayed out of Grandma's way. Much needed to be decided by the elders. Apparently, this was no place for a girl.

Chysauster had its own druid – a kind man named Genaius. After the older druid died (a man my grandma called Old Sel), I took him milk and cheese most days. I liked him. He had a good heart. I asked him about my mother too, but he wouldn't budge. He had to follow the code, he told me. Some things druids could not reveal. There were more interesting things I should pursue. Had I been to the coast? Could I see those animal shapes in the clouds? What new dolls did I have? He instructed me in learning too. In this way, he distracted me from my purpose, although I have to say, in his enthusiasm for my happiness, I enjoyed the diversion as compared to the dourness of others. For Cadreth's death though, another more experienced druid was called upon. I learnt he was coming from Carn Euny. At last then, I would see a real piece of this mythic land. He arrived with great ceremony, accompanied by both warriors (in ceremonial armour) and farmers (carrying symbols of the harvest). I saw him first when Melwyn held me in her arms, while she greeted him.

"Good Casvellyn, your presence here is much appreciated. My husband much respected you."

Do you hear her? Do you hear that word? Respect? From this distance now, I spit upon it.

"When I learnt of Cadreth's passing, I came at once."

His eye fell upon the young me. I remember him sizing me up, gaining the measure of me.

"Is this...? Is it hers?"

My grandmother nodded.

He smiled at me, but beneath the upturned ends of his lips was something dark. This darkness was hidden by charm and verve. It was what you found under a stone in the black month of November.

Preparations were being made. We had a fogou at Chysauster, and my grandfather (although to me, he was neither father nor 'grand') was placed within it. Ceremonies of his passing began. For someone so respected as he, three days would be devoted to his transition from this world to the Other. When not conducting events, this druid Casvellyn stayed in our roundhouse. He ate my grandmother's broth and bread. From my room I heard them talking. I now understand that this eavesdropping was the moment where I grew. It was where I would wrong-foot the past.

"It is true what you say. I can see she has his eyes," said Casvellyn sighing.

"Oh, she has his spirit too. Full of herself she is. She won't take telling. A proper little madam she is sometimes. The apple never falls far from the tree."

There was a pause. I listened more intently.

"Curiously, not his wrist though; nor the finger. Sometimes, such things are passed on, as I am sure you know..."

"True. Annown spared her that..."

The sound of their voices lowered as they ate. Then, between mouthfuls of soaked bread, came his solemn voice again.

"It was... for the best... you know Melwyn... that we did... what we did. The milpreve said it should be so."

"I know," I heard my grandmother say. "I accept what the glain says. Despite it all, I still have the old faith you know."

But I knew her voice. The way she said that didn't sound right. It sounded like what was done had never been for the best. Later this was confirmed, when I heard her alone in her room, softly crying. I knew the tears she shed weren't only for her dead husband.

That is why, that night, I entered the main room where the druid slept, and committed the unthinkable. I stole a milpreve (yes, a finely-swirled glain), from his bag. I did not know what magic they made but I did not care for the threat of them. I played with the rounded stone during the night, while I heard Casvellyn snoring. In the darkness, I was worried that the swirling snakes that made it might re-emerge, but in the morning, I took the stone with me onto the heather-coated purple moors.

Up there, I threw the glain hard at a rock over and over again until it shattered.

Do what you like to me Annown. I don't care any more.

4

Pipe-clay figurine, Mackenzie Creek, Massachusetts, 4th to 5th Century CE
This tiny pipe clay figurine was found preserved in the mud at Mackenzie Creek
by a hiker in 1963. Although probably of Gallic origin (and displaying some
Roman influences), such figures were commonly produced in the period 380
to 500 CE. Its provenance here suggests early trade or exploration by Europeans in this northwestern corner of North America. Courtesy of the Kingman
Tavern Historical Museum, Cummington, Massachusetts.

ALTHOUGH SPRING WAS BURSTING ALL around us at Carn Euny, the
immediate days after Eleder's passing were quiet and unremarkable. People
returned to their toil in the long fields, or herded boar, cattle, goat or sheep to
where they were to graze next. Pens and sties were cleaned, fences mended
and stone walls rebuilt. I had to admire Howel's organisational skills. He had
shaped a community where each individual seemed to know his or her role,
but more than that – they actually seemed proud of what they did. Most villages
I visited, I was always witness to the moans and gripes of the people there –
they seemingly thinking that a fogou-builder would be able to solve all the issues. There was no pride in what they did in such hovels. It mattered not if a
job was done poorly or incorrectly. Someone else would sort it out. Not here
though. Carn Euny functioned like a glowing hive of efficient bees: drones,
workers and warriors each knowing their place in the whole.

In the evenings, which were growing lighter by now, I noticed there was
great interest in making their food tasty and wholesome. Unlike other communities, where food sometimes seemed scarce and was hoarded, here people
shared, with much interest in other's recipes and dishes. Sometimes, two or
three of the courtyards cooked together, usually in a stone-lined pit. By some
standards, this was old-fashioned cooking – placing heated stones into the
trench to cook the meat or vegetables, but it had the effect of bringing everyone
together – both old and young.

I was party to some of these evenings. Gradually, the villagers' wariness of
me declined (we fogou-builders were still viewed as special connectives between the living and the dead – and therefore odd) and I was invited into more
of the courtyards, asked to partake in more of the feasting. There were moments, I must admit, when instead of my itinerant travelling, I began to think

about living this way – settling, and enjoying the passing of the years with others. There is much comfort in that. Sometimes as humans we never seek the mundane, but instead far horizons and adventures. Perhaps we should rein ourselves in and be happy with order and routine. As we sucked the juicy bones of the meat, and drank a thick and sweet mead, tongues loosened, gobs unfurled and more of the world of Carn Euny was revealed to me.

Leading the narration was Remfra the bard. Wise in some ways, in other ways he was utterly naïve. Clearly, he was a man obsessed by the greatness of the past, so there were long stories of Bran's marvellous deeds, layered eng-lynnion surrounding a slayer of giants named Jowan, and the great and varied sea voyages of Bryok. This kind of man had a thousand tales up his sleeve. I must say I learnt a little of my own patter these days from him. I saw how he used pause and reflection, wide eyes and gesture, to carry the tale. At the right moment, he would lean forward fiercely, scattering the children into their mother's arms. But they were soon back with him again, when evil was defeated, when there was fun and laughter, slapstick and chaos. Remfra had little time for modernity. It was too full of gadgets and fashion. People were less tolerant now, less loving, he would argue repeatedly, and his tales seemed to support these assertions. The stories were important because if he did not utter them, then they would be forgotten and no-one would know where we came from or where we were going. In this, despite my nearly nodding off in the thirteenth voyage (of some fifty episodes, which would follow later that week) of Bryok, Remfra had a point.

Not only came the stories of the epic past, however. Gossip and rumour emerged when the children went to bed, and when Remfra's words no longer held sway. As the moon rose high, tongues loosened.

"What's the latest on Howel then?"

"Well, I've heard tell that a maid's been lined up for un from Chysauster. A dowry's to be paid. Their chieftain has agreed. A deal's been done so I hear."

"Good. good. There's some comely maids from over there you knaw..."

The speaker made the shape of a woman's body with his hands, exaggerating the breast and hips.

"Time he get married, his todger won't get hard anymore..."

At this, there was much laughter and guffaws. A man stood up and raised his arm erect in the air, then dropped it as if a drooping member. The women cackled and nudged each other at the fun of it.

I knew of Chysauster. A team of builders and I (when still an apprentice) had put in a fogou there five years ago. There, I truly learnt what my withered limb could devise and complete. Lying to the east, it was a larger and more established courtyard community than Carn Euny, but probably less well-run. It was a sprawling metropolis compared to the rural intimacy of Carn Euny.

I continued to listen to their chatter, trying to hide a smile.

"A chieftain such as he should be married by now. He needs to protect his lineage. Have a son or two. His father had him when he was still a young man."

"Him living up there on his own, well it idn' natural."

"Not natural t'all in my view. He be more focused on his oity-toity plans and ambitions than he is on having some rumpy-pumpy. Howel d'not only want to rule here. If he had the chance, the bugger'd rule the whole of this horn of the world."

At this, again there was much laughter. Another round of drinks was poured.

"Perhaps he dun't want no maid. Perhaps he d'bat for the other side."

This was too much hilarity for some of the gathering and they laughed heartily.

"Shhhh," said one of the women, pointing at them all. "If we don't keep quiet, he'll be down here to see what the row is all about."

Each of the group tried to stifle their amusement.

There was then a sudden pause in the proceedings, as all gazed into the fire.

"What think you, Master Voog?" asked a man in his thirties who I had noticed bred goats. "They d'say they with physical limitations d'have great insight..."

"I think much, but say little," I replied.

This frustrated the man and he came back to me with, "You must have a view on it surely?"

"Maybe I do and maybe I don't..."

A villager stepped in to defend me.

"Don't push un," he said. "Let the man keep counsel on what he d'think. You wudn' run into someone's village slagging off its leader now would you?"

The baiter dropped his questions to me and acquiesced.

"Come, never mind Howel's love life," said the woman. "'Twas time we were in bed. We've all got work to do in the morning."

The men and women all finished their drinks and the fire was doused with water.

"Dunnee take naw notice Master Voog at all our jerks. We d'love Howel really... We just want the best for un, that's all. "

"I understand," I said. "I won't say anything."

I stood, and made my way back down to Kenal's hut. The sky was cloudless that night and the stars shone clear and bright. In my mathematical apprenticeship, I had learnt much about them and knew how to calculate their movements and understand the turn of the earth. It was true too, that things here were turn-ing. I could not quite work out which way though. These thoughts kept me awake that night. I know I didn't sleep deeply until the first traces of dawn came over Caer Bran.

Somewhat bleary-eyed, I met Howel the next morning deep inside in the of-ficialdom of the parliament house. He led me to a table placed in the centre of rows of benches. Behind the table a fire pit roared and smoke drifted upwards, out through the opening in the roof. The full dawn eased in through the tim-bering and the slight spaces between the wall stone, scattered bands of light across the floor. As ever, Howel greeted me with much enthusiasm and care for my well-being.

"Is Kenal looking after you down there? If he isn't, you must tell me you know..."

"The food and accommodation are excellent," I replied. "Everyone's very friendly and helpful."

"Good to hear, very good indeed. Now listen, have you been making any drawings?"

I nodded. I removed the sack from my back, opened it and reached inside for some clean white hides on which I had sketched with charcoal how the fogou would look, after its transformation. I laid them down on Howel's table and we each held the corners tight, so that the roll of hide would not curl up. Howel lowered his face towards the drawings. I had spent some time on them in the past week, sketching the fogou from each side, from on top, and from both entrances. The perspective was accurate and measured. I gave him two options, each considering the stone available and the cost of moving it here. The chief pored over my drawings, his fingers following the lines and angles proposed. At each alteration he sucked his teeth, drawing in the smoky air.

"I can see why you are considered such an outstanding architect – and why I needed you. These are fine drawings. I like the look of it very much. May I ask then – which option do you think is best?"

"Personally, considering what you want and the purpose proposed, I would go for the second option. In the long term, it will last longer and the entrance stones will be easier to place and remove."

"I see..."

"Option one is fine, but the movement in and out is not quite so easy. There are pinch points here... and here. The second option gets rid of that problem."

Howel leaned back from the table, and looked into the rasping fire for a while. In my head, once again, I checked my calculations, awaiting his re-sponse.

Finally, it came. He said, "Master Voog, I want you to construct the second option."

"Very good. Shall I begin right away?"

"Not yet..."

My face conveyed puzzlement at the delay.

"I have to run it by our parliament."

"But, as chieftain, surely you have the last say?" I said.

"I do. You know what they say about leadership though, Voog. Consult, consult and consult – and then do it the way you wanted in the first place... I've always found this the best way. I'll bring the elders on board steadily... you'll see."

Now, I was beginning not only to get the measure of the fogou here but also the man. Quite clearly, Howel's success as a leader had been in his politics and careful manipulation of opinion. Perhaps it was always so, and would always be so.

"We meet later today. I will let you know the outcome then."

This seemed the cue for me to leave. I took the drawings and placed them back into my sack.

"Don't worry about Casvellyn either," Howel offered.

"Casvellyn?"

"He will have had words with you I know. He doesn't want the changes. We have argued for many nights about my proposals. Change must happen though, Voog. You see that I know..."

I did not respond to Howel's words.

"If he is awkward, let me know."

In this, at least Howel recognised that, as so often, it was fogou-builder and druid who had to liaise about the reality on the ground, regardless of what leaders and chieftains wanted.

"I'm after a compromise you see," Howel noted. "Listen... I forgot to check. Will it hold everyone? In event of attack I mean. You have considered numbers?"

"I have. I calculated that all women and children, and all men not fit to fight, would enter. There is room enough for them all."

"Good."

I moved to the paved entrance of the house, where only a few days ago the procession had entered with Eleder's body. Back to the left was the fogou itself, the stone of it lit by the eastern sun of the morning.

"I have plans, Voog..."

I turned to listen.

57

"There is the small matter of my marriage. No doubt you have heard..."
I lied and shook my head.

"Much ritual lies ahead of me... But I have been thinking... you may be the man to help me achieve all I want to do. More fogous I think – a network of them, yes? From coast to coast. Let the *Ancredhor Mor* know we mean business... This way I can protect not only my people but others too."

At this philanthropic wish, I was surprised. No leader had ever requested that of any fogou-builder. This was news indeed. Any word of it that got out into the community would spread like wildfire, and there'd be guild members from all over the horn here to offer their services. That said, considering Howel's grand designs, maybe I would need them. Such a scheme would require fifty builders, not just one.

Before I left, Howel had some final words, "Play your cards right Master Voog, and you will have work here for years to come."

Suddenly, all I had thought about stability and being stationary seemed within reach. Finally, I could plant myself. I have to confess, as I trod back out across the pavement leading away from the parliament house, I felt that huge distances were going to be a thing of the past. How blindingly wrong could I have been?

Outside, cattle were lowing as the morning heated up. Steam rose from the grass and the dew gradually subsided. A few seagulls from the coast flew over and mewed to the sprawling world beneath them. That world today nursed a good many hangovers which might only be cured through penitent work in the fields. No doubt they'd still be gabbling about Howel's wedding: what his bride would look like and who she was. The day then, had brought me rest, and to an extent, some peace of mind. After all the surveying, measuring, calculations, sketching and precision drawing of the last week, I now only had to wait for the permission of the parliament. In my mind, I made notes about the best way of getting the stone in. As I thought through these processes I was greeted by Remfra, who seemed to be heading northwards towards the cairns.

"Part fourteen tonight Master Voog! You'll be there won't you?"

"Wouldn't miss it for the world," I responded.

"Good. You'll love that section. It's the one filled with sea monsters and the islands of fire."

"Sea monsters are figments of the imagination," I mistakenly offered.

"Mmm.... are they now? Are they?" argued Remfra.

He peered at me like I ought to believe. In the end, I had to compromise – and accept this bard's wisdom.

"I look forward to it very much," I said, nodding.

"Have you no work then, Master Voog?" Remfra asked.

"Not immediately. I am waiting for the parliament's decision about the works to be completed."

"Those idiots," said Remfra. "Don't worry. Howel will push it through. The elders know he is right. You'll know by the end of day?"

"I hope so."

Remfra considered me a while, then said, "Walk with me Master Voog. I am heading to Tregeseal – for inspiration. Your company would be most welcome. You can tell me all your stories along the way."

This offer was unexpected. Although now I am brimful of stories – thanks to my experiences – back then, I felt I had none to tell – that were worthy at least.

"No... Much as your offer is kind, I must make preparations here. Perhaps another time?"

"Very well. Not a problem, Master Voog... I will see you later."

Remfra pushed past the light scrub and climbed over a stile into the fields. Bards like him had a good life. They were not required to work in the way that the other villagers were; and yet it was their duty to provide for him. This was because, like the druids, their services were valued and considered important. This had been clear not only from Eleder's funeral, but also in the way the children and community delighted in Remfra's tales. In this sense, he was not just a teller but a teacher too. You see my point here? This tiny world is on a cusp. There are those within it who rely on superstition, prediction and prophecy still, but then there are those others who push for enlightenment, learning and understanding. Sadly, those who rely on superstition, prediction and prophecy want to hold on to their secrets so badly, that they do themselves a disservice by it. Their greed twists them.

All of this became very clear to me later that day and would become clearer over the ensuing week. In the afternoon, I was at work in the beehive hut, ensuring that all the stones were in place. In my plans, little change was needed here, except that stronger capstones might be required across the top of it, in order to make the refuge safer from attack from above. This was part of the plan I'd hoped the parliament would approve. I suppose my work was not noisy, and I believe myself to be a quiet and unassuming individual by nature. Regardless of this, in the shadows I sensed a figure move past the hut and enter the deeper chamber of the fogou.

Momentarily, it was perhaps as if the spirit of Eleder had returned, and honestly, I'd wondered if somehow he had returned from Annown, the Otherworld somehow unhappy with him (I have been told by some fogou-builders that this can happen and that they have witnessed such moments). What I saw, however, was much more of this world. Easing carefully between the hut and the chamber I crawled under the lintel to see who was there. Sticking my head out past the base stonework, a figure clad in black was reaching into the wall of the chamber. At first I wondered if they were ritually placing something there, but finally I realised that they were doing something that was quite the reverse. The figure was using an iron trowel to excavate one of the smaller stones. I could hear words being spoken under the figure's breath.

Because the figure was almost crouched double, it did not take me long to establish who it was. Clearly, it was Casvellyn. There he was, destroying the work that my father had completed many years ago. Because Casvellyn knew him, perhaps even helped him, maybe this gave Casvellyn, in his twisted view, the right to vandalise the sacred.

"What a complete bastard," was my immediate thought.

In our society, any destruction of a place so sacred as the fogou was punishable by death – druid or no druid. It was hard to resist immediately confronting him about his activity. I had to bear in mind too, that druids do the oddest things and that they have that right. It is why they exist, but this, this seemed a step too far. Casvellyn might have believed that having finished my plans and now waiting around for a parliamentary decision, that I would not be here: that I'd be in field someplace, gossiping and gabbling, just like the others. Casvellyn did not know me very well though. He never did.

Eventually, in a slow motion, he pulled out one of the upper wall stones, spoke briefly to himself and then placed the stone into a leather satchel he was carrying. He turned his head back up towards the eastern entrance and so I darted my head back. When I next looked, he had gone – no doubt crouching down further to ensure his easy passage through the western entrance. Quickly, I got up to inspect the wall. The socket of where the stone had been stared at me in the gloom, the earthy sides of the space compacted into position, but now missing their guardian. Small earthworms poked out from the soil. So it was said, such changes could alter our relationship with Annown. Birth defects could result. Even worse, could come non-acceptance into the Otherworld. Casvellyn knew this. What was he up to?

There was only one course of action. I had to follow him. By the time I had paused to look at the stone's socket, this had given him good opportunity to put some distance between himself and the village. My instincts told me that having left via the western entrance of the fug that he would head to the south west. This was the case initially. I could see a black-clad figure walking on the edge of the lower field planted with the last of the winter barley. His movement was rapid. I'd have to run now to keep up with him. Once through the field though, his direction changed markedly, weaving a course that was now more towards the south east. It felt almost deliberate, his zig-zagging to hide his movement. Where could he be going? Where was he taking the stone?

He was on lower ground now, moving past the groaning relic of a chamber tomb erected years ago. Every so often, he would stop and turn to see if anyone was following him. When he did this I had to crouch and hide behind the dense gorse that grew out there. Was it Trevorgans he was heading towards? There were settlements there I knew. There was no logic in that. Why lug a stone that distance, and to what purpose? I was gaining on him. His almost six decades had made him less sprightly than he thought. The closer I got to him, the more danger there was of being noticed. Care was needed. Under my breath, I was cursing druids and their stupid ways.

We were still in Howel's territory here. In my mind, I scrabbled around for remembrance of this landscape and what was held on its granite palms and heathy fingertips. Perceptively, at an instant, Casvellyn changed the rhythm of how he was walking. He became more reverend and then more studied in his posture and steps. Whether anyone was following now, appeared not to matter. Appropriate respect must be given. Then it dawned on me. Features in the landscape at Creeg told me where I was. I'd been past here before – on a building job we'd speculated on being down at Boleigh. Shit. This was Boscawen-Ûn; words which translate to the 'elder tree upon the downs'. In Remfra's tales, it was Beisgawen – one of only three major gorseddau or 'gathering' sites in the whole island. On occasions, determined by the planets' alignments, this was where all the surviving druids of the horn of the land met. Apparently, in its day, it had hosted hundreds. Now, by my reckoning, there were only a few left – but highly sacred the place still was. Unlike the fugs, stone circles such as this one had been erected thousands of years ago for ceremony and celebration. There were smaller local ones – of a variety of designs for community druids perhaps like the deceased Eleder or Casvellyn, but the latter's alliance with this site told me he was of greater significance and power than I thought. Was he the guardian here? Probably he was. Was he the one who called gatherings? Perhaps. Maybe it had been Eleder, but presumably Casvellyn was the one to carry forward the responsibility.

The circles were out of bounds to normal people. You'd never cross one. If by some reason you accidentally stumbled across one, you made sure you were outside its providence as soon as you could. They were powerful centres – up a notch from fugs (though the fugs still had their place for common people). Here there were, in fact, two circles. The outer circle contained some twenty stones which were waist high. It was one of these that I hid behind. The inner circle's stones had the same number, but these were slightly taller, the granite there more powerful. Casvellyn entered the circle through a gap in the stone rings in the west. It was a portal he knew well. Once in the inner circle, I might have guessed what would follow. He called the four quarters of the earth, and although I could not catch all of his words, spoke about his reverence to Mother Earth, and the trees and stones. He then walked around the circle, first north-wards and then to the east and south, finally back to the west. Here each stone was touched by his left hand, seemingly pausing slightly to let the energy enter him. For perhaps an hour then, he knelt before the leaning and phallic centre stone, speaking in a language I couldn't understand. Crouched behind one of the outer stones, there was nothing I could do. Any movement at all and he would have seen me. I was hoping he would soon finish though, because my knees and back ached from the awkwardness of where I was. No amount of claustrophobic stone positioning in the past could have prepared me for this. Finally when his incantation seemed to stop, he took the fogou stone from his satchel, held and turned it in the air, then placed it beneath the base of the centre stone. His words were not clear still but I could make out something about him wishing things be left as they are.

This was it then. Fucking druids again you see. They always think they know best. Here was Casvellyn hoping that this act, this placing of a fug stone here, might irrevocably stem the tide of change. His superstition, prediction and prophecy would thus have a place. He could still control the world with staff, tree and stone.

He was deluded, the poor sod.

Once the stone had been placed there, he bowed, turned and left the circle.

What was now unclear was whether he would at some point come back for it, or leave it there forever – just to spite me, and more importantly Howel, and for that matter, the rest of the Carn Euny community. It seemed he did not sus-pect anyone following him; otherwise he would surely have curtailed the cer-emony and waited for another occasion. There was a close call as he left. Momentarily, I thought he had spotted me but instead, his gaze turned on a scared bird scattered skywards by his movements. I kept low behind the outer stone and, despite his proximity, he didn't see me. Casvellyn looked as if he would be taking the same route back up to the village. I would follow later. For now, though, there was a decision to be made. Should I enter this space and rescue the fug stone or should I leave it there for the Beisgawen to commit its magic upon? If I entered the circle I would be breaking every rule that my culture, my lineage and my guild had taught me. This was my stone though wasn't it? Or rather it was my family's stone? – a stone once placed in its socket, and packed in the earth by my father's hands.

In the end I decided it was my stone and entered the circle to retrieve it. Maybe I expected some kind of change to occur. Maybe I would feel the energy of the earth and be struck down, as if an arrowhead had hit me in the back. But nothing came, nothing at all. Instead, I walked into the space, and reached for the fug stone now held here. Perhaps here now, the circle would by some force or magic pull it from my hands and reclaim it, dependent on Casvellyn's incantations. But no. Nothing happened at all. Instead, the stone parted with me. I cradled it, first with my left hand, and then with the right, as if it were a newly-born creature.

"Soon you will be back home, my beauty," I said. "Set back in your socket eh?"

In my mind I imagined Casvellyn's face at some later point in time, when he would note that it had returned. It was a moment I was much looking forward to. His face would be a picture.

Looking back now, I know I should never have been so cocky. Maybe it would have been best never to have crossed that space, never to have put a curse upon myself, never to have gone against the express will of a druid. I was asking for trouble. These were not my thoughts then though, as I walked back across the brown downs to the slopes of Carn Euny. Instead, I would show the druid what I was made of. It would not be stone or tree but human instead. Yes, I went to myself, he can tear himself a new kind of prophecy, the arsehole.

When I got back to the proximity of the village, I saw Casvellyn transform once again right in front of me. He was back in the role of civic dignitary. You could tell by the look of it that this was an important delegation. Whoever they were, they had brought several warriors with them, as well as their own two druids, with whom Casvellyn was shaking hands. A trail of people also followed across the moor, the like of which I had not seen for a number of years. From the parliament building, emerged Howel and a line of elders, their senate discussions having been interrupted. Howel was smiling though, with his hand open in greeting and signs of welcome. There was much nodding and embracing from both groups.

When I reached the hedge at the northern end of the lower field group, I could finally see the offering being made.

It was a beautiful young woman.

ARE YOU THERE ANNOWN? MAYBE you are, and maybe you're not. I'm here now, distant from you, but still trying to understand the puzzle that was my mother. It's hard to cut through the fog. Layers of concealment had been placed down in order to confuse anyone following. Obfuscation had been the plan. You know I need to admonish her. My earliest memories are of this: of me never giving up. It drove every part of me.

Nothing was ever said about the smashed glain. Maybe Casvellyn thought he had not brought it with him. Maybe he felt he had just lost it. He didn't seem to suspect me. The day afterwards he met with Genaius, but nothing was said. When the ceremony of Cadreth's passing to you was over, he left. This pleased me greatly since I did not like his presence around my grandmother. In the days that followed after Cadreth's death, Chysauster was so very quiet. Death still hung its black washing in the air. It felt like the village was falling into an abyss. It would have been wrong of me to have tried to lighten the mood of Grandma Melwyn. Perhaps the only difference I noticed was that, with Cadreth gone, if had I been important to her before, I was now her sole focus.

You might say during this phase of my life, I lived a closeted existence. I had no need to find anything or seek food or shelter. That is one reason I did what I did. Being headstrong, I took it upon myself to travel to Carn Euny. There, I knew I could find out what others wouldn't tell me. It would become my oracle. Deception was crucial in all of this. If Grandma had known of my intentions, she surely would have locked me away. Nothing was going to stop me though.

I knew the general direction I had to walk in. All I needed was someone to cover for me. In the end, one day, while she was pinning her tunic, I told her I would be staying at a friend's house on the other side of the village. Distracted by her grief and consumed with making right all that was wrong, she absent-mindedly let me go. I informed her I would be back tomorrow. I packed a sack with food and water, and put on a hooded tunic to keep out the cold. Then, I went into the west. It was November.

The old track that led across the sweep of the bay was well-established. It took me most of the day. Remember, I was still only a child. I was not the world-traveller I am now. The hood concealed me enough from people who I passed heading back to Chysauster from work or activities outside the village. I don't really know how I expected to enter Carn Euny. I suspect I hoped some magic would catapult me straight into its world, and that I would instantly find the answers I wanted. It didn't quite work that way. Approaching the village, a tall, armed man with grey hair and beard stopped me. On sentry duty, he was slightly stooped in his appearance, perhaps born of years looking down at everyone else. I could tell he had experienced the fear of combat.

"Are you lost, little one?" he joked to me.

"No. I'm on my way to Carn Euny."

"Looks like you found it."

He gestured behind him to where the roundhouses dipped down on the hillside.

"Odd for one as young as you, to be walking alone – in these times of Saxon raids... You need to be careful. I don't know your face. Who are you looking for?"

I couldn't answer him. He looked at me impatiently. Access would be denied until I was more forthcoming.

"Who are you then?" he persisted.

"I'm from Chysauster."

"You travelled from there on foot?"

"I did."

"You're a tough one then."

I had no idea how important this sentry would be in my story but he was becoming hard work for me. I was no raiding party. I had not come to steal and burn. Clearly, I would have to come clean. In the end, perhaps it was my honesty that opened the box that had been so tightly locked before.

"Whose daughter are you? What is your lineage?"

"I have no father or mother. I was brought up by Cadreth and Melwyn."

This information altered his response to me.

"You are Cadreth's granddaughter?"

"Yes."

"I know you now then... I was sorry to learn of his passing. What does the granddaughter of Cadreth seek in Carn Euny?"

But before I could answer that, his face changed again. His pallor altered and he became nervous. Another door was about to close. As soon as he had asked that question, he seemed to know what I was after. I had to act fast.

"Did you know my mother?" I asked him straight.

It was a question he was afraid of. I sensed it instantly. He moved his tongue over his lips before saying a word.

"What do you know of your mother?"

"Nothing," I answered.

"Are you sure you want to know?"

I nodded.

I knew from the outset I could trust this man. He was not about to harm me in any way. Yes – my grandmother had warned me of strangers countless times, but this man was no stranger. He had just been hidden to me before.

"You'd better come with me. Put up your hood child, when you enter the village. You already know why."

He was sensing my difference, my shame.

"Your timing was good. I was about to finish my shift."

He led me through Carn Euny's stinking, mud-coated streets. The settlement was no Paradise and all seemed unloved and slovenly. I peered up at this man. I knew he had the answers. All I had to do was extract them.

"Not that way," he exhorted, pointing me in an another direction.

"Why not?"

"The druid lives there."

"Casvellyn?"

"You know him?"

"Not really. I know of him. Best avoided eh?"

The man gave me a look of astonishment.

"Keep going. Down to the bottom of the village."

We entered his hut. What story was about to follow? I was about to learn who had walked here before me.

"Do you want something to eat or drink?"

I answered yes. It had been a long trek across the moor to the village. He brought me milk and a wheat biscuit. Outside, it had started to rain. He piled some more wood onto the fire; the smoke drifted upwards, staining the thatching and seeping through to the outside.

"Of all the people in the world, I'd rather not have chanced upon you."

A good start, I thought.

"You see, I knew your mother. I knew your father too. We are not meant to speak of them – but for your sake, I will."

The man wetted his mouth with a cup of water. What he was about to begin, seemed an epic tale.

"My name is Kenal, though you must swear not to reveal that which I tell you. Do you?"

"I do."

That's when he began. He told me of the romance between Orla and Voog. I learnt of the fogou there – the one built by my grandfather Donyerth, and intended for conversion by my father. I learnt that it was Kenal (who sobbed as he told me) who pushed my father out onto the ocean. Maybe he had gone to Armorica, he thought. At the end of it, I realised why I had intuitively smashed the glain.

I had met this Kenal, who was now filled with guilt and loathing about his life – and what he had been ordered to do.

I now had to find someone else: a man named Howel.

5

Weapons hoard, Mahone Bay, Nova Scotia, Canada, 6th Century CE
This hoard of weapons – comprised of three swords, two shields and sling stones (for use in a sling shot) – was found close to a shallow grave containing five skeletons. Buried hurriedly, lesions in the skeletons show signs of bone damage by flint arrow heads, clearly indicating a dispute of some kind. Radiocarbon dating of the bodies estimates them to be Europeans from the 6th Century. Chemical analysis of the metal and wood of the weapons indicates a Breton origin – probably from the Cornouaille region from a similar time, though this is not necessarily an indication of the warriors carrying them. The three decorated scabbards here are particularly unusual, having stylized animal heads and compass-beard abstract patterns. Courtesy of the Maritime Museum of the Atlantic, Halifax.

AT THE SIGHT OF THIS prominent delegation, my playful mind travelled back to the late-night gossip of the villagers around the crackling fire. From the sound and look of events in the eastern edge of the village, it was clearly a proclamation of marriage. Banns were being read. Orations about unity were spoken. Remfra clearly saw work ahead of him. Children became excited at the prospect of a royal wedding. I checked that the stone Casvellyn had relocated was still with me – delving my hands into my sack and feeling its warmth. He had set incantation upon it – always a problem, but nonetheless, it would be going back into its hole. There he was now, with these visitors, looking as if butter would not melt in his mouth. I decided to edge closer, having in mind that I would need some excuse for my absence. Yes, that was it. I had been sourcing local stone, testing its suitability for the rebuild.

When I got closer to the group, I recognised that I knew the chieftain. The group were obviously from Chysauster, just as the villagers had predicted – and their leader was a man by the name of Cadreth. By reputation – and in my brief encounters with him (when I was still a botch-jobbing apprentice) – he seemed a good ruler, but it was clear he had neither the vision nor ambition of Howel. Cadreth was a man in his forties, and though he still had the face of enthused youth, his body showed signs of ageing and he walked with a limp. If this young woman was his daughter, then there would be relief that she was to be married. Howel's status in our world was running high – and that made him the perfect choice for Cadreth's lineage.

I watched for a little while before making my presence known. The delegation from Chysauster would be housed in guest accommodation at the top end of the village, with Cadreth seemingly entering Howel's residence and staying there. I saw Casvellyn take the druids up to his quarters where they would no doubt fix their eyes and words upon the usual mistletoe and magic, not to mention offer his view to them of the changes to the fogou that Howel was proposing and I was about to execute. The young woman was chaperoned by older women from her community, as well as a bustling and talkative group from Carn Euny. This was the way things were done. I watched her graceful steps as she was led to the women's roundhouse. Inside, due preparation would be made regarding her enjoining with Howel. As in the ceremonies of life and death in our world, marriage too had its own rules and markers. No doubt these were now being extolled and examined. If Carn Euny followed the ceremonies of elsewhere (and I had no reason to doubt that they would be any different) then the fogou would be used for their ritualised union.

A thin weave of rain was coming in from the ocean by now – which brought down a blanket of chill on outside events. People scurried to their roundhouses to find more wood for their fires and to stay in the warmth until their next day's work. I had the option of immediately placing the stone back in the fogou. Right now, with the rain hurtling down, and the guffaws of laughter coming from the parliament house, there was perhaps no better time. But something in me told me not to do so. Something told me to hold onto the stone for a little while more at least – druid magic or no druid magic upon it. At this moment, I can tell you – I really needed the advice of my father. He might have known how to deal with such an incident. Then again, the world had greatly changed and maybe stone and earth wasn't what it used to be. Still, no matter if they are wrong or right, as you will know yourself, the words of a father can be comforting.

Kenal's roundhouse was full of energy when I entered. As a kindly host, he'd asked me to join his familial group, but instead I selected the peace of my own room. I made up an excuse about being tired from my excursions that day. My mind had been racing with the discovery of events at Boscawen Ûn.

"You fogou men – always on the look out for better stone, yes? I can't tell one bit of stone from the next..." he laughed. "Now, join us later, Voog, won't you? Remfra will be delivering his latest excerpt..."

At the latter, even Kenal raised an eyebrow, to indicate the nascent boredom that might follow.

"I'll be there," I had answered him.

"What do you think of Howel then?" he whispered.

"I don't know... I saw the delegation but..."

"His wedding will take place this week. To the maid from Chysauster. Some pretty from what they tell of her. Prepare yourself. No work, eh? Just feasting and celebration... It's about time we had a little of that here at Carn Euny. It's been too long."

I lay on my wicker bed and listened to the rain falling. The weave had progressed to a thick curtain. In the roundhouse, various excited voices discussed events. I got more of the flavour of what had been agreed. Cadreth was to pay a significant dowry to Howel. This included the lands of Noongallas, Trevern and Trannack. I knew their value. These parcels of land ran in a northeasterly direction toward Chysauster, and made a useful corridor between Euny and Chysauster. It was a considerable empire that would set other chieftains (in the north and far west) talking about Howel's growing power. No doubt with this increased land, Howel could expand further the defensive line of fogous that he'd discussed with me. They were profitable lands too – full of fruit trees and acreage from which could be grown cereal. Howel would be able to expand his herds of cattle and boar. There was talk of more deer on Noongallas – and the taste of extra venison was whetting a few of the appetites around the fire.

I have to admit in my limited knowledge of the ways of this world that small is often beautiful. Howel had a useful and productive kingdom already. Why did he need to expand? Why, for that matter, did Cadreth feel the need to align himself with Howel? There were perhaps a dozen other leaders who would have taken his daughter off his hands – tribes to the north and east that I knew of – and probably for far less of a dowry. The accumulation of empire was not always such a good thing. I had seen it many times before. It was the way we believed the 'sea pirates' and the Saxons worked. It was an ideology that seemed to say that whatever one group of people had, they always sought to gain and take more from someone else. It was always about not being satisfied with what one had, and being keen to sail over that horizon. Apparently, the grass was always greener.

The preparations for the wedding would also postpone my work. I was predicting the conversation I would be having with Howel over the next few days. He was bound to ask me to delay building works until his nuptials were over. If there was one thing a chieftain did not want to show another, it was an unfit fogou. I'd be kicking my heels then. The sort of weather outside was now ideal fogou-building conditions. I rather liked the work inside the belly of the structure when it was raining. It always gave me a good feeling – that nothing could touch me; that nothing could harm me. This, I suppose, is embedded in the fogou-builders' mindset. You will now guess how fundamentally wrong I was – but that is to come.

The wet also gave the right feel and shine to the stone. When it was wet, you could see its textures and form more clearly – employ the right stone in the right place more easily. It made the craft smoother somehow – as if the rain made construction fluid, and free from all obstacles. Speak to any fogou-builder and they'll tell you the same. I suppose, like any profession, we have our particularities, our ways of doing things. For now, though, this one stone occupied my mind. I had stowed it in my sack, and so then lifted up the item to feel its weight. Carefully, I slipped its form out of the material holding it and felt it once again. My extra finger rubbed against the surface. All stones carry an energy about them and this one was no different. Casvellyn had not taken that away from it.

With hands like mine, I could turn it easily between my right-handed menhir fingers and observe the slight indentations on its surface. I could rock it gently back and forth and feel its balance and line. It was what we fogou-builders call a good stone – a stone that will fit almost anywhere in construction. Some stones, well, they are like naughty children who won't sit still unless they are fully occupied. Others, like this one, seemingly have a natural affinity with other stones around them. They exude a kind of inherent cooperation and love in the hand of the maker. It is as though they have been shaped by the elements to serve and provide. This was one such stone. No wonder the enlightened Casvellyn had taken this one. He would have noticed its power too.

In the end, I decided it couldn't stay with me. It wasn't natural for it to be here. In the roundhouse, Kenal's family were huddled around the central fire pit. They had eaten, and so looked satisfied with their lot in the world. Remfra had assumed his storyteller's place on a chair before the children. In recollection, just as I do for you now, he had closed his eyes – remembering the bare bones of the next piece of narrative, upon which he would embroider and extemporise. Sensing my presence, he opened his eyes.

"Master Voog, I am about to begin..."

"I know," I replied. "But I must do something a minute."

"You will miss the best bit. The opening of this section, so all the great poets say, has so many wonders..."

"Maybe... but what I must do is important..."

At this Kenal, leapt in.

"You're not going to see Howel now, are you?" he asked.

I shook my head, but nevertheless, he came back with, "You must not disturb him and Cadreth. There will be much discussion.... much drawing up of tithes and boundaries. That is where the real wedding takes place, yes? "

"I won't be disturbing him," I said.

"But... the rain? Do you really want to go out there? It's blowing in hard now – from the ocean."

"There's something in the fogou I must attend to... It'll be dry there, once I'm inside. Don't worry... I'll be back soon to hear your tales, Remfra."

Remfra began his oration with a raising of his hands, and I slipped out of the roundhouse. In the wings of the courtyard, a few of the tethered animals nuzzled against the stone surround. They, as much as anyone else, were trying to avoid the wetness of the night. The goats bleated their own stories as I passed them.

Despite the rain, bright lights shone from the parliament building and the snap of the large fire inside could be heard. Now again, Howel's voice travelled over the lip of the land; a few seconds later that of Cadreth. This saddened me somewhat because what kind of a place was our world? It was one in which human life and fate was bartered over for land deeds. In all of what I had heard, no-one (bar the women of Kenal's roundhouse, who seemingly only had dizzy interest in what the bride would be wearing on the day) had talked about the forthcoming ceremony from the perspective of the bride. No-one seemed to care. I suppose when you observe my world, this was always so. Women were treated as second-class citizens, but this is not a view I have ever followed. You should know me by now. This isn't my way. By now, with ale inside them, I suspected, the conversations of both Howel and Cardeth's retinues had turned towards the bawdy ways of women. There were always good jokes to be had at such occasions. They were speaking about a prostitute who apparently lived at Porthinnis.

In reality, their talk had no interest for me though. After all, I was just a contractor at the village. The reality was that despite my wish to plant myself somewhere, I had no long-term affiliation to this place. As an itinerant worker, I had even less of a say. I had no political affiliation, apart from my own. As always, I would try to keep my mouth shut. Notice here I use the word 'try'. I am afraid – as you are starting to know now – I am not always perfect or successful in my aims.

That night, though, the stone slipped back perfectly into its socket inside the fogou. I breathed a sigh of relief as the wall regained its sacred status. I would have Casvellyn to deal with tomorrow or in the days that followed, but he could claim no connection between the stone's return and my movements. For certain, his wondrous druidic seeing (which all the fucking druids boast about all the time) could not see enough into the present world to see me following him or returning the stone to its rightful home. At this I wondered what Annown would think of his desecration of the fogou. Would it have words with him in the afterlife when it came? This was, of course, what he preached. This is what the druids constantly told the people – that their current behaviour would have an effect on their status in the afterlife. Perhaps Casvellyn would argue that what he did was a necessary evil – and that stone circles always have more sway than what fogou-lore says. He'd have justified his actions certainly.

It was back to Remfra's endless narrative then for me – or so I thought. I mentioned before that Kenal's finding of me at Halliggye was the life-changing moment, but in retrospect, it was probably what happened that night – there and then inside the fogou, that was it.

You see, that is when I met her.

This was where my future 'ocean of emotion' truly began.

Do you describe such moments as pre-ordained?

Is it fate?

Is there a time-line on this earth written down for you in which such occasions are meant to happen? I do not know. I still don't know. But happen it did. You see, it still could have happened – and nothing would have come of it. We would have been two beings who met and did nothing more. We all of us have this choice – and yet, I know why it happened. It happened because of her beauty. This, in my experience, is how all strong men lose focus. It deforms us all, and makes limbs go weak. And in the moments that followed, deep in the fogou – momentarily, I forgot who I was and became someone else. But do you know? – I liked that. All my life I had spent constructing dwellings which allowed transformations to happen. Now I would have my own.

Enclosed in a brown cloak and hood, into the fogou came the young woman I had seen earlier on. This was Howel's bride-to-be. It felt, at that moment, like she had stumbled into another world, fallen into a hole in the ground that had swallowed her up and wouldn't let her go. Though her movements earlier that I had watched at distance had been graceful, inside she slightly stumbled down the steps into the souterrain. She laughed at her own folly – always a good sign.

"Am I allowed in?" were her first words.

She startled me with this request for permission. Fogous weren't out of bounds for anyone. You could visit them day and night – any time you might want to converse with the as yet unborn or the dead. They were unlocked and unguarded. This openness made them what they were.

For a while I could not speak. She had silenced me – yes me, then a young man full of life, and she still does – when this now grumpy old teller of tales thinks of her.

She had an aura to her to which I was instantly drawn. She was a flame to the moth of me. The air inside the chamber, a little damp now from the rain falling, was infused with her perfume that ignited something I had not felt before. She was a world away from stone and earth.

"Am I?" she repeated.

"Anyone is allowed... The same rules apply here as at Chysauster..." I said.

"You know of me then?"

"Everyone knows of you here at Carn Euny. You are the talk of the town..."

She laughed at this, blushing slightly.

"The talk of the town eh? Well, I had to get out. I couldn't stand it in there any more."

"In where?"

"In the bridal house. So many clucking and fussing women. My mother, my aunts and all the women from this village who must oversee the preparations. Endless bathings and advice and what to do and what not to do. It was claustrophobic."

"I can imagine," I said.

"I argued I needed some air and then slipped away – to explore."

Such behaviour in a young woman would have been frowned upon by both communities. Young women were to be protected and not seen. They were certainly not allowed to wander an unfamiliar village alone.

"So this is where I am to be wed?"

I nodded, looking around at the walls.

"It's a fine fogou," I stated. "My father Donyerth built it."

"And you?"

"Well, I am here to change it, to enhance it so to speak – for Howel..."

"Yes, I have heard. My father speaks much about Howel's vision of them as a defence – a shelter in the event of an attack. He's greatly impressed by this."

I laughed a little.

"Then you know all about them?"

"I know so little really," she said. "All I know is that I am to be married to Howel, and that is that. A decision has been made. "

At this she turned her eyes down and then switched her line of questioning.

"What are you doing out here?"

This caught me off guard. I didn't answer at first, resting my left hand on the fogou wall.

She noted its unusual shape, but there was not the usual revulsion. Instead, she saw something different. I could see it her gaze.

"Nothing much," I said, telling a lie. "Just checking all is well... you know,

74

with the rain and so on."

"I see."

By now, the young woman had taken off her hood and I couldn't help but notice the beauty of her face and hair. She had skin as flawless as kaolin and her curly black hair tumbled down her back. I could see why Howel had wanted her as his queen. There was an awkward pause; a rooting around on both our behalves to say the right thing.

"You're Voog, aren't you?" she asked eventually.

"How do you know my name? You've not been here at Carn Euny for five minutes."

"Some of the other women were talking about you. They were joking about who they fancied.... Your name came up. They said the fogou-builder was quite tasty."

I laughed. My left hand jerked at the absurdity of what she'd just offered.

"Who said that?"

"Oh you know... just women.... There's nothing quite like a wedding to get women talking about men."

Already, I liked her headstrong nature. Although a piece of bartering between one kingdom and another, she was clearly no meek chess piece and no compliant offering. She had a lot of spirit to her. There was an edge of playfulness too. As you know, I have already explained to you that before this moment, I had – throughout my apprenticeship – no real interest in the opposite sex.

"He be too into his stone fur ee t'nawtice girls," my father had once remarked. "Besides what girl would want ee – with..."

This however, was different. I freely confess that from the moment I saw her, I absolutely wanted her.

All the rules then, of our community, were upturned in these moments underground. Was Annown watching? If it was, I cared little. I'd take any punishment in the Otherworld to continue this flirtation a little longer.

"How do you feel about getting married?"

She bent down to enter the beehive chamber and explore it. From the echo inside came her voice.

"What choice do I have? None really. As a chieftain's daughter I knew my path from a young age. Eventually I'd be married off – the same as my mother before me. Come, you know the ways of our people..."

"I do. I have seen a lot..." I said, "in my travels... But do you love Howel?"

"Love him? Love him! Now, let me see, I've hardly known him – so I don't think I can possibly love him yet."

She paused, becoming more reflective.

"We are supposed to grow to love. I may not fancy him now but in time, maybe I will. Maybe if he takes care of me, looks after me, cares for me, then...."

"...things will change," I interjected.

"Yes – things will change. I will grow to love this community, this place – and forget my previous life. It is all arranged."

"Do you want that?" I asked her straight.

She did not answer. For a few seconds we let the rain continue outside. Faintly, we could also hear the parliament building still at it. I realised how close the fogou was to it. At any second, one of the retinue inside could come outside and take a leak nearby (sacred space mattered little when you had a full bladder) and hear voices in the fogou. Her presence would take some explaining.

"I should go," I offered. "For your sake."

"For my sake, Master Voog!?"

"Yes."

"Don't you mean for your own too?"

This was a question that was unexpected.

"It's not right," I argued, "for you to be here... with me. I am contracted to Howel to rebuild this fogou. You know how these things might look."

"These things?" she laughed. "Master Voog, I have merely stumbled upon you here. I don't know what on earth you mean."

She brushed past me as she came back through the entrance portal of the beehive hut. The brush was so close to me I could smell her hair.

Shit. This was getting worse for me. Clearly, this young woman might come to cause me problems.

What fucking wasp's nest had I blindly stumbled into here?

Was it just me, or was she the same with other men? Either way, I knew that my presence at Carn Euny was now jeopardised. Compromised within the matter of a few minutes, I was wishing many things at that moment. I was wishing that I'd not accepted the job here, then that I'd not come out into the night to replace a stone some fuckwit of a druid had taken away, and that I'd not – absolutely not – engaged in conversation with this woman. I should have left sooner, before she had a chance to pry and talk to me. Most of all, I was wishing that I could kiss her, over and over again, and feel her delicious body against mine. Oh yes, I had noticed. Her legs, thighs and bottom all excited me. I could only imagine her breasts, but knew I would be fixated upon mentally recreating them for days to come. She would leave all this with me.

I couldn't see it then, but my ocean was about to wash over me.

The more I thought about her, the more assured I became in knowing I had to leave the fogou.

"I'm going," I said, my voice betraying every single stimulated nerve inside me.

"Suit yourself," she said flirtatiously.

But then I didn't go. I needed one more piece of information.

"What's your name?" I demanded.

She didn't answer.

"What's you name?"

"You really need that? I thought you'd have known by now."

"I need to know," I stated.

"It is Orla. I am Orla, daughter of Cadreth."

Orla. I instantly said it over and over in my mind,

"Orla, soon-to-be-wife of Howel," she sighed.

I knew right there and then that I didn't want her to become Howel's wife. I wanted her as my own. This came to me like a capstone whacking me in the head from a loosened guide rope. Although I wanted to say it, I couldn't. All the stones of the chamber tumbled about my head, clattering and turning. In that instant, I knew I was no longer just Voog, a humble fogou-builder. Something had changed that was far-reaching. For the first time, I could see into my heart.

"I'm going," I stated once again.

This time I meant it. Crouched, I walked toward the western entrance and left her alone in the chamber.

Back at Kenal's roundhouse, the collective were sleeping, Remfra snoring louder than most. On my bed, I replayed my conversation with this woman over and over again, looking for insight and understanding. Consequently, I slept little and thought much. This Orla, daughter of Cadreth, was about to turn everything upside down. She was going to make my secure land and stone turn overnight into the uncertainty of tide and wave.

OH ANNOWN, THE PIECE IN this puzzle that I had not fully understood nor fully contemplated, was that my mother had not been killed. This came as a complete surprise. My supposition was that between Casvellyn and this man Howel they had neatly had her executed. I had always felt that her transgression and the shame that she constantly cast upon the communities of Carn Euny and Chysauster would no longer be tolerated – but in fact, events were a good deal more complicated. In my younger years, I had put together a whole set of reconstructions as to how they had done this. Had they dumped her in the ocean – tying her to some weighty rock – so that her lungs filled with water? Had they dispatched her off the cliffs at Treryn Dinas, dashing her brains on the rocks below? Had they cut her up with wood axes and fed her to the boars? These and a thousand other scenarios had entered my mind. When Kenal informed me of the actual truth, for a moment I wished I had never asked. You will soon see why.

Given her situation in the aftermath of the discovery of her affair with my father, with 'him', my mother had been silenced. She would definitely not have been staying in Carn Euny. She had contaminated sacred ground there. She had offended the royal line of Howel. She had insulted the morals of the community. Well, let's be honest, she was a fucking devious whore, wasn't she? Thus she would return to Chysauster with her parents. She spent nine months with no contact from anyone else before my eventual arrival. Cadreth, in effect, locked her away. He put her into solitary confinement. That would teach her a lesson. All hope of alliance with Howel had to be put on hold.

I had suspected this. What I didn't realise though was that while she waited there, alone, and in the aftermath of my arrival, just how much she resented what had happened to her. I had assumed she just took and accepted what the male order of the villages said. She would have to have conformed to what the druids dictated (they dealt with all issues of morality). They certainly would have had a word with her. But all that suppression and restriction, all that shame and hatred, brought in her a new kind of energetic bile and, consequently, a need for revenge. She planned and perfected her assault. According to Kenal, and he told me this in hesitant tones, that is why she had tried to kill Howel.

Yes, my own mother was killer, murderer, assassin.

Whilst she had first tolerated and accommodated the community's wishes, in the end, I suspect, she felt it was Howel who had wrecked her life. He was the one to whom she'd been palmed off. He'd been the law towards her lover. He'd cast him into exile. It is easy to judge hate when we do not experience it, and although this information at first appalled me (each day now, dealing with my own love, as you shall shortly see), as I have grown older, I find it easier to understand. When something so precious is taken out of your reach, you can settle, and fester, and die a little every day, or you can react. You can clutch life back again. I suspect that is why my mother acted the way she did. I still have no real knowledge of where she obtained the poison. In Kenal's view, the arsenic had been gained from the moors above Marghas Vyan, where it was a by-product of the unscrupulous smelters. Given the grime and agony of work there, many would be prepared to sell on the substance for a few coins. Such tin-streams were always home to black markets and terror.

Somehow, when I was still a toddler, and unknowingly, placing me forever into the arms of my grandmother, one day, my mother followed the same track I did and, disguised, headed towards Carn Euny. There, by duplicitous means, she was able to enter Howel's retinue, and lace his drink with the arsenic. Kenal had not been there (he'd been on patrol, awaiting a possible Saxon incursion), but he heard of events. Howel had imbibed greatly of the poison, and it was apparently only through the swift actions of Casvellyn and his box of herbs and potions, that he was revived and saved. He had already been a broken man after the cataclysm of his wedding. Now, his skin had turned grey and his veins still raced with traces of the poison. In an instant, the kitchen staff were surrounded, and my mother revealed. Howel spent six months recovering from the attempt and, so I was told, would never be well again.

I cried at this – and still do, when I think upon it. The first revelation had been bad enough. Now, a second murderous transgression hung around her neck.

"You must understand, she decided her fate that day," offered Kenal. "It is hard for me to say it to you, but to the people, now she was both whore and witch. Not a good combination."

Further shame rained down on the stained house of Cadreth.

"So, what happened to her next?" I asked this Kenal.

"Do you really wish to know?"

Given what he had already told me, there was a moment, a tiny period of time, when actually, I wanted him to stop. He paused in his telling, waiting for permission to continue. I already felt tenfold the hurt of my grandmother. I understood now why Cadreth had disowned me. I was of that same bastard, murderous stock.

I had to resolve all this with what I now understood about myself. I was trying to unpick the aftermath of her passion. It is passion I have felt myself of late. It is that which made me want to know her true fate. That same passion ran through me.

You see, in the years that I had been alive, the world had changed a good deal. The Vikings no longer troubled us. In fact, we'd formed pacts with them – to work as one and resist the imperialism of the Saxons. Can you believe that? The *Ancredhor Mor* fighting alongside us. Men we once slaughtered now stood in our ranks. We fought shoulder to shoulder, arm in arm. The strategic issue was that the Saxons had given up on some of the landward assault. Instead, in fighting the Britons in the east who had left for Armorica, the Saxons had taken to the sea. And so for all the time I could remember, it was now they who attacked from the coast.

The whore and witch that was my mother had been a convenient bartering tool. Shamed and now ousted as poisoner, it was during one such treaty with the Saxons that she was handed over to them. You see, despite treachery, adultery and everything else, she kept her looks.

"Men adored her," Kenal had remarked. "And when the druids said it was the best course of action, her fate was sealed."

"The milpreve?" I asked.

He nodded.

The Saxons prized Brittonic women. They idolised them. Thus she was sold to them, as slave and breeder; a symbol of the conquest of the truculent west. Such pacts allowed Carn Euny and Chysauster to be left in peace. She was a sacrifice worth paying.

"Who traded her?"

"Need you ask?"

I knew it was Howel and Casvellyn.

As I learned of this story, I prayed that she somehow got through the ordeal of this. I hoped that she took consolation from my arrival and that somewhere out there in the world, my father felt her spirit, and continued to love her.

With all of this, although she was lost, I finally felt I had found her. Now all I had to do was find him.

"Thank you," I said to Kenal, "You have helped me so much."

But I had been impatient. Already I had romanced her. In my head, she was both martyr and heroine.

Then, he told me. A year later, news had come to Carn Euny that my mother, unable to cope with the rest of her life in Saxon chains, had taken her own life. Her body was never found. She'd not be placed in any fogou and be subject to ceremony.

She'd have no safe journey to you, Annown.

6

Carving of the Goddess Sedna on walrus tusk ivory, Nonortalik, Kujalleq Municipality, Greenland, 9th to 10th Centuries CE
From 986 CE, Greenland's west coast was colonized by Norwegians in two settlements on fjords near the southwestern-most tip of the island. Sedna is the goddess of the sea and marine animals in Inuit mythology. Although the image here is native, the work is characteristic of Norwegian carving from this period. A number of versions of the Sedna legend exist. In one, her father, the creator-god takes her out to sea and throws her over the side of his kayak. As she clings to the sides, he chops the fingers off her hands and she sinks underwater, becoming the ruler there. The carving is made on a section of tusk from a walrus *(Odobenus rosmarus)*. Courtesy of the Kujalleq Municipality Museum.

THE INTIMACY OF MY IMMEDIATE world at that time was both its triumph and also its failing. Lord Howel's bright kingdom was in so many ways the perfect vision of civilisation – and perhaps, as I reflect upon it from afar, I should have been more grateful to have been a part of it. Yet, it was also highly claustrophobic, in that everyone knew everyone else's business. Seemingly, each blade of grass newly grown was subject to gossip. You see, guarded secrets are impossibilities in roundhouses. One soon becomes acquainted with the nuances and events of others and their lives are etched in your own. Even the children of Kenal's retinue, I came to know well – which toys they liked carved (the wooden dolphins I made for them they adored the most) and all the places they liked to play (the woods towards Boscarn were always a popular destination). Once they came to know me, then my body became part of their fun (I was a stomping giant to the toddlers); they imitated my tools and pretended that they too, were builders of fogous, making camps and underground playhouses in the landscape all around. I soon became known for my generosity towards them and this endeared me to mothers, fathers and siblings. This intimacy had then, some benefit, but again, for the following few days, I could barely concentrate on anything. The erotic vision of Orla had changed all that.

From the start, I recognised that I had to conceal what I felt for her. I was desperately worried that a look in my eye, or a brief flicker of affection would be revealed if anyone mentioned her name. My secret feelings would soon be known. This was how roundhouses worked. Their thick granite walls surrounded you, and took away your individuality. To be honest, it was unlikely that I would see her again before the wedding day. Females getting ready for marriage were closeted away from the rest of society – to somehow ensure a kind of purity before matrimony. There was not much I could do.

Of course, the encounter with Orla had turned my world view upside down. I was going to find it hard to continue my work here at Carn Euny with her presence. In the days afterwards, there were several times when I almost went to Howel to explain how I felt I should move on. There were other builders who could be there in a day or so – craftsmen just as good as me. But then he'd require an explanation for the termination of my employment, and I had no reason to give him one. Perhaps I could make something up about the delay in starting the construction. In fact though, as you have heard, I was loved by the community. Such a leaving would instantly make him suspicious of my movements. I'd never work in his realm again – and now that meant the landscape from here to Chysauster. Perhaps I had to cope with it then, do the work wanted, and then move on. In the distant future, I was thinking of heading east again. There, I wouldn't easily forget her, but at least she would not be in my face every day. I felt I could cope with that. She'd stay a fixation; only one that I could not touch or reach for.

My immediate difficulty was that the community's wedding preparations were becoming the sole focus of everyone's activity. It was the kind of unwanted excitement that induced me to go walking amongst the cairns. There, whilst solitary, I could contemplate both life and death, and everything in between. This meant love and sex. I could also avoid the frantic activity of women preparing rich foodstuffs for the feasting, as well as the men assembling timber for a massive celebratory bonfire that could probably be seen from the western islands. Children completed mock weddings, anticipating the forthcoming festival. You only got this much fun normally around the midsummer, or the marking of the winter solstice. Remfra was hard at work too – preparing a brooding and passionate wedding epithalamion which he wanted to test out on any individual who would listen. He was comparing Orla and Howel's love with stories of the ancient kings and queens, who once ruled Lethowsow. I sought peace and solace away from all of this. I do not know what they thought of me in these moments. My only excuse was that I was out, sizing up stone – the fogou-builder's only excuse when he wanted to be alone and leave behind everything else.

Back in the fogou, Casvellyn and the two other druids from Chysauster were at work. In the beehive hut, they were making the sacred marriage bed for Howel and his bride. I discovered them there after my walk. Casvellyn welcomed me into the operation, and cautiously introduced me to his comrades

Selus and Genaius. Selus was a tiny and very old man, with no teeth, who could do little in terms of actual work, but appeared to be the chief druid of Chysauster. Genaius was a younger man, perhaps in his thirties, with a twitch in his eye, but with an eager attitude to please his elders. Whilst Selus showed some signs of senility in his ritual, clearly Genaius had much time for Casvellyn. It was going to be Casvellyn who, like Howel in terms of politics and economy, would be the spiritual leader in this new super-kingdom. Genaius clearly knew this. When introduced to the doddery Selus, he peered at me long and hard.

"Knew your father. Yes. Knew your father," he said. "You have his nose and eyes. His eye for stone too, I hear. I've heard that."

Genaius talked a little to me of the proposed changes to the fogou, which obviously Casvellyn had informed him about. His was a gentle line of enquiry, different to Casvellyn, purely questioning me about the ambition of the project. As we chatted, the druids carefully prepared the space. The whole of the souterrain began to smell of dried herbs, which partially had been brought here from Chysauster, and which would then be conjoined with those of Carn Euny. This was the way marriage was made. The union of smell and fragrance matched the union of the individual man and woman, but also of each family and tribe. When the druids placed each herb down onto the bed, they usually spoke an incantation suggesting its qualities and wishes for the marriage. Many had already been completed. On the floor were elder and fennel, meadowsweet and sage. Genaius prepared valerian and thyme, while Selus fussed over the quality of the burdock.

"Tidn' very good at all," he muttered. "Not good at all. It'll have to do though. Have to do."

In the next half an hour, further plants were produced and placed down. Among them was wolf's claw, which Selus insisted on calling druid's flour – its old name. Casvellyn worked on the arnica, while Genaius offered a generous posy of calendula.

"This is the most important of them all," a smiling Genaius said loudly, and then as an aside to me, "It is the herb of love magic."

He nodded, knowingly.

It was a magic I didn't really wish to think of, but it was one I was forced to accept was real.

Gradually, the smells of these herbs and others mingled. I had to admit, these two from Chysauster knew their stuff. Cumin had even been brought in (specifically to guarantee a happy life for the married couple). That was a herb you could only obtain from traders who came from the far south. It seemed that nothing was too expensive for this union.

Lastly, all three of them scattered lavender, the smell of which consumed me. I openly admit that it was a fragrance in which I wanted to dreamily cavort with Orla. At this thought, I found myself hardening in my undergarments. I would cover her body in lavender flowers and tenderly kiss the nape of her neck. For a few glorious seconds, I was in here with her.

My growing erection was soon quashed however, by Casvellyn, leaving the beehive hut and examining the wall of the fogou. I followed him. I managed to catch the look of surprise on his face as he discovered the stone so ritually placed at Boscawen Ûn was now back in its rightful surrounds. His hand moved to the stone, perhaps contemplating the surprise magic, or indeed, the human hand, that had brought it back.

"Problem?" I enquired. "Do you approve of the wall?"

Casvellyn didn't answer.

"I mean, will it be fit for Howel's marriage?"

Again, there was no response.

The druid felt his long beard and then brushed his right hand over his lips, as if having to carefully moderate what he wanted to say. Had he now recognised that I had followed him? Was I becoming a real problem for Casvellyn in his ambitions? If I was, he couldn't say anything, as by now the elderly Selus had shuffled out into the main chamber.

"Casvellyn – it is time for the milpreve," he said solemnly.

Selus jolted Casvellyn out of his gaze at the wall.

"The wall is fine," he eventually said; his tone only marginally indicating an irritation with events.

However, as he passed me, I noticed Casvellyn lowered his eyes. When druids did this, you knew you were in the shit.

So now, they were onto the milpreve. The milpreve were so sacred I was not permitted to stay. Selus made a gesture for me to leave, but I already knew what I should do.

"I'll go," I said to him.

Most fogou-builders deal with milpreve at some point in their career. Let me explain. Milpreve are sometimes known in my locality as the *glain*, and they are the druid's most sacred items. Each druid carried one – and so a total of three would be placed in the beehive hut. The *glain* is a magical stone, glassy in its feel, which has a naturally occurring hole through the middle of it. Some druids call them the serpent's egg or the snake's egg. As hard as it may be to believe, they truly thought that the stones were formed by large numbers of snakes congregating together; the perforation in the middle caused by their collective forked tongues. Such stones were difficult to find, though most often they could be found after rock falls near the coast. It was then that the druids sent out the *glain*-hunters to find them. *Glain*-hunters had to work by moonlight only. It was rumoured they were found in lands far away and specially brought here. *Glain* gathered in the daytime would lose their power. Such hunters were supposedly always well-paid.

Me – well, I was less convinced of their serpent origin. Any fogou-builder will tell you that the rocks of the earth sometimes twist and form incredible shapes: such crystals and myriad formations that one might think they are formed by magic alone. Any tin-streamer will tell you that. In my experience, the earth makes marvels at every move and so to my mind, they were just natural. Given their sacred nature however, I wasn't about to tell the druids that then. Later, I might have wanted to shout their foolishness across the expanse of an ocean, at gulls, guillemots and gannets, but today, their lore was too powerful and too prevalent for me to do anything.

I knew what they'd be doing. There would be some ritual peering through the hole, in order to see spirit traps or any difficulties ahead for the marriage. Their minds would be focused on Annown and what would be permitted in this life. Then the stones would be carefully tossed in the air, accompanied by hissing before being caught in their cloaks. They should never hit the earth as that would return them to their original state. Sometimes, ritual water (fetched from a local spirit well) would be poured through the hole; this always to indicate the passage of semen into the woman's womb, thus giving a blessing to fecundity and fertility. Depending on how long each druid had the *glain*, they might sometimes be encased in metal – or even gold. Frankly, it was for this weirdness that the druids of our world got paid and were provided for. Aside from the gathering of mistletoe, the *glain* ceremony was just about the most sacred act a druid could complete. After the ceremony, the milpreve would be placed together on top of the ritual herbs and plants and left there. Occasionally, they'd be examined by each druid for any cracks or even worse, for collapse, since this would surely mean the marriage was destined to failure. A broken *glain* meant a broken future; their power was that significant. These apple-sized rocks determined much in our ideology.

As a divining tool, they worked beyond such ceremonies as this. Often, their most productive use was before battles. The druids could supposedly see the future through them. They had been used at Gwithian when I fought there, and although it might seem like guesswork, the druids had advised on the strategy to be taken. The milpreve had proved right, and the method of attack suggested by the druids was correct. *Glain* were so powerful that once in a druid's clutches, the normal people of these villages wouldn't go near them. I usually avoided them, but in my line of work, as you will imagine, sometimes I had to deal with their presence. This was one of those moments.

The *glain* ceremonies usually lasted an hour or so, depending on how much weight was put on their divination. The likelihood here was that it would take a little longer, as Selus seemed much convinced of their properties. Usually, the older the druid, the more they relied on them. So I sat on the soft ground a few feet away from the fogou and let them get on with it. I heard the trilogy of hissings that accompanied the ritual and listened to their boring incantations and chanting. Compared to the dull and rainy weather of the last few days, a spring sunshine had lifted over the village, and I welcomed its warmth. From the fogou's location, I looked down to the women's roundhouse where I knew Orla would be. Just as the druids were completing their part in the wedding preparations, she'd be doing her own. Such lore was secretive to men, but there would be presents and kindly advice from the flabby-bellied middle-aged women who'd seen it all, and then wisdom from the bearded and lined elderly women, along the lines of 'give and take was everything in a marriage'. Orla's matron, and only her, would confer with the druids over the marriage chamber's preparations.

I was thinking through all of this, when a strong hand fell upon my shoulder, accompanied by the following words: "Voog, you look lost."

The playful tone was instantly recognisable. It was Howel. I turned to face him. Already he was sat next to me, his left arm wrapped around me.

"Lost?" I offered.

"Lost in your thoughts... I suppose a fogou-builder always has the right to do this..." he joked. "You do create other worlds in the midst of the real world."

"No... Lord Howel. I'm not lost. I was just enjoying the sun for a moment. I can't go inside. Casvellyn is at work with the milpreve."

"Ah. The milpreve eh? Magical snake eggs. Are Selus and Genaius with him?"

"Yes. They're both in there with him."

I looked at Howel. So, this was the man who was going to have Orla for his own. She could do worse, I imagined. Howel was kindly, generous and loving. This was part of the problem for me. If Howel had been evil and violent, then my situation would have been easier. I admired Howel. He had become a close friend, to the extent that an employer and employee can become friends. Joy pumped through his body. Here was a man entirely certain of his destiny. Not only did he know that he was about to marry the most beautiful woman in the peninsula; most likely his marriage would confer an air of respectability and status that within a few years would see him becoming overlord of the whole of the west. Greatness was his destiny. If any man could lead a people against the *Ancredhor Mor*, or the Saxons, then he was the man to do it. Such a thought twisted my already-gnarled guilt into further knots. I raged at him for not understanding this woman's position and for marrying someone who did not love him for the right reasons. I could do nothing though. I was helpless.

"Let's hope the milpreve's omen is good eh?" said Howel. "Otherwise I shall be in for a bumpy ride."

"It will be fine," I stated. "Don't worry."

Howel removed his arm from my shoulder.

"Voog, I've neglected you of late. My mind has been so filled with the ceremony and the agreements with Cadreth that I've not had time for you. Kenal says you've been out walking... Looking for stone eh?"

"Yes – well, I like to see what's available."

"Of course, and next week, when all of this marriage stuff is out of the way, I'll have every man in the village at your disposal to move rock here. I've rollers, pulleys and ropes all ready for you. Anything you want, and it's yours. Just let me know. You know how important this project is to me."

"I will," I said.

"Cadreth rates you, you know. I showed him your drawings – what we proposed. You should meet him later. I'm holding a stag night – to celebrate my last night of 'freedom'. You should come. I'd like you there. Plenty of free food and drink..."

"I'm not much of a drinker these days. Really."

"What? A young man like yourself? Come on, it'll be fun. Kenal's got musicians planned. Dancing and singing until the small hours. The beer we've been brewing will knock your head off."

"Perhaps..." I ventured.

At this moment, Casvellyn and the two other druids emerged from the fogou, somewhat saving me the further embarrassment of having to openly decline Howel's request. Howel broke off from his stag-night deluge and turned instead to the three white-clad figures walking towards him.

"Are the omens good my friends?" he asked them gingerly.

"Very good," replied a croaky-voiced Selus. "We have left the milpreve in there for you. They will bring you and your bride great fortune."

"The *glain* suggest all is well," added Casvellyn. "I would expect nothing less."

"Good... And is the fogou well-prepared?"

"All laid with herbs my lord," answered Genaius.

"Then we are all set. We must have Orla's matron look over the fogou. Shall we fetch her?"

Selus and Genaius nodded and bowed, putting their hands together to praise Howel and his wishes.

"Shall we?" said Howel, giving a nod in the direction of the women's roundhouse.

Casvellyn did not move. At this moment, I noticed he was carrying a bundle of plants; perhaps further herbs for the fogou.

"Casvellyn?" said Howel. "Are you coming?"

"In just a moment my lord. First I must speak with Master Voog."

"Very well. See you there."

Casvellyn nodded and both he and I watched Howel and the two Chysauster druids make their way to Orla's household. When they were out of both earshot and sight, Casvellyn came closer to me.

The druid was now my problem. He seemed to note a change in me. This was the problem with druids. Although the fuckers could not always be guaranteed to have second sight, they had a kind of wisdom and insight that was both scary and accurate. Like rats, they understood human psychology. That was their true skill. And it was as if that day, Casvellyn had a notion of me. It was like he magically passed his hand through my chest and grabbed hold of my heart. For that reason, I hated him. I hated the fact that he could see into me – as if my skin were a clear window. I watched his eyes. They could read my soul.

"Try this..." suggested Casvellyn, whispering his words.

He passed me a ragged bundle of vegetation tied with string.

"...if you want to escape."

"Escape?" I asked.

"From whatever it is that troubles you, Master Voog."

The bastard. He knew.

"What is it?"

"You've no doubt seen it before. It is watercress. Expensive. I have it brought here from the east. I use it to... um... alter my mind. Yes – for a trance-state."

"You think I need that?"

"I do. We all need trance-state at certain times," said Casvellyn knowingly.

I'd heard stories of the druids taking watercress for kicks, for insight, and for vision quests, but had always dismissed them as hearsay.

"Fast for three days, then only eat the cress. The whole lot mind. Then you will experience a different world – the world you seek away from this one, yes?"

I looked down at the bundle of peppery leaves and stems. This was it, was it? – the solution to my guilt and shame: a bit of greenery that would make me feel queasy for a few hours and then give me a hangover for the next few days after eating it.

"Think of it as one option," said Casvellyn.

"And the other?" I requested.

But Casvellyn did not answer.

"I don't need it," I said.

"Carry it with you – as a kind of insurance wherever you go... If things ever get bad, so bad that..."

Casvellyn didn't finish his sentence. Recalling this now, I wonder then if he really had already seen what would come to pass, or whether he was just testing my reaction. For certain though, he had noticed a change. It was if he could read my love for Orla as easily as if I had shouted it from the gorse-hatted top of Carn Brea.

"What do you mean?"

The druid shrugged his shoulders.

"No – come on, what do you mean?"

"Only you will know what I mean."

There they go again. Fucking mystic druid-speak. He began to walk away from me.

This time, I reached for Casvellyn's arm, and grabbed it aggressively. I pulled him back towards me. Instantly, I realised I'd offended him. People like me weren't meant to touch or disrespect druids in this way. It broke the code; the order of things. Casvellyn hardly needed to say anything. His eyes fell on my soil-stained hand that had grabbed his pure white sacking cloth into a fist. I let go of him. My father would have reprimanded me harshly for such a transgression.

"I will see you at the wedding," said Casvellyn, now dignified once more.

At once he seemed to know it was me who had replaced the stone in the fogou wall, and that it was me who was about to bring chaos down on Carn Euny. His distance and dignity said it all. I knew I was on borrowed time.

I was tempted to leave the watercress there, and let it mingle with the other plants and herbs ready for the wedding, but instead I took the bundle back to my ante-room and left it on a wicker rack. There, it beckoned me for the next few hours and throughout the night. The more I contemplated my situation, the more a trance-like state sounded a possible way out. A vision-quest might lock me out of Orla's gaze. Maybe Kenal would find me out of my head and cast me out into the misty wilderness of the moors as a true exile. Yet despite the watercress's temptation to take me away from the temptations of the flesh,

I resisted. I made an excuse for Kenal to explain to Howel that I felt unwell and that I could not be at his stag-night. Their singing, shrieks of laugher and drunken antics kept the village awake for much of the night. Such behaviour was tolerated for he was Howel, the King.

Meanwhile the hallucinogenic cress would come in useful, but not just yet. As dawn broke, a tide of light eased over Carn Euny the next morning. I knew it was the day of Howel's wedding to Orla, and I needed to keep the clearest of heads. I was trying very hard to not allow myself to go to a place that I shouldn't. This was both the ultimate terror and the ultimate risk. I was standing on a parapet. I was on the edge of a tilting logan rock. I was on a slippery quay, high above where the wild waves broke. It was a place where only fools went.

DEAREST ANNOWN,

YOU KNOW THE very dark of me now. You know my black interior. You know the shadows that cross my heart. You see the crows and ravens there, cawing their song. Will I still be fit for return to you eventually – all these long years on?

So far, I realise, I have been as slippery as a fish caught of a morning down Penberth Cove. I have not yet given you my name. I pick it for you right now: it is Blejan. It means 'flower'. My mother Orla gave it to me on the day that I was born.

Did you know that upon my entry into this world, I wasn't allowed inside your fogou? Neither the ones at Carn Euny or Chysauster were deemed appropriate. She had broken trust with you – so they said. Fogous were for women who conceived children in the right way. They weren't for slags like my mother. And yet, what was paradoxical about this was that I had descended from a line of fogou builders. My family built and maintained them. If ever there was ever anything that belonged to me, it was them. Thus, through my oppressed childhood, fogous were always just out of my reach. I could see them, smell them, even touch them – but I could not enter them. I was tainted. Despite knowing the finality of my mother's fate, although I did not expect it, Orla's tainted life, her beauty and her passion, were yet to have an effect in some unexpected ways. Howel's guilt would make it that way.

The night Kenal revealed all of this to me cleared away so much of the haze that had accompanied my early years. I was resolved, however, not to tell my grandmother of what I had discovered. For now, it would be better that way. I could test and observe her – and see how she might react. You may say that is cruel, but not when you consider how much I had demanded from her over the years, and how little she had told me. Kenal genuinely feared for his life over what he had revealed to me. I was not to say anything to anyone. He had put absolute trust in me.

He let slip that in times past, this Howel had been an impressive leader, one committed to development of the community. That had changed much of late, he indicated. His attitude had become bullish, dour and dictatorial. Whereas once he consulted with advisors and elders, he now made instant decisions. Sometimes, strategies in warfare had been undertaken that Kenal simply disagreed with. There was not much he could do: a village under a peace treaty with the Saxons would hardly be committed to any internal revolution.

Most of this I learnt travelling back with him on horseback, in returning to Carn Euny. He had been kind enough to take me over the moorland, both to ease the journey for me, and to make sure I returned to Chysauster for the following morning. If I didn't appear, I would have only caused my grandmother further anxiety and perhaps the generation of a search party; neither of which I wanted to incite.

"I dare say your father would not expect us to be having this conversation," offered Kenal. "The last time I saw him, I am afraid to say, I was very cruel to him. I wonder what he would make of you."

"My father doesn't know of me."

"Does anyone know if he's still alive? Does Melwyn speak of him?"

"I don't know. She won't mention his name."

"I have to be honest with you, Blejan. Let me level with you. I have asked after him. You hear things – about others. But nothing has ever come back to me about him. It is as if he has disappeared off the edge of the world..."

Kenal lowered me from his horse.

"He's out there somewhere," I said. "One day I'll find him too."

Kenal gave me a look that didn't hold out much hope.

"I'll come back sometime," he said. "Maybe to see your grandmother... In the meantime, you take care, little one."

It was with a swagger that I walked back into Chysauster, suddenly all grown up. Before, I was innocent. Now, I had experience. The issue was how I was going to put this information to use.

It now being night-time and the village still, I thought I would chance it and try entering the fogou I had been so long banned from and warned about. Kenal had delivered me at the southern end of the village, where the structure was located. It was only a little way from one of the roundhouses, in which a noisy gathering was taking place. In the darkness the vug-hole looked fearsome, a gaping mouth into the earth. I knew that it extended some distance under-ground. Despite what I had always been told, I was going to enter it. I was going to claim it and make in my own. In so doing, I would reconnect with my mother and father. Maybe, somewhere, they were watching. I stepped down into its space. The floor of this one ran upwards under the hill. Inside, I could almost feel the earth pulling me. Somehow, it was as it was meant to be. Kenal had helped me to reclaim it and make it resonate with me.

"Your father was the best fogou builder," he had said. "He was the one everyone wanted. That's why Howel got him to come to Carn Euny."

But I resolved not to be silent. I would not remain as still as this underground place. I readily tested out my grandmother in the days that followed.

"Grandma, what do you think of Howel?"

"What?"

"You know, Lord Howel – who runs Carn Euny. What do you make of him?"

My grandma nervously responded to this line of questioning.

"He is a good leader from what Cadreth said of him."

"Really? I heard he was poisoned... Someone didn't like him. Have you heard that?"

"No," came her response.

The harshness of this assertion was enough to make me stop for the moment. Later though, I advanced the questioning still further, now toying with her.

"Did Cadreth get on with him?"

"Who?"

"Howel."

"Yes, they remained good friends, despite..."

"Despite what?"

"It doesn't matter."

Occasionally, over the next few months I would mention his name again. Grandma Melwyn always shut the conversation down, though she was rapidly running out of ways of avoiding my interrogations. We had moved through the winter and Genaius had led the community's winter solstice celebrations. Com-pared to what they had been in previous years, these were somewhat sparse and bare. Even the bonfires were tardy and poor. The stories and poems the bards sung and recited were not a patch on previous times. Innovation had been lost. Our spirit seemed dampened by Saxon stewardship. I heard the druid's exhortations to the four corners, his hope for continued peace and that the com-ing light would bring us a good harvest. The way Genaius said those words, though, was as uncommitted as I had ever seen.

"He's useless," said Grandma Melwyn. "He's got no passion. It's like he doesn't believe any more."

So passion did matter to her? This was a revelation. Maybe deep inside her, there was something of my mother and me that I had not noticed hitherto. I even wondered if, at some point, she had been willing to help my father and my mother.

Then, some strange news came through. Genaius was the one to relay it to my grandmother. I was out weeding vegetables being grown in the courtyard. There were occasional glances over to me to see if I was listening. They were right to be guarded. I was never one to let anything pass me by.

"How strange," said my grandmother. "I never thought it would come to that."

Genaius confirmed that what he was saying was the truth.

He was explaining that this past week, Lord Howel had received some missionaries and, overnight, had converted to Christianity.

7

Thule Inuit artefacts from Iceberg B-19, Atlantic Ocean, 1998
Recent archaeological expeditions have focused on large-sized North Atlantic icebergs (B-19 is 5,390 km²) as sources for decoding the Inuit past. Because of the great age of some icebergs (the compacted ice may be more than 10,000 years old), ice core analysis has revealed a range of artefacts. The artefacts collected here – among them fish hooks, miniature ivory carvings and stone harpoon heads – demonstrate that Arctic peoples have subsisted for thousands of years on the resources of land and sea, prospering under some of the harshest conditions on Earth. The Thule Inuit period operated in the period 5th to 10th-Century CE. Courtesy of National Museum of Natural History, Smithsonian Institution, Washington D.C.

I MUST CONFESS, NOW THAT I know how things transpired that day, then you might expect me to have placed myself anywhere in our land but at Carn Euny, and yet, when I reflect upon it, there is in fact no wise hindsight. Veracious love was motivating me so thoroughly that I can honestly say I would do that same thing again. In life, so as I see it, there are momentary decisions, which flip you one way or the other, and they are decisions which mysteriously find you. You do not find them.

Sometimes you have no choice.

The choice is already made for you. Events of the topsy-turvy day of Howel and Orla's marriage are, however, so seared upon my obsessive mind that even now I constantly replay them when I wake, and when I am trying to sleep. They busily slosh around my skull like a spring tide in a rock zawn.

The wedding had been timed for the optimism of that year's Beltane. I had been so utterly consumed with my own thoughts and activities that I had forgotten the turn of the year. The showers of April were about to give way to fine summer mornings – ideal for building and construction work. Likewise, this was when the days became longer and when the darkness of winter was temporarily forgotten. That morning, the weather was clear – only the lightest of dew upon the ground, and this soon evaporated as the May sun broke over the mound of Caer Bran. It was good sailing weather as we were later to realise.

As you will know by now, nothing takes place in my culture without grave ceremony. It is ceremony that determines all – and marriages were no exception. In fact, when compared to the ceremonies of birth and death, marriage was right up there in terms of high pomp and hallowed circumstance. After all, you already know of the preparations made by the druids. Entry and exit to and from this life were held in high esteem, but so was union. This is why not only did the whole of the community of Chysauster make its way across to Carn Euny, but so did many of the surrounding minor estates. The people there were under the protectorate of Howel or Cadreth, and wanted to publicly show their allegiance to each ruler. A few had started to arrive in the days before, forming random encampments around the village, but many had travelled overnight, and the surrounds were now filled with skin tents and temporary shelters. A busy sense of preparation could be observed wherever one walked. All of this was leading to the day's initial activity of the processions. My world loved procession. Procession was public showing of private emotion. It was always a civil duty to declare love, war or whatever needed to be declared. Thus I knew what the morning would be. Usually, it involved the wedding guests separating into two groups: one male and one female. Each had their specific songs and their ritual duties.

I tagged on the end of the male group – as I knew this to be my duty. With drumming and singing, we made our way (with young boys assisting the elderly men) up around Bartinney Downs, giving praise to the Earth and wishing Howel much success and fertility. On the top of one of the highest tor stones protruding up from the Downs, he would strip to his undergarments and be handed a pair of antlers to wear all the way back down into the village. Whether chieftain or villager, this was the same. Kenal and other men of experience in the village would then tease and humiliate the groom for what he was about to endure, hilariously described in the songs as the 'woeful prison of marriage' and the 'yoke of one nagging woman'. Gifts were also given; this time being an opportunity for the men of Carn Euny to bind with those of Chysauster. In such events, there was always good banter and much amusement.

The women meanwhile – accompanied by the smallest of girls and the most elderly grandmothers – would take Orla to a local well. Men were not allowed to know their rites, and they were only discussed in hushed tones afterwards by the men – but it was thought that there she was bathed and anointed with perfumes and balms. Such an event was the fantasy world of many a man. Each of the women present had to speak, offering Orla their wishes for her marriage. Like the men, there were connections to deer as well. The women's party always wound its way through the deer enclosures. In my world, deer were special creatures who offered blessings to the bride. They were 'fairie cattle' – skittish animals whose dark eyes and shy nature expressed something of the vulnerability of us all. Apparently, the desired experience was that the women would sit in the enclosure and that after a while the more inquisitive does would come to investigate Orla. If so, then much fortune would fall upon Orla in her marriage and that she would be blessed with healthy and unblemished children. In my view it was all about reflection, about the women being still and quiet enough for the deer to come back (a tricky job for some of the gossipy women of Carn Euny and Chysauster). This was obviously something my mother had failed to do – probably because, like me, she liked a chinwag.

So, you see how my world was filled with magic and superstition? Perhaps, as I speak to you here, in this new land, not that much has changed. Indeed, were it not for magic and superstition, I may not have made it across the ocean at all. But let us leave that for now and return to these ceremonies.

By noon, both groups were to be back in the village in order to eat, drink and celebrate. The bride and the groom were not allowed to see each other during this time of preparation. That was strictly forbidden. Inside Howel's grand roundhouse, a great feast had been prepared. Expensive flagons of wine and ale were brought in. The very best meat, dried fruit and fresh vegetables had been assembled. Tasty cuts of boar flesh and venison were being consumed by men in their prime of life, as well as by young boys and old men.

Howel acknowledged me a couple of times that day: first upon Bartinney itself, while the antlers were being fixed to his head. He gave a look that I read as comic, Howel knowing the absurdity of what was taking place and wishing perhaps, that someone might take his place. Secondly, he nodded knowingly, as I took another plateful of food back to one of the benches and socialised with the men of Chysauster. Such food was rare and so it wasn't long before the whole of the serving table had been stripped of its initial offerings. It was clear however, from the frantic cooking over the fire pits that more was on its way. No-one would be going hungry on Howel's marriage day. Nothing would go wrong for him or his guests.

Like the consummate politician he was, Howel was moving between different parties, joking about the antlers upon his head – and expressing all his hopes for the union of the two communities. Times of peace were ahead, he kept saying over and over again, as if in some way to convince himself, if not others, that our world was entering a new era of stability and safety. Cadreth stood closely by him, the leader of Chysauster already a little inebriated from his nervous consumption of ale. As the father of the bride, he was feeling the pressure – to say the right thing, to give the right speech when the time came later that evening.

A festive energy bubbled throughout Howel's roundhouse. Old and wondrous stories were retold. There were tales of the ocean, of the beach, of the moor and of battle. Giant fish, wolves and bears all came into the conversation. This was the way it was. Men remembered previous celebrations and their own individual moments of glory. Then they exaggerated them still further. As more ale flowed, the stories got grander, the exaggeration greater. As I come to reflect now on events, I sometimes wonder if this is what I am doing – merely enhancing the truth of those times. All I can say is I that have tried to be honest with you. I have genuinely tried to tell it like it was. So yes – this was how it was that day. This is how I remember it.

The roundhouse got louder and louder in the afternoon. Soon, there were trials of strength from each party, bawdy songs and dancing; then some of the braver young men from Chysauster jumped over the fire pit for kicks. This rowdy behaviour only stopped when Casvellyn, Selus and Genaius entered. At the druids' collective stoical presence, the rowdiness ceased. Old Selus gave a few hard stares to the young men of Chysauster for them to calm things down a little. I could not overhear what Casvellyn said to Howel, but it was clearly something along the lines of "It is time". I saw Howel swallow nervously. This was it then: he was about to be married.

In my life, I had not always stayed long enough in any community to witness too many marriages, but the ones I had participated in gave me some measure of preparation for what was to follow. Depending on the couple's status and place, then one or more of the druid caste would officiate. Given Howel and Orla's status, it was therefore apt that all three would be present. Casvellyn led the way, followed by Cadreth, Kenal and the enjoined retinue.

The marriage ceremony itself would take place above the fogou. There had been placed on top of it a so-called 'marriage stone'. Most communities had one of these. It was normally a thin piece of granite or slate, which had worn indentations caused by weathering, or which had been carved for the purpose. The couple's feet would then stand in these indentations, placing them in sacred space for the ceremony. It was the men who first gathered above the fogou in a semi-circle. Kenal was helping the lame Cadreth up onto the bank. I stood back from events, some distance behind the men of Chysauster.

Selus and Genaius prepared the space in which the ceremony would take place by marking the north, south, east and west quarters and by uttering low chants. Casvellyn signalled to Genaius, who took a large curved horn from under his cloak and blew it loudly. The sound was guttural and deep, and echoed from Caer Bran all the way over to Carn Brea. The mouthpiece of the horn was intricately crafted from bronze and was probably centuries old. The sound reverberated through the crowd. Genaius paused for a while, and then blew the horn a second, and a third time.

"So – thrice blows the marriage horn," declared Casvellyn.

The male crowd became quiet.

"The first day of May welcomes the union of Howel and Orla."

At first, almost as if a dream, from the lower end of the village, wound a stream of white-clad women. Leading the way was a matriarch, holding the hands of several girls, as if plaited together. They moved like fairies, light on their feet, laughing and giggling at what they must do. I didn't want to look though. I had to force myself to observe events. I knew that when I would see Orla I'd die a little inside me. In the mass of women who followed, throwing yellow gorse petals and purple heather flowers high into the air, she would be in there, nurtured by them, but lonely. She'd wear a public smile but hold an inner grief. Female musicians accompanied the group as they climbed the slight hill of the settlement. These were harp, lyre and lute players, playing a light melody which transfixed the men already gathered.

Between the men of Chysauster I noted, first of all, Orla's mother. She was a good-looking woman in her early fifties by the name of Melwyn, who very soon would come to curse my name. Cadreth talked much of his Melwyn and how much she meant to him; his daughter Orla even more. Between the bob of the musicians' heads and the studied movement of Melwyn, I caught my first glimpse of Orla. Obviously radiant in the May afternoon's sunshine, she carried the hopes of the people of Chysauster. The men all around knew of her beauty but, of course, said nothing; their faces betrayed not a hint that she was so attractive; they could not in front of their chieftain, nor their new political ally, in the form of Howel.

She was a good distance yet from the platform on top of the fogou, and yet I swear I could detect her perfume on the air. Her brightness infected everything. If she had stumbled upon those blackened tin streamers I had encountered above the bay of the Mount, then a refreshing new light would have glowed about them. She had that capacity. I was wondering how she would react if somehow she caught my eye. I was both hoping this would not happen, and that it would happen. She brought out this extreme duality in me – like my left and right hands.

Howel was still wearing his antler crown, but was now dressed for the occasion. He was clad in the richest and finest purple cloak (the dyes for which had to be imported from the far south), tied at the corner with a huge bronze clasp, detailed with intricate knotwork. Such was its size that it seemed to catch the sun. They were suited I supposed at that moment: despite the 'arrangement' of their future lives, Howel and she would make a lasting couple. Both carried an energy which was lacking in others. They would do well – if no-one interfered.

Although Orla was now closer, I decided to take my eyes off her. I focused on anyone else that I could: first, Casvellyn and then Selus for a while. Next I watched the smiling faces of Melwyn and Cadreth. The problem with Melwyn was that in her features, I saw traces of Orla's, and soon I averted my eyes from her. The dull grass beneath my feet suddenly became more interesting. Orla surely knew I was there somewhere. She did not betray this knowledge though. In the end, I had to look up at her. By now, her back was towards me, which helped somewhat. I still wanted to be near her, close to her, to wrap my arms around her waist. I was the one who wanted to be bound to her. Her white robe clung to her figure. It was the same incredible figure I noticed not long ago inside the fogou. Her hair had been tied up revealing the nape of her neck. In the slight breeze, a few wisps blew out of place. These wisps tempted me like nothing else.

Casvellyn and Selus were conducting the majority of the proceedings – the union of two druids at the union of these two royal lines. Selus greeted the couple and asked them to stand on the 'marriage stone'. The couple shuffled into position; their bare feet placed in the stone's grainy indentations. Casvellyn meanwhile gracefully took their hands and placed them together.

"Orla... and Howel... come, hold hands firmly and fixedly," said Casvellyn.

Selus meanwhile, held up the fastening rope that was used for the ceremony. He turned it to the four quarters, blessing it each time and presenting it to the onlookers. The rope was decorated with flowers and tied with sacred jowds – the rags of their families before them to symbolise their joining. Old Selus then fastened their hands together with it to publicly declare their union.

"With this rope, may Orla and Howel be forever joined. They shall not part as this knot confirms."

Selus tied the knot strongly on top of their wrists. Knots were our people's symbol of unity. They were everywhere – on each blade, each breastplate, each brooch. Now they were here.

"You may now kiss," the old druid said, salaciously licking his own withered lips.

Orla and Howel leaned towards each other. You could have thrown a spear straight into my heart as I saw Howel's lips touch hers. The bastard.

At this, I checked myself. Was my face giving too much away? Maybe Casvellyn thought as much. He was watching me. Maybe I uttered 'bastard' under my breath. I did not know anymore. I wanted the earth to eat me up and bury me alive. I wanted to be encased in stone and left on the moor to rot. I wanted masses of fairie cattle to stampede over me. I wanted something to snap off my hands.

Their kiss brought cheers and smiles from the crowd. Cadreth and Melwyn congratulated them, followed more formally by Casvellyn and Selus. Genaius followed too, with his best wishes, after which he blew the horn loudly to symbolise the marriage was complete. I had to look down again. What was fate doing with me? Why had it brought me here? Why was it making my life so painful? These questions chipped away at my mind. I realised that although my father had prepared me well for my life of work, he had given me less insight into the workings of the heart. For that, at this moment, I detested him, and all that I was.

Howel was speaking now, and addressing the crowd.

"People of Carn Euny, and people of Chysauster, my wife and I welcome you to our marriage day. I have never been happier in my life than I am right now..."

I sensed him pause, and turn to Orla. He would be gazing into her eyes. Those eyes.

"Orla, you have already brought so much into my life. I know that our union today will prompt much cooperation between our communities. Already, I have come to know all your brothers and the men of Chysauster. And in time, as in all marriages, I will come to know you, and you will come to know me. Thus, I look forward to a new era of wonder and great happiness."

Right there and then was when I decided that I would have to leave Carn Euny, the fogou job incomplete and unfinished, but me a little saner. Events seemed to swirl about me then. The assembled crowd mingled with the bride and groom, kissing and congratulating them. Many hands were shaken and women cried small tears of happiness. With Casvellyn watching though, I had to keep up my pretence. When Orla stood for a while with her mother and father, I dutifully went up to Howel and shook his hand heartily.

"Congratulations," I said. "Now your life is complete... Lord Howel."

That is what came out anyway. Probably the tone of it held some sarcasm to it, but Howel, gracious as ever, accepted my wishes and told me to partake of more food back in the parliament building. This was where all of the wedding party would now celebrate, bringing both the men and women together.

I sensed Orla saw me but I did not stay to talk with her. Besides, this was now the moment when she and Howel would enter the fogou and consummate their marriage on the bed of herbs the druids had prepared. While the rest of the community would drink to excess and over-eat, they would make love, watched by Annown. Annown, and only Annown, would guarantee the long-term success of their marriage. In order to gain this guarantee, they had to follow the sacred way. Once this had been completed, only then would they return to the celebrations as true husband and wife. Casvellyn and Selus would lead them down into the fogou, say their words and leave them to get on with it. The earth would become their bedroom for as long as it took. While the rest of the community partied, the druids usually used this time for prayer and contemplation, helping Annown to approve the union.

In the parliament building, I drank too much. I was sat on Kenal's table, and there, I numbed my brain with excess ale. Perhaps this was what Casvellyn had meant the watercress for – to assist me in escaping. Kenal was a live-wire that evening, already full with beer and dancing and singing himself into a stupor. Both Chysauster and Carn Euny had to endure the opening section of Remfra's epithalamion too:

Howel in his court exercises his right,
the shadow of the Carn and the shadow of the Carn,
with the artificers serving Lugh,
who sing love who sing prosperity,
we dedicate this sacred space,
two households and two peoples heal a wound:
the hearth of the house, the hearth of the house
we sing love and we sing prosperity.

The thing was so epic and overblown with imagery he got booed off after the first few lines, and instead the music and drumming began again. Remfra and I were forced to dance with Kenal's children and family – as good a diversion as I was going to get, as opposed to thinking about events underground.

So maddened was I by the moment, that I could sense each thrust of Howel into her, his hip movement compounded by the agony of drums now. How long would they be together? Each minute they were not at their wedding party was a minute longer that he was alone with her; Orla forced to service his needs and Annown approving – all this in a dwelling my father Donyerth had built and which I would later have to adapt. I knew these thoughts were the way to derangement, a quick walk to insanity, but I honestly could not help them. I wanted to leave the parliament building party and spy on them. I wanted to protect Orla, but likewise, I didn't want Howel to be hurt. He didn't deserve that.

This madness was about to be changed and irrevocably altered. As late afternoon turned into early evening, the party atmosphere was to be swiftly curtailed. The actual moment is now a bit of a blur to me.

The years have made it so.

All I seem to remember were the doors of the parliament building flung open and the entry of two men whom I knew. These men had not partaken of the party but had been positioned outside the village as sentries. When the doors opened, I saw them silhouetted by the light behind them. They were shouting. I do remember that. No – more than shouting. They were screaming. But no-one was listening. Everyone was either dancing or drunk by now. In the end, despite their efforts, they could not make anyone hear in this way, so they elected to move over to the musicians. One of them kicked over a drum; the other grabbed a lute and dropped it on the floor. It took a little while, but the dancers eventually realised that the music had stopped. The other musicians stopped playing. Even the children who had been swirled about the floor by their parents stopped their innocent laughter.

The first sentry's heart was still pumping. Breathless, he only had to say two words for complete panic to break out.

"*Ancredhor Mor*!"

The words did not register for a few seconds. Disbelief reigned. How could the sea pirates come now when the community was in the middle of its celebrations? Couldn't they wait until it was over?

"Don't you hear me? *Ancredhor Mor*! Landed... here..."

Once this had sunk in, they wanted more.

"Where? How many?" asked someone.

"A messenger came to us from Penberth Cove. Five ships put in down there. Around twenty-five men each. They are heading north. You can see the smoke from their looting..."

This was all it took. Sobriety returned quickly, although finding military kit in the midst of a marriage event would not be easy. Men fumbled for shields and swords. Their heads were numb from ale. Their feet hurt because of the intensity of the dancing. Everyone pushed out of the parliament house and gathered on the hillside. In the distance, to the south, were the tell-tale signs of an invasion. Plumes of black smoke rose from settlements down near the coast. These weren't the normal grey trails of smoke from inside roundhouses or huts, but instead, the sign of pillage and plunder.

"Tell the druids," someone shouted. "They will pray for us."

That's all very well, I thought, but what was needed was men with strategy and arms. The *Ancredhor Mor* fought hard and well. They were no soft target. In my experience, the bastards were unstoppable beasts of war. They were physically bigger than the people of the peninsula. Sometimes, the only way to stop them was two onto one, and then you were still struggling to defeat them. They had an energy, a savagery than seemed to be beyond all knowledge here. It was other-worldly.

Kenal began to wrestle what normal battle-sense he had left inside him. He was instructing some of the younger men to look after the women and children.

"Put emergency procedures into place. You know where to take them?"

The young men nodded, most grateful that their duties would end there and they would not have to face the wrath of the *Ancredhor Mor* directly. They'd hide them up on the moors by heading north.

"We may need you later," said Kenal, temporarily destroying their hopes of non-combat roles.

The eyes of the crowd now turned right to the fogou in which Orla and Howel lay. He would have to be told – and quick, marriage bed or no marriage bed, eyes of Annown or no eyes of Annown.

"Vug-man," said Kenal to me. "Can you go down and fetch him?"

"Me?"

"Yes – you know the vug. The druids aren't here yet. You're the obvious choice..."

"Not really," I said. "I'm an outsider. Not really one of you. It's a sacred time for them. It should be someone from Carn Euny."

"Bollocks," said Kenal. "Just fetch him will you? You don't have to go in and catch him on the job. Just call for him from the entrance."

"Can't Cadreth or Melwyn go?" I pleaded, but my words were lost on the air.

Kenal left me to that job. He'd already moved on, marshalling his men and detailing what they would need for battle.

Remfra, who had gathered up the manuscripts of his writings, then gave an ominous observation.

"The sky is black over Boskennal... They're moving closer. They're heading northwards."

Being of the bardic class, there was no compulsion for him to fight. It was his job to write, to report and to observe – if he survived.

"Thus they come," he seemed to be composing on the spot, improvising verse. "Like a wave of ravens..."

The women and children gathered a few possessions: items of food and clothing that were always ready for an evacuation such as this. Howel had trained the community well. The women of Chysauster were less well-prepared than they would be if they were at home, but still had enough knowledge to always be ready for such an attack. The worry perhaps was that the sea pirates would travel to the east instead and attack an unprotected Chysauster.

Kenal noticed my hesitancy.

"Get him out of the vug you cunt! Hurry the fuck up," he bawled.

His anger forced me down the steps and inside the fogou. I stopped before I had sight into the cell.

"Lord Howel! It's me – Voog. You must come out. We are being attacked – *Ancredhor Mor* – to the south of us."

"Shit," came a voice from inside the cell.

I thought I'd give Howel time to get dressed. He'd probably now be utterly naked, but when he emerged from under the lintel, he was clad in the same clothing as earlier on; his cloak still fastened around him. The only item missing was his ceremonial antler crown.

"Annown has waited already," he voiced in a low, frustrated tone. "And may need to wait even longer now."

"Kenal is preparing the men..." I offered.

"See, Master Voog, this is why we need you. This is why I need these alterations... I have been observing my own pleasures when I should have employed you earlier – when you wanted to work..."

"I'll come with you. I have fought these bastards before."

Howel peered at me.

"You are a brave man, Master Voog, but you are no warrior. Kill with stone would you?" he laughed.

He was thinking of my gammy twist and stump of a hand.

"No. Stay here. Protect the village. But before that, take her to the moors – with the other women. She will know where to go."

Her? Is that what he already thought of her? She had a name. Didn't he recognise that?

"Queen Orla?"

He nodded.

"Orla, it looks like my patience will be tried even further today," he shouted back into the cell.

So, it was becoming clearer to me that Annown had not witnessed their consummation. Three hours they had been in the cell while the rest of the wedding party had celebrated, and in those three hours it seemed they had not been intimate. This was some consolation to me.

Howel turned back to me.

"Have they called for Casvellyn?"

"He's being fetched..."

"Good. I never go into battle without a druid nearby."

This was laughable in my view. This was Howel at his best and his worst. Although he was an accomplished military leader and strategist, he still needed the superstition to help him.

At that moment I felt that fate, religion, superstition, spell-craft or destiny made no difference. Only good and bad deeds alter events.

"Voog," he said finally, gazing toward the cell. "Look after her. I know I can trust you."

Outside, Kenal had unified the men of Carn Euny and Chysauster into a war machine. Men doused their heads with water to wake themselves up. They tested blades and shields to ensure their usefulness and durability in the forthcoming conflict.

"Friends," I heard Howel shout, "it seems the ocean brings us a new test. Let us chop fiercely and hack swiftly to save our kingdom. Let's tear their arses off."

This test, it has to be said, was nothing compared to what was to come. I went back down into the fogou and heard the fearful stomp of feet across the top of it. This noise was accompanied by the bark of Kenal's orders. Eventually, the sound of the combined army of Carn Euny and Chysauster subsided and the village became deathly still. It seemed the drumming and wild celebrations of Howel and Orla's betrothal were now a world away. I had to hope, like everyone else, that this army of Howel's would be able to resist any more incursions from the sea pirates. If the *Ancredhor Mor* got this far inland, then it would bode very badly for the future prosperity of the peninsula.

Ancredhor mor.

Saxons.

Where would it end?

For me, it was going to end right there, when, in the stillness of the evacuation I heard shy, soft breathing, as frightened and as skittish as any fairie cattle.

YOU ARE STILL HERE SOMEHOW Annown – in this new land. How did you get here – all these thousand of miles away? Did you run – just the same as he did? Maybe it was for the best.

I sensed you as I walked with these men. They were still talking to me in my own tongue. Back and forth the dialogue went. I explained – in brief – how I had found them: how I read the stones, how I had found the creek and how I had discovered clues. They told me it wasn't that far to their village. If we kept going, we would be able to make it there by the end of the day. They had gone out hunting, just the same as the men back home. Here, it felt like nothing had changed. Maybe that's why I felt you there, Annown. They moved fast, lightfootedly skimming through the forest as if a story sprite. Now and again, we startled birds which rose in a clatter from the peaty floor. When we came to a river they told me it was not deep. It would be safe to cross. When I seemed thirsty or hungry, they offered me water and food. I saw how humanity could be so kind, and so caring. As we travelled, I ached for information. I wanted to know everything, but perhaps I just had to be a little more patient. I gleaned snippets, just as I had done about my mother. Whereas those had been almost universally negative, here there was great respect. I hardly knew what to expect. I could barely contain my excitement. It put butterflies into my stomach. I felt light-headed.

"You will see him soon," they said.

"He will be surprised."

"Maybe we will see him smile," one joked.

"He has not smiled in a long while," another explained.

As we tumbled through the forest that day, I recalled further flashes of my youth. They came upon me as waves. Small tides leap at our hearts and minds every day, but occasionally huge breakers lunge and break upon us. I would have to meet the elders, the men said. The ruling women would be pleased to meet me, and to know my connection. At these words, I was back in Chysauster. I was with the elders there – among them, my strong-willed grandmother.

To her great surprise, one day – some time around the end of October – Lord Howel entered the village and asked for her. I was out at the time, gathering wood for the season's celebratory fires, but when I came back into the roundhouse he was there. I had not met him before, but I knew instantly it was him. He was wearing the regalia of a chief, and when I peered through the gap by the hinge of the door, I recognised all that I had been told. He was older than I had imagined. Youth had been sucked out of his body a long time ago. A few streaks of blond remained in his grey hair, but these too were losing their lightness. The eyes, probably once bright as sparkling tin, were dulled. And yet with him, there was now something more gentle and considered. Perhaps when the poison entered him, it had somehow changed his composition. I listened.

I heard him sigh, and then say, "I would entreat you to convert, Melwyn. Since I let God into my world, I have truly seen the error of my ways."

"It's too late," said my grandmother.

"Too late? It's never too late to take up belief in the Lord."

"I don't mean that Howel. I mean that whatever you say now is too late for me and my family. If you had this forgiveness fifteen years ago, then all might be well. But it has not been well, and now it is too late."

I read the desperation on Howel's face.

"Forgive me then? Please. I need you to do this."

"What? To make you feel better about what you did...?"

"If that is what you think..."

My grandmother had aged much of late, but she still had some vigour. Despite his status, she would take him on.

"You are the man who sold my daughter into Saxonage. You made her do what she did. You made her feel ashamed – not just for a while, but for eternity. You are the man who despised my husband and my people for what they had brought to you. You are the man who sold your soul to make peace with those who would destroy us. In his dying days my husband only knew you as a traitor."

"Melwyn, I did what I had to... for peace... for our future – not just for Carn Euny, but for Chysauster as well. In truth, I did it for the whole of the land."

"And now look at you... a lonely man, falling to pieces, and filled with regret..."

With that, Howel began to sob.

"Have mercy on me," he pleaded. "I can put right what was wrong."

"Say what you like. Nothing will absolve you Howel – not in my mind. You speak to this Johnny-come-lately god as if he will solve everything. Believe in him and you'll be fine... Well, Howel, it's not fine. It won't ever be fine. Don't you understand that?"

"I'm not the only one to convert," he explained. "Many others now follow the same path."

"No. Well, fools always follow other fools..."

For a few minutes they said nothing. I watched my grandmother hold back her tears. She was experienced at that. She'd been doing it for some years now. She'd have her say.

"And what does the 'great' Casvellyn think of your conversion? Been to Boscawen Ûn lately has he?"

"He has said little."

"I expect so."

"He knows of my decision...."

"I know his role in all of this. Don't go thinking I'm a fool. His hand is as blackened as yours is with this matter. As for you hoping – to come here today, after all this time – to reach a new union with us, and for you to rule Chysauster, as some Christian King, go... go... take yourself away from here forever... You put yourself into exile a long time ago."

My grandmother remained hard as stone. She stood as a menhir before the hearth.

"Agan Tas-ny, us yn nef... Benygys re bo dha. Hanow, Re dheffo dha whas-cor, Dha voth re bo gwres... y'n kepar hag y'n nef. Ro dhyn-ny hedhyu..."

This sobbing prayer came from Howel's mouth.

"Don't give me that," my grandmother warned him.

I had never seen her so angry.

"Stop your claptrap Howel."

But Howel continued. The prayer was chanted low and soft.

"....Rag dhyso-jy yu an whascor ha'n gordhyans. Bys vykken ha bynary. Amen."

At these words, I saw my grandmother push him to the floor. She kicked and pummelled at him. He did not fight back. I saw Howel's body wrench and twist in pain. I heard his yelps; his gasps. I watched his contortions and saw his limbs twist. Still, at her frenzy, he was asking for forgiveness. But there was no way she would give it. Annown was watching but she knew she was in the right. When she had finished, she spat upon his body and walked out, sharply forcing me back from the door and into the shadows.

With the ferocity of her attack, I thought she had killed him. I wondered if I would have to fetch Kenal and Genaius and explain to them what had happened. Maybe in that twist of his body however, something was now over. There was absolution and ending for him. For me though, there was only blame and the beginning of much more.

Still, I went over to his shaking form and cradled him. In his eyes I saw both the arsenic and the Amen. He knew who I was.

Softly, I spoke to him.

"I forgive you," I said.

8

Video footage of the Atlantic Ocean from the International Space Station, 2011
This video was taken by the crew of Expedition 29 on board the International
Space Station. The pass starts from Fogo Island, just north of Newfoundland,
then crosses over the North Atlantic Ocean moving to central Africa, finally
reaching South Sudan. The station has been continuously occupied for 11 years
and 303 days, having exceeded the previous record of almost 10 years (or
3,644 days) held by Mir in 2010. The International Space Station has, for this
period, been monitoring changes in the Atlantic Ocean related to pollution,
the Greenhouse Effect and changes in sea ice. These, alongside surface water
temperatures, currents and seasonal changes can all be mapped from space.
Footage courtesy of the International Space Station.

"I JUST DON'T FANCY HIM! Why can't people understand that? I mean, I
tried telling him but he just doesn't want to listen."

This was the first thing a breathless Orla said to me when I bent down under
the lintel and entered the cell. On top of the bed of choice herbs and flowers,
she had pulled the woollen clothes up to her flawless chin, hiding her body, so
that only her face was visible. Her face carried much fear and worry.

"Has he gone?"

"He's gone," I confirmed. "To repel the *Ancredhor Mor*."

"I know he's a good man. My mother said I should just do my duty and forget about my own hopes and dreams…"

As she said duty, she pointed down at her vagina.

"For the good of Chysauster?"

"Yes – for the good of my people."

The cell which the druids had prepared for the consummation of Howel and
Orla's marriage carried an incredible fragrance to it. Every sweet and sensuous
smell of our world seemed to be contained within its corbelled walls. An earlier
fire pit had taken away all dampness from the air. I was surprised that even
Orla hadn't been lulled into love by its passionate atmosphere. However, she
seemed to sense my awareness of the surrounds.

"It smells good doesn't it?" she said somewhat dejectedly, reflecting on her
own failure to feel any passion for Howel, and absent-mindedly trailing her
left hand through the herbs. "I have to say – the druids made it wonderful."

Fuck the druids, I wanted to say.

"We should go," I said instead.

"Go where?"

"To a place of safety up on the moors... where the rest of the women and children have gone. It was Howel's wish for me to take you there. The invaders don't know the moorland. They won't touch it."

"You?" said Orla, smiling to herself. "If only he knew, eh?"

There she went again – flirting with me. I had to try to resist this.

"He knows nothing of how I feel," I said. "Come on, that's all over now. Your safety is paramount."

"The moors though? What is safe about them?" asked Orla incredulously. "Surely inside here would be safer? Isn't that my Lord Howel's master-plan?"

"Only in the future. Right now, it isn't safe here. In times of attack the entrances would have to be rebuilt – and the creep passages shored up. You know that's what I've yet to do."

"Do you think the raiders will really make it up here?"

"I honestly don't know Orla... The men of Chysauster and Carn Euny are well-prepared – if a little hung-over."

There followed a small debate on the techniques of warfare offered by our people and the Vikings. In short, the Vikings had brute force, the peninsula men better strategy and more cunning.

"I'd rather stay here," muttered Orla.

You could see why. The cell was a wondrous place to be. As well as the fresh herbs, the walls of the cell had been lined with candles, gifts, food and drink, held in the community's finest pottery and baskets. All was opulent and luxurious, wholly fitting for this new May queen. It was rat heaven, I could not help but note.

"Your actions," I noted. "Will they upset the watchers from Annown?"

"Probably," said Orla. "But I don't care about them. I care about the here and now, not some mystic claptrap. Annown can chuck itself over the cliffs for all I care."

She paused. She realised she was speaking to a fogou-builder.

"I suppose you wouldn't agree... I mean, you make your living from building all this mystic claptrap. I'll be taking away your living next. Then you won't thank me."

It was true what she said, any way that I might wish to cut it. I did make my living in this way. There was not time to respond to her, though, since she was speaking again.

"We spend our lives ceremoniously thanking what happened before we began and what is to happen when we die... celebrating landscape, stone and tree.... when we ought to be just..."

"Living?"

"Yes, just living and enjoying the here and now."

Her words echoed many of my own thoughts, and yet at the same time, there was something beautiful, something wondrous about our people and their otherworldly obsessions. It made us who we were. It defined us as not being the *Ancredhor Mor* or – from what I had heard – the Saxons. It made us stand out against the bogeymen.

"You agree with me though Voog, don't you? I can tell from your face."

"More or less," I answered softly. "More or less..."

"I wish I could be more like you," said Orla.

"So speaks the Queen of the realm," I jested.

"No. Seriously. Your lifestyle is what I want. Not to be stuck in one place. To travel around. To experience new things. There is a whole world out there that I have never seen. How else do you think Remfra gets his stories? He gets them from people who have travelled out of this world of granite and gorse to find new experiences, to taste new foods, to hear different tongues."

"You make it sound as if I travel to the limits of the earth," I said. "I don't. I merely wander this small peninsula.. Besides, hearing different tongues isn't all a bed of roses. Look at those different tongues currently raiding our land."

"Even so," she interrupted. "Now with my marriage, I will be constricted even further – hardly able to walk free or unaccompanied anywhere."

"That, for your own safety," I argued.

"I don't want that. I want danger. I want passion. I want freedom."

Perhaps even then, she knew it was coming.

I hardly needed to say that she had sacrificed part of that when Casvellyn and Selus bound her and Howel's hands together. There had been the metaphorical fastening of wife to husband, but underneath there undoubtedly was a kind of tethering – as cruel, as inhumane as that which faced any farmyard animal. Knots then, were binding, cutting, tearing, constricting.

As Orla became more relaxed around me, she dropped the bedclothes pulled up to her chin and breathed more easily. She was still wearing her wedding garments. I could not help but admire the form of her voluminous breasts which pressed against the material of her bodice. These physical urges that I had for her previously were now matched by her passion for living. I had known of the former before, but had not known enough of the latter. Now that I knew of this independence she carried from head to toe, I wanted her even more. Outside, I'd likened her to fairie cattle, but she was nowhere near that. Instead, she was the whole of nature rolled into one beautiful form.

I started to leave.

"Where are you going?" she pleaded.

"Up top. I want to scan the horizon. I want to see where the battle is... I need to determine how close they are."

"Don't be long. Please."

I hurried out of the cell, and then turned right down the fogou passage. There was Casvellyn's stone, still in place. Had his power, his arcane incantations affected the way the world was twisting? Some believed the druids could do this. I couldn't entirely go with this – even more so now that I had found a compatriot in disbelief.

The entrance brought me back out into the village again. It was eerily silent. Even the dogs and pigs remaining from the evacuation stayed silent, as if not wanting to reveal their position to the enemy. On top of the fogou, the 'marriage stone' was still there. From there, I gained a good view to the south. I was looking for the tell-tale smoke that indicated how far north the invasion had pushed. Perhaps across the moorland and field systems I might be able to see the combined army of Chysauster and Carn Euny. I peered out for a while trying to discern any markers or clues as to their progress. My view was impaired by a slight mist that was starting to form in the valley bottoms. Perhaps the *Ancredhor Mor* had completed enough battle for that day, and were at rest. Maybe Howel and his army planned an ambush for the night. There would be no way of telling unless a messenger was sent back, the army itself returned, or worse still, the hordes of the *Ancredhor Mor* found their way to Carn Euny.

At that moment, I knew what I *should* have done. Even if I had to drag Orla from the vug hole to the moorland, I would have to do it. It would be better if she would come quietly, but she – being a new kind of woman – was never going to do that. How complex had my life become? I was wishing Kenal had never found me that day – and that I still had the uncomplicated life of a stoneworker back at poverty-ridden and lice-infested Kynance.

Looking back, it was possibly the silence that made it happen. Silence guaranteed that every look and every word would be heightened. The silence permitted what was about to happen. We'd atone for it for what seemed like an eternity, and we would pay a price so ruthless that it would rip us to shreds.

Nevertheless it was going to happen.

The silence transformed Carn Euny into the opening days of the world, when rock, tree, stone and sea had first been formed and we were the only beings upon it. The moment had, of course, been building in the silence for both us. It had been unspoken, but was tacitly understood since we'd met those few days before. So yes, it was my duty to have taken Orla to the safety of the moorland, but when I returned to the cell, it was clear that she too, had been moved by the silence. All around the cell, using burning oil which had ignited incense, she had lit candles (intended for Howel and her). I sensed their flicker as I bent down beneath the lintel to re-enter the cell. To do this, my eyes peered at the dry earth but when I was through and I was able to look up again, Orla stood before me. She had talked much before, but not now. Instead, she unclasped her bodice and let it and the rest of her dress fall to the floor of herbs and flowers.

I must have given a gasp of pleasure. Now I was the fairie cattle, breathless and skittish, as she took my left hand in her right and moved it so it touched her breast. I caressed the soft flesh, and then with my rough and five calloused finger-tips rolled her nipple. It became hard. She tipped her neck back at the intensity of it, and then moved her head forward in order for our lips to touch. The kissing was at first slow and gentle, unreal, as if in a milky dream, but soon became frenetic and passionate, sloppy and wet. Our frantic tongues felt for runs of pleasure between teeth and gums, while our hips and thighs became joined. We fitted flawlessly like the best stone. Skin was no longer granite cold though. Instead it was warm and fluid; each motion making the tiniest of hairs on our bodies stand on end.

This is what Howel should have been doing with her. Instead, he might at that very moment be lying alone in some desolate swamp, pierced with wounds, his skin a mixture of blood and mud. He was there, dreaming that such a moment might come, perhaps before death, before some *Ancredhor Mor* pummelled his head with a war axe so that all became black. His body would then become the food of birds. But I never thought of this, not at that moment. I was too consumed with passion, too selfish, too much in love with her to even think of the consequences (Show me someone who is in love – and tell me that they always think of the consequences – and I will show you a liar).

Silence still pervaded. Even the sounds of our pleasure were dampened by it. Soon we were on our knees and she was scrabbling to lift up my jerkin. She nuzzled against the hair of my chest, feeling each rib and the tight stone-shaped lines of my stomach. Ears, neck, cheeks and brow were all kissed by her tongue. Muscle merged. I had moved to her shoulders, her arms and stomach. All tasted sweeter than anything on earth. Obviously, I had heard stories of love and passion, and how wondrous such events were in human experience, but I had not expected this. If I was a man of unbending stone, then she was making me red and molten again. Desire cracked hard crystals and bumpy surface imperfections. She was carving me into a man; her body a chisel of sex.

From our knees we were soon down on top of the bed of herbs and flowers.

These were imbued with magic and wonder by the druids, but to us then, that did not matter. They could work their magic if they wanted. That was all mumbo-jumbo, mystic claptrap. Our love was real, a kind of care and passion that was rare on this earth. Although it was never spoken of at that moment, we knew this to be completely true. A line had been crossed but we were gloriously happy to do so.

A delicious fumbling followed. You have to remember we were both virgins. We just did what came naturally to us. My penis was hard now, erect as a menhir and she was wet for me. I took stalks of lavender and rubbed these gently over her stomach and clitoris. She used her tongue on the tip of my glans and sucked, sliding her hand busily around the shaft. This was a magical sensation and one that made my body contort and twist with pleasure. Soon my fingers gently broke their way into her wetness. I moved them gently around the warmth of her, trying to feel for what she liked. How I had desired such intimacy with her. Orla began to speak now, in gasps, telling me what she liked and when I touched her right. The same gasping affected me. I found my heartbeat increasing; my body seemed as if it might burst. From other men, I had heard of such feeling but never had experienced it myself. Our gasps became groans and these groans edged into animalistic sensation. All time was then forgotten, all taboo finally disregarded. We became one. Orla mounted me; her legs wrapped around the lower part of my back. My penis slid into her – a stone meeting its socket. The fit was perfect, a kind of glory that I had heard of in Remfra and other's tales – but never knew a man and woman could experience. This position, this lock onto each other we held for a long time, trying it in every way that we could. Despite our naïvety, our innocence, our inexperience, we fucked each other so hard that afternoon. Even now, after all these years, I can still taste her, still smell her hair, and still know the precise beauty and curvature of her back upon which I placed one shovel-like hand and one stump of oak.

"I wanted... you... from the... moment... I saw you," Orla managed to tell me, as each thrust of me separated the rhythm of her words.

"Me too," I managed to say.

Utter passion engulfed our bodies now.

"Harder," I pleaded. "Fuck me harder."

She complied, extending her body up and down to slide upon my shaft's length. Truly, by now it was as if it were no longer skin and blood, but iron. I could pierce deeper into her as our union became complete.

Any fear we initially felt – either about Howel or even the incursion of the sea pirates – was utterly dissipated. It was now only we two that mattered. If the *Ancredhor Mor* showed up and found us, and killed us on the spot, then so what? At least we had enjoyed one gloriously long fuck-fest which would endure (for certain, it was going to have be this one session which would endure, though we never contemplated that at this point in time). This was the moment when I could no longer hold on. I felt a rush of energy fill my body and I knew I was going to fill Orla with my white seed.

"Fill me with it," Orla said. "I want your seed Voog."

The raspy sexiness of her voice was enough to release me. One final thrust into her vagina brought forth a fountain inside her. I felt it gush and seep around me. I remained hard for long time. The space I had entered squelched with our combined juice and trapped air; each movement now making us laugh. When I finally removed my penis, it glistened with wetness, a glorious mixture of male and female, which Orla licked off me – a wild pleasure in her face. The last thing I remember was her eyes watching me, loving me, intriguing me. They were so dark, so wondrous that I never wanted to leave their gaze. She licked her lips and swallowed. We kissed again and I was able to taste ourselves. I knew its decadence and I knew its guilt as well, but nothing could have stopped us that afternoon.

After so many exertions and such wonder, the only thing we could do was to sleep. Under the bedclothes we kept a union; her bottom pressed into my groin and my arms caressing her breasts. I slept with the scent of her hair in my nose. When we had finished we never should have slept. In the end it was sleep that revealed us; that spoilt what we had. Were it not for sleep, then maybe no-one need ever have known of what occurred between us. We might have had only a little regret but at least we could have had our secret. Maybe if chance was willing, it could have happened again. Such was our energy though; such was the passion that sleep fell upon us all too easily. Deeds again you see. I cannot tell you the exact form of my dream and neither can I tell you what Orla imagined. What I do know is that I was imagining the conflict between us and them. Maybe, given the fact that I had been told to look after Orla, rather than fight, momentarily I had lost my masculinity within my subconscious mind. So there, in that place, I was hacking bloodied limbs from sea pirates, I was leading attacks on their camps, I was gaining revenge for all their slaughter. I was beside Howel and Kenal pushing through ripping bramble and spiky gorse to bravely meet this foe. I saw the faces of Vikings that I had encountered in the attack at Gwithian. There, mixed into this wrath, I was saving the blackened faces of exploited tin streamers, of other women and children I knew. Finally, in my dream it was Orla herself whom I was saving – thrusting a long sword into the stomach of a yellow-bearded warrior; his horned, ornate helmet toppling into fogou trench. And although my dream was of violence, it was the violence of a rage that paradoxically calmed and reassured – that in Orla, I had something to fight for, when for so many years, I had nothing and no-one to care about in this way.

It was this knowledge that gave the calm, uninterrupted sleep that sometimes we all crave, a deep sleep given not by the subtle fragrance of herb or flower, but by the complete knowledge and understanding of one's role in the universe. As Orla said, it went beyond Annown and all that it held. Our transgression was complete.

Awakening must come though, and come it did. The way it came might easily have been compared to an incursion from the *Ancredhor Mor*. But it was not their grim savagery that eventually discovered us. Instead, its vitriol and violence came from somewhere and someone much closer to home.

ANNOWN, ANNOWN, ANNOWN, I FEEL your vowels of power. They roll around my tongue. It is so strange to think that you are the land of souls that have departed this world. And now, Annown, it feels as if you are departing. It is as if you are waving a goodbye to me – leaving me as your orphan cradled within a fogou. I just hope you still have strength enough to send new life back to this world again. I was worried that if you weren't there, then who would I turn to? Around this time I remember praying for you to send me someone, someone who would look after me. I had had enough of having to look over my shoulder.

Back then though, I was with the controller of my mother and father's fate.

"Thank you. It's Blejan, isn't it?" said Howel to me, through his bloodied lips.

I did not answer.

I was face to face with the man who had destroyed my family.

All I remember doing is trying to make him comfortable and washing his wounds. As I wiped the blood, I noted large bruises forming upon his body as a result of my grandmother's ferocity.

"I understand her hatred towards me."

"Are any of your bones broken?" I asked.

He felt around his body. He shook his head. I could tell, however, that her strikes and kicks had hit bone deep.

"I had to come and see her. The holy men suggested it..."

He paused. His eyes lowered.

"I wanted to see you as well."

"What for?"

Howel coughed, and spat out a globule of blood-coloured spittle from his mouth. It landed on the kaolin floor.

"To tell you the truth..."

"I know the truth now – or at least, I think I do now that..."

Howel interrupted me.

"I wanted to tell you something. I wanted to tell you that despite what happened... despite the arrangement... I loved her. I still do."

"But you sold her?"

Howel put his hands to his head and cried deeply. He wrung out his innermost soul. Tears streamed onto his jerkin.

"I know. I know," he sobbed. "I realise my sin."

I looked down, not meeting his eyes.

"Your father," he continued. "The one your grandmother won't talk about.. You need to know: he was a good man. I was confused... I... never..."

He stopped, unable to contemplate the horror of his past.

In truth, I did not know what to say to him. As the years have passed, there was much I wished I had said. There have been times, when I have felt as violent as my grandmother and wished I had beaten him into a pulp. There have been other times when I just wished I had asked him more questions. But I saw what was left of him – and when I saw that, I understood and forgave him.

I understand now that we can still love things when they slip away from us. They may be gone, but that love is constant, despite time, despite change.

"Say something," he demanded of me. "Please... Tell me what you are thinking."

You have learnt how I can converse. You know me in this moment, talking to these people in distant Hyperborea. I can gabble and yap with the best of them – but there in front of Howel, I was rendered speechless. For so long, I had wanted this conversation. I had longed for this moment. I had rehearsed what I would say to him if I ever encountered him. But my mouth stayed shut. I tried to force out a response but it wouldn't come. It was shut in – buried deep in the earth. Perhaps I had entombed my feelings a long time ago.

Howel held out his hand in desperation, pleading for a response.

Being so tongue-tied, being so unable to tell him my truth, I got up and backed away from him. I left the roundhouse with him still lying on the floor in agony.

I ran.

I ran long and hard to anywhere that was away from him.

Breathless, I found myself high on the moors, surrounded by stone. Finally, my gob opened and I screamed a yelp, high to the moon, low to the black ocean. Back in Chysauster the bonfires burned.

In the morning, my grandmother and I re-entered smoky domesticity without a word. I watched her carefully, to see if she might give anything away of the previous night's violence. Sometime, while we were both gone, Howel – like a wounded deer – had limped home. When I returned, there was no trace of him on the kaolin floor of the hut. Any marks from the scuffle, or blood from his mouth had been removed. She was busy baking bread. I tried to catch her attention to make her eyes cast over the spot where she had attacked him. But she was too good an actress, too accomplished in the pretence.

We knew nothing of what Howel had told his people about his injuries. Perhaps he would claim an attack by robbers, or say he had fallen from his mount. Either way, we did not expect him back in Chysauster.

Several months passed. First of all, the Christians left us alone. Perhaps Howel had warned them of the response they might get. The next thing we knew was word from Genaius that all the druids had been called for a gathering at Boscawen Ûn. Survivors of their faith would come together for a senate to talk over the fate of 'we' Britons and what they were going to do about this new God and his prophet. It seemed like a line in the sand was about to be drawn. Though there would be other sketchers, scribblers and well-meaning prophets, Genaius explained that the master artist would be good Casvellyn.

"No doubt old Remfra will be hard at work," noted my grandmother sarcastically. "Some new piss and vinegar titled 'The Prophecies of Casvellyn' I expect..."

That evening, we sat by the hearth sewing together. There was a shared understanding that we'd reached a destination – though perhaps by different routes, different navigations, different voyages you might say.

"I want you to have this," said Grandmother to me.

She pulled out one of her pins she used to fasten her tunic.

"It's very special to me. It was given to me years ago by my mother when I first got married."

I twirled the length of intricate metal between my fingers and felt its disc-shaped head.

"Thank you."

"Good," said Grandmother. "Just don't lose it. That's all."

9

Hy-Brasil Island, Atlantic Ocean, 1572
A number of mythic lands are contained in the folklore and legends of Atlantic peoples from the 5th Century CE onwards. One of the most documented is Hy-Brasil, which appears on a map of Ireland drawn by the Flemish cartographer Abraham Ortelius (1527-98) in 1572. The etymology of the name *Hy-Brasil* is unknown, but in the Irish tradition it might be derived from the Irish *Uí Breasail* (meaning "descendants or clan of Breasal"), one of the ancient groups of northeastern Ireland. Hy-Brasil also features on *Còpia del s. XIX de l'Atlas Català de la Corona d'Aragó, de l'any* [the Catalan Atlas] of 1375. Image courtesy of Amsterdam University Library.

ONE DAY, ALL OF CARN Euny will be abandoned. Isn't this the way with all wondrous civilisations? They emerge, grow, develop, flourish, and then somehow fall into decay, chaos, dissolution and abandonment. One day, people will walk here and perhaps just find the stone foundations of the roundhouses and the fogou neglected, and fallen in upon itself. The corbelled walls will be ruined and the cell exposed to the air. They will have to use their imaginations to conceive of how we once lived. It is the way that we now think about those who came before us. We think about how strange their existence must have been. Maybe that process of abandonment began that day. Maybe this was the tipping point; the time when the order got inverted; when all Annown's wrath was let loose.

I mean, by now, you know we were guilty of adultery. I have confessed it all to you. This was not any average adultery. This was adultery between a queen and a vagrant. Worse still, it had been committed in a sacred place at a sacred moment, when the man cuckolded in all of it was out fighting for the life of Carn Euny, doing everything he could to prevent it from being abandoned. What folly then. Perhaps both Orla and I had thought this through. Perhaps we knew the consequences, but this didn't stop us – the mutual attraction was too powerful. It had been unstoppable. We knew it from the moment we first met. Love then, cannot be abandoned. It must find a way. You know this to be true.

We must have both heard the voice calling at the same time, because when I opened my eyes, Orla was looking at me. Her all too brief smile turned to shock. Someone was calling her name. Our bodies, which were wrapped together in harmonic convergence, suddenly became tense. Realisation came to us; that in our rapture we had fallen asleep and lost all track of time. The light in the cell had changed. The candles were extinguished. We'd been sleeping for some time. The voice came again.

"Orla?! You there?"

The tone of it was plaintive, full of worry and concern.

There was not time for Orla to say that she recognised it because before we knew it, the body that had shouted her name was crouching in the cell's entrance, hoping to find her. The form was instantly recognisable to us both. It was Melwyn. The shock of seeing me with Orla nearly knocked her off her feet. She physically stumbled as if her legs gave way. I cursed under my breath. Our sleeping had meant that there was no time to cover anything up, to hide, to pretend, to explain, to lie. Our nakedness told her exactly what had happened.

"So... the two of you...?" was all she said. This was deadpanned as if she knew all along.

At our discovery, Melwyn initially broke into tears, and collapsed to the kaolin floor in front of us. We watched her body crumple and begin to sob. But then her inner anger found energy, and suddenly she raged, first at Orla – slapping her hard across her cheeks – but then turned in a more violent way at me. I had barely time to get myself upright, before thick pummelling blows fell upon my body. They came with such ferocity that I thought she might kill me. I was still naked, so she kicked me hard in my testicles and used her hard fists upon my stomach. I felt her warm tears fall on me. I twisted in pain as Orla tried to pull her off. Melwyn's breathing sounded like a boar's. She was normally a gracious, controlled woman, but she hated what she had discovered, and knew the shame it would bring. Lines deepened around her eyes; her face transformed into agony. She had observed something she didn't want to. Life does that to us sometimes.

"I was worried, when you didn't come," she tried to say between her tears. "The other women tried to stop me for fear of the *Ancredhor Mor* making it up here – but I had to come back for you..."

The beatings had stopped now. I sat upright, out of breath and sore; my back to the wall of the cell. Orla was getting dressed. She nodded at me to do the same so I fumbled in the herbal bed and found my shirt and trousers, hastily putting them on.

"Why?" she asked.

Neither Orla nor I answered.

She tried again.

"Why?"

"We..." Orla tried to say.

"You had it all," Melwyn declaimed.

There was a pause; a moment where this seemed to sink in with Orla, and I thought that momentarily she was going to agree. Not her though. She was made of stronger stuff.

"I had nothing Mother," she stated.

"When I was..." Melwyn said in a low voice, "When I was..."

We listened.

"When I was younger, all I ever wanted was for you to be happy. Your marriage to Howel, it should have made you happy."

"It didn't though, did it Mother? It was political. It was an arrangement. Nothing to do with love."

Melwyn grabbed her daughter's arm.

"We are women. We cannot think of love. We can only think of protection, of security and what is best for the whole."

"Orla wants more than that," I said, but probably I should have kept my gob shut.

She turned to me.

"You? And who are you, Voog? Is my daughter just some fumble you couldn't resist? Just some occasional fuck in your fogou? You are employed by Howel to work here. He is your master and yet you betray him."

"I think much of Howel," I said. "But I love your daughter even more."

"He will have to be told." noted Melwyn. "Your transgression must be exposed."

"No," said Orla. "You don't need to tell anyone. You are the only one who knows. Don't ruin things mother."

"Me? You are the ones who have ruined things. If I have noticed, so will others."

"Please," pleaded Orla.

There was no answer from her. I felt the throb of hurt in my testicles from where I had been kicked. Already, I sensed purple bruises forming on my torso.

Melwyn sat near the entrance, thinking through the consequences. There was much to consider. Although unspoken, for all three of us, there was the worry of the attack itself, still going on, somewhere to the south of us. Guilt frantically wove around the inside of the cell.

Finally, Melwyn spoke to me.

"What do you plan to do next?" she asked, looking at my eyes.

"Plan?"

"Yes – now that you have committed this act with my daughter, what next? I mean, will she leave with you? Will you stay here? What will happen?"

"That depends on you Melwyn, and what you do."

"No, come on, Voog. Tell me. You are foolish enough to do this. Are you man enough to care for my daughter?"

"I am," I said. "If necessary, we will leave..."

"Leave now?"

"If we must."

This seemed to inspire Orla's mother.

"Now is a good time to go," suggested Melwyn. "If you leave, maybe they will think you have been carried away by the *Ancredhor Mor*... Another group reached up here and took you. I can say I saw it happen. Voog, you will stay but you will need to be wounded, and look as if you put up a fight. Then later, when everything has settled down, Voog, you can leave here after your work, and meet Orla. You will need to live far from here though."

At least Melwyn was trying to find a solution to the mess. We all thought through her words. There was a certain logic in what she said.

"What about Father though?" asked Orla, already knowing the difficulties.

"He will think you dead," Melwyn said matter-of-factly. "As will Howel – and the peoples of Chysauster and Carn Euny. If not dead, then a slave to the *Ancredhor Mor*."

"And I, the whipping boy for the loss?" I asked. "I will be forever the warrior who failed to defend the village, and allowed them to take Orla."

"You will be forgiven," said Melwyn. "That is no crime at all compared to what has been committed in the fogou. Your hand there will tell the story of your failure."

I knew she was right, but I didn't want to know it was true. I still wanted to be in the arms of Orla. I knew, though, at that very instant, that was not about to happen again. It was as if after being so intimate, we were now going to be stretched to the ends of the earth. I could feel it happening. Fate was holding a catapult and shooting us apart.

Melwyn had stopped crying now. She had become stronger. She replaced a pin that had worked loose from her robe, nervously touching its ornamental panels. I knew what she understood. She knew that our future was suddenly embroiled in her own. She was Orla's mother. What values had she taught her daughter now the dirty slag had betrayed Howel? This was the gossip of both home and Carn Euny. The break up of the states of Howel and Cadreth could not happen. Union was the future. The attack that day had proved it. Then there was Annown. That world would have to be placated – but how on earth could it be done? It would almost need someone to be sent there and talk to the spirits of the past and future. Then she made her confession.

"There was someone I loved once," said Melwyn. "Someone in my life who..."

She paused.

"...but it wasn't right. I married Cadreth – which was the right thing."

In her frustration, she turned back onto Orla.

"You should have done the right thing too."

I could see the agony inside Melwyn. She understood perhaps why Orla and I had happened, but then again, she wanted her daughter to have been stronger, to have resisted such feelings. She wanted her to pack them up and place them in a box, just as she had done. But Orla was no such woman. It was what I liked – no, it was what I loved about her.

There was a moment in this cell when a decision could have been made, but such were our fears, such was our agony, that it did not happen. Orla and I were still recoiling from our transgression, though in essence we still wanted to transgress further, whilst Melwyn was desperately trying to find a solution. Other ideas were discussed – whether Melwyn could keep their secret and whether Orla could live her life back with Howel; with me leaving as soon as I could.

"I love Voog," said Orla. "That is it. Nothing else should matter."

A practical woman, in the end it was Melwyn who made a decision.

"All right," she said. "For now, I won't say anything. It'll be our secret – but that's not to say it doesn't need sorting out."

Sorting it out meant, in essence, me leaving. I had already decided that this was the only way out (which left a deep sadness in my soul), but any kind of steerage on events we thought we might have was soon about to be swept away. Already badly bruised, I was about to receive a kicking that made everything else seem like a slight knock. Standing in the fogou we sensed a presence. It could have been something savage from Annown; something vengeful and filled with hate. Then we heard its low voice.

"I hear talk of secrets and love. Whisperings of such matters do not bode well."

Melwyn, Orla and I left the cell and entered the main souterrain of the fogou. I gave a slight glance back to the bed of love. It would be my last view of that forever.

Deep down in the chamber, was sitting a white-clad figure, apparently appalled, his hands weighted upon his knees. Clearly, it was Casvellyn, and the way he looked at me that day I shall never forget.

"Don't deny it, Master Voog, Queen Orla. I have heard every word. Clearly, there is a problem."

Suddenly, all of Casvellyn's earlier actions became clear. The seer had seen inside me. He already knew what I felt about Orla; it was the reason he'd given me the watercress – so I could escape somewhere mentally – before this happened. Worse than this though, the fact that Casvellyn was back signalled something even more alarming. Howel had gone into battle with Casvellyn close by. If Casvellyn was back, then so might be Howel.

"They are young and have been foolish," argued Melwyn. "Don't punish them..."

Casvellyn sat still, quietly confident that the universe was on his side.

"Annown will know," he grumbled.

"Where is Howel?" I asked.

"Worry now do you, Master Voog, now that you have had share of his wife?"

"I worry about him yes. Have the *Ancredhor Mor* been pushed back?"

Casvellyn turned to us.

"For now, yes. We pushed them back to the coast – and they fled... but as you know, they will be back."

"And Howel – and the others? Are they back?"

"Howel is back, but he was injured – an axe wound to this shoulder. The men are carrying him in now – as I speak. Cadreth is back too, Melwyn. You need not worry. He fought mightily today."

"I am glad," said Orla.

"All has changed though – has it not?" questioned Casvellyn. "You make love, while others make war."

"Will you tell him?" Orla asked.

Casvellyn pulled on his beard, wishing this moment would go away.

"I have to," he answered. "It is in our code to do so. I must tell the truth."

So fate was now pressing on us like a huge lintel stone, squashing every ounce of hope from us. The pressing would be even more complete now that Howel had been injured in battle. Here was serious salt to rub into the wound. Melwyn could do little to change the druid's terms. He had power. All she could do was to comfort her daughter. At that moment, I tried to work out Casvellyn's machinations. It seemed that recent events suited his agenda. The destruction of Howel's marriage would inevitably result in me not completing the architectural changes to the fogou – the thing Casvellyn had wanted to prevent. That was what his work at Boscawen Ûn had been all about. Now he had a weapon, a means of getting rid of me and retaining the order. And yet, all of Casvellyn and his fellow druids' herbs and flowers had meant to ease the process of consummation of Howel and Orla's marriage – though in fact, such magic had not assisted in their union. Therefore one had to question the power of their ways. Were they fading into the night – becoming just stone foundations and collapsed dreams? It certainly felt so.

Intuition took over now. I grabbed Orla's hands and yanked her from Melwyn. We would run from this place – all this agony of unknowing. We would become ourselves somewhere else. Perhaps to the east of here we would find peace. Bugger the Saxons. In Orla, there was a look of wanting that, of moving on, but then some slight regret – her hand reaching to her mother as well. She knew that her dreams had been shattered, perhaps by Orla's own selfishness. Then again, as she let go of the maternal hand, she also knew her world must change. If it didn't, then others in the future would suffer the same fate. Orla knew she must be strong. In seconds, her expression told me this.

"We're leaving," I said.

"I don't think so," said Casvellyn. "You can try, but I've already sealed both ends with men. Ironic, eh, that you should be jailed in the very structure that was meant, by your hand – with sharp chisel and blunt bevel – to one day offer our village security and protection?"

He was right. At both ends of the fogou entrance – west and east – Casvellyn had positioned guards, fresh back from fighting the *Ancredhor Mor*. The game was up.

"Master Voog, you will stand trial by our law," said Casvellyn, and then, asking one of the men, "Is Howel back?"

The man nodded and Casvellyn barked his orders.

"Put Voog in irons, and take him before Howel. He will soon know the measure of events and how he has been duped. Take the girl to the women. Ask them to examine her below – to see what has been done – and what has been left."

Fuck. That sounded awful for Orla. They were going to examine her vagina to see if she'd had sex with me.

Men who before had chatted with me, and who I'd deemed as friends, now put semicircles of iron around my ankles. Already, before I'd even begun to walk, they weighed heavily. A link of chain ran between the inner semicircle of iron on one leg to the other. The outer half was then clasped around my ankle and shut tight, held in place by an iron pin. My freedom was being inexorably taken away.

I just managed to see Orla being pushed roughly towards the western end of the souterrain. This was it then. This was where our chickens came home to roost.

Casvellyn was now in deep conversation with Melwyn. Maybe she too, would be up for trial for attempting to keep our secret. More likely, they would be discussing Cadreth's reaction. He would have to be told.

It was fully night outside by now, and news of victory over the *Ancredhor Mor* had been passed out over the moors. Women and children wound their way back down the gorse-valleyed pathways. There was some sobbing. Clearly, some of the men of Chysauster and Euny had been slain in the conflict. There'd be good use made of the fogou over the next few days, despite the transgression that had occurred in it. Already the wailing and mourning had begun. It suited my mood – I was already mourning my past life. The people of the village looked with surprised faces at me – this Voog, this Vug-builder now in chains. Why on earth was he in such a state? Remfra pleaded with me to know what had happened, but I could not say.

"Look to your tales," I eventually said. "They will tell you of true love."

All around, the decorations of the wedding feast remained, in mocking irony of my choice, and of the recent attack.

I was marched into the parliament building, which was buzzing from the energy of warfare. Soon, I saw that Howel was being treated by Selus and Genaius for a wound on his shoulder. Casvellyn was right. An axe had been brought down hard upon it and gaped a wound. Probably, the shoulder bone had been broken. Druids knew how to repair such injuries and they were at work upon him. Cadreth was at present nowhere to be seen. As the druids worked on Howel, the busy energy stopped. The people who crowded inside wanted news of their leader, of how the battle had been and whether or not the Vikings would be back. They wanted to see him and his bride as well, though already there were rumours. Guards at the fogou had told their wives, and their wives had told others. Some women had been called to make an inspection.

Although the elderly Selus and the quicker Genaius were keen to continue working on Howel's injury, he was clearly in no mood to lie down and rest. Instead, he made a sign, and the three Viking prisoners whom they had captured were hauled by their feet over the rafters so they dangled there in full view of the community. They'd been stripped and beaten and Howel was about to deal with them. Such a view of the world and such embarrassment make a man very vulnerable. He knows what is coming.

The first Viking – a young blond man in his late teens with barely a beard – looked meek and mild as he swung upside-down from one of the rafters. He swore at Howel in a lengthy diatribe which no-one understood literally, but all got the sense of, when the Viking spat a great green gob of phlegm at the chieftain.

"Mock me would you, bastard *Ancredhor Mor*?" said Howel. "Mock me in our Annown now."

Howel made signal to Kenal, who took an iron blade to the throat of the captive. He cut his throat instantly and a river of blood cascaded onto the floor.

He moved to the second prisoner, a Viking already shaking with fear – and around the same age as Howel himself. There was something about him that told you he was a father and a husband, but the chieftain was in no mood for forgiveness or platitudes.

"Tell your ancestors, your kin and your sons that you will not step foot again on my land. Tell them from the other side. Haunt them forever."

This time, it was Howel himself who took a blade and sliced it across the throat of the pirate. He did it the same way he killed boar. The man had tried to speak but instead his plea became a pitiful groan of agony.

The third man they'd captured was older. He was probably a grandfather. This had been the bastard who'd located the axe into Howel's shoulder. The resolution here was nastier, and expected by the audience. Such a man needed to die in a more agonised way – not the swift end of the others. Howel reached high and cut the bollocks off the man, stuffing them globe by globe into his saliva-dripping face. Then with one slice he ruptured his ribcage and out fell his organs. The man saw this before he slowly and agonisingly died.

The fourth man tied upside down was no Viking. It was me. When I spun into Howel's face, it was almost as if he had seen a ghost. Initially, he made a sign to cut me down, thinking there had been some horrific mistake, but then Casvellyn appeared from the crowd, placing a caring hand upon Howel's and obviously telling him what had occurred. I knew Howel could take it. This was a day for slaughter, not for sensitivity. In some senses, perhaps he was even glad: that bitch Orla had not wanted him. Casvellyn, masterminding proceedings as ever, then signalled to the women to bring in Orla. The rope I was strung up with creaked and turned, the rafter I was hung from bending slightly. I surveyed all the people of Carn Euny and Chysauster from my upside-down state. In this position, you notice only legs. They show expression. Faces are almost beyond your vision, so you watch walking instead. The moment Orla was brought in, I recognised the milky skin of her inner thigh – which only an hour ago I had touched. With her, came Cadreth and Melwyn, both pleading to Howel for forgiveness for their daughter. Ah, it was becoming clearer now to the masses watching. This Orla, this 'babe' from Chysauster had gone and fucked that Voog – ee who repaired the vugs. Still the rafter creaked with the weight of the spinning blood of the dead Vikings. The third man had now given up the ghost, his testicles falling on the floor as his jaw muscles relaxed. I looked at them. This was my fate now, it seemed. I was going to be flayed, punctured and split into two like a cow carcass, and forced to eat my own pleasure.

Howel had retreated into himself. All of his plans for the future had fallen by the way. When in battle, he had been dreaming of fighting alongside his future sons, of securing a free state between Euny and Chysauster; perhaps even fairly ruling the whole of this peninsula. That had been completely fucked up by the attack, and now this situation. Clearly, he could hardly make sense of it – that his new wife would find this stonecutter, this clicky-handed Vug-hole builder more attractive. He had put trust into me, fed me, homed me, fetched me here, and now I had repaid him with complete betrayal. And not out on the moors, or on sand by the ocean, but in the very space that was so sacred to him and his people that he could hardly bear to think about it. The wound in his shoulder was nothing compared to the mental agony of this. Even worse, the whole of the community was watching. Their leader's laundry was out in public. On another day, in another Age, this might have been solved in secret. Not now though. His tragedy would be talked over for years to come. He knew there and then that it might even define his reign. All was public now. There was no point in trying to pretend none of it had happened.

The stench of the dead Viking next to me was become overwhelming, his organs giving out the gasses of the digestion, and the smell of his dangling entrails was very powerful. Casvellyn fussed around some of the women. Here they were clearly telling him that Orla had consummated her relationship with me. They had reached into her vagina and found traces of my seed.

"She must be tried by fire," shouted Selus. "Although she is from us, deceit must always be rooted out."

I knew what this meant. Either she'd be asked to walk across a hot bed of burning wood, or perhaps to carry a heated iron poker. If her feet didn't burn or her hands remained unscathed, then the focus would fall back on me. Then the charge would be that I had lured her into the cell and raped her. All guilt on her behalf would be exonerated. The problem was that such a trial was hardly fair. Human flesh melts and burns when it comes into contact with fire. I couldn't allow that to happen.

"No!" I screamed at Howel. "Please don't do that to her. I am the one who is guilty. Not her. Take me instead. Slit my throat, but not hers. I seduced her. Yes – that's what happened. "

Howel gestured for the men who were holding me to raise me up slightly. Then my eyes came into contact with Howel's piercing vision.

"If I cannot trust you Voog – one who knew my deepest thoughts about the future – then who must I trust?"

"Trust her," I said. "Don't hurt her. She... we... made a mistake. It should never have happened."

You see, I said all of this, but I didn't believe it. I was just trying to save Orla. I was hoping the provinces of Euny and Chysauster weren't about to go to war.

Somewhere in the crowd I could hear Orla sobbing; the other women with her trying to comfort her. Me lined up with the entrails, slit throats and disconnected bollocks did not look good.

"What do you think, druid?" asked Howel, indicating Casvellyn's presence to be close.

"The law is clear on adultery, good King," I saw the druid noting (he'd brought along, for purpose and show, a scroll detailing the legal basis of the code). "Both participants are to be sentenced to death."

"Death? Are you quite sure?" asked Howel, looking over at that young woman he had pinned his hopes on.

Howel looked at his crowd. Many were from Chysauster. A sentence of death on their most prized daughter would be a declaration of war, adultery or no adultery. He knew of Orla's popularity. The women may have thought little of her at this precise moment, but she was Cadreth's daughter. He could hardly sentence her to death on his land. Besides, this kind of legal system was not really the one he wanted to run. The druids' system was inflexible and intolerant. He wanted a world more forgiving, where punishments would be given and taken, but in which integration back into society might follow. He felt himself a fool clearly, because in acts of revenge he had swiftly cut the throats of these pirates. Therefore now, a guilt that he did not like ran through his veins. I knew Howel and knew how he operated. This was my one advantage. There had been enough bloodshed in the last twenty-four hours.

Then there was me. But if he wasn't about to sacrifice Orla, then perhaps I would become the target of his revenge. I was ultimately expendable. His fogou might not get its overhaul, but I was transient – a drifter who would not be missed. Punishment would thus be dealt out and the matter would end. My death would show he had not been compromised. Shit happened. It was the way you dealt with it that earned you the respect of your people. Perhaps there could be a middle way. Thieves sometimes had their arms lopped off. Perhaps my useless left hand might be sacrificed for this piece of adultery. I knew the wider issue though. Events here had cosmic consequences. This is what Casvellyn meant. The fact that the marriage had not been consecrated would probably be used to later explain why enemies descended and were victorious, why crops would fail, why cattle would die, and why rats and other such creatures would kill people. I'd be scapegoat and I would come to know the consequences.

At that moment though, when Howel was deliberating, I was still fully expecting his final act on me to be a slice through my member and to shove that protuberance into my gob. When you encounter death in this way, you have accepted though. You know what will pass. You have already seen it. You are out of your body looking down. You are in the fogou awaiting, for me at least, the horrors of an unforgiving Annown. You will not be laid there though. You will just be tossed into a field and left for the crows and rats. See what I was expecting?

"I have considered much," said Howel. "In these last few hours I have lost colleagues I have fought alongside, and I have lost my wife. Somewhere I hope to regain her again – and you Voog, one in whom I put so much trust, you have betrayed me beyond all measure. If I were a leader who had not seen so much blood already today, then I would run you through. By this sword, I would do to you as I have done to him."

He pointed at the stinking *Ancredhor Mor*.

"I am a better man than that though. So I will not do that."

The pain in his shoulder was hurting him I could tell. He was breathless, wanting nothing more than peace and rest. Twirling and twisting on the rope, I sensed Casvellyn's disappointment. Clearly, a dead fogou-builder was a good fogou-builder.

"I cannot kill you Voog. Killing one of my own is not my way. Instead, I draw on the wisdom of my father – one who knew Donyerth, your father Voog – all those years ago... He told me once that a man betrayed him too. He killed him in a different way. This, I do to you, Voog. I send you into exile. I declare that not only do you leave this peninsula, but that you leave this island of Britain too – and make your way in the world upon the horizon."

The crowd listening gasped at the unusual nature of this punishment. They did understand though. Exiling me would avert cosmic disaster and secure the safety of Howel's people. Future prosperity would be guaranteed: there would be a harvest, cattle would not die, and our enemies would not be victorious

"There you will be able to think back on all you have lost. You will think each day of your romp in the fogou, and think of her and you growing old – and yet apart – and that way will your suffering continue until you die. To kill you – well – that would just be swift and too quick like these sods...."

He pointed to the gaping Vikings.

In the crowd, Orla sobbed softly.

"But know you, Voog, if ever you set foot on these islands again, I will hunt you down fast like a dog, like an eagle, like a wolf, and there will be no end to the agony that I will give to you."

The ropes continued to creak on the rafter.

"Cut him down," ordered Howel. "In the morning, take him to the ocean and set him upon it."

I fell onto the earth, still roped, and still bound in shackles. It was perhaps the last time I would look at the community so closely for some while. A sack was placed over my head. Instantly, I understood that I would not see Orla's face again. Annown's wrath was banishment and not death – and yet, as you will see, banishment can sometimes be worse than a death. And this friends, was how the ocean became my ocean.

IN THOSE TIMES, I OFTEN sat in your sacred space Annown. I absorbed you in the earthy warmth of the fogou. Maybe that year, there was a final ember that burned bright. They say that, don't they? Fires have one final gasp before they are extinguished, before they become ash and dust. While others began to ignore the fogou, I made it my daily habitation. There, I found a peace. There, I could contemplate all I had discovered. There, I could think about my own future. What has come to transpire never for an instant entered my mind, but maybe you were secretly working, Annown – churning the waters and bringing to the surface things that had long been lost.

The gathering came in the spring. From all over they came; those that were left. Many had been in hiding, or had disguised themselves; only here could they wear their white robes. Some had ended their isolation and moved back into their communities. Others now refused to train ovates – it was too dangerous. You could see it in their eyes: they knew their Age was over. These were the last fragments. Whereas before, such figures moved with confidence, perhaps even arrogance, they now walked with heads bowed. The Romans had given them one holocaust. Now they faced another. They came from other parts of the horn of Britain, where the arm of the Saxons had not touched. They came from Armorica, where both native and refugee communities still carried this old faith. Some had crossed from Cymru in the north. There were even rumours that two druids from Hibernia might arrive. Every couple of days, word reached us that another arrival had managed to make his way to this final peninsula of belief.

The arm of Casvellyn spread far and wide. He was well-respected amongst their order. Messages had been sent out to those whom he knew would respond. Despite the Christian presence at Carn Euny, he had continued to practise there, ignoring the emerging crosses and still putting faith in the fogou, the stones and the stars. So it was said, despite Howel's conversion, he tolerated his old druid, though the two no longer spoke. Probably Howel hoped that Casvellyn might fade into the mist. All of this I gleaned from Kenal, who kept me informed of events at Carn Euny.

The druids had camped near to Boscawen Ûn. A city of tents and temporary dwellings surrounded the periphery of the stone circle. Daily, the druids would rise to greet the dawn, and then spend their days sat in discussion and thought over the future. Nights brought further ceremony. Although many people of Carn Euny had followed Howel's lead, still a residual respect for them remained. The gathering had brought well-needed economic benefit to the village – with many people supplying the druids with food, water, wood and their ritual requests. For the elderly, it had something of the old days about it. A familiarity returned.

Despite having no love for Casvellyn, Kenal and his men had been employed to guard the events. Such a gathering might prompt reaction from watching Saxons, and the druids could not risk attack. Casvellyn however, must truly have known the danger. Perhaps this was his one last gesture of defiance. He would not be told who he could and could not meet.

Snippets of information came back to the surrounding villages about what had been discussed, and what they planned to do. The need for secret training of new ovates was deemed necessary – otherwise the order would completely collapse. The young were, after all, its future. Apparently, some of the Cymric druids wanted them to engage in more open debate with these Christians. If ideas were put before the public, they would soon see who was right. The Armoricans were suggesting more militant action: years ago the druids had led warriors into conflict with any who dared to oppress them. Maybe that time had come again. There were more controversial ideas. One surviving member from the peoples beyond the Great River had tabled a motion that their order should vacate the mainland and move to Silura. There, they could leave their life in peace and practise their faith undisturbed. According to Genaius, such a wish was quickly defeated: the druids were there for the people. What use would they be if they separated themselves from them?

My grandmother had little time for such discussion.

"Talking won't solve anything," she said to me each day. "They need to get off their fat arses and so something."

"What can they do?" I asked.

She didn't respond to that, only saying, "Too comfortable by far, that lot. They've had it too easy. Casvellyn won't be caring any more. I know him – he'll wheedle his way out of anything if he can."

Around this time, I was cheeky enough to say what I liked. It seemed the moment to recognise all that we had jointly endured.

"I know what he did," I said. "I know what he and Howel did..."

My grandmother stopped her cleaning.

"You and Howel," I explained. "I saw what you did to him last year."

"You did?"

"Yes. All of it."

"Then you'll know I won't ever forgive him..." she said matter-of-factly

132

"I saw him afterwards," I continued. "After you had left. I forgave him."

She turned to me.

"Have you? Then you're a better woman than me, child..."

"Do you think ill of me for doing so?"

"Not at all. If I could forgive, then perhaps all might be well. But I cannot."

"He told me about my father. He said he was a good man – but you don't seem to think so..."

"Blejan, listen... I have been wrong about Voog – all these long years. The truth is I barely knew him. But I have come to understand him and what manner of a man he was."

"Tell me about him. I want to hear what he was like."

"Very well," she said.

That evening, as the druids celebrated their dying faith in the clutches of Boscawen Ûn, for the first time, with honesty and with joy, she told me her version of my father's life.

A few days later, after I had contemplated events, I decided that I would pay a visit to Casvellyn. I now knew my grandmother's take on the tale. I next needed his. In this time, I no longer needed permission to travel across to Carn Euny. I awoke, borrowed a pony and rode there.

At the village outskirts, I jumped down and led my ride through the courtyards to where Casvellyn's roundhouse was located. I would finally have my moment with him, just as I had done with my grandmother, and with Howel. When I got there, however, the door was ajar and rocking in the morning breeze. Carefully, I pushed it open, expecting to find the druid peering at me and all of his pots, potions and paraphernalia upon the shelves. Instead, the roundhouse was empty and the shelves cleared. I had imagined his sanctum as being filled with objects of wonder and prophecy. Now, there was just emptiness.

"Are you looking for Casvellyn?" came a voice. I recognised it as one of his neighbours.

"Yes."

"You are too late," said the woman. "We're moving in here..."

"And Casvellyn?"

"He has gone my dear. Went yesterday. After the gathering down Boscawen, he decided to make his way to Armorica. His two ovates went with him."

"Not coming back?"

She shook her head.

"For the best I expect," offered the woman, knowingly.

10

Oracle Bone fragment, Skellig Michael, County Kerry, Éire, 6th Century
This fragment of turtle shell plastrons, has an obscure Latinate script upon it.
It was probably used by a pre-Christian community who lived on the Great
Skellig Island in the 6th Century. Fragments of bones in such communities
across the world often indicate their use in prophecy. *Skellig Michael* lies some
11.6 km west of the Iveragh Peninsula. A Christian monastery was founded on
the island at some point between the 6th and 8th century, and was continuously occupied until it was abandoned sometime in the late 12th Century. This
fragment was discovered as part of an archaeological investigation of the island's midden (domestic waste tip) undertaken in 1999 by the Department of
Archaeology, National University of Ireland, Galway.

IN THE IMMEDIATE AFTERMATH I knew not the fate of dear Orla, nor of
Cadreth's political allegiance to Howel. I was told nothing. They kept me in
the dark – figuratively and literally – with the rough sacking still covering my
head. No-one spoke to me. I was given no food or water, but left alone to contemplate my sinful transgression. I had lost all sense of place and purpose, having been cut down from the rafters and bundled into a locked side room. There
I remained. I had been stripped of my clothes; a good thing in the sense that it
allowed me to shit and piss in this cell at will without soiling my garments. I
tried to do this in the corners of the space so as to keep clean the central area
where I lay. My hands were bound (that blasted knot-work again) – because
of my error, I was being managed more like an animal than a man. I could tell
that I was becoming dehydrated – and even longed for some of the hallucinogenic watercress Casvellyn had recommended, to mentally take me some place
other than this. Perhaps the greenery might even satiate my hunger, which was
also starting to bite hard.

Somewhere, Orla (she was never really *my* Orla; she belonged to Howel)
was doing the same thinking as I was. I contemplated her fate over and over
again, wishing and praying that she had not been harmed. Deep in my mind, I
knew that forgiveness could not ever come to her from the communities of
Chysauster and Carn Euny. She'd probably live amongst them, but never, ever
be fully accepted again. I imagined her as an old woman of faded beauty, mad
with loathing for what she'd been forced to accept, ruing the day she clasped
eyes on a gammy-handed, pathetic stonemason. To not see her any more, how-

ever, broke my heart – and thus, from this time onwards she became a kind of recurring dream. On some days, though, it was as if we had never touched or felt each other. It seemed as if it had all been nothing but a story – one of Remfra's extended romances – only a tale cut far too short. All the while, I tried not to forget what she felt like, what it was like to kiss her and how she had made my soul feel so alive.

This, you must understand, was the overwhelming thought in my mind, despite the many events, places and creatures I was to witness over the coming months and years.

In short, no matter what I faced or saw, her picture was seared into my eyes. There would be days ahead when I felt her spirit watching. Maybe, in the wilds of the ocean, it was she who protected me. See, I can dream of having a better functioning hand – and I can still dream of her.

Of Howel himself, I knew even less. That he had saved me and kept me alive told me something of the man and his mercy. He was not going to allow his baser instinct to be enacted on me. The Vikings – well, that was a public act. It had to be done – to demonstrate his ruthlessness against them. Me – well, there had been too much friendship between us for him simply to cut me through the torso like a stuck boar. He hated me no doubt, hating the fact that I'd come into his world of his own wishes, and wrecked it. In the cell, I could almost feel that hatred oozing through the granite walls. My act with Orla would not only have stolen his marriage, it would also possibly have taken away his empire, his vision for a line of defensive fogous across the horn of this land – and it would have taken away his relationship with Casvellyn. That was one thing – the druid might actually have sat back down in his hut, glad of my error, since now the fogou's sacred space would not be compromised. The bastard probably thought his placing of one of its stones at Boscawen-Ûn somehow influenced events. Why, anyway, should this village trust a man with a stump of a left hand and an extra digit, who'd come through to this world from Annown already cursed and blighted? Now that Howel had crumbled, Casvellyn could pour more poison in the chieftain's ear. Howel had been visionary. This incident with Orla might make him pull back, rethink and no longer engage with a world at change. In a way, this was what saddened me the most: that reliance on superstition, divination and prophecy might return once again. That was surely the true way to abandonment, the true way to oblivion.

Perhaps Howel could remarry. He was young enough, powerful enough, and perhaps stupid enough to do so. Besides, he would be able to argue with the druids that the marriage was never consummated. If he did, then he might be wiser in his next choice of bride, and select a woman who wouldn't be as head-strong. He'd wanted compliance, not the kind of resolute feistiness that emanated from Orla. Much would depend, of course, on whether further Viking raids would take place. Despite all the other dire issues facing him, this would still be Howel's central concern. In the confusion of the previous days, although I knew they had been successful in beating back the Norsemen, it was less clear whether they had departed these shores. Maybe they had – trying now the other less well-guarded inlets to the east. Despite my situation, it was still a fear I felt. I shuddered at the sea pirates' collective fate in Howel's hall. Their bodies would have been cut down and dragged to the fringes of the village, there to await the fate of picking crows and gnawing rats. That would be their learning.

The learning of my own fate came in the dawn of my third day in the cell. From gaps in the stones, I sensed light breaking through. This I could see from the small perforated squares in the sacking material. It was the first day since the wedding when it had not rained. Perhaps this was what they were waiting for – a break in the weather. All I could tell was that a group of men came into the cell. A heavy iron clasp was undone and the door creaked open. It seemed as if they'd had orders not to speak to either me or each other. Only one of them betrayed this when he eased back into the corner of the cell and accidentally stepped in my overnight defecation.

"Ah... fuck!" he went, giving me a juddering kick into my thigh as punishment. "Your shit is all I need."

I tried to recognise his voice, but could not. Others I tried to discern by their breathing, their coughs and grunts, but none was so distinctive I could make them out. I pleaded for water and food, but none was forthcoming. At this request, they just laughed. I suppose I deserved their inhumanity. Instead, the four men lifted me up, two at my feet and two carrying me under my shoulders. In such a position, a man is very vulnerable – his pissle and nuts exposed – but there was nothing I could do. I let them do their work. Inside the sack, I noted how the surroundings first became darker, and then, as the men grunted up some steps and a door was opened, we eased into a bright morning light. Despite the sacking, my eyes needed to adjust to the light and for a while I shut them tight, daring not to be blinded by the morning sun. Despite my circumstances it was good to breath a fresher air now.

"Where are you taking me?" I had to ask.

There was no response. They had been well trained.

There was a pause in proceedings as I sensed one of the men move away a little distance, to some longer grass, in order to wipe my shit off his shoe. This left one man at my head, to take care of the whole of this end of my body. I felt him struggle with the weight of me.

I tried to sense if others were watching; if this was a public event for the amusement of the community. It seemed very still however. There were no murmurs of conversation or even shadows above and around me that indicated such an event was being observed. In many ways, this made me more fearful. The eyes of others guaranteed a certain respect or 'safe' passage. The present situation could only indicate this group were doing what the hell they wanted, or whatever the hell someone wanted them to do. Maybe it had been organised this way. Maybe Howel had declared that everyone should stay in their round-houses and not watch the proceedings. It was perhaps part of an organised way of wiping me from history – not seeing my final moments would make for an easier and more convenient disappearance. It was always the same way – with all humans. What they want to remove, they do it when others don't see. That way it is tidy, less messy for the instigators.

Seemingly, my shit wasn't coming off easily.

"You should have given me a bowl," I argued. My hunger and thirst were beginning to affect me. These words came out slurred, as if I were drunk.

There was no response.

At last the fourth man returned to carry my weight. This assistance made the other three breathe more easily. I was brought down a slope, and there, a sensation of them inverting me. I was adroitly turned over and lifted up, to be placed on the rear of a shuddering creature. My bollocks dangled against its flanks as they levered me across. When my nose came close to the animal's skin, its smell became familiar. I soon recognised the scent. It was the pony I'd taken as payment from the Halliggye job. Kenal must have at least have been spoken to as they'd have needed to obtain the pony from his stabling.

This was it then – this was how I was to be taken to the coast. To prevent me from falling, I was bound with ropes, dangling there like a piece of caught meat. I sensed the others mount upon their own horses, and within a matter of minutes we set off. They'd take the quickest route down to the coast no doubt. It was a road I knew well already despite my lack of eyesight, and as we continued I could sense potholes and dips that were familiar – places where the gorse grew thick, and later, the rocky ground at Lisadell.

All the while, the familiar odour of the pony was a comfort to me, but I knew that I was being taken further and further away from Orla. She was becoming distant, a ghost, a split stone, a sketch – in a life I once had. By my calculations, we were trekking past where the Vikings had pillaged. Seemingly, at points, there were moments where we stopped to survey the damage. A little distant from me I could hear the men talking in grievous tones. The precise nature of what they spoke of I could not make out, but I could tell from its gravity and angst that people here had not been so fortunate. They had been at the full mercy of the *Ancredhor Mor*. At Trevorgans – I am guessing – there was still a stench of death in the air.

When the sun was at its highest point, the party stopped for food. A fire was lit and some boar meat cooked. My pony was fed and watered but I was given nothing. By now, the banging of my penis and testicles against the flank of the pony had started to bruise them. This was due punishment, I suppose, for what I had engineered. I could hardly complain to the men with me. The cooking meat made me ravenous though. In order to cope, I tried to mentally take myself to other places – earlier parts of my life, where things were better. I was even wishing I was back down at Kynance completing the rebuild there. At least there, I had food and water. There I was not naked or prostrate upon a pony.

What was worrying me the most was that although I had accepted my fate, this lack of nutrition would not be a good start for any push out onto open water. One needed to be satiated, well-organised and have supplies at hand, if one was about to go out on the ocean. Were they about to just drop me in a boat and let me go? Would they untie these knots or leave me as I was? Bound and blinded was no way to steer a course. This uncertainty caused me as much angst as the lack of food and water. All was unclear to me. Although I had seen most of the punishments doled out by chieftains in this horn of the land, this method of exile was new to me. I was, so it seemed, a test case.

In my delusion, Orla's name kept coming to me.

Or... la.

Ooor...laa.

Was she now high on Bartinney looking out for me?

No. More probably, she was back in Chysauster in disgrace. Shame would forever be hung around the neck of their family. Disgrace would be a yoke she'd take to her grave – and beyond it.

Ooor...laa. Ooor... laa. Ooor... laa.

Her name matched the movement of my pony's strides as the party moved off again. The name still tempted me. The O of it enveloped me – just like the wonders of her vagina. Despite all this hardship, I could not stop fantasising about her.

Whilst my guards' bellies were full, mine ached with acid and bile. In the summer heat, my lips cracked. My pony was tethered to the saddle of the first guard again, and we proceeded onwards. From the sun's position, I felt that we were heading to the south west now – probably over the tussocky downs at Pendrea and on to the ash wood at Silena. These I knew well. If this was their route, then they were thinking of taking of me down to Penberth. That was where I would be cast off, shook like a bastard of a cow tick, into the blue. I was scum to be sent upon the foam and brine. I'd be food for fishes, a dish for sharks, and in the bardic tales not yet composed, a hearty meal for the sea serpents.

I noted a change in the air. Inside the sack I could taste the salt of the ocean. We were dropping as well. The pony's steps were more ragged and less assured now as we followed the groove and dip of the valley stream, heading toward the cove. Navigating streams was often the best path to a location as it was more or less the most direct route. The guards had chosen well.

The hooves of the many horses made splashes upon my back. This cooled me but I was praying my ordeal might soon be over. This really was no way to travel.

Penberth stretches south east, and by mid-afternoon the sun had moved its rays further to the west. The western cliffs left the cove in shadow. I could feel this foreboding as we came to the cove itself. Here, the beach drops steeply. Just as it was a good landing site for the *Ancredhor Mor*, here it would be my departure. I knew the cove well, of course. A few years ago, a settlement had existed here. That had long since gone, following the growing threat of brutal raids from the sea. Now the walls of that settlement had probably most recently been adapted for Viking use. Their recent presence seemed to startle the horses a little.

"Get him down," one of the guards instructed.

Hands reached at the ropes and untied the knots that bound me to the pony's back. I fell to the floor. I heard the swash of the ocean cut onto the pebble-crammed beach. Gulls yelped somewhere out to sea. They expressed my panic to the expanse.

Around me I heard the struggle of them lifting an object off one of the horses, which with some weight, banged down onto the pebbles. Wood banged against it.

A pair of hands reached around my neck and undid the string of the sacking. The material was yanked off me. At my back, another man undid the knot binding my hands together.

"Here, these are your clothes...."

Silhouetted by the sun, I made out a familiar face. It took a while for me to adjust to my freedom and to regain my full sight. Soon, as the figure in the silhouette crouched down to me, his face became frighteningly clear. It was Kenal – but not the old Kenal I had known. He was different somehow – or perhaps

I had tainted him. Yes – that was it. I had changed him. There was no smile anymore. Once we had been comrades. Now, I was a bit of flotsam about to be tossed back into the tide.

"I didn't mean..." I tried to express my regret to Kenal, but these were words he had no wish to hear.

"Your children – did they ask...?"

Kenal spat his distaste.

"Go fuck yourself with your excuses, Voog," he said, grabbing me by the chin. "Everyone knows what a bastard you are.... Here's your future friend."

He gestured to what they had positioned on the pebbles. It was a coracle. Like half of a nut shell, the oval boat (if you could call it that) was being readied for me. I knew of such vessels of course. They were used all over the south coast. I peered at the framework of split and interwoven willow rods, felt the strength of the willow bark knots holding all together.

"It's a good one," noted Kenal. "Of bullock hide, and tarred all over..."

"They're for inshore use – for fishing," I quipped. "Not for the ocean... not for journeys..."

"These new holy men use them, so Lord Howel has heard... to cross great distances. Hibernia to Armorica it is said. If it is good enough for them, then it should be good enough for you."

I started to dress. Although my undergarments and clothes stank of sweat and earth, they were good to feel on me again. Nakedness makes a man more vulnerable than anything else. Slipping on my shoes and tying their laces felt satisfying. Despite this, the men and Kenal noted my unease at the prospect of life in the coracle.

"Would you rather suffer the fate of the *Ancredhor Mor* at Carn Euny?"

I hardly needed to answer. They knew my choice.

"There is food and water within it – enough for some twenty days of jour-neying. That should get you somewhere far from here."

At this, I moved to reach into the interior of the vessel and pulled out a skin of water which I drank from liberally, and untied leather pouches of goat's cheese, stuffing cubes of it into my mouth.

"Eat now," went one of the men, "and you'll go hungry on the waves..."

I didn't care. I knew I needed to regain my strength again. Besides, the ocean was a larder. There, I knew I wouldn't go hungry.

"Suit yourself," Kenal offered. "Here... don't forget this..."

I peered up at him in puzzlement. He threw my sack at me. Inside were my tools and drawings thankfully untouched and undamaged.

"Maybe another land will offer you work, mason, eh? Build another civilisation perhaps? This time, you might use the right 'tool'...."

Kenal laughed at me, pointing to his own knob.

I delved further into the sack. The dusty tools saddened me. They were the devices by which I might have helped Howel's empire grow. They were the tools that should have offered me stability and safety. Now they symbolised all of my failing, my lack of precision, my lack of control.

Kenal symbolically drew his sword. This was a sign for the other three to do the same. It was my cue to take the black coracle down to the tide. I placed the skin and pouches back into the willow work, tucking them in behind straps, and then, like a turtle, turned the structure upon my back. I waddled, carrying it and my sack across the pebbles to a new watery frontier. This was the sacrifice I must make for my past pleasures. The coracle was heavier than I had reckoned, and it took me a while. All strength seemed to have gone from me. Besides that, my bollocks were bruised from my time on the pony, and they ached to buggery. Finally, I was able to flip over the vessel onto the water.

Kenal and the other three men had followed me down to the shoreline. As I stepped into the coracle, Kenal prepared his final statement to me. He spoke it like a warrant that reinforced the solemnity of my exile.

"You shall be always be known to us, Voog. Do not think you can return. Do not have hope of this. Howel has sent messengers north, south, east and west, saying that if any man finds you, then you are to be killed on sight. They have been told to watch out for a traitor who has a backwards-facing wrist, like that of twisted oak. They will know you by this, and of course, your extra finger."

"That the one he used to nicely finger that slag Orla, eh?' guffawed a man I had once reckoned on being a friend.

I shook my head.

"One quick shag for this, eh? I've met some fools, but you, Voog... you don't know when your cup is full.... Worth it, was she?"

"She was," I said under my breath.

Kenal resumed his opus: "Word will spread. The whole of these isles will know of you. Nothing spreads better than news of a liar and cheater. You are a marked man."

I knew this. I knew it the first moment I realised my difference. I pushed off with the paddle.

"Don't come back," advised Kenal, a little kindlier this time.

I'd forgotten: coracles were utter bastards to control. These so-called holy men must have great patience and endurance to work them. You had to keep swapping sides in order to maintain a constant direction. Penberth's water did not help.

That summer had brought about a growth of twirling kelp into shore, and this hindered my progress away. I'd paddled for around two minutes and was already tired. I turned back on my old life. The four of them stood there – as solid menhirs of control. Howel had obviously instructed them well. They'd watch until I became a dot in the distance. They'd stay until the horizon and I merged.

Kenal's loyalty to his chief meant that our friendship had sunk deep like a weighty stone. We had once fought alongside each other, but now, seemingly, I was his enemy as well. Truly, I was snake and rat combined. What venom and what pathogens did I carry with me?

I sculled at the front of the vessel twisting the paddle in a figure of eight motion. Now I remembered that this was the best way in which to pull the vessel forwards. That day the ocean was reasonably calm, so once out of the seaweed, I started to make good progress. Since it was keel-less, the coracle glided neatly on the skin of the water. That was why the fishermen used them – they offered little disturbance to the fish below. I had seen pairs of coracles cast a net between them to catch a decent haul of fish.

My distance from the shore meant that I could now see the uplands from which we had come. The green vibrancy of the cliff tops and zawns trailed into the brown of the moor. Still there in the porth, stood Kenal and his men – monitoring my leaving. Since they were observing still, I had no choice but to make a course south. Let them think I am heading for Armorica, I told myself. That was perhaps my most logical course. Let Kenal return to Howel and tell him that. The Channel will be enough distance perhaps. He will be satisfied and eventually come to peace. There, the people speak like us, dress like us, and have the same fears. Maybe even Orla will hear word of this. Maybe that would comfort her in my leaving.

But you see, in fact, this was not my plan. Any mason, any mathematician, any engineer like me will not follow an illogical course. As you know, I am most often not one to let fate decide for me. Oh no. I may be withered physically, but inside, I remain strong. Inside, I plan, calculate and navigate. Water is as malleable as stone. In fact, the more I think about it; the more they are similar elements.

Thus, there comes in each of our lives a moment where we choose to leave. Sometimes we have to go. There remains nothing for us in one place. This choice was the only way I could cope with the situation I found myself in. If I might turn exile into my choice, then things might be well in the long term. So I work upon this – upon *my* ocean. See, even now, I am claiming it, making it my own, so that no-one can claim they have dropped me here. Even though I know the truth, I am pretending for my soul, for my mental well-being, for my future, that this salty excursion is my chosen path. It is as if some arsehole of a druid has foreseen it. To do this, I believe, is what makes us human – it is what defines us above being rats and snakes. They just accept circumstance. We do not. We try to cope, we try self-belief: willing that things will get better.

My plan is not down to chance. Oh no. You see, as I told you before, I am not inexperienced in the ways of the sea. When times have been hard, when my father was not paid, we too came to the ocean. It sustained us, loved us and nurtured us like we were its very children. Even though I come from a line of underground workers, the sea has proven my friend. To that end, ever since I was a much younger man than I am now, I have kept a boat. At that, perhaps you will laugh, not seeing my intent. You have a boat you say. You have a coracle – a vessel good enough for these new holy men, and so why is it not good enough for you?

My answer to you is that coracles are too small for my choice. If I am to follow what I choose, then I need a larger vessel.

There. Now you see my journey. Now you see I am no little fish wiggling in the womb of the ocean.

I have a larger vessel. This coracle will keep me safe and dry for now, but when the wild westerlies crack and storms brew I won't survive in this – just as I told Kenal. Ha – I will chance my arm (my withered wrist, at least), and return to the land. This I will complete now that darkness has descended.

For a while, though, I disappear into the fusion of sky and water. I am no longer even a dot on the horizon. Kenal may wait to see if I come back, but he will not find me. As I came to know all too well, the sea's blackness holds too many secrets and sounds for even him to hunt me down. It is black out here. Only the moonlight gives shape to where the land rises, and thankfully the stars are bright enough for me to know my position. I have sculled far enough south for them to believe I have merged with the ocean forever. Probably they already wish me drowned.

That night, my coracle's silence proves useful. I hear the loud splosh of creatures who normally would not dare to go near men upon the sea for fear that they might be caught and eaten. Do they know me as someone who will not harm them? Do they sense in me the malformed flipper of my left-hand? In my stupor, I look over the side to see nuzzling, whiskered faces, the membrane of their eyes black as coal. These are what my people term *ruen*. They come to be called seals. That night, around five of them swirl about my coracle, spinning their sleek and barrelling bodies in the spray. They are bundles of ergonomic granite slipping through the weed and wet – three males and two females I think.

143

After my lone silence in the cell, and the abuse from Kenal and his men, these creatures seem to want to communicate with me. Their grunts and slaps upon the water seem to tell me all will be well. I listen to their moans and motion, and in the moonlight watch their furry hides melt in and out of the water. They come close enough for me to see how their nostrils close when they dive under. Others snort, exuding tiny flashes of water. If only I might train them, they might fetch me fish, shellfish and squid from the deep. But I've no wish to control them – to make them slaves to humanity. I know all too well what that is.

I knew it in the faces of tin-streamers.

Had I a mirror, I would see it in my own face too.

Our people believe such creatures can dive straight to Annown. It is their rolling, their barrelling, their swift foray through the wet that makes them think it so. For some they are magical signs, magical creatures. I know them for what they are. They are like us all in the world. They try to make their way as best they can, and not upset anyone. Right now, it seems they are placed here for me. These seals are my oracle. They will see me safely back in from this night, for the rocks of Porthgaurnon are where they bask, rest and nurture their young. In a cave, in this cove, is where rests my boat. All I must do is follow these mammals in.

Seals are good swimmers – faster than my slow sculling. They know my weakness, and seem to pause for me, waiting to guide me in. I must be careful though. Possibly Howel will have positioned men along the coast to make sure I don't return. Perhaps he has visions of me turning up as a leper and sneaking through cowl and bell back into the warmth of Carn Euny. This is what the englynnion would have me do. But I am no poet. Instead, I am a practical stoneworker, trying, like these seals before me, to make my way in a watery world. It being summer then, light comes early, so there is not much time for me to put ashore, survey my own choice of vessel and put to sea.

When we arrive at the cove, the moon is already starting to wane. The seals assume their positions on the low rocks, while I negotiate the coracle around their grounds, to where my vessel should be. I left it here because access from the shore is tricky. Anyone wishing to find it would need to cross the angry seal mothers who will defend their cubs at the first threat. Even now, they bark and hiss at my movement. All the while, I check to the cliff tops above. I am heeding Kenal's words. My banishment is non-negotiable. About me is a good tide. It takes me with a long thrust of weed and flotsam far into the cave, but landing takes a little more effort. I use the blade of the paddle to steady the coracle against the eastern wall of the cave. All is subject to echo. My vessel should be far enough back into the upper reaches of the cave for it not to have been harmed by higher tides. The worry is perhaps more to do with the dampness of this world – as you will see.

I gasp when I see her. I gasp in the same way as I did with Orla. She is that precious to me. She will allow me to make my choice.

She is hidden under layers of hides. Steadily, I walk about her, first surveying for damage or holes – caused by crabs, rats or gulls. Some guano is encrusted on the hides but seemingly there is nothing more. I look above, and make sure that a run of water from the wet interior of the cave has not weakened her anywhere. When I am satisfied, I unfurl the heavy hides to reveal her hull. This I now look at with precision, pulling at each hide to check the sewing.

The coracle presented to me by Kenal I knew very little about. This vessel is one I am intimate with. Did I foresee this moment when I constructed her? Not at all. She has been there for me as a welcome diversion from earth and stone. In her, I could experience sea and light. She is built to my own specifications. There are adjustments in her rigging, her ropes, her pulleys and spars – otherwise, with this weedy wrist, I'd be unable to work her. The full hull is now revealed to me. It took almost sixty oxhides to cover. They had to be hand-stitched together. By the time I'd finished, my right thumb and forefinger had become as hard as brass. I had bought the oxhides from one Enyon – a swift-talking shyster who ran a tannery near the dock at Lulyn. Knowing his reputation, the purchase had worried me but I should have trusted him. Sixty was a big order. He wasn't about to let me down.

"It'll be the best you're wanting then boy? Not calf, sheep or goat – but oxhide... Es – oxhide..."

He'd asked if I required it oak-tanned. Of course, I had argued. This was the most resilient leather to the wet.

I was recalling a murky day inspecting the tannery. The entire process created a stench that made all other smells (even the stinking innards of the discarded fish on the quay) seem like sweet fragrances from Phoenicia. The old bugger Enyon rounded the tanning pits, poking his testing stick at the leathers already dressed, then stepped back into his hut to begin the process of scraping further hair off newly-delivered hides.

It was at Lulyn I constructed her – when I'd made a bit from a rebuild job on the north coast. But I'd known for some time that I'd set her at Porthguarnon. I'd completed a few drawings first. I applied the same knowledge on building her as I did upon constructing a fogou. To an extent, boats were just fogous in reverse – and made of wood and leather, instead of stone and earth. Under the hides lay the frame itself. This was perhaps no conventional build. Unlike the vessels of the *Ancredhor Mor*, or even the fishermen further to the east, she had no keel, so in this sense, she was more an extended coracle. I had gathered the ash for her frame from the north-facing slopes of woods at Silena. These were chosen because they were the strongest and hardiest. Little should break them. Under the hides I felt their longitudinal run from bow to stern. The frames and stringers then, were the colour of druid robes – pure white. I used leather thongs from Enyon to bind them. These were soaked in sea water for a week beforehand. That way the lashings would hold tight when she hit the water. The oars, thwarts and masts were made of the same, and then the heart wood of an oak growing at High Treverven was chosen for the double gunwales.

The hides themselves went on next. These were the real bastards to fix. Enyon helped me, showing me first the plain back stitches, and then as my skill improved, how to do the two-handed ones. You had to be skilled with an awl and needle to have any impact on the hardened leather. For thread, Enyon swore by rolled flax dipped in wool grease and beeswax. He knew his art. As well as tannery products for the fishermen of Lulyn, it was he who was commissioned to make saddles for the chieftains. He employed that skill here.

She was twin-masted. This was unlike most of the other vessels that sailed to and from the horn. Such advice came from my father.

"Always have two. When one breaks, there is always another..."

For the distances I intended, this was good advice. As I peered up to her masts, I felt Donyerth's gaze. I wondered what he would think of me now – rat, snake and mariner.

Just like the seals who led me back here, she has her own blubber, this vessel. She is coated in tallow and sheep wool grease. It stinks like a bastard, but there is nothing better to keep out the wet. This is the smell that will endure the miles with me. I spend much of my night in the cave smothering her hull with woolgrease. The substance works well but never leaves your hands no matter how many times you try to wash or wipe it off. The same oak-tanned leather is used to make the sails. There you seek a different kind of strength.

She was near ready. I loaded what food and water Kenal had given me into her. Already she is stocked with dried wheat and cereals, salted roots and cool water from Alsia Well. Not only will the water be needed to quench my thirst, it will also act as ballast. Here too, was a stove of iron upon which I can cook in a cauldron. For it, are supplies of wood which will at least last me a while, until they can be replenished. For the cold are sheepskins. There is nothing better to keep out the chill on frosty nights. These, Enyon gave me for free.

She comes with a host of other features to engender her endurance. There are spare hides for ripped sails or for holes in the hull. I have lines of string and hooks for fishing, spare steering paddles in case some should break. Like the coracle, this vessel moved low in the water, and such a paddle is the best way to determine its direction (at first, I used a rudder, but that proved ineffectual). My pride and joy is an iron device my father constructed for me. It allows me to measure the angle between any two objects. On board this vessel, I can make use of it to determine the angle between the stars and the horizon, which can help me to understand my position and determine my direction. I used to think it was magic when he used it. Now, I know it to be science. I use the same way to calculate the positioning of souterrains, if the commissioners wish the midwinter or midsummer sun to rise through an opening in the structure. This device is not the only way to cross water. I take advice too from the fulmars, terns and storm petrels. When the latter put in to land, or island, you know to proceed no further.

The other item the vessel carried was a bell. I had it made for me by a smithy and iron craftsman in Lulyn. He'd formed two decorated beast-heads over the yoke that made it an impressive feature. In fog, bells were necessary. They told others you were there. Their sounds could be calming: a dull strike of the clapper upon the rim meant you were somehow not alone. For luck, I had set my talisman upon the mainmast. This was a stone pebble from Porthquarnon carved with my symbol – me holding a staff and a snake. Thank Cernunnos and all the other flaky gods of my people that I had done this, for there were times ahead when pure luck was all I had about me. And now, given this coracle handed to me by Kenal as my 'vessel of exile', for the first time I had a liferaft. I tied her tightly to the stern and hoped that she'd remain there, despite what the ocean might throw at me.

Just before the darkness of the night was swept away in the east, I pushed hard into the slippery shale deep inside the cave, and managed – with the aid of stinking wool grease – to ease her down over a run of wood planks, pebbles and seaweed into the wash of the Channel. By the time dawn properly arrived, I had unfurled her mainsail. So busy was I with my preparations overnight that for the first time in three days, I forgot about who I was and what I had become.

And so I have my ocean. And now I have my ship.

Her name?

Come, it is obvious – she is *An Ruen*: The Seal.

She will be my compass..

It is she who will navigate me across time and space to new worlds I could not yet imagine.

ANNOWN, MY LOVELY, I FEAR for you.

I fear not for my own survival any more, but for yours.

The land altered. These Christians converted not only us, but the Saxons and Vikings too. They built cells and they reinterpreted our wells and standing stones. Crosses were carved on the stones I knew once as unchanging symbols of life. In my view, they were being vandalised. Pagan heroes became Christian warriors. Dragons and monsters were products of this Satan. The old battle lines faded, and our words altered. We used more terms from the enemy. We used our own tongue a little less. I summarise this change here now. Perhaps it took some ten years or more, but as it happened, it was barely perceptible. There were, at first, tiny tremors of alteration, but then came more fully vast earthquakes which upended all we had known. What was familiar seemingly got sucked into the earth and what was new and unfamiliar got planted. It grew like a weed in a wet summer.

I came to a new sense of myself. Howel's life of penance for what he had done altered my view of him. There were times when I understood his earlier hate, his need to act, his need to exile my father. And yet, I had begun to understand his position. I also understood how much he loved my mother. I knew that his absorption of Christianity had happened as a reaction to his guilt. He had eventually hated himself for what he had done to my mother. He had despised the fact that he had traded her for peace. He could not find any peace within himself, without undergoing conversion. It is perhaps fair to say that you, Annown, could no longer offer what he wanted or even needed.

After his conversion, things did change. In his thoughts of forgiveness, he forgave others and realised what meaning he still had. Despite his loneliness and his poor physical condition (a result of my mother's poisoning attempt), he smiled more, and became the leader he once was. The past was a different place now; it had long since disappeared. Perhaps if this was what this new God prompted, then was it such a bad thing?

Genaius, in comparison to the departed Casvellyn, was working to fuse the two belief systems. He saw the similarities between the new and the old and tried to unite them. In this, I believe, he was to find his passion. My grandmother would have been pleased. Gradually, others followed in their footsteps. Baptisms took place at holy wells and crosses replaced older gods.

Howel encouraged and paid for further missionary work – from the horn of

Britain, southwards to Brittany and Galicia. He welcomed those passing through, on their way to Cymru or Hibernia. Was it any better? In truth, I did not know – not at this time in my life at least. Young people are not fixated with one view of life. Instead, they float and hover, and see what is available. In my thinking, this is the way to be – and the way I consummately was. I would observe and learn, pick and choose. Perhaps I was like Genaius, synthesising something new.

It was for my ranging and as yet unknown father I felt compassion. All his family had worked so hard to retain and keep our tradition of fogou building. It had been his life's work, from what I had been told. Now, that was all decaying. The fogous fell into disuse and neglect. Weeds grew on their floors. Earth trickled out from being compacted between stones. The cap stones remained, although some poor farmers raided the walls for building materials. Tradition that is spoken of now as age-old was established in a finger-click. Deep in their recesses, collapses occurred. No-one bothered to say anything any more. Neither did anyone prepare the old and infirm for passage to the Otherworld.

In this Christian world, the dead were simply given prayers and buried in wooden coffins. There was no mourning, no ceremony, and no acceptance into the fogou, no cremation, and no instilling in a cist. Stone no longer seemed to hold any power. It was perhaps a good thing that my father was not here to witness it.

This was the time of my young womanhood. I discovered that my body altered and changed. I noticed young men observed me differently.

"What are you looking at?" I asked them.

"Nothing," they'd say, smiling.

Did people forget and forgive my shame? Perhaps so. Some, who cared little about class and divide, and thought more of an egalitarian future, talked to me, and treated me as normal. They started to see that lineage was no mark of a person. It was instead how that individual behaved, how they responded and how they cared for others. This was something of that new era I embraced. I began to smile more, I know that. I became more open about what I said and whom I talked to. Within the constraints of Saxon stewardship, there was still some freedom. We were perhaps so small, and so far in the west, that we were left alone.

Most of all, I shed the bitterness that had followed me. Maybe that is what this new era brought the most. Perhaps that is what Howel had discovered. In my mind, I made plans. Maybe I could continue to live here. I had hope. There were young men who liked me and asked me to walk with them. No longer were there the taboos of arrangement and preferment. I was in no hurry though. If I say I wanted to see a little more of the world before settling down, I may give you the correct impression. It was still unlikely women of any type could be so bold, but somewhere inside, there was just enough of my father's spirit to make its mark on me. I didn't want the drudgery of other women. I knew that.

Looking back now, that era of my life seems so woefully carefree, it makes me smile to myself. I have already spoken of great change. I have told you too about homogeneity with people a long distance away from me. I will now explain how the collision (or was it collusion?) of these two aspects of my tale come together.

One day (I believe it was in the March of that year), I saw two horses ride through the southern gate of Chysauster. One of the riders I recognised. It was Kenal. Now an old man, and recently widowed, he let his horse take the route of least resistance upon the slope of the hill to where I was sat. I was embroidering, enjoying the morning sunshine, and its nod to warmer spring weather. Now, Kenal was a man whom I had come to trust and care for deeply, no matter what evil he had once committed on my father. He looked after me, and offered wisdom when I sought it and laughter when I did not. The other figure with him was at first indistinguishable. I could tell however, from his garb, that he was not a local man. He worked his horse harder, pushing her up the steepest ground to make better way. In time, I understood him to be a man in his late twenties. His manner was urgent and forthright.

"Blejan," shouted Kenal. "I've a visitor for you."

I put down my embroidery and adjusted my grandmother's pin holding my tunic. Whoever, it was, I wanted to look tidy.

The two riders came close. I felt the breath of their horses.

"You won't believe what this man has to say," enthused Kenal, "or how long it has taken him to get here."

"Why – what is it?" I asked.

"He has news of your father, Blejan. He came to Carn Euny from Lulyn, enquiring after Orla..."

"My mother?"

The man stepped down from his horse and knelt before me. He had the twang of a Breton accent.

"If what Kenal says is true, then I have much to tell you. My name is Tigernus and when I last saw him, your father was far across the western ocean."

"Where?"

"Hyperborea..."

I cannot remember my response. This man, Tigernus, witnessed my mouth fall open as wide as a vug-hole.

VOOG'S OCEAN

Dew

"I bear witness that the waves are happy."

> From *The Prophecy of Merlin*
> by John of Cornwall, *c.*1150

"Po rez deberra an bez, vidn heerath a seu;
po res dal an vor, na oren pan a tu
Thuryan, houl Zethas, go Gleth, po Dihow.

[When you leave the world, longing will follow;
when you begin the way, it's not known whether
it is to the East, West, North or South.]"

> Traditional Cornish Engylyn, collected
> by Thomas Tonkin, *c.*1732

VOOG'S OCEAN

11

Detail of a boat carved on a Standing Stone, Connonagh, County Cork, Éire, 7th to 8th Centuries CE

North of Connonagh, on the Skibbereen side of the River Roury, is a standing stone made of old red sandstone. Carved upon it is the image of a seagoing vessel. Examination of the image shows that it was probably constructed of stringer framing (most probably of ash) with the exterior of the hull made of oxhides tanned in oak bark. The vessel has two masts and was steered by an oar paddle at the stern. Such a vessel would have considerable stability and remain watertight in strong Atlantic seas. Image courtesy of the National Museum of Ireland/Ard-Mhúsaem na hÉireann.

INTIALLY, I HEADED INTO THE west. There was nowhere else to go. I mean, subconsciously, I was probably following the alignment of the fogou, but I didn't purposely think of this on that particular day of departure. Besides, all that was evil in my present world seemed to come from the blackness of the east and the north, so this direction chose itself. The western horizon was my destination. I knew very little of what I should find there. There were many theories. Wise men like Casvellyn still categorically argued the world was flat, and that if one travelled far enough west, east, north or south, one might encounter the broad edge of the earth and cascade off its torrent. My imagination always gave me a picture of a vast, unstoppable waterfall tumbling downwards into unrecoverable darkness. For the druids, this was another, more physical route to Annown, though never was there any way of coming back.

To be honest, this view surprised me because the druids supposedly understood the stars and their movements, and intimately knew the way the sun and moon rose in the east and fell in the west. They knew their cycles and waning. They even talked of distant planets – gave them names – but still, it suited them, this story – for it meant they had control. It meant that we would not try to travel too far, out of their clutches and philosophy. Perhaps because of their lack of druids, of bewildering mystic priests like ours, the peoples of the far south had no apprehension of travelling so widely. They were never put off by fear of waterfalls cascading into nothingness. They knew of vast lands to the east and to the south. They knew of different peoples – humans still, but of new forms and kinds.

My incorrigible father would never argue with the druids on such matters, but he had clear views on the absurdity of their arguments. The mathematician in him had calculated that such a theory held little credibility. He proved it to me by showing that the seasons and the daylight hours were dependent on both the axis of the earth and our proximity to the sun. The stars did not move, as the druids posited, but it was the globe on which we were situated that moved. I remember him marking this entirely out for me on a patch of wet sand, scratching hieroglyphs and mystic lines into its surface. Not only did this show me that if one was able to sail far enough around the earth then one might eventually come back to one's starting point, but the more incredible view that each of the stars in the blackness above represented further examples of our sun. If you followed this logic, then maybe there were other worlds, other moons, other lands and peoples far from here. Somewhere out there, others gazed at us.

Such theories often swallowed up my father's time. Let it be said that I think he drove himself mad thinking about them. These questions made his eventual senility much worse, brought on by his infirmity. Cognition, which once controlled his mind, had to be let loose. Let it also be noted that he was never one to accept what he was given. Instead, he would always question, always articulate difference. I know where this trend in me comes from then. Likewise, in the sand, he was able to draw for me the world as he saw it. Despite what I have heard from far cleverer men, it is his cartography that I am now reliant upon. My own maps and sketches of the earth and ocean follow his.

Where then, was I travelling? I had no purpose, unlike the Phoenician tin traders who came to the horn of Britain. I suppose, lurking in my mind, and let us be honest, lurking in the mind of any explorer, was the possibility of some undiscovered paradise, some finer land, some place filled with fruit, gold and wonder that would see me set for life. There, I should find new flavours, try delicious vegetables, encounter cute animals, maybe even meet dreamier, sexier young women than dear Orla. Who needed that cramped granitic land of damp and mould when one could live in luxury as a king every day? There, it would be sunny and never rain. There would be rivers of milk and honey (it was that hope that kept me going this long time upon the ocean).

There were stories though. I'd met enough travellers and sailors to know something of what was said to be out there. Perhaps it was bullshit – bravado born of long, hard days at work on the sea – that gave rise to such notions. But they were spoken of in such hushed tones and utter respect that somehow one believed of their existence. The names of these fabled 'Islands of Bliss' flickered back and forth across my mind. Let me list them for you. Mayda was one;

sometimes the land was called Asmaida – and she was rumoured to be not that far into the great ocean, and a place of abject wonder. The Vikings, so it is said, talk of a revered place called Frisland, somewhere in the same ocean, but further to the north. Though colder there, tales are told of its herds of fine cattle and sheep.

The name that most frequented the lips of the fishermen I knew though, was Ogygia. The banks near there were said to be full of fish. Usually in these tales, back-along, someone's great-great-grandfather or uncle had sworn to have landed there. Locating it again had proven more difficult. However, given that most of those buggers hardly dared go five miles beyond the quay at Lulyn, this was perhaps not really surprising. See how we like to think there is something there – but equally, see how we do not always wish to encounter it. This is the true paradox of discovery. On reflection, it was something I was soon to feel.

In my lengthy discussions with Remfra, occasionally he had spoken to me about the lands of the west, purely because they were such good starting points for his tales. Unlike the druids, who preferred the words of nature, Remfra was better read. Like most bards, he had travelled beyond our islands, to Gaul and to the rest of that continent. There, so he recalled, he had encountered, I think, the work of one Hecatæus of Abdera. So he informed me, Hecatæus' writings told of an island opposite the coast of Gaul, not smaller, in his words, than the island of Sicily, which was inhabited by a people he named the Hyperboreans, so-called, because they dwelt beyond the North Wind. According to Remfra's take on it, this land of the Hyperboreans was of "a happy temperature, rich in soil and fruitful in everything, yielding its produce twice in the year..."

Although Remfra was a man committed to embroidering and enhancing reality, this small snippet stayed with me – especially during the early phase of my voyage, when ambition, hope and promise followed me like the trailing gulls at the stern, after my daily cooked fish. This Mayda, Frisland, Ogygia and Hyperborea may seem perhaps fictions, travels into pure imagination, but I ask you not to judge them until my tale here is complete. Sometimes the reality is stranger than fiction. Sometimes, these old spun tales turn out to have not just grains, but a thick slice of truth to them.

These thoughts occupied my mind fully as I completed the more practical task of sailing *An Ruen* in my chosen direction. From Porthguarnon's clutches, and with chirping seals accompanying me, I had run the boat a fair way out to sea, so as to not be noticed by any prying eyes of Howel's men. Perhaps the most important location to stay clear of was the complex fortification at Treryn Dinas, a jut of granite into the sea that served as the first warning post of any raids on the south coast. I knew the location well; had often walked down to its double ramparts and stood upon the *logan* – or rocking stone – which topped the rocks there. Although it was not within Howel's lands, the people there had good alliances with him, and my movements would surely be reported back. An oxhide sailing vessel, towing a coracle, would make for an unusual sight. Thus, I headed further out to the sea, not following too closely the line of the coast. Arm's length was enough.

Still the majestic outcrops of Pedn-mên-an-mere and Carn Scathe guided my route. To be quite honest, too close a route around the shore was something I was not comfortable with anyway. Beneath the threatening form of Carn Bargas lurked the rocks known as the Vessecks, and many an experienced mariner and naïve fisherman had come a cropper there. The land began to fall away from me as I rounded Carn Guthensbras where I charged properly into more open water. Here, making a crab-like movement around the space, I roamed the vessel, testing the seaworthiness of the hides and stitching. Enyon had apparently trained me well – I could find no leaks. She was creaking a lot as the waters became choppier off Nanjizal. This didn't bother me though. She had been designed to have some flexibility within her frame and stringers. Rigidity was fine to an extent, but within this kind of vessel – and understanding what she would endure in the full force of high seas – you needed some give.

As any lone mariner will tell you, one needed eyes in the back of one's head. There was the constant check of her performance, and how the hull was standing up to the force of the waves, but also I was noting the land I had been exiled from and the presence any vessels of the *Ancredhor Mor*. For the former, and the leaving of one life, I must confess to shedding some tears. But as I say, I was now in control. I was making the choice. To the latter, I would be smallfry, hardly worth the effort of boarding I suspected, but nevertheless, one needed to be wary. Usually the Norsemen put into bays such as those near Greeb Zawn, and await their prey – springing from traps like golden-haired spiders. Although not known for attacking single vessels like this, they had sometimes boarded fishing boats simply to raid their catch. Care was needed.

You will understand by now that I am not, by any stretch, a natural sailor. I usually proceed with trial and error. It is not difficult to understand the main principles of sailing though. In reality, it is the notion that by changing the rigging, sail or steering paddle, I will be able to best manage the force of the wind. That is sailing in three words: managing the wind. As I see it, sails work in two ways for the mariner. Firstly, if the boat is going in the same direction as the wind, then the wind simply pushes on the sail. The problem for me is that, as any mariner will tell you about conditions off the horn of Britain, the wind tends to come from the south and the west, and thus one is naturally pushed to the north and the east. For the most part though, I would be travelling across the wind. Here lies the trick. What happens is that the sail must force air to the rear of the boat, which means the sails should experience a force in the opposite direction.

These were the very conditions I experienced as I headed off Pedn an Wlas, and further into this west of my making. In effect, I was like the seagulls above – generating lift by allowing the air to flow around the sails, just like a bird's wing. As my father might have told me, the important thing was creating the perpendicular to the sail in order to pull the vessel forward. Thus, I would not be 'in irons' – trying to sail head on directly into the wind. It cannot be done. Therefore, one finds oneself continually working at the points of sail to opti-mise the vessel's performance. Now I was tracking in a close haul, which was perhaps the minimum angle the wind and its sail could manage in the morning. Nevertheless, as I eased further out into the afternoon's ocean, I turned the boat and moved to more of a beam reach, at 90° to the wind. This eased the effi-ciency of my passage.

I knew what would follow further out. I'd need to work her windward. This required me to proceed to an upwind destination, but sailing her close-hauled with the wind coming in from one side, then tacking her – turning through the eye of the wind – and sailing with the wind coming from the other side. Thus, by these changes I could zig-zag westwards through the wind. Such a way of working was tiring though. I tell you – it seemed like you sailed for twice the distance at half the speed, and three times the discomfort. But no matter: if it needed to be done, then I would do it. All the time you pray for a lift where hopefully the wind shifts in your favour. If you are not in luck, then you face a header and then the only thing to do is tack on through it. Such a beating was facing me now, on my first day of voyage towards the slippery rocks of Tal-y-Maen. Of course, if there is an inlet or harbour to be put into, that is when you should realise that nature has beaten you. But I knew there and then, that such havens would be rare indeed.

At least I was managing to keep a good course and keep *An Ruen* – as they say – 'in trim'. To this extent, to assist the wind, you, as the crew, also shift and move according to need. The core aim was to keep her flat to the water. With the sail itself, it was more complicated. I aimed to pull the sails in until they filled with wind, but having said that, it needed to go no further than where the front edge of the sail is, exactly in line with the wind. All of this came to me eventually.

I cussed several times at my initial incapacity to work the lines and ropes on her. On all aspects of this, I was certainly out of practice. Mainly I struggled with the forestays on the mainsail. These were great lengths of beeswax and sheep wool grease-soaked flax, that were tough as stone, but which seemed to slip out of my hands each time I tried to grab them. Thus, to improve my handling of the lines I employed good use of knots (them again); sometimes the same figures of eight that had bound me back at Carn Euny. Then I remembered the others – clove hitches, round turns and reefs – that eased my work. They were not easy for me – my left wrist and hand seemed to turn to floppy kelp, when I tried to tie them. Occasionally, though, the extra digit came in handy. Cursed I might well have been on land, but perhaps at sea, it was a different matter. Perhaps Annown's reaches did not extend here.

You have to remember that for the most part *An Ruen* was an open vessel. This meant there was no decking or overheads. Perhaps, of all things about her, this was what worried me the most. In squalls or storms, she'd be subject to the pounding of water, and potentially, of course, flooding and sinking. On rolling high seas, waves might easily inundate her. Bailing water then, I knew would become a necessity at some point. To prevent some of this splash into her, I had covered the bow with a tight canopy of oxhide and installed a similar structure at the rear. This meant the steering paddle was actually starboard at the rear, and this position, just before the stern's oxhide canopy was my main position at sail. My quarters – if you could call them that – were located just aft of the mainsail, and consisted of an ash wood frame, again covered with oxhide. In there seemed to be stored what remained of my life. Certainly, my sack of tools was in there, as well as all the food and water I had laid beneath the warming sheephides. So far as I could note, this was the driest place on the whole vessel.

That morning, then, I had tacked towards the Tal-y-Maen. This was the southern part of a rocky reef that poked through the ocean. A little further to the north were the two other parts of the reef – what was known now as Carn Brâs, and then the frightening finger of Meinek. Although now submerged, these outcrops were said to have once been part of a land that lay here known as Lethowsow. Low lying, it had sometime been overcome with waters – said to have been generated by the retreat of the last great Age of Ice. People still spoke of some forty communities that lay beneath the waves. You see now just how easy it is for fantastical places – once thriving and significant communities – simply to be swept away, to become folklore, to become myth. This was knowledge I could not help but reapply onto Howel and his vision for Carn Euny.

On the upper reaches of the foaming black mass of Tal-y-Maen might be found many bird colonies. At my presence, the throaty guillemots and mewing herring gulls circled me, protecting their young from what unknown threat I offered. Around the reef the waters became more rolling, and skilful use of my steering paddle was required to negotiate them. I had hopefully given myself enough distance from them, and any more that still lay crouching, submerged beneath the waves. Although *An Ruen* sat low in the water, her bottom was gently and purposefully curved; for negotiating such difficulties she had a short draft. I hoped that this might not only help here where depths were somewhat unknown, but also with whatever I was to encounter later on in my voyage.

When Tal-y-Maen was passed, and the seabirds realised that I offered no threat, that I suppose is when real loss set in. A loneliness and fear came upon me that one doesn't see coming. It is sneaky and sly and hits you in the heart, stomach and head. Before, I had purposely not looked back on the land from which I had been exiled. I knew what it looked like didn't I? I knew its lines and curves, its corbelling and its earth. I knew its dwellings, its people, its food and its ale. I knew – or imagined I knew – how far it extended to the east and north. I knew what was there.

Also, I thought I knew what was coming, and how it might change in my absence. In such moments come flashes of your past life. I have not talked much of my mother Athwenna in this tale. But now, she appears in my memory. She died when I was young (this accounts for her absence you see) but at this moment her face was clear to me. I remember my playing beside her, while she spun wool. I remember her gathering up my wooden toy animals and counting them with me. This is when fate aches, when your heart is caught unexpectedly. You feel it miss beats, contract, make a fist tight inside you. You rage inside but there is nothing you can do. You either control that rage, or you burst.

Alone, you can stay morose at such thoughts, or you can talk them through with yourself. I thus had the first of many conversations with myself – this time about her, but of innumerable other subjects during the times that followed. Following me, if you were, say, a herring gull above me, on the beg for a scrap of fish, then perhaps you'd deem me mad. I found it helped though. Changes in tone, expressing anxieties out aloud, comforting your fears – they all worked for me. Talking to yourself is a way of both remaining sane and of keeping faith. I began this process (I suppose I would eventually come to see it as a process of healing) as I began to come to terms with my banishment, and as *An Ruen* made a course toward the isles of Silura.

The wind was not altogether in my favour and I had to beat a zig-zag motion into the west as the afternoon drew on. The likelihood was that I wouldn't be putting into Silura's translucent bays that day. I'd be spending the night alone out here. There were not even seals for company now. Through the day, I'd dragged some spinners on a line, and brought in a fresh supply of mackerel. I eased back on my need to cover water, and instead concentrated on cooking. Although now distant from land, the smell of the grilled fish seemed to focus all the gulls of the western world upon the rear of *An Ruen*. Some of the cheekier fellows even landed on the crossbeam of the mainsail, to express their interest in my activity. The lazier buggers gathered – like grinning children – in the towed coracle itself. Cooking on board was easier than I expected that evening, but at present the ocean was relatively flat. It was unlikely that the fire would tip over or extinguish; even worse that it should burn through the stringers or hides.

The gulls were not, however, the only company I would face on board. This I was to find out after I had eaten. The port side of the stern, I had decided early on, would be the heads for this voyage. I'd carved an arse-shaped round of wood that fitted onto the vessel's walls, and in the centre of it – a hole. Through it my bodily waste could easily be expelled. After the enforced fasting and dehydration of the past few days, my body was now finally coming back into its more regular metabolism. It was while I was sat there that I saw the stowaway.

It was no human or child, but you will understand my revulsion. I have already expressed it to you once at the start of this tale.

Head down and looking at the movement of one of the cross-braces, my attention was brought onto him through a blur of noise and feather. The stowaway had taken it upon himself to try to devour the remnants of my meal of mackerel. To be honest, I had cooked too many – and, already full, I set about leaving the uneaten pair for breakfast. Unexpectedly, this stowaway's joy in finding his supper was at the same time experienced by the lead male herring gull, who then simultaneously made a dive for the fish.

What the gull faced was my most hated of enemies – a fucking rat.

Logoson. That was what we called them.

Curiously, the two of them went at each other. To be honest, the rat had some balls to him because he was not big (not as large anyway as the huge bugger I'd discovered in the fogou at Halliggye), and with a little effort the herring gull might have been able to toss him aside, or even carry him away. Such sheer ferocity was shown by the imp however, that it was the herring gull who eventually backed off, signalling his brothers and sisters to follow. In this momentary process, not only had the gull squawked a fear that hurt my ears, but the rat too had produced a squeak that seemed low-pitched and full of control.

"My food. Now piss off," it seemed to suggest.

This stowaway had seemingly forgotten about me. He obviously knew of me. For a fact, he had travelled with me for a day, and had managed to escape being found as I checked the knots and hides for their seaworthiness. For the moment, there was not much I could do. I was still, so to speak, finding my normal metabolism. He, on the other hand, was successfully reaching for great gob-fulls of grilled fish upon my wooden plate, using both his teeth and claws.

Of course, his presence was easy to explain. He had found warmth and possibly food in the comfortable surrounds of my vessel. Why dart off into the predator-ridden forest or dig for putrid chough eggs on cliff-tops when comfort could be found here? There was something about him though. He looked the kind of cheeky little bastard who might even cast a line out and fish for sprats off the rocks at Porthguarnon. For a moment, watching him was all I could do. He stood on his shanks, occasionally sniffing the air, awaiting the return of the crazed bird he'd done battle with. That was it – most of all, he was a confident fucker, full of himself. That, initially, is what drove my hate more than anything else.

The irony of his presence didn't go unnoticed. For much of my life I'd been wary of them. I knew their ways down in the damp, dark of the earth amongst stone and offerings. Down there, you could barely catch them half of the time. They had bodies that seemed covered in wool grease. Halliggye? Well, that had been a bit of luck to be honest. Size had been his undoing. This one was smaller, more mouse-like, and sneakier too, somehow. Now I was in the open air, in the wind and sea of the ocean, and there he was, happily tucking in.

Wasn't he even frightened of me? Had I lost, perhaps through my recent encounters, through woman's witchery, through betrayal, every stroke of manliness that I once held? Was the bastard even now eyeing up my left hand, already spotting my weakness?

As I eased myself off the heads, and wiped, he still seemed comfortable with his position, still happy that his intimate world was safe. My instinct was to force him off the boat as soon as possible – in effect, to get him to walk the plank. Me sharing my quarters with this most nasty of mammals was not something I wanted to contemplate.

"Logoson," I mouthed.

He continued eating for as long as possible. That's their instinct, their way. I grabbed a spare steering paddle and took aim. Squashing him flat dead with this was probably my best hope. Easing closer though, the rat's whiskers sensed a change in the air. The paddle was almost down on him, but he was off the plate and onto the floor of the boat. The paddle rammed down onto the plate, and came up with the remaining fish on it.

There followed comic absurdity. For at least ten minutes I chased him, first through the warmth of the sheepskins and then up to the bow, where for a while he cowered in the canopy there. But he seemed to sense my weakness. I couldn't reach that far under the hide to pull him. He knew too, that I was scared of his teeth, scared of what his bite might carry. Various pieces of equipment became weapons against him but none seemed to be able to force him out. My other worry was that he'd find a weakness in the sewn leather and bury behind it, hiding in the space between the internal and external leathers. There, perhaps he'd sacrifice all, biting through the skin and sink us both. Please don't let him go there, I was saying to myself.

Eventually it was my mason's crowbar that forced him out from under the canopy. He came out in a split second, faster than an arrow, and knowing that perhaps the hull was unsafe for him, he decided to proceed upwards, climbing one of the flaxen lines that held the headsail in place. There, out of reach of me, he remained, thrusting his small claws into his mouth, and licking them. In his way, he seemed to be blowing me a raspberry like I was a gormless buffoon.

Perhaps, it must be said, I was.

Given our position, and time of the day, the sun was beginning to set in the west. There it was lighting lands, people and creatures I did not yet know. Here, it silhouetted this rodent's body, high on the flax and twirling around it, his tail correcting balance and position.

I was to have the last laugh however. Following Enyon's advice, the upper parts of the line were greased more thickly (where the sun might dry them out). That's when he slipped. That's when I had the paddle ready for him. As he slid down the line, unable to stop himself, I eased the paddle forward as a bat and nudged him off easily. He instantly fell into the ocean.

The cold of the seawater shocked him. A few moments ago, he had been tucking into glorious fish meat. Now the possibility of drowning was very real (I didn't know if rats could swim). But as I have suggested, he was plucky, this rat boy. Despite the cold and shock, he manoeuvred himself towards the leather skins of the boat frame. There, he managed to grip.

"No...No... Not there, " I heard myself say.

His actions posed a real danger to my survival. Annown was speaking to me. Even the druids and the importance they paid to all creatures in the tree of life came home to me. Despite all my loathing, all my fear, all my prejudice against his being, I scooped him up in my arms – a sodden mass of brown fur and skin. He had the same innocent eyes as the seals – black and fathomless.

"My friend, it seems you are destined to be saved," I said to him.

This Rat, being who he is, which I now come to realise is a creature of special note, chitters and sings back to me in his own rodent tongue, drawing seawater off his long whiskers and shaking it off his body.

Complicit, I scrape what is left of the grilled mackerel off the paddle, and feed it to him. I realise, for the first time, that I now have a crew.

This then, is the way one rat saved another.

I note that although my people put much mysticism in the lives of horse, deer, bull, boar and dog, they do not show the same appreciation for his kind.

This day, on the outset of my voyage, the symbol of this beast shows just how far I am leaving them behind.

DEAR ANNOWN,

LIKE THE WORLD around you, I too seem to be leaving you behind. As this young man stepped in, you stepped away from me a little. I had seen it coming. I just didn't realise how final it would be. Now that I had word of my father, my dulled heart was enlivened. Somewhere, at some time, he had been alive and had impacted upon this young man's life. There was no longer a nothingness, a gap, a void. Now there was something tangible.

"Please forgive me," said this Tigernus. "I expected to find your mother alive. Sorry to hear that she was used in some pox-ridden treaty with the Saxons. Now I know I should have come sooner... much sooner..."

I had so many questions for him that I hardly knew where to begin. My tongue failed me.

"Why didn't you?" asked Kenal, sensibly taking up the discussion. "I mean if you had come sooner then..."

"How long have you got? We might need a while to explain all that. My journey here has not been easy. I got delayed. I can explain..."

"But my father – he is still alive?" I interrupted.

"He *was* alive – when I left him, some years ago now. How old are you now?

"Nineteen."

"All of that then...I travelled with him you see. He picked me up from Scathynys and from there we proceeded across the ocean. I knew all about him – his exile from here, and so on..."

"Scathynys?" asked Kenal. "Do you know it Blejan?"

I had an idea of its positioning – to the north of the horn of Britain – between here and Cymru.

"Viking land these days," offered Kenal.

"So I gather," responded Tigernus, revealing little of his past – a past I would come to know well.

"But you've not come from there now have you?" I asked.

"No. I have not yet been back, but sometime it is my aim to do so. These past years I have been in Brittany – and elsewhere..."

"For how long?"

"Too long," he said, his face serious – a pain behind it.

"But tell me, where did you leave him?" I asked.

"It is hard to recall everything now. You have to understand, I was still a young boy. Off the coast of Hyperborea, he advised me to go back. He carried on southwards. I know the coast though – I knew where he was heading."

"Did he ever mention coming back?" I enquired.

"Why would he? He had been excommunicated. He knew nothing of you... Blejan – is it?"

I confirmed my name for him and asked, "Did he mention my mother?"

"All the time. She was on his mind constantly. He truly loved her."

"How do you know?"

"Ha," said Tigernus. "You've obviously never been in a boat with someone for that amount of time. You get to know everything about them, how they think, how they dream, what fires their soul. How could I not know?"

"Was he well?" Kenal asked.

"Yes – when I left him. We knew of hard times – starvation even – in the middle of the ocean, but when I left, he was in good health."

"So..." Kenal continued, "... he went on to live in this Hyperborea? That was his plan? That's where he was headed... I always had him down for Armorica."

"I believe so," Tigernus offered.

"You've not been back?"

"It has not been possible to go back."

So far, our interrogation had been thoughtless. We had not been concerned for this young man one bit. We had only thought of ourselves. He had become a solstice morning's light into the life of my father. Already he had given Kenal and me much to contemplate.

"I have long heard of these villages of Carn Euny – and Chysauster," Tigernus said. "It is strange. Although I had not been to them before today I felt as if I knew them. It is good to walk their paths, and understand the place your father talked about so much."

"I have been rude. Please – come inside. You must be hungry and thirsty"

I gestured towards my grandmother's roundhouse.

"A drink would be much appreciated," said Tigernus. "It has been quite a ride today up from Lulyn..."

Kenal tethered the horses and we made our way into the courtyard.

"I know you will have many questions. I will attempt to answer them all."

"Don't worry," said Kenal. "I am sure you'll be kept talking until the small hours."

"Grandma!" I shouted. "Grandma. There is someone here you need to meet."

From one of the anterooms, my grandmother poked out her head.

"Who is that?" she asked.

Tigernus overheard.

"Greetings lady. I am Tigernus of Scathynys. I come to Chysauster enquiring after Orla..."

"Orla?"

"Yes... but I..."

"My daughter?"

I nodded to confirm to Tigernus she was speaking the truth.

Tigernus lowered himself to his knees.

"I am truly sorry to learn of her fate," he said.

"He knows my father," I interjected.

"Blejan," said my grandmother, "Quick – fetch a stool for this young man – and bring him meat and ale. He must be hungry and thirsty."

When the seating and victuals were arranged my grandmother sat straight in front of him. Eager to know more, she cajoled him to explain what he knew. Kenal drew a flagon of ale for him.

"Begin," she entreated. "Tell us all you know..."

Looking back, knowing what I know now, I saw much of my father in this young man. It was not only his mannerisms, but the way he told his tale. It was something I was to notice much later. We learnt so much. Tigernus filled in the missing pieces from my father's life. In the general sweep of the narrative, we learnt of his ocean, and how it had shaped and made him. I learnt of his tools and his mason's mark. I came to know more about his twist of a wrist and his extra digit. It made me re-examine my own bones and hand.

"You'd be amazed how he used it," was what Tigernus said. "I'll tell you more sometime."

I learnt of creatures and people whom he had met along the way. Some made my eyes stand out on stalks. Others gave me more questions; so many questions that I could barely sleep that night. If I had craved knowledge before, now it was knowledge itself that was consuming me. It ate at me like a monster from the deep.

In the night, I got up and walked around the hut. Kenal's snoring dominated, but in Tigernus' bedroom, I found him sweating and having nightmarish delusions. His uncontrollable turnings and rantings scared me. I had not witnessed anything like it before. When I spoke to him, he awoke and smiled; now more calm and serene.

"Sorry," he said. "I have suffered from this for some years now."

"How came you by this condition?" I asked.

He sat up. By the morning, I knew about the curse.

12

Carriglada Gorget, Carriglada, County Cork, Éire, 700 BCE
A boy hunting rabbits in 1932 found this gold ornamental collar (or gorget) close to a wedge tomb. It dates from about 700 BCE but was probably used much later, since the tomb it was placed in originates from the late Iron Age. The raised bands were created by detailed *repoussé* work. The marks that run through the ridges on the right hand side show that it was roughly bent in two before it was thrust into the tomb. Given the rarity of such finds, it was obviously worn by a high status individual. Courtesy of the National Museum of Ireland /Ard-Mhúsaem na hÉireann.

WHEN AT SEA, YOU ALWAYS sleep with one eye open. You are at the mercy of the wind and tide and, sometimes, what unexpectedly lurks beneath. Boats like *An Ruen* have their own sounds too. They creak and rustle. There is often some mysterious clamour or worrying din in the ash wood stringers; some unidentifiable racket in the oxhides. The sea seems to make it so. Water laps and the wind, no matter how slight, always threatens the silence. You sleep in this broken way because you are afraid. You worry that in a moment of deep slumber, some catastrophe will ensue. You will hit bludgeoning rocks. You will spring a gaping leak. You will lose a full sail. This pattern of sleep is the curse of every lone mariner. On other vessels, where there are many of you, then you take turns on watch. On your own, you must both sleep *and* watch. You cannot do one without the other. For the moment, my sole 'crew' member (if you could call him that) was my Rat boy, and he didn't appear to want to take the middle watch, or any other watch, come to think of it.

All of this said, I did sleep. I needed to. That last forty-eight hours had drained me of energy. I had swapped one life for another – the land for the sea, security for danger – and the changes were many. It was high summer, and the nights were not long. I soon found myself disturbed by the early sunlight in the east, poking through the stitching of the hide canopy beneath the mainsail. I was actually too hot in the night, and so had pushed the warming sheepskins off me. There had been dreams; always with me on this journey there were dreams, and in the few first few seconds of awakening I could recall them. Orla was here with me – naked and wrapped in the sheepskins, ready to sail with me, smiling and certain that her runaway with me was the best course. I woke then with a hard erection. But this glorious fantasy was soon shaken from me, and the reality of my present world returned. I stifled a yawn and recalled my progress.

In the late evening of the previous day, the wind had died down, so it seemed the right moment to pause. In essence, I was adrift. I would remain this way for many nights of my voyage when the see-saw of the ocean was all I had. The sea was too deep here to even consider dropping anchor. I had such a device ready – a holed piece of granite, tied with a good length of thick flax. But you know the size and immensity of this ocean. You know its end will not present itself for a long while yet – if at all. All you can do when you are drifting is to pray. You have to hope that you have not moved much from your intended course and that you'll not come to any harm.

Aside from the creaking of the hull, outside, the ocean itself seemed still and calm. Nowhere could be heard the sound of gulls, or other bird life. I had temporarily entered a realm too distant even for them. The only natural life that was with me was Rat, and now, let loose on the boat, he seemed to have found his own sleeping quarters distant from my own. I listened for him, but could hear nothing that told me he was active.

"*Logoson*? You there?" I called, but there was no response.

I laughed at myself. There I was, trying to have a conversation with Rat, and actually caring for his well-being. I'd obviously lost the plot.

Beneath the canopy I stretched and tested my back for aches and pains. Though somewhat cramped, the shelter was overall much more comfortable than the cell I'd last seen at Carn Euny. I began to rummage for various items I needed to keep myself clean. I was in the minority in this Age, in that I saw the need to clean one's teeth on a regular basis. Sow boar bristle, cut off her when pregnant, and pushed and tied between a cleft stick, was good for this purpose, and I used my mother's remedy for a paste. This was of chalk and kaolin, containing mint for flavour, and tiny crushed bone as an abrasive. I swilled the paste away with a minimum of drinking water (not wishing to waste any) and spat the white mixture over the side. Then I took a small thread of flax and ran this between my teeth. Such procedures took time, but I always tried to follow them. Too many men and women of my age had lost their teeth but perhaps because of this daily ritual, mine remained. The yellowing breath of old Selus of Chysauster told me to maintain this cleaning.

You have to understand though – and perhaps I have not emphasised this enough before. Maybe you are even thinking my world is full of only roses and pinewood. Keeping clean this Age is not easy. It was not easy on land. Most colleagues I knew rarely washed. Dirt and sweat became part of who they were. They embedded themselves in men and women's skin so as to give them a dark hue and the rancid, yet familiar and homely smell of the armpit and gusset. To some, it barely seemed to matter, for notionally everyone smelt the same. To appreciate the stench of it, perhaps you had to be out here – far from it. Suddenly you realised your nose had a set of different olfactory sensations to encounter.

The land did not make it easy though. The world of Carn Euny was one of mud, shit, piss, perspiration, blood, soil, drudgery, grime, fleas, mites, filth and squalor for about three-quarters of the year. Only in summer, perhaps, did the mud alone cease. At the same time, the fleas and mites doubled.

Despite, or perhaps even because of, my occupation, I had always felt the need to stay clean. After all, in my line of work – now I suppose, my previous line of work – I spent my days close to the earth, in the very thick of soil and sweat, and so it seemed to me that I should combat these smells above all else. Besides, I was dealing with the holy and revered space of the fogou. When I was not directly building, or shifting stone or earth, cleanliness there was a by-word. The druids declared it so. Therefore, you might say that I have been trained by my profession. It didn't seem to matter as much to those who frequently worked with animals or planted seed. Perhaps they considered the process of washing pointless. Why bother, when you wake up the next morning and deal with the same muck you did yesterday? With me though, it was a basic requirement. Maybe Orla sensed this, smelt something gracious about me. Maybe as a male, I not only had an extra finger, but an especial smell.

Like the druids then (who were required to wash twice a day, every day), I too sought places to bathe and cleanse myself. To me, it seemed the most natural thing to do. After all, we humans were just following what animals did. At Carn Euny therefore, I had found a stream at the bottom of the valley that pooled slightly before running down to the coast. There, most days I was able to strip and wash. When that was not possible – sometimes due to the poor weather – Kenal (aye, he who eventually came to force me upon the ocean) provided a jug and bowl of water, with rough, woollen towels.

I had stowed a round of soap made of tallow and ashes on board, and used a jug and bowl of seawater for the same purpose, dangling my torso over the side to allow the used and dirty water to fall directly into the sea, instead of on the floor of *An Ruen*. The cold brine certainly woke me, and the invigorating wash made me feel more human again. I have found with travel that it is easy to lapse into the mode of the men of Carn Euny, and not bother, when in fact, such ablutions not only cleanse the exterior of one's body, but the inside too. I have to tell you such things because in the tiny world of this boat (in effect, this mere piss in this ocean) such actions are important.

Likewise, I used an apple-based ointment for my hair. As is our way, my long braids remain in place. These denote my origin, my place, that I am from the horn of Britain. They are beaded with blue and green glass, and are iron-clasped to ensure they do not impinge upon my view or work. Now that I have left, they seem less important – appendages of the past no longer necessary for the present. I do not have to denote anything to anyone. But for now, this early morning, I keep them – perhaps because there is still something in me that belongs there. There is still something that I am unprepared to let go. I ask you – is that the way with all of us?

As I washed, the day opened up around me, and carried itself to the limits of the horizon. It would be a scorcher today – I'd need to be careful not to be burnt. Like everything else, a coating in wool grease would shield my skin from the sun's power.

My plan was to make the inlets of Silura.

It should be possible, but let me first explain about Silura. No one much ventured there. It was, how can I put it? – a place for vagabonds and thieves, otherwise grumpy hermits and recluses who enjoyed the solitary life. On days like this, it was very beautiful there, but I knew too that the *Ancredhor Mor* sometimes favoured it as a base for their attacks on the west of Britain. So it was rumoured, the place was haunted by the ghosts of those who'd perished in the waves that engulfed Lethowsow.

Put together, this made it somewhat daunting. Like the rocks of the Tal-y-Maen which represented the pinnacle of its most easterly hills, the isles of Silura were its most western heights. I had never been there and, to an extent, despite the ghosts and Vikings, the prospect of arriving there excited me. For certain, I'd be able to refill my water skins, perhaps find new food, maybe even barter for work. There, I could study maps and contemplate possible directions and courses.

Momentarily, I even considered the fact that Silura might become my new home – perhaps one of the distant western islands – but then reality set in again. It was too close; not nearly far enough away. I might survive for a time there, but word of a five-fingered mason would probably get back. All it would take would be one fisherman from Silura and one from Lulyn to meet. Howel would send a hunting party across. Silura was too close. It was probably even in his sights as an eventual part of his growing empire.

I tested the wind. It was slight but just enough to raise sail and track towards the low form of islands ahead. I settled on my block and took the hefty steering paddle in my right hand. With the left I reached into a pot for some wheat grains as a remedy from hunger, realising that now, due to the actions of another, I was unable to anticipate the cooked mackerel I'd caught yesterday. Another spinning line out the rear of *An Ruen* should haul in a few more for later though.

The tranquillity of the early morning made me smile. I relaxed and let the vessel and waves guide me. The lull of the water and dip of her movement made me shut my eyes. The sun felt good on my face. When times are this good, be wary. I should have known this. I know that when a bladder grows large, something is always ready to prick it. My mother used to tell me one of my people's favourite sayings: *En Hâv, perkou Gwâv*. In summer, remember winter.

The prick in fact, was a gentle nudge. Here, I thought, came the initial traces of winter in my summer.

At first, it was no more than, say, the ninth wave, a crest bigger than the rest that made the hull thump down a little harder. It was as if we'd picked up a bit of speed. But then I realised the lift was higher than that, and that no wave could have made that movement. Recognition came slowly to me at first. There was then another bump, a tickle from beneath like something was playing with us. Something liked our company and wanted to engage.

On this second bump, it was Rat that unnerved me. I heard his voice, his squeak from behind me. Night time it seemed, he had decided to spend in the coracle tied behind. This he had declared would be his nest alone, his own vessel for our voyage. I imagined him sprawled out on some seat, sunning himself. His commandeering had not altogether gone to plan though. Whatever had brought this bump had frightened him out of solitude. He again sought my company. I turned to watch him perilously swing upside-down along the rope, one paw and claw gradually put before the other to make his way across. It was a move practised on many previous occasions, but perhaps even he did not always expect the sea's motion to jerk the rope as much as it did. There were moments when he lost grip and had to use the entire strength of his body to reattach his feet to the rope. All the while, he was squeaking with greater intensity, warning me of what had bumped us. I got up and scanned the ocean on both sides of *An Ruen*. Frustratingly, I couldn't see anything.

By now, Rat had managed to get back onto the hide canopy at the stern and was gesticulating and speaking loudly.

"Out there, you fool! Something big. Something terrible," he seemed to be saying to me. "Are you so stupidly blind that you can't see it?"

I watched his whiskers twitch and scan the air. In this sense, this Rat was quite a useful device to have on board. His perception was sometimes beyond my human senses. I had to trust him. That's it. I was now trusting, of all things, a rat.

We were both on edge. The land of *Pedn an Wlas* was becoming a tiny, charcoal smudge in the distance. Silura was not quite in our grasp. We were utterly at the mercy of whatever it was that wanted to play with us. Driftwood maybe, I considered for a while. You found it in the ocean sometimes. Not just flotsam and jetsam, but larger trunks of timber brought down by cliff fall or high tides. Yes – that was most probably it.

Rat, sensing my concern, had decided enough was enough. He jumped off the rear canopy and headed into the sheepskins, to burrow and nest there – away from the fright of the ocean. But this was *my* ocean, I told myself. I had put myself into it. Whatever it was that was out there I could deal with. This positive ideology controlled my heartbeat a little, and began to ease the sweat.

"Show yourself," I finally mouthed.

There was still nothing. Only the lap of water onto the hull could be heard.

I tried to imagine *An Ruen* from below – to consider what form we appeared to the world under the waves. There was the extended oval of the hull itself, but then behind it was the coracle. That's when I realised we might have looked like some creature with its youngster trailing behind it, shepherding it through the water. On the one hand, protection might be offered; on the other, attack. At this, I felt the port of the front hull section lift slightly in the air. Something had nudged it, beyond just a floating tree trunk. Whatever lifted it was organic and moving, producing a swash in the sea that I could now hear.

I moved as fast as I could over one of the slippery gunwales and peered over the edge of the boat. So close that I could touch it, a vast, long form eased itself against the hull. Considering its impressive dimension, I first thought it was a whale, but half way along its torso stood a flopping dorsal fin that told me it was not that kind of sea creature. Mottled in complexion, and gentle in its movement, it was clearly some kind of large shark. At that word, many people I know would run scared, but I began to realise this was no killer in that way.

"You can come out Rat," I shouted, vocalising my relief.

I knew of such creatures. The men of Lulyn sometimes called them the 'wonderful fish'. This was because when they washed up dead upon the shore, they'd cut them open for their huge, oily livers. Bartering with that might last for six months. What they were referring to was a kind of shark that sought not prey in the conventional sense. Instead, it basked in warm waters around our land – and hence its name – a basking shark. They did not seek fish as quarry like you or I, but instead opened up their vast jaws to filter the water for the smaller creatures of our world, such as sprats and shrimps, and some, I supposed, I could not see.

These creatures came to the horn of Britain in the summer, when the water temperature rose. I had observed them feeding in groups before – glad perhaps that I was onshore, and that they were distant at sea. Rat and I need not have feared though, for they were the gentlest of giants. This one – I could not tell if it was male or female – was probably curious at our crossing. For certain, it dwarfed us. I could not see its complete form, but I estimated its length at around thirty feet. While we proceeded forwards, the shark circled around us, still inquisitive. Occasionally, it dipped down into the blue, so that the fin disappeared, then poked up again, running close past the hull, and nudging us with its girth. Here, you could make out its conical snout, and just below the waterline, its vast gills for raking the ocean.

This then, was probably one of Remfra's sea monsters. It was nothing more than a curious visitor who, I suspected, was momentarily enjoying our company. You could see though, that in the imaginative mind it would be easy to transform it into a fearsome kraken or man-eating beast beneath the waves.

Considering the heat of the early morning, there were probably more of them out there that day, enjoying the food and tranquillity of these waters. This one appeared comfortable with me, not seeming to feel any need to return to its school. As it brushed past again, now feeling that no harm could come to me, I leant out my left hand and felt its grey-brown surface. There, my fingers touched its skin – noting the rough scales and a layer of mucus. At point of contact, it noted no difference, no mutation in me.

"Come, look at this," I shouted in to Rat, but there was no response from him. He had already decided that this terrible beast was a threat and that no amount of cajoling was going to bring him out.

There was though, a poetry in their movement, I decided: a kind of mathematical grace and precision in the way they pushed through the water, perfectly adapted to their environment. Although change was certainly on its way for we humans, I contemplated that these spiritual beings had probably been here for thousands of years and would be for some thousands more – so long as we allowed them to survive, and didn't hunt or kill them out of existence through some irrational fear. Such fears were always based on selfishness and self-loathing, fear of transition and growth, the need for one to tell a better story than the other. Perhaps instead, there was pure learning in the life of these creatures. Perhaps, I, this simple vug builder, who'd spent his time underground and had little real contact with the natural world, was coming to a new sense of myself through such encounters.

It was clear that the ocean was teaching me. It was both my new druid and bard. To think – only a few moments before, I had thought such an encounter could be the true winter of my summer. This creature had taught me something else: whatever the season, I needed to remember my own personal summer.

The basking shark stayed with us as we made our way to Silura. The wind was not altogether strong that morning, but there was enough of a breeze to make some progress. It was only when the water depth began to decrease that the shark bid goodbye to us. Such moments in the ocean would be common enough – temporal diversions from nature that would make me marvel – but would be often over in seconds. The basking shark seemed to sense our going as well, and as we proceeded into the west, it made one final breach that scattered spray across to us. This was like writing a farewell in the brine.

Care would be needed on Silura.

The many islands held many traps.

The white-sanded bays with azure waters conveyed a beauty that was deceptive. Many a mariner had warned me of such duplicity. Rat was out again, sniffing the air. He clearly sensed the disappearance of the shark, as well as the appearance of land. We first encountered the easternmost islands; these were great piles of brown and grey granite, the former tors and mountain tops of a lost world. This close in, it was possible to observe the bottom of the sea. The water was crystal clear; the only thing breaking the clarity was *An Ruen*'s wake. These easternmost islands seemed a good place to put in. For larger vessels, there were probably not enough supplies there anyway. They would have preferred the islands further to the west; there would be deeper water, and a place for fuller bellies.

The duplicity of the islands also came with the climate and seascape. Although on this day, all looked very inviting – so much so that you wanted to run and explore each of them – the weather here could easily turn. A mistake could leave you foundering on rocks, or lost in the sea mists that could continue for months at a time. With the mists had grown stories of witches and wrecks – sirens who purposely conducted missions to deceive and plunder the wares of vessels. In this way, such sea bitches existed – knowing the stupidity of men upon the ocean. Whether beauteous or ugly, it seemed not to matter. Men still fell for their songs and charms.

One of the easternmost islands I knew to be named Menawethen. I had not been here before, but I'd known that this was the first island mariners from the east encountered. I pulled down the mainsail and only worked the headsail – she'd be more sensitive for steering in this way. I'd need to negotiate a clever course through these outer isles. A neck of water ran across to two smaller islands to the north of me, joined by a rocky isthmus. The neck was not deep but was reasonably clear, with little risk of grounding.

Rat watched our progress, sat on the canopy of hide at the front. He was confident on board now, like a rodent figurehead, occasionally barking complex but indiscernible navigational orders back to me at the stern.

To the southwest, a ragged run of rocks pointed to the north and so I avoided these as best I could, to ease around a larger island to the northwest. Because she was still lit from the east, her form looked foreboding; the nearest shore still cast in shadow. I tried to perceive features there: settlements, enclosures, and homesteads – anything that might give a sign of life. The geography of it, however, seemed to indicate more a place of burial: cists and cairns, just as the line of Bartinney did back at Carn Euny.

Annown was present then and this made me a little fearful.

What grotesque and multi-headed sirens might the Otherworld throw at me?

I dropped anchor at the northern end of the island, watching the splosh of the stone into the sandy waters beneath. As I clambered into the coracle, black-backed and herring gulls darted overhead. They remained curiously silent though – as if watching me for some other force. Rat barked at me, wishing to come ashore, but I believed it was best he stayed on board, and I indicated so with a flick of my left wrist. He seemed to understand. Such an unexplored, vast world would be no place for a tiny creature. Inside the coracle, I had a basket for gathering food, my crowbar as a weapon, and a few empty water skins ready to be filled.

Sculling these calm waters was much easier than the ocean out of Penberth and I was soon levering the frame onto my back and carrying it up the beach. It was strange to be on land again. I walked oddly. Usually, on the ocean, there was the need to continually counter-balance, to lop and rise, to measure and predict the fall of the hull. Now that things were strangely so solid, it took a while for my legs and feet to adjust.

The granite here was coarse grained. Whoever worked it had a hard job. This stone didn't break or allow itself to be cut easily. The sunlight made the crystals in it dart and flicker. Once past the stone of the beach, I was in grassland of bramble and bracken, merging into plains of heather. This was the territory of Rat's cousins – shrews and mice, though all scattered at my stomp across the peaty earth. I steered a course northwards, ranging in and out of the bracken, sometimes stumbling over figwort and spurge tufts nearer the tideline. The bracken smelt warm, laced with the tinge of salt. Back in the bay, I looked onto *An Ruen*. There seemed no sign of trouble, but I kept an eye on the more distant sky-scape to ensure no storm beckoned.

From brambles I picked early blackberry fruit, and found edible tuber roots of the spurge. These were tasteless when eaten singularly, but made a good base for soup and broth. They would serve me well when the ocean wouldn't give.

Having traversed the grassland, the vegetation temporarily disappeared as a field of boulders lay on a causeway – leading to a higher point of the northern-most end of the island. Making my way there seemed the most sensible thing to do. A close scan of the landscape though, showed me human life had been here, for on the lower slopes of this hill I could see a group of eight round-houses. They'd long since been abandoned – modernity telling the residents that this drop in the ocean was no place to eke out a survival. It took me another twenty minutes to reach them. Their form acted as an instant reminder, of course, of my previous life. In their stone surrounds I perceived the previous life: the chatter of children, the bleat of goats, and a flickering hearth. These were the real ghosts of Silura. What eased out in front of me was the future of Carn Euny: abandonment and decay.

Lone travellers such as me are vagrants. We have to take what others leave; find hope in others' debris. That is why I scanned each of the dwellings in de-tail. I searched for anything that might be useful and stowed them in my basket. I debated whether to take some left stone querns, but in the end dropped them again, fearing their weight was too great. Likewise, within an alcove, I found abandoned scraps of bronze. Meanwhile, scattered on the floor were hundreds of crushed limpet shells – clearly the main diet of whoever once lived here. The bronze I took. That kind of metal was always valuable regardless of me being at sea. The rest seemed worthless. Perhaps the surrounds here had already been subject to scavengers beyond the wiles of the cormorant and the gull.

The sixth hut, though, offered me more reward. There, half-buried in its re-cesses was a clay figurine, not much bigger than my extra finger. I scrabbled at the earth, my spade of a right hand being useful to ease out the delicate form. Carefully cast, she was probably of Roman origin – perhaps ending up here via Gaul and Armorica. When dusted off, I traced her serene shape and held it up to the light. It was nothing like the carvings found back in Carn Euny. Al-though my people were skilled with iron, able to scratch and sear the most complex knot-work across the surfaces of metal, this was something far more delicate. She'd travel with me, this statue, as my new Orla.

That moment of serenity was not to last long. A thick wallop of something hard fell across my neck, and in an instant I was unconscious on the floor of the roundhouse.

I hadn't been out for too long, but enough time for me to have been moved into the surrounds of another of the roundhouses. My neck ached and the fall had caused me to bang my head on the house's hard floor. Whoever, or what-ever, had taken me, had managed to drag my body here. The clothes around my knees and elbows were stained with grass, and they ached too, from all the abrasion against the floor.

On wakening, I initially stayed completely still, trying to understand this new environment. My mind was full of affirmation – those tired old mariners had been right for me to have been wary of Silura.

How could I have been so foolish?

How could I have been so arrogant in letting my guard down?

I had thought the place unoccupied. From floor level, it was clear that this roundhouse was undergoing a reoccupation. In essence, whoever lived here now had taken the shell of the old building and was trying to rebuild it. The only problem was that they'd failed with the roofing. No large structure covered the entire house. Instead, temporary framed canopies of browning ferns were draped outwards from the walls, and supported by wooden poles in the old interior. A fire was burning in the central area, and I had been shoved under one of these canopies. I had not been bound, but I could not feel my possessions close by – my crowbar, basket, or the newly-found statue. The fire lent out a smell of incense of some kind – which sweetened the air and gave the house a perfume. It was a perfume that I was later to learn clearly hid an awful stench.

I turned in order to see what was opposite me. My first view was of the dusty soles of someone's shoes. At the same time, the voice was female and she was chanting something before a stone altar. There were words being used I did not recognise, though she spoke in a tongue that was understandable to me. The phrasing was somewhat different though – an unusual dialect compared to what I was used to beyond the great river. Seemingly, she sensed my movement, for after the chanting stopped, she addressed me.

"Bah. What brings a dull Pagan such as you to Nornour?"

Her voice was old and gnarled. She had croaked the question at me. Nornour, she had said. That was the island I was upon. I had heard tales of this place, but never thought I'd step upon it. Why was she calling me a Pagan? This was a term I didn't understand.

"I mean no harm," I spluttered. "I was journeying west and put in here for fresh food and water."

"Where do you come from?"

"From the horn of Britain, close to *Pedn an Wlas*..."

"I saw your boat in the bay. Bah. I followed you from the moment you arrived. Wondered what you wanted..."

Between these questions, this old woman talked to herself, mumbling her joys and pains at once.

"I am Voog, son of Donyerth," I stated. "Who are you?"

She didn't answer.

"I had to knock you out. Sorry about that. You have to be careful. The bastard Vikings see? You had that look about you."

She turned to me. Instantly, I saw that she wore a patch over her right eye. She pointed at it.

"They took that. One of their raids, see... Hard to forgive that is – but I try. It is my way now – or should be my way. "

With a grunt, she eased herself up. She was hard to age precisely because of her dirty skin and filthy clothes. Her hair was long and grey though, and some of it had transferred from her head to her chin, where it remained coarse and black. She wore clothes that even the poorest women of my world would have discarded.

"You called me Pagan. What do you mean by that?"

She laughed a cackle that echoed over the causeway leading to the south of the island.

"Bah. Bah. Well, you are, aren't you? You worship Annown still, no doubt, and with a name like yours – I daresay, you must have something to do with the old ways..."

"Eh?"

"Vugs... Voogs...Voogery buggery. I saw your crowbar. The only men I know who hold that kind of device build fogous – bah – ways in and out of the Otherworld."

"Your intuition serves you well, old woman. Do you know my people? Have you travelled there?"

"Probably not, but I know enough of the world to know what you are."

She laughed again.

"Do you have it – my crowbar?"

"That – bah – and your other items are over there..."

She pointed to a pile, holding the iron rod and the basket of food.

"The statue you found is there too..."

"Was it yours? I mean, I thought it was abandoned."

"It was... The people who once lived here left over a hundred years ago – tired of eking out an existence on an island with no future. A parliament they had too you know. Eight families they say."

She paused for a while, and let me absorb this information about Nornour. Then she reminded herself of my question.

"I have no need of such statues. They are as well to be buried in the earth and forgotten about as far as I am concerned. They followed the wrong god."

The nameless old woman then moved away from her altar. There I saw what she had been chanting before. It was a stone cross.

She saw my curiosity.

"Odd you think, yes – that I pray before a cross?"

"Not odd. You choose the gods you want," I offered.

"There is only one God..."

This statement I found harder to believe. For one thing, my people already had many gods, and for another, I knew the Saxons and the Vikings followed different deities. There were as many different ones as there were tribes. and this discounted all other people in the south and east. Even the people of Armorica, who were like us in so many ways, had their own. The Phoenicians too, decorated their vessels with all kinds of creatures they venerated. What amazed me was her certainty – the absolute insistence that her way was right, and the rest of the world was wrong. I didn't know it then, but we were to have many debates about this.

Then I realised. This woman was one of these new holy types who were spreading about the world. These were the types the druids loathed. If they were right, then this belief seemed to be the way of the future. It was an odd call though – a single, all-knowing deity in whom people put their whole faith. The phrase 'All eggs in one basket' came to mind and this didn't seem a good system.

"Why are you out here?" I asked.

"Bah. I am closer to God here, don't you think?"

"I don't know."

For me, rocks and the sea, and the natural world always enlivened me (aside perhaps from the day I was enforced upon it) but she seemed to mean something entirely different.

"Voog," she said. "You think I chose this place? Oh no. I didn't choose it at all. Bah. God placed me here."

She spoke in riddles this old woman. I considered the bedrock of my own belief again. It was Annown who placed us. Annown chose our beginning and our end. Annown selected our appearance. Although I was listening intently, her words turned my safe world upside down.

"There are surely better places to be... placed?" I argued. "Although this Nornour is beautiful... you must agree that it holds nothing but cormorants and ragwort."

"My boat took me here. That was God's will. The coracle smashed though, down on the rocks there. Bah. This told me I should stay..."

I was beginning to understand this woman's logic now. Fate or destiny was whatever the fuck her god wanted. It seemed a bad way of living to me; not that I was going to say that to her now.

"Where had you sailed from?"

She thought about this before answering.

"Ever-y-where," she cackled with a glint in her remaining eye. "Lands you wouldn't even have heard of, or even dreamt about..."

I wanted to ask her then about Mayda, Ogygia, and Frisland. Maybe she was so crazed she had also visited Hyperborea in her quest to extol the virtues of this solitary god.

The more I spoke to her, the more I began to be amazed at her life-story. She had, so it seemed, covered half of the known world, just by putting to sea in a small coracle. From what she'd said, she'd already had enough encounters with the Vikings for them to have partially taken her sight, and now she had been shipwrecked – forced to live out her remaining years on this rock that was named Nornour.

The design of her roundhouse was now beginning to make sense. Finding this old community here had, in essence, been a blessing for her. She at least had walls to keep out the wind, but what more could she do? There weren't many resources on the island, and she probably didn't have the tools or skills to manufacture any roof. She kept faith, kept alive, kept surviving through her belief in this strange, new god. I shook my head. What bizarre world had I stumbled into?

"You hungry?" she asked.

I nodded.

"Then I'll cook. Bah. Food that's better than roots eh?"

She began filling a pot with an unidentifiable fish and then added herbs and water. She blew out the incense that had perfumed the air and raised the whole above the fire on a triangular stand made of what looked like driftwood. The pot dangled above the flames. As she leant over, then I noticed her stench – a mingling of urine, fish, smoke and dung.

"What are you called?" I asked again.

She stopped what she was doing.

"You asked me that before. I don't know," she said.

"Come – you must know what you are called..."

I stopped, because I knew what I was forcing her to do and then I realised that I too, did not know my own real name. Instead, the name I had gained had mutated onto me.

"I cannot remember it for the moment. Bah. It's been too long since anyone else used it."

I wanted to ask how long but didn't. I was afraid of the answer she might give and how solitary her life must have been.

But being who she was, she heard me anyway.

"Twenty years," she said. "It's been twenty years."

I realised then, that she must have a completely different sense of time than me. How does one spend such an amount of time in just one place? How does one cope? How does one not wish to see the edge of the sea again?

"Here?"

She gave a nod, almost imperceptive, but a nod nonetheless, as if she didn't really want to contemplate it.

As she relaxed with me, knowing that I wasn't going to harm her, she allowed me to move around her house more. I gathered my belongings and offered her the berries I'd picked. We'd eat them as a sweet treat after the fish.

"This is *barfus*," she explained. "Good eating. I catch it off the northern point."

I knew the fish. It was cod. The details of what we were about to eat interested me less than her beliefs and motivation. I wanted to look closer at this altar of hers. I wanted to understand its difference, but also wanted to see where our worlds fused and melted together. The same offerings were there – these might have been found at the bottom of any fogou – but there was also something clearly beyond the symbol of the cross, her most treasured possession: a book in a language I could not read. Here then, were this god's stories, this god's tales and his englynnion.

"You read this?"

"Every day."

I turned some of the pages. Some were now so fragile by continued use that they almost blew away in the breeze. I could smell the fingertips of this old woman amongst the ink, where she had scanned along the lines over and over again. This was a god whose power clearly rested in language, and not feeling. I wondered what Casvellyn might have made of it. Probably, he would have burnt it, or cast it from a high cliff into the ocean. After all, that was what Carn Euny did with anything it didn't like or approve of.

Solitary living makes one mad. While cooking, this woman sang to herself. They sounded like lullabies for children. She seemed to be singing not for my benefit, but instead to keep away fear, to stop Nornour finally grabbing her. Their rising hope annoyed me, given her circumstances and mine too (though truly as yet, she knew little of them). But she seemed to have hope here – that was the biggest surprise. Despite the filth, loneliness and emptiness of her world, she embraced life.

"Bah," she spat a globule of the fish stew across the space. "Not cooked. Not nearly enough..."

And then back to her lullabies she went.

"What did you hit me with?" I asked. "My neck's throbbing now."

She stopped stirring the pot, and pointed to a weighty length of driftwood. The cudgel could have easily taken out an ox, let alone a man. She would have to have used both hands to operate it.

"Use this," she mouthed, throwing me a pot of a black clay-like substance. "It'll take away the pain..."

Clearly the tub contained some herbal antiseptic that I rubbed into the skin around the place on my neck where the cudgel had caught me.

"Bah hah. Shouldn't sneak into the houses of old ladies, eh?" she laughed.

The bruising on my neck eased somewhat, and I moved closer to the fire. She carried on cooking as if I wasn't there – as if I was some kind of wailing ghost who had temporarily entered her life. It was odd not knowing her name – conversing with a person who'd lost their identity through time and travel.

"Woman..." I tried calling her, but she seemed to ignore me.

I tried again with her.

"Woman, do the *Ancredhor Mor* ever land here?"

That made her stop her stirring and singing.

"*Ancredhor Mor*?" she checked.

She nodded; her face full of woe.

"They used to," she recollected. "When I was younger and they wanted pleasure... Did what they wanted then. I had no choice."

So she'd been raped too; gang-raped by the sound of it. My imagination was appalled at this fate.

"Not any more though. Bah. Not now my tits are saggy and my cunt dry... They leave me alone now."

She laughed.

"They seek fresh, young fanny on the other isles... the place they call Marluhöfn,... and on Bryher... I don't know what they call that in their despised tongue."

Such knowledge made me think that Howel had been right to have ended those Vikings' lives back at Carn Euny. They could be vicious animals. But for the stench of her, I wanted to comfort this old woman – for her to understand that not all men were the same. She seemed to have already recognised this in me though – despite me being a child of Annown.

We sat silent for a few moments, contemplating this evil.

"There were children... babies..." she revealed.

That, I had not expected. Again, she predicted what I was going to ask.

"They are buried... in graves over there."

She pointed across the causeway to the southern section of the island.

"I'm sorry..."

"The winters," she stated. "They didn't survive them."

The fish broth seemed ready now. Using a ladle, she eased some of the grey-white mass into a bowl for me. She gestured for me to eat.

"Do you have any children?"

"No," I said.

"No wife?"

"No."

This was emphatic.

"No love?"

"No."

My answer to this was more emphatic than the first.

Although she had revealed part of her past to me, this was not the moment to share my own. It sounded like her god would not approve of me.

There was a pause while she thought about my own bachelorhood.

"Your arm?" she ventured. "Does it put them off?"

Straight in, this old woman then: a cut to the chase.

"Maybe," I said nonchalantly.

"Bah. How did it end up that way then?"

"I was born like it."

"I see."

"This too..."

I showed her my fifth finger. She hadn't noticed it before.

"Marked for greatness then," she mumbled, chewing on a bony piece of cod.

I laughed.

"I have not heard that before..."

She spat out a white bone across the floor.

"It was something a teacher of mine once said."

"What does your book and your god say on such matters?"

She looked over at the altar where her book lay.

"I know what yours says," she said. "Annown believes your spirit did something wrong in a previous life – that your disability marks you and that you must work through it to eventually become reborn with it gone..."

"That's what the druids say, yes...."

"Bastards," she mouthed. "Those floundering idiots know nothing."

"Come – I asked you, about your god... What does he or she say?"

"He says you will be healed."

"That all?"

"That's all – if you believe, that is..."

"If I believe? And if I don't?"

The old woman tipped up her bowl and swilled the rest of the broth into her mouth. Then she belched.

"I don't have all the answers," she snapped. "That's what I try here. I think a lot. Meditate on such questions. Islands are good for that."

"You're saying one day – I will be healed?"

"I sense it, yes, I suppose. Look, stop all these questions will you? I don't see anyone for twenty years – and then you turn up out of the blue, and start interrogating me. Bah!"

"I didn't mean to..." I offered. "I'm just interested – that's all..."

"Well, be interested – and wash these dirty dishes and pot... There's a stream down there..."

She pointed a short distance away from the roundhouse. I took the spoon, bowls and pot to the sparkling water, and used a hardened fern stem to scrub away the detritus from the pot. The woman went back to her stench and songs. From the stream I could look out over the bay. In this aquamarine paradise, I contemplated the many horrors of existence this woman had faced here. It put my own situation into a new perspective. Despite the smell, the gabbling tongue and her irritation at me, I was strangely comforted by her. Whatever odd religion she followed – well, that was her choice wasn't it? Out here, she could do what she wanted.

I wandered how Rat was faring on *An Ruen*. If he was now as worried about me as he was the placid basking shark, then presumably he'd be squeaking frantically. He'd also be calling for food and water. To the west, I observed the cloud formations. They grew low to the ground, black and ominous. This meant rain and the wrong kind of wind.

"You have friends aboard your vessel? Are there more of you?" she asked when I got back from the stream. Her good eye missed nothing.

"No. Nobody else. Just me."

When I said this, I rethought what I'd said.

"Well, there is something else on board..."

I explained the rat situation. She cackled so loudly I saw the deep recesses of her mouth, where her teeth were rotted black.

"You'd better fetch him up here," she advised. "The weather's worsening."

I viewed her skin more closely. Under the grime, under the aging, there was something more beautiful. One time, this woman had stopped men in their tracks. No more now though.

Rat then came to the world of Nornour, cradled within my sack. I warned him not to shit in there – like the last rat who was inside it – or I might even leave him behind. This, he seemed to take notice of, and then enjoyed partaking of the remains of the fish this woman had cooked earlier. Like most rodents, he was wary of this new presence in his life, and therefore kept close to me.

Whether sleeping here, high on Nornour, or back on board *An Ruen* was the more comfortable, I did not know. We'd have had to endure the swell and the rain battering down on the central hide canopy on board the vessel, though things here in this semi-covered relic of a roundhouse were not much better. At least here there was a large, warming fire, which would endure through the night, despite the downfall. I carried the sheepskins up from the vessel and packed these under one of the woman's improvised roofing sections. The weather had deteriorated during the last throes of the afternoon and into the evening. A horizontal rain pushed in.

Before sleeping, the old woman bowed before this stone cross and said a prayer. I watched in a kind of rapt amazement – as one does when one sees something one does not understand. After the prayer, she read to herself from the book – and seemed comforted by the words. If I was her, then I would not have let a man sleep as close – but then I remembered her words. She knew she was no longer a temptation and that I was not a threat.

At least my sleep in the roundhouse was not broken. For the first time since my exile from Carn Euny, I was able to sleep soundly. I valued this greatly, for in the weeks ahead, it wasn't to be repeated very often. I could not yet class this woman as a friend, but her new ways intrigued me, and I supposed my presence intrigued her too.

We were opposites finding magnetism in our collective pain.

In the days ahead I resolved to help repair the roof of her shelter, and make a positive contribution to her life as thanks for her hospitality and company. In the winter of that year, she'd at least have a roof over her head.

The sun had just poked up over the horizon when I woke. The night's rain had cleared, and already the peaty earth had started to dry out. Over where the woman should have been, was a pile of ferns and bracken in which she'd been sleeping. She'd already risen and was about her business somewhere on Nornour. Near blinded by the rays of the sun streaming through the entrance of the roundhouse (they knew how to greet a morning these ancients), I peered down to see her sat atop a rock. This was her meditation I presumed – her praise to this bookish god from the east.

I wound down through the boulders and ferns to where she was.

Eventually, the mossy floor merged into hard granite and I was with her on this natural altar.

"I'll make a start on the roof today for you," I declared.

There was no response from her.

"The trees to the south are probably tall enough for me to cut down and fashion into rafters."

She turned to me – smiling.

"Last night," she explained. "You got me thinking. I retraced all the steps of my life, and when I got up I finally remembered."

Clearly, she was ignoring me.

"Remembered what?"

"My name. Who I am."

"Who are you then?"

"I am Warna," she mouthed. "That is who I am. Warna. Bah. And now it is time for me to leave this rock... to go back to where I am from."

"But you have no vessel, no boat, no passage. Who will take you there?"

She turned to me, this Warna of Nornour. I knew what was coming. She purposely reached for my left hand to lift her up; clearly her old bones were filled with rheumatism. She wanted to feel the touch of my extra finger.

She laughed a laugh that resonated over the still causeway.

"You will, of course," she said, " – or shall I ask Rat?"

DEAR FATHER AND DEAR ANNOWN,

I need both of you to listen. You are each with me. I know more of you now father. Part of your life has now been mapped for me. I can see it laid out before me. Please listen to what happened next. Try to see how I was digging for you – working the land like a tin streamer. I was seeking the ore of humanity – for you both.

While Kenal and my grandmother spent time absorbing all this new information in their own way, I took Tigernus for a walk on Carnaquidden Downs. There, I explained all that had happened to me – and how I had discovered the fate of my mother – as well as my father (I was open with him – I even told him about the poisoning). He explained how he had travelled across from Brittany, and had tried to find, on the recommendation of my father, a tanner named Enyon. He had anticipated that by now the old man would have died, and found it to be so, but the tannery had continued, and its new owner had shown him the direction to Carn Euny.

"Voog's boat," said Tigernus. "*An Ruen* – that was its name. Enyon's tannery was where he got the oxhides from."

I had been past the tannery a hundred times. I had not known its connection to my father. From the tannery, he had hired a horse to allow him to travel up to the higher land above the bay.

"You're quite a horseman," I noted. "I saw the way you rode up through Chysauster."

"I've had to be," he explained, but said nothing more for now.

As we pushed through the dark ferns and bracken, I learnt more. I came to know of the cave at Porthguarnon; what my father had done to avoid being seen by Kenal and his men; how he had first made for Silura. I learnt of his love of animals – I heard of his rat companion, and Tigernus explained his own fascination with puffins. Both of us confessed that we were amused by their antics. His stories made me laugh – in ways I had not known previous to this time. I was enjoying his company.

It was unclear how long Tigernus would remain with us. I asked him straight.

"Are you planning on staying?"

"For a while, if that is all right?"

"Of course – but where were you headed?"

"Home. Scathynys. You see, I told a lie many years ago – to my family there – in order to go with Voog – er, your father. I have two sisters you see. Probably, my mother's still alive. But not my father. He was failing fast when I left as a boy. They think I'm dead though. There was – how can I put it? – a convenient event you might say. I timed my leaving well."

"How do you know if they're still there?"

"I don't. I have no idea what became of them. All I can hope is that they carried on somehow – without me."

"Wasn't it cruel to have made them think that?"

Tigernus did not answer. Perhaps he knew his guilt already.

It was strange. Although some information about his past was forthcoming, other phases of his existence were sometimes glossed over. Was this something else he had picked up from my father? If so, it was a feature I disliked.

"Why don't you tell me the truth about you?" I eventually asked him.

"I do."

"You don't, Tigernus. There is much that I don't know; or rather, much that you don't, or won't tell."

"Tell me what you need to know..."

"You've told me you made it back to Brittany. I know all that. But what happened to you there?"

"I see," he said. "I see what you are asking."

"Is it so bad? Is it as bad as the curse?"

"Maybe," he said.

"Trust me then... I want to know. I won't judge you. I promise. Believe me, I have had enough of being judged myself."

"It is not that."

"What is it then?"

Tigernus absently-mindedly stripped a fern of its leaves, and scattered them into the air. Minutes passed while he contemplated the landscape in front of him. I knew what he was thinking. This was Voog's world: Voog's land.

"You were right – about my horsemanship," he finally said. "The Bretons taught me how to ride well and how to fight. I was still young when I returned. But they had much to be angry about. You see, they were refugees, and slowly, over time, they wanted revenge..."

"Against the Saxons?"

He nodded.

"I joined up with the resistance. I was good with a bow and arrow – your father taught me. With mathematics and strategy too... They saw it in me. I had learnt of war in Hibernia..."

"But you were across the Channel? They didn't raid there surely?"

"They didn't. We did though. We headed back across and raided the peninsula at length. There were missions to wreck the Saxon push to the west."

"With you leading them?"

"Not first of all. Initially, I just went along. They saw my potential, shall we say? But gradually, the boy turned into the man... I forgot about voyage and exploration and became solely concerned with combat and annihilation."

"So tell me, were you successful?"

"Very. We stopped great slaughter. We halted their advance for many years. They came to hate us."

"Who were 'we'?"

"My comrades – the people whom I had come to know in Cornouaille. Some were those who had brought me back from Hyperborea. Others were their descendants. They became my family – just as Voog had once been my father..."

Here was a confession indeed. I was talking to my father's adopted son. We were both his children. Despite this, I could sense a tragic tone in his voice. There was something he did not want to reveal. I had to ask him. I could not bear the unknowing.

"What happened then?"

"One night, a raid went wrong. Hundreds were killed. They were corralled in like cattle. The Saxons picked them off one by one... Most were stoned to death."

"Was it your fault?"

"No-one ever said it was, but I must confess to you, it was all my doing..."

"Stone, war and death – it is the way of men," I offered, hoping my grand-mother's words might console him.

He looked to the ground. I realised he saw safety in it – after so long on the ocean.

"Is that all?" I asked.

He shook his head.

"No."

"Tell me. I will not judge."

Tigernus did not want to talk, but eventually, I got it out of him. Not only had he been ashamed of his failed tactics, he and several of his men had been captured. They'd spent several years in a Saxon slave camp. There, he had re-learned living – if you could call it that. From the way he described it, it sounded more like the hell these Christians talked of.

"I would have come before – just as your father had asked," he said. "But..."

"I know."

I would come to know later of what he endured. In knowing this, I became closer to my mother – and also to him. He had survived what she had also wit-nessed.

As we took the tight path off Carnaquidden Downs, I stopped walking and he was forced to halt.

"Don't ever be bothered by shame," I stated, turning back to him. "I have wrestled with it all my life, and I know it to be a thankless ghost, a deceiving phantom. Don't even think of it. Promise?"

"Yes."

Light streaming across from Mulfra Hill silhouetted Tigernus' head. Read from this angle, he looked holy. He was a man for this new Age. He smiled at me.

Father, Annown, I was beginning to like him very much.

13

Peat-preserved wooden shepherd's crook, Reanscreena, County Cork, Éire 5th to 7th Century CE
Sheep form the lifeblood of many communities around the Atlantic. There are numerous native breeds which are highly suited to the wind-blown climates of headlands and clifftops. This carved wooden shepherd's crook has been preserved due to the unusual conditions of the peat in the area surrounding Reanscreena. These conditions include highly acidic water, low temperature and a lack of oxygen, combining to preserve and tan the wooden object. Courtesy of Cork Museum.

IT TOOK ANOTHER WEEK BEFORE Warna was ready to depart. Unbeknown to me, all around the island of Nornour were various makeshift encampments in which she kept items ranging from rusting fishing tackle and a considerable hoard of salt-stained Viking swords and axes, to bizarre smelling darkened stores of seaweed and smoked fish. Given her twenty-year isolation, she had hoarded much and was finding the process of selecting what to take and what to leave behind difficult. In essence, she wanted to take it all, and there were times, I suspected, when she may have rethought her entire plan to leave. At her age, perhaps it was easier now to stay on this island prison and be comfortable with what she had. Maybe in some senses she wished me to stay, to give her company – and not continue on my journey. But I could not do this. There was no possible way that I was going to remain on Nornour and, like her, accept that fate had brought me there.

Before we left, there was also the issue of her stench. I wasn't about to get into close proximity with her on board *An Ruen* unless she decontaminated herself. Beyond the sheer dirt and grime, she had lice – and the latter were something I did not fancy acquiring. I already had one creature that might carry disease on board. I did not want another.

The prospect of sharing my journey with an old woman was not one I had really considered before. She was hardly going to be the best crew-mate, considering her rheumatism, claw-like fingers and aching frame. She was also curmudgeonly and annoying on almost every aspect of life. I felt she might also judge my actions, and talk about the punishment in hell I might have to accept from this new god of hers. In all, the omens for a happy voyage did not look good.

I persevered however. I showed Warna just how much of her life she could take with her. As with me, whatever she wanted to take had to be bound within a sack. She didn't have any changes of clothing, but now wanted to take souvenirs of her time on Nornour: odd pieces of wood, shells and stones which she argued were visualisations of her god's glory. All the time, these had to be whittled down and sub-divided, or else the hull would be full of nothing else but her knick-knacks. It was a daily project, so to speak, helping Warna select symbolic pieces from her life. I thought of my own life as we completed this task, but soon realised my path had been very different to hers. As a vagrant, a traveller across the peninsula, I had no need for possessions. Possessions only come with an established hearth and home. I had neither. At various decisions I sometimes had to make for her, she shrieked and cried, and angrily contested their importance. Some days what I had thrown out, she had decided were now essentials to take with her. Then we began the process all over again.

In the end, the only way I could have her understand the limitations was to paddle her out to the boat, and for her to physically see what room she would have. Out there, the reality of leaving shocked her. She saw the roundhouse from a distance, and realised that it was slowly passing from her reach. However, knowing that she would never come back seemed to invigorate her preparations, which was part of my purpose.

A few days before we left, I had managed to raise the issue of her cleanliness with her. How do you tell someone they stink? Do you tell them face-to-face that they reek? I went about it in the following way. I made a big deal of my own clothes needing to be washed before we left, and hoped that psychologically, this might induce Warna to do the same. I also took a naked swim down in the bay so that she might learn by example. If she would do this, then I would have the pleasurable job of washing her clothes in the nearby stream. The worry here was that once off her body, the clothes might disintegrate altogether. Looking at her it seemed as if material and skin had almost grown together. Purposely, I had brought soap up for her to use. She had not encountered such a substance before – or at least not for a long time. I showed her how to use it. Initially, all these techniques failed. It seemed that she was refusing to follow any of my wishes here, but then the next morning, she left her rags at the roundhouse entrance, and as I looked down to the bay, I saw her in the water, waving at me, enjoying her naked freedom. Thankfully she was submerged enough for me not see too much of her lined and wrinkly body.

I must have washed out decades of filth from her clothes. Touching these items was not something I particularly wanted to do. Instead, I took a couple of lengths of discarded wood from one of the abandoned roundhouses, tied them with a knot of flax at one end and placed the material into an area where the stream pooled and swirled. The wood formed a pair of improvised tongs so I could squeeze and push out the dirt on stones along the bank. When held for drying and placed on tall ferns in the vicinity, the resultant clothing did not sparkle in the sunshine. Some stains and ingrained filth would probably never leave the material. But still, instead of black grime, I could make out the blue and green colour of the original dress and cloak. Gradually, the true colours of this woman's life were revealing themselves to me.

"You did what I wanted, Warna – you took a wash..." I laughed.

"What *you* wanted!? Bah. Oh no – it was not what you wanted. I read it from the book – the prophet Christ does say that washing and cleanliness are noble endeavours. I was unclear on this before, but see it now."

Thank fuck for this Christ, whoever he was, I said to myself. If Christ, and this god of hers caused more people to smell better, then maybe it was not such a bad thing.

Her hair was the next job. I'd perhaps resigned myself to never fully ridding her of the tiny white beasts that found their home within it, but at least if some of the mass was trimmed, a start might be made. The curls of grey had formed knots and twists close to her skull, and those older that ran down her back had fashioned themselves into matted coils. Almost while she was not looking – and after putting on her newly-washed clothes again (with her rediscovering their original hue and feel) – I took a sharp knife from my sack and made a swift cut along the length of her hair running down her back. The coils fell to the floor. At first she gave an exclamation of surprise, but then let me continue – trusting, I suspected, someone for the first time in so many years; trusting that he was caring for her. I was no expert. I could only think back to the time my mother cut my own hair, and hope that such movements as I was making would not leave her looking like a badly shorn sheep. I'd elected not to scalp her, but leave her hair at a shoulder length. I applied the same apple ointment I used on my own hair. She liked the smell of it. Supposedly, the tiny mites did not like the acidity of it, so again hopefully, they would depart.

When the treatments had finished, Warna turned to me. Now, I could see her properly and see what lay beneath the weathering of Nornour. Sat in the front entrance of the roundhouse, the sun made a slight aura around her head, and she was instantly serene. For the first time, she smiled. At this, I could only think that her story might make a good tale for bards like Remfra. Just recently, his type had been writing more radical stories that people acted and showed instead of just being told or recited. Admirable women – whether holy or not – might make for good theatre in times ahead. Warna's narrative might never reach him – but it was certainly as good as any I had encountered of late.

I had to remember the reality though – Warna's suffering. Just before we left, I caught her on the skyline of the hill beyond the causeway. It was twilight and her silhouette merged with the land – but her ungainly form was instantly distinguishable. I knew what she was doing. She was saying goodbye to her children – those placed in the graves there. Others might have labelled them as bastards – formed of Viking seed – but this was clearly not the way I saw them; nor did Warna, who had begat and nursed them. It seemed Warna was now not following our way of cremation. Instead, her evolving faith believed that the bodies were best placed whole into the ground, at the mercy of the worms. She told me she hoped – as innocents – they'd go straight to this strange heaven she spoke of. I had difficulty understanding the concept – and didn't ask her too much about it, for fear of another lecture, but it seemed in her reasoning that the afterlife was split between two places. Whilst we had just one – our Annown – she had two: heaven and hell. Whichever you went into depended on what kind of life you had led. When I pressed her on where these places were she could not say though. For heaven, she merely looked at the sky. For hell, she looked at the ground. Perhaps I could understand heaven. It was where the clouds formed swirls of wonder in the western sky – perhaps where we placed Annown as well; hence all of my fogous looking to the west in order to transport the spirits of the dead there. Hell, I could not understand though. It seemed to be a combination of a huge underground mine and great fire all hosted and organised by a character named Lucifer. I switched off when she told me he was once an angel, and had fallen from heaven to hell. The ludicrousness of this descent swayed me to keep my faith in Annown.

"What of the earth then?" I asked, as we sat eating our final meal of smoked fish on Nornour. "Who created it?"

"Do I need to tell you, Voog? Don't you know by now?"

"Your god?"

"Precisely. It took him seven days."

I laughed.

"My apologies, Warna. I do not mean to be rude, but clearly that's impossible. No matter how strong and powerful this god is, he could not have made the world in seven days. It can't be done."

"Is it really that impossible? You talk like a druid. Sometimes, the most complex things are easy. "

"And all the animals, and plants, and people? This Adam and Eve you've told me about?"

She nodded, reaching down for more fish. Although she was now cleaner and less lice-ridden, the absolutism remained. I hadn't been able to wash that out of her.

The conversation stopped. I was back being a child again and hearing my father Donyerth talk about the world. For him, humans had not been created – they were not made of clay. Instead, they had come from other animals, and all other animals had merged and formed from others; each an improvement or adaptation from the last. That way, nature learned and grew. According to him, this was how the world came to be and it took millions and millions of years – time that was inconceivable to human beings and that only the rocks comprehended. Even the druids knew the interconnectedness of things – that all life was dependent on that which surrounded it. There was no word for it – but it was understood. This debate burned inside me, but perhaps there would be time for more of this discussion whilst out at sea. There, an endless horizon always gave rise to debate. The polarities of our views were sure to prompt further contestation over Annown, this new god, and their respective places in the modern world.

The ocean was testing me in ways I could not have imagined previously. My common sense was being upturned on a daily basis. Events on this next stage of my voyage made me question the world once again – but Warna and I could not have possibly predicted this when we pulled out of the clasp of Nornour the next morning.

"It is best not to look back," I suggested to her, drawing on my own experience of exile.

Warna had settled herself on the port side, distant from the view across to her roundhouse. There was much she was going to have to learn. Although she had once made her way in a tiny coracle across great distances, her sea legs were now slightly shaky. She had to adjust to the roll and bank of the hull, and be willing to move when we needed weight or resistance on one particular side. Initially, everything was slow with her. The new environment provided her with new challenges every minute. On her face I read that she was uncomfortable and uncertain, and yet this did not match her words.

"I am glad to be leaving. You came as a blessing to me. Bah. Memories there certainly, but not all good ones... it is time to go back."

We had established that the route *An Ruen* was to follow would take us in a direction that I had previously not contemplated. Whereas my initial plan had been to plough steadily into the west, Warna had convinced me that there were far safer ways of reaching my eventual destination.

"There are places to stop off... islands and larger lands," she had gone, "if you follow this route."

I saw the logic. My route into the west would now follow a stepping stone approach that would see me first gain enough experience and enough supplies for the final push to the horizon. Islands to the north existed, so Warna said. The Vikings mentioned them. That was often how they crossed great distances, holing up on many locales while winter passed, before making spring strikes to the south.

Warna's home appeared to be a land somewhere to the northeast of Silura. It was as accurate as that. She would know it, she said, when she saw it – which wasn't the most fantastic piece of navigational help.

"Bah. I know you think I am useless," she explained, "but the land will tell me. I know the shape of the coast. You will see."

I was uncertain about Warna's memory. Twenty years away could deceive the mind – but I had little other choice.

The early morning start was important. The tide, this time of year, only covered the watery neck between Nornour and the larger desolate and unnamed island in the north, for a certain time. Any later in the day, and we would be beached before we had even begun. The strait successfully negotiated, *An Ruen* found her way easily past the rocks of an island Warna named and cursed as Hanjague (it was there that her own coracle had first caught a reef and foundered). When out of the archipelago and in open water, we were ideally placed to catch the western wind which blew at exactly the angle we needed it. I unfurled both the main and head sails and we picked up good speed.

Rat and Warna were wary of each other to begin with. Each edged around the other, seemingly staying – within the small confines of my vessel – as far apart as they could manage. On the island, I had been somewhat worried that he might run off and not be seen of again. As if he were a child, I felt responsible for him – and leaving him on Nornour seemed cruel. He, though, knew when the going was good, remaining around Warna's shelter and feeding off our scraps.

The rain that had fallen had pooled in the hull of *An Ruen*, and for her first task, I had Warna take a cup and hastily bail water overboard. This, she seemed happy enough to do – perhaps having had experience herself of what havoc the weather could cause.

I had no notion of what day it was. On such a voyage, days become immaterial because they are irrelevant to sailing. Time merges. Day becomes night, morning becomes evening, and the routines that are taken for granted and not noticed on land, become the only markers of regularity. Only now and again on this long voyage did some passing individual or community offer up what day they considered it to be. In our Age, that in itself was not very trustworthy, for different lands and peoples had their own distinctive frames of time. When you realise this, you understand how driven your own normal life is by this tyrant named Time. When you forget him – and push him overboard, so to speak – you come to gain a heightened sense of freedom.

Do you see how I am trying to forget Orla?

Because I had become so involved with the story of this crotchety god-obsessed hag Warna, temporarily at least, I lost sight of myself. There were some hours at least, when busied by necessary activity on Nornour, I stopped thinking about her and life back in Carn Euny. The gossip was continuing now no doubt, somewhere across the land we were about to pass again. On the north coast, the cliffs were higher; the sea rougher. She was up there somewhere – being chastised for a love that was smashed and broken like the breakers edging in on these northern zawns and promontories. I felt in my pocket for the figure I had found at Nornour and this reminded me of her. My regret was that she had nothing of mine to call her own. My father's fogous I suspected were put out of her reach as well. They'd have now been tarnished by my own actions, both at Euny and at Chysauster.

Warna knew nothing of my past, but now that she knew me a little better, she probably sensed my grieving.

"You can speak to me you know?" she said, sometime just after midday.

"About?"

"Your past... about why you came to me alone... upon an ocean."

"There is nothing to say," I lied.

She cackled.

"What – a glum-faced young man like you... pissed off with the world. It must have been a girl. With a face like yours, she must have been both pretty and pert."

I concentrated on the steering paddle, occasionally lifting my sight to look at the fortifications on the northern coast.

"Don't look at them. Stockades and trenches won't give you answers," she stated.

Some distance away on the waves was the complex at Kenidjack. This was my mother's old community, safely compacted behind the ramparts and high over the ocean, the huts there were set to stand fast against any *Ancredhor Mor*.

"Dump you did she?"

I ignored Warna.

"Either that or her father didn't like the look of you... The left hand maybe?"

"Get on with your bailing old woman," I said, to make her loathe me.

"By your silence, I see I have touched a nerve."

"Does this god of yours encourage such forceful questioning?"

"Bah. Only if it is to seek the truth," rued Warna. "The truth is all that matters..."

"Really?" I said sarcastically.

"By your tone then, maybe she was married... Maybe another man and she were betrothed before you chanced upon her. Such is the power of love sometimes."

"Sometimes," I said, "we cannot have all that we want... You know that, all too well."

"Bah. I know much," Warna continued. "But if you wish to keep your mystery, then so be it. I cannot force it from you. But, as you know, a trouble shared is often a way of easing the burden. Keep it if you prefer, but in my experience, young man, it will eat away at you... That carcass is something you do not wish to be."

Warna was right, but I was not about to let her have the satisfaction of knowing it. I kept a stony face, and ignored her pleas for information. I decided she could think what she liked about me. Although her body was frail, clearly her mind was still sharp. She was as quick as Casvellyn at piecing together clues.

This temporary difficulty in communication between us was only relieved by a pod of dolphins that broke the sea's surface on the port side. We both expressed our pleasure at their arrival. On the wind, we could discern their clicks and whistles of communication to each other. At one moment, the full group seemed to arch as one over the surface of the sea. It was strange in my view that my people named these creatures *morhogh* (literally 'sea-pigs') because they carried a grace and wonder that no land hog bore. Maybe it was their rounded beak which reminded land-dwellers of the snout of hogs and pigs. They were bright, these creatures, displaying an intelligence lacking in others. They could not be described as fish at all. No, these were mammals that lived in the ocean; they gave birth to live young.

"I've seen them many a time on Nornour," Warna recalled. "Sometimes when one is fading, and knows his time is over, only to wash up dead upon the strand, they will not leave him. Bah. They seem to mourn their loss in ways I know no other animal does."

"They are clever fishers too," I noted. "They will corral a shoal together and let each take its turn to enter and eat."

They had circled the horn of Britain for many centuries. There were dwellings I knew that were hundreds of years old, that had images of jumping dolphins carved upon the walls. Their behaviour seemed to attract humans. In seeing them, it seemed that they were watching something of themselves.

"Aren't they a good omen?" Warna asked. " – especially if they follow in our wake."

I affirmed this, drawing upon all the sealore I knew, and watched the pod (there were six of them) delay their movement forward and swing around to be in the trail of *An Ruen*. Closer now, we could see their joy in playing with us.

"You are smiling, Master Voog," announced Warna. "Omen or not – they are good cures for depression."

I smiled and knew I was warming to this crone. Rat too seemed to sense joy in them, and sat proudly on the canopy at the stern.

The ocean easily shifts though, and what was coming was a mighty change that the three of us never anticipated.

As quickly as the pod appeared, very suddenly they disappeared, scattering out singularly to the south and north of the wake.

"Something's spooked them," I noted.

Clearly, the pod formation was now something unsafe for them. They had sensed a presence under the sea that they disliked. Swimming alone gave the rest a chance to survive. It was a simple survival strategy for the whole. Maybe it was a shark; the bigger, more aggressive ones were known to take dolphins, but then, despite their size, the basking variety offered no threat.

Rat went quiet. This was unusual for him. Considering his reaction to the basking shark, I'd expected a sustained hubbub. He was shivering though, which seemed odd. Something encouraged me to keep sailing; not to halt and see what was there. Anything that scared dolphins (sizeable creatures in themselves) was probably best left alone. I also gave off a fear, which was noticed by Warna.

"God will see us safe..." she said, clutching her book and cross.

Instead of these tools, I elected instead to keep my crowbar handy, just in case.

Both of us scanned the ocean intently. I noted how far the north coast of the horn was from us. In case of trouble, could I swim it? Perhaps I could, but I was less sure about Warna and Rat. I kept the coracle close, making the knot looser in order to allow for an easy escape. Given this unease, maybe the land would have to host me again, despite everything. Facing Howel's law might suddenly have been better than facing what was out here.

And then it passed. Gradually, the Awen-like rays of sun passed through the cloud ahead of us and the atmosphere changed. Whatever foreboding had accompanied us for that half hour after the dolphins scattered, it had evaporated.

"It seems your mighty god has his uses."

"Only if you have faith," Warna responded.

I let the crowbar loose and checked our heading. To the right opened up wide beaches. I knew them intimately. This was where Kenal and I had together faced the *Ancredhor Mor*. I recalled the battle, and the men lost – their ashes now buried in the dunes. I became lost in this triumph, and knowing Warna's tale, it pleased me even more. Satisfaction is a terrible emotion though. It leads directly to complacency. I knew it more than most. It was that which led to my discovery – to our transgression becoming public knowledge.

Complacency then.

That is how I came to meet my worst fear. I recall the moment exactly. Warna was inside the canopy resting; with me hoping that not too many of her head-lice would transfer onto the sheepskins. I tell you as clear now as on that day: the neck and head of it came from nowhere – like nothing could have predicted its presence. You will know this creature. You may not believe it – but you will know it. You label it a plesiosaur. It rushed up into the air on the starboard side, its flippers splayed out to support its rise out of the water. There it sniffed and tasted the air, and peered down on the vessel. We must have seemed tiny to it, though the whole of *An Ruen* was slightly longer than this creature's body. My whole body quaked with fear in ways I never knew existed. The unpredictability of the neck was what scared me the most. It was snake-like, forever twisting into a new position. When it felt uncomfortable with any angle, it flipped its entire body, so that the long neck dictated the turn of the spine. This created a wave that engulfed the hull and flooded it.

This had been what had spooked the dolphins and what had tracked us up the coast. I never really believed such beasts existed. Surely they were the stuff of mythical legends. What was Remfra's tale called? The Voyages of Bryok wasn't it? It had featured there as one more hurdle for him to defeat. His imaginative proclivities now had an urgent reality that made me wish I had listened more carefully. How did one go about defeating such a reptile? But they weren't just the stuff of tales or bardic fancy. Oh no. Sailors and fishermen both had sworn their existence to me. They were a rare sight, but according to them, they were out there, left over from some past Age. What was the word they used for it? *Mor* – something wasn't it?

Morgawr, that was it. It meant 'sea giant' and at this point, the nomenclature seemed apt. Now myth was becoming real on my ocean.

Despite its immensity, I could tell this was a juvenile still. There was a playfulness in its manner that suggested it was comparatively young. I sensed she was a female. All of this knowledge, of course, increased my concern further. If the juvenile was this close, in just what proximity was the mother? I couldn't think too much about that for the moment though. Instead, I spent my time dodging her inquisitiveness and tried to discern what she wanted from us.

After scanning *An Ruen*, the neck lowered again, allowing me to see the creature's mouth in more detail. Although I counted numerous teeth, they didn't look the kind that would devour dolphins. Instead, I suspected they were bottom-feeders, after squid and crustaceans rather than larger mammals. That said, its bite might well have carved up larger species which it could then devour in sections.

Its eyes were the most frightening part of it. They were tiny yet unreal orbs – so black I saw my doomed reflection within them.

All this happened in seconds.

I shouted for Warna to come out of the canopy.

"We need your god!" I yelled "I thought he was granting us safe passage. Look at this thing!"

Warna mumbled something in the canopy, still unaware of what it was that toyed with us.

By now, my crowbar was back in my hand. At least, I had something to batter it with should it become more aggressive. The strength of its neck muscle alone could easily upturn us.

At sight of it, Warna froze. All her experiences and her time alone at Nornour had not prepared her for this. But nothing could have. Despite our difference, we were united in horror. Seconds later, she had fainted and I felt the boat lurch as the full weight of her body fell into the hull. There was nothing I could do. I had to watch the creature that was watching us. Warna might be best off unconscious anyway. The monster might then seem like a dream to her – it'd be better that way. Rat meanwhile, was made speechless. With this sea beast towering above him, he suddenly seemed to realise his place in the order of things.

The plesiosaur's body was breathtaking in its design. Whilst I had earlier marvelled at the dolphins' ability to jump and dive through the waves, this creature could turn on a coin with incredible ease. Curious at what we were, she headed towards the bow, trying to make sense of the vessel and what we were doing in her domain. At the bow, she became noisy, vocalising her interest in our passage – a sound that only lurked in my imagination before. It combined the rich throatiness of the cormorant with the high-pitched scream of a hunted boar. The tone of it was painful to my ears – so close was I to the source of the sound.

I could not make my mind up about it. All I knew about reptiles was based upon the few tiny lizards I had ever seen that skittered over granite on the top of tors. To operate, they needed the heat of the sun to warm their bodies. But this creature had something of the mammal about it too – tufts of hair poked from its head and neck, and the way it behaved conveyed intelligence far brighter than dolphins and their ilk. When I say there were moments of humanity within it, I mean it.

How many of them were there? Not many I first thought. They were predators at the top of the food chain and normally these were fewer in numbers. Then again, the ocean was an undiscovered realm. Much was out there that we knew nothing about. There were bound to be creatures like this that, from time to time, encountered humanity, but then disappeared again. The ocean was deep enough to conceal many a strange occupant. In that, I include me.

As it became clearer that the plesiosaur was not going to devour me – in one go at least – I began to observe her behaviour further. Her movement was so fluid it was seemingly magical; her two pairs of flippers worked as both paddles and fins at the same time. With such a design, manoeuvrability and speed were easily achieved. The body itself was broad, with a wide ribcage, but the tail a mere stump. Like seals, her nasal ducts closed over when she submerged; any water absorbed snorted out when she emerged from the deep.

My fear gradually subsided into pure excitement. What I was witnessing was a species of animal that few men or women had seen, and that those who had, instantly judged it as a dragon to be slaughtered. She would never be trained, not like oxen or a horse. She was too wild, too full of nature's power for her ever to be reined in, but she might be placated and kept happy. My mind turned to this as she reared in front of the bow. Maybe feeding her might show that we meant no harm. A sack of smoked fish was one item that I suggested Warna did bring with her on board. Such preserved flesh would not rot or smell, and might be stowed for some time. Now however, I believed I had found a more urgent use for it.

I shouted an obscenity to grab the plesiosaur's attention, and she flipped a roll around to the port side. From this angle I could toss her fish. She was adept at seeing them coming – most being caught by confident snapping movements of her neck and mouth. Others that fell into the sea she quickly retrieved. The ferocity and viciousness of these captures seemed to show there was something of the snake in her – something of the devil in serpent form – which mad Warna had explained to me. Perhaps this was disingenuous. She was, after all, like any other creature – just trying to survive the best that she could. If this small being on board this vessel offered her free fish, then why not accept it.

That was it – I understood her anatomy more now. The lower half was turtle-like. The tales said such creatures buried eggs on the beach at night. Some even linked these to the magical *glain* stones of the druids. I, for one, did not believe it, but then I believed so little they said about the *glain*. On all the beaches I had ever walked upon, I had never discovered eggs of this creature. More likely, they gave birth just as dolphins did – to live young. They did this far from the prying eyes of men in order to protect themselves and their young.

The upper half was the snake. This reminded me of being back in the fogou as a boy – finding my first adder. I could still feel its coils around my misshapen wrist. Those muscles were strong in the adder, and were strong too in the snap and nuzzle of what was now twisting on the port side. Although this *Morgawr*, this plesiosaur, now seemed to enjoy me feeding it, I still felt vulnerable. This feeling increased incrementally as the supply of smoked fish decreased at a rapid rate. Would it, could it, turn to other foodstuffs of a more human nature to satiate its hunger? The snaps it made now were lower, more confident and assured – closer to where Warna lay. At present, she was perhaps safest there. If she was conscious in any capacity, she'd hopefully continue to play dead.

My fear rose to new heights, however, when the stock of smoked fish ended. I had nothing more to give it. Would it sense or smell the wool grease and hide of the oxen and think that was worth a bite? I prayed that the stench offended it and that its appetite was, for the moment, suppressed by my actions. Its continual coiling and movement made me nervous and soon my anxiety increased when she bent her neck lower, so that the bristled head and damp nostrils could examine Warna. Smell was key. I watched, appalled, as the head of the plesiosaur passed slowly over the frame of Warna. A watery saliva, composed of sickening stomach acid, chyme, brine and desiccated fish parts dripped onto her. The creature had no tongue, but instead nudged at her, trying to make sense of what lay there. At any time, its sheer weight may have tipped us clean into the water, and our ocean voyage would be over.

I eased back, away from the horrific scene unfolding in front of me. I could smell the whole of the ocean in the plesiosaur's putrid breath. Its exhalation was ancient and inescapable. Again, the creature scanned Warna's body and at any moment I expected its jaws to jump forward and clamp around one of her limbs, or her neck. She could break either in one adroit move – toss the rest over, or drag the entire body into the deep. My crowbar could do no good now. This thing was in control. She could do what she wished.

Ten days ago I had been at the mercy of men. Now, I was at the mercy of a giant of the sea.

Just as I expected this to be the last seconds of Warna, the creature turned its head to me. It snorted one last time, seemingly unwilling to make anything else of Warna and to leave her alone. *Morgawr*'s eyes though – they seemed to note every part of me. Did she sense in me my respect for her or simply my fear? It was hard to tell, and once that moment was over, the neck withdrew as the flippers churned the water once again and dug into the depths. Revolving, the whole cage of her body turned to the left, and the neck descended, her stump of a tail showing briefly as she disappeared beneath the waves.

Her sound – both her breathing and her cry – had been so domineering that nothing else could be heard. Now, all was still again but I could hear my own panting and feel my heart beating wildly. It must have been a minute before I moved, before I gained enough air to fill my lungs and appreciate my survival. Had I been one of Remfra's broad-shouldered and square-chinned heroes, I would have taken a broadsword and cut off its gibbering neck at the base with one deft swing. Instead, there had been no heroics – just feeding time from out of our larder.

Warna was back to being stinking again; this time though, through no fault of her own. I reached in for a bowl and filled it with fresh water, rinsing the sea creature's chyme away from her face and torso. I listened for her breath, trying to sense her respiration. It sounded weak. Within seconds I had clamped my mouth onto her lips and exhaled air to inflate her lungs. It only took one breath. She spluttered and coughed her way back into consciousness – a tough old boot, this new kind of holy woman.

"Has it gone?" she asked.

"Looks like it."

"Why do I stink?"

"It drooled over you."

A look of despair crossed her face.

"You ever seen one of those before?"

"Never. Heard about them – but never thought I'd see one. The bugger's had all your smoked fish Warna."

"Better that than me," she croaked.

"Indeed."

"I don't understand why it didn't take you... It looked like it might."

Warna shuffled in her position. She reached into her clothing and pulled out the stone cross which had been on her breast all the while.

"Protection," she said.

I smiled, laughing and crying at once, mucus from my own nose falling upon her.

"No cunning serpent's going to deceive me," she asserted.

I cared little for her belief, but I was happy she was still there. For the first time, and without hesitation, I hugged her.

FATHER ANNOWN, ANNOWN FATHER. SEE how you both merge and become part of me. In my mind you are inextricably linked. You are fogous both that burrow deep into me. I am walking still with these men, who gaze at my skin and talk of the moon. In this new land, I am running with them past rock and boulder, and past tree and shrub. In my head I am running towards you and away from you at the same time. You are future and past.

The arrival of Tigernus had done much to change all of us. For me, I had found a companion, but as well as this, he had brought a future. He had given me continuity. For my grandmother, it had reaffirmed much that she knew but which she had suppressed. Despite her infirmity, knowledge of my father's survival gave her hope. He had defied Howl and Casvellyn. For Kenal it was harder. Although under the orders of Howel, he had been the one who had actually forced my father out onto the ocean. The guilt of this ate away at him. Kenal was, however, not a man to become a Christian overnight. Instead, he had talked to me and reasserted how sorry he had been. With hindsight, if he could have done anything to have altered the course of events he would have. I entreated him not to worry, for what had taken place was unalterable. If he had not followed what Howel had wished, he himself would have been executed. I had learnt much from the way the chief of Carn Euny had dealt with the *Ancredhor Mor*. After a few days, Kenal rode home to Carn Euny. He would tell nobody of the arrival of this young man from Scathynys – or the information he had.

Tigernus and I talked about the druids. He was aware of one called Casvellyn, and another named Eleder. Eleder had been talked of by people they encountered. My grandmother knew him well. He was praised as an honourable man. Casvellyn, though, had been spoken of in more scathing terms.

"I feel the same way as my father about him."

"Does he live here still?"

"No – in fact, he has travelled south... to Armorica. Perhaps you may encounter him if you go back there. I am just glad that he has gone."

"It is the same there," offered Tigernus. "The druids are not strong any more but some survive at least. Holy men and women come – like this Warna I told you about."

I nodded. The fact that my father had found her intrigued me. It was hard to imagine him sailing with her. From what Tigernus had offered, it was even more incredible to think how she had eventually departed from them.

"Did he put any faith in this new religion?" I asked.

"Not really... well..."

I saw Tigernus mull over what I had asked.

"Go on."

"Well, one time, he did give me a cross to carry... I think it may have helped. I'm not sure he believed it though. It was more for Warna's sake than anything."

I watched Tigernus turn the pages of time.

"And then he gave it to somebody in Hibernia..."

He stopped. The young man realised he was probably revealing too much.

"Who?"

"A woman."

Tigernus became uneasy.

"There was someone else? Someone else who he loved? I thought you said..."

"No. Listen. Don't take that the wrong way. There was no-one else for him. This woman thought much of him though. He saved their people. Maybe she loved him, but I tell you honestly Blejan, he only had thoughts for your mother."

"Perhaps he has remarried by now..." I contemplated.

"Perhaps so," chipped in my grandmother, "and who would blame him if he had?"

"I don't think so," said Tigernus. "He had to let go of Orla, but he never forgot the love he felt for her. Time doesn't alter that, in my view."

I persisted.

"Who was this other woman?"

"I cannot remember her name."

"Let it go," said my grandmother.

There was an awkward moment when I still wanted answers from Tigernus about her, but then again, what more could I expect? My father had been put into exile. He would have to have contemplated a new life. I had no right to pursue this line of questioning. I stopped my onslaught.

"Wait," said Tigernus. "I forgot. I've something to show you. Hang on a minute..."

Tigernus ventured outside of the roundhouse, to find something in the saddlebags of his horse.

"You could do a lot worse," my grandmother said, looking to where Tigernus had vacated the dwelling. "If I was thirty years younger, I would."

"Gran!" I said, reprimanding her.

"Just being honest... He obviously likes you. He was dead keen to walk with you. Has he a girl back home in Armorica?"

"He hasn't mentioned any."

She tapped her nose.

"Make your move then..." she advised.

"Stop interfering!"

"I know, I know. I promised not to. I won't say another word."

"What did we agree about arranged relationships?"

"All right. You've made your point. Just saying. That's all."

We must have been red-faced when Tigernus came back in as he asked if there was anything wrong.

"No, nothing," we both said, trying to hide our discussion.

He carried with him rolls of parchment and hide.

"This is what I wanted to show you. Look..."

Tigernus unfurled a set of maps, positioning their corners with the weight of pots and stones from my grandmother's house.

"What are these?"

"Look... On the back here – sketches of the extended fogou at Carn Euny... See where he has calculated the angles and the leverage needed... But on the front, see these maps of the ocean. He drew these based on ideas from his father Donyerth."

I pored over the ragged edges of lands. I took in the islands and the currents.

"This one though. This is the last one he drew. He did it when we reached the coast of Hyperborea. Said he didn't need it any more. They've been with me all this time."

I traced the faint charcoal lines embedded in the hides and parchment. Here had traced my father's hand. I bent down to smell the charcoal, hoping for a whiff of him.

"This is Ogygia. Voog and I never found it," Tigernus continued, "but I added it in when I came back. We stopped off there. It does exist."

He pointed to a set of islands off the coast of Iberia.

"Were these maps what you used to get across?" I asked.

"Yes. Your father, he used the stars as well – to calculate our position and to see how much progress we were making. He taught me too. That's why the Bretons valued me as a leader."

"What's that there?" I asked, pointing to one island.

"That? Oh, that's Hy-Brasil. I told you about that."

I nodded. Now I understood.

"What do you think?" enquired Tigernus. "I was hoping you'd like seeing this."

As he pointed his hand to the north, his hand accidentally touched mine. The warmth of it felt good to me.

I couldn't answer him. I marvelled at the map, but I was now also marvelling at my own feelings. I wanted him to touch me again.

Other thoughts also tumbled around my head. If they had made it across, then why couldn't others? Why couldn't I too see the coast of Hyperborea?

14

'A Most Strange and True Report of a Monstrous Female Fish', Skomer Island, Pembrokeshire, Wales, 1602
Many Atlantic peoples tell stories about mermaids. From the 5th Century CE onwards, they appear in numerous folktales and mythological narratives ranging from Galicia to Greenland. This illustration of a 'monstrous female fish' comes from a unique pamphlet telling the story of an alleged sighting of a mermaid near Skomer Island, Pembrokeshire in 1602. The creature was first seen by William Saunders, a yeoman from Hasguard who then summoned others to keep watch for three hours. Thomas Reynold of Hasguard later examined Saunders and some of the other witnesses. A reference to the sighting of mermaids is found in the journal of Christopher Columbus (1451-1506) for 9th January 1493. Belief in mermaids, fairies and other mythical creatures persisted around the Atlantic Ocean until the eighteenth century. Gradually, opposition from the Protestant Church, greater levels of literacy and industrialisation led to the demise in the belief in such creatures. Image courtesy of the National Library of Wales/Llyfrgell Genedlaethol Cymru.

THE JUVENILE PLESIOSAUR PUT US on edge. They might do this in whatever Age humans make contact with them. The heroes of Remfra's tales knew it, and so now, did I.

In the aftermath of the attack, we could barely function, and hardly speak. We became irritable with each other. Warna decided I was both morose and unfriendly; I told her she was bitter and that her cloying faith was a guising myth. This vitriolic abuse was unfair to both of us, but our personal circumstances had altered. Whereas before, I had set out reasonably confident that I could voyage wherever I wanted, I now knew that I too, was frail and vulnerable. I knew that if I was lost, wrecked or perhaps – Annown forbid – even eaten, there was no-one to mourn me. Perhaps that is why I was so morose.

Warna said little really, but I could tell that she too imagined this journey very differently. On Nornour she'd come to view me as her protector: a kind of surrogate 'son' of sorts, who might look after her. Now, she seemed less certain of me. She put distance between us. I tried explaining to her – I could deal with a lot of things, but huge-necked sea monsters of that kind, well, that was something very different.

How on earth do you combat forces that powerful?

I was no brave and mythic Bryok.

In the midst of this silence on board the vessel, Rat played his cards carefully, vying between us. He had got closer to us, so that even Warna (who, like me, despised him at first) would pick him up and cradle him, and with me, he was sometimes confident enough to sit atop my shoulder as I worked the steering oar. Up there, he was captain of everything – perhaps even of *Morgawr* herself. He seemed to even fancy the plesiosaur pulling us along – a sea horse for our chariot of the ocean. He'd be skipper of six dolphins next, drawn astride them in a cave fresco.

We tracked up along the fearsome north coast. The ocean was choppier here; the wind stronger and, accordingly, the grey waves bigger. The angle at which the bow hit oncoming waves increased, and the whole of the hull dipped up and down more steeply. It was a motion that might easily induce seasickness. Feeling green, we both kept our eyes fixed on the horizon and tried to ignore the heave of the vessel. Warna had to wash her own clothes this time, following the plesiosaur's digestive juices dripping on her, and I spent some time looking the other way (to shore, in fact) so that she could complete this. However, given our close proximity, when on board a vessel of this size, practically no nakedness or bodily function is hidden. It is the way of things.

For three days and three nights, nothing much altered, aside from the land we went by. We passed estuaries, wide, sandy beaches and thunderous cliffs. On these jutting cliffs were villages. These promontory settlements I tried to place and connect in my mind. There was a web of them. Some were vast communities; others on a much smaller scale. All seemed set to face invasion of one kind or another. We lived in that kind of an Age. The logic of these promontory settlements was simple. They were impregnable from the sea, which meant the *Ancredhor Mor* would find them difficult to attack, and likewise, because they were often built beyond a thin neck of cliff, defence of this from the inside was relatively easy. In such ways, they were prepared for attacks from the land as well. Only a small group of invaders could ever reach the entrance and these could be dealt with easily.

Beyond these cliffs was the high moor: Brentigia, it was called in my people's tongue. I had touched upon its boundaries one time, but it was a desolate place and hard to cross. Even the normally thorough and well-disciplined Romans had been defeated by it. This tract they failed to manoeuvre across, as well as the much higher land further to the east, that fed the waters of the river they called the Dart. Bog-ridden and isolated it was, full of looming mountains and jagged tors – a foreboding ocean of land that no-one wished to pass across. The Romans went around such obstacles, and if they had need of tin from these underground idiots of the west, they sailed straight to the trading source at *Carrack Looz en Cooz.*

The Saxons were said to be more ambitious though. Maybe even now they were crossing it, preparing for colonisation and integration into their growing empire. So it was said, the way the Saxon hordes worked was different to the *Ancredhor Mor.* Whereas the Norsemen just slaughtered anything that moved, took what they wanted and burnt what they would rather not leave behind, the Saxons rounded up the men, put them into detention camps and then redeployed them as slaves – using them in their war machine. The women they quickly impregnated so as to assimilate them and their resultant children into their world. While the *Ancredhor Mor* colonised by death, the Saxons colonised by lineage. You see, my world was a harsh one and right now, there seemed very little to choose between Saxon, Viking and a plesiosaur. When I thought about it though, I was starting, even now, to prefer that monster of the depths to men.

The wind was bringing us in close to the coast in what travellers call the North Country, where the high chieftains of Cornwall were said to dwell. On a jutting island was their majestic fortification. These were men of military might and power; the kind that Howel admired and wanted to be. His gaze was set on these North Country lords, but they squabbled often, and there was said to be great dissension between them, when they ought to be standing as one against their common foes. No-one, as yet, united them. In fact, union seemed impossible. Besides that, they probably thought little of my people (perhaps I mean my former people) in the far west – where they were still bound up with ritual and ceremony, pretending all might be well again by putting all hope into the sun and moon, the oak and the elder. The chieftains there probably viewed us in the distant horn as impractical and as men who likely didn't even know how to draw a sword, still innocently happy with their fishing and farming. That is it with us people of the west – we are too busy fighting amongst ourselves to agree on the common enemy. It will be the curse of us I am certain.

We avoided the harbour. It was a cosmopolitan place. The Phoenicians traded there and there were probably boats in from Africa swapping pottery, silks and jewels for metals, wool and skins. Certainly vessels from Hibernia crossed to here, though, so it was said, tension was always rife between the men from there and those of this peninsula. It was the usual arguments: over beer, cards, games of nine men's morris, gambling – and of course, women.

Stories travelled fast. The banishment of a five-fingered fogou-builder would already be known around the pontoons there. I could hide my hand, but me showing up with a crazy old crone who thought she was on some evangelical mission would certainly generate interest – precisely the wrong kind of interest. No, it was a place best left alone. In time, its own greed and stupidity would bring it further notoriety. It would only take some chronicler with a bit of an imagination to make it so.

The way things started to pan out onboard *An Ruen* was that Warna took charge of cooking. Her speciality (or do I mean her only dish?) was broth – usually a variant based around the degrees of fish and vegetable, and other unrecognisable and unidentifiable barely chewable substances that went into it. It was warming and somewhat nutritious though, and on a voyage such as ours, this is all you can really ask for. Culinary delight could be found back where the Phoenicians, Africans and Hibernians partied and feasted on the profits of their trading.

Whereas I gulped mine down, she always said a grace before spooning the morsels into her mouth. In this way though, we managed to coexist. She was even beginning to wash on a daily basis, regaining a sense of her womanhood perhaps. Rat often just slept, aside from when scraps were on offer.

The maps I had redrawn from memories of my father's view of the world turned out to be accurate. Although he had not visited it, he swore that there was an island set in the middle of this part of the ocean. It was a jewel, he recalled: an emerald stone set in the bright blue. Warna knew of it too. She had visited it on her crossings many years ago. Supposedly, there we might find a plentiful supply of eggs, as well as fresh water.

"What did your father call it?" Warna asked.

"Scathynys I think."

"He is right. It is a paradise of birds. Yes – 'Puffin Island' is what it translates to. I had forgotten."

Our course then, was for Scathynys. How it came to be in this part of the ocean was unclear, because the dark, granite batholith of it rose starkly from the sea. Few rocks or other reef formations surrounded it. It was as if some giant of the past had accidentally dropped it there, and now could not be bothered to retrieve it. Scathynys had been on the horizon for some time now. At first, it was a low slung stretch of land in the distance, but as we drew closer we realised its height and majesty.

"Many stop here," Warna said. "It is on a direct path from my land to the peninsula. A day's sailing each way I think."

"And by 'many' you mean?"

"Anyone."

This was ominous. Warna knew it too.

Although seemingly a useful watering hole it could easily turn into a trap. We'd need to be cautious.

We were uncertain who lived on the island. A scan of the clifftops provided few clues. The people here were about as isolated as they could be. It perhaps even made parts of Silura look like a fully functioning civilisation by comparison. On the one hand though, this knowledge was a good thing. There was no point in raiding a community if it had nothing to pillage. Why too, take out resources and structures that you yourself might need? There was a logic in leaving it alone, and using it only when you needed to.

"I'm going to sail around it first," I said to Warna. "I want to see what we are dealing with."

"I am sure I put in to the south last time I was here," she replied.

At the island's southwest corner, we thus turned and sailed up, along its western shore. As Warna mentioned, it was a paradise of birds. There were so many different species who inhabited the cliffs: black-legged kittiwakes, guillemots, fulmars and herring gulls. There too, amongst these larger birds, the tinier, cuter forms of curious puffins – a whirling collision of blacks, whites, blues, reds and oranges. Those returning from the ocean had beaks filled with sand eels as food for their chicks. Like the plesiosaurs, left alone by humanity, here they could flourish. In these birds though, I saw a link back to *Morgawr* – the same line and form somehow, and definitely the same piercing eyes – as if all had some similar mother, some amalgamation in times long before these.

The puffins were a delight to watch and encounter though.

Warna was elsewhere. The landscape of Scathynys had cleaved off a quarter of a century for her. Memories tumbled out.

"I was here with them," she said dreamily.

I had been given to ignoring Warna when she was like this. Sometimes it was for the best. She had these vacant moments all the way, usually before uttering a prayer.

"Yes – with all of them," she mouthed.

"Who?" I asked, frustrated at her lack of precision.

"The children of Brychan: Adwen, Wenna, Nectan, Yse, Clether, Endelienta, Menfre, Tedda, Kenhender.... All together and then all dispersed. Their lives were torn apart. Scattered they were... or martyred..."

The litany of names recalled came out as if these souls were fairies or spirits of the past.

"Who were they?"

"People of my kind. People of the new faith. They were as seed heads of the dandelion... carried to the south of here I think."

"Why were they scattered?"

She didn't answer. She didn't need to say. I knew she was thinking of other monsters, beyond plesiosaurs.

"And you?"

"To Nornour."

She needed holding, comforting, telling that the world would be all right again, but that could not come from me this time.

"Some were only young girls..." she continued.

Instead, I nodded at her story and concentrated on our route around the island. The land and cliffs to the west were rocky and barren; those to the east more verdant and luscious. As we rounded the top end of the island, it was clear that the milder climate could be found on the sloping mounds of the east. Most of the marine bird life was to be found in the north and west, though puffins still occupied burrows on the eastern clifftops, scattering a hello to us as we proceeded. From out here, Scathynys resembled a resting beast, the foreshore of land to the south like an extended flipper pointing to the south east.

There, the rock formed a natural harbour. Warna had remembered well. Sometimes, she was worth trusting.

"Bah. I told you," she griped.

It didn't matter. Sometimes having the measure of a place is worth the delay in landing. I was to discover this many a time in the future.

It was drawing into the early evening by the time we had dropped anchor, and put coracle to shore. Interest in our circumnavigation became clear as a young boy aged around seven or eight years old ran down the steep path from the summit of the island. He pummelled enthusiastically across the pebbly beach towards us. Warna was just stepping out of the coracle, and I suppose he saw just a bit too much of her. This put him off his mark slightly, but he soon recovered and began a well-rehearsed speech, hardly stopping to draw breath.

"Welcome both to Lund-ey. My name is Tigernus and, for a small fee, I will be your guide to this wondrous place. Should you require fresh water – then I have this all ready for you... and if you require eggs or bird meat for your long voyage, then this too can be arranged. I also have a variety of freshly picked vegetables on offer – the very best on the island."

"Lund-ey?" mouthed Warna to me, leaning in. "What means he by Lund-ey? This is Scathynys isn't it? It was when I was last here."

The boy looked puzzled, aware that his prepared declaration had somehow offended these two new visitors.

I knew enough of the Norsemen's language to realise what it meant.

217

"It's the same thing, Warna – Norse for 'Puffin Island'..."

This was not what either of us wanted to hear, but then again, this boy had a name like ours. He had not been named by the *Ancredhor Mor*.

"Young Tigernus, we will take up your offer but my people know this land as Scathynys," I said. "What has happened?"

Tigernus looked faintly embarrassed.

"It's the old name for it – but since we mainly get visits from the *Ancredhor Mor*, I was told not to use it... Judging by your vessel there, I thought you came from the same line – but now I see you are..."

"Different?"

"Yes – different."

He paused for some seconds, and then began again.

"Welcome then both of you to glorious Scathynys...."

I interrupted him.

"Your sales pitch is fine as it was, Tigernus. Here's money for you."

I tossed him a coin – a currency he was probably not used to these days, but he smiled and pocketed it nonetheless.

"By the way," I said. "There are three of us."

Tigernus' eyes bulged as Rat sniffed the air atop Warna's shoulder.

"Has he come home then?" asked a surprised Tigernus.

"Home? No – he is a hundred miles or more from home."

"Why do you ask?"

"Over there," Tigernus pointed to the southeastern protuberance of flipper-like land, nervous with his words. "We don't go down there. We call it Rat Island. It's where they all live."

"Do you hear that Rat? Your very own *Logosowynys*." I said to him.

He seemed nonplussed about this prospect.

"We have to watch them," said Tigernus. "They steal all the eggs.."

Now much began to make sense about this Lund-ey.

I had questions for Tigernus. So did my companion.

"How often do the *Ancredhor Mor* put in here these days?" asked Warna, Tigernus keeping a good distance from her.

Tigernus thought about it for a while.

"It depends on the season, but right now... most weeks."

"Most weeks you say? And this week? Have they been here this week?"

"Not yet," replied Tigernus.

Warna and I looked at each other.

"If they come, you will let us know?"

"Of course I will."

"It's just that..." Warna tried to explain.

"...you don't like them," continued Tigernus. "Don't worry. Most people don't like them. You must understand though, that isolated as we are here, a boy must make his way in the world as best he can..."

"And?"

"I have a special relationship with them. I know... their needs, so to speak," Tigernus said confidently.

This conversation made me want to leave the island as soon as possible. Given Warna's experience of them on Nornour, and the scattering of Brychan's holy children, not to mention my own encounters with them at Carn Euny, they seemed best avoided.

"How long do you think you will be staying?" continued Tigernus. "We have excellent accommodation here you know. New roundhouses. Good-sized fire pits. Wicker-framed beds – comfy as y'like."

"Bah. I don't think... bah.... we'll be here that long," mouthed Warna, puffing as we climbed the tall steps to the island's summit.

As we continued, I warmed to this boy. He reminded me of myself as a youngster, trying to make his way in an adult, and sometimes hostile world. Along the way, he pointed out features in the landscape; things apparently that Scathynys was revered for. To us though, they looked nothing more than hillocks of grass or rushes of bramble and weed. He assured us they were bar-rows of the dead of an ancient race that once lived here.

We'd come quite a distance now from the harbour.

"Most people come for the isolation," Tigernus continued. "You can get away from it all. I promise you that."

Getting away from it all was something along the lines of what I wanted, if not Warna.

"Where are you three from?" he asked.

"From the southwest, from the horn of Britain."

"From all over," interrupted Warna. "From God's glory..."

Mad woman, Tigernus indicated to me, raising an eyebrow at her words.

"We get a few in from there... not very often though... not much these past few years."

Tigernus spoke as if he was a seasoned owner of a hostelry – not a lowly boy.

The summit opened out into a generous plateau that could not have been ap-preciated from the ocean. Emerald undulations of grass and fern stretched to the north. I could see now why Warna remembered it as a paradise of birds. Even now, although the sun was setting, the sky was filled with different species, all intertwining and weaving their stories together. Below, other birds cast out across the waves, heading into the distance.

"*Morgawr*," I stated. "You know the term. Do you see any?"

This boy barely altered his stride at mention of them.

"Most months. I see them out to sea mainly, but they sometimes come to the waters here to feed. They like the lobsters and shellfish the most. Their babies are funny..."

He paused, and then came his enthusiastic question: "Why? You see any?"

"No," I lied. "Just wondered. That's all..."

Warna kept counsel too.

"They won't harm you, you know... No-one's ever been eaten by them. I don't see as many now as I used to. They seem to be disappearing.... swimming elsewhere maybe. Hibernia perhaps."

He shrugged his shoulders.

"My father calls them *Tebel Bryv*..."

"Terrible worm?" I translated.

Tigernus nodded, "But he doesn't mean it."

The boy walked backward to face us. He was bursting with questions.

"You do want accommodation don't you?"

"Yes," agreed Warna. She'd clearly had enough of the choppy waters these last few days.

"Got anything to trade, or will you be settling with cash?"

The boy glanced us over. We carried nothing. We owned nothing.

"Cash it is then..."

He held out his hand for more currency. At this rate, I was going to have nothing left. Still, it was perhaps one of the last outposts of civilisation that would take money. Most places to come probably even hadn't invented an economy like this. It did amuse me though. Where on Scathynys could one spend money? There were no markets or fairs. He'd grow to gain a horde of unspendable money.

"Were you wanting a double?"

I gave him a hard stare, while Warna gazed out beyond the roundhouses and into the west. A golden ocean opened up before her.

"Two singles it is then," Tigernus said, hastily reconsidering the precise relationship between us. "Absolutely not a problem at all... Your mother can have this room and you this one..."

I gave Tigernus another much meaner stare. He got the point.

He soon settled us into our respective accommodation. The island life of this cur intrigued me. I wondered why he stayed, why this young man hadn't seen fit to follow the horizon. Where were his friends? Where in the future, would be girls?

"You don't live here alone do you?" I asked.

Tigernus shook his head.

"Down there, that's where I live – with my mother Resgeuta and father Tigernus – and my two younger sisters..."

He pointed to a set of courtyard dwellings of somewhat similar design to those at Carn Euny. The stonework was cruder though, and less accomplished.

"Are you the only people here?"

Tigernus seemed unsure of how to answer that.

"The only ones who speak... There are farmers, in the north, but they engage with no-one. They just farm and shut up. Then sometimes, people come from the mainland – for a while, to collect eggs and bird meat – but they don't stay."

"Have you ever left?"

The boy shook his head.

"We have no boat."

"Do you want to leave?"

He seemed unnerved at this question. Finally, while plumping the fulmar feather pillows for Warna, he answered with, "I've never thought about it."

"You should," I said.

But as soon as I had said it, I wanted to retract it. Why shouldn't this boy continue his life here? Here on this Scathynys, this Lund-ey, this paradise, it seemed he had peace and tranquillity; a family and apparently a thriving business.

"My father, he has been across, but he came back. He said across there was too much war, too much hate. We don't have that here. He needs me here I think. Like this lady, he grows old and cannot walk the steps down to the shore – nor climb the cliffs for the best eggs."

Tigernus thought for a little while, then he pressed me with a question: "What do you think of the rest of the world? I mean, what is it like?"

I laughed to myself at his request. How could I answer that without giving him my life story so far?

I wanted to tell him it was full of deceit, disappointment, confusion and procrastination. Maybe too, it held momentary flashes of love, hope and forgiveness.

"Maybe it is best you don't know..." was my eventual answer, but I could tell that, like all young and enquiring minds, it was not what he wanted.

His focus though, had to transfer back to the present.

"I'll bring you breakfast in the morning and then your eggs and water... Do you want some bird meat too? The guillemot is good this time of the year."

"Is it smoked?" I queried. "So that it will last?"

"Not smoked," Tigernus said, "but salted..."

"That will be fine. Some of that too then..."

I reached into my pocket and paid him once more.

Tigernus waved a goodbye and ran down over the primitive field systems to his parents' dwelling. No adult ever emerged from there. They seemed content to let their son do the work. Perhaps the Norsemen and other such travellers were best avoided. Perhaps they knew the fate of the children of Brychan.

I had not realised the roundhouses we were bedded down in were so near the middle of the island. While having our conversations we had covered good ground. As the night came down, a bank of cloud came to hover straight along the western cliffs obscuring my view. This not only confirmed how high up we were, but also made me realise what distances were still to be travelled. These I saw beyond the cloud, toward the east and north of where I stood.

Warna's exhaustion was obvious. A bed like the one provided by Tigernus was a rarity indeed and I fully hoped for a change in her mood in the morning after lengthy and uninterrupted sleep. Let it be said that she probably felt the same way about me. One should never underestimate the importance of sleep in travelling great distances. It is needed for survival and revival, but also for reflection, for dreams, for fantasy and for wonder. As humans we need all these things, so as I have come to understand.

Scathynys then. I never thought once I would make it here. Already, it seemed like the edge of the world.

I talked earlier of complacency – how it caused trouble back at Carn Euny, and then once again with the plesiosaur. That was not the feeling I felt as I drifted to sleep. No, it was more a satisfaction that I'd come this far. If this was possible, then so was the larger ocean. Howel, Kenal, Cadreth, Casvellyn – they wouldn't be able to see me, but it didn't matter.

I'd still show them all.

The room in the roundhouse was luxurious compared to the grime and poverty of Warna's home on Nornour. Maybe it was troubling to think who had slept here before. I had to dismiss this though and not think too much about the manner of men who had long since gone. Whoever had slept here previously had still sought the same delicious rest as I did.

When trying to sleep though, images do come to you. Often they are the very ones you want to cast away. They are the kind best jettisoned but the silence seems to bring them on. I had to turn over frequently to ignore them – the jaw of the plesiosaur, the past life of Warna, and the imagined scattering (body parts too) of Brychan's children. By the sound of Warna's snoring next door, she seemed to be having less trouble. Perhaps her new god gave her comfort.

Eventually I went to sleep, and for some long hours revelled in it.

I was unexpectedly woken by the roundhouse physically shaking and the earth beneath it somehow moving. Smaller stones embedded in the structure of the walls fell to the floor and two of the roofing timbers crashed down. It was not bad architecture alone that caused this though. It felt like we were being attacked by a terrific force of some kind. I was awake enough to hear Warna scream at the power of the event. Whatever was happening to the island felt catastrophic, and that within minutes we would assuredly tumble into the ocean. This first shock lasted for around a minute or so, and then subsided. Everywhere the dust settled and the ground became stationary again.

"You all right Warna? You there?" I shouted through the wall to her quarters.

"Yes," came her frightened voice.

"I don't know what it is," I shouted.

" I do," she shouted. "It's one of those underground thunderstorms."

"What!?"

"You heard. It's the air in the cavities of the earth moving...."

I had not heard of such cavities. I had heard of earthquakes though, but usually these were said only to be experienced around the sea in the far south. The Phoenicians told of them. There, they were common, and usually associated with the formation of volcanos and lava. There were no such volcanos here surely?

I hastily dressed and entered Warna's room. She was still lying in her bed.

"It's the earth," she went. "Below this island, it's still liquid... I've felt them before you know. We had them on Nornour a few years ago. Broke all my best pots they did."

"They're natural aren't they? That's what I thought – where two pieces of the earth rub together. Like friction," I said to myself.

Warna overheard.

"They happen when God is mad...."

He was a vindictive bastard, this god of hers then.

"You mean when he's annoyed with earth's residents..."

She nodded.

"But you told me he only did flood and plagues when he felt that way."

"Not always..."

"Then what have we done to offend him?" I argued. "Why us?"

She wouldn't answer me, but perhaps there was no need to. Events dictated that theories no longer needed be discussed. A second tremor hit the ground, more fierce and intense than the first. This time, it was accompanied by the roar of the earth splitting – somewhere much too close to us. We could both feel the land slipping, changing its angle, so that it was becoming an ocean of movement. The angle wasn't large, but it was enough to alarm.

"Get your clothes on quick Warna. We're leaving!"

I re-entered my room, grabbing my sack, and stuffing my shoes and jerkin into it. Rat nudged his way into the space of the sack too, knowing the danger. I could tell we hadn't long. I'd be having words with this Tigernus. What kind of place did he run here? Didn't he know what was coming?

The earth groaned again. It seemed in a kind of agony. I knew the possible consequences of such events, even though as yet I had not seen the reality outside. If the rock here fissured enough, it would slide into the sea and produce a great wave that would run to the shores here and maybe even the coast of the peninsula. My mind ran to *An Ruen* and her ability to ride it. She could be swamped and battered out of existence. Likewise, already in the flooring of the roundhouses the soil was becoming liquefied. This was perhaps the scariest sight of all. The fine, granular, dried peat on which it was built seemed to be turning into a black sea. Roots and rocks were exposed, tunnels of rabbit burrows instantly opened. Waves of energy seemed to be running through the whole island, stronger than a plesiosaur, stronger than even an army of warriors could repel.

"Fuck me," I mouthed to myself.

Fortunately, the quake had occurred on the turning of night into morning, and the first streams of sun produced a red light on the eastern horizon. There was enough light to see the ongoing devastation. From where the roundhouses were located, fissures ran up the island in a south-north direction. Not far from where we were, great chasms had formed; part of the western side of the island had split into fragments, the stone like cut cheese, crumbling and cracking. One of the fissures ran about as close to the roundhouse as it possibly could, the brown peat snaking away into its depths. Only at the wall of the dwelling did it decide to stop, perhaps forced to halt its expansion by the rigid stonework that lay across it.

The second quake continued to shake us. Clouds of dust formed further to the north, where we could observe columns of rock and soil falling into the chasms. Runs of earth and grass tipped over, as if they were a child's game upon a sandy beach. It did not take us long to take all of this in. In these situations, the mind can process much information. It knows what is happening visually, orally, audibly.

We ran.

Neither Warna nor I looked back.

Half-dressed still, she was useless. She had the speed of a slug and kept tripping on tussocks of grass. Her one eye and rheumatism prevented her from being nimble.

"Run!" I screamed at her. "Don't stop!"

The earth still shook – and us with it.

The fissuring of the ground appeared to be affecting the northern end of the island more than the south, though right now, although unspoken, we both had the sensation that the whole mass might fall and crumble into the ocean, and that the sea would overwhelm us.

I was making for the harbour where *An Ruen* bobbed.

Having made our way down off the higher land, the plateau then dipped slightly before we could pick up the steps down to the ocean. Close by were the courtyard dwellings where Tigernus lived. There was no sign of life from them. Perhaps they had just chosen to cower inside the houses, or maybe they had already risen, knowing the calamity and effects, and relocating to the south of the island where it seemed safer. I felt that checking them would be endangering us further, and I already had Warna with me. I was aware of the limitations of Tigernus' father from what he said, but just prayed that he knew the landscape well enough to avoid being sucked into the chasms.

"Is it you who brought this upon us?" mumbled Warna.

I couldn't believe what she had asked me.

"What do you mean?"

"Your sin Voog?"

More of her god claptrap.

"Perhaps if you repented for whatever you did, then God may not have enacted his revenge..."

A vengeful bastard this god was then.

"Don't talk such rubbish Warna!" I shouted at her, trying to make her hear above the din of the cataclysmic activity behind us, but just as I shouted this, the shaking halted. We both stopped running, checking to ensure the island was not going to sink any further, and that solid land still lay beneath our feet.

"I have no desire to follow any god who is vindictive and vengeful – and besides, this was not our doing. If the land decides to quake, there is no man or woman on earth who can stop it. Don't you understand that, Warna?"

Warna let go of my hand, shaking it off her grip.

We stood above the steps now – devastated at what we had just experienced. We caught our breaths. Warna stood gazing out over the ocean, muttering to herself, re-tying the patch over her useless eye. Is this now what she thought of me? Was I some bad luck token that she had mistakenly aligned herself to? Seemingly I was some talisman of evil. This sin she alluded to suggested that humans should not follow their hearts but instead some false set of morals. It was a concept I could not adhere to, or promote.

Like the broken land behind us, wide chasms of belief and faith were opening up.

"Come on," I said. "No point in debating all that now... We need to leave."

"Bah. But what of the food and water we were promised by the boy? We'll make poor progress without it."

She was right. The whole point of our time on Scathynys was to resupply *An Ruen*. It was not to discuss the punishment of humanity's sin via catastrophe.

I'd even paid Tigernus for what he had promised. Still, it was hard keeping promises when the land beneath one's feet disappeared.

"I am sure he will keep his word."

I led Warna down the steps. It took some time. She couldn't step down one foot after another. Instead, she had to stop on each level, then step gingerly down to the next surface.

"Bah. My legs," she moaned.

Rat had been shrewd throughout the whole quake. At the first shaking, he had jumped into my sack and bounced around in there amongst my tools and supplies when I grabbed it. I dare say the prospect of banging against some of the iron in there was preferable to what was going on outside. Thus he had managed to sneak his way out of disaster. To this extent, he was reminding me more and more of me. He was an arch-survivor. Whatever he faced he would somehow endure.

The harbour, being distant from the middle part of the island where the earthquake had first struck, seemed idyllic in comparison. It was a world away from liquefied earth and collapsing columns of granite. Golden morning sunlight danced on the lapping water, along the beach. The coracle and *An Ruen* hadn't been harmed in the slightest.

"A miracle," Warna declared.

I was less ebullient in my declaration.

"Thank Annown."

Although the land had shattered, it seemed it might not have toppled into the ocean on the western side, to cause any massive surge in the water level. Maybe even if it had happened, there was enough of the ocean stretching out to absorb its force. See, I was still calculating, still making sense of the voyage with mathematics, engineering and calculus. The architect in me hadn't quite gone yet.

I was going to have to make a decision about water. I'd have to go back and find some. We could probably survive on caught fish which would mean our diet would be rather dull, but at least they were there. Water, however, was a different matter.

"I'm going to have to go back."

Warna understood. Although she was cursing me and just anything else that moved at the moment, she already knew the importance of a supply of drinking water. Without it, we could do nothing.

I didn't tell her, but I was worried about this boy Tigernus as well. What had been his fate overnight? Had he been sucked into the clutches of the earth?

As I eased Warna out of the coracle and into *An Ruen*, a wet face appeared from inside the hull and looked over the gunwale.

"See, I got your water.... and look, a basket of eggs, and salted meat. Good eating."

The face held up a tun of sloshing, preserved flesh.

"Tigernus! You made it," Warna noted, as if she'd fully expected him to be dead.

"I refilled your skins and these are the very best eggs. Fresh as the morning."

I eyed him carefully now, this boy. He sounded like a farmer at market.

"And the earthquake?"

Tigernus shifted on his feet nervously.

"We've been getting a few tremors... I forgot to mention it.... They happen here sometimes. No-one knows why."

"You forgot to mention it? Are they always that bad?"

"No. That's the worst I've seen..."

"And your family?"

"They just stay inside and hope it will go away."

"You didn't think to come for us.... to tell us....?"

"No point," calculated Tigernus. "I couldn't do anything anyway. I was up early fetching eggs for you – down on the southern cliffs. You seem the sort of man and woman who have their wits about them. I knew you'd head back down here."

He was a cocky little bastard, this Tigernus.

"Well, thanks for the supplies. You can go now... I'll take you back in the coracle."

I indicated which way he should proceed with my left hand. His curiosity got the better of him and he stared intently at my bent wrist and extra finger.

"I never saw a man with a hand like yours," he said softly. "Does it hurt?"
I laughed.

"Not any more," I answered.

He was in the coracle now, and I started to scull with the paddle to nudge the boat back to the beach. Meanwhile, in her one-eyed way, Warna set about sorting out space for the eggs and salted fish on board *An Ruen*. Tigernus' eyes darted about as I paddled. Back and forth they went, between the shore of the island and our vessel.

"Thanks," I said. "There you go..."

I gave him another coin. He face beamed at me.

"Thank you, Voog."

"Scathynys is your kingdom, boy. You serve all mariners well that land upon it. Annown bless you."

He seemed pleased at my words, stepping out of the coracle and onto the swash of the beach. Somewhere in his folk memory, he knew of Annown – and that it was a force of good.

In the aftermath of the quake, he'd now have to rebuild his empire. I had no concerns. This Tigernus was a bright lad.

I sculled back to *An Ruen*, tied on the coracle and stepped into the hull.

"Time to go," I announced to Warna, and she muttered something indecipherable back to me.

I unfurled the head and main sails and checked the wind direction. It was not altogether favourable. We'd probably have to zig-zag into it in order to make progress. Warna did the best she could to help me by pulling up the anchor. That was it. We were leaving Scathynys. There'd be no breakfasting for now. We would eat once we were on our way. I was going to pull *An Ruen* around this so-called Rat Island, as I wanted to see what damage had been caused to the western cliffs. We'd take that route northwards.

As the vessel turned, I looked back to the beach where I had dropped Tigernus. He was not there, nor was he making the steep climb up to the plateau. He was quick that boy though. Maybe he'd already run up to survey the damage, to start rebuilding his world. I was surprised he hadn't waved us goodbye though. He seemed the type to do so.

I assessed my experiences on Scathynys. Obviously they were marred by nature's fury but beyond that, it seemed a place where one could exist in harmony. A peaceful trip to the land in the north was what I now pleaded for. Warna and I had both had enough of adventure for the time being.

Once beyond the wide flipper of land at the foreshore, we started to make good headway.

It was Warna who noticed a movement up in the stern. At first I thought it was a herring gull that had landed. They were weighty birds whose motion you could feel. From time to time, they liked to land on us, curious at our expedition.

"We've picked up another rat," said Warna. "Bah. A drowned one, by the look of him."

I peered beyond the central oxhide canopy and there saw a small, dripping mass of clothes, skin and hair. The mass lifted its head when he sensed we were both looking at him, and instantly gave a cheeky smile. Obviously, he had decided to swim out to us.

"I'm coming with you," a wet Tigernus said.

So it seemed then, on my arrival at Scathynys I had gained a 'mother'. Now on my leaving, I had also acquired a 'son'.

I hadn't, so it seemed, managed to leave my rodent companion back on Rat Island. He was still there, twitching his long nose at our new crew member.

Clearly, my adopted family was growing day by day.

DEAR FATHER,

I UNDERSTAND NOW. In my travels, I have often wondered how you and my mother first found love. I think of this now as I run in this vast forest. I know much about you both, but those initial moments of intimacy are lost to me. Maybe if my mother were still alive, she would have told me. We'd have had the kind of mother-daughter chat I have craved for. You see, I have had questions. How is it that love walks into our lives? When do we know it is real and not just infatuation? Maybe both of you had doubts even at first, like I did then. I know though, that you then quickly let yourselves into each other's hearts and found union. Love is a cleft apple reuniting – pip and core of identical halves coming together, fitting to make something whole again.

And Annown, do you know love? Surely you must do. You both give and take lives and their loves. You know its power. You know its force. It is as vast as an ocean; deeper than its darkest depths.

All I am trying to say, father, is that I understand.

When I think back, there is much in my life that I might have prophesied. I knew that I would discover the truth one day. I saw me finding it. I had a notion that one day someone would arrive who would enlighten me. I could have predicted that in the long term, I would leave Chysauster. Just how, though, I really had not contemplated.

There is one thing I have not yet told you: that is how Tigernus arrived at Lulyn. I wondered if he had travelled with some of the holy men or women who now crossed so frequently between the Britons and Bretons. This Warna he talked of, she was one of them. Maybe she had inspired him. They used coracles to travel vast distances. He had informed me of the inspiration she had given him during certain times.

"When things got bad," he had said earlier, "she was there – watching over us. I know that sounds strange, but even now, I believe it to be true."

Every day, you see, was a new gleaning, a new piece of illumination.

"So tell me, how did you get to Lulyn then? She wasn't accompanying you – was she?" I joked.

"No. Well, probably not... But let me explain. I built my own boat to make the crossing. When we finally escaped from the slave camp, it was the thing most on my mind – to get to Carn Euny, and then to return home to Scathynys. I could have caught one of the hulks the fishermen use. The crews from Cornouaille put into Lulyn sometimes – but no; I purposely choose a different way..."

I looked at him intently, pleading for more information.

"When we stopped one time, we had to rebuild *An Ruen*. That's when your father taught me boat-building. My vessel – moored down in Lulyn – well, I used his design. I made a few modifications, but it's basically the same kind of boat we crossed in."

"You'll show me?"

"Of course. It's down there now, moored close to where old Enyon's tannery is located."

I had heard so much about this vessel they had travelled in. At this point, I felt I would never see the real thing, so this was as close as I thought I might get.

"What's her name? What did you call her?"

"It's obvious isn't it?"

At that moment, it wasn't clear to me. I shook my head.

"*Warna*," he said. "I named her *Warna*."

Now I understood.

"Take me out on her," I pleaded. "Take me fishing. I want to know what it was like on board *An Ruen*."

This then, is how I first came to board *Warna*. We went out a day later. I was incredulous at what he had built. I felt the hide hull and the way it had been waterproofed with wool grease. I wanted to feel each leather knot, each stringer of wood. I wanted to use the steering paddle the way he did. I could reimagine the rat and the puffin. There was an intimacy on board Tigernus' vessel. The isolation of the ocean forced us to work together and to find commonality in the tasks. I shiver now, at his hands guiding my lines off the stern. I knew this was no infatuation. I could hear my grandmother's advice. Yes – he was slightly older than me, but did that matter? No. Not now. All that mattered was our connection. Was it just my father uniting us? No. That helped, but I would have been attracted to him anyway. I know that.

You know you don't decide.

You don't ever decide.

Our journey was no epic voyage. We kept close to the shore, only traversing around the headland to the south. But it was enough of a taster for me. We had caught a good supply of mackerel and scad, and when we returned to Chysauster, I resolved to take some across to Kenal. Older now, the prospect of fresh fish would have pleased him. He made it down to the coast less these days. In the evening we rode across to Carn Euny, laden with these gifts from the sea. In the same way that we had travelled down to Lulyn, I rode in front of Tigernus, his body cradling me. The warmth of his form consoled every part of me – and yet, he was distant still; perhaps scared to express his feelings too. The conversation was formal, clipped even, as if we were still strangers.

"Do you see much of this Howel these days?" Tigernus asked.

"No. He keeps himself to himself. Devoted to prayer they say."

"I see."

"The fish are smelling a bit," I noted.

"We need ice," offered Tigernus. "That's what the Bretons use..."

At Carn Euny we were well-received by Kenal, who immediately began creating a fish stew. We told him about *Warna* and our fishing expedition. Kenal invited over an old man named Remfra to eat with us. We were intrigued because he too had known my father. A former bard, he was now hard of hearing – and so interest in his skills as a rhymer and storyteller had declined. In short, he could no longer hold an audience's attention, but there was still enough of the poet in him to lament the old days.

"Do you reckon on him still being alive?" he asked Tigernus.

"I like to think so," I answered before he could respond.

"That boy – from what I saw of him, he had the luck of Bryok about him..."

Kenal leant in to explain who Bryok was.

When we had eaten, I suggested to Tigernus that he came with me. I was on tenterhooks now. I had never walked through Carn Euny in the way I was about to do. Now however, Tigernus had given me a confidence to do as I wished. Had Kenal known where I was heading, he might have shook his head and tried to warn us off. But I was intent on doing what I wanted.

Given our time on board the vessel, I was now bullish enough to grab hold of Tigernus' hand.

"Come on," I whispered. "Let's go up here."

I was worried he might let go, but the way his fingers curled around mine, I knew that the moment was right.

"Where are you taking me?"

"To see something," I said, flirting with him. "Trust me."

I led him to the fogou. It was not how I had imagined it. Decay reigned. What we witnessed was a scene of abandonment. For all its dereliction however, the beauty of the structure remained. The souterrain itself was still whole – and the space could be negotiated. A slight fall of rock blocked some of the way into the northern cell. As I led him through, Tigernus was still holding my hand.

I knew we were not far from Howel's roundhouse. Here, in this moment I would right many wrongs.

I made a prayer to you Annown. It seemed like you were listening. I wrapped my arms around Tigernus and kissed him. When his lips met mine, I understood. I felt whole again.

<h1 style="text-align:center">15</h1>

Coin found at the Holy well of St Gofan, Bosherston, Pembrokeshire, Wales, 5th to 6th Century CE

The giving of tokens – financial or other – into the waters of Holy Wells has long been a practice of communities on the Atlantic seaboard of Western Europe. Coins placed in wells offered protection or combatted ailments. Horse motifs were popular, as exemplified here. Coins were formed in two ways: the first way involved engraving a blank disc. After forming the blank, it would have been flattened out before striking with a die made from iron or bronze. The tiny details engraved on dies were just a few millimetres in diameter. Casting a coin required a different technique. They were produced by pouring molten alloy into a set of moulds which were broken apart when the metal had cooled. This coin appears to have been engraved with the name of a local chieftain named Rhydderch [Richard]. Courtesy of the National Museum Cardiff / Amgueddfa Genedlaethol Caerdydd.

"I THOUGHT HARD ABOUT WHAT you said. I realised there's a bigger world out there..."

"You know, I'm not intending on coming back," I said. "I can't... I'm..."

I stopped myself from saying anymore. Warna's ears had suddenly pricked up. She really wanted to know my tale.

"I understand," said Tigernus. "When I want to return I'll catch a lift with some Vikings. It'll be fine. Don't worry."

He had an answer for everything, this mite.

"What about your family?"

"Oh, they'll be all right... My sisters aren't bad at finding eggs... They're pretty nimble actually..."

"And your father?"

"I know that he's not long for this world. I have said my goodbyes to him. Annown can now welcome him."

"It is the son's honour to cremate his father and place his ashes into a cist... Do you disregard our traditions?"

"Maybe," he went. "Perhaps it's now time for women to do that."

"I mean... do they know you've gone?"

Tigernus had no response to this.

"No? You haven't told them... They'll think you were lost in the earthquake."

The boy pushed out his lower lip. Shame was not an emotion he felt. "And?"

I could see his cunning. He had timed this just right. With such an event, there'd be no need of explanations. He'd just conveniently disappear.

"You'll break your mother's heart," chipped in Warna.

Warna knew this pain.

"Imagine how amazed they'll be when I come back though," offered Tigernus, grinning from ear to ear. "Maybe in year or two, when I'm grown up."

"I hadn't counted on picking up anyone else," I said. "I already rescued Warna there..."

"I won't be a burden, Voog. I promise."

His smiling lips turned more serious.

"Have you ever been in a boat before?"

"Not really..."

"Not really, or not ever?"

"Not ever, but I can learn," Tigernus went, tipping his head to one side, and pushing his eyes upwards to see my reaction.

It seemed now I had a crew, but none of them had any experience. I was not really a seasoned mariner either. The blind were leading the blind here.

"Come, you'd better dry your clothes," I said, "before the cold you catch is the death of you."

Tigernus stripped off his garments – more or less, just a tunic and some trousers, with pads of thong-tied leather for shoes. I attached these to some lines so the sun and wind would dry them, and then pulled a spare oxhide from the storage space at the bow. He could wear that over him for now.

"This world you so want to see," I suggested, "is not always a place of harmony and peace... Evil lurks everywhere. I bet you are as handy with a weapon as you are with a boat..."

"I'm good with a sword," he boasted. "The Vikings taught me..."

At least then, we now had a warrior on board. Annown be thanked. I wasn't sure if one who had learned the ways of Vikings was exactly the kind of companion I had in mind.

I gave Tigernus a lecture on the rules of the boat: what to do and what not to do. Most of these rules he broke within the next ten minutes. I also explained where he must sit, and how for now at least, he'd have to cower under the front canopy to sleep. To give him credit, he took this entire talk well, and seemingly was prepared to suffer discomfort in exchange for travel and adventure.

"Should you go back?" Warna asked. "Tell the rat's parents what he's done... I know how his mother and father would feel."

Tigernus went timid, almost starting to cry.

"Please, don't do that. They don't actually need to know do they? It's easier this way – really... I don't want to live there any more. It's actually boring. "

"He may 'actually' be right Warna. Even if I chucked him off right now, he'd probably climb back on again.

"Bah. Do you eat much?" Warna asked. "We hadn't planned on feeding an extra mouth."

Tigernus showed us his bony ribs and breathed in to make his stomach smaller.

"Not at all," he said. "Besides, I am an excellent fisherman..."

"Really?"

"I'll catch some beauties for us... This big."

He opened his arms wide, gradually moving them inwards, to make the pretended catch more realistic.

"Provide for us, and you will be welcome, Tigernus."

There were now four of us on board *An Ruen*. I continued to check whether she was still watertight, and that she had sunk no lower into the ocean. In all honesty, the boy weighed little and despite the earthquake and the 'terrible worm' she was still in good shape.

"Where are we going?" asked Tigernus.

"North – to Warna's lands... She is returning home."

"Do they speak funny there?" the boy asked. "The crews who put into Lundey from there all have weird words."

"Does Warna sound funny to you?"

Tigernus peered over at the old woman, who glowered back, one eye fixated on this skinny boy to see his response.

"No. She doesn't," he said, hastily correcting his former intuition.

"They'll be no funnier there than the way we speak, boy, and the other tongues we will encounter."

Rebuked, Tigernus placed himself on the port side, near the bow, and occupied himself with fishing. Warna began cooking.

We passed the western cliffs of Scathynys. About halfway up the island, many of the birds were circling wildly. You could now see the devastation of the earthquake from sea level. Several cliff faces had toppled. Below them were soft cones of debris. Behind that, the land was mottled, where wide gaps appeared in the land surface. Some of these zawns opened straight down to the cliffs. They had not been there twenty-four hours ago. The birds were circling because they had lost their nests. They had no homes to go back to. Their eggs and young had toppled down with the collapses. You could hear their pain and frustration in their shrieks and whoops. There was nothing anyone could do to make it better for them. They just had to carry on.

I understood their loss.

Nature could be cruel and unforgiving.

Aside from the trauma of this, the rest of the island looked to be intact. There had been no submersion into the water, and the northern end (where Tigernus had informed us people farmed) seemed to still be there, the ruptures fracturing the western side, if not the east.

"It must be on some line in the earth," I said aloud so all my crew could hear. "A weakness in the seabed..."

"Yes," went Warna. "Just like I said – thunderstorms down there."

Thunderstorms down there now worried me less than any that might appear on the horizon of our pelagic world.

While we were having this conversation I noticed Tigernus was holding out his right arm and wrist. With his tongue, he was making clicking noises and guttural caws deep in his throat. In amazement I watched as, from behind the boat, a bird, after hovering a while, skilfully landed on the boy's wrist. It was a *scath* – in the new tongue, a puffin: the very island's namesake.

"Who's that?" I shouted.

"Nobody," Tigernus shouted back. "Just my pet, that's all... I trained him."

The puffin turned its head towards the stern and peered at his owner's new surroundings. Here, you could clearly observe its stocky build and large beak. Its orange-red pads of feet seemed to slip on the boy's skin, and so he moved his arm, the puffin stepping onto the hard surface of the gunwale. There it wobbled slightly at the bob of the ocean, and stretched out its wings to steady itself. Out at sea, the bird was less vocal than on the cliffs, and appeared to find comfort in locating Tigernus. He seemed to have a way with it – a bonding existed between them.

"I met him while I was collecting eggs. He'd fallen out of his nest. I nursed him back to health again. You should have seen him. He was tiny then – when he was a puffling."

Although smaller than stories ever said of them, this puffin was of fair size.

"I think his colony must have been destroyed – in the earthquake..."

"I hadn't planned on having a boy, neither had I planned on refugees," I argued.

I thought about my words. Always too mouthy I was. One day my gob would kill me. I went back to the knowledge about our people having to trek into the west, away from their homelands. They had dispersed before they could be assimilated. It was not by choice they had left. They had to – for survival's sake.

This small creature, too, was now at the mercy of others.

"Will he pay his way?" I asked more gently

"Surely," said Tigernus. "He will catch fish and be our eyes in the sky."

"Don't they come in pairs?"

"Don't be silly. He is too young for a mate yet."

"He may get lonely."

These words might as well have applied to me, as this Puffin.

"You'll see," offered Tigernus. "The ocean will find one for him."

I was glad this boy had faith in the ocean. I had lost mine in it, and Warna had put all of hers into a book and a cross.

"He has to come. He is a symbol of Scathynys. When I am homesick, he will remind me of being there."

This boy was more complex than I thought. Clearly, his interaction with other travellers had given him astute knowledge of the way distant voyages worked. He had already anticipated homesickness. It was not really an emotion that I felt. When your people kick you out, a different passion emerges.

"Yet another passenger?" questioned Warna. "Well, I suppose God will provide."

The boy and I ignored her.

The sea north of Scathynys started to open up and the island became visibly smaller. I kept my eyes open, peeling the surface for these *Tebel Bryv* as Tigernus' father called them. In short, although the boy remarked on their harmlessness, I would rather avoid another encounter of that kind.

The morning sun had dried out his clothes and so he dressed again, stowing the oxhide back in the bow. Warna provided a meal for us all of boiled eggs, salted guillemot meat and the remains of the small turnips she'd managed to bring from Nornour. Tigernus purposely didn't eat much, trying to show us he was no burden.

"Eat," I advised him. "Go on. You will need your strength."

When he first came back to the stern for his dinner, he offered up a handful of fresh herring. Warna started to like him better then. She had started to talk to him about this new god of hers, evangelical as ever – but Tigernus made his excuses and made much of intervening in a dispute between Puffin and Rat over the leftovers. In the end, Rat got the eggs which, for safety's sake, he carried back into his coracle, while Puffin devoured the herring. Far from this being *my* ocean – it was now in fact, a community.

With bellies full and the afternoon sun beating down upon us, the voyage to the north was sometimes idyllic – as one might imagine a leisurely skim across the sea. The wind was slight though, and while Warna had suggested her lands were merely a day's sail away, we were not making the kind of progress she wanted. By mid-afternoon, the wind had dropped completely. We were on a millpond. Being static was something you never wanted. Our stationary position was about to become our problem.

Puffin had gone to scout ahead. He seemed to have been out of view for an hour or more.

"Aren't you worried where he is?"

"No. He'll come back. He always does."

Rat didn't seem to like us sitting still. He was noisy and vociferous.

"Row if you want to my friend," I said to him. "Feel free."

He barked something sarcastic back, and decided to sleep.

"We won't make it today, will we?" Warna observed, articulating what we all knew.

"Not with this stillness."

With a loud thwack, Puffin suddenly arrived back on board *An Ruen*. He was now more vocal, cawing and croaking his observations. You wanted both him and Rat to really speak at times. This was one of those moments.

"What's up with him?"

"There's something heading our way. This is the way he tells me..."

Tigernus tossed him half a herring in reward.

"Do we know what?"

Tigernus shook his head.

"I'm not that good at understanding Puffin," he said seriously.

Warna and I smiled at each other.

There were lots of possibilities. Although the ocean carried its evil, there were other vessels which bore all kinds of travellers. There was a fashion to trek from the northwest to the home of this Christ. Most died on their way – either getting lost or catching disease. As we had already noted, the traders were prepared to go far around this land of Britain, but again none of us were quite sure how far this extended to the north and east. Sometimes, there were organised fishermen – not just the coracle men of the west, but bigger boats which serviced the larger promontory forts.

Perhaps our worst fears were realised however.

Given Tigernus' view that the *Ancredhor Mor* were due in at their Lund-ey sometime this week, it was not surprising that when Warna spotted something ahead of us, we realised it was a fully-laden *drekar*. These boats were the big bastards, usually elegant in form, but geared up for plunder and pillage. It seemed so large, and we so small, that it might even miss us – as if we were a piece of seaweed just floating there. But no, it wasn't to be so. Someone on their crow's nest had observed us. We could see the course of it altering, following a line down to Scathynys. There was a grace to its movement that *An Ruen* never really had. The thing was double-ended, with a symmetrical bow and stern, allowing her to move in any direction as she so wished. Powerful rowers (who worked her in shifts) augmented her huge oxhide sails. Unlike *An Ruen* it was a great load carrier, the wide hull stable enough to endure rough seas. These ships were the result of hundreds of years of evolution, of craftsmen perfecting each component in a way that we West Britons had not managed. Good enough, was how it was for some of our builders. Not for the *Ancredhor Mor*. You had to admire them for it. It was partly the reason they had been so successful. The fuckers lived for it. You could almost smell the oak of it. It made my own skill as a shipwright look utterly pathetic. This was the kind of vessel you needed to cross an ocean – not this extended and bloated coracle. None of your bound leather thongs there; they used great treenails and bow saws.

You'd think for its girth, it would be slow and steady in reaching us, but in fact, although we first saw it on the horizon when Puffin came back and Warna had noted its form, it took only half an hour to row this way.

"I know that longship," said Tigernus.

After all, he was perhaps the boy to know. Warna and I were helpless. We had to let fate decide for us now. No god. No Annown.

"It's heading for Lund-ey. They had been making for their Hibernian raids in the summer, but they said they'd be back."

"Who captains it?"

"Aw, they don't have captains. Usually they are managed by three chieftains. One takes control of the navigation, another of provisions; the other oversees the pillage they make. If it's the one I think it is, then this one should have Swein, Þorbjörn and Eirik upon it... They are based on Suðreyar in the distant north."

I wondered if these were the same bastards who had put to shore to attack Carn Euny. This was no time for Warna's forgiving god. I wanted revenge. These men were the progeny of that same line that had massacred the children of Brychan. It was their fathers – and maybe some of them still on board, who had taken out Warna's eye and robbed her of her virginity. It was her body they'd abused again and again.

"Don't do anything," said Tigernus. "Let me do all the talking. I know them. They often land on Scathynys. They enjoy the puffin meat I provide for them. It's their national dish. There's nothing tastes as good as Lund-ey meat so they say."

There I was then, at the mercy of a boy, facing a fully-laden longship of the *Ancredhor Mor*. I did not usually believe in fate, but here it was, slapping me around the face.

"You there Swein?" shouted up Tigernus. "Þorbjörn? Eirik?"

The hulk of the longship dwarfed us. The success of the Vikings was their incredible skill at constructing machines of war. Although we had skill with stone, it was with wood that they clearly had most affinity. The craftsmanship was incredible, beautiful gods and animals carved into the planking, in fearsome praise of Thor, Odin and their ilk. At the front prow, high in the air, a huge dragon figurehead reared, supposedly to put fear into any sea creatures they encountered.

A gallery flap lifted along the hull, and an elderly man put his head out. He was balding with a straw-coloured plaited beard. Warna wrapped a scarf around her face and looked down.

"Þorbjörn!?" questioned Tigernus. "Where is Swein? I thought he controlled your navigation..."

"Sadly, Swein is dead," said this Þorbjörn, dejected in his tone. "He was killed six days ago in Hibernia. An arrow pierced his heart. We carry his body now – back to Yggdrasil."

"I am sorry to learn this," said Tigernus. "He was a good man."

All the while, Tigernus translated what was said. He was remarkably skilled at the Norse for one so young. He had grown up with it as a toddler.

"Why are you off the island?" Þorbjörn asked. "You never leave... And we were hoping you would provide for us tonight. You gave us your word."

"I know, but you see this man..."

Tigernus pointed directly at me.

"He is my uncle and this decrepit and crazed woman, my maternal grandmother... She is dying and we are taking her home – to the north..."

Warna played along with the act, making a heart-rending groan.

Tigernus was trying hard, though I was unsure the pretence was working. What could I do though? I could hardly reveal our true identity to this chieftain and tell him where I was from. The three captives at Carn Euny who had not made it back to their vessel made sure anyone from the horn of Britain might be of especial interest. Bollocks and penises stuffed into one's mouth tended to do that.

I hoped Warna wouldn't show her face; otherwise this Þorbjörn might recognize her. Her tale was probably known on board. All of the crew would know that a one-eyed new kind of holy woman lived on Nornour. Someone might even know her by sight.

"I see you have a snack for me," joked Þorbjörn. He had noticed Puffin on the gunwale.

"Ah now – that one is not good eating," responded Tigernus. "He is diseased. You are welcome to this tun of salted guillemot meat though."

"Throw it up," commanded Þorbjörn.

I took the tun and lunged forward to throw it up to the chieftain. I gulped as I looked up at the immensity of its hull.

Shit, now we'd lost some of our food. I had to hope it would be worth it for them to leave us alone.

"Will there be water and provisions for us?"

"In the usual place," said Tigernus.

"If the rats don't get there first," guffawed Þorbjörn.

"You know the cave well enough."

Interrupted by one of his men inside, Þorbjörn shouted this information back, then turned once again to look below.

"So we may continue then?" tried the boy, his wits still about him.

Þorbjörn did not answer immediately. The gallery flap closed. Clearly there was some discussion inside the longship. I eyed Tigernus, who looked back at me, raising an eyebrow, wondering if his deception had worked. Þorbjörn returned.

"That coracle of yours," he said, his long, tied beard back through the hole again. "One of my men knows its type of construction. It is not of the Hibernian type but of the kind made by the men of the west. How did you come by it?"

"Fuck, fuck, fuck," I went to myself.

Our cover was being blown here.

Tigernus seemed unable to mouth anything. Spit flew from his gob but non-sense accompanied it. I interrupted.

"We found it... a vessel wrecked on the western cliffs... some fool of a new holy man I expect... Tell him that Tigernus."

Tigernus translated, with Þorbjörn listening intently.

Þorbjörn laughed.

"Good pickings then? They come to convert us. We tell them where to stick their new god."

He turned around, dropping his kilt to show us his hairy arsehole.

"In there...!"

Tigernus and I feigned a hearty laugh.

This Þorbjörn was no fool though. He was suspicious. Something was telling him that I was not right, the boy was not right and this old woman was not right.

Þorbjörn spoke again to Tigernus. This time, the language he used was faster, more aggressive – like a command.

"What's he want?" I whispered.

"He says he wants to see this woman. He says she seems familiar to him... He thinks he knows the fabric of her clothes."

Shit. An earthquake went through me.

Warna would now have to show him her face. We were backed into a corner that we could not wriggle out of. I didn't want him to see her eye. All would topple then. Just as much, I didn't want Warna to see him. The vision of that ghost now back in her life was something she didn't deserve.

"Tell him she's got leprosy," I said to Tigernus.

"Leprosy? That won't work. Why would we be travelling with her? If she had leprosy we wouldn't go near her..."

This sharp boy had a point.

Above, Þorbjörn was not following our argument. The wooden gallery flap had closed, and clearly something on their starboard side had gained the attention of all the men on board the longship. Whatever it was, it had distracted their chieftain nicely and, for the moment, he had to deal with it. We could not sense what was going on. At first, there seemed a kind of euphoria and intrigue – but this was followed by a disturbing silence – and then a lilt in the vessel to port, as all crew members ran to this side of the boat. The great oars, which had until now been gripped hard, fell and scattered in different directions. The thick oak wood clumped down in their rowlocks. Watches were left, weapons abandoned and some men even seemed to be preparing to jump overboard. It seemed liked the longship was being attacked; perhaps by a rival band of *Ancredhor Mor*. If it was, they'd chosen their moment perfectly.

We were wrong though – but we had faced what they now feared. The longship had clearly been tracked by a mother plesiosaur.

We could hardly not notice this, when her huge neck and head careered into the bow section of the hull, wrecking it in an instant, and forcing, ironically, the dragon figurehead to crack into two.

"Some protection that offered," Warna chuckled.

Splinters of wood and debris fell into both the water and into our hull. We desperately flung the larger sections overboard before they dragged us down.

Activity on deck was brisk now. The longship was turning in the water, her spinning forcing us to be catapulted away from her.

"I thought you said they were peaceful," noted Warna, her voice not betraying her panic at all. "This thing's not very peaceful. Voog – come on, can you make a start on rowing? We need to get away from this."

I took a pair of oars, holding one out for Tigernus to use. Although he was not trained as any kind of mariner, he soon got the gist of it and ploughed away.

As we looked back on the scene of devastation, it now became very clear why the mother had enacted this revenge. There, on the now tilting deck of the longship were the butchered body parts of her offspring that Þorbjörn was obviously going to use to feed his warriors. *Morgawr* flesh was cheap and would last for a long time no doubt. It was more than a herd of ten cattle. I could not tell if it was the same creature that we had encountered, but I certainly understood the mother's hatred. Most obviously, the neck had been cut into thick steaks; the deck was bloody with bone and entrails.

"A terrible worm," I noted.

"Good timing though," said the boy.

At such catastrophe, at such pain, you don't really want to see anymore – but, like times before, I could not help myself.

When I turned again, I saw a barely alive baby plesiosaur crucified on the mast of the main sail. It was screaming in agony. The source of this plaintive screech was the mother's sole aim now. Maybe if she could sink the *drekar*, she could release the infant.

Men were jumping into the sea now – flashes of leather and yellow hair and beards which did anything they could to escape the terror. The mother creature battered the survivors down with her flippers, not allowing them to surface. She'd have her way. Further wreckage of the longship was caused by her forcing her full body into the hull. It ruptured and split, and then let the ocean ooze inside.

Panicking voices came on the air.

"They are shouting for us to rescue them," said Tigernus. "They are pleading with us to come back."

"Are they?" I said sarcastically. That was one of my harder moments.

We pushed on.

Maybe the luckier ones might get upon some of the debris. Upon the larger vessel were tied smaller *karvi*. These were rowing boats for journeying back and forth from the larger *drekar*. Some had been launched and survivors were being picked up.

"They won't last long," said Warna.

We knew it.

Twenty more minutes of rowing and we were out of the debris and chaos. The vast *drekar* no longer existed and we were alone again. Puffin had decided to take a look over the wreckage, before landing back on the gunwale. He had nothing to say, which seemed entirely appropriate.

This time, nature got her own back.

We passed on and reflected on this.

It was Tigernus who broke the silence.

"They made it across, you know," he chirped. "The strange land you speak of in the west..."

"Annown?"

"No. Not that...That is a fairy tale for the dead and unborn. I am talking about a real land – a new world."

I suddenly took more interest in what the boy had to say.

"Swein – the one who was killed with the arrow through the heart – told me lots of stories about his people. They headed to the northwest, from the far side of Hibernia. His grandfather made it right the way across the great ocean. There he found a bounteous world with forests and fruits, bear and deer. Vines and berries too."

These Vikings had some uses then. At least, this tale confirmed what I had thought. If the *Ancredhor Mor* could make it across, then there was no reason why I couldn't as well.

FATHER, DEAR FATHER, SEE ME now. I am filled with the same love as that which you once felt. Deep in the fogou we dissolved and became one. I took him there because of you and my mother. Can you imagine that small boy, whom you once nurtured, was now tightly holding your daughter's hand? He was the one who wrapped his strong arms around my waist and nuzzled his breath on the nape of my neck.

Both of us are your offspring. We are son and daughter. We are man and woman. We are lovers.

After our time in the fogou, we returned home the next morning. Tigernus was now becoming used to the routines of Chysauster. Grandmother had him clean out the boar sty and make repairs to the roundhouse roof. While he completed these tasks, between cooking, I contemplated the maps Tigernus had brought here. I viewed them from all angles, imagining their reading of them years ago on board *An Ruen*. In truth, I wanted my father to walk out of the sheets of parchment. I wanted him to see us in the here and now – and view what he had made. I wanted to show him his legacy. At the midday meal, there was initially not much conversation. I suspect we were both still enraptured by the confession of our love. I know I was. It didn't stop me trying something out on him though.

"Take me there," I said.

"Where?"

"You know where..."

"Do I?"

"Don't play games with me Tigernus. Isn't it obvious?"

"You mean you want to go to Scathynys with me?"

"Yes. Well, no. One day, maybe. Not just yet though."

"Where are you thinking of then?"

"Hyperborea."

"There?"

"Yes. I want to meet my father. I want to see if he's still there."

Tigernus looked uncomfortable at the prospect.

"You? You really want to go there?"

"What – you think I can't do it?"

"But your life is here – in Chysauster – with your grandmother..."

"Is that what you thought – when my father first found you? Did you want to stay on Scanthynys for the rest of your life, serving Vikings puffin meat?"

"Well, no."

"Come then. Why is my request so different?"

He chose not to answer me.

"Come on. Be honest. Tell me."

Tigernus looked down and away from me. He knew I wouldn't like what he said.

"The ocean is filled with danger. The crossing is not easy. It almost took my life on several occasions. I love you too much for it to harm you."

"It won't though, will it? Not if you come with me."

"What? You and I together?"

"Yes – in *Warna*."

"You've got it all planned out haven't you?"

"Not really. I've just been thinking through the possibilities. We don't have to go via Kembry and Hibernia. We can go south instead – and stop off at the islands of Ogygia you've told me about. You said it yourself – that would be a better route."

"I don't know... I mean, let's be honest here Blejan – and sorry to say this – but we've no idea if Voog's even alive..."

"But you know where he was heading to. We've the maps. You can remember the coast there..."

"Can I? I don't know. It's been almost twenty years. My memory of it is blurred. Maybe I have even romanticised it. Blejan, you can't contemplate the harshness of the crossing... Besides, even if we found where he was heading for, the country is vast there. He could be anywhere. He could have gone further inland. How would we find him?"

"Faith," I said. "Just have a bit of faith..."

"Isn't that from this new religion?" he asked.

"No," I said. "It's always been there. Listen, I had faith in me finding the truth. I found it. I had faith in someone – you – arriving, and helping me. You arrived. Now, I have faith in this..."

"I admire this trait," Tigernus said. "But maybe it is blind faith only. Maybe it will lead you into a darkness you don't want to meet."

"I have to take that chance, just as you once did."

"I thought..." said Tigernus, struggling to cope with my new-found desire. "I thought we had a future. After that time in the fogou last night, I felt that finally I had met someone whom I might..."

"Might what?"

"Might settle with... Have a future with. This aim of yours – it throws that all into doubt."

"Why should it?"

"Blejan, I spent so long incarcerated. You will not believe what agonies I witnessed. I spare you them – but you don't know of the suffering. When I first met you, I wondered about you. I wondered if you would be my salvation."

"I am," I stated. "I still want to be."

Tigernus walked away from me, turning his back to me.

"No. I realise what you want. I know how much your father means to you. But I cannot go back. I can't spend that amount of time on the ocean again. There are things there that haunt me. I must be careful – you know that."

"Must I choose?"

"It seems so," Tigernus stated. "Me, or him?"

"It doesn't have to be that way..."

"Doesn't it?"

"No."

"You've made your choice, Blejan. I can see that it's the ocean that has won."

Tigernus hurriedly left, leaving me alone; the weighty cartography still leering at me.

16

Objects from a Viking Drekar, Bristol Channel, 6th to 8th Century CE
Objects recovered from the wreck of a Viking *drekar* (elegant and ornately decorated long-ship) in the Bristol Channel include arrowheads, winged spear-heads (*krókspjót*), larger headed spears (*höggspjót*), and broad axes (*breiðöx*). A section of chain-mail armour known as a *byrnie* or *brynja* was also recovered. Shipwrecks such as this are important for archaeology because they can form a kind of accidental time capsule, preserving an assemblage of human artifacts at the moment in time when the ship was lost. Evidence on the sea bed suggested this vessel endured a catastrophic event of some kind; possibly collision with another vessel. Remote sensing has indicated other wrecks of such vessels in the Bristol Channel which will be explored in the coming decade in a joint project instigated by the Jorvik Centre, York and the Bergen Museum, Norway.

PUFFIN, RAT, WARNA, TIGERNUS AND I. This was our ship's company as we plodded to the northern lands from where Warna originally came. Extracting the exact location from her proved somewhat impossible. She continued to say that she would know it when she saw it, and that she was confident it would all come back to her. These weren't great coordinates for travel.

All I could do was to measure the horizon, and keep our boat in alignment with the North Star. She said it was precisely due north of Scathynys, so I had to pray she was right. Tigernus and I realised we both knew the lands there collectively as Kembry (even the Vikings called it that, when they weren't eating plesiosaur, or rather when plesiosaur wasn't eating them), but Warna had a different take on it. Although she knew that term, she preferred to use the more specific name of Deheubarth for the region she wanted to return to.

"Deheubarth," she kept saying. "Yes – that's it... Make a course for old Deheubarth."

To reach it within a day's sailing had been overoptimistic. We had also sat on a windless sea for several hours, and had dealt with what Tigernus began to comically refer to as the 'worm incident'. These two words covered up the agony and trauma of that moment for the rest of our passage. His witty take on just about everything amused me though, and he brought a gentle humour to the vessel that perhaps had been missing before.

Having survived the 'worm incident', we rowed for a while, but soon became tired from the effort. There was no new shift to replace us and the wind was still light. We could only rest and chat. At least now there seemed less prospect of an attack, so we slept a little better. One eye was not quite so open. Puffin made a lulling noise that conveyed his satisfaction at being there, and the rhythm of this, combined with the motion of the sea, induced us to sleep.

When I awoke, Warna was close to me – her one eye tracing my form.

"What are you looking at so much?"

"Just wondered who I am with," the crone said.

She sat up and turned her face fully toward me to gain my complete attention.

"Why were you banished? I have been thinking about it and couldn't sleep..."

It took me a while to realise what she was asking.

"Come, Voog. There can be no secrets on board a boat such as this. You know it. Bah. I have seen your bits and you mine and still, you haven't told me the truth..."

"It's a long story."

"And we have an ocean... I *am* listening."

She said this kindly. It felt like she truly wanted to understand and help me.

I took a mouthful of water, and looked to the bow, where Tigernus was still asleep. Rat and he had become good friends, and the rodent was curled into him. Tigernus used him as the plaything he was meant to be. We were into the night now, and perhaps it was time for a story.

The confession that came out was not quite the way I had planned it. It was filled with pauses, relapses, circumlocutions, corrections and retractions. Still Warna patiently listened though. What I tried to explain to her was how unstoppable the feeling of love was and how wholly truthful it was. Although it was masked by deception, fundamentally the force of it was good. She seemed to understand that.

"Knowing what you know now – would you do it again?" she asked.

"I would. Unquestionably."

Warna nodded and, unembarrassed, with her thumb and forefinger plucked a black hair out of her chin. She contemplated it for a while, perhaps reflecting on time and aging, and then flicked it overboard.

"I grow old, Voog. Hairs appear on my body where I do not want them. Still, even at my age, I understand true love, deep love – a love that is binding and complete. It sounds like you found that – even though it was over so quickly... I am so glad that you have been able to tell me."

I listened to her words carefully now. Most of the time I ignored Warna, but she did have moments of clarity – clear now, as the moon that shone above us.

"Hasn't your god something to say on this?"

I was expecting judgment.

"There is no faith in the world that can judge such love," Warna replied, "let alone my God."

It seemed from these words that we had reached commonality – an understanding, a fusion of both of our Christian and Pagan worlds. I began to think that we were not so different.

Warna got up, picking up the head seat, and hiked her dress high in both hands. She sat on the edge of the vessel and took a long piss.

"I've thought about what you told me..."

"And?"

"You'll find each other again. I can tell. No distance can separate a love like that."

"Really?"

"It may take time Voog, but if you search hard enough – it will come again."

The way she spoke these words sounded very final. There was no point contesting them because she was so definite about them.

It seemed that the closer we came to Deheubarth, the greater clarity Warna had. Something seemed to be calling her back and illuminating all. Just as Howel's words would haunt me forever, so too would these optimistic lines from Warna. She was giving me hope when hope seemed an ocean away.

With great satisfaction at the emptying of her bladder, Warna shuffled off the head seat and yanked down her dress.

"You hungry? I am... Tigernus... you want something to eat?"

A bleary-eyed Tigernus woke from his slumber, and nodded, affirming he was hungry.

The moon was now high in the night's firmament and above us, the stars burst out of the clear sky. If there is one wonder that the ocean can give, then it is this: a lens to the heavens. From my position at the stern, Ursa Major and Minor shone forth, and to their right, the Pleiades. Below them the twinkling mass that was Orion.

"That's Sirius isn't it?" asked Tigernus, pointing somewhere wildly into the sky, but hoping I'd make out the form of it, just to the bottom right of Orion.

"Yes – and just above it, see there, is Canis Major."

"Who gives these stars their names?"

"Great scholars... men who know much more than you or I will ever know..."

"The druids?"

"Ha... no, not the druids – although they do use the stars..."

249

"Well, I think they're stupid names. Why can't they use a normal language like we speak?"

"Most of them sound a bit like your name," I offered.

"What?"

"Yes – I can see some new star being named after you. Tigernus..."

I moved my left hand to point to a dark space in the sky where I imagined it might sit.

"Me? What, named after me?"

"Yes – fitting I think. Your name sounds like a star, Tigernus Minor..."

I left Tigernus to contemplate light and distance. He was no fool, this boy. Someone had taught him about the night sky. Mesmerized by the cosmos, he seemed to temporarily forget he was at sea, and stumbled over one of the bulwarks.

While we sought solace in the heavens, Warna was experimenting with our diet. Realising that our general intake was fish in its infinite forms, and because we were now lacking guillemot meat, she had managed to grind flour and made a wheaty dough which she fried on a pan. Digging into her own supplies, she pulled out a small pot of honey which she spread upon this bread. It tasted so good we asked her to make more.

"My mother made these for me, when I was little..."

She said this joyously, as if she were young again herself.

Her memory was opening up; the cloud of isolation was falling away from it. It was as wonderful to behold as the night-sky stars.

After eating we rested a little more, with Tigernus telling us of his prior days on Scathynys – and all the odd, interesting, crazy and diseased travellers he could remember. It was quite a litany – some even from as far as Almayn and Ytalek, the latter whom he described as being very fussy eaters.

"Probably they weren't much used to the wonders of guillemot or puffin meat..." I offered.

The men from Almayn had been studying the flowers and plants, drawing them on swathes of paper. Maybe through such encounters was how this boy had become so world-wise, how he knew of homesickness and the names of the stars. Warna and I laughed at his tales.

The pre-dawn time brought a wind from the southwest. It was not of the strength we hoped for, but was enough to catch the main sail and push us forward. A sense of relief crossed Warna's face. Like the magic of magnetic stone, she was being pulled back to Deheubarth.

Pre-dawn transformed itself into a generous morning of sunshine. By mid-morning, all three of us shaded our faces from the sun, such was the heat and power of it.

"Make the most of it," sparked up Tigernus. "It won't always be like this."

He had a point, knowing well the weather that afflicted most of the west of the islands of Britain. Generally, it was fog, mist and rain – and then more of it.

The run to the coast of Kembry seemed endless. Before midday, we spotted land on the horizon, but it seemed to keep its distance from us. Sometimes, the ocean is deceptive that way.

Warna became animated though, no longer seeming to suffer from aches and pains in her joints as she nimbly moved around *An Ruen* to get the best view.

I remembered my father's words about this place called Kembry.

"They say it looks like the head of a great boar."

By my calculations we were hitting the tip of its snout. To our right was its mouth, and above us, stretching north were the nostrils.

The people of Kembry were in essence that same group as those of the peninsula. A few hundred years back, we had dominated the whole of the land to the east as well, but invasions and occupations (the Saxons being the latest in a long line) had pushed us back. We had seemingly been separated for some time now at the great river near the neck of the boar, but there was enough commonality for us to understand each other. Aside from these new holy men and women, the bulk of the people worshipped Annown, and saw life in and life out the same way we did. For the most part, they ate the same, dressed the same, listened to similar stories and felt the same way as we did about the *An-credhor Mor* and Saxons. In essence, we were one people, separated by the ironies of geography. As Tigernus had noted though, they spoke our tongue slightly differently – especially these people of the boar's snout. Warna kept a tinge of it within her accent, but had lived so far to the west for so long that she spoke more like us.

As the afternoon continued, features in the forthcoming landscape became clearer to us. Distant – to the east – was a wide strand on the edge of a peninsula, and in the bay above it a wide estuary. An island lay closer to our heading.

"Caldey," Warna confirmed excitedly. "I remember it you see. There, lived a hermit when I was young..."

I glanced at Tigernus. He knew what I meant. Hermits were two a penny in our Age. You were nobody if you weren't a bit of a hermit. I was even considering myself as one, truth to tell.

The cliffs of Deheubarth were unlike those of the horn of Britain. They were lower in height, and their rock was yellowy-grey. They were certainly more welcoming than those we had already seen. The landscape above them was isolated. We observed no settlements or single dwellings. Instead, the flat rolling green of the clifftops seemed to last forever.

"Do you recognise it?" I asked Warna.

"Of course," she replied.

Compared to the horn, where zawns and promontories broke up the cliff-line into a pattern of undulation, the same thing could not be said here. For the uninitiated (which I suppose was Tigernus and I), one part of this coast looked very much like another section of it.

"This part follows the new God," declared Warna. "I first learnt of him from missionaries from Hibernia. They came from over there."

She pointed to the west. Clearly, it was our next direction.

"And the rest?" I asked. "Further inland?"

"Oh, they follow the old ways – your ways I suppose. Stone, darkness and oblivion..."

Warna's past was opening up. Just as I had told her my story, now hers was beginning to come to light. You could tell that she had rejected the old ways of her people and set out herself as a young missionary all that time ago. She had not meant to spend the bulk of her life marooned on Nornour. Such missionaries were supposed to travel the known world weren't they? – not stop off at such shit-holes as Nornour.

She was scanning the coast intently.

"What's she looking for?" asked Tigernus.

"I really don't know."

I levered the steering oar so that *An Ruen* turned to the west from her northern course and we followed the line of cliffs.

"It's here somewhere," Warna was mumbling. "Voog – don't go too fast..."

From close by, the toll of a bell rang out.

"Over there.... That's him.... Look..." said Warna. "Tigernus, ring our bell back to him..."

The boy took the decorated bell-shrine and rang it loudly.

The shore bell and our ship's bell then rang intermittently, each offering a call and response.

I eased the boat into the water close to a fissured part of the cliff. In the horn, we'd call it a zawn of sorts. The water here was not deep, and Warna seemingly could not wait long enough for me to use the coracle to take her into the shore. Instead, she jumped overboard and waded inwards.

This close, the shore bell-ringer became clearer. He was a very, very old man bent near double, and who walked with two sticks. The silver bell he rang seemingly had perfect tone and clarity, unlike the dull thud of ours.

"Gofan! Gofan! It's me..." Warna was shouting.

At sight of her, the old man Gofan seemed to tense up. We could see him wipe his eyes to check that what he was seeing was no dream.

"It's me! Warna!"

Tigernus and I dropped anchor. Puffin flew high above the boat, and found a perch on the surrounding cliffs. There, he could gain a new perspective on the story happening below. Rat had now made himself a regular feature of Tigernus' clothing, and rummaged in his right-hand pocket.

Warna had reached the beach by now, stopping briefly to bend and kiss the earth of her homeland. She paused to smell the sand. Then with a speed that I had not thought her capable of, she scrambled over the rock debris up to where the bell-ringer stood.

Although I was intrigued at what was transpiring, I was not about to get wet.

"You coming?" I asked Tigernus.

"Of course."

I lifted him into the coracle and we spun into where rock met ocean. It was by no means an easy paddle. The swell was quite fulsome; the reason why Warna had got soaked. We nurtured the vessel in, and roped it off around a boulder.

So Warna's journey then – her return home – had been to meet with this old man whom she was now showering with kisses and hugging at the top of the cove.

When we caught up with her, she was breathless; the old man also seemed virtually speechless. Warna explained to us.

"This is Gofan... My old teacher."

Warna was in her sixties, and so this Gofan was probably ninety years old. She had to talk loudly, because Gofan's hearing had declined.

"So good to see you again, my child," lisped this deaf Gofan.

"He helped me understand," said Warna. "He was one of the first converts..."

"Though I am an old Pagan," Gofan chortled.

"I had a hope you'd still be here."

"I have not moved since the day you left," observed Gofan. "I had already done my travelling and seen enough. Since that day, this place has offered me peace."

"Where does he live?" asked Tigernus.

Gofan overheard the boy and pointed.

Warna took up the story.

"He was chased here by pirates... Not Vikings... but others. And when he commanded it, in the name of God, this cave opened up for him..."

"Amazing," I mouthed.

Neither Tigernus nor I were very impressed with the prospect of cave-dwelling. Surely that went out fashion hundreds of years ago?

"Ha... Ha... I will show you," said Gofan.

He moved slowly and this gave Warna the opportunity to properly introduce Tigernus and me. By the way he spoke, he seemed to sense we were from the horn of Britain.

"I know your accent," he went. "I knew a man from where you are from. We trained together once – under the old code... I will remember him shortly. Old age, you know, it is a terrible thing..."

He tapped his head.

As we entered Gofan's cave he looked at me intently and asked, "What is your profession?"

The question caught me slightly by surprise.

"You are not a trained mariner. I could tell from the way you brought your boat in," he laughed.

"I am a fogou-builder – a stoneworker. I dabble in architecture too...."

With these words, Gofan halted.

"What is it Gofan?" asked Warna.

"Now – fogou. That is a word I have not heard for a bit. Takes me back that..."

He thought intently.

Puffin circled and came to sit on a rock close to Gofan's cave, almost listening to the dialogue.

"Your people still use them?"

I nodded.

"For Annown..."

"Birth and deaths?"

"Yes."

Gofan laughed a little.

"The world has not changed so much. We have much to do Warna eh? Ha, ha."

Inside Gofan's cave, I saw Tigernus' eyes bulge with interest. He scanned the dwelling (if you could call it that) from top to bottom. Much of the furniture inside it had simply been hewn from the rock. It must have taken Gofan an Age to complete. Then again, it seemed he had been here an Age to work on it. In the seat where he placed himself, a black layer of wear had formed from its daily use. The stone gave the cave a cold feel, and yet the audacity of this old man much intrigued me. For cooking and for winter, there was a hearth, and for his sleeping, nothing much more than a length of stone, which must have hurt, but which – if he followed the typicality of these new holy men – he would swear was as good as anything his Christ had lain upon.

"Are you hungry?" he asked us. "I have a leek soup ready..."

Warna assisted him in moving the pot, and helped him light a fire in order to warm the soup through.

Warna and Gofan had history and there was much for them to discuss. Tigernus and I sat patiently, overhearing snippets of their dialogue.

"How did you lose your eye, child?"

"*Ancredhor Mor*... They took a disliking to my belief..."

"I see. *Ancredhor Mor* – of course..."

The fire was lit and Warna was stirring the soup.

"And where have you been these past years?"

"Silura."

I saw Gofan try to remember where that was.

"The islands off the horn... What remains of Lethowsow," she explained, drawing them in the air for him.

"Ah... Lethowsow. I see."

"I am so glad you kept faith..." Gofan said, his face almost in tears.

"You made me that way..." Warna responded.

"And have you children?"

"No."

"You kept chastity?"

Warna delayed answering. She knew I was listening but I understood why she lied. It was easier.

"Yes."

Thinking about it, Warna was quite right. She had not chosen her fate.

There were further questions for her, but these I could not hear as well, since she moved to the rear of the cave to find spoons and bowls. Somewhere in the dialogue, though, there was a discussion about her mother and father – and I saw Gofan shake his head sorrowfully. By the way they were talking, I also came to understand that Warna's father had once been a chieftain of this Deheubarth – one Rhydderch – but that was as far as my overhearing went.

Warna returned with soup in the bowls and we ate.

"There is a village nearby," said a coughing Gofan. "They bring me vegetables each week – and look after this old man of the cliffs... I ring the bell wildly if I see pirates; slowly if I see a friendly ship like yours."

All the while, this Gofan peered at me. His mind was at work.

After we'd eaten he took us into the far recesses of his cave. The stone here was completely dry and so paper and parchment survived. There, he showed us a collection of books and papers he had assembled.

"Can you read, boy?" he asked Tigernus.

"A little," was his response.

Tigernus looked at the words but they were in a language he'd not encountered.

"These I have collected – or else written."

"Do you know much of the lands to the west?" I asked.

"Hibernia, you mean?"

"No. Beyond that..."

"Beyond that is Hy-Brasil."

"Hy-Brasil? Is that the same as Ogygia?"

"I don't know of this Ogygia you mention. but Hy-Brasil – that exists... Why anyone would want to go there though, I do not know. No-one lives there. There is nothing there."

"You've been there?"

"Oh yes."

The answer was definite.

"It is past Hibernia. You will find it past *Na Scealaga*."

"What about Hyperborea?"

"Ha, ha. Someone's been feeding you rubbish there," said Gofan. "Is that where you are heading?"

"Sort of," chipped in Tigernus.

Gofan laughed.

"You may as well try looking for Annown," he then said more seriously, dramatically altering his tone.

Gofan was starting to get the measure of us now. Most probably, he thought us deluded: innocents abroad who would one day wish they had not started out.

A short while later, we were outside Gofan's cave watching the sun settle. It had been agreed that Warna would spend the night inside the cave with Gofan. The comfort and chatter of her old teacher was something she had longed for. Tigernus and I decided to sleep back on the boat; otherwise we'd only have had the difficulty of transferring sheepskins across the debris-strewn foreshore. Rat and Puffin came back with us.

All seemed well, and then an odd thing happened. As I began to leave for *An Ruen*, Gofan grabbed my sleeve and yanked me down to the rock he was sat upon.

"I remember now," he whispered in his lisp to me. "The man who spoke like you – his name was Eleder. He was of the old faith. Swore by Annown he did."

A shiver went through me. This Gofan and Eleder were of the same generation. One had not altered, but one had changed much.

"Did you know him?"

"I never met him, but I prepared his passing... not three weeks ago."

"I would dearly like to have talked with Eleder again," said Gofan wistfully. "We had much in common."

I wanted to add, "But not now..." since both their paths had now diverged. But I would not insult him with this.

"It is good to meet you, master Voog, and your boy there," Gofan confirmed.

"He's not my boy," I explained. "But he's a stout mite."

"That he is."

I would like to have learnt much more of this man Gofan, or as my people named him, Govan. Clearly, he was a man of the world, who had seen much, and now seemed comfortable here, watching the horizon from this zawn.

I started off again, but as I scrambled down over the rocks, Warna caught up with me.

She seemed different.

She'd been different for a while now.

Momentarily, I was back with her on Nornour. I could still feel the bump resulting from her thwack to my head. It was as if she wanted to tell me something, but couldn't. I knew how this felt – until I had confessed my own story to her the previous night. Our telling had changed things somehow. The ocean had made it so.

"Thank you, Voog," she said. "Thank you for saving me."

At this, she kissed me on both cheeks, bowed, and climbed back up to be with her teacher. When she reached the cave, she waved at Tigernus, perhaps a little longer than she should have.

Night came in. Again, the stars rose. This time, I had a long and untroubled sleep inside the canopy. Tigernus did the same beneath the bow's hide. I must have dreamt that I had borne a gift back to this Gofan. It was a fragile, complicated gift of love and wonder. It held insight, compassion and hope. I had grown very fond of it.

It was late by the time I woke. Our excursion had forced exhaustion upon me and my body needed rest to replenish itself. My waking had been induced by the shouts of Tigernus. It was his voice all right, high-pitched and as shrieking as his puffin.

"Voog! You've got to come out here. Look... Look..."

My mind felt it had a hangover, though it had been a long time since I had drunk any alcohol.

"You should see this. I told you it would be weird here. This is weird. And I mean really weird."

"Can you keep it down a bit!? What are you on about?" I said croakily as I eased my body out of the canopy.

It took a while for my eyes to adjust to the sunlight. Gradually, they focused, and I saw Tigernus up near Gofan's place. Initially, all seemed the same. The coracle was on the shore, his bleddy Puffin was still circling, and then Rat, who had shuffled inside with me for the night was opening his own eyes to the light.

Then, what had transpired fell upon me like a loose boulder from a tor top. The cave had sealed itself. Where once there had been air, light, and the whole of Gofan's world, now there was just a wall of stone.

Tigernus was testing it with his fists, working his way around the face.

"It's solid," he shouted.

I threw on my trousers and jumped into the water, swimming across the shore in seconds; then picked my way through the rock clutter.

"What the fuck happened?"

Tigernus shook his head.

"I've never seen anything like it. Perhaps it's another earthquake?" he suggested.

"This is no earthquake," I said. "This is magic."

"But it's real," deadpanned Tigernus. "Magic's for *pobel vean* and fairies. This has *really* happened."

"Have you checked? Are they anywhere about?"

"Nowhere here. I've looked. Not on the cliff though... Perhaps they've left."

"They have indeed left," I went.

What was it Warna had been speaking to him about? The cave had opened up for Gofan by God's will. Perhaps it had been closed by God's will too.

"You see this too?" noted Tigernus.

He pointed downwards.

There, a spring had burst forth, that had not been there the night before. I followed the run of glistening water down the zawn. It took my eye to where Gofan's bell stood – or rather had stood, because now it too had gone. On the rock, where the headstock had been, were purposefully placed Warna's cross and her holy book.

"I reckon she left them there – for us, er, for you I mean."

I collapsed to my knees, smiling and crying at once. From this position, her cross poked up over the ocean, the head of it silhouetted in the sky.

"I don't put much into her faith," went Tigernus. "A bit too crazy for me, but it seems like she wanted us to take this."

"Where have they gone?"

Tigernus shook his head.

"Check, will you – up on the cliffs?"

The boy did what I asked him and trekked up the winding steps to the top of the zawn. He went quickly, disappearing over the top of the land mass, and spying in each direction. Within ten minutes he was back. This had given me time too to consider the rock that covered the cave entrance. It was nothing that could be moved in a few hours. Such lifting would take a dozen men a week or more to move – and then only with rollers and ropes.

"So where've they gone then?" asked Tigernus. "I mean that Gofan, he was a bit crippled up too wudn' a? I don't think he'd be going too far."

"Last night, when you were on the boat – when she waved to you – she said goodbye to me. These last few days, she had known. She knew she was departing."

"Departing for where?"

I shook my head.

"Maybe *Pow Sows* – the occupied lands of the Saxons... She told me she thought they needed missionaries."

"I don't think so."

Tigernus thought about it.

"Annown then? I mean, Annown doesn't say no does it? – despite what anyone might believe."

"This cave – a bit like a fogou eh?"

"Wrong alignment," I mouthed back.

I stood up, and stretched my back. I wiped the tears from my eyes. Warna's presence with us would have to come to an end at some point. It was just that I hadn't expected it this soon.

"Where've they gone then?"

"Up there somewhere."

I pointed to the way the clouds in the sky made beautiful shapes – like undulations of soft sheep's wool in the west.

"Heaven," I said.

I took the cross and the holy book and began stepping back to the vessel.

"Come on," I shouted. "The tide's good. We'll make our way to Hibernia."

Tigernus quickly followed.

With good timing, I hitched off the coracle, just as the boy stepped into it.

"This heaven," he went breathlessly. "I never heard of it."

"Don't worry about it. No one has."

We tied the coracle at the stern, and checked that Rat was on board. Puffin landed on the main sail's yardarm and vocally announced our leaving to the whole of the lands of Deheubarth. I stowed the holy book and cross inside the canopy. A little piece of Warna was coming with us.

"Hibernia then? confirmed Tigernus.

"Yep..."

"Holy shit," said the boy. "I haven't heard one good thing about it."

Facing those delights were now the four of us: Puffin, Rat, Tigernus and I.

OH FATHER, HOW QUICKLY DOES love sometimes seem to rot and sour? You must know of this. Maybe you knew it that day when you were caught and exposed. Perhaps my mother felt it when the women examined her. I have felt it too of late. I wanted more harmony to begin with. Difference and antagonism can come later in life. There is time for that. But maybe too, I came to understand more what true love was about. Sometimes it is about argument and dysfunction, but it is also how you resolve a difficulty. It is loving someone enough to understand their difference and be accepting of it. So often, we disregard others for their different views. Such disregard leads to the kind of hate that daily battled around the islands of Britain. As I have told you, I care little for it.

Annown, you watch me and my ways. You watch how I conduct myself. Please understand what I was trying to do. Do not punish me in the next life, I plead.

Our heated discussions continued the next day.

"Lend me *Warna* then. I will make my own way. We've money enough to pay you for another boat for you to return to Scathynys."

"Are you serious?"

"Tigernus, I am not joking. You know that I love you. I would do anything for you, but I must find my father. I can only know who I am if I can find him."

"No. I won't lend you *Warna*," he said bluntly.

"You would deny me?"

"No. Please, Blejan, listen to what I have to say. I have thought much overnight. I do understand. I know why you would wish to make the crossing, but *Warna* is not the boat in which to do it. I am certain your father would not have crossed such distance had he known better. Do you think he might return in *An Ruen*? He won't. The boat was in pieces by the time we had reached Hyperborea. I won't have you do it. There is, however, another way..."

"What are you suggesting?"

"We will cross to Armorica. I will find the man who brought me back. All the energies of the Bretons these past few years have been channeled to fighting the Saxons, but perhaps, only perhaps mind, they might consider another trek into the west. Before things became so violent, and there was such peril at sea, they crossed often. The grounds over there were rich in fish. That way, you might at least travel to the position your father departed from me."

"And will you come with me?"

"I swore that after my escape, I would do two things. First, I would come looking for your mother. Second, I would return home to my original family. Would you have me break that promise?"

I couldn't answer him. The simple fact was that yes, I would have him break every promise he had ever made.

"I need to think carefully," he continued. "I had no plans to return to a place I thought had long since faded into memory."

It seemed that now that I had found something special, I was about to give it away again. I needed to be careful. It was unstoppable though: my wish to swap land for ocean. It could not be controlled. There was too much of my father in me – that was clear.

Did I have doubts? Yes; there were so many that they kept me awake at night. I dreamt of plesiosaurs attacking. I had nightmares of us being subject to boarding by marauding Saxons. I dreamt of drowning. I had visions of the coldness that Tigernus had described. The mix of these galloped through my mind. What was worse though, was imagining my father never knowing me; heading to Annown in old age, and not seeing what he had created.

Other doubts too, raged inside me. Did Tigernus love me a little less now that I explained my wish to voyage? Had he seen something in me he did not like? Did he conceive of me being part of the lineage of a witch and whore? In retrospect, I should not have worried. I shouldn't have had any doubts. But when they come and meet you, you have to confront them. I talk much about faith, but it is there and then that I should have embraced it.

It was also unclear when such a voyage might be undertaken. Were we talking days, weeks or months away? Or was it more likely to be a year or more before we ventured? The indecision of this made me nervous. Although I had travelled across the horn of Britain with my grandmother and Cadreth, I knew I was ready to leave the peninsula. I wanted the stone and the mist to remain behind. I wanted new horizons. I wanted to see the view from where my father stood. Even if he was dead, at least I would have walked in his steps.

The opportunity for departure might well have drifted on and on. Tigernus and I could have enjoyed further time together, and he might even have become more closely embroiled with life in the village. Chysauster needed a new chief, and given how he was proceeding, perhaps it was upon him that fate might fall. You could tell the other villagers were thinking the same thing. Such a man had not ruled here in many years. He was handy with a weapon but had intelligence too; the two rarely walked hand-in-hand – Howel had proved that.

Things altered one morning though. A date for departure became more obvious when I entered my grandmother's chamber. I had called her name several times, explaining that I had made her morning porridge. She had not responded with her usual fussy request about it being the right temperature. You sense things sometimes don't you? I knew it. I called Tigernus and we entered her room together. He felt her pulse. I clasped her hand. She was no longer breathing and her body was as cold as stone.

17

Four Inscribed Memorial Stones, Lundy, 6th to 7th Century CE
Replicas of four inscribed memorial stones found on Beacon Hill cemetery, on the Island of Lundy, Bristol Channel. The stones have the following inscriptions upon them:

OPTIMI, or TIMI, the name Optimus is Latin and male. Discovered in 1962 by D. B. Hague.

RESTEVTAE, or RESGEVT[A], Latin, female i.e. Resteuta or Resgeuta. Discovered in 1962 by D. B. Hague.

POTIT[I], or [PO]TIT, Latin, male. Discovered in 1961 by K. S. Gardener and A. Langham.

IGERNI [FIL]I TIGERNI or—I]GERNI [FILI] [T]I[G]ERNI, Brittonic, male i.e. Tigernus, son of Tigernus. Discovered in 1905.

THE DAY BECAME HOT AND sticky, and in the afternoon looming clouds of thunder had formed. The whole of the sky took on a raven-black form, but initially only a few teasing droplets fell on our heads as the firmament thought about exactly when precipitation should fall. At one stage, we thought it might pass us by. Then, by early evening, it absolutely pissed it down like it does sometimes in these islands. It wasn't to fully stop until we reached Hibernia, but we had a good few days sailing ahead of us yet. You could see great sheets of it falling down ahead of us, and there was no possible way to go around it. Both of us knew we should be prepared to bail frantically. That much intense rain was sure to swirl around the hull's struts and stringers. At best, we could cover the bottom of the hull with hides, so that the rain might pool, and then we could just flick it overboard. Any that seeped beyond these skins would need to be captured with a bowl or bucket and heaved into the sea to begin the cycle again.

Tigernus and I had little to say to each other in the immediate aftermath of Warna's going, but gradually – through chores and responses to the wind (flax and knot tying, letting in and out sails, and by steering) – we began to speak again. To be honest, I was glad he was there. If I had been alone at this point, I am not sure I would have carried on. I might have just let the boat drift, sink into a watercress-induced state and accept my fate upon the rocks or reefs. There was no point in thinking about Warna too much. She would not have wanted us to do that. As so often in life, as I have found, our lives had momentarily collided, and then each of our paths immeasurably altered again. It was the way of things. In some ways, she was still with us – in spirit, so to speak.

Now, the way of things had to be conducted in the wet. Because it was summer, the rain had some warmth to it and, although intense, it was not coming in from the west as a driving front. Instead, it fell in thick globules which coated all four of us. Even Rat, who was usually good at finding dry spots, shook out his fur because the dampness seemed to seep everywhere. Puffin, unperturbed, stood on the canopy at the front bow occasionally shaking the water from his wings. Tigernus remained in the front section, making sure all was well there. We began to realise how fortunate we had been with the weather thus far on the run from Scathynys to Kembry.

Under these kinds of conditions, my aim of pushing back the infinitude of the ocean seemed less of a priority. One lived minute by minute, always in the present, always trying to steer the best course or set the best sail. I postulated that this was the reason some men loved the idea of sailing. There was no past or future – only the present. I could tell that Tigernus didn't like the rain very much. He hated the fact that it was inescapable, and that there was nothing else one could do. When all was well, there were infinite dreams a boy could contemplate on the ocean. Not now though.

When we settled into the canopy for some food – the usual stern-caught mackerel and some surviving eggs from Scathynys – he was questioning me about the wind. Tigernus sometimes saw me as a kind of oracle of wisdom, which I freely confessed to him that I wasn't. Nonetheless, I had become the adult steering his existence, and he sought understanding from me.

"Is it right that the different winds have different personalities?"

"Who told you that?"

"I don't know. Just something I have picked up from travellers."

"What winds do they speak of?"

"Zephyrus mainly, but also sometimes Borea..."

I corrected him: "It is Boreas. It means the wind from the north."

"Zephyrus is from the west isn't it?"

I nodded.

"Who taught you all this Roman rubbish?"

"Dunno. I just know it that's all."

"Come on then – what are the other two then? – those from the south and the east?"

"It is Euros – from the east?"

"Yes," I answered, and sensing that he was struggling with the name of the one from the south I offered it to him.

"The other is Notus."

"Ah – yes I remember now."

Tigernus contemplated these concepts for a while, as he delved into another mackerel.

"So should I pray to them?"

This surprised me.

"What for?"

"So they grant us the best passage."

"I don't think it works like that. They are not gods."

"But right now," argued Tigernus, "We need Euros right? I mean, that's where we need to be blown from."

"Yes – well you can try it."

"Should I give an offering? Would that help?" he asked naïvely.

"You can try if you want," I smiled, "but the winds are not like Annown. Whatever you give may have no effect at all."

"I think I might."

"Better you pray for this rain to stop."

Being the kind of boy he was, Tigernus thought he would give it a shot. It was, at first, comical. He stood with Puffin and Rat at the bow, making up some incantation to the mighty Euros. His thinking was that if Euros puffed a little more, then we'd get to Hibernia more swiftly and be out of this infernal rain. I could understand his theory – though I was unconvinced it would work. After the incantation (some mumbo-jumbo from Scathynys) he then began a plaintive melody – something old that he had learnt as a child.

The chanting of his sweet voice was to have another effect however.

Had I known what would transpire then perhaps I would have thought more carefully about allowing him to speak to the ocean and winds the way he was. You need to think before you undertake such actions. As I should have known by now, there is much in the deep that is not understood, and I am certain now that it was his melody that did it. The tone of it was so full of innocence and kindness that it was bound to attract attention.

I have to say that I was lulled into submission by it too. I began to believe that even Euros might respond to his request.

Had you said to me that we would encounter what we did before I set out from Kembry, I would have dismissed you as a storyteller – another Remfra, bored with reality and thus transformed into a bard. But as I say, it was Tigernus' sweet singing that caused his downfall. Song sometimes leads to tragedy, as you will see.

The rain was continuing to fall, and no discernible wind had picked up in the east. I was observing Tigernus, and at one moment I saw him jump back from the bow; Rat and Puffin were disturbed too from what they saw. I dismissed it initially, thinking that we'd hit a harder wave and, that as so often, it had forced him to lurch a little. But then he seemed more timid and the song stopped for a while. Tentatively, he began again and as soon as he had completed another verse, he jumped again.

"What's wrong?" I shouted. 'Something scared you, you wuss?"

Tigernus turned to me.

"I saw the face of a girl, in the ocean! She was smiling at me."

"Are you sure?"

He nodded his head. Rat squeaked affirmation that Tigernus was speaking the truth.

"Stop singing! Right away!"

Tigernus stopped. We were back to hearing the rain thud on the oxhides; the stringers creaking in the sway.

"Tell me, what colour hair does she have?"

I could see Tigernus looking over the side again.

"Don't look again. Just tell me."

"Ginger. Red-coloured," he mouthed.

"Fuck," I went. "Now you've done it..."

I made my way through the central canopy to the bow where Tigernus was standing.

"What is it? What have I done?"

"Don't you get it?"

"Get what?"

"Your singing... If you sing at the ocean you attract things you shouldn't..."

"Like what?"

"Like mermaids," I said, my face grim with worry.

Tigernus smiled at me.

"But she was beautiful. I mean, really beautiful..."

"That's the whole point you fool. Of course, they're beautiful. They are meant to be beautiful to tempt the strongest man of the stoutest heart."

"But I am a boy," argued Tigernus.

"It makes no difference. They are sirens, ready to lure you below. Is that the fate you want? Do you want to be transformed into a merman – never to return?"

Tigernus didn't answer.

"I can see she has gripped you. Did you look into her eyes?"

Tingernus gazed at me, helpless – his own eyes darting.

"You did, didn't you?"

I shook him hard by his shoulders.

"I don't remember."

I raised both hands to my face and clasped it in frustration.

"I've sung to the sea loads of times around Scathynys. The only things I attracted were guano-dropping herring gulls – on my head!"

"It's different out here – on the wide ocean. You know what the open sea can bring. You have seen it with your own eyes."

I was beginning to wonder how long this mermaid had been following us. Mariners sometimes confused them with other creatures: seals and dolphins mainly. This was perhaps understandable given their form in the water. True as well was the fact that many was the time that a lonely sailor had fancy for a woman's love and came to be deceived by other elements of time and tide. The menhir of their loins always led the way.

This was different though. The bitches loved innocent boys. They were the kind of victims they sought out the most. If Tigernus had made eye contact with her, she'd be unstoppable. She'd seek him out and lure him under. If that failed then... well, I didn't want to think of that for now. She was ginger-haired too. This was the worst kind, so it was said. It was all to do with the contrast of this bright hair with the white of their skin. Then, of course, the hair hid what all men and boys seek – her breasts.

"Did you see anything of her tail? Think, Tigernus..."

"No. Only her face."

If he'd got sight of her tail, you could perhaps work out what type we were dealing with. The scales and form varied. They usually echoed the fish found in the locality.

"I didn't mean to, Voog, honestly..."

He could tell how angry I was. So far, I had not had to raise my voice with him once, but this was different. I was angry because I knew I could lose him. Sometimes, it is hard to avoid panic inducing this kind of anger, and although I knew it was not helpful, I could not control it. My only hope was that Tigernus was too young. Sometimes, boys got away with it. If they had not conceived of girls and their charms, then there was hope. But this Tigernus, he was too world-wise. He was too curious. I was sure she'd come back for him.

I peered over the bow and scanned for her. There was nothing there – but this was not unusual. In most incidents of this kind, the seer was the only one who really saw the mermaid. Others witnessed splashes, stirrings, seaweed gathering as hair, before it morphed again.

I could not be too hard on Tigernus. He was, after all, just like me. My eyes had fallen on beauty and I too, had been seduced. But he was so young. I didn't want him to make the same kind of mistake as me.

In my head, I went over all I knew about these sirens and their ways. So it was said, some men loved being taken away – and spent the rest of their days happy at the bottom of the sea. Lured individuals often reappeared to mariners they knew; complained when anchors dropped on the merpeople's doors below. There were many good stories of them around the horn of Britain, but not only there. As far I could tell, they crossed all seas.

"You'll have to be blindfolded," I suggested. "It's the only way."

Tigernus nodded.

"That way you won't be able to look at her... You stay under the main canopy now – in the sheepskins. Whatever you do, don't look over the side."

"How long for?"

"Until we reach Hibernia... Until you make it to dry land at least. Maybe there, we can reel the bitch in and be shot of her."

"But I don't want her killed," Tigernus protested.

This was a bad sign. He was already caring for her; her poison was already in his blood.

I was trying to think through any times in the stories when these water spirits were a kind of boon or offered benevolence. I could not think of one. Usually, they were harbingers of storms. Many could swim up rivers too. If Tigernus was to be really safe, I'd have to get him as far away from the water as was possible. It didn't escape my notice of course, that this was presently impossible, given the fact that we were now half way between Kembry and Hibernia. I didn't know how to counter the power of such a mermaid. It seemed like they always got their way. They were unstoppable.

Hoping that Rat would not have his eyes affected in the same way, I asked him to patrol the gunwale, and for him to squeak if he saw her. With Puffin, Tigernus and I got him to fly around and above us. I wanted him to survey the ocean. Sometimes, mermaids came in packs – whole legions of them – love hounds of the ocean. If this were the case, I wanted to know what we were facing. Tigernus meanwhile, cowered in the canopy. I had tied a length of leather around his eyes, forcing a hard knot at the back of his head.

"I only wanted to please Euros," he was pleading.

"I know, I know."

Tigernus turned in my general direction.

"I know you were in love once," he said.

This was unexpected.

"I heard you talking. You thought I was asleep. You told Warna what happened to you. How you met someone called Orla and how you were separated, how you came to be on the ocean. You were pushed out here by a man named Howel."

He was telling me this to make sure I did not judge him in the same way.

"It is true," I said. "You know my story – so there is no more to say."

Tigernus paused for a while, perhaps thinking now of his own fate. The rain continued to fall. He could no longer bail the hull, so I was forced to do this on my own.

"Why didn't you fight for her?" he asked. "I mean, if you really wanted her to be with you."

I sloshed another bucket over the side, minding that I did not look into the sea.

"I had no chance to. You weren't there Tigernus. You have to believe me."

"But what if this girl in the ocean..."

I interrupted.

"Tigernus, do not think of love at this time. Think of anything but love. It is the only way you will get through this. These creatures are not like normal girls. They are the vampires of the depths. Don't you get it?"

These words seemed not only to be advice for the boy, but also, I realised afterwards, for me.

Night came upon us. The rain eased a little, but it was no longer now just a summer thunderstorm. We were into bad weather. The boat was rolling more. It felt like the mermaid was playing with us, teasing us with her reach.

"It's her isn't it?" asked Tigernus.

I could tell he was frightened.

"No. It is just the weather. Don't pander to superstition. Rest a while."

I knew that sleep for me would be impossible that night. If I dozed, that was when she would pounce. Tigernus needed watching too; otherwise he'd do something foolish. Rat continued his patrol, and Puffin reported back – a silent satisfaction from him that there were no further creatures for me to be worried about.

There was a lack of other vessels on this part of the ocean. Yes, it was hardly the trading route to Ictis, but one might have expected to see other travellers. Perhaps that was it; perhaps we had strayed into enchanted waters. If this was the case, then this could be my fault after all. I should have used better navigation; should have consulted charts; maybe have had a word with Gofan about the risks.

The night rain continued and the damp caused me to feel cold. The mermaid was on my mind. What did they represent for us humans? Perhaps because of their form, they were the ultimate link between us and the ocean. They were both human and fish. Warna would say they were like her faith – both this God and this Christ. What I found on my voyage was that although hybrid creatures may be hideous and strange, they usually tell us something about ourselves. My extra finger twitched. When I considered all of this, I realised I too, was a half-breed. Just like these mermaids, I was mutated, hybrid, and cast imperfectly. Maybe that is where their frustration came from. That is why they had to tempt, to cajole and to offer intrigue.

Tigernus was asleep now. He'd had to endure much on this journey of his. Already, he'd witnessed death, destruction, duplicity and deceit. I had warned him though. I was reflecting on this as I tried to keep my own eyes off the water. This is no easy task in a boat of *An Ruen*'s kind. One must look low all the time, and not out across the pelagic wilderness.

I hoped that my love for another would prevent me from being caught here, but there was no guarantee.

There never was with mermaids.

Somehow I made it through the night, but there were, I have to admit, moments when my eyelids closed. Temporarily, I shook myself back into life again, jumping in my skin at the avoidance of sleep. A light rain continued throughout the darkness and the sea remained rough. We could expect this all the way to Hibernia, as I had suggested to Tigernus.

The boy awoke.

"The blindfold's hurting me. It's on too tight. Can I take it off for bit?"

"No. Keep it on. It's when you are least expecting it, she'll strike."

"Strike? You mean like a snake?"

"Sort of... She'll just grab your arm and pull you under. Here, eat this..."

I passed him a plateful of wheat and grains to stave his hunger.

"No cooked food?"

"No. No fire on board. They are attracted by it. Besides, nothing would ever catch alight in this rain. It's too heavy."

Tigernus picked at the grains. He looked vulnerable now, all of his eight years old. Before, he'd been tough, but now the inner child was clearer to see.

"How long do I have to stay like this?"

"As long as it takes."

"And how long will it take?"

I scanned the circle of horizons around us. Dawn was glowing in the east, cascading red and orange across our swash. I could see no sign of land before us.

"A while... I estimated three or four days to take us across. We're on schedule, though this confounded rain's not helping."

"Do you think Hibernia will be any better?"

"I doubt it. They say they get a drop of rain there."

"You mean it rains all the time?"

"Pretty much."

This knowledge furthered the gloom on board. We were no longer facing armed warriors with a penchant for pillaging, but instead a new kind of threat – a desirable siren with the hots for this boy.

Another day passed. I could see Tigernus was becoming bored and frustrated with his position on board. I tried telling him stories – some I'd learnt as a child; some that I'd come to know through my travels; and some direct from Remfra. It was the only way to keep him occupied. But perhaps I was no great teller really; no embroiderer. Still the rain forced its way down. There seemed no possibility of a break within the weather. It being hot as well, conditions were about as uncomfortable as they could get. I felt sorry for the boy, but I was merely doing my best to protect him. Out there, she was sure to be following. In my pocket, I felt and turned the clay figurine from Nornour.

Had I been a little more organised, I might have pleaded with Tigernus to stay awake and allow me to rest for a while during the day. But me being me, and thinking I could do everything, I didn't. Trouble came during the night. Initially, I felt fine and was able to keep awake, but the ocean was talking to me, pushing me into slumber. I almost had the sensation that the mermaid was singing back to us: an irresistible melody being thrown up from the depths. Its power seemed to charm Rat and Puffin too. My slumber had to come. No man can sustain such wakefulness for forty-eight hours. Senses are nulled; the world becomes a rushing current of lethargy.

In the middle of the night, I woke to the sound of a splash – something sizeable re-entering the ocean – and my eyes opened enough to see a fish tail make entry into the water. At the bow was Tigernus. He still had the blindfold on, but was clearly holding something in his hand. The jolt of this made me jump across the boat as fast as I could, my motion upsetting its buoyancy.

"What's she given you? Tigernus? Wake up..."

"She kissed me..."

Shit. That was very bad news indeed. If only I had been more watchful.

"...and gave me this."

I had a notion of what might be in his palm. When he opened it, my thoughts were confirmed. It was a comb made of coral. Intricately carved, the object was beautiful to behold; aquamarine in colour.

"Did she speak to you?"

"Yes – but not with her mouth. Through my mind."

This was getting worse. If she could drill in there, she probably had him.

"What did she say?"

"Only for me to go with her – and that she wanted me. If I wanted her, I should use this comb upon the water, and she would come."

Fuck. This was going really well now. How do you snap an eight-year old out of a mermaid obsession?

I tried to wrestle the comb out of Tigernus' hands but he clasped them tightly around it.

"Give it to me."

"No. It's mine."

Annown forbid. She had him now.

"Tigernus. Look at yourself. Look at what you've become!"

"You're just jealous – that's all," the boy went. "Just because I've got a mermaid, you want one!"

This was going even worse than I had first thought.

"Nothing could be further from the truth."

"Let me keep it then."

"If you keep it, you will use it. She will come for you and you will be taken."

"Maybe I want to be taken..."

I hardly knew how to react to this.

"Maybe I want to be taken. It's so wet here that I may as well be beneath the ocean than on top of it."

Accidentally, my eyes caught the surface of the water. She was upright in it – watching us. She held a wooden-framed mirror in the form of a paddle, intricately carved with spirals and knotwork, which she was gazing into, but the glass also caught the light of the moon which burst outwards over the ocean like a falling star.

She was glistening.

I knew I should look away but I couldn't. She was something you know you must not look upon, but to gaze was unavoidable, unstoppable. I knew just how Tigernus felt. She was now using me to get at him.

Dazzled by her beauty, I barely saw what was happening to Tigernus. Oblivious now, he was standing on the gunwale, his arms wide open. Despite the blindfold, he was feeling his way into the ocean. Rat squealed his anxiety, and Puffin landed on his arm, pecking at him to regain his life force. By the time I had averted my eyes, I saw him tip in one precise movement into the sea, pushing his feet against *An Ruen*, and letting go of one world for another. The entry into the ocean was certain.

When I looked down, I saw the form of the mermaid circling around him; her long hair almost touching the motion of her tail. The swirl of her form churned the ocean and cast a glitter into the depths. Still afloat, Tigernus was reaching out with his right arm, dragging the comb through the water. She had him, exactly where she wanted him. Recovering from the way she had dazzled me, I was not about to let him go that easily. I lurched backwards to grab one of the oars we carried. Now standing and trying to balance myself on the sway, I gave a lunge and sharply pressed the oar's paddle into her body. I noted her scream which came upwards as a gurgle of air. Again, I hit her body – this time targeting her tail, trying to manipulate her direction away from Tigernus. She was winning though, because Tigernus was slipping. She was dragging him down. I did not know the full magic such creatures possessed. All I could do was to use every ounce of my humanity to try to save him. I dropped the oar in order to reach for him; the siren used her tail to flick the length of wood into the sea. Her playful laughter echoed around the ocean as the oar swiftly sank.

She was trying to speak to me now – through my mind. I was having none of it though. She was teasing me, trying to seduce me with promises, offering me bounteous jewels, ordering my vision of her realm, but I could switch them off. I was looking to the west – following the light of Annown on a midsummer morning entering the fogou. This resistance lasted against her charms, and I was able to reach down with my left hand to grab Tigernus. When I touched him, I felt no life. He was as cold as a dead jellyfish that had misjudged the outgoing tide. The sea too, was cold and black, almost making me drop the weight of him. The only finger that could still move was my extra appendage. While the other four gripped Tigernus' wrist, this one was free – able to sense his skin. I manipulated it, trying to nudge him out of this induced state.

"He's not yours to have!" I shouted at the mermaid.

I saw her more closely now. I could understand why Tigernus had fallen for her. There was something of Orla in her too. Stories said that. Mermaids shape shift in order to resemble those we have loved and lost. She was using that against me. She was a clever girl.

I was resolved to save him though. She had now, like a snake, wrapped her tail around his legs; the coil wound tight so that he could not flail, and that I might lose grip because of the downward drag. But I knew I had dealt with snakes before. I had pitched them out of the deep of fogous and I knew their form in the Paradise that Warna had spoken of so often.

I kept trying to nudge Tigernus out of this state with my finger, but it was getting harder. *An Ruen* was leaning markedly on her hull, and the gunwale was nearly in the water. Any more and she'd completely capsize. This was the mermaid's purpose. She knew how to destroy the boats of men. She'd done it countless times: immortality and experience were just two of their tricks. The rain was not ceasing either; her doing no doubt, just to make me as miserable as possible.

The struggle had to end soon. Our forces were pulling Tigernus apart, both physically and mentally. It was Rat and Puffin who knew the way forward though. Unbeknown to me, the conniving Rat had pulled up a length of fishing line from the stern, which had a row of hooks set upon it. He cast it out over the bow, and encouraged Puffin to circle the mermaid with it. As happy in the sea as he was in the air, the bird was able to swim around the tail of the mermaid. When I pulled Tigernus from her clutches, and her tail rose in the water, the puffin tightened the circle line of hooks. They pierced her scales instantly and the coils relaxed in their agony. Blood stained the water, and she screamed from the pain. It was a noise I will never be able to forget. The release of her tail coils meant I could pull Tigernus onto the deck. In an instant, due to his weight and the lack of strain on me, *An Ruen* righted itself. I undid the blindfold on Tigernus and slapped him in order to wake him from this trance. Out in the water, I sensed the mermaid endeavouring to pull the hooks from her tail, each struggle only embedding them more and more. It was a cruel fate for her, but mirrored her cruel passion to take this young boy.

When she submerged, I thought we had got away with it. Tigernus opened his eyes and breathed normally again. I checked his hand. The comb had been returned to the ocean. She could no longer work her magic upon either of us. Or at least that is what I thought.

But in that instant, I had forgotten what mermaids do best. They are good at vengeance and revenge – even better than the worst of humanity. What they cannot have or own, and what they cannot love or take, they curse. And thus, that is what I believe she did. She wanted to take this Tigernus so much that she wasn't prepared to allow him back to this world. That is why, I believe, over the next two days he went into a decline.

He had now perhaps seen a little more of the world than he had wanted to, and maybe, in his innocent mind, he wished he was back on old Scathynys. I nursed him all I could, using every herb and potion I had at my disposal. Willingly, I would have given him anything to have made him better. Sometimes though, stories do not turn out they way we wish them to, and by the time the coast of Hibernia stood before us, he was suffering badly from a fever.

In three days the curse had fully taken hold of him. I would have to find help urgently. For luck, for belief, for anything, I clung to the clay figurine.

TAS – THAT WAS OUR WORD for you father. The men I am running with use it now. Fatherhood is important to them. *Tas*, I need you now, but I needed you then, when my grandmother died.

Genaius presided over the departure of her. She lay in the deep of the surviving fogou at Chysauster for five days and when we felt Annown had accepted her, the body was taken up on Carnaquidden Downs and burnt upon a length of stone. The pyre sent a plume of black smoke high into the air. Her ashes were placed in the same cist that contained those of Cadreth. In you Annown, maybe she would be reunited with him. Old Remfra and Kenal came over from Carn Euny for the ceremony and lamented her passing. Remfra spoke an elegy. I was now the sole survivor: my mother and grandmother were in the Otherworld. *Tas*, maybe they were seeing us and believing in us. I had to think so.

Grief fell upon me hard. You never know quite how. It runs beside you all the time, and then sometimes it turns and trips you up for gain and mastery. When that happens you cry and collapse, and need someone to hold on to. You cannot stop it. It is there beside you all the time. You just have to know it and try to anticipate when it will conquer you. Its invasion never quite leaves you.

Although my grandma and I had had our differences, of late we had been reconciled. Maybe now that I was in the arms of Tigernus she felt she could let me go. In more positive moments, I wondered what conversations she might have with my mother (if she was there). They'd have much to tell each other. That's what I tried to make myself think about them. It didn't always work. Sometimes, I found this hard to imagine. Sometimes, there was just a void, a blackness, a nothingness, where life ended. I imagined myself there with them one day as well, though I was not sure then what might transpire.

It took a fortnight to sort out my grandmother's clothes and chattels. I raked through her life. I gave most things away. Unfortunately, somewhere up on the moor, I lost the pin she gave me and this distressed me more than anything else. Tigernus and I looked endlessly for it, but found nothing. The pin's loss and the giving away of my grandmother's life did, however, lead to the final decision for me to leave. I had little left to keep me in Chysauster. I told various people my intentions, and sold on her roundhouse. It was bought by a family with two children. Maybe they would find a new happiness on its kaolin floors. The money I got for it, I would put towards my crossing of the ocean.

I left Chysauster without negotiating new leadership. It had, for some time, remained chieftain-less. The role, of course, was not to fall on Tigernus. No-one seemed able to step up to the mark. Perhaps this was a sign: a signal of future decay – of its final abandonment. I had to hope new leadership might emerge, but under the dictate of the Saxons perhaps others considered it pointless. Why lead, they argued, when there were already others leading? We weren't the only village to feel this way. I was running away from a world where our every move was policed and monitored.

Looking back, I understand that now.

I see the freedom I have gained.

Not surprisingly perhaps, Kenal took my leaving badly. His own children now lived in the northern villages of Bosullow Trehellys and Porthmeor. There, they made their own lives and wrote their own stories. His wife could not walk far. His paunch hid a warrior's body. Tigernus and I had become his daily interest. When we announced our departure, I could see the deep sadness in his eyes. He knew he would never see me again.

"When you see your father, tell him I am sorry. Do this for me Blejan, please."

"I will... He will have already forgiven you."

"Forgiven me? I don't think he will have become one of these Christians. Not over there – not in that Hyperborea – or whatever it's called."

"Maybe not, but he knows your worth – as do I."

"Tell the bugger to hurry up and come back. That fogou up Euny needs a bit of work on it..." he joked, nervously.

He paused, realising that this would never happen, and then said solemnly, "Goodbye then."

"Goodbye Kenal."

We hugged.

"Look after her, boy," he said to Tigernus, shaking his hand. "She's valuable cargo."

"Don't worry," said Tigernus. "I will."

We mounted Tigernus' horse and set off.

"Wait!" shouted Kenal.

Tigernus turned around the mount back in Kenal's direction.

"I have something for you."

"What is it?"

"It's not from me."

"Who then?"

Kenal came over.

"I let it slip you were leaving and..."

"To who?"

"Howel. He needed to know of your departure. He was grateful for me telling him."

Howel needed to know nothing of me. For a moment, I was angry with Kenal that he had told him. But then, things altered.

"What does he give me?"

"This..."

Kenal handed me a book.

"It's one of these new holy books," he said. "You know what he's like."

"For me? From him?"

"He says he hopes you might read it. I know you can read. Says it will offer you protection and hope. He's marked passages for you to look over."

I hesitated. At first, I wanted to throw it back to Kenal, and for him to return it to the man who had ruined so much. But then I thought about what Tigernus had said about Warna and her ways – how one time, that God had saved him. Maybe it would save me sometime too.

"Take it," encouraged Tigernus. "It will do no harm."

In the end, the book slid from Kenal's hand into my own. I opened up my sack and placed it in there.

Although I didn't realise it then, in that moment, you Annown rose upwards and forced your way out. You went stumbling and turning over the moors like a windblown piece of gorse. I never saw you again until I reached Hyperborea.

18

Buhez Warna [The Life of St Warna], 15 th Century CE
This recently discovered manuscript was found in 2005 in the papers of the late Emeritus Professor Gwennol Hamon, Department of Celtic Studies, University of Brest. Unknown before, it was handed by his widow to staff at the Bibliothèque Nationale de France. The manuscript is incomplete with much of the later section of the life missing. It dates from the middle of the 15th Century but appears a copy of an earlier copy. Although composed in Middle Breton, there is evidence that the original version was first written in Old Cornish. The drama tells the story of an early Christian Brittonic female saint who is mentioned in other earlier *Vitae* and probably originated in Wales. During the course of the play Warna uses cunning to defeat Romans and Norsemen who try to prevent her missionary activity. She then founded a Christian community, though the location of this is far from clear. Courtesy of National Library of France /Bibliothèque Nationale de France.

HIBERNIA WAS ANOTHER COUNTRY. WHEREAS Kembry was just another facet of us (indeed, we were the same people who'd only recently become separated by a large river estuary), it immediately became clear to me that I was now dealing with a land and a people who were quite different to my own. But there was more learning for me here. As with all new cultures first visited, they can seem a world away from one's own to begin with, but once their broader humanity is understood, then one realises a commonality.

However, despite knowing this difference, I was to learn that Hibernia did have three main similarities to the horn of the Britain: firstly, the weather. It was as utterly shit here as back home. The whole time I was on the island, it never stopped raining. As you might expect, this induced mud – of which there was a lot. It was a constant in my story here. For each word I speak, attach a filthy layer of it around each syllable. Secondly, the people relied on the ocean as much as we did. The hinterland of their island seemed to give little of value, so they were dependent on the sea giving food, trade, and life. Thirdly, they feared the ocean as much as we did – in the sense that they too, had witnessed the ravages of the *Ancredhor Mor*.

You'd be wrong to think I found all of this out in one go.

No, it took me many days to understand what I had stumbled upon, and then all this time to realise that which I had found; perhaps I wish I hadn't. You will have noticed this by now: it is always the way with me.

My priority was Tigernus. The curse of that bitch of a mermaid had given him a fever that I could do nothing to stop. What do you do in the middle of an ocean when someone becomes sick? Where can you find help? In Carn Euny I'd probably have taken him to Casvellyn. Although I despised the druids on so many levels (and especially his hypocrisy), given my profession, you know I had to work with them. Despite all their *glain* bullshit, about the one thing they were good at was medicine. Their arcane ability to diagnose illness and offer treatment was borne of years of studying herbs and plant lore and their effects. I had a small kit on board with me for common ailments and problems, but this fever I could do nothing about. Where was mighty Casvellyn when you wanted him? If I could have magicked him here I would have done.

Tigernus was sweating badly and I could tell that his condition was worsening. It was becoming harder to keep him awake, and for him to accept food and water. Indeed, the former had become a real problem now. If he didn't eat, he would not recover. He would take on water, but he was also becoming dehydrated – somewhat ironic considering what we were surrounded by. Tigernus was already skin and bones before he became cursed. His body was now wasting away – and it felt that his soul was going along with it. Again and again I damned the mergirl who had fixed her eye upon him. If only I had thought to warn Tigernus of such sirens then things may not have transpired the way they did. I consoled myself with the knowledge that they were always hard to predict: mermaids – slippery as eels.

In desperation, I had done the unthinkable as we first began to trace the mist-strewn coast of Hibernia.

All that I had been taught about Annown, I temporarily left behind.

I wrapped Tigernus in the warmth of the sheepskins and got him to hold Warna's stone cross against his heart. Then, with faltering words, I read a passage at random from Warna's holy book to see if that would help. I did not know what the words meant, and I probably pronounced them incorrectly. I daresay Tigernus was ignorant of them as well, but you have to understand my desperation. I was willing to try any god for help. Looking back, I like to think this was Warna's wish; that I was doing right by her for the boy. Perhaps it helped. It is hard to say. In this voyage, gods come and go.

Cormorants, with their diabolic black wings, cawed a cautious welcome to *An Ruen's* form as she emerged out of the grey. Aside from these birds there was no sign of life. We watched them gulp down sprats and dive the waters for more. I let out Puffin in order for him to circle inland to see what was there, but I knew the problem: the mist was so opaque that nothing could be discerned under it. The rain, too, tended to hide human habitation as people retreated into the warmth of their homes. Hearths were always busy when it rained back at Carn Euny. This was summer still. I just hoped I wouldn't find myself remaining at this desolate spot in winter. Rat seemed to sense the situation with Tigernus; his normally selfish behaviour stalled for the last few days as he spent time with the boy – performiing mad acts of acrobatic ingenuity inside the central canopy, which at least raised a smile with him.

I suppose I had a choice to make. Either I was going to have to leave Tigernus on board *An Ruen*, and head inland myself in order to seek help, or I would have to take him with me. The former had advantage in that I would be able to be swift, and perhaps find people who might help, bringing them back to the shore. The disadvantage was that I would not be able to nurse and monitor him. He'd be left to his own devices. With the latter, the disadvantage was that I'd have to carry him but he would be with me, so I could continue to care for him. All the time, I didn't really know the kind of world I was about to face. It could be a hostile one, which would be no use to either of us. I was going to have to rely on the sympathy of strangers.

I checked my sketch map of the world. Although there were some core locations labelled on this island of Hibernia (as you'd expect, *Baile Átha Cliath*, *Sí an Bhrú* and, not to mention *Na Scealaga*), there were no labels or key for this part of it. As well as that, you can tell with remembered cartography which parts are 'known' and which parts look to be guesswork. I was on one the guesswork sections of my father's notion of the world. Perhaps I should have been grateful to have something to go by. Had I gained a little more time with Gofan, I might have asked for his perspective, but that had not passed.

With my right forefinger, I traced the land around to the southwest tip of Hibernia. We were not far from it. There, the coast became fragmented into long bays (estuaries similar to the ones back home) running in a northeasterly direction. Where I estimated we were, the coast was smoother, but clearly much less was known about it. To the west of those bays lay this Hy-Brasil and then a vast nothingness: the latter location where I was finally heading.

All of this limited knowledge encouraged me to make the decision to take Tigernus with me. What there was, we'd see together, curse or no curse. I put into a small, seaweed-strewn bay that looked like it would offer good shelter for *An Ruen*. Anchor was easily dropped and I loosened her sails. I used the coracle to put ashore, and chopped down some straight tree branches of birch. With these, I was able to make an improvised cross-frame sledge on which I would place Tigernus. Thus with two longer pieces of wood tied to the frame

I could drag him across the landscape. In this way, I felt I would be able to cover more ground, rather than carry him upon my back or in my arms. I knew speed was of the essence. I used spare flax to tie the frame together and then managed to scull a floppy Tigernus across in the coracle.

By this time, his eyes had grown dull and seemed to cloud over. This was worrying. I kept talking to him, trying to nudge him out of the illness (just as I had done with my extra finger when the sea-hag tried to take him), but he (perhaps like myself) was becoming more incoherent. I'd keep talking though, whatever the cost. Rat came with me in my pocket, while Puffin was given orders to watch over *An Ruen*. He seemed comfortable enough with this, having already sought out a new supply of sand eels. I told him to watch for the cormorants; they'd probably view him as something of an interloper. In my sack, I took enough supplies of food and water to last me for a couple of days. Beyond that, I was not sure what would happen.

It was still pissing it down. The damp and mould made Tigernus cough and splutter, and me slip and slide through the landscape. The surrounds were green and luscious; the shore quickly transformed into low-canopied woodland of mossy oaks and ash trees. How odd it was to be trekking through a world without naming. It made me realise how much you normally rely on place and memory to exist (this was a sensation I was to experience again on this voyage – but did not know at this stage). Even on the ocean, where there are few markers, you have a sense of yourself. Now here, I seemed to be losing who I was in a land that knew itself intimately.

I steadied myself with the knowledge that removing Tigernus from the water was a positive move. The moment he hit land, his spirits lifted a little. The curse would find it harder and harder to operate the further he was from the ocean. For this reason, I drove onwards sharply away from the coast. For all I knew, the mermaid may have continued to follow us into the inlet. Some of her progeny, it was said, could come ashore, transforming fish tail into legs and deceiving men some more. I checked Tigernus was carrying Warna's talisman. His hand still held it, which gave me some reassurance. Any magic would do.

I continued to drag the frame up the dank valley. Here the land became more difficult to pass through because large sandstone boulders punctuated the woodland. There was no discernible path. The effort required was immense because I had to keep stopping to turn the frame so it would pass through gaps between the stones. Hard rain continued to fall. After an hour of this terrain, I was exhausted. I was stuck in it though, and for both of our sakes had to persevere. At the top of the valley, the trees thinned and the land here altered its shape, running into wide fields, divided by drystone hedges. There was a familiarity to these fields; they were the kind we used back home. Howel, of course, revelled in their construction – part of his growing empire. Mine was a more practical understanding at this point in time. If there were fields demarcated and enclosed, then there would be life. At this, I breathed several sighs of relief.

The mist had not risen. I could not see very far in front or behind me, but looking back, I suspected that on a clearer day, I would be able to see the ocean by now. The wetness lost me all sense of timing. I was hungry and so rested and ate for a while, making sure that Tigernus drank, and that I washed and cleaned him. The colour of his flesh was worrying me. His skin had gone utterly white – the colour of fish meat, and in places I sensed it scaling and peeling. Most ailments I knew, but this magic was something that defeated me.

The field systems allowed me to cover more ground. I followed the line of the walls, pausing a few times to admire the architectural skill of them, and the sheer time it would have taken to move the stone here from the valley below. This was through the efforts of previous generations of men who worked these lands. Their agricultural and architectural skill was a good sign: I may not have to deal with an aggressive group of warriors – perhaps, up until now, my worst fear. The systems at first housed relatively few creatures (an elderly bull in one and a ram in another), but as the land rose, we traversed a field of snuffling and grunting pigs, and then further up, I found an enclosure of sheep. Most were lambs beginning to transform into adulthood as the summer pressed on. The snouts of the pigs (a species I hadn't encountered before) had churned up their field, and walking through the quagmire was not a pleasant experience. The sheep came as something of a relief. They scattered to the uppermost reaches of the field as I levered Tigernus over a stile in the wall.

At the top end of the sheep enclosure I noticed a dwelling of some kind, poking through the mist. Given the weather, I would have been mad not to make for it. A fear had come over me by this point in time that my decision to go to shore with Tigernus had been a stupid one. Maybe I should have followed the coast a little further and put into a populated harbour. Then again, I could literally see the ocean killing him – mermaids' curses used the waves. The final effort to reach this dwelling was immense. The land increased in steepness and became even more slippery. There were several times where I lost my footing and dropped the whole frame. If he felt the judder of its fall, then Tigernus said nothing. One time my face fell onto the wet soil, my forehead coming close to stinking sheep shit.

Eventually, the dwelling came into better view. I had temporarily swapped the ocean for land, but here the ocean seemed to return. The architect in me revelled in what had been constructed. This building resembled an upturned boat made of drystone corbelling. Every stone was laid at a slight angle: lower on the inside than on the outside, thus allowing the rain to easily run off. I briefly examined the stones. They had been cut, but the builder has been reliant on the stone's natural form as well, to help engender the slope upwards to the 'keel', which in fact was now the ridge of the roof. No mortar appeared to be used at all, not even earth that I would normally have used to pack the stones. Even I had to admit, the load-bearing was exceptional; the corbel vaulting a triumph of ingenuity. Whatever people lived here, we would at least have something in common: our love of stone.

Inside, the purpose of the dwelling became clearer. It was a building designed for the sheep to stay warm in during winter. The wet, as it was, appeared not to trouble them, but perhaps when colder winds blew (Tigernus' northern Boreas), then this shelter would offer respite. A stone trough of stagnant water was located at the rear, while the floor, although of the same sandstone as the walls, was now coated with sheep dung. A small, rear window let light into the room of this stone boat. Despite everything, despite the wet, and the fact that Tigernus was still so unwell, there was, I must confess, a sense of peace that I reached within this humble building. Tigernus himself cared little for the stonework, but appreciated being out of the rain. This would be our accommodation for the night.

In order for this animal house to become habitable, I kicked the dried dung outside, and then placed Tigernus to the floor, gently removing him from the wooden frame. Before I lowered him down, I moved the sheepskins to make a bed for him. I hardly dared to look at his skin. I didn't need another sign to tell me how unwell he was. I knew it was blackening and becoming disturbingly mottled. Through the doorway, I looked at what we faced.

We were nowhere, but we could have been anywhere. The mist was deceptive, and in union with the rain, it made for a miserable vision before us.

"You should have left me," croaked Tigernus. "It might have been easier..."

He may well have been right, but I was not about to agree with him. We had come too far together.

"You're better here with me. I would have hated the not knowing. Besides, I don't think our friend Puffin would have been able to offer you much care..."

I said before that I did not believe in superstition and fate. I had hoped I had left those concepts behind a long time ago, but as we waited, I knew I was going to need them. One of Warna's so-called miracles might come in handy too.

The form fate sometimes takes can deceive us. We want it so much that when it comes, it disappoints – or at least, is not what we ever imagined.

It was my lighting of a fire that did it. I'd gathered a few twigs of broken gorse and used these to make a small hearth inside the dwelling. I made it close to the window, so that the smoke could rise from it. The fire would give us hope, as well as dry us out. The blaze took a while to ignite. I used tiny strands of flax upon which the spark from my flints jumped. Then I had to blow carefully so as not to extinguish it, but assist combustion. I was just trying to keep Tigernus warm. I had not realised that by doing so I was making smoke signals. I was making our occupation known.

Gradually, I became aware of the presence of someone standing in the doorway.

"Voog," went Tigernus nervously. "Someone's here."

I peered at the shape. It did not speak for a while, but instead surveyed the scene.

Then it laughed and spoke: "Crét dogní inso i n-ainm an diabuil?"

I shook my head. I did not know this language. I assumed it was what was now spoken in Hibernia, but could only respond in my own. The figure shook his head, appearing not to have understood what I said either. Despite time and space throwing us together, we were incommunicado.

He had another go: "Is áitt inso do na caírib issin gemrud."

Again, there was silence.

I held up my hands – palms forward – showing the figure I had no weapons.

He nodded at this, and gazed at my clothes. They were of interest to him, presumably, because they were so different from his own. The man who appeared at the doorway was dressed in the grey and white hides of wolves. The head-skin of one particularly ferocious beast dangled as a hood across his shoulders. He carried with him the crook of a shepherd, while on his back was a quiver of neat arrows, alongside a large longbow on his shoulder. In his left hand, he carried a net and inside it were some freshly-caught salmon, still twitching. Clearly, he'd hunted them using the bow and arrows. I could see the arrow marks in the shimmering sides of the fish. This man was not a patient fisherman.

The salmon were a good sign. According to the druids, these fish were to be seen as liberators and carried with them great knowledge. It was their ability to swim upstream and return to their origins that made them so. Dead or alive, I took their appearance as positive. Wolves I knew less about. They had inhabited the moors of Brentigia at one point but had been hunted to extinction because of man's fear of them. By this man's appearance, they were clearly still present in Hibernia. The fact that he was decorated by them meant that he was unafraid to kill them.

He was hard to give an age to. He might have been in his thirties, but equally he could have been in his fifties. It was difficult to tell past the lines of layered wolf fur and the thick hair and beard on him. I examined his hands. They were like mine – or at least, my right hand. I sensed he was the builder of this dwelling. He was gazing at me too, trying to work out what kind of creature I was. He noted the stump and twist of my left hand and the experience of the right. He must have wondered how this mutant came to be in his sheep shed.

Given that verbal communication seemed impossible, from my bag I took out an instrument (carefully demonstrating it was no weapon) and drew on the floor of the dwelling. I outlined Hibernia and then the boar's head of Kembry, which he seemed to understand. In the ocean I drew our boat, and then took time in drawing the mermaid. I worked carefully on the tail and hair. At the form of it, he gasped, and then gave knowledge that he wanted to use the crow-bar to etch with. I saw him test the weight of it – perhaps recognising the stone-worker in me. He drew an arrow coming from the mermaid towards a representation of a boy on board the boat, with the taller figure of me standing next to him.

"An mhallacht ar cailleach farraige?" he asked.

He pointed to the mermaid and her arrow.

Whatever he was saying, it seemed to show a mermaid committing harm to the boy.

I nodded in approval. We were getting somewhere.

Although we could not communicate with words, his shared humanity saw my predicament. He noted Tigernus' condition, and bent down, almost to view him as if he were a newly-born lamb. I saw him look closely into his eyes, check Tigernus' pulse and then examine his skin. From a pocket, he pulled a clay bottle, not bigger than my extra finger, and while lifting Tigernus' head, had him drink from the vessel. Tigernus didn't like the taste of it; that much was clear, but this was good medicine.

I thanked Annown.

I thanked the clay figurine.

I thanked Warna.

I even thanked her god.

This man was a shepherd and we were about to become his sheep. I had no choice in the matter. I was utterly dependent upon him and his crook.

"Más eslán in maccán, tic limm ocus do déntar linn a leigeas," he said.

It was Tigernus who picked up on the tone of what he was saying.

"He wants us to go with him."

"Corcu Loígde?" he asked.

I didn't have the slightest idea what he meant, though I nodded.

The shepherd smiled and spoke again, saying, "Sil Lugdach meic Itha."

I was to come to know what all of this meant, but if I told you now you would not believe me.

The fire, which I had taken some time to ignite, was put out with an instant crush of my foot, and then I strapped the sheepskins and Tigernus back onto the frame. I saw the shepherd briefly touch and smell the quality of the skins, to see what manner of man I was. I could only hope they met with his approval. I then began to drag the stretchered Tigernus out of the boat-shaped dwelling. Although he was already laden with fish, the shepherd picked up the two ends of the frame that had previously dragged in the mud. Two of us carrying the boy made a considerable difference and lots of ground could be covered. The shepherd pointed to a path, speaking to himself, if not to us.

I was very glad he was with us. The mist had now become so thick that we could barely see a few paces in front of us. If I had tried to continue any further, I would have ended up walking around in circles. By now, the shepherd had observed Rat in the midst of my pockets, and clearly pondered our mental state. In his world, such creatures would be eliminated. He tapped his skull with his forefinger indicating the madness of our inclusion of our animal friend.

For the first time in a long while, the ocean felt no longer a part of me. In fact, it was very odd to be continually walking on land again. The shepherd, whose name I had not yet grasped, walked at quite a pace and I found myself forced to move my own legs faster. I still had no idea where we were taking Tigernus. This man had certainly given him hope though, and there was a cheer in him that I had not seen since before the encounter with the mermaid.

Out of the mist, a circle of stones appeared. There were seventeen in total.

The shepherd gestured towards it with his hand.

"Drombeg," he noted.

This seemed to be its name.

Although not as large as the circle at Boscawen Ûn, here some of the stones were taller, and more tightly packed. Like at the horn of Britain, the people here still worshipped the old faith.

"Annown?" I asked the shepherd. "Annown?"

He shook his head. Clearly, their word for the Otherworld was different. I would have to investigate and find out their practice.

What I was observing, though, was a very similar culture to the one of Carn Euny. When we stopped to rest, there was even a boiling pit, just like the ones back home. Clearly, when ceremony was conducted here, in order to cook, people filled the trough with water, and added heated stones. I pointed at the arrangement, and the shepherd responded with, "Fulacht fiadh." This was clearly his word for the cooking place.

As we rested I thought I would try to learn this man's name. It had not been forthcoming yet, and it seemed strange for Tigernus and I just to refer to him as the shepherd as we had done so far.

I pointed at myself, and said my name. When I spoke the vowels, it sounded odd, like I was no longer the same person.

"Vo-oog," the shepherd went, and I nodded.

I pointed at Tigernus, saying his name slowly at first: "Ti-ger-nus."

He tried this, almost getting it right.

I said it faster, and he repeated it: "Tigernus."

In the circle, we were now onto him. I gestured at him, before I did so, repeated both of our names. He understood

"Caera Mac Nia," he seemed to be saying.

I repeated what I thought he had said, and he nodded an agreement.

For us then, he was Caera from now on. Maybe we got it wrong and perhaps he didn't even know we meant our names. All this experience of translation and understanding would be of great use to me later on when I was to encounter other peoples. Right then though, I was merely trying to be friendly. At some point in our discussion over the cooking pit, it seemed like Caera was ready to boil up some of the salmon, but I indicated that we should concentrate on Tigernus. He seemed to realise my concern and allowed the three of us to push on.

I was sodden. Not only had the ocean coated me with wet brine; now the land too had decided to dump as much earthy rain on me as it could manage. It dripped off the end of my nose as a kind of waterfall. There was now nothing I could do to keep Tigernus warm. He was either going to make it through the next hour or so, or not at all.

"How far?" I asked Caera.

But the question was not understood. What was the word he had used inside the sheep's winter dwelling? Tigernus had remembered the sound of it.

"Something like Cor-cu Loígde I'm sure."

I tried it.

"Corcu Loígde?"

Caera beckoned me to step forward slightly. I stepped up to the brow of the hill we were currently climbing and looked below. At first, the view was unfathomable and indistinct, but when the mist momentarily departed, what emerged almost took my breath away. Formed on an island, in the middle of what appeared to be a lake, was an entire city of thatched huts.

The more I gazed, the more I understood its construction. In order to make the island, they had dug a wide ditch which had now been flooded. The lake then, had been man-made. A generous bank of this material then led to a wall made of sharply hewn wooden posts forming a strong palisade around the entire compound. A drawbridge lay across the ditch at present and although it was as wet now as at the start of the day down by the ocean, the people here were conducting their normal business unperturbed. Rain, it seemed, stopped nobody in this country.

"What is it?" asked Tigernus, expressing a wish to see what was unfolding before me.

"A city," I said.

"I haven't seen one of those before," he said, adding "Have I?" as an afterthought.

We levered him up so he could see its vast spread. Despite his fever, Tigernus might at least have seen a little more of the world at sight of this community. Rat too, breathed a sigh of relief. Here was a world of food and fine gnawing close at hand.

Aside from its enormity, two other things instantly engaged us. The first was the central point in the urban sprawl of this place. It was a huge forefinger, built of stone which pointed to the sky, and was topped with a conical roof of slate. There were perhaps six storeys to it, each with a narrow window. Its immensity was beyond any construction I had seen in the peninsula of Britain. Even from this distance, I could see the neatness of the stonework and how much care had gone into its crafting. It took a little while, but then I remembered Howel's words – that the Hibernians had perfected these structures as refuges, just like he wanted our more humble fogous to become.

From this hill, it was easy to see their defensive strategy. The outer palisade and ditch of water would keep out most marauders, but if they should break through that, then the entire community would relocate behind a second line of palisades; here with pikes of wood sticking outwards, ready to pierce anything that tried it on. Inside that circle was the last resort – the round tower. It required no explanation. A ladder allowed access to a door far and away above the normal height of a man. When everyone was stowed inside, the ladder could be kicked away, and the people could stay safe in the refuge for so long that the enemy got bored. Presumably the tower would be stocked with food and water, and there would be space enough for everyone. An outer chute looked like it provided sanitation for each of the layers.

Although this spectacular round tower took much of my gaze, I could also not help but look at the brightly decorated wooden carving above the main entrance. It was a bold statement of who these people were, what their lineage was and how they saw themselves in the immensity of the land that was Hibernia. The carving depicted a fearsome warrior queen or goddess (I could not tell precisely which), standing above four calves.

Clearly, we had entered the lands of the people of the Calf Goddess.

Caera caught me surveying this public monument and statement of intent. He nodded and smiled.

"Corcu Loígde," he affirmed.

So that's what he meant: the tribe of the Calf Goddess. See, I told you that you wouldn't believe me. That is why I have saved it to now.

It was clearly my hope that her bovine descendants could heal Tigernus.

I HAD BEGUN MY JOURNEY back to you, dear Father. I was leaving everything else behind. I was on a cusp. I was leaving land for sea and swapping hard granite for soft salt. Wherever you were, I wondered if you dreamt of me. I knew you didn't know of me – but maybe there was something telling you I was coming. Sometimes, there is that physical journey, but there is also one in our minds. Journeys can come both with and without us moving. It was clear to me that the far away was becoming nearby. The nearby – step by step, wave by wave – was becoming far away.

Winter was still clutching the peninsula when we left, but the first signs of spring were pushing through. In the hedgerows, small flowers poked out their heads. On trees, buds had started to form. It was the right time of year to set off. Tigernus and I did not say much as we rode across the downs towards Lulyn (we would make up for this silence later, as you will learn). I dare say he had not expected to pick up the cargo that was me. He had come to Carn Euny only to find Orla and relay my father's message – and now, he was leaving with her daughter, going back to him again. That village, that place, that time, were behind me. I did not look back. I had no wish to. Instead, I kept my eyes focused on new horizons, and the fact that hopefully, I would soon, like you once did Father, head into the west. With each step, I was getting closer to you.

I didn't contemplate it that day, but as well as my journey opening, I came to realise that the door of redemption I had opened with Howel now followed me. It clattered over my footsteps. Maybe it was my transition into adulthood, my necessary maturation, but there was something else too. You see, I thought about the world in different ways – which anticipated this moment now, with the people who I am running alongside. I saw opportunities. I contemplated much about faith and belief. I realised what united people rather than what divided them. I was starting to see the Druidic in the Christian; the Christian in the Druidic. I was humbled by its union. I came to realise that what I had undergone in my childhood had instilled in me a sense of wonder and respect for the world and its differences. I was about to find more of this on the ocean. I was going to find needles in watery hayricks.

In Lulyn, Tigernus returned the horse he had hired, and then we set about obtaining provisions for the crossing to Brittany. Tigernus knew what to get. He knew what would last and keep best on the ocean. He knew the foodstuffs that were easy to cook upon the steady bob of waves. We spent a day around the market finding these items. We bought extra sheepskins for warmth ("You'll thank me when you reach the northern latitudes," he had said) and spent time re-greasing the hull of *Warna*. At the tannery, he bought more ox-hides as spare linings, and showed me the stinking tanning pits where my father had once stood. The stench stayed in my nostrils long afterwards.

That evening, for the first time, we would sleep together on *Warna*. We had already transgressed the normal expectations of our society, but then, who was there to point the finger? In another time, we might have married but that now seemed irrelevant and alien to us both. We were two orphans who thought we had found love. You see how I use the word 'thought' here. I use it here because I thought that not everything was as wonderful as I had wanted it to be. I suppose I had wanted it to be romantic. I had dreamed of this moment for many months – years even – but when it came, I became fearful and paranoid. Tigernus was somehow not close to me, or at least, I thought he was not. Instead, he was contemplating what had to be done, what was necessary in order for me to find my father. He understood better than most the immensity of what I was proposing. I read this concern in him, as we all sometimes mistakenly do with those close to us, as disdain, unresponsiveness, and cruelty.

"Why are you so cold to me tonight?" I asked him.

"I'm not," he said defensively.

"You won't lie with me – or hold me..."

"I am planning what we must do. I have to concentrate. There is a lot to think about."

"Really?"

"Yes, Blejan, really."

I left it a while, to see if he would move closer and respond to my need. When he refused to be intimate, it was then that I let loose a spear. I fired it straight at him, aiming to pierce his heart.

"It's her, isn't it?"

"Who?"

"The mermaid. I see she is really still your love – even after all these years. That's it, isn't it?"

"No. Not at all..."

"But you've told me when you first arrived at Chysauster – the effect she had on you. Her love was much stronger than what I can give you. You are still charmed by her, aren't you?"

"I still think of her, if that is what you are asking. I cannot help it. It is part of the curse. Daily, I have to face her – and then face my own demons."

"And do you still love her?"

"No."

"I don't believe you."

This was the second spear I shot into him.

"Blejan, I can't believe you think this."

Retrospectively, I should have stopped then, but I persisted.

"You've lied to me haven't you? All these years – you said you were en-slaved, actually you've been pursuing her..."

Despite my taunt, Tigernus maintained his composure.

"If I were pursuing her, I should have gone back to the ocean where I found her long ago – when I was with your father. Then I would have dived in and dwelt with her for eternity. If I had wanted her, I would have been a merman by now."

I started to cry. Grief for my grandmother came out, as well as the fact that I discerned Tigernus not to be fully committed to me. I was questioning whether he was the one to help take me across the ocean. I was wondering if what I had felt as my destiny was now mistaken. I had put my trust in him – and now, it seemed like I had misread everything. I had tried to wrong-foot the past and now I had wrong-footed myself.

"You are talking nonsense, Blejan. You know I am devoted to you. Whatever has messed up your mind in your childhood, you must not apply to me now. I am not like others you have met. I will not betray you. I am not in love with the mermaid. If I had my way, I wish such creatures would die and never re-emerge from the depths. Can't you see that?"

"I need to hear it," I said.

"I've just said it."

"Say it again, please..."

"I want you, not her."

Tigernus dropped the maps and navigational device he was holding. He moved to the bow of the boat where I was sat and kissed me passionately.

"Never think of me loving you other than utterly and completely," he said. "Your father taught me about sailing and the stars – but he also taught me much about kindness, humility and most importantly, love."

I had been stupid. Is this the way of women sometimes? Sometimes, they chase and cajole when there is nothing to hunt. In these moments, I hated my sex for what we were. Why did I behave in such a way? I abhorred the fact that I had questioned him; that I had ever doubted his feelings for me. I resolved that I would not let fear or jealousy enter my mind again. I kissed Tigernus and on *Warna* we made love. Between our hot breaths of desire, I managed to mouth, "Forgive me."

As we caressed, I rethought the mermaid. Hopefully, this combination of woman and fish maybe could one day be perceived as being just like this new Jesus, who was both man and god. In our love, which now was utterly complete and understood (and I now knew did not always need to be spoken, or declared), Tigernus would help redeem me too.

19

Kitchen utensils and food from a roundhouse community, Island of Nornour, Isles of Scilly, 6th to 8th Century CE

These implements include spoons, ladles and plates — mainly constructed from wood (from Pembrokeshire, Wales) and the bones of sea birds. They were discovered buried in this isolated roundhouse community by a team from the British Museum working there in 1973. Although used in this period, the utensils could well have been made during an earlier time. Direct evidence of diet consists of preserved food remains, both plant (paleoethnobotany) and animal (zooarchaeology); and coprolites (fossilized faeces) also give us a picture of life in this community. Collection and analysis of plant remains is often futile because most decay. If, however, they have been charred (burned), perhaps during cooking, the material is preserved indefinitely. Once salvaged, these items can be dated by the system known as radiocarbon dating, based on carbon's known rate of very slow decay. The diet on the island included cod, limpets, herring gull, spurge roots and blackberries.

BY THE MANY GREETINGS THAT Caera was given as we entered the fort of the Calf Goddess, it was clear that he was well-respected. We had been fortunate in him locating us. I could sense his hurry to have Tigernus seen by someone who might be able to cure him. The fort was busy with energy, and as we proceeded through the paved streets and huts, I began to notice that steady preparation was being made for war. By this, I mean that the townspeople seemed to be readying themselves to defend their fort against some as yet unnamed enemy. Even the smallest of children were being trained with spears and shields. Getting them trained up young was clearly important. Tigernus and I were a curiosity, however: travellers of a kind they hadn't seen, and large, slobbering grey-hued dogs sniffed us, and those same children gazed at us in wonder. As we continued, men and women chatted about us, asking Caera questions as he pushed through. He seemed to be giving them the occasional answer, which at least satisfied some of their curiosity.

I began to understand the community we had entered a little more now. It was clear that it was completely dedicated to the rearing and production of cows and cattle. Outside the main fort had been great pens of long-horned, shaggy-coated cattle, while inside, virtually each hut had its own cow grazing nearby. Milk and beef were highly valued items. It seemed that whatever eco-

293

nomic transactions were completed hereabouts, the base unit of exchange was a calf. I was now beginning to understand why they conceived themselves to be of the progeny of the Calf Goddess – but who was she? I even wondered if I should meet this Calf Goddess at some point.

Tigernus and I were taken to a large-sized hut that would have covered the entire village of Carn Euny, and the boy was encouraged to lie down upon some furs. In different sections of the hut were other people, all lying in beds, and gradually, I understood that this dwelling was dedicated to looking after the community's ill or infirm members. Amongst its inhabitants were some small coughing children who looked undernourished and weak, as well as more elderly faces who peered up from whatever condition they were suffering from, reaching out with their hands for compassion.

This was all unexpected. Never in my life did I think I would be led to such a place. If Howel wanted to see how a community organised itself for the benefit of others, then he should come here. These were a people collectively working together for the good of the overall community. I thought back to home: any illness there was generally a family thing. You sought to be home with your people and hoped that you'd recover. If you were lucky, your family would call on a druid to work his medicine. Sometimes they were difficult to find – and so you put your faith in Annown, and prayed for the best.

Caera went out of the subdivision of the hut, clearly seeking help for Tigernus. He gestured for me to stay. Tigernus was delirious now, and I tried to comfort him as best I could. I could only hope that what help was coming would end his curse. I was still blaming myself for not taking better care of him on the ocean.

When Caera returned, he had with him a woman who was in her mid-forties. She was black-haired and upon first seeing her, I felt she looked hard-hearted. I was proven wrong though. She, in fact, had a kindly demeanour, and this apparent hard-heartedness was rather her brisk efficiency at her work than anything else. When she arrived, instantly seeing the state of Tigernus, she called out for another woman to enter. This woman was younger, obviously an apprentice, and she carried two wicker baskets full of equipment.

The first woman spoke to me in broken British: "Caera here... says you are from Britain... Is that right?"

This was unexpected.

"You speak British?"

"Badly," she said. "I learnt through my training – and some time spent on the Llŷn peninsula... On Ynys Môn as well. Do you know it?"

I confirmed I knew where it was – somewhere in the north of Kembry.

From the outset, it was clear that this woman was smart.

I introduced myself and quickly explained what had happened.

"I am Aimend," she said, "daughter of Oengus."

She said it like I ought to know who Oengus was. I would soon come to understand.

"I need to examine him."

Aimend and I gently stripped him of his clothes and she set about looking over Tigernus. I had never seen a woman work in this way. I had so many questions for her, but knew these would have to wait. Saving Tigernus was the priority. My culture would most likely have labelled her a *wra* – a witch. Those kinds of witches were not evil; they were just women who had knowledge of the lore of plants and assisted with the birth of the young in the fogou. Even this gives the wrong impression of her. She was nothing like that.

Caera stood by, and occasionally she had questions for him, which he duly answered. At other times, she shouted orders to the young girl with her, and this individual passed Aimend various items. At Aimend's command, she began to take pots from the baskets, and from them spoon various ingredients, which were mixed by pestle and mortar. Water was then added to this paste, and Tigernus was then encouraged to drink the solution. It was not altogether successful at first, with some of the medicine spewing from the sides of his mouth. Another white-coloured paste was then mixed and applied to his skin. This seemed a coolant: something to take down his temperature.

"I am not sure what he has," Aimend said, "but it has the properties of a disease... how do I say this?... transmitted through sex.... It's unusual in a boy this young, yes?"

"But he's not had sex."

"Yes – but this is what I notice mermaids often give."

"What kind of disease?"

"It is a form of syphilis," she explained, "though one I have not seen before."

I knew of such ills. I knew what she said was serious.

"Will he get well?"

"I have to be honest with you. This kind of disease, it can be controlled, but he will never fully recover from it. I've given him a solution to kill the infection, to make him well from the inside out, and this cream should help cool him – and ease the scaling of his skin."

"So he is going to be all right?"

She looked at me more hesitantly.

"Do you have any god? If you do, then now is the time to make offering.

Here, this man will go now and make offering to the Calf Goddess for him. This boy is now in her care."

She spoke to Caera in her own tongue and he understood what he needed to do.

"You were lucky to have found us I think," observed Aimend. "He would not have survived much longer. These kinds of curses are very powerful."

Aimend washed her hands in a stone bowl presented by the younger woman. It was intriguing watching her at work. Although she seemed to follow a new kind of science and logic in diagnosing Tigernus' condition, still there was superstition and magic. In her was a curious mixture of the new and old. Perhaps she had been conditioned to use both. It was safer that way.

"Annown isn't it?" she asked.

"Pardon?"

"What you believe in... It is what all the British believe in..."

Now I understood what she was talking about.

"Yes – what most of us believe still."

Aimend dried her hands in a towel. She obviously saw how much the last few days had taken out of my body. Though her face still had traces of that hardness (derived perhaps from years of making the sick better) underneath was a tender concern.

"You should rest," she said. "You need your strength to help look after this one. When Caera is back from the altar, he has plans to cook you a meal of that fine salmon. I'll show you to his hut."

I noticed that Caera had given this woman two of his fish to help pay for her services.

Aimend escorted me to Caera's dwelling. As I might have expected, the inside was covered with wolf and bear skins, but this did make for a warming atmosphere, compared to the gusting rain and mizzle being experienced outside. I wanted to talk more with this Aimend, but she clearly knew her place in this society – she had further patients she needed to attend to. You see, I had wider questions for her about the world I had entered that I felt Caera could not respond to at present. There was still a language barrier.

Then I thought back to what she had said about Annown. If there had been a fogou nearby, I would have gone there and meditated, and thought on the breath of Annown reinvigorating Tigernus. But there were no such structures here. All power would need to come from my own mind. I thought on it. Some time ago, back when I built fogous, I would have done this naturally. In fact, it sometimes came to me on an hourly basis – as part of my day's endeavour. I suppose I assumed it would always be there. Now, distant from the source of my beliefs, I had to work harder to give it energy and presence. That's how it felt anyway.

Caera came back from his offering made to the Calf Goddess. I knew not what he gave her, nor if this Goddess was a living entity. I hoped however that she was benign and not vengeful. Considering she was the goddess of calves (which seemed to me to be sweet creatures) I had a hope that she was kindly.

Communication between Caera and I remained difficult. We both stumbled with words; me with the few survival phrases and words I had gleaned from the past day, and him with everything about my tongue. He did, however, introduce me to his family: his wife, and seven children – and although he carefully told me all of their names, my mind was too full of other thoughts and hopes to remember them. All I knew was that they were kindly and that between Caera and his wife they cooked delicious salmon. I have to say that when the final fish was offered to me from the boiling trough, I leapt upon it, well, like a bear in a stream.

In it, I hoped I ate liberation and knowledge. They seemed as good a motto to live one's life by, as any other.

The night's darkness allowed me to meditate further. I had many questions but these needed to be stilled and forgotten about. Instead, I had to focus upon Annown and its ability to assist Tigernus. I knew he was at a door, and could travel in either direction. I did not want him heading to the darkness though. He had to be pulled back into the light. That is what I thought upon. Somewhere, I hoped the Calf Goddess was doing the same.

When I released myself from this meditation the sounds of the surrounding fort nuzzled into me. Distant was the bleating of Caera's sheep, but closer were the laboured lowings of cattle. It was as if I could hear them chewing cud; their gentle ruminations rocking me to sleep. I had become a baby again, in the caring hands of the Calf Goddess. Rat, normally as inquisitive as they came, was also brought to a peaceful state.

Aside from waking once to empty my bladder of the mead Caera had insisted I drank in the evening, I slept well. The morning brought no lull in the rain and its patter on the thatched roofing was the sound I awoke to. The hides warmed me, and nestled here, amongst these people, I was beginning to dread returning to the ocean. Bleary-eyed, I stepped to the front of the hut and observed the wider metropolis of this fort of the Calf Goddess. To the left of me, the round tower extended skywards – a triumph of design, perhaps built on the money of cattle.

The breakfast Caera's wife offered me was a milky porridge, which warmed my stomach. There was plenty of blood sausage and 'boxty' potato bread too.

The potato bread I fed to Rat and he chirped his approval at the sustenance. By the fact that Caera's crook had gone I assumed he had gone back to his herds on the hills. I therefore almost jumped when he appeared at the doorway ready to escort me somewhere (it felt like he had a habit of doing this). After I had eaten, washed and dressed, he gestured me to follow him. We crossed the town, darting past a marketplace and a well, which was busied by children with over-filled pails fetching water for their mothers' daily duties. Caera checked I was still following him as we entered the inner perimeter of the town, and, from there progressed to a grand structure.

The stonework was different here, almost taking my breath away. Huge kerb stones at the base of it provided a strong foundation. All of these – there must have been a hundred of them – were decorated in triskeles, spirals, lozenges and serpentiform images. They made my own carving back home look woefully naïve. My father would have been in ecstasy at the sight of such work. Caera clearly knew I would find pleasure in such work. He traced some of the forms with his own hands and gestured for me to do the same. I felt its glory and revelled in its creative wonder. Every so often, between these decorative marks, came similar images to those I had seen at the entrance to the fort – the goddess atop her four calves. This structure then, was perhaps their equivalent of our fogou. It was their holiest of places – hosting an altar to the Calf Goddess.

What stuck me was how long-established this cult was. These stones had been in place for hundreds, perhaps thousands, of years. Despite all my skill as an architect I was humbled. If ever I were to return home, then I would take this knowledge with me – and show men and women there what was possible.

Caera beckoned me away from the kerbstones and towards the entrance of the dwelling. He took his own shoes off and I followed suit. Bare-footed we entered what was a vast hall. I suggested that Rat enter my inner pocket, so as not to offend anyone. Hides and straw lined the floor. In recesses made in the walls burnt beeswax candles, and at the far end sat a great sandstone altar. Above it was a vast wooden statue of the Calf Goddess herself; her four calves outlined in the stonework surrounding her, their etching lined with white paint. The statue was as tall as three men, and it had been carved from a single oak. The carving flowed with the knots and lines of the wood, giving the Goddess a tenderness and grace.

Below the altar were many offerings – flowers, fruit, toys, messages and objects as beautiful as any I had seen on my travels. There too, were stone crystals hewn from the earth. Upon the altar were what I supposed were the skulls of four calves. The room smelt of frankincense and combined with the fruits and vegetation left there, offered up a kind of sensual experience that I had not known before.

I wondered where these people's druids were. There seemed no-one coordinating events here. It felt like they just happened – an organic desire for communion and worship.

Close to the altar an early-morning group had already assembled, kneeling towards it, and when we approached they rose and turned towards us. All of them were dressed in fine skins and hides, but one wore a spectacular gold collar. It denoted his power. At its end were two terminal discs – hiding his shoulders while the collar itself had raised bands decorated by rope motifs. Caera knelt before this man; knowing my place in these circumstances, I followed his lead, bowing deeply before him.

"Oengus – is é seo an fear na Breataine Dúirt mé leat faoi," said Caera, arm extended towards me.

I looked up and noticed Aimend in the rear of the group. This Oengus then – he seemed to be the chieftain. If that were so, then Aimend was his daughter. Oengus stepped forward to greet me, placing his hand upon my shoulder. Grey-bearded now, but clearly once flame-haired, he began an oration that seemed long and complex.

"Abair leis go bhfuil sé fáilte roimh anseo, agus go bhfásann sé go raibh maith agat buachaill láidir leis an Corcu Loígde."

Aimend stepped forward.

"He says to tell you that you are welcome here, and that your boy grows strong – thanks to the Calf Goddess."

"Please thank him for me, and tell him I am in her debt."

This seemed the right thing to say. Aimend duly translated my words back to him. Oengus smiled and pointed to where Caera had moved to. There, fashioned from corn and flax, was an image of Tigernus, nurtured by offerings on either side. The same care that I had seen in the stone carvings was here given to accuracy of his image.

"Anois tá mo dhualgas a rinneadh anseo – in iúl dúinn leanúint ar ár n-ullmhóidí cosanta," declared Oengus fiercely.

Those surrounding him affirmed his wishes, and Oengus left.

Aimend leant in to me to translate.

"Don't worry. He was saying that he must leave to continue working on the town's defences."

"Was what he was saying about Tigernus true?"

This was the more urgent matter to me.

"He has made good progress overnight. You will see him soon. He is presently being bathed and cleansed."

Once I knew this, my mind came back to being interested about the town.

"May I ask who is it you are worried about attacking you? Is it the Vikings?"

"Ha ha," she laughed. "If it were just Vikings we should indeed be happy. Besides, Vikings rarely come this far inland. They like to be able to see the ocean. We have not had Viking raids here for perhaps twenty years."

This intrigued me. Whilst the Vikings still pressed fear into the people of the horn of Britain, here they were being dismissed as no threat at all. What were they fighting then? Could it even be Saxons coming in from the north and east? This seemed illogical though, because they had not yet crossed fully into Kembry.

"What we fight you will not want to know," she said. "What we fight claimed my brother Conall earlier this year. It is why we are on guard. It is why, like other fortresses in Hibernia, we built the refuge tower."

"Tell me who you face then..."

"It is not easy to explain," said Aimend, a grace and charm exuding from her lips. "Do you like stories?"

Considering my own tale of late, I wasn't sure I much liked stories any more. I used to think that stories were fictions and fantasy to delight the ear. Most often now, they were coming true.

"Fire away. I can take it," I replied.

"Like most of the troubles of our Age, it relates to the distant past. We are in conflict with the descendants of the Fir Bolg. According to all the books of the invasions, the Fir Bolg were the first people to populate Hibernia. But the lines of our people came from the north. We are Gaels. Gradually we took over the southern lands of the Fir Bolg. The Fir Bolg became weak and dispersed, but over time they have reunited, formed new armies against our occupation here. Their line was broken – but now they recruit mercenaries and the disaffected."

"But this took place hundred of years ago didn't it?"

"It did. But memory is long in our world. Perhaps you know this too."

Aimend had a point. It was the same in the horn of Britain. Events that happened a thousand years ago may appear to have occurred just yesterday.

"It has become more complicated of late. We formed an alliance with those who, each season, arrive from Galicia – these are the children of Breogán. These migrants, the Fir Bolg hate more than ourselves."

"I understand, but surely you are not stuck on some small peninsula. From what I know of it, this land is massive. Isn't there room for all?"

"Perhaps, but it is not just about that."

The conflict here was making what went on in my own home peninsula seem like a futile schoolboy disagreement.

"You see here the way the Calf Goddess defines us. The Fir Bolg strike at that. When they come, they attack not just the people, but raid our cattle. In times before, they have taken our entire herd. We starved in the years that followed."

The practicality of the situation now became clear to me. This was a civil war conducted over the ownership of cattle. It seemed absurd but when cattle defined a people as much as they did here, then it made sense. I imagined what might happen in my own prior life if such descendants of the Fir Bolg dared to take our production of tin away from us. Tin defined us, just as cattle defined these people here.

"But what of these descendants of the Fir Bolg? Why do you fear them so much? They are just men aren't they – not monsters? – and your father seemed to have a well-trained militia here."

"You do not know?" asked Aimend, puzzled as to my innocence.

I shook my head.

She laughed, although the joke was clearly not funny. She changed the direction of the conversation.

"Come, I will take you to see Tigernus..."

"No. Wait. What is it I need to know about these people?"

I could not help but use my left hand to grab her wrist as she walked away from me. She then noticed its deformity.

"Voog, they are not people," she said, drawing breath. "They are giants."

That shut me up. Now I understood.

I had more questions, not just about giants, but about her.

Instead, she struck off towards the entrance of the building, pausing only to put on her shoes. I had been too inquisitive though, too demanding.

Caera, who had been watching and listening to this conversation, saw the importance of the exchange in educating me about the tribe of the Calf Goddess and what they faced. He had heard the terms Breogán and Fir Bolg and knew what we were discussing.

"Mná!" he said, shaking his head, and I knew instantly he meant 'Women!'

He grinned at me; us both knowing the ways of men and women were sometimes very different, despite each trying to please the other.

Aimend didn't look back at us but continued striding towards the medicine hut in which Tigernus lay. The rain had not abated one iota. Around the outside of the fort, I noted Oengus' men making further preparations for defence. Now I knew that we were facing giants, the work they were doing seemed noble, but perhaps less valid. If they were facing giants of the kind I was imagining, then surely they might just step over the palisades and get on with gathering up handfuls of cattle. But then, there was still much more for me to learn.

Inside the medicine hut, I was uncertain about what I was going to find. I had to hope Annown had assisted this Calf Goddess in making Tigernus well again. Maybe even this god of Warna's would have helped too. In the subdivision of the hut where he had been placed, I was relieved to find him now sitting up in bed, alert and with brighter eyes. The whiteness of his skin had dissipated, though still it flaked and scaled. I felt this as I hugged him.

"How do you feel?"

"Better."

I sensed the medicine working.

"Do you know what they used?"

I shook my head.

"Was it druid magic?" asked Tigernus.

"I don't think so. They don't have druids here from what I can see."

"What's it like here? Tell me about it..."

"That can wait," I said, trying to calm his expectations. "You need to get well before anything else."

I did not yet want to mention the word 'giant' either. He'd had good share of mythical beings already.

"Will I recover fully?" asked Tigernus, his tone more serious.

I would have to be careful with what I said.

"The curse she gave you – I have to be honest – it was serious... There may be times it will affect you, but the women here, they seem to have eased the poison from you."

"I see," said Tigernus glumly.

It was a lot for his young mind to contemplate.

"My skin feels better. Before, it was as if it was tightening on me – like I was wearing too small a coat."

"She was turning you into a fish my friend."

"I will be able to come with you, Voog, won't I? On the ocean again, I mean."

In truth, at this point, I didn't know the answer to that.

"And leave me with Puffin and Rat? I don't think so. Rest and you will be back on board."

At this point, I realised Puffin was still fending for himself down at the coast. I had to hope he had not annoyed the cormorant community there. Rat had been with me, but I transferred him over to Tigernus now, who looked like he could do with the company. When Aimend came back in, the rodent hid beneath the skins. She might object to him in terms of hygiene, but maybe not in the sense that his presence would please Tigernus.

"Looking better isn't he?" she said.

It was as if our earlier conflict had been forgotten.

"I am grateful to you," I said.

"There is more medicine for him to take later. Right now, his blood needs to absorb what we have given him. I am glad that the fever is passing."

"If it's not a rude question – where did you learn such skill? My people have nothing like it."

"It's not a rude question but I don't get asked it that often. I am, as you know, the chieftain's daughter. You know the way of our Age, women are second-class citizens. I don't agree with that. The only way I knew I might gain status was to learn medicine. This I did by travelling in Hibernia – and to Llŷn."

"So you trained with druids?"

"Yes, but there, you will find not just male druids, but female ones too. These were of the same lineage as those who cursed Caesar from Ynys Môn."

"Then – why no druids here?"

"We used to have them but their ways declined. People lost faith in them – when the Fir Bolg returned."

Now more was becoming clear. Hibernia was changing in precisely the same way as my homeland.

"There will come an Age when women are equal," I stated. "I know it."

"Will there?"

She tucked in the hides of Tigernus' bed.

"A fine statement from a man. Are you being sarcastic?"

"No," I said. "I honestly believe it."

"I know I told you stories earlier. Perhaps this is one too..."

Whether she believed me or not, at least now this Aimend was gaining a greater sense of who I was. Maybe she was even learning to trust me. Considering what was about to happen, this was to be even more important than I thought.

Dear Caera had become important to me in so many ways. I longed to converse with him properly; to discover more about his life and ways. We got through with grunts, drawings and learning a pidgin-version of each other's tongue. Throughout these conversations with Tigernus and Aimend he had been there – and was, like her, trying to make sense of the man he had found among his sheep.

I understood too, that both of them were offering me liberation and new knowledge. In this I was coming to understand the true nature of travel and further forgetting that I was banished.

I stayed a while with Tigernus that morning to ensure he had everything he needed, and then in the afternoon Caera indicated he wanted to show me something.

Before I left though, Aimend passed me Warna's cross.

"This belongs to you I think. We found it in Tigernus' bed. I don't know what it is or what it means..."

"It's a gift from a friend of ours."

"What does it do?"

"It brings hope."

"Do you believe in it?"

"Does it matter if I do? I asked her back.

I weighed the stone cross in my hand then passed it back to Aimend.

"You have it," I said. "Given these giants, you may need it."

She reluctantly accepted the gift and smiled. Her face told me she didn't know what to do with it. I had to hope she would discover a use for it.

Caera led me outside the fort to where the pens of cattle were housed. Clearly, they were not always placed here. When it was a safer time, they were left to graze in open grasslands – and the men of the Corcu Loígde rounded them up when they were due to be sold or slaughtered. I admired the quality of the cattle they had developed. Some were marvellous beasts of great power. He pointed out their bulls and indicated that this was a strong line – perhaps going back to their original arrival in Hibernia. Caera showed me how astute horse riders looped and circled rope and were able to precisely catch the calf they wanted to look at. I had never seen such skill before. When caught, the men would all run to sit upon the struggling calf, but they meant not to harm it. Such actions were to ensure the beast was well. Out here, the stench of cow dung was obvious. It pervaded everything in the town of the Corcu Loígde. I suppose it was a smell you became used to. Maybe for them, its odour indicated safety and security.

The way the community worked these beasts was as incredible as anything else I had seen there. No man held individual animals. Instead, all the creatures were held by the wider community. Within this system, it meant that no matter how good or bad conditions were, everyone had the same products. There was an equal distribution of meat, milk, hides, horns and bone. This seemed a good way to conduct a society's work, for it made all individuals within it equal – or at least, as equal as they could be. That said, the system allowed for a specialisation of labour, where each knew their place within the society and provided a different service. Thus, as children became adults, they were encouraged to take different paths – but always to realise the significance of cattle in their well-being. I could see now why Oengus and his men would fight to the death for them. I understood why Caera was not only a skilled herder, but also a deft bowman. This society was well-trained for both war and peace.

The principles I learnt here were to travel with me many miles. As you will learn, they will come back to me in new forms for the forging of just such a society. I was coming to much admire the people of the Corcu Loígde.

A few more days passed, and I divided my time between learning some of the skills of corralling cattle and looking after Tigernus. One day during the boy's recovery time, when the mist finally rose, Caera took me back over the hill and down the boulder-strewn valley to the coast. There, I was able to check on *An Ruen* and see that all was well with her. Caera seemed impressed by the vessel. She was fine, aside from rainwater that needed to be bailed out. The eggs from Lund-ey also had to be thrown away as they had rotted in the heat. Puffin applauded my return and seemed to want to come inland with me, but I suggested that he was best suited to the environment of the shore. It felt slightly mad, but I spoke to him, telling him that Tigernus was recovering. With another man, I may have been shy of doing this, but I was sensing just how Caera viewed the world. He saw the creatures as beings and would offer the gentlest words to them in order to soothe them. It did not matter if it were a tiny insect or a snorting bullock.

But it was with a hunter's view of life that he did all this. There was a pecking order to experience in his view, and humans needed to survive just as much as other creatures. With bow and arrow, he then taught me how to hunt woodland deer (these were the shyest variety, of a kind I did not know from home). I explained that we labelled them 'fairie cattle' but I am unsure if he understood. I had used a bow and arrow before, but never with the accuracy or the efficiency he showed me. Likewise, his way of harvesting salmon relied upon the adroitness of wrist and fingers on the bow. Kind as he was, he saw my difficulty with my left wrist, but noted too its extra finger power in pulling back the string. Just like my stone-work, these skills would travel with me. Then I had no knowledge of how important they would be – or what they would come to represent. I suppose too, this weapon would always be handy in times when the descendants of the Fir Bolg might attack.

Tigernus was recovering well. He was able to walk now, and on occasions came with me to visit the altar of the Calf Goddess. I showed him the offerings left for him, and we left further gifts to thank her, and to engender his continued recovery.

Meanwhile, tension in the town increased. Word had come from riding scouts that the Fir Bolg were marching toward us. Oengus' preparations had been justified.

"Should we leave?" asked Tigernus. "I mean, with the Fir Bolg arriving, maybe it's best that we go."

On many levels, Tigernus was right. We had stumbled into a civil war that we had no vested interest in. Were it the Hibernians versus the Saxons, now, that would have been a different matter.

"It depends on how well you have recovered," I argued, "and how you feel. I will not leave until Aimend believes you will endure. You know how careful you must be."

The real difficulty though, was perhaps not Tigernus, but me.

You see, the Corcu Loígde – for all its stench of cattle dung and mad devotion to the Calf Goddess (whose genesis no-one really seemed able to explain to me) – had become important to me. I had learnt to love again here. The people had shown us great kindness. We had been strangers to them, but now – although they knew we came from Britain – we lived amongst them, and knew of their desires and dreams, their frustrations and foes. In short, I felt like I owed them my allegiance. I couldn't just walk away at the prospect of this world being attacked. To tell Tigernus this would perhaps have been fairer, but I thought maybe it would show him my weakness, and he didn't need any more of that. He had already come to know of my lost love and of my banishment. As we were to discover however, our wish to leave came much too late.

Our indecision would turn us into warriors.

DEAR FATHER, I BEGAN MY crossing to you on the first day of March. We left Lulyn as dawn broke, its light silhouetting the triangle of *Carrack Looz en Cooz* across the bay. I know you know that island. The tide was right for our departure, and at the island port there, the tin-laden ships were already taking the same advantage of its height. Compared to us, these ships were huge vessels that dwarfed our form as they passed us. My mind ran to the ships of the *Ancredhor Mor* that Tigernus and you had faced. These vessels and their crews, however, were benign by comparison, and some working on board acknowledged us as we passed between them. These people's different-coloured skins were a taste of what was to come.

I had noticed how cramped things were on board when Tigernus had taken me out fishing in *Warna*, but now I understood the reality of this a little more.

There would be no privacy. Neither would there be any room to relax and enjoy the journey. In fact, this thought was knocked out of me within hours. Tigernus was keen to train me in the ways of mariners, and I did my best to learn and absorb what he asked of me. I made many mistakes.

"I was just like that when I first began," he laughed. "You'll get used to it. I won't tell you how useless I was."

To reassure me, he often held me as we sat in the stern. He understood how the ocean was a daunting place for the uninitiated. I knew I had to stick with it though if I was to accomplish my objective. I already viewed myself as tough, but this voyage was going to harden me further. I felt I was prepared for what it would bring. Even if certain things were to surprise me, I had enough resolve to cope with them. These thoughts swirled around my mind as the coast of the horn of Britain first showed as a grey and green rise behind us, and then fell to a distant, thin line. Eventually, in my work on board, I noticed it was no longer there. When it finally disappeared from my view, much of my past seemed to fall overboard. I cast it into the wake – and there, it could remain. I realised I was now away from all those that had kept the truth from me for so long.

Tigernus caught me smiling.

"What's up?" he asked.

"Nothing," I said. "Just happy – that's all."

In all that I did on those first few days on board *Warna*, I felt I was becoming closer, not only to you Father, but also to Tigernus. I learnt more of his understanding of the ocean, and he began to teach me how to read the weather and the signs and signals of the natural world. I already had respect for the sea, but now I gave it more veneration. Occasionally, Tigernus would release a snippet from the past about the previous voyage. It was something tiny he had forgotten to tell me before. Activity on board *Warna* encouraged this.

"It's funny. Sometimes, it's like I am back on *An Ruen*," he would say, "and your father was sat there, instead of you."

The isolation of the ocean impacted on me. Even though there was considerable daily traffic between the horn of Britain and this new Brittany, we encountered few others. It made me understand how lonely and vast the sea can be. Paradoxically though, it was drawing Tigernus and me closer. That is what travel in such intimate conditions does. We talked about our plans for the future: what we hoped to still accomplish in life; our dreams and ambitions. As sails were unfurled, so was our future. It became clear that what we sought was something very similar. Maybe after the quest for you, Father, had been completed, it would be possible.

The nights were when I became most frightened. Sky and water then merged into a blackness that was overpowering. It consumed me like a drug. Tigernus sensed this in me, and lit the stove, to give out some light in the dark. It was apparently something I would need to get used to; there would not always be the wood for such luxury. Here I was challenged again. Such blackness gave rise to internal questioning. When there was nothing else to view, the only thing you could do was to gaze into yourself. Sometimes we do not like what we see. I was always therefore enlivened by the first lines of light from the east each morning. Each sliver of dawn gave me hope. Then I could stop peering at myself.

In the daytime I had pored over the maps we had from you. The coastline of this Brittany was well-annotated with detail of the names of places and peoples. Tigernus pointed out to me the differences between them – and where their origins had been, back in the peninsula of Britain. Each wave of migration was explained, alongside the power of the Saxons. He traced lineages for me, and explained how the Bretons operated. In a new land, new traditions and customs had emerged.

"Watch for how they speak," he said. "It's different somehow..."

Already it seemed that their tongue had started to shift away from ours.

"Nothing major," he said. "But you'll see what I mean..."

This made me laugh. I had already heard the signs of it in Tigernus' own speech. Twenty years spent with them had shaped this – though he himself seemed quietly oblivious to it.

As well as the maps of the lands nearest us, I also gazed at what was more distant. I tried to gain a sense of what it would be like to travel between them. What would the ocean be like there? Were those islands of Ogygia peopled? What creatures might I encounter? Were they friendly or fierce? Yet, you must know that fears and doubts did not come to me all the time. Sometimes, I was genuinely excited by the newness of everything. But when I became scared, there was not much I could do but reach for Tigernus' love.

One night though (we were perhaps five days into the voyage), I reached for something else. In changing my clothing for something warmer, I noted Howel's book at the bottom of my sack. I had not thought much about it these past few days in the Channel between Britain and Brittany. At first I ignored its form, but there was something in the blackness that made me reach for it. Such books were rare items. The words on the pages had been hand-copied, translated from some other source – Latin probably – and then expensively placed into our own tongue.

I brought the text closer to the stove, so light flickered on the writing. I felt the hide pages and smelt its distinctive odour, born of leather and ink. I traced its string binding where the pages had been tied together. Here, was different knowledge – not that of Remfra's tales or of Casvellyn's faith in the natural world or the glain. I read some from the passages Howel had marked – noting a distant world of characters whose lives were good ones. It made me think of the place I imagined my father was. In the short sections I read, perhaps I could now see what Howel had found, and what this Warna that Tigernus had known, so believed in.

Was I finding comfort in those words? At that point, I did not know.

Tigernus mumbled that he was awake and hungry.

"What are you doing?"

"Nothing," I said.

I slid the book back into my sack.

"Look," said Tigernus, gaining his senses. "Up ahead. Looks like we've found Brittany..."

The pre-dawn revealed a coastline in front of us. We had found old Armorica – but maybe I had found something else too.

20

Interactive Model showing Changes in Sea Level, Cornwall, unknown date
Sea levels rise and fall as the ice sheets advance and retreat, and raised beaches
now mark the interglacial periods when sea levels were higher. Either side of
Penzance, on the beaches at Ponsandane and Wherrytown, evidence of a "submerged forest" can be seen at low tide in the form of several fossilised tree
trunks. Geologists believe that a forest may have existed here before the most
recent sea level rise. Trees identified include hazel and ash. This correlates with
the Cornish name of St Michael's Mount, *Carrack Looz en Cooz* – literally, "the
grey rock in the wood". Large amounts of submerged wood and peat can still
be observed at very low tides, and now form the homes of bivalve molluscs,
piddocks and shipworms. Press button to show sea level changes over time.
Images courtesy of Photomarine.

KNOWING WHAT THE SCOUTS HAD discovered caused a sea change in
the whole organisation of the town of the Corcu Loígde. An attack was clearly
imminent, and under the direction of Oengus (now in armour and without his
statutory gold collar) they set about preventing these fearsome giants from
raiding their stock. The outer pens were hurriedly emptied, and all the cattle
were herded into the rear of the central fortification. There they were corralled
and given enough food and water to last many days. With this, I sensed that
the forthcoming bombardment would be intense.

Likewise the refuge tower was also stocked with food, water and medical
supplies. The sick and the elderly were already placed inside. Anyone who
could handle a weapon was dispatched to the walkways of the outer palisade.
This meant some women and young men, as well as more experienced adult
bowmen. In the hours that followed, many offerings were made to the Calf
Goddess in order to grant protection. I meditated once again upon Annown.
Maybe Aimend looked to Warna's stone cross and hoped it might offer her survival. The rain hadn't ceased, and I got the impression that the townspeople
believed the Fir Bolg liked such conditions for conflict.

Tigernus was out of the medicine hut; his skin was starting to lose its scaly
feel, but I felt he was not strong enough for full combat yet. I had insisted he
went into the tower. There he could do some good; perhaps helping Aimend
with the other needy. Rat, maybe feeling the tension rise, elected to stay with
him – perhaps to Aimend's horror.

If you are laying siege to a town of this kind, you think carefully about when to make your first move. You do not, for example, attack at nine o'clock in the morning just because you feel ready. No, you are sly. You come when humanity is at its lowest ebb. You come when the night offers its own Morrigans and Banshees. Thus they kept us waiting, and in this way tried to tire us out. A night and a day passed, and we were into the second night of the watch. To be honest, by this point, although I feared what was out there, I wanted to physically see what these Fir Bolg were like. I had formulated a plan: if they were giants, then I would aim to ride upon their shoulders, firing arrows directly into their neck, where the blood vessels were thick. In this way, I could take them down. How many of them there were, I could also not derive from Aimend or Caera. No-one seemed to know.

"Sometimes one, sometimes many," was the only response I got.

According to Aimend, I'd know the attack was imminent because the descendants of the Fir Bolg always screamed a battle-cry that resembled the screech of a barn owl. It was this sound that I listened for. Of late, I had faced sea monsters, Vikings, sea witches and earthquakes. Could these beings really be any worse?

Well, on my first encounter with them – perhaps the direct answer would be yes.

There was no battle-cry; only a resoundingly hard set of thumps as somewhere in the gloom of the early morning of the second night, a succession of catapults, trebuchet and ballista launched their swings and projectiles. Their payload was a form of warfare that was meant to melt the brain if not the body. Carcasses of rotting cow flesh showered upon us. The cadavers had been purposely cut open to scatter organs and intestines as they flew through the air coating the defenders of the Corcu Loígde in the body parts of the very animal they worshipped. Subtle it was not, but even I had to admit, it was highly effective in putting the wind up us. The women fighters screamed; men let down their guard. The bombardment went on for some time. To take it up a notch, whatever was out there, next used the heads and body parts of rotting calves. I myself had to scrape the stringy ligaments of a decomposed leg off my shoulder. Now the place not only smelt of cattle dung, but also of cattle death. If their target was the whole of the herd at Corcu Loígde, then probably a few sacrifices of this kind could be made.

I was beginning to understand now why Oengus' preparations were so thorough. Although our enemy was in the dark, we were encouraged to release a hail of arrows to let them know we meant business. From inside the fort, one of Oengus' commanders gave an order to launch their own slingshots of burning fire out into the attackers. These were boulders of sandstones around which were wrapped hides soaked in oil. They burned brightly and had the dual effect of giving light to proceedings and clouting many of the attackers and their machinery. With the flames heading skyward, finally, I could see what we were facing.

The descendants of the Fir Bolg were no giants in the sense that they were as tall as trees or even the kind that Remfra had in his tales of Bryok – able to crush the whole of a man in their fist. No, these were not the creatures of romance. Instead they were just men. What was striking about them – and perhaps where Aimend had conflated fact and fantasy – was that they were extremely tall and muscular. Although I was glad to see that they were not magical beings, I could perhaps see how popular folklore had instilled in the tribe of the Calf Goddess a desire that their foe was superhuman. Although the bombardment coming at me had now turned from dead cow flesh to boulders, I could see that these men were just opportunists; in essence, bullies who sought to not work the land, but instead grab meat and milk from others. That was how they existed, moving from one raid to another. When they had devoured the meat of one settlement, they moved onto the next.

The stones being slung were already ripping gaping holes in the outer palisade. This was exactly the effect they wanted. A number of the Corcu Loígde men were already crushed; flattened dead by lumps of rock. This realisation was the exact moment I heard them scream. This was Aimend's barn owl screech. I could see why she said it resembled that sound, although it was much louder – not just one creature, but from the sounds of it, an entire nation state yelling in unison.

Another way in which the myth of their giant stature may have been accentuated was the fact that this group wore body armour made of metal. Although the Vikings had plates guarding their most vulnerable organs, no force I had encountered completely encased their bodies in metal. This made our arrows useless, unless one caught them behind the knee or at other break points in their exoskeletons. As fighting machines however, I now began to understand the fear expressed in the fortress. I was beginning to wish that Tigernus and I had deserted.

I had no choice now but to leap into the fray and give the best I could. At close quarters, clearly my bow and arrows were useless. I swapped to a sword and shield. Although the Fir Bolg warriors attacked with a ferocity that I had only seen elsewhere in Vikings, their weakness could soon be identified: they moved slowly and turned at a snail's pace. You could jab them several times before they realised where the attack was coming from. You had to time it right though, or else a heavyweight poleaxe fell upon you. We had no armour to match that. In the breach of the outer palisade, our speed and agility proved their downfall. I probably took out eight of their warriors before I was forced to retreat. The normally gentle Caera was a fearsome fighter in this situation. As he swung yet another stroke into one of the Fir Bolg I knew he was doing it for his wife and children. Even a gaping axe wound to his arm didn't stop him. The problem with the attack was the Fir Bolg had the numbers. They could sustain losses because their leaders had recruited many to step up to the front and fill the ranks. Oengus knew this, and once we had beaten back their first line, we retreated.

Who can describe the chaos of war? I certainly cannot. Our numbers were lessened by the release of so many crossbow arrows which cut down the retreat like a scythe through corn during harvest. Men and women fell and scrambled. They looked to colleagues for help but the fallen could offer them nothing. Still the Fir Bolg ploughed through. Some now arrived on horses, and they unlocked the front gate, putting the image of the Calf Goddess and her four calves to the flame. I imagined that this was what it was like for my people in their encounters with the Saxons.

I saw the panic in Oengus' eyes. He knew preservation was impossible now. Perhaps he had tried to develop this location to be one of strong defence, like his ancestors had done before him. Now it seemed to topple so easily. Even the water of the outer trench was easily displaced. The army carried enough wagon-borne stone and earth to fill it and make their own road across it. The Fir Bolg then combined engineering skill with their ferocity. It was a mixture I was not sure we were going to escape from. In these moments, I wanted to be back on the ocean's spaciousness; not condemned to a tower that may as well have been a tomb. This was Howel having his own back: I would see first hand now what it was like to be in a refuge whilst an army attacked.

The cattle sensed the flames and the stench of death. In the inner compound, they were restless, some shoring up on each other, kicking wildly, and snorting their terror and confusion. This fearful animal noise made those in the tower lose a little more hope. I prayed that Tigernus was doing his best inside there.

Caera and I were doing our best to repel the onslaught but we knew the hopelessness we faced. Again, the sheer numbers of their men were pressing against us. The warriors of the Corcu Loígde could take out individuals, but not the whole mass. The whole was too strong; too intense. Already, the inner defensive line was beginning to fail and crumble. Where it had been weakened, men knew their only chance was to make it back to the round tower and climb up the ladder on the outside to achieve safety within the core of the tower.

I was trying to work on a strategy that might help the situation. For certain, the Corcu Loígde were going to lose their herd. It was a given. Knowing this, I wondered if the tribe might use the cattle against their foes, rather than just let them be taken. If we could cause the cattle to stampede, the whole herd could scatter as well, and the thieves may not be able to round them up. In the aftermath, maybe the people here could eventually locate some of their stock and begin once again. How could I get Oengus to enact this plan? How could we startle the cattle enough to make them stream towards the Fir Bolg raiders?

I couldn't communicate verbally with my fellow warriors. I would have to enact my plan individually and hope that others might follow. My rage only increased as I saw the Fir Bolg torch the altar dwelling of the Calf Goddess. In minutes it became a burning mass. Within the corral I selected the biggest, meanest-looking adult bull I could find. He was certainly wary of me, but seemed to welcome his freedom when I kicked the fencing down. Oengus had already stopped fighting, seeing the Calf Goddess burn. It was like an arrow had already entered his heart. But then he saw what I was proposing and this snapped him out of his stupor. He watched intently as the massive adult bull steamed his way down through the town. It scattered the Fir Bolg warriors in different directions and for a while they gave up the conflict. When the bull halted and expressed its desire to rage again back through their lines, another group departed from their duties.

The whole herd had to be let loose. Oengus understood now. He left his own position and beckoned Caera and me towards him. With effort, the three of us could open the main gates. If we made enough racket the cattle would get the message and stampede over the Fir Bolg. The strategy was difficult to enact. At first, none of the cattle seemed to want to move. In fact, they stood as far away from the incoming conflict as they possibly could. We'd have to get in there amongst them and frighten them to scatter. This was a prospect that didn't entirely thrill me. These were large creatures with long horns. In enacting our plan, we ourselves might be gored.

In war there is not much time to think. One just does. One follows one's instincts for survival. This is how I operated. I kept myself low and tried to steer clear of their sharp horns. Yes – their heavy hooves bruised my legs and we were forced to slide and walk amongst the wet dung, but the herd were becoming anxious at our presence and were gradually starting to move out of the compound. It would only take a trickle of some to leave, before the rest would follow.

When it came, it was like an ocean of cattle opened upon the Fir Bolg. Some were instantly crushed. Others were gored. Most ran because they knew they could not stop that many cattle. The Fir Bolg had their cattle handlers, but even those men were rendered useless by this bovine wave. Many were pushed into the earth never to see the sky again.

The lunge of the herd allowed the remaining warriors and Oengus, Caera and me to make it to the ladder entering the round tower. We ensured as many survivors as we could were back safely from the defences, but the ladder rungs were now slippery. It took time for each man to step upwards – time we really didn't have. The Fir Bolg, although stunned from the recent onslaught of cattle, and now blinded as to where their prize had dissipated, were starting to recover and regroup. They were priming crossbows again, ready to not let us rats clamber up into our safe retreat.

Events of the past few minutes had allowed Oengus to see my valour. At least there was one chieftain in the known world who appreciated my endeavours. He made a tight fist at me, showing his approval of my decision with the cattle before climbing the ladder. Being elderly, he was not a swift climber and another ocean of violence was starting to engulf the tower. From here, I could really see how tall these men were. I had thought all humans were much the same size in stature. Now, I knew different. Now, I had encountered giants.

Thick arrows were whistling past the slow Oengus as he made his way up. It was inevitable that he would be hit. He was punctured in the thigh but fortunately, was far enough up the ladder for some of his men to yank him inside. I saw them cut through the arrow, drawing the bladed end out of his leg. He screamed in agony but it was the best thing they could do. Caera was next up the ladder, and being nimble he was up it quickly. Crossbow arrows hit him but they lodged into his many layers of wolf-skins, and he emerged intact at the top.

When my turn came, I had a feeling I was not going to make it. These attackers knew nothing of me; knew nothing of my journey or of my transgression. There they were, pursuing me as a quarry – like some hunted deer or salmon. I prayed to Annown they would not be lucky in their shots. I was a slow climber though – certainly not as quick as Caera. My left hand made it so. Neither was I very adept at dodging the arrows. One fast length lodged itself in the wood of the ladder between my forefinger and second finger just missing skin and bone. I knew what was happening below as well. The Fir Bolg had made it to the bottom of the ladder and were trying to release it from the wall, aiming to flip me backwards. In an instant, I realised I had no control over the ladder any more. I was now in an aerial tug of war between the Corcu Loígde and the Fir Bolg. It swayed so far back away from the wall that I thought I would lose my grip. What had brought me here? I was asking myself why had life presented this moment to me? Even if I got inside, what on earth was to happen next? Why, of all the muddied and random places upon the earth, had I ended up here? Wasn't there a whole ocean to explore?

But then, in that time, I suppose I was experiencing that very moment of panic when, under attack, the village of Carn Euny might seal itself away safe and secure from its marauders. That was what I was being tested for. That was why I was here. I was coming to understand how the world placed me.

The decision I made was momentary but life-changing. I knew the only way to get the ladder back to the wall of the round tower was to swap my weight around. Therefore, on the top of the ladder, I stepped around the side of it and lowered my rear. The Fir Bolg below could not possibly support it, and with my spine I banged back into the hard wall of the tower. Two sets of hands reached down for me, and first grabbing one set and then the other I let them pull me up, kicking away the ladder at the same time. It tumbled to the ground, knocking over a couple of the Fir Bolg. In seconds, I was inside. The iron door was being pushed outwards on its creaking hinges and huge bolts were then rammed across it into their shackles.

At this sealing of our tomb, everyone inside went quiet. Aimend was at work on her father's leg, trying to stem the flow of blood. The crossbow arrow had pierced it all the way through.

"Rinne tú go maith go bhfuil fear le cúig mhéara!" he shouted across to me. Aimend translated.

"My father says you did well there, five-fingered man..."

I nodded.

"Smaoineamh maith a scaoileadh ar an eallach."

"Good idea to release the cattle."

No-one seemed to much care about the cattle. Instead they were now gazing at my strange hand. You did all of that, with that 'thing' they seemed to be thinking.

From the second level of the tower, Tigernus descended down one of the moveable ladders, landing stoutly onto the wooden floor. His relief at my survival was obvious and he immediately hugged me.

So this was it. This was what it would be like in the fogou I had designed for Howel – only, I had to say, probably this tower was more comfortable. Given the way we were sealed, we didn't have much idea as to what the Fir Bolg were up to outside. Perhaps because of the frantic nature of the last few minutes both of these warring parties needed to regain their breath and consider their next move. Perhaps already the Fir Bolg would be corralling up as many of the herd as possible. To an extent though, this was inevitable.

Aimend explained that the tribe of the Calf Goddess had already sent for help some long weeks before. Hopefully, they would only have to survive in the tower for a few days. The Fir Bolg would then grow tired of waiting and push off. That was if they didn't rope off the stone and start trying to lever over the foundations, using the strength of the captured cattle.

"We know Breogán's children will be on their way," she observed. Everyone seemed to know what that meant except me. Clearly it gave the people inside some degree of hope.

My further fear was that the Fir Bolg would manoeuvre their various catapults, trebuchet and ballista closer to the round tower and try to take it out. Aimend explained that she thought the walls were too thick, even for those heavy weapons. The tower had been built with this in mind.

"Let's keep an eye on what they're up to, shall we?" I said to Tigernus.

Although better, I noticed Tigernus had slightly lost some of the spring in his step. A mermaid's curse can do that to any man or boy. We still climbed the ladders to the top of the tower though, passing the various levels of civilisation of the Calf Goddess people. The elderly and the young all gave us a look of fatigue and fear. There was no time to comfort them. We had business to attend to. Tigernus was small enough to clamber into one of the window slits and observe what was happening below.

"They're rounding up as many of the cattle as they can, and looting the huts."

"Stay there. Keep watch. Let me know if they start working on the tower itself."

A couple of hours passed. Inside the tower, there were so many sad and miserable scenes I do not wish to see again. Some of the women learnt they had lost their husbands; children discovered their fathers weren't coming back. Sisters were unaccounted for. There was always hope that some had escaped to a bolt-hole, where they might survive, but most knew the grim reality. Tears flowed and woeful laments and elegies were sung.

On the lower level though, there was a new development. A voice was shouting in to the chieftain.

"Oengus – oscail an doras. Ba mhaith liom labhairt leat!"

"Who's that?" I asked Aimend.

"It's probably their leader – a man called Sreng. The bastard wants my father to open the door so that he can speak to him."

"Is that advisable?"

Oengus shouted something back to this Sreng. Aimend translated.

"He has told him that if he wants to speak, he can do it without the door being opened."

317

"Wise move," I noted.

There was a pause while Sreng considered the offer. Then came his bellowing voice: "Tar, seol amach do curadh chun aghaidh a thabhairt dom?"

I beckoned for Aimend to allow me to understand.

"It's an unusual move – but one of honour. He wants my father to send down his champion to face him."

"You mean in one-to-one combat?"

"Wait," hushed Aimend.

The discussion between the leaders continued. Everyone inside the tower listened intently.

"Not with weapons though, Sreng has said," offered Aimend.

She listened some more and then gave me the gist of what was said.

"He wants to do it like the heroes did in the past: a wrestling match to determine today's outcome. Sreng says that he will still take the cattle, but that if he loses a wrestling competition he will leave us alone – and the Fir Bolg will go back to their lands."

Aimend listened again to what her father shouted back.

"My father says he will think about it."

"Bí gasta faoi. Nach bhfuil mé fuair an lá ar fad píosa tú de cac."

From the tone of these words, it seemed Sreng was in no mood to be waiting around.

This was a turn up for the books. I had not anticipated such an offer, but it seemed by consensus to often have been a way in the past for leaders in Hibernia to resolve a quarrel or dispute. What was with the Hibernians and their champions? This was always the way they did things in the old stories that I knew.

Now coming where I am from, you will know that those of us born in the horn of Britain like, as we say, 'to try a hitch or two'. It is impossible, if you are a boy, to ignore wrestling. Wrestling trains youngsters into warriors, teaches them discipline, cunning, and how to use leverage to shift a weight (ideal, you might say, for the young stone-worker). Some romancers say our very origins are derived from the sport, when those broken refugees from ancient Troy – Corineus and Brutus – arrived at Langoêmagog just over the great river, and that the champion Corineus faced off a huge bugger by the name of Gogmagog. The latter thought he was in with a shout, but Corineus gave him a good scat and knocked him off the edge of the cliff, breaking his jaw bone off. Since then, we boys of the horn have always thought we had a way with the sport. I tried to summarise all this for Aimend but from her puzzled expression I suspect it came out as a blur of folklore and fanciful myth – not fully demonstrating my inherited skill.

"You?" she went. "You really think you can take on Sreng?"

"I will do my best for the Corcu Loígde, I promise."

"Your best may not be good enough. If you lose, they will wreck this tower and us with it."

"Do you have another option?"

She didn't answer. Aimend instead went across to her father, and she, Oengus and others had a heated discussion about the offer Sreng had made, with all of them occasionally stopping to size me up.

I didn't care any more. I had very little to lose – unlike them. I started to speak aloud, so the whole of the tower had to listen to me. I suppose they had become used to this mad Briton around them. This time, they would have to listen.

"Most of you don't know me. Most of you don't understand me – but I have fought for you, because you took it upon yourselves to help. My boy Tigernus has recovered from his illness so I am in your debt, and although you probably judge me by my imperfections (*at this point I raised my left hand*) my people have a fine tradition of wrestling. Maybe this Sreng has expectations about the moves a champion of Corcu Loígde will pull. He has none of me, and my appearance might even be an advantage. It will make him complacent (*this was a feeling I knew well myself*). Let me become your champion, good people of the Calf Goddess."

Aimend took a deep breath and translated for them. They listened carefully and afterwards clapped. A few of Oengus' warriors nodded their approval. They had fought with me now and knew my mettle. I could not really think too much about the rest of the community's thoughts over my volunteering. As an outsider, a loner, a man who would not be missed, perhaps I'd make a good sacrifice. Hearing the uproar, Tigernus came down the ladder into the lower room. He had news that the Fir Bolg were gathering in a circle outside. He was soon brought up to speed by Aimend about what had been happening here.

"But are you any good?" he asked.

"I reckon so."

"When was the last tournament you won?"

"Does it matter?"

"Come on, when?"

"I don't know, Tigernus – when I was your age I suppose. What do you want me to say?"

Tigernus looked at me woefully.

"Don't do it. I've seen this Sreng from up there – and he's big. Looks like he could squash you a like a fly."

"I've got a few moves," I argued.

"I really hope you have."

Oengus was starting to come around to the fact that I would wrestle his foe. For the first time since I had been in the court of the Corcu Loígde, Aimend looked pained. She knew Sreng's strength, but there was something else there too. Aimend was older than me, but there was perhaps a mother's love in her eyes; perhaps maybe even a desire to be young again, and embrace and feel the warmth of this strange-armed fool.

Oengus could barely stand, but he held me by the shoulders and blessed me, speaking once again of the Calf Goddess. Caera shook my hand, shaking his head at me.

"Fool," he said in faltering British, "But a good fool."

Caera undid the locks and pulled back the iron door. I stood in the doorframe and looked down at this Sreng and a circle of Fir Bolg warriors. They had removed their armour now, stripping back to their filthy jerkins and ugly undergarments in the early morning light. Caera and other men helped to lower me down the face of the tower wall. From half way up, it was a reasonable jump down. In my arrival, Sreng sensed Oengus had taken the bait.

"Cé é seo bod?" went Sreng, taking off his jerkin to reveal his barrel of a chest.

He was hairy as a boar and with the breath to match. Close up, I could now see why the Fir Bolg were different from the other Hiberians of the Corcu Loígde. There was something earlier about them – more primitive somehow – in their faces and in their eyes; perhaps even the shape of their jaws and brows. However, he was just a man. He was no giant – just tall and full of muscle.

Sreng noted my mutation and laughed, pointing to the circle gathered around the wrestling space. They peered at my deformity.

Oengus and the Corcu Loígde dared to watch from the open doorway of the tower. I could see other faces crammed tight to the window slits high above.

"An chuid is fearr de thrí?" asked Sreng.

I think I knew what this meant. Aimend confirmed it. The match would be the best of three.

He started to circle around me. We were fighting in a cattle pen, and the floor had been churned by a thousand hooves and mixed by water and dung into a crucible of slippery muck. Getting a hitch would be hard. As ever, it was raining, with the water pooling into green and brown hoof shapes. Sreng reached into the earth and pulled up handfuls of the black-green muck, smearing it over his body and face. In this way, he wanted to make himself as hard as possible for me to get a grip on.

Close up to him, I realised how high he was. Now I understood Aimend's words. Sometimes folklore and yarns were reality. He was a giant. I was no short man, but he dwarfed me. I went for my first hitch by treating him to the best 'hugg' I could manage. I seemed to only really get a grip on his oak trunk of a leg. The move must have looked poor and pathetic from above. Meanwhile, this Sreng was playing with me, so it felt. With one hand I felt he could easily get four points of my body down on the floor. His hand on my chest, the shoulders would be easy – then quickly followed by my lower back and legs. I wasn't going to make it easy for him though. Although he had the grip I was nimble and with some twisting could manoeuvre out of his clutch.

I darted under his legs – a move he did not expect. Then, with some agility I was able to mount his back, me aiming to put weight on one of his hairy shoulders and pull him down. The force required for this was immense, and without too much trouble, he was able to shake me off. I landed hard in the mud, covered in the shit of a thousand cattle. At least in terms of slipperiness to the touch we were both equal. The bastard was unstoppable though, always ready with moves that would be deemed illegal back home. Here, of course, there were no referees. We weren't contesting for pride either: I was fighting in order for the Calf Goddess people to survive.

The Corcu Loígde shouted their support from the tower. People who could see events offered a commentary for those who were still imprisoned.

In the next phase of the match, Sreng found my weakness. In his huge palm he gripped my left hand, and when he had enough leverage he was able to flip me to the ground in one easy motion. I tried to use my feet to trip him but he was solid. The way he won the first fall was easy: he just bent back my extra little finger. The pain of it meant I had to release my grip on him, so he could enact his move and floor me. The way I went down utterly winded me. I could tell by the pause in the cheering in the tower that the audience felt he had almost snapped my spine. I was regretting my choice. I should have listened to the boy. You know me now though. You know I never follow advice.

Advice was being shouted at me thick and fast from the tower above. It being unintelligible to me, I went my own way. In order to bring Sreng down I needed to trick him and perhaps let him think he had the advantage on me, He'd already stomped around the circle soaking up the glory of his supporters. I'd try a flying jump at him and at least try to get some weight on his body. If I could twist his arm behind his back, then I might be able to make him less steady on his feet. The more I twisted, the more it would hurt. I didn't let him go down this direction first of all though. No, instead, I made him feel like he'd got me again – even to the extent of letting him start to bend my extra finger. But I could release the digit this time. Completing it so quickly that I became a blur of energy, he didn't see the jump. That is when I enacted what I had planned. He fell like a freshly-caught mackerel on *An Ruen*'s stringers. The stickiness of the mud and cow-shit wouldn't let him up and I was able to press four points of his body to the floor. While his supporters were muted, mine cheered. It was one all.

In the match, I could tell my body was taking a severe beating. Bruises were already emerging. Much more and I'd be concussed. It was the way he was pummelling me that made it so. Sreng was using his weight and power to grind me down. I could resist, but I was sliding in the shit so much that it was hard to maintain any resistance against him. I had at least tried, but in the final thirty seconds or so of the match, I knew instinctively that I wasn't going to win. Those above me knew it. I could see it in their faces. They were preparing for Sreng and the Fir Bolg boys to destroy all that they had built. Enslavement and abuse would follow. Perhaps further agony and death.

As that final moment of resistance disappeared from my body, I suddenly felt Sreng's body alter. It was as if he became feather light and airy – inflated with some new fascination. I was probably the last to see it of everyone gathered around the ring. Marching down the hillside that I had first walked with Caera on my entry to Corcu Loígde was an army of warriors. Leather-clad, their oval shields were decorated with ornate swirls and triskeles. In their arms they carried both vicious bardiche and lengthy iron-forged morning stars. This was no small rabble of supporters – perhaps from another tribe dedicated to the Calf Goddess – but instead a consummate battalion of soldiers, who looked ready to encounter anyone who stood in their way. Their presence was heightened by the bluster of bombards, bagpipes and war drums.

Sreng left me; his gaze utterly fell onto what was approaching – knowing that their spoils would need to be left. Slowly, he grabbed the pieces of his strewn armour, encouraging his men to do the same. They realised it was too late though for the approaching army was gathering speed, blocking their exit along the entry escarpment to the north and already seizing their machines of war.

"They have come," shouted Aimend. 'I knew the children of Breogán would not let us down..."

Already, some of the Fir Bolg were surrendering. Sreng's demeanour changed and in frustration he punched at the round tower's wall, badly grazing his knuckles. Others more loyal tested these new warriors' mettle, with a show of opposition as they reached the burnt gates of Corcu Loígde. Fresh, and well-equipped, any last bastions of anarchy were soon dispatched by members of the army of Breogán.

The Fir Bolg were rounded up; their weapons seized and their armour shaken off them. It would be molten very soon, and used for better purpose. They were then tied in prisoner lines to be herded into detention pens just like the cattle they had once wanted to steal. I chose not to discuss their eventual fate: the Corcu Loígde would decide that. Although many of the cattle had scattered, several had stayed close to the fort, their capacity to herd had not yet been extinguished. Pillage was taken off the raiders and redistributed to the families from whom it was originally stolen. A new ladder was put up to the round tower, and gradually the people who had taken refuge there returned to their homes. There would first be much mourning and the Calf Goddess would have many souls to lead into her cowshed. The bodies were placed on carts and brought before her scarred remains. They'd be cremated and then placed into nearby passage tombs.

In the immediate aftermath many of the Corcu Loígde hugged and thanked me for my efforts. Aimend did not hug me for I was coated in cow-dung from head to toe. Tigernus also declined, but at least he helped me up out of the mire. In the next few days I was introduced to the leaders of the army who had crossed from far Galicia. These were two brothers: good men named Ith and Bile, who swore an allegiance and union with Oengus and his people.

I learnt that Ith and Bile hailed from the town of Brigantium, and that they had crossed in open sea, avoiding Armorica, Britain and Silura for fear of encountering Viking ships. Any Armoricans I had ever met spoke highly of these men of Brigantium. Their joint power watched over the ocean between them. The bards of the Corcu Loígde were already making stories up about them and me. Apparently, in the tales, the brothers would see the need to travel to the green isle of Hibernia, after standing on a tall tower in their homeland. This green would entice them across to save the people of the Calf Goddess. Such a story was twaddle. It had been Aimend who had sent men across to fetch them – knowing the danger and knowing how close the Fir Bolg really were.

What stories they made up about me I do not fully know, nor perhaps even need to know. In the feasting and dancing that followed I was told one night there would be an epic romance dedicated to my endeavours. Its recensions would be told down the years. Oengus declared that my time here would live on in the memory of the people of the Calf Goddess for thousands of years. I thanked him for that (see, not all chieftains throw me into exile). I could have whatever I wanted. The very best cattle and their finest stud bull were on offer. I chose very little in fact. All Tigernus and I needed were some provisions to set us on our way. Plenty were provided but if we had taken all of them, then *An Ruen* would have sunk with the weight of them. The feasting continued long into the night, accompanied by much piping, drumming and dancing. It was hard to join in, so we remained as onlookers – two souls who had already committed themselves to another beat, other steps.

Caera provided more sheepskins for us. He tried to explain his were softer and that they would keep us warmer if we headed north. There was also a hefty sack of fresh salmon to keep hunger at bay and a new quiver full of balanced arrows, accompanied by a finely made bow. I tried to explain that my journey on the ocean and my time with them had given me great liberation and knowledge. Aimend gave Tigernus a pot of medicine: magic to fight against the infection if it ever came back. She had become very fond of him. It seemed she was not destined to have children – and though we had somehow stumbled into her life, I sensed now that our going would distress her. There was nothing for me except words.

"Whoever she is, she is lucky," Aimend whispered.

She seemed, for a moment, to want to say more – but knew she shouldn't. Perhaps in another life – another trip back from Annown – we might have been together, but she had already sensed my love was elsewhere.

"Never accept fate," I told her. "You have the ability to alter a mermaid's magic. Your abilities can change what is pre-ordained."

The day before, I had noticed Warna's stone cross had been given a place in her hut. She was welcoming change.

I leaned into her.

I whispered into her ear: 'You were our true Calf Goddess weren't you?'

She backed away from me shyly.

That was the last I ever saw of her.

There was no public farewell. I did not want it, and I suspected that if we had had it, Tigernus (now sentimental about his experiences here) would never have left.

When we were finally ready to depart we headed up over the hill to where we had first met Caera. There was the abandoned stone circle of Drombeg; there the upturned boat of the stone sheep shed. I picked my way through the valley in which only ten days ago I had struggled with Tigernus' body.

I had to mark our time here. It seemed appropriate. Tigernus assisted me in levering up a ragged length of sandstone at the head of the valley. There upon it, using a hammer and chisel, I carved an image of *An Ruen* for those passing here to remember us by. Maybe one day, Caera, Aimend, Oengus, Ith and Bile and their children and grandchildren would see it too – and recall the time we two stood by them.

Puffin gave a caw of welcome at our return. Rat buried into the soft new sheephides. The inlet had a peace that contrasted markedly with the earlier clamour of battle. Both Tigernus and I knew our respective tasks in order to make *An Ruen* carry us once again.

Not far away from us, in the deeper water of the inlet, were the vessels that had carried Breogán's warriors across to here from Galicia. They waved an acknowledgement, learning over the past few days who we were. For the moment, their travels had reached a conclusion. In so doing, they had saved a civilisation. Their odyssey had been a noble deed.

We both felt we had come far in our odyssey upon the ocean. In truth, we were just beginning. I let out the sail and we left the inlet, pushing onwards towards an unknown west.

CAN YOU HEAR ME? I hope you can, Father. I have much to tell, just as you have much to tell me. Let us listen to each other. Let us talk. Let our memories work like fishing lines. Let us catch our stories.

I am talking to you now as I run towards you.

Although we had located the northern coast of Brittany, it was not here that Tigernus had in mind as our initial destination. His ties in the country were much further to the south, where many of the Britons had set up new colonies. We did, however, put to shore on one of the white beaches to seek fresh water and firewood. Stepping onto new land after the ocean was an experience I had not encountered before, and in the seconds when we emerged from the breaking waves onto the sand, I savoured the moment. The land felt strangely secure after our five days at sea. I gazed back across to the north from where we had come. It seemed so distant now. It was only a short distance compared to what we planned, but it could have been a world away.

On the rocks we found mussels and boiled these on the beach to make a midday meal. The flesh of them made good eating.

"Always make use of what is available," said Tigernus. "Save the long-lasting foods for when you really need them."

Later that day, we pushed off and travelled in a westerly direction following along the northern beaches and cliffs. By nightfall we were starting to turn south, rounding the head of land that jutted into the ocean. Tigernus pointed out places to me but these I have now forgotten. I kept looking into the west, expecting to see something emerge; expecting the land I so desired to step on, to somehow be close. I wanted it to rise before me in an instant, but I knew I had to be patient.

The seas around this coast were not entirely calm. I experienced my first taste of the true rise and lull of the swell, and the continued spray of salt water in my face. The upward and downward motion pushed my heart into my mouth, and there were times when I wished I could have reached for words of comfort from that book. Instead, it remained stowed in my sack – away from the damp and wet. You will notice that you, Annown, were not travelling with me at this point. I had seemingly left you behind. You hid alone, back in the rear of the fogous of Chysauster and Carn Euny, or maybe unaccompanied high on the moor. There and then, I doubted very much that I would find you again. Perhaps I should have more faith, though admittedly it was hard to find it sometimes in a vessel as small as *Warna*, on so vast a bowl of water.

The state of the sea meant it took us two more days of travel to reach a good-sized sweep of a bay further to the south. This was after passing the western inlets and several capes which were dotted by British settlements. I realised what journeys these people had made in order to gain their freedom. What faith they must have had.

Tigernus pointed to our destination. He seemed to relax more. These were waters he knew intimately. Maybe he knew that mermaids did not exist here. He was enjoying more of the romance of the journey. We became Voog's children once more. We headed towards a now long established settlement tucked in to the east of the bay. It had been some twenty-five years since migrants had first moved here, and now they had carved out a lasting piece of Britain in old Armorica. The house designs were familiar.

We docked at some wooden landing jetties and tied off *Warna*.

"This way," said Tigernus, pointing up to a run of houses that watched over the harbour. "We'll see what we can do about getting you across."

At first, Tigernus held my hand. Our presence raised a few eyebrows. Clearly, they knew Tigernus, but not me. I heard mutterings questioning who I was. I could tell they were talking about him and this new girl.

"In here," said Tigernus. "This is whom we need to talk to. For a minute though, just wait there."

He let me go. I stood by the door, and watched Tigernus creep up on a man who was sat with his back to me, warming himself before a fire. Tigernus placed his hands over his eyes to surprise him, and then jumped in front of him. The man stood up and hugged him. Clearly, they were old friends, although the way the man spoke to him was more in the tone of a father.

I overheard snippets of their conversation.

"Son, what brings you back so soon? I thought you were headed for Scathynys."

"Well, I was – but my plans have changed."

"But it was your heart's desire to return there, was it not?"

"It was. But I told you. I first went to the horn of Britain to seek Orla."

"Eh?"

"You remember? This was Voog's woman. Don't you recall? All those years ago when you took me back here..."

I listened while cognition and memory worked together in this man's mind.

"Voog?"

"Yes. The man who was with me.. Don't you remember? His wrist..."

"Ah... Ah.. Now I know who you are talking about: that madman who wanted to push on alone. He's probably long dead by now."

"Maybe not," I interrupted.

"Who is this?" the man asked.

"This is Blejan – and she is Orla and Voog's daughter. Voog knew nothing of her."

"Voog's daughter, you say?"

"Yes."

"What do you want with me?" the man asked.

"I want you take me across the great ocean so that I can find him," I said, taking control of the conversation.

The man laughed.

"What's so funny?"

"You – and what you ask for. You'll never find him. Not in a million years."

"Why not?"

"Who on earth knows where he is? He could be anywhere."

"I want you to take us to the part of the coast where you left him. That's a start."

"What – just like that? I've got enough problems here without traipsing half-way across the world."

"I will pay," I said. "I have money."

"No matter. I'm too old now for such crossings. When we were young men – yes, we believed we might sail around the world. What fools eh? Not any more though. See this limp ? – That's where some Saxon impaled me. Tigernus here knows. He knows what we have been through."

"I know what you have been through. We have been through some of the same nightmare at home – but Tigernus tells me that if anyone can make this voyage, then you can..."

"My crew from the old days have long since scattered. Loic's passed on. You know this Tigernus – and my coxswain Rosparzh, he seeks only the peace of farming these days. Times have changed. Sometimes men have had enough of adventure."

"But you are the fabled Corentin are you not?" I said, flattering him. "This man here has told me much about you..."

"I am that Corentin," he said. "once of Caresk, and now of Douarnenez."

"You once sought your son didn't you, who got left behind?"

"That I did – and this man here helped rescue him..."

"Then if you know the love a father expresses for his child, then think too of the love a child has for their father. Help me."

This man Corentin was put into thought. I could tell he viewed me as brash and outspoken. I was speaking words that only men normally got to say. Who on earth did I think I was? No doubt he was viewing me a maid with a big gob. Yes – a maid with a vug-hole for a mouth.

"Time for one more adventure eh?" Tigernus put to him.

Corentin did not respond but remained in contemplation.

Finally, he responded with, "I suppose idle hands are not good for a man. Perhaps I have one more puff of wind."

"Are you sure?"

"Of course I am. Beats sitting around waiting for some boiled mackerel head of Saxon to turn up..."

"Good. Good. Now, where is she?" asked Tigernus enthusiastically.

"*Azen*? Oh, she's still about," said Corentin. "A bit older, a bit wiser... like all of us."

My face revealed my puzzlement as to what they were discussing.

Later, it became clear what was being gabbled about. It was my ride across the ocean.

VOOG'S OCEAN

Try

"The natives of Pretannike who live on the promontory called Bele-rion are especially hospitable to strangers and have adopted a civilised way of life because of their contact with external traders."

From *Peritou Okeanou* [*On the Ocean*] by Pytheas of Massalia, *c.*325 BCE, quoted in Diodorus of Sicily.

"And thy seed shall be as the dust of the earth, and thou shalt spread abroad to the west."

Genesis, 28:14

21

Harness fitting, Penwith, Cornwall, 5th to 6th Century CE
Held within a private collection, but currently on loan to the British Museum, this elaborate bronze plaque was found some time before 1804 on the Penwith Moors. The design on the piece is more or less symmetrical and would have been worked in a wax model before being encased in clay to form a mould and then cast in bronze. The size and shape of this piece suggest that it was more suitable for a pony than a horse.

THE COASTLINE OF SOUTHWESTERN HIBERNIA was jagged and ominous. Low, swirling cloud covered the lichen- and algae-encrusted rocky peninsulas that jutted into the flat ocean, sometimes obscuring them completely, sometimes releasing them, and so the land mysteriously disappeared and reappeared again.

Such closures and revelations were to be all part of the next phase of our voyage.

Like a long slingshot, we knew we were being catapulted around the bottom of the island, and that at some point we were going to be released into the full fury of the wide ocean – a place about which we actually knew very little. The ocean here seemed to be grabbing us, reaching out underneath our vessel and willing us forward with eight fingers. Despite the huge vistas that opened up before us – distant black mountains, long heron-populated estuaries punctuated by momentary breaks in the damp cloud and thick moss that coated the timelessness – there was an incredible stillness to our progress. *An Ruen* itself seemed to calm the very waves, and the water lapped less, broke more softly on her bow. After the clamorous events inland, this peace was welcome, and yet it also seemed to herald something else – isolation and loathing perhaps.

We skipped then from shadowy headland to shadowy headland, each poke into the vast sea followed by a succession of low islands that had fragmented from the whole. Human life was completely absent; here there were not even grazing cattle or hardened sheep. I had to remind myself that we were at the very limits of the continent we knew. Somewhere in those days we witnessed the summer solstice: our *Howlsaf*. We could not be sure of the precise day: there was no stone to mark it, no entry point in a souterrain for the sun's rays. Back at Carn Euny they'd be lighting roaring midsummer fires upon the moor; Casvellyn would be conducting due ceremony at Boscawen Ûn – gathering all of his order from over the peninsula. But at this, I remembered my mother's words: *En Hâv, perkou Gwâv.* In summer, remember winter.

The weather too did not indicate the height of the year, yet still we praised Annown and marked the time with ritual and observation. Knowledge of this was important: we knew that whatever part of the voyage we now faced, the days ahead would grow shorter; the nights longer. Neither of us needed to say it – we knew we were heading northeast, and that certainly meant our lives were going to get colder. We were going to meet snow, ice and frozen seas. I could barely contemplate what these looked like.

Smaller bays were echoed by larger ones: whole oceans in themselves – where nature had escaped the hand of any human. Creatures showed us no fear at all. They knew nothing of the bow and arrow, the net or the hook. Keeping fairly close to the birdlife, fish shoals and shore helped us feel safer I suppose. It was one last handshake before the vacuous horizon.

I had wondered if this was indeed far enough away from Carn Euny? Was this the safest limit? This world looked like it could sustain a man.

Perhaps I could fit in here.

But I couldn't stop.

That was the irony. I had to push on and discover now. This was my new role. Before these days, I had not realised how much it burned inside me; how much this quest was now a part of me. This turned in my mind as I turned the clay figure in my fingers; the fragile item somehow surviving the attack of the descendants of the Fir Bolg.

I looked at my crew. Tigernus was transforming from a boy into a man. He had been an innocent. Now he was experienced. Rat – the very soul of whom I had detested and hated not so long ago – had shown me the importance of not making rash judgements, the very thing I always hoped people would not do about me. And then there was Puffin – this dear creature entertained me more than I can ever say. His flight, his persistence, his wonder – they were the same mottoes I was living by. Because of this there were some days on this stretch where I genuinely forgot who I was. Fogous and stone became fictions. I had to think hard about what I once did. I suspect I had trained my mind to feel no homesickness; to live only in this present.

Conversation on board *An Ruen* had been routine. We might have reflected further on the events at the muddy fort of the Calf Goddess, but not enough time had yet passed. I kept my eye on Tigernus, watchful of the ocean too. I wanted him to suffer no further curse of the deep. I have told you how Tigernus was now experienced in the ways of the world. That moment of understanding of this shift I can easily recall. We had rounded one of the longest peninsulas and we were about to pass between two forsaken islands north of it. Tigernus was wistful, thoughtful, sat at the stern with me.

"You should definitely have gived her one," he said, offering me the benefit of his wisdom.

"Who?"

"That Aimend..."

I had to ask him to repeat what he said. He did so.

I was shocked, but listened.

"It's obvious you liked her," he continued. "And she liked you. She wasn't married. No kids. No ex around – and good with medicine. What more do you want?"

I spluttered my disbelief at this boy's assessment of the situation. I shook my head at him.

"You sorting my love life out now are you?"

Satisfied, Tigernus put his hands behind his head and stretched out.

"Someone needs to."

"She was much too old for me," I offered.

"Pretty though," countered Tigernus. "Some older women are hot."

I glared at him.

Where had the guileless boy of Scathynys gone?

It was another five minutes before he spoke again. By now, we had sneaked between the two islands, our baited lines pulling a good-sized crab from the depths, which would make for tasty eating later.

"You have a lot to learn about life and love boy," I said.

"Why's that?"

"It is more complicated than you make it out to be."

"It's not complicated though. She told me she liked you."

I raised an eyebrow to him.

"I cannot be *fixed* in the way you wish."

"You over women completely then?"

It sounded like Tigernus now had plenty of experience himself.

"Over?" I laughed.

"Yes – like the reason you voyage to the horizon?"

"Well, when you put it like that Tigernus, yes, I suppose you are right."

"How can it be resolved?"

I could not answer him.

"Warna said you will find her again."

"Let me remind you: Warna said a lot. Most of it was gibberish. Don't put too much measure in what she said. The ground snatched her away – what more can be said?"

There was a pause again, as each of us thought through past conversations. These pauses said as much as the words we spoke. This is the way it was on board a boat.

"I wish I had the chance to meet this Orla," said Tigernus.

"Why's that?"

He thought about it.

"So I might better understand you."

On days like this, Tigernus' insight scared me in its accuracy of understanding humanity. Not wishing to deal with this right away, I gestured at the pot and we lit a fire. For our lunch we would have the crab, dressed with herbs and seaweed. As we ate, we traced the curvature of a bay that had a sandy beach to the distant northeast. A bright rainbow bounced across it. The boy's words and the beauty of the landscape made me think further. Although there might have been good reasons (and, if I am completely honest, Aimend was one of them) to have remained at Corcu Loígde, I had to stay true to myself. Beyond that was oblivion and apocalypse.

"I have to stay true to myself," I said.

"Just testing," came the boy's response, and he smiled as he fed the last of the crab meat to Rat.

Later he asked, "Will you teach me how to wrestle some time? You were pretty good you know – *considering...*"

"What do you mean *considering*?"

Not much more was said that day. The cloud lifted, but the wind dropped. Our progress started to slow down. Possibly, it was an indicator that we needed to rest, and this bay seemed as good a place as any to halt in.

We still had the salmon Caera had provided for us, and this river fish made a change from the salty variety we had become accustomed to. *An Ruen* was well-stocked at this point, and we perhaps revelled and ate a little too well that night for our own long-term good. Sometimes though, the frugal nature of our life on the ocean had to be sidestepped. In the back of our minds, we knew more parsimonious times were ahead of us.

"Tigernus, you've no regrets at coming with me?"

I asked the boy this because he had suffered much. So much was still uncertain.

He shook his head.

"I'd only be facilitating the bastard *Ancredhor Mor* to make further raids," he said.

"And do you think much of your father and family?"

"Often," he said, "but not so much that I would rather be with them than here."

We started to settle into the sheepskins. The night was now a little muggy, but the sky was clear of cloud.

"As I see it, none of us can remain as islands or upon islands," the boy reflected. "If I had stayed any longer, I would have gone mad. This life is what I always wanted. To see other people, to meet new people – whatever they're like – that's what I need."

This seemed a good point to conclude our conversation. Every day the boy was not only growing physically, but mentally as well. It seemed he was turning into an adept philosopher. Some days it felt like I was travelling with Plato. Back home, a boy like him would have been selected for entry into the druid order. He had the kind of insight they liked; though perhaps not the discipline they required. I eventually reflected that he was better off without them.

Markers come in different ways in the world. Signals come at us from so many angles. Most times, we fail to read them or if we do see them, we fail to act upon them. Sometimes those markers come when we are not looking for them – or when we least expect them. Only later do we understand their meaning – their liberation, their knowledge. It was to be the case that night.

An excited and nervous Tigernus woke me.

"Look, look," he said frantically, pointing up at the night sky.

Only half awake, I did as he wanted and looked upwards at the bright cosmos.

Tigernus' finger was tracing a fiery shape as it moved across the sky. This was no usual star, nor even anything falling from the firmament to the earth. The moving object was glowing, and behind it trailed a tail of luminescent material that almost seemed to spark and phosphoresce. Its presence in the night sky was overwhelming; all other lights became dulled.

"What is it?" the boy enquired. "I've never seen anything like it."

I watched it for a while, sitting up straight, trying to confirm in my own head what I thought it was. I had never seen such an object before myself, but I had heard tell of them.

"Is it Warna's God throwing weapons at us? Or is it a Fir Bolg of the sky?"

"No, it is neither of those. What you see crossing the sky there, is a comet."

"A comet?"

"Yes. *An steren lostek...*"

Tigernus knew what this meant. He translated it back to confirm he was right.

"Long-tailed star...?"

339

"It's not really a star, not quite..." I tried to explain. "The druids say it is a piece of rock – perhaps a broken star – moving through the sky. For them, it is the 'hair of the head' in the sky."

With my hand I drew in the air a disc with three strands of hair emerging from it; the strands imitative of the comet's tail.

"That's the symbol they use. I've seen it in their writings. They sometimes carve it too."

The celestial object had an incredible beauty and wonder to it. I was glad Tigernus had woken me so that I could observe it. I explained that such sightings were few and far between. Most people only ever saw one or two in their lifetime.

"Is it from Annown?" asked Tigernus.

"Not likely," I replied. "Not up there..."

"What do the druids say?"

"They say a lot, but don't put too much measure in what they offer. You know that."

"How do you mean Voog?"

I waved my hands in the air, simulating a scary prophecy.

"Oh you know... *Signa*! *Portenta*!"

I exaggerated these last two words, saying them in the Latin (oh, how I would eat such words the next day), but also sarcastically, so hopefully the boy would understand that no value could be put into their presence.

"They're just a natural phenomenon, Tigernus. Like the earthquake, yes? Like plesiosaurs?"

Tigernus watched it again. Distant, his eyes saw a burning ball of fire, perhaps heading to earth. Always curious, he had to respond to me.

"So they are signs then?"

"People have read them that way... but it is nonsense."

"How do you mean?"

"Well, my view of this kind of thing is that always in prophetic literature and stories, it was easier to write about prophecies after certain things had happened. Noticing a comet was far easier once something major has occurred. Noticing before is a bit of a problem if nothing scary comes to pass. You can go on waiting for days, months, years."

I thought of Remfra, whose fantastical tales often featured the arrival of a comet.

"For what?"

"Oh, you know – bad omens... Look, don't let any of that nonsense seep into your head. Just enjoy it for what it is."

Perhaps later I would eat my words, but then I could see nothing that was remotely malefic in intent. You must decide if my words here were true or not.

"Go back to sleep now."

I shut my eyes and when I next opened them the comet had long since passed overhead. A blue sky had returned, and Tigernus was at work in the canopy cooking wheat cakes, and plating up a piece of smoked herring for me.

"I was hungry," he managed to say, swigging deeply from one of the skins of water.

"Go easy on those," I said. "We don't know where the next lot will be coming from."

"Eat your fish," ordered Tigernus. "Good last night wasn't it? I'm glad I saw that thing in the sky. I just hope it won't jinx us."

"That thing won't offer any curse, don't you worry," I said, taking the fish, and then pushing the plate back for Tigernus to place one of the hot wheat cakes onto it. Puffin and Rat were also breakfasting; Puffin on some freshly caught sprats and Rat on a plateful of un-ground wheat grains. After gulping these down, the bird went on another food mission, flying out to sea.

"I thought you said that bird of yours would find a mate," I said.

"Don't you worry. He will."

Puffin's clean flight over the waves focused my attention in that direction. Obscured yesterday, but now possible to see in the clarity of the morning were two islands sat to the northwest of us. They were not like the other low rocky islands that we had traversed in the bays. Instead, these two were mountainous, huge pyramidal forms poking out of the ocean. In that light, they seemed snow-topped, but this was not really the case; the white was merely the guano of thousands of seabirds who constantly nested and to be absolutely frank, shat upon them.

"Perhaps over there," I suggested.

"Where's that?"

"*Sceilig Mór.*"

It was a name Tigernus recognised. We had been talking about making it here since Deheubarth. Old Gofan had known of this world. It had been the limit of his understanding; the very edge of his map.

"No point in waiting around," said Tigernus. "Let's go."

Small islands he seemed to like. Well, they were embedded in him. They were manageable worlds I supposed.

With breakfast still in one hand, he was unfurling the head sail and testing the wind's direction. It wasn't perfect. It was coming strongly from the northeast and too much of it would track us back to the southwest. We'd need to cut across it, which as we found was difficult in these waters. There was quite a current operating, and the swell was immense. At this, the breakfast was not sitting in our stomachs quite as well. Still, as ever, we persevered, not really knowing who or what we would encounter there. For the first time in a while, on the main mast, I saw him notice my mason's mark. I could see him contemplating whether what I told him about it was true.

Perhaps my aim in reaching the islands was different from Tigernus'. The boy liked islands for islands' sake. He loved their isolation and their wildlife. I saw a different purpose. I was hoping it might be occupied. If so, then whoever lived there might be able to give us clues about what lay out there – beyond the islands' peaks. You will know I was seeking directions and coordinates. I was seeking somebody to show me the way (though might it be said that all along it was always Orla).

The scale of the two islands that formed *Sceilig Mór* was not possible to assess at distance. Far away, they looked innocuous and easily surmountable. Up close, they became thrusting mountains of the kind that we had not seen so far. We reached the smaller of the two islands first, and this was enormous enough. Upon its cliffs was an array of birds that we had perhaps not seen the like of since Scathynys. Most noticeable were the gannets – flashes of bright white plumage and orange heads, but there too were large colonies of fulmars, kittiwakes, razorbills and gulls.

Nestled into some of the crevasses and nooks were puffins. Our Puffin kept a steady watch on the communities above him, seemingly almost overwhelmed with the world emerging around him. Given that birds seemed to own this island, we expected no form of human life upon it, and in our circumnavigation of it, we found none. A few plants clung to the rock – sea pinks, campion and spurrey. None were particularly nice to eat, but if we were desperate enough they would do. Foraging here would be impossible though. The swell was so great that we could not possibly have brought in *An Ruen* close enough. Neither would it have been possible to have used the coracle. That vessel had enough difficulty remaining attached to us anyway, given the conditions. We were constantly re-securing its knot to us.

"Have a look," suggested Tigernus to his bird, but despite his encouragement the *scath* would not fly. It seemed frightened of the size of colony that existed here.

"That seems to have shut him up," I argued.

"He's looking," protested the boy. "Sizing things up."

Rat – who often travelled in the coracle – had come up to the main vessel for this part of the voyage. He had noticed that things were rocking a little too much back there, and found solace in the larger vessel. He was up on the bulwark sizing up all the egg-devouring opportunities of this place. I warned him to be careful; the conditions could easily knock him clean into the ocean.

Tigernus turned to me. He looked green.

"What's wrong? Not the curse is it?"

"No, sea-sickness," he mouthed.

This was the first time I had seen him affected in this way. It wasn't a good sign considering we should soon be out on the wide ocean. The waves were rolling here though.

"Sit more in the middle of the boat," I suggested. "It doesn't roll as much there."

He tried taking my advice, but before he could reach the centre-point of the vessel, he had to retch over the side.

"You all right?"

I wondered why I asked this. He was most definitely not all right.

"Better out than in," he managed to say, spitting out the rest of the bile.

If this was a taste of things to come then it was not very flavourful.

In these kinds of conditions, *An Ruen* was difficult to manage. Tide, current, swell and wind all seemed to be pulling in different directions. In order to offset their battle for control of us, I suggested we made use of our oars. One had been lost in our fight against the mermaid, but there were still enough spare ones to put out on both sides. To be frank, initially Tigernus wasn't much use, but as his colour came back, he worked the blade better.

The second, larger island gradually rose before us. This close, it eclipsed the sun and we saw its immensity. Perhaps one time it had been some outpouring of lava from the ocean: a volcano erupting from an unsteady sea bed. At its very peak, the rocks divided, so that there was a kind of pass between them – but down here, we were a very long way from those heights.

"You sure you want to step on there?" asked Tigernus.

His words did give me some doubt. The effort of putting into one of this island's coves may not ever justify our presence on the rock. There might not be anyone, or anything there.

We actually brought up *An Ruen* into a reasonably protected cove – coming in from the northeast. The swell here was still gaping, and I did not know how we would step across from the vessel onto the shore without falling in and being carted off by the ocean. I was worried too about the stress on her hull, but given the situation and her present position, there was not much I could do. If she were wrecked, at least there was something we could scramble onto.

"Let's leave it a while," I said, "and get the measure of it before we do anything."

This was a wise move. We noticed that the ninth wave usually offered the largest swell. The one that followed in the next count gave less height. It was on this beat that I decided I might be able to make the stretch across to some of the low-lying rocks, which were sometimes engulfed by the swell, but also led back to safer, dryer land.

"Rope me," I suggested.

Tigernus was still looking a little queasy, but as if an experienced Corcu Loígde horseman, he wrapped a length of beeswax encrusted flax around me, and tied it to the main mast. If I went into the blue, at least I wouldn't be swept out into the open sea.

"Onen, dew, try..."

I made the leap across, slipping slightly, but nevertheless making it into the shallows of the rock shelf. I tied the flax that was on me to a nearby rock column. This would help hold *An Ruen* in place.

Tigernus did not look comfortable making the leap. He had already delayed his jump by throwing across some equipment: my sack containing food, water, Warna's holy book and my scrawled maps.

"I'll stay here," he offered. "And look after *An Ruen*..."

"No," I asserted. "You're coming with me."

I had to remember the size of him. Although Tigernus had grown, he was still tiny compared to me. What was a tricky jump for me was a wide chasm for him.

"I'll catch you," I said. "Just make sure that you're roped to the mast and you'll be fine."

Tigernus was triple checking that the knots he had tied were secure enough.

He closed his eyes as he made the leap. He was stretching into realms he'd really rather not see. Perhaps out here on *Sceilig Mór* he knew it.

The boy timed the leap rather badly, catching the end power of the ninth wave. He was anticipating the next lull, but in his desire to make the jump edged forward a bit too quickly. I caught him with my right hand; my left would not have the strength and would have lost him.

"See," I said. "Not too bad was it?"

I noted Tigernus look at the wash below him, glad that he had not succumbed to it.

"Rope that one off will you?"

He did as I suggested.

We had to hope *An Ruen* would survive the onslaught. Otherwise, we were about to become this island's latest permanent residents.

What greeted us initially was desolate rock. Its immensity is difficult to convey now, but in order to climb the pyramid we wound our way around its base towards the west, trying to gain altitude alongside our longitudinal path. A direct vertical climb seemed impossible. Were there pathways here? It was hard to tell. Occasionally, it felt like certain routes had been crossed many times before us; other times, it seemed we were quite alone. The push upwards was hard. Both Tigernus and I were reasonably fit, and you would think that after our encounters with the Fir Bolg such a structure would not defeat us. However, the climb was both difficult and treacherous.

"You sure this is worth all the effort?" puffed Tigernus.

"Someone'll live here," I huffed back. "Bound to."

The climb to the summit could not be completed in one day. Given the hard sailing and the rowing we'd had to endure since passing the smaller island, and now this punishing trek toward its high altitude, we were exhausted. Certainly, this was no easy horse track from Lulyn to Carn Euny. I might have gone on further, but I could tell Tigernus was exhausted. I had to be careful, knowing his fragility; knowing what Aimend had said of his future. I needed his companionship and he needed my care.

I contemplated how this place was like something out of a myth. Why was I here? Why wasn't I safe – still building dwellings at Kynance?

The night was warm enough for us to rest without too many layers of hides. One each was sufficient. From here we could look back to the coast of Hibernia, and halfway across sat the smaller island, now bursting with roosting birds. We ate blood sausage, boxty and hard bread. Skins of water slaked our thirst.

To our astonishment, Puffin arrived. How Tigernus knew him from any other bugger I will never know – but perhaps there was a quickness to him, a sharpness in the eyes that others lacked. He had been busy, so it would seem. Another female bird had obviously caught his eye, and he was dallying with her; showing off. Puffin completed a few aerobatics and then danced before her.

"See," went Tigernus. "Told you."

"Looks like I'm going to be one crew member down again."

"Hope she's a good mate for him."

"My friend, this Puffin seems to have reached his horizon, his destination – that rock in the ocean. He has found what he sought."

Probably Tigernus wanted some lasting goodbye, some final hug, but animals do not really show love in this way. They stay with humans because they have a food source. Life becomes easy. They really offer no loyalty. We may think they do, but we just project human emotion onto them. They are sharper than that; better survivors. And so the pair took flight. Puffin's time with us was over.

After this leaving all we could do was marvel at the life of the puffin colonies on both of the islands, and hope all was well – both at that moment, and over the coming time. Puffin's going was another portent of Tigernus' inescapable passage to maturity; of leaving one known world for something utterly different. This was Annown's way, I believed.

When night drove in, we scanned the heavens once again to see if the comet was still winding through the blackness. There was more cloud cover tonight, and so it was hard to even discern the normal stars. We resolved to rest for a while, and then look again when the moon was higher.

"There!" I nudged Tigernus to eventually show him the disc and its trail once again. "Do you see it?"

Tigernus was sleepy but had enough wit about him to view the orb's crossing. Tonight its tail was brighter, fuller.

"Did it prophesise Puffin's leaving?" he asked.

"Good point," I said. "I see you're understanding this prophecy thing. Always work backwards – that's the key to it. Nice one."

I reflected upon what dark, undiscovered oceans there were in those heavens – ones that, inevitably, I would never come to see. Still they watched me though, and I made connection to them somehow: oceans fell into each other and time fell apart.

The philosophy I had drifted into was sharply halted by the sounds of voices. Tigernus' body went rigid. He heard them too. We both listened, and could make out only two voices on the wind. Each sounded strange and affected – like there was some pretension and authority. I was trying to make out the tongue they were using. Here, you might have expected it to be the same as the Corcu Loígde but it certainly wasn't that. The voices were excited, though in them you could detect traces of nervousness and fear too.

"What are they saying?" Tigernus asked, frustrated at his incapacity to understand them.

"Shhh... I'm trying to make it out."

My ear tried to pick out their musings.

"They are definitely talking about us. They are talking about the arrival of our boat on the island. They are connecting it to the showing of the comet... They seem obsessed with the comet."

"How do you know? How do you make that out?"

"Easy," I said. "They're speaking Latin."

See how my earlier joke at Tigernus' expense backfired upon me.

"Latin – out here? But I thought only –

" – What? That only the learned use such a tongue?"

"Mmm."

"They seem fairly learned," I noted.

"Are they holy men – of Warna's kind?"

"No. Not so I can tell. They are not invoking her God."

I was beginning to know how Aimend had felt when she had to translate for me. It slows down emotions. There is less time.

"How do you know Latin anyway?" asked Tigernus. "You're not a scholar..."

"No. But I know enough to get by."

"Hush... They are measuring it – the comet, that is – tracking its movement, and trying to connect it with events on earth. They are speaking about what it heralds, but I can't make that bit out... They're speaking too fast. Their dialect is odd."

"Worse even than Deheubarth?" joked the boy.

"Much worse."

Hesitantly, and making sure no harm would come to us, we left our temporary site of rest and climbed a steeper section of the island, to present ourselves close to where they stood. They themselves had come down to a midway point on the natural pyramid, where it seemed there was good sight of the nocturnal sky. As yet however, we could not see them properly: only their two heads, silhouetted in the moonlight.

I could no longer stand the duplicity of hiding. I made my way forward, and standing alone greeted them, holding out the palms of my hand in peace.

"Abyssus ego sum accersitus Voog quod ego sum viator ut vestri Insula."

What emerged wasn't what we were expecting at all. These astrologers were not druids or magi – at least not of the conventional type (as you will know, we must be careful not to make judgements). At my words, and knowing no-one was about to fire a crossbow at him, Tigernus stepped forward out of the shadows.

There was then about a minute of absolute silence when not one of us spoke. Each group was as surprised as the other.

What they saw was a man and a boy, dressed in unusual garments (certainly not from Hibernia). In the blinking of their eye, they had already noted my twisted wrist and finger. What we were staring at were conjoined identical twins – both so short of stature that Tigernus both met and exceeded their height. It was hard to decide whether they were one body or two. If we say two, then both were men in their thirties with lines enough to show experience of life, but not yet full wisdom; though clearly it was wisdom they sought. Both of their bodies were joined together at the base of the back: there, organs and skin became one; and then below legs, knees and feet as any man. Perhaps they shared both their kidneys and liver. They were black-haired and bearded with the earliest flecks of grey running through these. What they saw in us caused great altercation and alarm in them, as if something momentous had occurred.

Tigernus had not seen such men before, and was thus instantly afraid of them. I assured him however, that there was nothing to fear.

"Such a body is natural. It is a chance thing during pregnancy. If Annown decides upon it, there is none who can alter it. It is the same as my wrist and finger."

The twins talked to each other constantly, and began a new line of discussion upon seeing us.

"What are they saying?" asked Tigernus.

"Hold on. Let me listen..."

The pair continued discussing events apace.

My translation is perhaps not fully accurate, but I tried to give to Tigernus a sense of their debate.

"They are saying that it is foretold that a man will step into the west – and that he is to found a new land, and plant new seeds there. He will come via this island – and that one day, to celebrate this achievement, a community will grow here. This, they have known was coming for many years, but recent events have confirmed its occurrence."

"What events?"

I asked them and translated for Tigernus.

"Oracle bones mainly – but also the flight of birds, the way fish shoals have swum, the way the clouds have been forming..."

Tigernus shook his head.

"Anything really then..."

"There is something else. The prophecy says that, like them, he will be a different kind of human. He will be flawed."

Yes, flawed. That is the word they used.

"This a bit creepy," suggested Tigernus. "It seems like you were drawn here too."

"How could I have known this? No-one can!"

"Prophecy?" suggested Tigernus sarcastically.

Here, my destiny was beginning to take shape.

So it started to become clear to me. Although it took some hours to discover who they were and where they had come from, eventually I began to understand. The two twins were both named Ir.

"What, both of them? They have the same name?"

"Yes – so it would seem. They are joined and therefore are one person, according to their people's beliefs."

"Who are they though? How did they end up here?"

These were complex and difficult questions for me to ask them. In my limited knowledge of Latin, I made many mistakes and clarification had to be sought. They beckoned us both forward, and in the dawn we climbed to their quarters, almost at the top of the island. We were shown to steps carved in the rock, although these were sometimes uneven and steep in their cut. This made them difficult to climb. In toppling back (especially with a weighty sack on one's back) you felt like you might fall hundreds of feet to the sea's surface. They led firstly to a high plateau, exactly where the peak we had observed divided itself, and then through an ancient arch of rock onto a primitive enclosure, nestled between one cliff edge and another.

I explained their story to Tigernus. The two misfits had been educated on Hibernia in the kingdom of one named Milesius. They knew nothing of the Corcu Loígde. I believed their education had been conducted in Latin and that is why they used it now. It seemed through isolation that they had forgotten their original language. They were placed here because people feared them – not only for their appearance, but because through learning, they had become excellent astrologers. But – and here, this part of their tale made me laugh – the people first liked the fact they could predict the future, but then after successive years of predictions, omens and portents, they got fed up with them, and thus made representation to Milesius to put them forever in isolation here.

Like me, they were banished. They were exiled to this rock.

In short, the community would rather accept surprise than know precisely what was coming; otherwise, life was always led in fear. Now they predict to each other and contest the accuracy of each other's insights into the cosmos. Sadly, their gift had become a kind of curse on them.

"Don't they get bored out here?"

"Apparently not."

"Do they survive on puffin meat then?"

"No – a vessel from Milesius brings them supplies every month. They have no vessel of their own to go fishing or return to the mainland at will."

I knew what Tigernus was thinking: these two had been condemned for knowing too much.

We both realised that their insights were no fluke either. In fact, they wanted to prove this to us, to justify their profession. Key to this was their use of oracle bones. I wasn't quite sure of what was meant by this myself until Ir and Ir led us to their huts. Although they lived in relative poverty, their stone dwellings were filled with parchments, costly astrolabes and diagrams depicting the heavens. It was these that they devoted their days to. All their dwellings were half the normal height and certainly I, if not Tigernus, had to crouch and bend to fit inside them.

We learnt that the oracle bones were derived from animal waste. Cattle scapulae brought out from the mainland were good, but at present they were using sea turtle plastrons. Ir and Ir carved questions into the bone with a thin, sharp knife the size of a quill. Then the bones were heated quickly in a fire. The way the bones cracked and broke determined the answer to their questions. These answers were then inscribed in the bones too, and stored for future reference in a pit they had dug. They showed us the pit – and it contained thousands of broken fragments of bone (such seeing – and yet such isolation). Divination was easy this way, they seemed to say, and coupled with this comet (only the third they had ever seen) – which only enhanced, so it appeared, what the bones said – it was the most successful form of prophecy going.

If this were not enough for Tigernus and me to take on board, the next day I learnt that there were many days when the twins did not speak to each other. So the left Ir said, he could communicate with the right Ir just by thinking about passing the information across. Tigernus was amazed.

"Magic," he went. "Proper magic."

I was less impressed, since I had heard that 'normal', separated twins have a second sense. Maybe their especial joining took this communication to a new level of understanding. Ir and Ir were also both fascinated with Rat. In his movements, sniffs and tail twists, they seemed to note all kinds of future events, which they duly wrote down. I was asked if I wanted to see them, but I declined. They already knew that not all humans liked to know their fate. Perhaps, I was already carrying too much weight of expectation for them to release any more. I daren't ask them about Orla – though perhaps, on reflection, maybe I should have. For certain, while most human beings saw nothing in the slightest movements, or the smallest changes, they saw huge alterations.

We did not so much live with Ir and Ir; rather we stepped around them and let them continue their work. They seemed never to sleep. The comet absorbed their energies all night, and then they returned to other studies during the day. Amazingly, they brought the comet closer to their eyes by peering at it through a tube, with glass lenses in it at either end. Neither of us had ever seen such a device. Peering through it made Tigernus jump back, for he thought the comet was drawing frighteningly close to him. This made Ir and Ir laugh heartily.

Tigernus reminded them of their own youth; perhaps a more innocent time when they weren't quite as obsessed with portents.

I learnt that the prophecy about me was as old as they were. It had been known for some years. But this was prophecy that I was considering: let's face it – it could have been made up last week. What saddened me was that even though my travelling was proposed to be a good thing, if I was not careful, there might be a later disaster.

Actually, left Ir didn't put it quite like that.

In fact, he said, there would be much joy, but equally, there could also be an apocalypse. Obviously, I questioned him on this. He replied with, "Vestri factum muto fatum plures."

I understood: my actions could alter the destiny of many others. One day, I would come to know what he meant – but not quite yet. The pressure was on then.

Tigernus had been quiet during this conversation. All the Latin was hard for him to take in. He felt excluded.

"Dio vos volo scio vestri posterus puer?" asked right Ir.

"Do you know what he has asked you?" I enquired.

"I think so," said Tigernus. "I'd rather not know."

I shook my head back at Ir. Tigernus preferred to remain ignorant of his future.

"When are we leaving?" questioned Tigernus. I could feel his youthful impatience. All this talk of prophecy was getting to him, gnawing away at his security and sense of himself.

"Soon. I need to find out what Ir knows of Hy-Brasil."

I translated my request into Latin and waited to hear what the twins would say. I showed them my map, and noted the island with my finger. The two heads spoke at length on the subject, too quickly for me to understand. Tigernus looked both bored and puzzled and, I suspect, tried to see how his now departed Puffin was faring somewhere out there, flying over the vista with his female mate.

What came back was intriguing.

"Sometimes it is there; sometimes it is not," I shouted across to Tigernus. "They've shown me the direction though. We have to go directly northwest from here."

I could discern nothing else from Ir about it. What I might find there or what people inhabited it, they could not say. At my continued questions, they shook their heads. Sometimes, it seemed even prophecy was not much use.

I dug into my sack to pull out Warna's holy book. This place and these two seemed a perfect destination for it.

"Here, have this," I said to Ir and Ir. "It's about a prophet. A friend gave it to us."

Ir an Ir had my full attention.

"Most of it is in Latin – so you should be able to read it. You never know, it might start something here...it might not. Either way, I believe some of what it says is worthy."

The twins accepted the gift and began consuming its pages, nodding to each other.

I called Tigernus over. I pointed at the route we had to take from high on this sea-surrounded mountain. It felt like we were standing on the top of the world. Foam burst onto the rocks below, and spume frolicked in the distant waves.

"They already know we're to leave in the morning," I laughed.

"How come?"

"The oracle bones told them last night."

We began to make preparation for leaving.

"Don't they want to leave with us – and get off this rock?"

I gave him a puzzled look, like he ought to be able to work it out.

"Don't tell me," said Tigernus. "The oracle bones told them not to go."

I nodded.

We both smiled.

I AM NOT CERTAIN WHAT I should call you. Of late, everything has been turned upside down. It is topsy-turvy. It is arse-about-face. What was once solid is now liquid. What was land is presently ocean. Granite is seaweed. Earth is water.

Let me be honest. It was in Douarnenez that I decided to read more about you. I spent my time engrossed in the holy book Howel had given me. I found the text addictive. It consumed me. At night, I had hallucinations about it. They left me sweating and panting, but I still wanted to learn more. Sometimes I felt guilty in picking it up – not only because it had been handed to me by a man that I should have hated, but also because I felt like I was betraying my lineage, my people, my grandmother, and all that had conceived me. I was worried too, that I was corrupting all that you, Father, believed in.

Believe me when I say that I hid it under linens and blankets, and then reached for it again in moments when I needed its comfort. Its binding called me. The pages were a drug to me. I read alone, in secret. You have to understand that in this Age it was not the done thing for a young woman to be reading – especially this. A woman with ideas? Surely that was not in the natural order of things? Some days, I tried to ignore its messages and words, but they roamed around my mind completely, testing and reformulating my ideas about the world. There was much that I found difficult to absorb and understand (these passages I would have to re-read), but again, there was much too that was obvious – that seemed to match precisely what I thought. It helped me to make sense of what had happened to me. I read stories of prophets, of disciples, of missionaries, of miracles, of wonder, of compassion, of forgiveness – and of hope.

In the end I resolved to call you Lord.

Can you believe that? I would never have said in my youth that it would be this way. But here, to an extent, I was letting a 'man' – or a 'god' boss me about. In some ways, alongside this I craved discussion. I wanted to converse with Warna even though she was a distant soul far from my own life. In the end, I came to realise I would not find that discussion with people. In the end, I would have to have it with the ocean.

I did not share many of my thoughts during this time with Tigernus. He would, I think, have been sympathetic to my leanings. After all, we often chatted about both our different and similar understandings of the universe, but this was not the right time. By day, his sole concern was assisting Corentin and Rosparzh in readying *Azen* – and I did not wish to distract him from his purpose. One task recently had been to mount *Warna* on board as a small inshore vessel that could be lowered by ropes off the stern. By night, we cooked and cleaned, washed and slept, and began to get to know Corentin and his people. I would also become acquainted with the crew. A call had gone out that Corentin again planned to sail and men and boys arrived in Douarnenez. Some came with experience from the first voyages; other were signing up now for the hope of new adventure.

Tigernus had his own roundhouse in the village there. It was strange to stay in his domestic environment. The dwelling had not really been prepared for habitation because he had expected to be away on Scathynys for some time. All had been stored and packed away. Therefore, just as slow preparation was made to ready *Azen* for the voyage, we ended up making his place homely once again. I enjoyed the home-making we shared, but also knew of its temporary nature. One day, I promised myself, we would have it – but not just yet.

Things didn't alter overnight or in one day. Instead, an unease that I had noticed for a few days now, was confirmed.

"Blejan, listen... There's something I need to tell you about," Tigernus said, as he came back from the harbour one night. He looked tired and pained.

I gestured for him to sit and passed him some of the vegetable broth I had been cooking. I wondered if our journey might be delayed for some reason – but this was not the line of his words.

"I'm not quite sure where to begin. Look, Corentin – he reminded me... when we first arrived. Do you remember? – he mentioned a man named Loic. I had forgotten about him these past few months, though it has to be said, at one point I knew him well."

He stopped to spoon in a mouthful of food.

"This Loic. Your father sensed something about him. It was hard to see at the time, but after I travelled back with him, it became clear. When your father was first exiled, Howel sent out word in all directions for people to watch for a man with a deformed wrist. No-one, the message said, should offer him help. This way his exile would be as far away as possible. As the message spread, so would it be harder for him to find a new home. That is the fate he wanted to inflict on your father. That message had travelled across the Channel to here – and Loic, well, somehow Loic remembered it."

"I see. Did he hold this against you?"

"No. Not at all. He was just a gossip – a man who loved to hear the pain of others. That way, it made his own, sad little life feel better. You know the type. He wasn't malicious – not really. He just liked tittle-tattle. The woe of others fascinated him. I fought alongside him and he was a good warrior – when his gob was shut."

"So why do you tell me this now?"

Tigernus seemed reluctant to answer this.

"It's something I overheard of late," he said.

I became more frantic, wishing that he would tell me whatever it was. He clasped my hand.

"A couple of days ago, I was working with the shipwrights. We got talking. They told me. It is on Loic's land that Casvellyn and his order came to settle..."

Suddenly, the world toppled in upon itself again. The high crests of waves fell on me. The name of Casvellyn was one that I thought had been purged from my life. Now, again, he would come to haunt me.

"I could not prevent it," said Tigernus. "Word has spread about our arrival. You know, they are intrigued about us. The people here know you are from the horn of Britain, and this knowledge has reached Casvellyn. It was bound to."

"He knows where we make for?"

"Possibly."

"Does he know we seek my father there?"

"I don't know."

"We need to find out."

"When you mentioned his name to me before, I am sorry that I didn't make the connection. I knew a community of druids had moved here, but not that it contained this man who you told me about."

I had more questions for Tigernus about Casvellyn's presence. We talked long into the night. Apparently, his order had found revival here. This is what his gathering had wanted. While Britain seemed, in their view, to shamefully collapse into this Christianity and Saxon overrule, clearly here they had found sanctuary for their particular vision of Annown. I wondered much about what Casvellyn would do. Had he now understood what had become of my father? Had he realised that I considered him still possible to find? Had he understood that the world did not begin and end in the horn of Britain? I knew he was too old to do anything about it physically. The sense was, though, that my father had once wreaked terror – that his arrival in Carn Euny all those years ago had heralded all the pain and change that occurred. Fogou-builder he may have been, but he had also been a harbinger of doom.

He would, of course, never contemplate travelling there. He was too old for travel now. The struggle relocating here would have been hard enough. But I had other fears. Druids were powerful beings. I learnt from Tigernus that Loic's land was filled with powerful stone circles just like the one at Boscawen Ûn. Revenge was something Casvellyn was accustomed to. If he knew the sole daughter of Voog was here in Brittany, about to make a sea crossing, he would use any malediction possible to ensure we were wrecked by tempest, or sunk by sea monster.

Even now, I sensed him reach for his milpreve. With the glain he would try to do his work.

I would deny him though. For protection, I read the holy book aloud. I think I said my first prayer.

22

Disc-headed pin. Chysauster, Penzance, Cornwall, 6th Century CE
This silver pin, 10.4 cm long was a dramatic statement of the importance of its wearer. The finely incised ornamental panels were probably originally inlaid with enamel. Unprovenanced, other similar pins have been found across other courtyard villages in Cornwall, Brittany and Wales. The pin was first discovered in 1873 by the Cornish antiquary William Copeland Borlase.

THE LAST THING I REMEMBER was Tigernus giving me a brim-full bowl of warming soup.

Yes – innocuous soup.

Seemingly, that was all it took to knock me out for a while.

I knew we'd made progress upon the ocean though.

Let me explain.

When I came around I was still in *An Ruen*, but Tigernus was nowhere to be seen. By the motion of the boat, I could tell we had temporarily stopped. The sails were furled and there was a stillness that seemed to suggest the vast ocean had been lost; that it had somehow been tipped away. My head hurt, though I was not completely sure what had caused this phenomenon. My mouth was also extremely dry so the first thing I reached for was a skin of water; our supply newly filled from *Sceilig Mór*. This satiated my need for my saliva to return. The colours of the world still seemed odd, unreal and intimidating – forcing themselves upon me. It was an experience I'd never had before. The only thing that I could possibly equate it to was having a very bad hangover; and I had not had those since being a young man who thought he could handle his drink. At any movement, each nerve seemed to quake and jar.

I slowly sat up and began to make sense of the emerging world around me. For any money, I felt I would look up and find us grounded upon a sandbank (I realised Tigernus had been at the steering paddle), but this was not what I saw. It was somewhat foggy, but we had moored next to an island of layered barnacles and rock, set low in water. The bell clapper gave a steady toll according the rhythm of the water. Where the barnacles were fully established, small fronds of seaweed had made themselves at home. A gentle wash pushed itself against the edge of this form. From this, my eyes followed the undulating curve of the island to its ridge, and there sat a lone Tigernus. He was active, having moved our small stove there, and was aiming to cook a breakfast of some kind. While he was at work, he was singing to himself – no doubt some old ditty of Scathynys – as he was accustomed to do.

Scanning around me, I saw that the small island he sat on was not the only one of this kind surrounding us. Almost as far as the eye could see were many more – some larger; some smaller. We had come to nestle in the middle of an archipelago, so were sheltered from the wider pressing winds and waves of the ocean. Channels pushed through these islands; all of them watched by steely grey rock. Because of the fog, they came in and out of focus. Initially, on occasions, I thought their forms even changed – slightly new angles, some set higher, some set lower in the sea, some even disappearing – but I first put this down to both my own hazy condition and the fog. I knew how the latter weather condition could deceive the mariner's eye so very easily. Their solidity was confirmed by the way colonies of birds (a long way out from the Hibernian coast now – but perhaps migrating south to warmer climes) put down upon them in order to rest, and conduct fishing trips into the deep.

What had I dreamt? It seemed that ever since I had started out on this path, I had not experienced such strange dreams and visions. That morning, I considered that they had been part inspired – or perhaps even conditioned – by the duality of the brothers Ir; that somehow they had induced in me a kind of divination. Such forms I had never encountered before. Much was recalled and remembered, but much was also forgotten and scattered. Most of all, the pleasant dreams I had seemed to take away the pain of Orla. They sucked her love from me and cast it into a midden. They also warmed me – giving a feeling of euphoria that most of the time in life, we never, ever encounter. It was as good as falling in love, as making love for the first time, as dying with those you love around you.

I had gone on such a journey inside of me so that my ache and heartbreak were completely nulled and cast long away. Senses of heightened perception had overtaken me. A multitude of doors opened in front of me. I opened them all to enter new rooms. I knew I was still on *An Ruen*, safe in her clutches, but I was travelling too – fast above the waves, as if I were flying in the air. I was seeing other countries, other people, other stories, other creatures. I had even heard Tigernus talking to me but I could not answer him, I was too ensconced in wonder. I was too busy forgetting.

"You're finally up then?" observed Tigernus from the island, shaking his head in dismay.

This time I was cogent enough to respond to him.

"What do you mean? Finally?" I shouted across.

"Voog – you've been out of it for three days."

This was news to me. I hadn't realised.

I had been on an epic journey then, inside my mind. That is where the ocean had gone.

"I put it down to exhaustion," Tigernus said. "You've had a tough old time of it really, and I reckon that climb up *Sceilig Mór* really knacked you out... that an' the wrestling, of course. Whatever I tried to do, you wouldn't wake up. I was beginning to get a bit worried. Not much I could do though, except carry on."

Was this boy right in saying this?

Had I really driven myself to the point of exhaustion? Perhaps it was the case, though when we left *Sceilig Mór* I had felt as right as rain: rested and in good shape. Maybe, I pondered, events catch up on you. I had thought on the physical challenge but maybe I hadn't fully contemplated the mental strain of this voyage.

"You know where we are, don't you?" asked a pleased Tigernus. "Look at your map. Go on..."

I scrambled around in the canopy where I had stowed my scrawl of the map of the world. I found *Sceilig Mór* and traced the route to the northwest we had planned. I looked at the island we had been heading towards. The exterior I had just witnessed confirmed the drawing. My father had told me he thought it was supposedly criss-crossed by waterways between smaller islands. On the map, it looked whole, but on closer inspection, it was exactly what we appeared to have found – small islands grouped together, similar to Silura. The difference was that whilst Silura's isles were scattered and could sometimes be fairly expansive, here they were smaller, islets almost, safely contained in a round.

"Got to be Hy-Brasil hasn't it?" Tigernus shouted. "Do you see the map? It's exactly like it says. And do you remember what Gofan said? He told us there was nothing here. Look at it. He was spot on. There's nothing but rock, barnacles and the odd sea bird. Not even a well – or some new creature for us to observe. The old man was right."

Gofan appeared to have known where we'd reached. The prophets Ir and Ir had got it wrong though. They had said that sometimes it was there, and sometimes it was not. It was here right now though. Tigernus was sat upon it. I wondered though – maybe because the islands were so low, sometimes the tide overcame them – just the way it had with the flooding of old Lethowsow.

This knowledge pleased me. What once had been speculation was now reality. If there was a Hy-Brasil, then maybe there was Ogygia, or Mayda. Hyperborea might even exist perhaps, and maybe then, other worlds beyond that.

"Looks like we found it then," I noted. "Or rather you did. You were the one who navigated us here my friend."

"Piece of cake," Tigernus said, "when the wind's in the right direction."

I made a quick calculation from the map. Three days from *Sceilig Mór* to here. Using my callipers I was able to judge the distance we would need to sail to reach the edge of the map. I did not like what I saw. It would take a month; perhaps even more. That would take us into August, and then a great, unexplained autumn. Clearly we would have to find landing by winter. We would not survive that season on the open ocean.

"Do you reckon Ir and Ir got it wrong then?" questioned Tigernus.

"Maybe... I don't know. They seemed to indicate it appeared and disappeared... Perhaps they were referring to the fog?"

"Seems pretty solid to me."

Tigernus gave the rock a stomp with his right foot.

Nothing moved or gave way.

"You coming over here for some food then?"

"Why didn't you stay on *An Ruen*? We don't normally cook outside..."

"Thought I'd take advantage of the stop-off. Stretch my legs a bit."

I stepped across onto the rock. It was of a curious kind that I don't think I had come across before. It was neither granite, slate nor sandstone, but instead was partially crystalline, and it seemed to be still fusing together, as if it were young still.

"Strange stuff," I noted.

Tigernus ignored me.

Perhaps I was being paranoid, unable to accept new experiences. He didn't seem to be worried.

"Look, I have some cod for us – fresh caught this morning – and eggs that Ir and Ir gave us. There's some of that soup left too if you want some. I kept it, as you seemed to like it so much."

Rat had already joined Tigernus on the island. He was comfortable wherever he was, so long as there was a good supply of nourishment. He'd already found a space down the slope of the island, after securing two eggs for a meal.

"The fog's dulling the fire," moaned Tigernus. "Can't seem to get it alight this morning."

I was still nursing my head and my aching body when I happened to catch sight of the cooking pot – still filled with the past days' soup in it. What startled me now was its colour. It was green. Since Warna's leaving we had very few green foodstuffs with us. I knew it when I had spooned the soup into my mouth but had been distracted – or rather it had distracted me – and then, well then, it seemed to work its way without me noticing. I began to understand more now. My questioning of Tigernus was instant.

"What's that soup made of?"

"Why? Want some more? I'll heat it for you in a moment..."

"No. Tell me – what did you make it out of?"

Tigernus stopped what he was doing and thought back to three days ago.

"Bits and pieces really..."

This was the way all cooking took place on *An Ruen*.

"I want to know about the leaves. Where did you find them?"

Tigernus didn't seem to want to answer. He recognised that there might be a problem.

"Did you pick them on *Sceilig Mór*?"

Tigernus shook his head.

"Nope. There was barely anything edible on that lump."

"So... where did you get them then?"

"They came out of your sack. It sort of fell over, and I saw them and I thought you'd probably forgotten they were there, so I used them up. That's all. No point in letting them go to waste. You're always saying that to me..."

I sighed. All was now clear to me. My exhaustion and mental journey during recent days was not down to anything I had done myself. Instead, it could be put down to what I had ingested. Tigernus had managed to make a soup out of the watercress given to me by Casvellyn.

"You made me a hallucinogenic soup, y'fool."

"What? It was a kind of drug you mean?"

"Watercress is very potent – more so after fermenting in my bag during this summer."

The boy considered what I said. His reaction surprised me.

"You some kind of dealer then? I mean we've had them come through Scathynys. Lots of potions. Crushed horn from Africa. I heard of some that makes your pissle grow large..."

"No, not at all. I was given them by someone whom I'd rather forget."

"Who? Who supplies this sort of stuff?"

I didn't want to be having this conversation on Hy-Brasil. Right now, I wanted to be anywhere but on Hy-Brasil. This island was meant to be a goal: a half way point between one world and the next. Tigernus was talking to me as if I was an addict of some substance.

I wouldn't lie to the boy though.

"A druid named Casvellyn gave it to me."

"Casvellyn? Now, that's a crazy name. Good with drugs was he? I hear a lot of druids use them."

He pointed to his ear and turned his finger, indicating their madness.

"I don't know..."

"Why did he give them to you? Did you pay for them?"

"No. I gave him nothing for them. He gave them to me in case I needed them – to – ah – escape from things."

Tigernus' questioning paused for a while.

He contemplated what this meant. He realised that at some point we might encounter something that might induce us to want to escape instantly; some horror beyond comprehension. This watercress could bring instant oblivion judging from my three days of internal journeying.

Tigernus put his hand into the pot and pulled out one of the surviving leaves. I could see what he was thinking. He was finding it incredible that so innocuous an object could induce such delusions and aberrations in the mind.

"What's it do to you – like? I mean, how do you feel when you take it?"

"Depends on who you are, I think. In me, it gave me hallucinations – some quite beautiful – past, present and future all colliding – like in dreams, only much wider and fuller than we normally experience. That's where I've been the past three days."

"I thought it was a bit weird."

Tigernus had forgotten about breakfast, forgotten that we had found this set of islands and that we were now sat upon one of them. He ached for information from me. I was honest with him.

"The druids grow watercress for ritual. They cultivate it in vast ponds just for this purpose. They use it for vision-quests – to prophesise, just like Ir and Ir with their oracle bones and malefic comets. But it has been known for some warriors to imbibe it before battle. They say it can make him into a berserker and feel no pain."

Tigernus was wide-eyed and agog. Thinking over all of this, he went back to trying to light the fire, and then suddenly asked, "Can I try some?"

As he lunged his hand in, I pulled the pot neatly away from him. He made a scowl.

"Food best not served to boys. It's probably good to let the sea have it."

I stood and made my way down the rock to the water, about to throw it away.

"No," said Tigernus. "We should keep it – in case of..."

He didn't finish his sentence but thinking over his words, and still not knowing so much we might encounter, I stepped back from my desire to get rid of the drug. I said no more, but instead scraped out the mass and stored it in a pot. I sealed over the lid with some hide and a short length of flax.

"There," I said. "We just have to break the hide in case of... an emergency."
I placed it back into the safety of *An Ruen*.

I hoped Tigernus wouldn't be too tempted to give it a whirl. The aftermath of its power was still affecting me. It was going to take me some time to recover.

The fog continued to pass over the archipelago. To be honest, it was a lonesome place. One could understand why most mariners avoided it. Why come to anywhere when there was nothing there? The only reason I could think of was for tranquillity – like all those other hermits that seemed to populate our Age. From time to time, there was, out in the fog, a few bursts of water, like as if the ocean had snapped up quick on one particular cove or inlet, so sending a spattering of spray into the air. I gave it no thought though, since we had seen such spray on the rocks of *Sceilig Mór*.

I should have known. I should have thought it through a little more – but you see, my mind was addled. It was still in the land of watercress.

Tigernus was now having some success with the fire and while he continued to cook, I explored a little further along the length of the island. I touched the rock a little more and noticed that a kind of algae was coating it. Again, this did not worry me, for algae was, after all, the very spirit of the sea. It was everywhere. It had even started to accumulate on the hull of *An Ruen* – nestling into the wool grease.

A little further on I discovered something more curious. In the rock was a pot hole; perhaps twice the size of my foot, and v-shaped in design. I peered down into it and shouted an echo. The hole seemed to go deep down beyond the waterline of the island and into some cavernous space below. I could work out the geology better now. Clearly, these rocks were on pillars of some kind, standing on the shelf of the ocean. I was fascinated. Looking back, I suppose, it was an odd thing to find and maybe I should then have questioned our presence there.

There was not the time to do so though, because as I saw the fire start to blaze, both Tigernus and I felt the island shudder slightly. It was only a small tremor but it took both of our minds back to the earthquake on Scathynys. As you might expect, it was an uncomfortable feeling and we looked to each other for understanding.

"Did you feel that Voog?" Tigernus shouted to me. I could feel the fear in his voice.

I looked at the rock below me again, seeing if there would be any more tremors. Then I noted something else: on the edge of the rock were some overlapping circles, in effect wounds, where something had one time attached itself here. I recognised them as being sucker marks from either a squid or octopus

– only a very large one. Retrospectively, I suppose, that is when I first put two and two together. We were not walking on something lifeless, but instead, something organic.

In this instant, I looked back to where Tigernus was cooking. He'd set quite a blaze going for the cook-up. At this moment, the rock moved again, and with it came a loud and melodic moan. I looked back to the pot hole, and noticed the rock moving. Stone was turning into flesh, pulling down skin to suck down air. I noted mucus forming that had not been there before.

"Tigernus... put out the fire," I said calmly. "Right now."

I knew the heat was searing the skin of this organic mass.

He stared at me.

"Put out the fire!"

The second time I shouted, I felt the end of the rock tip into the sea. The distinctive U-shape of it was gradually submerging, and taking the pot-hole under.

I had to push forward to stop my feet from getting wet.

"Shit, shit. shit. shit shiiiiiiiiiiiit!"

Not only was the island moving under at the front end of it, it was also turning on its side. Tigernus had no choice. He completely lost his legs and landed on his back. If the boy couldn't put out the fire on the surface of this object, then the object was going do it for us. A low moaning melody came from under the waves, like nothing either of us had heard before. The tip of the object made the fire slide off into the ocean; our cooking vessels clanked together as they were lost to the depths.

We were standing on no island, but upon the back of a gigantic blue whale. Hy-Brasil was not an archipelago at all but the established feeding grounds of a pod, who had clearly been congregated around the whale we were stood on. The plankton was good here – warmed and nurtured by currents from the south. That is why they returned year on year. That is why maps and mariners spoke of this archipelago.

Tigernus was being rolled into the sea. My first thought was for *An Ruen*, and whether in a moment of diligence, he had somehow tied her onto the rock. If so, she was going to go under as well. Fortunately, because the waters around them had been so calm, there had been no need to moor her in that way. Perhaps too, there had been nothing to attach her to; so smooth was the 'rock'. At least that needn't be worried about. I was still standing though, trying to stay stationary by keeping my feet moving, as the whale's body was flipping. Although the plesiosaur and the basking shark had been huge beasts of the ocean, they were tiny compared to the mass of this creature.

Given the speed with which it now twisted, it was quite obvious Tigernus was, like the fire and cooking vessels, about to enter the water. Meanwhile I was trying to counter the tip upwards of its peduncle which led directly to the tail. Between where I was jogging and the fan of its two flukes was the dorsal fin, which needed to be sidestepped as the whole mass plunged downwards. In the end, it was moving so fast, I had to jump it. Whilst the plesiosaur had offered one kind of terror, this was another kind – born of our naïvety and re-alisation that we could be sucked under from the vast creature's downdraft, drawing us into the sea.

I was still riding the tail as it receded, but noticed Tigernus was now swim-ming towards *An Ruen*. Annown only knew where Rat was. He had been down this end, but had probably been swept into the depths. That was sobering enough, although what was now happening worried us even more. The whale we had been on tossed *An Ruen* away from its surge, hitting another nearby 'island' that also decided to move. We then realised that if this whale was the mother; then the one next to it was probably her calf. Shit – where was the Calf-Goddess when you needed her? The creature let out a higher-pitched moan which triggered the rest of the colony to become restless. The archipelago upon which we had a few moments ago felt so secure was becoming fluid and volatile. Hy-Brasil was disappearing before our eyes and re-imagining itself in new ways. Ir and Ir had actually been right. Maybe Gofan had been too – soon there would be nothing here but fog.

In all of this, I was still clinging to the tail of this creature. On the peduncle I had been tipped forward to lie with my hands attached to the notch in the middle of its tail. Behind me I heard the pot-hole turn into a blow-hole, and the whale let out an expulsion of air, water and mucus that showered us, such was its force. This creature continued to make a noise, singing to the others around it. I was above the surface long enough to hear its plaintive wonder, and to understand that these were social animals who worked together; and protected each other. Unfortunately, I did not want to be socially attached to its tail. When this part of its body hit the surface of the water, I let go, and hoped I wouldn't be sucked too far under.

This mass and speed created a vast fusion of foam and bubbles, and for per-haps thirty seconds, I was clueless as to my depth and ability to survive. When the foaming and turbulent water cleared, I was a few lengths of the human body below the surface. From here, I could observe the full mass of these won-drous creatures – and learn how their rock and barnacle became efficient under water. To the right of me, I could see the distinctive throat pleats of the calf, and then its filtering baleen plates open to the water. The whole of this temporal land mass was moving, shifting, and realising its complete lordship of the ocean.

Under the surface, still came the clicks and song. Here, it was as hallucinogenic to the ear as the watercress soup was to the mind. It drew me downwards, wanting to immerse myself into the sound of it. It was like being back in the womb once again. As I re-birthed at the surface, the fog was still present but in the middle of all this movement, sat *An Ruen*. Tigernus had managed to scramble aboard her, and acknowledged me, glad that I had returned from the depths. Both he and the vessel were now at risk as, everywhere around us, individual whales turned and dived, clouting the surface with their tail flukes. At any moment, *An Ruen* could be hit by their blowholes or these tails but – even more dangerous – I knew that sometimes, with enough speed and power, they could lift up large parts of their bodies and breach into the air. Maybe our fire, our chatter, our exploration of them as some pretend island had upset them, and they may want to see us smashed apart.

All the while, I was wishing I had heard what other prophecies Ir and Ir had for me. Maybe I could have averted this. Maybe we could have taken a different route – directly east perhaps? The people of Milesius's kingdom had been fools. Who wouldn't wish to know of such moments? If we had known, we would have been more prepared. Gigantic sea mammals are something I want to know about.

In the heaving ocean, I began to swim, and made my way toward *An Ruen*. I would never classify myself as a strong swimmer, and the effort exhausted me. Each stroke hurt and juddered a mind still weak from the hallucinogen. At times, the bitter water even made me think I was still inside that inward trip; and that these whales were figments of my elongated imagination. Maybe I was even wishing it to be the case, so that I could escape this grim reality.

Tigernus was already unfurling sails and trying to evacuate us from this thriving pod. Although the islands had disappeared, still, these living rocks slid before us. I contemplated their cavernous bodies, and hoped and prayed I would not be sucked into the fogou of them. These were creatures that no magic could sort. Their dwarfing of humanity was complete. As I swam, I began to recognise their gentleness though. Even if I was engulfed inside them or crushed by their movement, that was not purposeful on their part. They were simply being themselves and, unfortunately, we had got in their way. We had stumbled into their society. We had to accept that.

Although I had glimpsed smaller whales off the horn of Britain, I had not come this close to them. My tide of fear was turning. It was becoming a privilege, a kind of gratuity, that nature had served us this spectacle. Maybe this was her thanks for us serving the Calf Goddess. She was not only Goddess of the land calves but of the sea ones too. I swam with awe.

Quite close by me, a medium-sized whale turned to its right, throwing its left flipper skywards. The wash of this movement pushed me in a wave towards *An Ruen*. I was thankful for its decision, for it decreased my time in the water; and my limbs already ached from effort. My limbs were flippers; my feet a fluke. Tigernus put his hand down and I reached up to grab it with my left hand. He couldn't help but feel my extra finger. Making sure we didn't capsize, he yanked me over the bulwark.

Their song continued to serenade us. It was eerie, with their music filtering in and out of the fog.

"They've told us," I said, "how places can appear and then disappear in an instant. We'll be more wary now. Hear them. Their singing wants us to learn this."

A tail fluke flipped up, dangerously close to us. We sculled *An Ruen* away from it breathing a sigh of relief.

"Did you save any of the stove?" I asked, knowing what he'd say.

"No," answered Tigernus.

We both knew it was a pity. We'd have to find another way to cook from now on. Things were going to get tricky.

"Hold on," said the boy. I saw him scramble to the port side of the boat. "See who I've just found..."

Tigernus reached over the gunwale and pulled in one of our pots that had somehow survived the onslaught and had been afloat.

He tipped the pot forward so I could see. Inside it was a shivering Rat. Lucky wasn't the word for it. Rat was drawing the spray from his whiskers and trying to get dry.

"Fancy some boiled Rat?" asked Tigernus.

"At least he's not vacating a sinking ship. A good sign perhaps."

Rat chittered back, chiding us for our stupidity to think that a whale could be an island.

We paddled out of the pod, though for a while the whales still seemed to be toying with us. We were their temporary playthings in a life given over to the finding of plankton.

Looking back on it, it felt like the moment we had stepped onto Hy-Brasil, we had created an earthquake. We had split the land up and made it ocean again. That is when I realised that oceans would always be more powerful than any land or people.

Water would always find a way.

Now, we just needed to find ours.

SO, DEAR LORD THEN, THAT is the way it is. How strange is the tide of life? It comes and goes so often, giving reflective striations in the sands, pools of marine life – anemones and seaweed – and yet at crucial moments leaves us bright new shells on the shoreline. We pick them up and listen to the sound of the sea. We hear its swash and think over our existence. We hear ourselves roaring back. This roar says that I am running out of patience now. I want to be with you, father. I want to hold you. I want to see this twisted wrist of yours that so many have told me about. Let me be there soon. Let this dark forest canopy of red and orange leaves be over and let me see your face. I don't care if it has lines and wrinkles. I just want its love.

As I run this hour though, I contemplate my journey and arrival here. It is late March and I am back in Brittany on the wood-planked jetties of the small harbour of Douarnenez. The strong vessel that is *Azen* was now ready to depart. The scene was filled with the busy energy of last minute preparation for our voyage. Not only did the community of Douarnenez come to watch, but so did all the surrounding villages. Nothing like this had been tried for many years now. Old men and women stepped up to Corentin and reminded him of the voyages he had made years ago. They sourly warned him not to go too far. You never knew what you might find: monsters, madmen, tribes of people who ate human flesh.

"I will go where the wind takes me," said a joking Corentin. "I fear nothing. Not even cannibals."

I believed him. In fact, I had already come to understand him as a careful and well-organised captain. Time had not dulled his understanding of good preparation nor his planned navigation, which I had talked through with him and Tigernus on several occasions. We had looked over the maps during several of our evenings together.

The hull of *Azen* allowed for plenty of food to be stored – mainly salted boar and lamb. Barrels of water were also loaded on board. There were no rooms on board her, but at least I was given sufficient privacy to not have to dress or wash with the men. A length of curtain made of sacking demarked where Tigernus and I would sleep. Around twenty men had agreed to crew her, and they were now being briefed by the equally experienced Rosparzh. *Azen* was the size of the Phoenician vessels who came to pick up tin and she was built for the open sea. I had every faith in her completing the voyage.

"You've no doubts?" I asked Tigernus as we boarded.

"No. None. It'll be good to see him again..."

Perhaps what Tigernus did not say was, "...if he is still alive."

Those five words did come back to me every day, but I had to ignore them.

"Just don't let me get too close to the waters out there..." he grinned.

I knew what Tigernus was indicating. He needn't have worried. I was not about to let any mermaid come between him and me.

"And Scathynys?"

"Plenty of time for that... We'll get there one day."

I wondered about this. I wondered whether he and I would come back. We said nothing because we both knew we were thinking about it. We both knew it was one of those life-changing decisions that would, at some point, have to be made. What is understood however, does not need to be said. Perhaps the ocean would decide for us. Maybe we both even wished for that.

Rosparzh blew a horn signalling our departure. Ropes were untied and the crew let out *Azen*'s sails. They cracked and billowed in the morning wind. This was it then. This was the moment when I was truly to meet the full force of the ocean.

Had my prayers worked? I did not know. I scanned the populace watching the hulk depart. In them I tried to look for Casvellyn and any of his order. In the old days, such a voyage as this one was bound to have been blessed by them. In fact, there might well have been a ceremony at a stone circle to guarantee success – perhaps had I not been upon it. Tigernus knew what I was thinking. He knew who I was looking for.

"Try not to let him bother you," he said, aiming to calm me. "Perhaps I shouldn't have said anything..."

The trouble was I knew how they worked. Sometimes they didn't work openly, but in secret. Tigernus knew that too. I knew about the stone Casvellyn had removed from the fogou and taken down to Boscawen Ûn. I knew what geomancy and magic he would have put upon it. My father had told him about how this happened years ago. Somewhere distant, maybe Casvellyn was doing the same. Perhaps he had already scraped some small piece of wood off *Azen* and used it for magic with malicious intent.

I took solace in thinking about my mother. I became her in that instant. I was, in that moment *her*, travelling to see her love. I was being spirited across to the man that loved her. This was what this was all about. It was rewriting our family's story. It was putting right a wrong that had been committed twenty years ago. In some way, I was turning back time, yet I was forcefully grabbing a future as well. We pressed out of the harbour, and past fog-coated rocks and small islands.

"Come down below," said Tigernus. "Brrr. It's cold up on deck here. They're cooking up a huge breakfast. It's a tradition... plenty of eggs and ham."

He was right. The morning fog had a chill to it that bit into your bones, but I wanted to enjoy this moment of departure.

"I'll be down in a minute... I promise."

I stepped forward to kiss him. The meeting of our lips was long and sweet.

"I read a bit of that book of yours last night," Tigernus said. "I recognised some of it from what Warna told me years ago."

Then he smiled, turned and left me alone.

So. He had noticed.

I watched young cormorants dive and return to the seaweed-coated rocks. I thought over all that had happened to me since my grandmother's passing. These black-feathered birds' antics made me smile.

The fog made the land ease in and out of focus. One minute the granite cliffs lifted out of the sea to their heights; the next minute they were shrouded again. *Azen* pushed on through the waves, creating a long wake that also disappeared and then reappeared in the fog. This is how it had been for them when they had encountered *Azen* for the first time. I imagined that moment.

Then, on the cliffs, I spotted something. It was a white-clad figure, first moving, and then becoming stationary, apparently stopping to watch the ship passing. It carried a staff. The white was clearly his flowing robes. And then as the fog twisted back in, the form was lost again. *Azen* was pushing on, picking up speed, but right then, I needed it to slow down and for the beguiling fog to clear.

"Please Lord... Annown... I need you to show me the truth here," I said to myself.

I kept watching that spot on the cliffs.

No.

No.

No.

Maybe.

Then yes. There it was again. I knew right away. The form was definitely him. What was he doing? That was no milpreve being tossed in the air. No, instead, I am sure I saw his hand was making the sign of a blessing. But before I could see for sure, the fog consumed him again and my view of the cliff was lost to me. Whatever message he'd been making was to remain hidden on that side of the ocean.

23

Bronze Flagon, Carn Euny, Penzance, Cornwall, 7th Century CE
Decorated with coral and red enamel, this flagon was found in excavations at Carn Euny in 1931 completed by the Office of Works under supervision of Dr Hugh Heneken of the British Museum. There would appear to be an oriental influence on the dogs or wolves located on the handle. The native component is symbolised by the duck on the spout. Such flagons were high status items and were probably imported specially for a wedding or coronation. Courtesy of the Royal Institution of Cornwall.

COMPARED TO THE PREVIOUS WEEKS of travelling, the seven days and seven nights on the ocean that followed our encounter with the whales of Hy-Brasil were, thankfully, non-eventful. Tigernus and I settled into the tedium and routine of sailing. At this point, a tedious routine was seen by us both as a positive thing because we did not want events to take us to the limit of our physical and mental capabilities. To serve time on the ocean without fear of catastrophe was indeed a pleasant change. We embraced the newly-found tranquillity and forgot the immediate past.

You will understand however, that unlike those periods I have already relayed to you, such times are harder to recall. In all of our lives, we continue to note the markers of difficulty – not the pauses where things run smoothly. Whether for good, or for bad, the markers punctuate our existence. It is the same as the ocean. On the ocean, time pauses. It is the coasts, the lands, the islands, the people and the creatures that mark it. Even the seaweed, the sand and the shells locate us. Forgive me then, if now I forget the exact detail of those days. That said, some individual moments are illuminated for me back across the years. The flame of a reading candle burns bright and lights up the long parchment of the ocean.

Some things I do recall vividly. Much of the wildlife that had always followed us seemed to stop. We knew that below us the sea teemed with life (inquisitive leatherback turtles were the one kind of creature we frequently bumped into) but aside from the occasional migratory bird – and on one day, a V-shape of trailing geese – the skies were empty. Being waterfowl, we hoped their presence in an otherwise lifeless sky might bode well. If Ir and Ir might have observed them, they would have known the omen and relayed it to us; that is, if they hadn't yet been converted by Warna's holy book.

The young mariner Tigernus was becoming highly proficient in just about all aspects of sailing. This left me the task of navigating our passage. Given recent events, there were often points where I wondered if taking a more southerly route would have been easier. The line on the horizon I was pushing towards was still to the north east, and I wondered if a radical change of course might have served us better. Maybe I already wanted to swap the cold for the heat of the sun. In the end though, I held the line we were taking, praying that this decision was the right one. My father's navigational device was a primitive object but, all things considered, I felt it served us well. The stars and it continued to dictate our route.

Given the hallucinogenic soup, I freely confess to you that I was still feeling its effects some days later. Every so often, unexpectedly, my mind would disconnect with the reality of the waves, and head to another place that was somehow both comforting and enlivening. Knowing me well by now, Tigernus was able to spot these moments of relapse and nudge me out of them with some urgent task that required my immediate assistance.

"You all right?" he'd asked. "Your eyes have clouded over again. Can you trim the head sail for me?"

There were times too, when I must admit I was tempted to locate the sealed pot in which I had placed the soup and imbibe some more of it. The worst days were the grey ones when the ocean and sky merged, and formed a union of destitute air and water which made our position seem the loneliest place on earth. Then, the horizon disappeared. I had to keep reminding myself. Although an exile, it was my own choice that had put me this far into this watery world. I had made my choice and I had to live with it.

Is it so bad to say I struggled with hope during these days?

Don't we all create a façade in our lives so that others perceive no weakness?

I believe this to be true. No one on *An Ruen* was about to confess their fears. Not even Rat.

Looking back, maybe we should have been more honest; maybe that would have been a better way. But this was no normal trip from point *a* to point *b*. We had started at *a*, but knew no other letters of the sea's alphabet. I had already found that if you started to predict them, their order became impossible to discern.

When few events punctuate your life, it is hard to tell one day from the next. Each day is a repetition of the previous one. This has the effect of making you realise the peace of your existence, but also makes you clamour for more. Maybe that was what was wrong with Orla and me. We knew the order, but clamoured for more. That clamour was our downfall. Maybe it was Howel's too. He had ambition and clamoured to be known: to go down in history, not just to go down.

I suspect that young men like Tigernus clamour for more disorder and chaos, as it enlivens the soul and turns one strong. It is invigorating and exciting. But as age comes upon us, we actually crave more order. We have made sense of the world and wish it to confuse us no longer. Ha – we can always wish...

Being in the middle of a vast ocean is a huge leveller. You come to understand your lack of importance in things. You realise that although you previously felt your life was at the centre of the cosmos, out here, that ideology must be reformed. You are a tiny piece of flotsam that is gradually being eroded away by time and tide. You are dead jellyfish and shrimp. You are torn algae and seaweed. You are lifeless crab shell and mermaid's purse. Your life is one tide of swash and swirl – and then, it ends. Best find the right shore to wash up on then.

All the while that was my dream: the correct shore that I might wash up on.

This section of our journey was tough. Many things contributed to its intensity. Since our stove had sunk, we had to improvise a new way of cooking food. After experimentation, we found the best solution in the form of a quern stone. Before, this had been used solely for crushing grain, but we now needed its solidity to act as a base in the vessel, otherwise any heat would have simply burnt through the hull bottom. The solution did work, but it was hardly as convenient as the device we had before. We cooked for longer periods of time now, experimenting with the sea-found resources and doing our best to invigorate its tired flavours. This longer period devoted to cooking was partly to combat our boredom, and partly because our tongues craved old tastes not available here.

I suspected I was growing thinner. My trousers and jerkin seemed to hang more loosely about me. Tigernus was certainly growing taller, but remained taut and bony. All this made me realise that we would need to ensure we didn't compromise our food intake. Although the larder was dull, it was still important to eat in this listless and endless blue. Without food, we would have no energy. Without energy, we would not function. In the week that followed though, some days one did not always feel like eating. Tigernus had some experience of this malady before at *Sceilig Mór*, but in the mid-ocean, the swell became enormous. No matter how experienced we now felt we were, such motion swirls the stomach and makes one never want to eat again. The sway makes one lose one's hunger.

Our progress on such mountainous seas was difficult. In fact, it was hard to discern that the vessel was moving forward at all, such was the dip and rise of her. Such conditions not only took away our appetite, they also exhausted us. One person needed to work the steering paddle and ensure the course was still being followed. The other needed to bail out water. Tigernus had a touch of ingenuity to him though. An island-childhood had shaped him that way. He had managed to construct a wider driftwood framework of greased hides over the hull which allowed more of the water and spray to dissipate. For many hours, we faced difficult squalls where the wind constantly spat water in our faces, and seemed to soak us from head to toe. On such days, our intimate world was utterly damp; the up and down motion from wave crest to wave bottom unforgiving and constant. Because of the intensity of such squalls, neither of us slept. In the morning we peered at each other with dark bags under our eyes. We became irritable and moody; each a critic of the other.

"Are you sure we shouldn't change direction?" asked a yawning Tigernus one morning. "We seem to go two steps forward and three back."

I knew exactly what he meant. The criticism still felt harsh. Any pilot or navigator will tell you that.

"Which way do you propose then?"

"I don't know. Any way but where we're heading at the moment."

I peered around the vessel. Voluminous seas rose and lurched in every direction – north, south, east and west. As bullying towers, wave tops flicked their foam at us, continually spitting their dislike of our form.

"We're not going east," I said. "I can take a more westerly course but according to my maps, we need to head north really in order to make land fall. The west may be more direct but that way we risk running out of water."

The issue of our water supply was a key factor. It determined everything. In the north, I anticipated ice. Ice meant fresh water.

"Can't we go south?" asked the boy.

South was possible, though it seemed even more undiscovered than the north. I had in my mind still the fact that the Vikings had found passage in the north. I reminded Tigernus of this. No-one knew of the south. Besides, the further south we went, the more we would drink. It got hotter there. He acquiesced and let me continue.

I could see Tigernus tiring. I was becoming worried about him. We had many conversations about his curse, and how he felt. Like an angry parent, I sometimes chided him for dipping his hands too far into the sea. Some days, I checked his skin to see that it was not scaling. Always he pulled down his jerkin, pulling away from me and asking me to leave him alone.

"Sorry," I said. "I just want to check there's no re-occurrence. You do know what Aimend said... It's for the best."

After such moments, he'd shift to the bow and stay there for a couple of hours, quietly sulking in the spray. Only Rat kept him company. Usually then, the seas would twist and reform in some new configuration which would prompt us to begin talking again. There were as many types of waves as there were clouds.

"We are like a married couple some days," I joked with him, but perhaps he did not see the funny side of it.

Tigernus raised his middle finger to me from the bow. A little more sensitivity with him may have been a better plan. You will see why.

For a fortnight, the sea had not relented, and though when the lull decreased somewhat, I was able to snatch a couple of hours of sleep, never was there opportunity for deep rest. You do not know it, but you become careless, happy-go-lucky; then I start to follow my own personal nemesis – complacency.

I woke and we were still victims of the sea's lurch. Bow became stern and stern forced our stomachs into our mouths as the wave receded. My eyes told me Tigernus was in a strange place. He was standing on the weak hide of the front canopy, arms outstretched to the ocean, beckoning somebody or something towards him.

"What are you doing, you daft fucker?"

There was no response.

"The hides are not very strong there. Get off, or they'll rip!"

He didn't turn to me, or respond to my chiding.

Still around us, the seas roared; banks of water appeared in front of us. They were cliffs of churning brine; at first pushing skywards, and then falling in upon themselves as they broke. Each crest fell directly onto Tigernus. He was getting soaked.

At that point, I was sure the curse had returned to him – some malevolency was reaching for him below. Could the mermaid have tracked us, followed us all the way out here? It seemed, in that instant, a possibility. Again, had I listened more to Ir and Ir, I might have known.

Despite my wish to hold the course, I had to do something. Any more of this and he would be washed off the bow and be completely at the mercy of the ocean. He'd be lost in the blink of an eye. I would never be able to pull him out. Another crest could rise and he'd be lost.

I reached the front of the boat, trying to suppress the churnings of my own stomach.

"Tigernus, come down! Please..."

I pleaded with him. He didn't even turn to me.

Then, over the wash of the waves, I heard him speaking to someone. Again,

I wondered if this was the mermaid back to entrap him. No, this was much more benign, though in its own way, it proved to me further how little we know of life, death and Annown. Maybe it also showed me the ways of this new god.

His speech was ranting, low and filled with capitulation, as if he was trying to make things good again.

"Who are you talking to?"

At first he put his finger to his mouth to try to shut me up. I asked him again; then came his response, which almost knocked me off my feet.

"Warna," he said.

"Where?" I asked, incredulous.

"Can't you see her? She's right there look – in front of the bow."

Tigernus pointed at some imaginary form in front of us. He was seeing a vision, encircled by a halo of light. Warna had an aura and glowed back at him. She was as all deities are depicted in art. She was saint and virgin, martyr and shepherd.

"I don't see her."

"That's because you choose not to."

"No. It's because she's not there."

This was all I needed: for that old hag to show up right now, and frighten the living daylights out of us.

"Warna's gone Tigernus. We left her – or rather she left us – in Kembry. Don't you remember?"

"Yes. I remember," he said. "But now she's back."

There was no arguing with him. I tried a different tack.

"What does she want?"

"She has come back to see how we are getting on. She's come back to tell us to keep going. She's talking about you, Voog: talking about what you are to become. She's saying the future will view you differently. The future will manipulate you."

This was now officially as weird as fuck. Maybe the boy had lost it. Maybe I had pushed him too hard. I didn't want to hear any more of this claptrap. I took a more aggressive tone.

"Is she smiling?"

"Yes – she is happy. She is at peace."

This was something at least. The tough old bird was rarely happy in her previous form (perhaps for good reason). It was good to hear things had improved.

"Does she look the same?"

"No. Here, she is younger. She has both eyes. She is flying. She is beautiful. There are children around her..."

"What's she doing there? Why has she decided to make an appearance now?"

"She's pointing in the direction we're going. She's telling us to keep to this course."

"That's it?"

"That's it," he confirmed.

This was charming. Tigernus appeared to be putting trust in some oddball vision rather than the logic of modern navigational methods. Had I taught him nothing?

I waited a few seconds.

"Is she still there?"

"No. She is going. She is walking across the water away from us. The ocean is forming steps for her."

This was getting better and better.

"Do you see her god?"

"No. Only her. The children have gone now."

The force of each wave was starting to worry me now. Tigernus was slipping. In his ecstasy of renewing contact, he was losing his grip on the canopy (not to mention reality). I had to grab him and force him down off the bow. Thankfully the hide had been just strong enough to hold him.

He fought back at me, pummelling his fists into my chest.

"Get off me! I want to speak to her again."

He managed to look out again, over the front of the bow.

"Is she still there?"

"No. She has gone," he spat. "You bastard Voog! You made her go. You never liked her, Now, she's left us alone again."

A globule of Tigernus' spit landed on my face. He continued attacking me with his fists, and kicked his legs at my shins. I wondered where this vision had come from. Why now? Why had this very practical boy suddenly lapsed into some strange fantasy? This was completely out of character for him.

As I wiped his spit from me, I noticed its frothy colour. It was green tinged, and not just from his phlegm and the ocean's rasping dampness.

Tigernus became calm, and he seemed to note a shift in my face.

"What is it?" he asked.

"You idiot. You had to try it didn't you? I knew I should have thrown it away. This is my fault."

Rat noted the anger in me and scurried from Tigernus' pocket toward the stern. I watched his form move through the hull, back to where I had stowed the watercress. With both hands, I let Tigernus drop; his head falling against the bow. In the middle canopy I dug for the watercress, in the position I had stowed it. It was no longer there.

"How much of it have you had? Tell me!"

Tigernus' eyes were cloudy and unresponsive.

He was still mumbling Warna's name as if she was above him, looking down on the scene within the hull.

Shit. Although I knew the watercress probably wouldn't kill him, this delirium could continue for days afterwards. It had worked on a young mind. Maybe it would frazzle his brain forever. Maybe he'd be unable to escape its power. I had found it hard enough to cope with, so who knew what effect it could have on a boy? The druids never gave it to their ovate apprentices. No vision quests were completed until any student had turned at least twenty-one. Knowing this, I decided the only thing I could do to help him was to make him sick. That way, at least some of the hallucinogen wouldn't enter his system. I scooped a bowl over the side and pressed down Tigernus hard onto the hull. I forced the seawater into his mouth and throat, using my extra finger to widen his lips. He gagged and struggled, biting at my twist of a hand, but in the end, the brine did its work and he sat up, retching over himself. The toxic soup re-emerged.

"See what you've done Warna," I shouted, half in fun, half trying to hurt her presence.

"It's not her fault," he frothed. "I wanted to try it."

"You're a little arsehole Tigernus then, aren't you? Don't you ever listen?"

He gazed at me.

"I'm just like you then. You never listen either."

This conversation was not going in a positive direction and we both wanted it to end. Its finish came because of something else. Rat began a set of squeals at the stern of *An Ruen* that were so intense it made both of us freeze.

"What's up with him?"

In a crab-like motion, I made my way back to the stern. My concern for Tigernus ended right there and then. Rat had noticed that due to the constant lull, one of the hides had ripped, and whenever we lunged up the face of a wave, water was gradually making the hole in the hull larger, and cascading inside us. What had probably begun as a trickle an hour or so ago, had now developed into a dangerous stream. It was a well no-one wanted.

What was I saying about a tedious routine?

I now had a drug-crazed eight year old talking to the ghost of a one-eyed god-botherer.

Nice.

I also had a hole the size of my fist in the hull.

Even nicer.

"Get back here Tigernus. You need to start bailing us out!"

Above the roar of the ocean, I heard him.

"I'm wiping the sick off me!"

"Never mind the sick. If you don't get back here, you'll have nothing to be sick on or in any more. We're holed!"

To his credit, Tigernus did what I asked. It was as if the drug made him stronger and able to endure the pain of the continuous work. If this was the case, then maybe his temporary intoxication was a good thing. Floating in the water, he located the pot in which I'd placed the remains of the soup. In an instant I'd swiped it from his hand, gave him another glare, and flung it into the waves. It could now mix with the primordial soup of the ocean.

What I really needed to do was to get *An Ruen* out of the water, and discover the true nature of the damage. This would have to wait. Nothing had poked through her though. It had purely been a slightly weaker piece of hide, which had been pushed to its tensile limits by the stresses and strains of the wave's motion.

My mind was not yet really running to the solution for this problem. Its sole focus was perhaps more on what we were going to do if *An Ruen* sank. Our only hope was the coracle, though, given the heights of the waves here, we would probably not last long. If we evacuated, we would need the sea to stop its surge to have any hope of survival. If *An Ruen* sank quickly enough, it would pull down the coracle with it too. We'd be able to do nothing but swim; perhaps clasp at some floating piece of debris. But then would come exhaustion; then would come the slip under the surface and then would come drowning. These thoughts flashed through my mind in seconds. Perhaps Tigernus (if he were at all back in the real world) was thinking the same. We had to make preparation for the inevitable. With this overriding thought I pulled in the coracle, and loosened the knot of her flax, tying it instead to my waist. Then I dumped my sack, our fishing lines, the weapons, our food and our water into its surrounds. At least then, we'd have hope.

This took perhaps a minute all told. Once I was satisfied there was an escape route, I began to focus more fully on dealing with the repair. Tigernus was continuing to slop out more water.

"Go faster," I said. "Use that pot and the bowls as well."

He recognised that *An Ruen* was slowly tipping backwards; that the water was starting to make her lose her buoyancy.

You hope that such an emergency never happens, but I have to say I was prepared from the outset of this voyage for something like this to happen. You have to be. You know the vigorous checks of her hull that I normally made. I was talking to *An Ruen*, nursing her back to health again. I was telling her how hard we had pushed her; how wonderful she had been in keeping us afloat in these cliff-like waves. For these long weeks, she had been our refuge and fogou. I needed her not to take us back to the waters of Annown. I looked for the clay figurine to hold. I couldn't find it.

The re-stitching of the hull required both dexterity and persistence. It also needed hands of pure iron in order to push the needle through the new piece of hide that I hoped would mend the skin of the hull, as well as connecting it to the remainder of the original hide. The stitching needed to be tight and close together. I was back in Lulyn again, taking on advice about her construction and ways of keeping her watertight. Stitch over stitch was required, both on the outside and inside the hull. Wool grease would then need to be forced around the stitching and over the hide itself.

The inside run was comparatively easy because it was accessible; though the frantic nature of the task left my right thumb bleeding with the task of pushing the head of the needle through the leather. I got Tigernus to seal this set of stitching with one hand using grease, whilst bailing with the other. His task was not helped by spray scattering over the vessel from the breaking crests. At each lift, we could feel the stringers bend. I was hoping that they had enough flexibility to ensure they would not snap. That really would be the last straw. Abandonment would be inevitable.

The outer run of stitching necessitated me going overboard. Not being fully confident in the water (and remembering the strain of swimming close to the whales), this was not something I really wanted to do. There was, however, no choice. I jumped into the cold water. It instantly numbed my body and I felt the sea's motion want to drag me away from the hull. The ocean wanted to claim me. Out here, it was the chieftain. For this reason, I had tied myself to *An Ruen*'s main mast. Then there was the pull of the coracle around my waist, but this was no choice. I had to ensure this opportunity was there for us. From inside the hull Tigernus passed me the needle and thread. In order to stop it from slipping out of my fingers, he wrapped the remaining thread around my arm.

There was no shortcut though. I'd have to endure the swash; its power sometimes physically swamping me. Such energy made Tigernus' task unending. One of the hides had to be used for the repair, whereas before it had stopped some of the spray entering the hull. His vomit on his jerkin merged with it, making for an unpleasant bath. If the hallucinogen was still powering around his body, then Tigernus would not truly know if he was in this world or Annown. All I could hope was that he would carry on with his bailing and try and keep *An Ruen* afloat.

The outer repair took much longer. There were only some occasions when I actually had enough time to sew, before being deluged again, or being pulled back from the site on the hull. I dropped the needle into the sea so many times; locating it again, and then once again losing it. I had to stay focused though. The hull had to be made good. Our survival was dependent on it. You may wonder how I managed to stay there (the immersion may have lasted some three hours or more). Bah! Perhaps it was Warna. Perhaps her persistence was with me. Although Tigernus' vision had been chemically-induced, maybe she had been there all the time: the drug only leading to a fuller perception and visualisation of her. Maybe her spirit (knocked about and raped by the *Ancredhor Mor* as it had been) was somewhere ahead of the bow – dragging us on through stormy waters, pulling us towards a new paradise. It had been her way. Maybe she was making it ours.

"You anywhere near finishing yet?" asked Tigernus.

He sounded drunk. I might have sounded the same when I came round at Hy-Brasil.

"Coming on," I replied. "How are things inside the hull?"

"Wet," came his answer.

"Are you still feeling the effects of the watercress?"

"I don't know," the voice said, "whether it's the ocean's swell or the swell of my stomach."

I imagined it was probably a bit of both.

It was night by the time I raised myself out of the water with some degree of satisfaction that I had averted our sinking. Just how long the repair would last remained to be seen. The hull had been breached and when that happened, it seemed to have a net effect on the rest of the structure. Sometimes, as hard as you work to repair one section, another starts to disintegrate before your eyes. We had to hope that *An Ruen* had the seal's persistence about her; that she was not yet ready to be released to the depths.

"I could do with hauling her up on a beach," I said. "Then we could really investigate the problem – maybe reapply a full skin to that section, instead of a patch. What do you think?"

Tigernus was in no mind to think. I saw the grazes on his hand, where he had caught it on the bulwark from so much bailing. I noted my own bloodied fingers from the sewing. His mind was probably racing still, not only from the narcotic effect of watercress, but from the mermaid's poison still creeping around his body. There was not a guiltier feeling man on the sea at this point than me.

In the moonlight we did the best we could to clear up the inside of the hull. We used spare hide to soak up the remaining sick and water, and used some alcohol (remaining with us from Caera) as a disinfectant. The night was clear. We both looked above to see if the comet was still tracing overhead, but it had long since gone; perhaps trailing to some new part of the black ocean up there. We realised nobody or nothing could predict the future for us now. At a fundamental level, we were purely in the hands of some wool grease and oxhides from the horn of Britain.

When the moon was at its highest, the swell started to decrease. It was as if we had passed a median or boundary, and that the sea was marking it for us. Our frantic hope that *An Ruen* would remain watertight continued throughout the night. Despite Tigernus' weariness and drug-infused state, we both got down to greasing as much of the inside and outside of our vessel as we could. I was taking no chances. What remained was the hull beneath the waterline. There, I was hoping the algae growing might serve a similar purpose.

The final task was to pull in our lifeboat – stocked as it was now with all our provisions. There was a comfort in transferring them back into the hull of *An Ruen* and then familiarising ourselves with a new on board layout. We agreed to stay away from the port section of hull. This necessitated moving the heads to the port bow. It was probably nearer dawn than midnight by the time we got around to sleeping. For all his testing of the adult world – of drugs, and love, and prophecy – Tigernus was still a child. When I woke in the morning, he had nursed himself into my arms and had curled into a tight ball. My body had become a temporary fogou in this tumult of an ocean.

Our latitude was getting higher and we both sensed a new chill in the air. Tigernus was shivering, and when I cleaned my teeth I felt our stored water had got colder. Cirrocumulus cloud punctuated the sky and instead of the grey, uniform tapestry, there was a distinct horizon once again: a blue sky and a green ocean. This was going to be a cold, clear day.

To my delight, on our route that day we were being escorted by a leatherback turtle at our bow. Tigernus' vision had been drug-induced, but looking back now, I like to think this turtle was the spirit of Warna. Just like this lowly creature, she had a hard exterior, but was soft inside. She already knew both my direction and her own. She knew it before I found her. Not even Ir and Ir though – with their various oracles – could have foreseen that, or what extraordinary events followed next.

DEAR LORD, I HAVE FAITH in your ability to deliver me across this blue void. You should know that by now. However, I still have doubts. I still need convincing of your power. I have read much, but are you as reliable as An-nown? Will you grant me safe passage? I have so many questions. Perhaps if you will return me to my father, then I will fully believe. I will be converted like Howel was. Only then will I let go of what was there before, and believe. As yet, though, I cannot do it. I need the security of knowing. On an ocean of uncertainty, I need certainty. How will you show me? Will this vessel *Azen* show me the way?

Azen had the sturdiness that had been lacking in *Warna* – and, by extension, how I imagined *An Ruen*'s passage. I was glad of this as we voyaged between the horn of Brittany and the northernmost tip of Iberia. Corentin had told me that the area was notorious for its storms. Part of their creation seemed to derive from the fact that the rock shelf and seabed under the ocean extended far into the bay here, and this made the waters shallow. I knew that many ships had foundered in its waters. The Bretons spoke guardedly about the positions of wrecks – commenting on how even the Phoenicians took great care over this stretch. I suppose I was glad that my father had not chosen this route – or he may well have been one of those vessels to have been sunk. I prayed that the mariners I sailed with were skilled enough. The weather too, was not easy. Westerly depressions tracked across us every day and brought constant rain. Some days there were powerful windstorms which formed when the air changed its feel. I noticed these transitions.

"You are so like your father," Tigernus would say. "It's scary."

As we steered southwest, dolphins raced alongside us. Gannets also followed our progress, hoping the Breton crew would throw them any fish they didn't like. Some of the braver ones of this species even dared to sit on the stern, and waited to be fed. I found myself asking for the leftovers from the catch, and tossed them to the birds sitting there. I marvelled most at the beaked whales which frequented the waters here. Tigernus had told me of his own encounters with whales – and they had generally been enormous beasts which, frankly, he hoped never to encounter again. These were smaller, seemingly more playful creatures, which were characterised by their elongated beaks and the presence of teeth instead of baleen plates. I had to be careful in mentioning them to Tigernus. I knew what he thought about whales. I still loved to see how the ocean revealed its life to me. I took your maps, Father, and marked upon them what I saw.

The crew that Corentin had assembled were a ragbag of mariners. Most were middle-aged men who had seen too much conflict in this world. They were

Britons turning into Bretons – renegotiating their identities. They came because it allowed them to escape the bloodshed; to perhaps have some faith in the order of things again. On the ocean could be found solace. Out here could be located a peace that was sometimes impossible to find on land. I understood now. I would catch them each day taking a break from their duties, standing, wondering, and contemplating the immensity of it all. I found myself doing the same. I conversed with it.

Being on *Azen* was not the same as being aboard *Warna*. *Warna* rocked with every step and movement its crew made. *Azen* could power through strong waves, and still remain stable. This stability comforted me. It made me think what I had set out to do was possible. My complacency in this and the natural world was only shaken when Rosparzh noted a black form on the horizon. It was another vessel, pushing up from the southwestern tip of Iberia. Stillness bore down on the crew. Although the Bretons devoted most of their time to fishing, they never stood very far from their weapons. Experience had taught them that the agony of war might come at any time, at any location. A hoarse Corentin shouted orders to prepare arms.

The men on board advised me to go down below, where I could not be seen. If there was conflict, then the decks would be no place for a woman. I contested this with them, in order to show my worth. One reluctantly handed me a bow and arrow.

"I can fight as well as the rest of you," I stated.

"Maybe as well as you wield your mouth," he responded.

Admittedly, I had not trained like the boys of Chysauster, but Kenal had advised me of how to shoot and fight while I was a young woman. Maybe if my mother had been taught the same skills, she would not have received her fate. It is why I had trained with him.

"Steady," Tigernus was saying. "We don't want any conflict if we can avoid it."

As we edged closer to this other vessel, discussion became focused on her lines and forms. Was she of the *Ancredhor Mor*? No. That was unlikely these days. Since the Saxons assumed control, they had retreated into the north. It was not likely to be Saxon either. They were still trying to hold their control of the island of Britain without venturing further to the southwest. I began to feel the fear of everyone on board. On the ocean, there is nowhere to run and hide. There are no refuges, no shelters, nor towers. You may wish for the comfort of the earth, but you will only find the brine.

The ocean was large enough for us to each pass by comfortably. What was it about men on the sea? Why did they seek control of it? Why look for power and tyranny when it cannot be administered? The only power is the ocean. It is that which has ultimate control. Can't the fools see that?

Tigernus picked up on my concerns.

"They want to make sure they are not headed for Brittany."

The vast size of the enemy's vessel drew closer. We noted their armoured warriors on board. The metal they used was far more sophisticated than that of the Bretons. It was then, in watching the flashes of metal, that I saw Tigernus' head move. He had noticed something on board the other vessel.

"Halt! Don't shoot," he urged. "Don't engage them in any way. I know this crew..."

"They are fearsomely armed," said Corentin. "I will not let them pass our way without a fight."

"They seek no fight with you, or our people," said Tigernus. "These are the descendants of Breogán. Good men – they fought alongside me in Hibernia."

Tigernus waited no longer. He ran to the bow and stood upon it, waving a length of linen as a white flag. The ships drew so close now that we could almost touch the ornate wood of the incoming vessel.

"Ith? Are you there? If you are, speak to me," Tigernus shouted.

Clearly this name ignited some concern on board the other vessel. I saw men dart from their positions.

"Bile? It is me, Tigernus. We fought alongside each other years ago. Do you remember me?"

From some inner sanctum on board the ship opposite, a heavily-armed middle-aged man made himself known. He wore a different head piece to the other soldiers on board, denoting his command.

"I am Bile," he shouted across, adding, "of Brigantium. You know me?"

"I do. You may not remember me – but we helped Oengus to defeat the giant descendants of the Fir Bolg... I was then but a boy. I am now a man..."

This Bile took an eye glass of some kind, and held it up in order to look across at Tigernus more closely.

"We come in peace. We aim to cross the ocean."

"Oengus is long dead," Bile shouted, "but the Corcu Loígde prosper. We trade with them much. Our peoples have united."

"Do you remember me?"

"Of course I remember you – and your father," shouted Bile. "A great wrestler wasn't he?"

Tigernus laughed.

"It is time we caught up, my friend."

Both ships halted their courses. We had launched *Warna* and crossed over to the Breogán ship. Within a few minutes, much had been gleaned. They had met the daughter of Voog. I learnt more of my father's heroism. Ith, it appeared, had died of disease when still a young man. Nothing could have been done. It had been one of those things; the disease was beyond all present knowledge. The Bretons learnt that they could always call upon the children of Breogán's help in their fight against the Saxons, whom they had come to loathe.

"There is someone else you must meet," said Bile. "You know her, Tigernus..."

We were led deep into the ship's hull where a grey-haired woman was tending to those men who were frail or unwell.

"Aimend," called Bile. "Someone to see you."

24

'Milpreve' stone, Bartinney Downs, Cornwall, unknown date
This naturally-formed stone was apparently much valued in early Britain by druidic orders; Milpreve meaning 'a thousand snakes'. The fragmented example here was dug from Bartinney Downs in 1962. Elsewhere across the archipelago of Britain, they are called 'Serpent's Eggs' or 'Adder Stones'. The stones were supposedly formed by the twisting together of the saliva and slime of snakes. Milpreve were well-known across early Europe and are mentioned in Book XIX of Pliny's *Natural History*. Mineral comparison data suggests that this particular stone originated from Dänholm, Germany close to the Baltic Sea. Courtesy of Penlee House Gallery and Museum, Penzance.

ALWAYS BEFORE, WE HAD FOUGHT others – other beasts, men and obstacles; or, of late, even the ocean itself. This is where we came to fight ourselves. Up until now, Tigernus, Rat and I had been a nation state, a people who refused to be compromised by those who wished to see us fail; but civil war (as we had witnessed in Hibernia) and its brother – internal division – could utterly destroy us. These twin evils had been stalking us for a while, though we had not recognised their presence. Like gawking vultures, they had positioned themselves on the gunwale and were watching our every move. How could I have let this happen? How could I have been so utterly selfish? After all, I was only dealing with a small boy and a tiny rodent. But if I tell you, perhaps you will understand. Maybe you will even forgive.

For a long time now, partly through his own endeavours, and partly through my own need for companionship, I had stopped viewing Tigernus as a child. Although a boy, on this voyage he had to mature in ways that most children of his age would never need to. Those back playing their games at Carn Euny would never have to endure what he had witnessed. Yet at the same time, he seemed to revel in the responsibility of adventure. Only the hallucinogen and its effects had caused him to revert to a needy state once again. In the aftermath of that, he had been embarrassed I believe; ashamed that he had temporarily compromised his manliness. I told him not to worry, but the boy kept his pride.

It was different with Rat. For a creature I once loathed, I had become fond of his tenacity and humour. When we became morose or bored, Rat always did something to amuse us; to start us talking again. But after the storm and the towering ferocity of those waves, when we seemed to cross a line into a new phase of our travels (led initially by the leatherback turtle, or Warna – I know not which) I reverted back to my original fears. Forgive me Annown. I did so, even though it pains me to say it now.

Although calmer upon the ocean now than in the days preceding this time, a storm was brewing inside *An Ruen*. There is no other way to put it.

Because of our higher latitude, both the air and the sea were getting colder. For perhaps five days we had pushed on, and each day seemed to bring a new gust of chilling wind on board. Oxhides which had once acted as resistance to the spray from towering waves swapped their positions on board. We both sat in tents made of them, storing up our own body heat. Sheepskins from the horn of Britain were dug out from storage in the bow to insulate us. Thus we combatted the cold: the sheepskins kept the heat close to our bodies, while the hides sheltered us from the wind. We looked like curious beasts – our heads atop these pyramids of wool and hide.

I had watched Tigernus carefully these last few days to see if the watercress was still affecting him. He denied its presence whenever I asked him, though I suspected that, like I did, he might have had flashbacks and relapses. Maybe he saw Warna again – but if he did, he didn't say. This, and my concerns for the mermaid's curse upon him, made me worried about the boy, and sometimes this anxiousness came out too sharply, too dictatorial. The moment I said something, he would go into denial, and then I would push further, dig deeper to double check that he was well. You understand, I did it out of concern, though perhaps I should have held back and realised he was mature enough to make his own decisions.

Was I being too much of a parental figure? Probably I was. He had left Scathynys to forget his parents. The last thing he needed was to gain a new one out here on the ocean.

Was there one moment when all this internal conflict came to a head? Probably not, but I do remember one key argument.

It was a day when the temperature dropped a few degrees once again. In the morning, a fine film of ice formed on the gunwale – delicate enough to be scraped away with the heat of a finger, yet telling us that we were now fully entering the realm of the frozen. I had been resting. As it got colder, I found that my left wrist ached more. I knew not why – perhaps the cold just found it easier to enter the bone there. The angle made the cool air gravitate towards it. Likewise, it was my extra finger that seemed to feel the chill more than the rest. Maybe the blood flow to it was not as good. It was always sensitive to mood though. I had known this since my childhood.

When I woke, Tigernus had lit a fire on top of the quern. It was not massive, but he had used some of our wood that we generally used for cooking. He was sat over it, pleasurably warming his hands over the flames. I overreacted.

"What are you doing?"

"I lit a fire."

"But you're not cooking anything."

"No. I just thought a fire would warm us up a bit. I was freezing last night."

"Us? Looks like just you..."

"No – for both of us... Here, warm yourself..."

He pointed to where the flames danced and licked.

"Very well, but if you use all the wood for that now, we will have nothing to light future fires to cook with."

I tried to say this in a calm way, but I could tell by the end of the sentence that I had raised my voice.

"But I thought..."

"You thought wrong, Tigernus. Obviously, the watercress is still affecting you. You've clearly lost your mind. Either that or you were stupid enough already."

A gust of cold wind bit into both of us.

"The wood stock is low enough as it is. Would you rather eat raw fish for the next week or two? I have no idea when we will make landfall, or even if there will be a supply of wood there."

In response, Tigernus took a cup of water and uncaringly, without thought, tipped it over the fire drenching the burning. The splash put out most of the flames, but an ember or two jumped off the quern and fell onto the bottom of the hull.

"Sorry," said Tigernus.

"Sorry won't be good enough," I barked, "if those flames burn a hole through the bottom."

I let Tigernus sort out the mess, but in my nostrils I could still smell something burning.

"There, look. You've not put that one out. It's on the stringer beside you."

He had neglected to see a length of wood still aflame on the bottom of the hull. I had to reach forward to suffocate it with a piece of oxhide.

"You fool," I shouted. "Why can't you be more careful?"

There was a brief pause and then the boy came back at me.

"Why don't you just shut the fuck up?" Tigernus pouted, kicking the quern stone and moving himself to the bow. "I was only trying to help."

"Just don't touch anything," I bawled. "Go back to seeing Warna – or whatever else you like – up front!"

This was how all wars began – a question over resources; about who helps oneself to what; about lack of parity; about a lack of trust.

"If you hadn't taken the stove off *An Ruen* and decided to cook breakfast on the back of a whale, we might still have something decent to use."

"Yeah, and if you hadn't been so obsessed with crossing an ocean, we might have had a good life with the Corcu Loígde."

"Don't bring that into it... This is not about that. It's about you being a selfish brat."

"Selfish? I'm not selfish, Voog. You're the selfish one – always so fucking self-obsessed with your past. You think you're the only git on the planet with problems."

"You don't know what you're talking about! You're just a boy."

"A boy, eh? Well, maybe I am, but if I was in love with a girl, like you say you are, despite everything, I'd fucking go back and get her. And not run away."

"I'm not running away, you ignorant little arsehole."

Tigernus cast a line into the ocean to fish, in order to distract himself from the argument.

"Well, that's news to me," he said, as the hooks bit the water.

I halted my vitriol for a while, in order to check our position. The arsehole had been right about the cold. It was chilly now. Pausing in an argument usually allows you to devise another verbal wound, another knife in the side of your combatant. I should have resisted, should have let it stop there and then. But being a fool, I didn't.

"If it weren't for me you'd still be stuck on a rock licking the arses of hairy Vikings!"

"Yeah well, at least I had a life there..."

"What? And you've not got one here?"

"Not any more. I should have gone with that mermaid. She loved me, and I loved her. I would have been happy then rather than out here in the middle of nowhere with no prospect of anything except more and more ocean."

"You're more of a tool than I thought Tigernus! Mermaids are not real love. They're just temptresses. And you'd have your fair share of ocean life with her – so don't give me that."

The real ache poured out.

"If it weren't for you, I wouldn't be cursed, and I'd be with her. It was you! You! You were the one who stopped me from going with her. You were the one who hit and hurt her. She never did me no harm."

All this had been boiling inside him these past few weeks. Now it was coming out. Despite the cool air, our words were fireballs launched across the length of *An Ruen*. We may as well as have had catapults, ballista and trebuchet lined up at each other.

"Want to go back to her do you?" I asked him, poking a stick into an unhealed wound. "Well, if you do, just put your body in the water enough. She'll find you – even all the way out here."

Tigernus didn't seem like he would commence this, as I well knew, but it didn't stop him responding with, "Perhaps I will! Leastways I could get away from you then."

At this, the argument ceased. We laid down weapons and an uneasy peace broke out. I wasn't sure if things were ever going to be the same again. I suspected Tigernus felt the same way. Despite my intense anger, I felt sorrier for him than me. I hated myself for some of what I had said. Some of the advice was still valid, however hard it was for him to swallow.

Very little else was said that day, and because of the earlier incident, we both ate separately. No fire was lit and we relied on the nutrition of handfuls of grains: a dull meal to suit our mood. I noticed Tigernus offering Rat some generous amounts.

This started to get to me as well. There was a niggle inside me about our resources. We couldn't afford to keep feeding our crewmate in this way. Rat was growing fat on our supplies, while they were dwindling. I wanted to say something but elected to bite my tongue for now. It was sure to come out. It had to.

In these moments, I had to stop myself and wonder if something was biting away at me inside. What gnawed my own soul in these waters? Probably, it was a twofold fear: firstly that we would run out of supplies, and gradually starve and die through lack of food or drinking water; secondly, a more worrying fear that the whole voyage had been a waste of time, and that we'd find nothing – no Hyperborea, no land of promise, no new world for us. This fear had been quietly induced by the discovery that Hy-Brasil did not really exist. I was trying to control these worries but found that I took them out on Tigernus.

There was a third fear building though, I have to tell you. It was one that Tigernus had already addressed: that none of the above things would kill us, but that we might just freeze to death.

I suppose that is why things developed as they did over the next few days.

In these waters, our supply of fish started to dry up. We relied on it as our major food source. It was hard to tell why shoals seemed to stay away. I knew fish could happily survive in very cold water, but the haul was definitely decreasing. Joking about Tigernus' ability to fish didn't seem the right thing to do today. He was already fragile from the previous set to that we'd had. The last thing I needed was another confrontation. Still, however, it had to happen.

When people feel their lives are being taken away from them, that is usually when they react violently. For all of us, there is a fine line to be walked. I saw it at Carn Euny. When Howel felt I took his future life away from him, he did the only thing humans are capable of: he reacted with vengeance, He wanted his own back. Warna had tried to teach me a different line, but I suspected it wouldn't catch on – not in the long term at least. By our nature, we are vengeful beings. We are also oceans who want to wash over and claim everything for ourselves. We do not want lands, islands or shores. We want to drown and flood. All of us are repressed empires.

That is how the argument about the fish happened.

Where were we?

Yes, the recall is easy here. One morning, Tigernus shouted for me. I'd found the clay figurine again and was feeling it in my pocket.

I remember his exact words.

"Look. The ocean is curdled."

What did the boy mean – how could a sea be curdled? Curdling occurred in milk if it was induced, or when it was left to go bad. The people of the Calf Goddess had been experts with curdled milk. They used it to make cheese, cream and butter – all of which we had consumed with great relish. How could it be so out here?

I looked at the view Tigernus held. I now understood why curdling was the only metaphor he could use to describe the state of the ocean. We were moving into a field of broken ice. It was nothing massive, but the sea all around us contained lumps of ice which had coalesced in the cold. This flocculation reminded us both of cheese and cream making in our respective homes. It signified for us a new kind of terror. It meant the ocean itself was freezing over. The fear was that if we went any further north, eventually the ocean would flocculate so much that it would render us immovable. We would be stuck in the ice like a leather ball in the middle of a pond.

"Go south," said Tigernus, after I had explained the process to him.

This had been a bugbear of his for a while now.

"If you go south, then we'll be out of this lot."

He paused and looked over the icy flocculence.

"It's still summer, Voog. Think what it will be like when winter eventually comes."

I tried to explain to him again that I was making for a land mass I thought existed in the north. It was the one the Vikings talked about. We needed to go there in order to rest and find new food. The hull also needed proper repair.

"I think we can manage it still," I argued. "The sea will stay unfrozen enough for us to pass through it. This curdling doesn't harm *An Ruen*. She just eases past it."

I could see the panic in the boy. It was the same panic that greets one on a winter's morning when the air takes away one's breath, and one sees that the world has overnight transformed from being green to white. I could see that he wanted a land filled with berries and fruit, dancing virgins, and cute animals; not a snow-filled wilderness. Tigernus knew of snow and ice. He had heard the tales of its power from the Vikings. I knew what he meant as well. We were innocents from the isles of Britain who found February frosts hard to take.

"Trust me," I said.

It was the wrong thing to say.

I should have said, let's give it a whirl; if we die, we die – no problem.

"Trust you? What, after all that's happened to us? I've watched you navigate Voog. You might as well throw a rock into the water and follow that. You haven't a clue."

"Compared to who?"

"Nobody," he mumbled, realising his argument was going in an unwanted direction.

"No, come on. Who do you mean?"

Tigernus moved away from me, his face still full of fear from the curdled ocean.

"Vikings."

"*Ancredhor Mor* did you say?"

He nodded.

"At least they know what they're doing. You don't..."

Knowing what had already happened between us, I decided to sidestep this argument. The boy seemed to be gunning for me because of his own fear.

"I'll ignore that remark..."

You see how I was trying.

Again, the boat went silent and we pushed on through the churning ocean cheese.

But I mentioned fish.

We had a battle over this: not just a verbal ding-dong but a physical fight. The trouble was, we became selfish. Hunger induces that. As we proceeded, the fish became less plentiful. We both struggled to catch decent meals. Although we had some days of competition to see who might bring in the biggest haul, before this time it had always been sportive and fun. That all changed when our bellies felt empty. You are both hoping that your lines bring in something, but if it's a nice sized fish, that does not become a shared meal. No, it becomes yours.

The metaphorical vultures sat with us caused this shift in our consciousness. We stopped sharing. We watched what the other was eating, trying to deny how much we were devouring, when we knew the larder was getting emptier and emptier, day by day. The cold made us want to eat more, not less. That was a key difficulty that we were both struggling with. I had not accounted for the coldness increasing our appetite. To ease the problem, I had suggested a process of rationing the food a while back, but neither of us were self-disciplined enough to see it through. I should have tried calculating days at sea, trying to work out just how close we were to land. The problem was that the accuracy of my map didn't seem to match our position in relation to the stars. Obviously, my father's accuracy was much more questionable here. He had drawn myth and question marks, not rock and reason. I was questioning and doubting myself. Maybe Tigernus was right. Maybe I was a shit navigator.

Cold and hunger bit down hard on us in those days. Without food, at times, I felt faint; sometimes delirious. I have no idea how food becomes blood and flesh (I leave that to druids and women like Aimend) but my growing lack of focus I put down to emptiness of my stomach. I could tell that Tigernus was experiencing the same feelings. He was trying to combat his feelings of hunger by keeping busy. If the mind was occupied enough then you hope you will forget your cravings. I can tell you, it doesn't work.

All of this is why I lashed out at Rat one day, when I caught him gnawing into the last of our grain. We'd been rationing him too, but he didn't understand the dire circumstances we faced. With his teeth, he had cut his way through the sacking, and when we lifted it to find him there, some of the grain was spilt as well, landing in the small pools of water inside the hull and rendering it useless. This made us both angry with him. I picked up the fat little fucker and cruelly dangled him by his tail over the edge of the boat.

"Drop him in," said Tigernus. "I won't miss him. Make him drown."

Looking back, you could tell the boy was not himself. In prior times, he had nourished this creature to become his plaything. Even I, who feared his kind, had come to recognise his use as an early warning mechanism. Were it not for his chittering about the hole in the side, *An Ruen* would have been utterly lost.

"He is a bit of a selfish little bastard isn't he?"

I realise now that my words might be applied to any of the three of us.

"We're a sinking ship anyway..." said the boy, with a tone of sarcasm. "He's going to be leaving anyway. May as well speed up the process."

"Do you really want me to throw him overboard?"

When the reality of what we were suggesting really hit us, then we retreated. At that moment, we gained clarity, as if all that had come before had been dulled and had clouded our judgement. Epiphany followed. I contemplated how cruel it would be for him to drown here. The cold would shut down his body instantly and even if he made it to one of the ice lumps there'd be no food. He would both starve and freeze at the same time.

You must see the limits though – of how close we came. Hunger was devious, manipulating us in ways that we had not previously contemplated.

We compromised by stowing Rat in a pot, and sealed it with a lid of hide, poking breathing holes in the top of it. At least there, his hunger could be managed. If he wanted to eat, he could gnaw into the thick oxhide. His random attacks on our store of grain would not be tolerated any longer.

If we were in union about what to do with Rat (I suppose he was a mutual enemy) we argued to the point of utter oblivion, as I say, over fish.

I don't know why it came to pass, but one day I managed to hook a fair-sized cod (they were rare this far north), and on its landing, instantly took its life with my crowbar, and began to light the fire to cook it. Tigernus had no luck that morning, and was struggling to give anything enough time and effort. Maybe he was delirious, maybe broken, from complete lack of food. I cut the cod flesh up into fillets, casting the head, skin and bones overboard, and began to fry them. I was shaking as I did this, both from the cold and from lack of energy in my blood. The cooked flesh tempted me. It entered my nose and ravaged my senses there. I had caught the fish; therefore, I deserved all of it.

Fuck the boy and Rat, I was telling myself. They hated me now. The boy was probably going to die anyway and no one would miss the rat. I confess. That is how it was. That is what I had become. That is how those vultures had manipulated my mind. This was my ocean and I was going to live on it.

I was talking to myself, telling myself that all of this was true. I cared for nobody now. Orla had completely gone from my mind. Hunger was now the hallucinogen: it became the only thing I cared about. I stopped thinking about our heading; ignored the stars, and paid absolutely no attention to the waters or the horizon. Nothing mattered but fish flesh falling upon my tongue and nobody else's.

"You cooking?" I heard Tigernus shout.

"Yes," I answered.

"Good."

This was the run of our conversations now. We only spoke one or two words. Anything else absorbed too much energy. See, even our language had become selfish.

"Tasty."

"Food."

I could hear Rat squealing. The fried fish was tempting his nostrils. Inside the pot, I imagined his whiskers twitching. Bastard. This was my fish. I'd caught it. I was eating it.

I only felt guilty after the last of the fillets had slid down my gullet. There had been four of them; each one tastier than the previous one and their chewy flavour never lasting long enough. The moment your hunger is satiated, you transform back into being human again. I don't know what I had been, but the speed at which I had devoured the cod left no room for me to defend my actions or make any apology. Hunger leads you across seas you never wish to go. I think I had barely licked the last of the fish off my lips when Tigernus came at me.

"You bastard!" he was yelling. "Bastard! Bastard! Bastard! You said there would be food."

He lunged at me with a knife; the same knife he used for gutting his own fish. If he could not have fish, then he was going to split me open. In that instant, I really felt he was about to slit my stomach, reach in and pull out my meal. I had a vision of him doing it pass through me. If not that, then perhaps he would like me to have regurgitated it for him. Otherwise he was going to lob off my twist of wrist and boil it up.

"I'm sorry," I shouted. "I didn't realise what I was doing..."

"You said we'd share what we caught!"

"Go easy Tigernus. Don't do anything you might regret."

"What – like slitting you open? That would teach you wouldn't it? Let's see how you'd like that, eh?"

I had stepped back toward the see-sawing stern now. He was crouched, ready to pounce. He had a length of flax in his other hand, looking like he was ready to tie me up like a joint of meat. I was back in Carn Euny again, suspended from Howel's rafters.

"I'll catch some more cod. You can have it all. I promise. There's plenty."

Tigernus was no boy now. He was a man. All I had taught him was now coming out in this instant. I was rebuking myself for making a monster. Underneath though, I knew I was the monster. I had been the selfish one. I had deceived myself into thinking my actions were permissible. They weren't. I had failed. I had left one place in failure. Now, at the edge of the earth, I had failed again. Just like the ocean, our relationship had curdled. It had rotted somehow, born of too little space in too long a voyage.

I could see it in the boy's eyes. He wanted me dead. I suppose, once lifeless, he'd go about eating me. Human flesh is as good as any other. Could this have been my end then? Maybe I was headed on a course to become a bloodied mass of bone and meat to satiate the hunger of a ravenous boy. That's it Tigernus. Feed my eyes to the gulls. Let me be nuzzled in the deep by a thousand crabs.

An Ruen rocked as Tigernus forgot all other desires. He teased me with the knife initially, holding it above his head, readying to bring me down. His first stab was accurate. It almost caught my stomach. I had to arch my back to avoid it. I tried reasoning with him but, as I knew myself, there was no reasoning with a man who needs nourishment. Nothing else will motivate him and nothing will stop him.

I was recalling the time when I had wrestled Sreng. Similar moves would have to be employed here, if I was to have hope of living. Unfortunately, in moments of boredom, I had been tutoring Tigernus in the ways of useful hitches and moves, so he knew a few avoidance strategies as well. He was able to dart back from my grasp. Again, Tigernus hooked the blade towards me. I ducked but the tip of it caught my shoulder. The metal was sharp and although its penetration was not deep, the skin parted and oozed blood. He was getting me. We had been friends. I had been his father. I had been his teacher. Now I was his enemy.

"You won't survive," I said. "Not without me. Not out here."

Tigernus peered over the cold, curdled ocean. It was far from the safety of Scathynys. His own dreams had rotted away.

"I'll be all right," he said. "Don't you worry."

The ocean was quiet here. All you could hear was our breath, each exhalation generating a hot mist from our mouths. We had faced so many storms, so many squalls, and now, at this final leap into the future, we had failed. It had been a long way to come to have learnt the skill of hatred. It shouldn't have been this way.

"Leave me then," I reasoned. "Put me in the coracle, and desert me here to float amongst the ice. You push on in *An Ruen*. Go south if you like – take whichever direction you want. What do you think?"

A flicker of hope passed through his eyes. Right at this moment, leaving me here – abandoning me – could be a quite exhilarating thought. That would be due punishment for a right cocky bastard who ate all the food.

"I accept it Tigernus."

But the boy knew the pleading. He knew I was trying to buy time, to turn this course of events into something positive.

"No. I don't think so."

I didn't see him responding to all of this quite at the moment he did. His lunge forward was bang on target, aiming for my heart. He knew the way to take out a man. I wasn't going to a let him have me though. Just as a survival instinct had come to me before, it came again. Although Tigernus had the anger and the energy, it was me, as adult, who had the strength. I caught his knife-wielding hand and grabbed it tight. That blade was going to do no further damage. Tigernus had a different idea though. He was twisting through the air, and aiming to bring it down on my fifth finger. He seemed to be thinking: I'll have that off, you freak.

The tussle continued for a long time. It was too much time. We should have realised the lack of control we both had, and stepped apart. I needed to knock him out of his unreasoning. I had to stop hunger eating him. Whatever may have happened here, we could recover from it, I was certain. It would take time, but it was possible. Though our bond had been broken, it was salvageable, surely?

You will see then, I had no choice.

When we broke, Tigernus fell backwards and dropped the knife. It fell into the hull. Without it, he was less of a danger. I could have him now. My own weapons were beyond him, back in the middle canopy. Necessity is the mother of invention though. I reached overboard and with both hands picked up the largest clot of ice I could. The mass was dense and compact. The cold of it instantly impacted upon my hands, but I still had enough energy and fortitude to use it. I brought the clot hard down on Tigernus' head and in an instant he crumpled to the floor.

I didn't know if I'd killed him. In that second, I had wanted to. It was a matter of survival – me, or him.

The attack had been so unexpected that it took me some time to collect myself; to even stand up and try to save anything from this situation. If I had killed something that I cared for and loved so much, I would never have been able to forgive myself. I'd have attached myself to the anchor and let it pull me under. The great clot of ice had no blood on it; I could see that. I took this to be a good sign. Perhaps it had the effect I wanted – simply to stun him. The great ball of it lay in the hull, weighing us down. I put my hands around its circumference and threw it back overboard. There it was returned to floating as mere ocean curd.

Close up, Tigernus was nothing but skin and bone. He'd always been thin. Now he was skeletal. I'd not been watching closely enough.

I moved anything he could hit or stab me with though. I was having no repeat of what just happened. Only then did I listen for a breath. Only then did I check for a pulse. You see what I had become. Survival had overtaken me and removed from me any compassion or mercy. I knew I needed to get it back, pull it out of the abyss. He was still alive, fortunately, and had only been stunned by the blow to his head. He was starting to come round.

"Tigernus. I'm sorry, I'm so sorry..."

I was crying; my tears falling onto his face and chest.

In the end, I was the child, hugging him – and yet, I was so childish as to ensure there would be no further attacks on me that I tied his arms and legs didn't I? I then tied his body to the main mast, just where I had positioned my mason's mark. I was crucifying him, just like the Vikings and the baby plesiosaur.

"Sorry," I was saying. But I have to do this. For your sake and for mine."

Tigernus was mumbling some apology to me, regretting what had transpired. There was no way I could let him go; not yet though. I didn't have the strength. If there was one thing I was going to do, it was to find Tigernus a decent meal. Guilt and pure hatred of myself drove me in this way. I had multiple lines dangling through the clotted ocean, praying that some creature might take a bite. He was aware of my activity, but said little. He could do little in fact. I saw the signs: his stomach had become distended.

The quality of fish that came in was very poor, but there was enough of it for a meal. I used everything I could to make it tasty for him.

"Get me down!" he was shouting. "Cut all these fucking ropes off me will you!?"

"You going to attack me again Tigernus?"

His eyes peered at me. Was there still a threat?

"No. I've come to my senses. You've nothing to worry about."

Using the same knife he had threatened me with, I cut away the rope and let him down. He soothed the marks on his wrists and ankles where the rope had cut into him. I hadn't realised. I had strung him up there for nearly twelve hours. Those hours would calm him though even if he was lying to me. When he was back down, the lunacy of hunger had sidestepped him and he was more placated. My cruelty to be kind to him had worked. It was now time to be kind again. I placed a large bowlful of fish in front of him. I needed him onside again. I had much to make up to him. While, he ate, I redressed my arm where he had drawn blood. Salt water would help its healing so I dabbed at it with a rag I had dipped in the ocean.

As he chewed the fish and spat the bones overboard, I sensed his guilt at what he had done. He was sobbing about it. I could hardly complain. I had gained a small wound for the massive injustice I had served him. Although sore, it would only take a few days to mend. Our healing would take a little longer. At least the two of us understood what had been driving us, what had turned us from men into monsters. We knew that both the fire and fish of hunger had so far been our downfall.

In the next few days though, it was water. I had tried chipping off the sea ice and melting it to see if it was drinkable. One taste was enough to make me retch, and not want any more. Tigernus tried it too. He suffered it a little more, but we knew we needed an urgent solution. Nothing though, was presenting itself as being very helpful.

The skins were empty. I squeezed the last of them into Tigernus' mouth and told him not to swallow it for a bit.

"Let it coat your mouth and bring back your saliva. You'll feel better for it."

I cannot tell you how many days passed with us in this state. It could have been one or two; it could have been ten. All I could manage to do was to cast a line over the back, and hook in whatever fish I could. We had wood for a while, which meant the fish could be cooked – usually just lightly frying it, but the wood soon ran out. There was nothing but a few pathetic twigs left. I considered cannibalising bits of *An Ruen* and, one time, took apart a food tun to give us more wood, but this was an unsustainable direction. What next, I wondered? Would I be pulling apart sections of the hull? Would we end up in the coracle cooking bits of oxhide? Would that then be burnt too – so we were like Rat, cast out in a floating pot? This course would lead us to an upturned skull drifting alone.

No. It could not be done. So we proceeded with very little. Fish had to be eaten raw. At first, the taste is instantly vomit-inducing. It feels like you are eating chunks of salted meat that the ocean has excreted just for our benefit. But when you are hungry and there is nothing else, it is a flavour you become used to. You never like it, and when you eat, your mind is back chewing some favourite delicacy of your childhood. And yet, it was the way we survived. It was the way nature survived, and as we were now indistinguishable from nature, it would be our way too. We were just two bigger fish.

Delirium had set in though. In all honesty, it probably had before. We just hadn't recognised it. We were both so weak that nothing strenuous could be done. Hours passed when neither of us could even move. We shat our pants; and without hesitation pissed in these too. We stank to high heaven, never washing or feeling the need to help each other. I had long since stopped cleaning my teeth, and felt a burr of food build up on them. Had it come to this? Yes, we had reached complete oblivion. Abandonment had already set in.

An Ruen, in effect, just drifted. We were no longer piloting her. She was piloting us. The ocean was curdling more intensely. Gaps between the ice lumps became tighter; the lumps bigger and more ferocious. The larger ones growled at us while we shivered in agony. Whereas only recently we had been attacking each other with the ferocity of a mother plesiosaur, we were now huddled together, finding raw comfort in the shape of another life.

I was so dehydrated I could not speak. Drinking our own urine seemed our next option. There was, in the end, thankfully, no need for this though.

"What's that?" croaked the boy.

He was pointing to something ahead of us, rising out of the ocean.

"Is it land?" he asked.

"No."

I was trying to perceive the vast form of it.

"It's a crystal column," remarked Tigernus. "It's got to be magical."

The structure certainly rose out of the ocean as a pinnacle.

"It's not crystal," I explained, coughing for breath. "It's not magical either. It's ice. Looks like crystal though..."

Tigernus had noted hundreds and thousands of shimmering ice crystals sparkling at us.

The moment he spotted it, I knew we'd be saved. The crystal column had not been constructed in the sea by some god or new race of men. No, this was a huge naturally-formed iceberg, and where there was ice of this kind, we were certain to find water. I'd never seen one of these formations before, but knew its presence was a blessing from Annown. Now there was new hope. Our pelagic nadir had ended.

LORD, YOU ARE FULL OF surprises. You bring me hope when there is none. You bring me a light in the dark. In you, I can see much of me. In you, I see the future. In you, I see humanity. Did you happen to place this woman in front of us? Was it by your all-knowing design and clever arrangement that she stepped into our lives?

Oh father, I wish you could have seen her. Maybe just as much as my mother – you would have wished to see this woman again. I sail and run towards you.

Aimend turned around to face us. Tigernus said nothing. He expected instant recognition.

"Yes?" she asked sharply. "What can I do for you?"

This was the woman Tigernus had talked about. This was the woman who perhaps had loved my father. Maybe he had broken her heart. I saw her beauty. Maybe there was something of my mother in her too; the thing that attracted him to her. Under the harsh exterior, I could already see a kindness.

"You don't recognise me, do you?" said Tigernus.

"Should I?" she snapped. "I don't know any Bretons. Never had much to do with them."

Although from Hibernia, the first thing I noticed about her was how well she spoke our tongue. I already knew why.

"Let me take you back twenty years," said Tigernus. "I was then nothing but a wretch of a boy whose agony you healed. The shepherd Caera brought us to you. I was no Breton then. I came from Scathynys."

The woman's face changed. It suddenly softened.

"Ti...ger.. nus?"

He nodded.

"No... But out here, now?"

"It is me, I promise."

He explained briefly his path since leaving Hibernia. He retold his journey across to Hyperborea; his time with Corentin and then his imprisonment and escape. She was sorry to learn of his incarceration.

"What do you remember?" Tigernus asked.

"That rat!" she went. "You used to sneak him in – when you shouldn't have... What became of him?"

"He remained with me through the years. They can live long, you know... I had him at least until I made my first raids back on Britain."

"Such a character!"

Aimend moved to hug him. It felt like he was the son she never had.

"Who is this then?"

She pointed at me.

"Your intended?"

Tigernus blushed.

"We are together," he explained, "and she is the love of my life."

Aimend moved to examine me closely. She was used to such activity and scanned my face.

"I recognise your eyes," she said. "Where do I know them from?"

"My father," I said.

"You know him," interrupted Tigernus.

Aimend looked at me again.

"Not Voog? Really?! Voog is your father?"

"Yes."

"He never knew of her when we first met you."

"I am glad that he has had a child. He deserved to pass on..."

She paused, not continuing what she was about to say.

"Pass on what?" I asked.

Flustered, she changed direction.

"His love. He would have made a good father."

"I have not met him. That is why we travel now. I am travelling to find him."

"I'm sorry. I didn't mean..."

"Don't worry. It's just the way things are."

Aimend thought over what knowledge she had just gained.

"And your name?"

"Blejan..."

"Blejan, sometimes it does not matter that a parent is not there. It only matters that they send you their love."

"I don't think he knows of me..."

Aimend stopped her present line of questioning and diverted the conversation back to the two ships meeting in the way they had done. She quickly realised Bile and Tigernus had renewed their connection. Introductions were made to her by Corentin and Rosparzh. Tigernus asked after Caera.

"He's getting on in years... but still strong as an ox. Still goes out to tend the sheep. He talks often of that time. He is a grandfather now you know."

We learnt why Aimend was onboard. A sickness had taken hold of the people of Brigantium and the Corcu Loígde had recommended that Bile take her back to his state for her to work her healing. She had been only partly successful though; the disease had been too virulent.

"I did pray," she confessed, "but it did no good."

While Tigernus introduced Corentin and his men to those of the Breogán – via much boar and ale, Aimend and I chatted long into the night. I learnt of her feelings for my father and how she perceived him. Before then, I had only really received negative views. My grandmother, although she had eventually come around to viewing him positively, had spent most of her life trying not to think about him. And Tigernus, well, Tigernus only spoke about him in a certain way. From Aimend, I was able to discern more. When Tigernus had first told me about her, I had been concerned that another should love him above and beyond my mother. Now that I had spoken with her, I understood.

There was much discussion about faith. It seemed Aimend and I had developed similar views. She knew of Annown, and then of the Calf Goddess, but also of this new God. Her heart, she said, had become split between them. Hibernia had become a centre of this new learning. She had met monks who were travelling to *Sceilig Mór* in order to establish a monastery there.

"I cannot let go of the old ways though," she said. "They are ingrained in me."

I told her I understood. I absolutely understood.

"You should see this though," she said, reaching into a basket. "This cross – Tigernus knows it well. Your father gave it to him to hold. From the missionary they met..."

"Warna?"

"That's it. Yes. That was her name."

I felt the weight of the stone cross. So this is what they had been given in Cymru and carried across to Hibernia.

"Has it been a good charm?" I asked.

"More than a charm I think. There is power in it... I just don't understand it – that's all."

Aimend sat thoughtfully looking at me.

"You know what you said before about your father not knowing you. I wanted to say more then – but I couldn't. Listen, in my experience, sometimes, that does not matter. Sometimes it is not about the length of time we spend with someone; sometimes it is the quality. You have so much to catch up. This time is coming for you. I can feel it."

I held out my hand to Aimend and clutched her.

"I told your father it wasn't over between him and Orla. You have proven that..."

I clasped her fingers hard. I knew what she was thinking of; my father's extra digit.

"Come with us," I said.

I saw her face alter again.

"I cannot," she said.

"Why not? Is it your duties here? The work you do for the people of Breogán?"

She shook her head.

"No," she cried. "It is not that."

"What is it then?"

"When you are older, then maybe you will understand... Sometimes a love is so strong that it kills you on the inside. This, I've lived with for twenty years. After that time, it won't grow back. Let me put it another way... It shouldn't grow back. Do you understand?"

Things growing back, I would come to understand much better in the future. For now though, it was clear Aimend was not about to alter her course to Hibernia. In the morning, we parted, knowing more about the way the world worked. Bile nursed a hefty hangover, as did Corentin, Rosparzh and Tigernus. The ocean had made it so.

25

Brooch, Chysauster, Penzance, Cornwall, 7th to 8th Centuries CE
Both men and women wore brooches such as this to fasten outer garments. Made of bronze, this is typical of the bold open-ring (or penannular) brooches of this period. It is inlaid with red enamel and millefiori glass, and has a complex incised decoration on the back. Its surface may originally have been made silvery by tanning. The brooch is unusual in having a doomed circular boss on each terminal. Considering the detailed decoration of this piece, it would have belonged to a local chieftain or his wife.

TRANSFIXED BY THE PINNACLED FORM before us, we gained enough strength to pull up alongside it. Tigernus' eyes were wide open. He had never seen such a vast conglomeration of packed ice. We felt the walls of it. They were dense, almost as hard as rock. I explained to him that, like the whale he had sat upon, over two-thirds of it actually sat beneath the surface. In the water, we could see where the white crystal dipped down into the depths.

"Who makes them?" asked Tigernus.

He saw an artisan at work.

I smiled at his question. It would take a hefty artisan to craft this work. He still appeared to disbelieve that nature formed them. I gave him my theory – that they were broken pieces of compacted ice that had run down to the ocean from mountains. It was on those mountains that snow and ice had gathered, each layer adding to the next, gradually pushing the whole along. I explained how snow and ice could creep – very slowly – perhaps over hundreds and thousands of years, and that when it reached the sea, it broke off. The ice was buoyant because it was filled with air bubbles. The surfaces of these bubbles were what reflected the white light from the sun, which is why they glowed white. These bubbles made it appear as crystal.

We found a lower edge to the iceberg we had chanced upon and positioned our anchor stone upon it. *An Ruen* nestled into a temporary harbour of ice. We stepped off and, still wrapped in sheepskins and hides, we marched across its surface, wary of any cracks or fissures upon it. We need not have worried. The ice was so thick and dense that nothing could pass through it. I tasted the ice near the waterline, and it still contained salt. Further up, the ice had been unaffected by the sea water and tasted pure. We slaked our thirsts by chipping off cubes of it and sucking them in our mouths. Although slightly gritty, the water was fresh and invigorating. We loaded some blocks onto hides which, as sledges, could then be pulled back to the boat. Perhaps we overloaded them in some ways, but then we were fearful of going without fresh water again.

The ice was not totally pure white. We both noted coloured streaks of black and brown running across the plateau. On closer examination we saw this was a run of rock and soil trapped in the ice, which had no doubt been pulled off the earth as the river of ice crept along. For me, this was a good sign. It meant that somewhere, relatively close, there might be this supposed land form.

As we walked on, we began to understand the full size of this iceberg. Over a ridge, and where the heights of its pinnacle began to rise, we noticed a long tail to the plateau. The iceberg was no small structure. Back home, it would be the size of a small kingdom. Although sitting lower in the water, I estimated it to be around half the size of Scathynys. That was indeed considerable.

"Where's it going?" Tigernus asked.

"They drift south usually, I think. The currents move them along."

It didn't feel like we were moving at all, but then, as we both knew, the earth itself was moving in space and we didn't feel that either. The larger the object, the slower the motion feels.

"Eventually, it will melt and return back to the ocean again. The sun will shine and evaporate the water into clouds, and if it is cold enough, the water will fall as snow. This is the way this cycle works."

"I never knew... I mean, I'd never thought about it before," said Tigernus.

It seemed we were back on track. I'd become his teacher again. He trusted me once more. The wound was healing.

"I wish I had that lens of Ir and Ir," I noted. "Then we might look upon the horizon, and see what was there."

To foresee in that way would have been good. We both wished that Puffin was still present too. His ability to cross distance would have been helpful. I checked our position by observing the sun's path, and quickly found north. Out there were other ice masses; some tabular, others domed or block-like. Beyond that, just perhaps, the low form of a land mass. It was hard to tell. I hardly needed to say it to the boy – he intuitively knew it was in that direction we needed to sail.

The purity of the iceberg made us realise how much filth and grime had gripped us. We began a process of both cleaning the vessel and cleaning ourselves. Although it was hardly the ideal environment to get naked in (our pissles shrank to mere holes), we needed to wash our clothes. They were soiled and smelt of urine and shit. Our hunger had stopped us thinking about our hygiene and appearance. For the first time in a long time, I cleaned my teeth and, using the fish-gutting knife, trimmed my beard and did my best to cut Tigernus' hair. This grooming was socially important, as well as giving both of us a better sense of ourselves. In brief ways, we started caring for each other again, in ways we hadn't over the past fortnight. We remembered the small things that each of us liked, and endeavoured to do that for each other. For the first time, we released Rat again and enjoyed his playfulness, realising how important he had been to us. Rat shouted abuse to us initially though, for locking him away. We found a few fish scraps which he was happy enough to plough through. Both of us had a word with our conscience about what past misdemeanours we had committed.

An Ruen's hull was tidier now. Things had gone adrift. Before, there had been a system but during the nadir of our voyage it had been forgotten. Now we tried to ensure all the systems were back in place. I was very proud of this vessel. She had nurtured us all the way, and was still intact. Yes – she'd been battered, and needed repair, but given what we had crossed and what obstacles we had surmounted, she had been a wonder. In this time, *An Ruen* became a person, upon whom we lavished praise.

We stayed one night beside the iceberg. In its purity we found some comfort and relief. The day had been still, but in the nighttime we noticed that the icebergs groaned and heaved. Their low moaning seemed to be generated by the melting they endured, and by small blocks fissuring and entering the sea. These were the clots of ice we had seen further south, which caused the curdling effect in the water. Occasionally out there, two domes might collide, and this brought further noise: the rasp of two hard surfaces brushing against each other.

Tigernus had altered his attitude towards the voyage. Of late, he had been dismissive, a tone brought on by fear. Now he was more positive.

"I don't think we're far from land," he was saying. "I reckon those icebergs have broken off recently."

I was praying he was right.

Hunger continued to be a problem but the vultures that threatened us had flown away. The fish haul each day was not great, but it was enough to keep us going. We were still eating it raw. By now, we'd become connoisseurs, knowing which species tasted better.

The next morning, we'd planned a push north through the ice field and bergs within it. Care would be needed. We did not want to be crushed in a collision of these enormous white blocks. The noise they made overnight told us to plot a course that avoided the largest ones. In daylight, all of them shimmered like jewels set in the crown of the ocean. The whiteness was sometimes so intense we had to shield our eyes. Despite this, we managed to negotiate a course through and around these icy platforms.

Things markedly altered when we found a sentinel. All along, enhancing my navigational efforts, nature had lent us a helping hand. The sentinel was completely unexpected, especially out here, where there seemed little life. How it came to happen was like this: we both heard a sploshing sound off the starboard side. As usual, Tigernus was both intrigued and appalled at any new kind of creature. He loved to see what wonders nature might offer, but was scared of what they might do. This creature, perhaps like the juvenile plesiosaur, was merely curious. It had observed our form in the water – and perhaps saw something of itself in us. To this extent, it was not far wrong.

"It's surely a monster of some kind," deadpanned the boy. "We keep meeting them."

"I doubt it."

We both scanned the ocean to the right of us. Clots of ice still churned, and immediately beyond that was a wide tabular iceberg.

I had moved to port, to pull in the main sail slightly, so we could catch the wind better, but I saw the face of the creature at the same time as Tigernus. Inquisitively, it popped its head out of the water and gazed over.

"Look," said Tigernus. "It's a sea cat."

I leaned over to see a whiskered face bobbing in the water. My first impression was that it was a seal – hence its attraction to us – but then I realised its girth and skin were different. It had a greater bulk too and when it turned in the water, it pulled its two long tusks into the air.

"See them! If we're not careful, he'll puncture our hull."

The tusks looked dangerous but the creature seemed unlikely to use them in this way.

I could see why Tigernus had called it a sea cat. The bristles on its face gave it a cat-like appearance, and the tusks gave it a certain ferocity.

"I think they are called walruses. They're a bit like seals."

"Do they eat people?" Tigernus asked.

"I don't think so. It's a good sign that it's here," I offered. "Where walruses are, there'll be decent fish."

"How do you know?"

In reality, I didn't know. I tried to recall where I had seen images of these beasts before. Sometimes they had dotted the leaves of parchments – purported as being some kind of mythic horse whale – or were they called sea elephants? Usually, if imagined, there was some thread of reality within their depiction. There could not be many people from our part of the world who had encountered such creatures, but as you know, stories always travel. Maybe once, when the ice was lower around the world, perhaps they were found closer to our homelands.

The creature's head was back out now. It grunted a low sound at us.

"I don't think it likes us much," said Tigernus.

"He's just saying hello. I don't expect he sees many mariners of our kind."

Tigernus seemed to understand that the walrus was like a seal. He'd observed plenty of those off the shores of Scathynys, and of course, we had seen several along the way during our passage. This knowledge made him have a more benign reaction to the beast that watched us.

"Are they old?" he asked.

"Why?"

"Well, they're all wrinkly – like old people."

"That's just their skin and blubber – that's all. It keeps them warm."

The walrus dived again and left us alone for a while. He was perhaps under the surface for ten minutes, before re-emerging a little way off our bow.

"Keep your eye on him."

"Why?"

"Well, this kind of creature can't survive forever in the ocean. They need to rest on land. Follow him, and we'll find the land we're looking for."

Although our voyage was now more erratic and slow, this aquatic sentinel appeared to be leading us through the icefield. A few times we had to wait while he dived and fed, but we remained patient and waited for his return. When he came back, he swam quickly; almost teasing us, waiting for us to catch up with him.

"Is he just playing with us?"

"Maybe... but the general direction seems good. He knows where he's going."

"Are you sure about putting our faith in a sea-cat?"

I couldn't be sure about anything any more. Surety had long since gone from my experience on this voyage. Faith was different. You needed it now more than ever.

And so we followed.

As the walrus continued, the water changed its consistency. The curdling became marginal; the clots were smaller, and clearer water began to push in from the northeast. The icebergs slowly subsided, although far to the northwest we could see a new distant line of them tracking toward us. These were the ones that had broken off more recently. The fact that the water was becoming clearer thrilled us, and yet more thrilling was the fact that we were no longer heading towards icebergs, but instead, a line of land. I had been right all along.

Although the territory was not as far south as I had anticipated, I reckoned this was the land that the Vikings had spoken of. This was the resting point – a jutting stop-off into the larger spread of the ocean. We were about to encounter another strange, new world.

"Is that Hyperborea?"

"No. I don't think so. We're not far enough west yet. No-one knows the name of this place."

"What about Frisland?"

"Maybe," I offered, just as uncertain as Tigernus was.

We looked at the land ahead of us. It looked green, though in the distance grew snow-covered mountains. As we drew closer, it seemed that we were encountering not just a new land, but a vast continent. We were putting into just one speck of it. Given our resources and energy, there was no possible way that we could venture too far into its domain, and yet on its shore we would surely restock and rebuild.

The walrus was still with us – groaning an acknowledgement of his colony, which sat on a rocky island close to the shore of this new land. We noted other 'sea-cats' in the water now, many of them turning south towards where we had come from. The icebergs clearly held good eating grounds for them. Some of the walrus population were larger than the one we had encountered. These were bullish males who tussled with each other over domain and female interest. They wrestled and fought, locking tusk against tusk. We were glad we were not passing them any closer. Assured that he had safely led us to the shore of this new land, the walrus we knew returned to his colony. His inquisitiveness had been our saving.

From our position now, we could look back to the south and see just what we had passed through. It was an icefield that stretched as far as the eye could see. To the east were icebergs that towered more than twice as high as the original one where we had washed and found water. From here, these crystal columns seemed impenetrable, but somehow we had managed to find a way through.

Aside from the barking of the walrus colony, and the swash upon the pebble-strewn beach, we entered a realm of eerie stillness. Although both still weak from lack of food, we manhandled *An Ruen* out of the water, and using lengths of driftwood, forced these under her bow and stern to keep her upright. In some months of travelling, this was the first time she had been out of the water. The next few days would allow me to examine her hull and to better understand what repairs needed to be undertaken.

Tigernus left me to make my initial assessments, and plunged into the immediate surrounds. If the Vikings knew it, they must have hated it. This was a bare place. The cold restricted the growth of plants. Most noticeable was a permanent frost which permeated the ground and made it harsh and unforgiving. It being the last throes of summer however, some plants had managed to drag themselves out of the earth. These were most often low-slung variants. When he came back to me, Tigernus had armfuls of various crops, which he hoped might invigorate our diet.

"I don't know what this place is," he said, "but I'm calling it 'The Land of Herbs'. Look, see how many there are..."

He dumped down his haul in front of me.

"Very nice," I said. "Now see if you can find some wood... and some berries..."

We needed the latter kind of food. I knew from the sailors of Lulyn and from the Phoenicians that mariners needed fresh fruit and vegetables. Partially, this is why we had been so ill and delirious. I feared the effect of it upon us. Malaise and lethargy had already come upon us, and a few curious spots had formed on my hands and skin. I had noticed the gums of Tigernus had become spongy and red. According to the Phoenicians, this was a sign that the body needed certain fruits. I had not noticed them until we had bathed and cleansed ourselves. This was a concern that needed instant address. The long-term effects of this condition were something we did not want to suffer.

Tigernus though, came back with some wood. It was damp and stunted but there was enough of it for us to make a fire; the first one in a long time. With fire and water, we could properly cook. The fire also offered us warmth. There would be no more raw fish. Over the next few days, Tigernus and I found trout and salmon in nearby rivers, and I used some of the hunting skills that Caera had taught me, to bring down some white-furred hares. These were delicious and, given our circumstances, we feasted well. We explored as far as we could – or rather as safe as we felt – away from where *An Ruen* was beached. There were low forests of dwarf birch, alder and willow. Cotton grass, sedge and lichen grew vigorously wherever we strolled. And, as Tigernus had discovered, the climate here facilitated herbs to flourish. He found mint, roseroot, yellow root (of which we ate copious amounts) and saxifrage. Nestled in decaying leaves, we found mushrooms and fungi, which we also cooked up. We left alone anything that was orange or red as usually this was a sign of it being inedible. It was moss, however, that dominated the entire landscape here. It rose in green and purple masses – seemingly well adapted to the cold. As we were in summer, thousands of flowers poked from its tufts and provided an array of colour. After the white surrounds we had become used to of late, their hues were bewildering.

Tigernus eventually managed to find some red berries for us to consume. I didn't recognise them, and I was careful to begin with, to make sure they were not poisonous. They grew on a plant of leathery leaves, encased by silky hairs – no doubt to protect them from the frost. Once we realised that they did us no harm, we consumed as many as we could find, and stored some for the next stage of our voyage. This would help our condition. I monitored Tigernus' gums and skin more carefully, as well as keeping track of changes in my own health. We were not about to leave this 'Land of Herbs' until we were both better.

I have mentioned the nights we had endured on board *An Ruen*. Our latitude being high here, of course, they did not last very long. Sometimes, we only marked a slight dulling of the light before the sun rose again. It made sleeping difficult at times. We used the ever adaptable oxhides to construct tents in which we could escape the long hours of light. Sleep was important. The open ocean had exhausted us. Our exhaustion and delirium had been part of the reason we had antagonised each other; why we had almost turned to cannibalism.

Sometimes we noticed that the sky glowed in waves. Shimmering lights could be observed in the northern sky. They were bands or ribbons of colour dancing across the night. We knew no god associated with them, nor knew how they were formed. We could only marvel at their forms, which each night wove a tapestry across the sky. I know Tigernus wished to learn more about them, but I could not answer his questions on this occasion. I was as entranced with them as he was. No doubt Ir and Ir would see some significance in their revelation, but we had no way now of either showing or telling them. They were an ocean away.

"It is just one of nature's stories," I said to Tigernus, "that she wants to keep secret. Sometimes, humanity is best kept ignorant. Once we know everything, then we will be complacent, and mess up this world of ours."

"Maybe it is that Heaven that Warna spoke of," suggested Tigernus.

"I doubt it," I said, still being cynical of this new faith.

The herbs we discovered took my senses back to my fogou days. Some were of the kind that we placed inside for rituals of birth and dying. Because of this, I felt Annown was with me in this land. Of course, their fragrance reminded me of a certain bed inside a certain chamber. Now that we were off the ocean, I realised its distance. I realised there was no going back. For this reason, I avoided those herbs. They say smell induces memory more than any other sense.

In the daytime I began to work on *An Ruen*. Out of the water, we could now see how her hull was faring. Barnacles had formed on the underside of the bow, and so these were scraped off. The algae I also removed so that I could test whether the hides remained watertight. Once we had gradually levered her upwards using a system of stones and branches, I could nestle in under, and examine the stitching. Considering the distance and the weathering she had endured, I was satisfied with much of the hull, though one section, just after the main mast shelter, I felt needed replacing. Thinking about it, this was the part of the boat which received most wear and tear. It was where we conducted much of our daily business and where we cooked. I wasn't going to put to sea again until this task had been completed. The job was bigger than I thought though. We had to unfasten so many of the knots tied around it, and lift up the surrounding skins. I kept some of it which I felt was strong enough still, and then replaced a broad section, perhaps with around half a hide. The stringers inside looked fine, and the oak bulwarks had survived anything the sea threw at them. They looked brand new. This was heartening to find. I had not built *An Ruen* to encounter some of the seas we faced. Now that I knew what was out there, you could be sure I was triple stitching the new hide. I knew better what she had to endure, and so tried to make her stronger and more rigid. Tigernus proved himself to have nimble enough hands to tie good leather thong knots, and even became reasonably adept at stitching.

"This is good instruction for you," I said. "One day, you'll make your own vessel. You'll know what to do then won't you?"

Importantly, the rebuilding of *An Ruen* rebuilt us. We had been undone for a while now. We had unravelled, but now we were becoming stronger again. With better eating, our health improved. We grew physically stronger, and the rest onshore allowed us a mental break from the strain of the ocean. We laughed again. We skimmed stones. We messed around in the coracle inshore. With pebbles, we had contests to see who could build the highest tower. My stone-building skills had obviously become weak. Mine invariably toppled before the boy's did.

"It's all right here," Tigernus said to me. "I mean, if you were dropped here, you could survive couldn't you?"

I knew what he meant. The question was whether he wanted to travel any further. This was no Hyperborea. It was no imagined paradise in the way that we had quite conceived of it. Had Tigernus had enough? Did he want to stop – or even go back? They were questions that needed answering.

"This 'Land of Herbs' has been good to us," I declared, "but it is not my destination. I am looking for something else."

Tigernus did not respond, but I did note a change in his feelings regarding our adventure. Perhaps he had seen enough. Perhaps the ice and walrus were a frontier too far for him. Maybe he was longing to return to Scathynys where horizons are more limited. I knew it was quite possible. Sometimes, those who have explored when still young in their lives, are content to remain stationary for the rest of it. Perhaps these were now the thoughts of this boy.

I examined his gums and skin. They were better; less swollen and red. His stomach too, looked a better shape. His skin had no scaling. The cold had obviously put off the curse.

That night, we settled to try to sleep. In our individual hide tents, I sensed Tigernus' restlessness.

"When are you thinking of setting off again?" he asked.

So he was with me then. This was pleasing to hear.

"How does the day after tomorrow sound? Tomorrow, we'll stock the boat with water, food and wood, and then we'll set off."

"Good," he said. "That's what I wanted to hear."

After this, we both slept well.

Our hunting and gathering continued in the morning; our aim being to assemble a larder of food and supplies that would last the next stage of the voyage. The skins were filled with ice-cold water from a nearby river, and we pulled in a good quantity of wood. More edible herbs, mushrooms and roots were extracted and then stowed. We collected a brace of hares and stored both salmon and trout we had caught. In the evening, we put another layer of wool grease on the hull hides and prayed for good sailing. I showed Tigernus the pot I kept the wool grease in. It was now empty. We kept it for other uses, but recognised that wherever we went next, we'd have to make that our final destination – or find a new supply of the waterproofing gunk. At this point in time, the former seemed a more realistic accomplishment than the latter.

The last few days we had watched the tides and currents off the beach, and in the next hours we removed *An Ruen* from her dry dock and, through lengths of wood, rolled her back into the ocean. We gave it a while before we pushed off, because confidence in her seaworthiness was essential. If she leaked just off the beach, then we'd have to go back. I used Rat to sense this. He was useful that way, spying into the crannies and crooks of the hull that human eyes could not see. In 'The Land of Herbs' the rat had been quite content to stay around the boat. He seemed to sense many dangers out in the woods and streams, so kept close.

Once we felt all was secure, we let the tide take us out, and then turned towards the southwest.

"How do you know which way?"

"*Portenta*! The colours in the sky last night told me..."

"Really? They didn't speak to me."

"Come on, Tigernus. I'm joking... I just sense it that's all. If we have come over the curve of the ocean to the north, we can't go any further in that way – and 'The Land of Herbs' was never Hyperborea. It stands to reason that we must now progress in this direction."

We both knew we were dealing with some mumbo-jumbo here. We could carry on and not find a thing. Hope was with me though.

"I suppose we can always go back to 'The Land of Herbs' if we don't find anything."

Tigernus nodded. There was safety in this; and now, a familiarity.

An Ruen felt sharper in her handling that morning, like she had a new breath to her. She had perhaps needed the rest as much as we did.

We crossed past the long, pebbly beach we had put into and watched this wilderness fade away. Moss, herb and rock passed into memory. As we progressed, we kept good distance from the rocks where the walrus colony nestled. Their blubbery skins were being warmed by the morning sun. The lead males barked warning to us to stay away. Rat ineffectually barked back.

To our right, we could trace the coastline of 'The Land of Herbs'. It reminded us of Hibernia – long inlets of water enclosed by dark and gloomy headlands. We both wondered if any people lived there. We suspected not. Anyone who did try and survive there would have to have been hardy. Life seemed impossible in the distant mountains where the icesheets grew. How odd it was then to have been a small part of this nameless world. In our time, we had come across so many that maybe we were getting used to it.

From the ice world, strong winds blew in a southerly direction, and we made good sailing. In tracking towards the southwest, we skimmed the edge of the curdled sea, where shimmering icebergs floated in the east. But the water here was warmer and the current better. We had forgotten how fast *An Ruen* could be in open sea. For days before, we had slowly picked our way through growling ice. Now she was skimming, flying across the ocean, in the way I had always imagined her.

There were five days at sea in total. From our starting point at 'The Land of Herbs' I had wanted to measure more accurately our speed, and try to correlate this with both the stars and my imagined sense of where this new coastline might be. We both worked at this, enjoying the stars again, and noting our position. This time, I actually taught Tigernus how to do it. I calculated that some day soon, he'd have to do it himself. The air became slightly warmer, whilst the sea lost its ice blue tone and became grey again. The cloud cover matched its reflection, but it rained only a little. To be honest, the fishing didn't improve much; but as we were well-stocked anyway, it mattered less. I watched the boy carefully. I knew his health was improving. In the reflection of his well-being I noted my own.

In the grey gloom, sea and land merged together again. They worked to deceive. On day four, I noted that the sea seemed to lose some of its fury. This was always a sign that land was nearby. Birds – gulls and terns – circled us again. You did not need to be a prophet to explain what this meant. Very slowly, out of this gloop of a day, the sea pulled back its cloak and finally revealed a length of land to us.

In truth, I can barely remember the moment when we first saw this new world. I remember exhilaration and excitement, mixed with joy and wonder. But I suspect most of all, I felt relief. So many paths, routes and crossings all seemed to fall in on one another, collapsing into this one moment. We had found a new land. It was a land that others only talked about and mythologised. It was a land that we were going to walk upon, taste, smell and touch. I could tell, there and then, that it was a land that would shape the future. They had all led us here – Orla, Howel, Kenal, Casvellyn, the *Ancredhor Mor*, Warna, Gofan, the Corcu Loígde, Ir and Ir, and the ocean itself.

We, of course, knew nothing of it. We knew not if it was truly Hyperborea. It could have been Ogygia or Mayda or somewhere completely different; somewhere as yet unnamed. We knew nothing of what peoples lived there or what creatures populated its forests. All we knew was that it was now within our grasp.

"You were right," said Tigernus.

That was all he said. It was seemingly all he could say.

"Thank you for believing me," I said back to him.

Sometimes when you want something so much, when you actually have it, you do not know what to do. You are frightened that you will break it, destroy it in an instant and never get to hold it again. I felt this way. I almost wanted to revel in what we had found for a bit longer. I wanted to observe the coast for days and let the land reveal itself to me in gentle fashion. If we put in, maybe all promise, all hope, and all of the future would be put in jeopardy. Such was my pride and my wonder that for a long time, I forgot all hurt dealt to me. The names of Casvellyn, Howel, Kenal and Orla were, in that instant, utterly forgotten.

The ocean had done its job.

I have no memory of why we made for where we did. Perhaps it was because we simply held our course, and did not deviate to the land that emerged to the west of us. Instead of turning into the west, we kept our course south. An unassuming horizon emerged before us. If it were another day, maybe you would not have even noticed the land that lay there. You see, the ocean and sky had fused again here, making for a grey template at our arrival. *An Ruen* beached on a stretch of sand still wet from the tide. We eased her up out of the tide's reach and contemplated what we had stumbled upon. Birds sang in the inland trees but we didn't know any of their names or forms. There was no welcoming party. The land seemed desolate. In some ways, I am sure both of us wanted someone to step out of the low scrub, and congratulate us on our achievement. But there was no one doing that either. We were alone.

There was still time and light that day to explore. Maybe in our excitement we should have reined our joyousness in a little. There was no need to do everything in one go. How many months had we waited for this moment? If necessary, we could easily wait a little longer. But I was enthused by Tigernus' energy. He wanted to see what was out there, and went bounding across the beach. Initially I followed, but then deviated when I found some holes in the rock formations. They had been formed thousands of years ago, and there were several of them – perhaps almost twenty, of varying sizes and widths. Tigernus turned back to where I had stopped.

"What have you found?" asked Tigernus.

"Some caves... vugs... They're not very deep in length, and they're naturally formed. Still, interesting to see though..."

"I can't believe you've come all this way to peer into a fug-hole. Didn't you have enough of them at home?"

"I suppose so," I said. "Well, maybe not as many now that I'm a long way away..."

I felt the walls of the caves. They had been shaped by water when the sea was higher than it was at present; or perhaps the 'thunder storms' inside the earth had pushed up the land here making it higher over time. Either way, they were fascinating for me to explore. I felt their comfort, their dryness, their earthiness. I sensed some union that I had not felt for some time.

"Come on. Let's see what else is here."

It took a while for Tigernus to drag me out of them. He was seeing a side of me he had never encountered before: my true fascination with earth and stone.

We explored the land further over the next few days. In peaty bogs, we found a kind of red-coloured berry. It thrived in these dark watery ponds. Their taste was slightly bitter, but they were edible. More amazing though were the groves of grapes that grew on the southern slopes of the island. Such fruit was sensational upon our tongues. We must have stayed there an hour picking them and placing them in our mouths. There was no better sensation than to crush their skin with our teeth and feel their juice. We forgot about raw fish.

"I like this paradise," said Tigernus. "It has been worth the wait."

Using hides as bags, we filled them with the grapes, and took them back to the beach. That night we gorged upon them again. Rat was in heaven. There were so many new experiences he wanted to try. He seemed to feel safe here.

We looked back across the ocean, and felt the sun set on our backs instead of on our faces. There and then, it looked so benign, so loving, and so calm that we must have forgiven it for everything that it had thrown at us: for every squall, storm and wound. Both of us slept well that night.

In our discoveries, we found that we could circumnavigate the island within a couple of hours. On such missions, Tigernus was always a little wary. He felt there might be strange snakes lurking in the undergrowth. There were none on Scathynys but after our on board discussions, and me telling him of once finding one in the fogou, he became a little more cautious.

"I just don't want to meet any 'terrible worms' out here," he declaimed.

We had landed in the northeast of the island, and our march around its circumference gave us a good understanding of its geology and fauna. The island was low set in the water, but had several rocky outcrops. Two inlets forced their way into the island's heart from the northeast, while to the south of it were two smaller bare islands, which seemed stepping stones across to the wider peninsula. To the west, we discovered another longitudinal island that again looked across to what seemed to be the mainland. One could see that at the end of summer the climate here was relatively warm, though by winter those hard oceanic winds might make your eyes water and your cheeks burn. As we had tracked down from the north, using charcoal upon the back of a hide, I had drawn, as best I could, what we were observing. Our time on the island allowed me ample opportunity to sketch it as well.

There was a strange kind of deer that we found herded in the interior of the island. These 'fairie cattle' were like no others I had seen. They moved more slowly, and had larger, more fanciful antlers, covered in fur (I later learned that they were called 'Caribou'). It seemed cruel to take an arrow to one of them considering this was our first time here, but again, we were now hungry and the venison led me at least to remember a forgotten taste of home. Together we dragged the carcass back to our landing site, and roasted the meat. I will return to this deer in my story, for although what I did then was perhaps only natural – part of our ongoing survival, as you will learn – in my later life I revised and rethought such opportunities.

We must have remained on this island for some ten days before we decided to leave. Considering the geography of the coastline, it looked like it would be better for us to continue to the south, and round the larger headland which clasped this small island. If we stuck close to the coast, we could see what other possible landing places were available to us. Tigernus was making preparation on board *An Ruen* for this mission. We had already shifted her into the surf. He was hopeful of good fishing in the coming days, and was checking his lines and hooks. We stowed some good thick slivers of the deer meat.

While he was at work here, I found a flat piece of natural stone at the edge of the beach. I carved my mason's mark into it – my figure with one hand holding the crowbar, the other with the snake. The chisel made good progress through the stone, the mallet offering a precise groove to the blade's force. The ocean wind blew away the small fragments of stone and dust.

I knew what I wanted to carve underneath it. I wanted to write *Fogoynys*: 'Island of Caves'. I considered this translation. It would be even better if people might one day see it as 'Island of underground chambers'. You see, considering our discovery *and* the discoverer, I thought this was more fitting. Of course, I realised that the likelihood of anyone passing this way who knew my tongue was slim. Sometimes though, as temporal, transitory beasts, we crave remembrance. I worked slowly and carefully on the letters, chipping neatly the F and the O. Being a more complex letter, the G took a little longer. By the time I had come to the second O, I noticed Tigernus was shouting at me from *An Ruen*. He was pointing to the steering oar, which he'd somehow managed to drop. I'd only finished four letters before I stowed my tools in my sack and ran back into the surf to retrieve the oar from the waves.

I grasped the gunwale and swung myself onboard.

"Thanks. I didn't expect the surf to be that strong here..."

I dumped my sack in the central canopy and let out the main sail.

"What have you been doing?" asked Tigernus.

"Nothing," I said. "Don't worry about it."

I looked back at my brief handiwork and smiled to myself, hoping that the future might find it.

LORD, I HAVE TO ASK: Will I burn in fire? You see, when my mother transgressed, that is first of all what people wanted to do with her. She would face trial by fire. But Howel wouldn't do that to her. Perhaps he was too soft, too in love with her still. He knew what he should do. Famine, invasion, destruction and harvest failure would all follow if he didn't act. But even then, perhaps his eye was on forgiveness and not punishment.

But I worry still. For what she did – the sin, I mean – might she not have made it to Annown and now be rotting in Hell? That is what your book seems to say. It says that if we sin, if we break the moral rules, we will go there. It puts fear into me. I worry. In your speak, in your terms Lord, I have already sinned, though I only thought I was doing right. I was just following my heart. Is that really a sin? I'm confused. I don't know any more. Why do all these holy men and women insist on isolation and celibacy? Surely union is what we all strive for.

I have talked to the ocean about all this but all it does is to give me more questions. It doesn't give me answers. Perhaps my father had the same thing.

It took us five days after our encounter with the people of Breogán to reach Ogygia. Ogygia was not like Hy-Brasil. It really existed. It was not formed by a school of whales, but instead, as we were to learn, by the very earth itself.

"What do you call it again?" asked Corentin.

"Ogygia, I think," answered Tigernus.

Corentin laughed.

"That is a very mystical name for such a shithole of a place. You read different maps than I do. You know as well as I do what it's like – or what one island's like..."

"What do you call it then?" I asked.

"Ynysow an Oves," he said assuredly. "It's always been called that. Don't you remember? – we stopped in on our trip back with you."

"I think so..." recalled Tigernus.

To describe the archipelago in front of us in this way seemed absolutely right. The islands here were indeed 'Islands of the Blacksmiths'. We soon understood why. We had come into the nine distinct islands from the northeast and first passed between one larger island on the port side and, to the starboard of her, a smaller rise of land. However, ahead of us loomed a lengthy island running from the southeast to the northwest, and beyond that lay an island made solely of a volcanic mountain. Once around the long island we were able to see the magnificence of the lava running out of the earth and solidifying and cooling in the sea. There, it bubbled and solidified into rock.

"That's the same eruption as twenty years ago," noted a surprised Rosparzh. "Do you remember, Corentin? It's been forming the land here all that time."

Ynysow an Oves made me think of furnaces and fires, huge anvils and hammers hitting lengths of forged metal. Perhaps it was a premonition of what I was to find. I did not know at that point.

"He's right," said Corentin. "This place was half the size it is now, all that time ago."

So in the twenty years since my inception, nature had just carried on here, undisturbed, fizzing and fissuring without disturbance. Twenty years here had made an island. Twenty years had also made me.

"Where is the red matter from?" I asked, for I had never encountered anything like it.

"From inside the earth," said Corentin. "The druids say that is what lies beneath us. The red matter you talk of once formed the earth."

"Not God?" I ventured.

This should not have come out then. I'd been too bound up with my reading. They looked at me.

"Not gods I mean?"

"Maybe," ventured Rosparzh. "It would take a lot more than Annown to do this..."

I understood what he meant.

"Do you remember when I told you about Scathynys and the earthquake there?" Tigernus asked.

"When you joined *An Ruen*?"

"Well, this world is much the same. It is a place where the earth is not so solid, and even though the ocean covers it, the red matter still spills out."

I was fascinated with what I saw. It reminded me of this place called Hell I had read about. There, supposedly, was great heat and fire. It felt like in all its smoke, fire and sulphur, I might find the Devil walking and at his work.

"Why do the other islands not steam in the same way?"

"They did, once upon a time," answered Rosparzh. "Now they have cooled, and wildlife has spread upon them. Then the tide washes and wears them away."

"This is how islands can come and go," noted Tigernus, wanting me to understand much of what he had learnt. "Not all of them are whales see..."

"Do people live here?" I asked.

"At one time," said Corentin. "In caves... vug-holes – especially on the islands in the east. We entered them one time. There were drawings on the walls."

"There are sheep there," confirmed Rosparzh. "We used to pick grapes too."

I knew what Tigernus was thinking. I could tell by looking at him. He was thinking that perhaps in the past, people had viewed these islands as the furthest limits. Perhaps indeed, this, at one time, had been an imagined Hyperborea. Now, however, it was a stop-off point for our crossing. It was just like his Scathynys.

"Are you seriously landing on there?" I asked Corentin, pointing to the eruption.

"Of course not. We'll head to the western islands. The best produce grows there. I know of a stream as well, where we can re-stock our water."

As we proceeded I looked back on the 'Islands of the Blacksmiths' and observed a plume of smoke and steam rising. I had never known of the power of the earth in this way before.

"Is this route any better?" I asked Tigernus. "I mean, should my father have come this way instead?"

"Hard to say. I always asked him to go south, but maybe I was wrong."

I knew why Tigernus said this. He was hot and bothered. We had all noticed that not only did the Ynysow an Oves look like a blacksmith's forge, we could also feel the heat. This came from the molten earth but also from the sun above us.

"You both feel the warmth?" asked Corentin.

We nodded, gulping down skins of water.

"We are closer to the sun," he said, pointing to the bright disc in the sky. "Here, the earth is wider. Drink well, or you will dehydrate. You can't afford to do that."

Tigernus and I wiped the sweat from our brows and arms.

"Make the most of it," said Rosparzh. "In a few days, you'll be wishing we were back here again. When that northern wind bites, look out."

I saw Tigernus take note. I knew that he had bad memories of when the ocean was cold. I'd have to watch him carefully.

On the western isles, we took *Warna* and another couple of coracles ashore. There, Corentin's crew indulged in swimming in some of the beautiful streams and gathered early fruits from the trees. The hot weather made them ripen more quickly than in the damp of west Britain. Everywhere grew interesting plants and exotic trees. Birds gabbled their languages in the trees and strange lizards darted past my feet. It was a very different world to that of Ynysow an Oves.

"It's like the Garden of Eden," I noted.

"The what?" asked Tigernus.

"Eden... Don't worry."

Several bullfinches crossed over us, chittering their love of life.

"I imagine this to be like Annown if you finally get there..." Tigernus said wistfully.

He was correct, I had to admit. Indeed, it did seem the right place for my grandmother and mother to meet (if the latter were not in Hell). My mind ran to my reading though: if this was just a taster of God's arranging on Ynysow an Oves, then I became even more excited about what I would find in Hyperborea. There, my father and the Holy Father looked set to meet. I wondered too about that white-clad figure on the cliffs at Douarnenez. Perhaps it was Casvellyn, and perhaps finally, he had given us his blessing. I thought about it for a while: perhaps too, you Lord, and you Annown, are one. If this ocean had taught me anything, then it was that.

26

Full-Scale Reconstruction of a Roundhouse, based on those found at Carn Euny, Penwith, Cornwall

This piece of reconstructionist archaeology demonstrates the conditions in which the people of 4th Century to 6th Century Carn Euny lived. Traditional rab (granite sub soil) was used for the mortar, and woods such as oak, ash, holly and hazel for the roof. Experiments in Cornwall and Wales have shown that a conical roof with a pitch of about 45 degrees would have been the strongest and most efficient design. It has been theorized that although a central fire would have been lit inside for heating and cooking, there could not have been a smoke hole in the apex of the roof, for this would have caused an updraught that would have rapidly set fire to the thatch. Instead, smoke would have accumulated harmlessly inside the roof space, and slowly leaked out through the thatch.

THE MORE WE SAILED, THE more we realised that we were not just encountering an island, or even a country, but instead an entire continent. I was sketching an outline of what we saw, trying to depict the geography as best I could. Every day though, there was a new revelation: some new rise of land, some incredible estuary, or some vibrant colour to the trees and woodland. This blissful world unravelled before us in ways we could not ever have imagined. What amazed us the most was how pure and untouched the land looked. I was, of course, comparing it to back home, where the raw and black scars of tin excavation had ruined so many moors for centuries afterwards. Here, nature was left to do its work uninterrupted. Man's hand was simply not present. Both Tigernus and I had grown up in barren places where trees were a rarity. To see so many here, and of so many different types, ensured that the woodlands were a constant focus of our conversation. Since 'The Land of Herbs' we had lost track of the time of year, but both the air and the turning of the leaves here – from luscious green to yellows, reds and browns – told us we were heading into autumn.

I did not know it in those days when we rounded a horn of land and followed a long line of the coast running from the northeast to the southeast, but this was also the autumn of Tigernus and me. Something had happened in him. He was not well. There were many things wrong: the gums and the spotting of his skin had not much improved and I somehow felt the daily presence of his proximity to water was bringing back the effects of the mermaid's curse. There was something else too. For weeks, I think, he had kept quiet about how he truly felt; he had held on to allow us both to make it here, but now that we had arrived and the initial wave of joy was over, his body seemed to go into a malady born of the anticlimax of it all. His very organs seemed to be saying, "Good. We've reached Hyperborea, I can now collapse". He knew it of course, but wouldn't be told. That was the way with him. He had a young man's arrogance of thinking that the body is inexhaustible: that it will always be there.

"It won't be," I told him. "Something has to give."

I nursed and nurtured him as we tracked this long line of coast, trying to cajole some spirit into him; and perhaps realising that sooner or later, I was going to have to find somewhere to stop more permanently. He needed real rest and long-term care. We had put into a few coves along the way to find more water, but none seemed to hold any precise reason for us to stay there. Did I know what I was looking for? Perhaps I did. It had to be a place as good as the horn of Britain; but preferably, it had to be better. I suppose also though, before making such a decision, I wanted to explore. I really wanted to see what the possibilities were.

I had no idea then – but as you will see, clearly, inside me, I had architectural designs on this place.

The fog over Tigernus and where we might settle was matched by a real fog bank that we ran into. We had been lucky not to have encountered such conditions so far on our voyage, and when this one came upon us, I was thankful it had not been mid-ocean. Despite the climate, fog puts a freezing layer onto everything and seeps into every dry space. If it lasts long enough (which this run of it did) it renders your navigation impossible. You cannot see the sun or stars, and the coastline (even though it may be quite close) completely disappears. You can pick your way along, carefully negotiating the ocean, but it is not very safe. Fog deceives the eye. It turns great distance into an arm's length; and then magnifies the lowly and small into something frightening and foreboding.

On one day, Tigernus did not seem up for much work. Rat was keeping him company in the gloom. I had him keep watch, but it wasn't easy. From the bow, it was difficult to make out activity in the stern, let alone anywhere else on the water, or what we were running into along the coast. We had pulled both sails up and were reliant on only the oars for our propulsion forward. The blades dipped quietly into the water. After our initial joy at discovering this new continent – filled as it was with all kinds of possibilities – this slowing down of our progress was both irksome and unwanted. My heart (it was hard now to speak any more for Tigernus) was filled with ambition, but at this instant it was thwarted.

We'd actually shifted our course slightly in order to avoid some of the reefs off the coast. Tigernus had spotted our steady drift inshore, and had suggested we pull out into deeper water. After all the work completed on the hull, we didn't need it to be damaged at this point. One hole had been enough. The ship's bell tolled with a dull clang.

Perhaps, if we had stayed more inshore, what happened may never have happened, and yet happen it did.

The fog had not dispersed. If anything, it had got thicker. As I recall it, we had been cooking: the last few steaks of venison seasoned with some of the remaining herbs. This was going to be paired up with some boiled roots. Afterwards, we planned on a handful of grapes each – those which we had saved from the island of caves.

Despite the bell, that was just when the nudge came. It was gentle enough, but a nudge nonetheless. Before anything else, both of us thought of a new risk from some lurking deep sea creature. We had become used to this by now, and imagined all sorts. We need not have bothered though. No, the nudge was from another vessel. As we turned to see precisely what it was that had shifted our angle in the water, we both saw a large-sized, clinker-built vessel; it was so high in the water we could not see its gunwale or its masts. In the gloom, all we could make out was a run of sealed planks brushing past our oxhide hull.

Once we realised it was a vessel, I suspect our minds ran to thinking it was of Viking origin. This was the only people we felt who could have made such distance (aside from ourselves, of course). Perhaps they now had the technology to push further than 'The Land of Herbs'. Maybe they had their own minds set on conquering Hyperborea in their usual manner: rape and pillage, followed by more rape and pillage. Grapes would always tempt them as well: anything that could make alcohol was worth invading. These wine and berry lands could suit their bill. It was quite possible that we had chanced upon them, or them upon us. I gave Tigernus a look. He was the Viking expert. He knew what I was thinking.

He shook his head.

"No. Not their kind of vessel. You can tell from the structure."

I glanced at what was passing us again. He was correct. The vessel did not have the usual flowing lines of the *Ancredhor Mor*. As we had noted before, their hulls were usually marked with gods and icons. There were none here.

Who was it then?

Because of the fog, it was also moving slow in the water. Although we had noticed it, it hadn't, as yet, noticed us. This changed when *An Ruen* ran into a set of oars on its starboard side. Their wooden lengths (which were presently out of the water) clattered against our masts. We tried hard to avoid them. The damage they might inflict on us could have been catastrophic, but there was no escaping the line of them. We ducked as they passed over us. Fortunately, no real damage was committed; only some slight dents on the two masts.

I tried looking at the way the oars were carved. Such knowledge often gave insight into different peoples. These, I dismissed as not being Phoenician. Although they travelled many miles across the oceans, they weren't known for getting this far across. Therefore, I was beginning to come to a conclusion that what we were facing was some ship built in the new world – and that on board it would be a new kind of people. I was preparing to gesture, to show that we came in peace; although given the situation – them massive, and us small – it hardly mattered. If they wanted to kill us, they would.

The noise of their oars clattering against something had caused concern for them on deck. We were about to have an encounter that might alter everything – and I suppose, in so many ways, it truly did. All the while, I was trying to work out what was being said. The fog was reshaping the sound though; twisting it as it was spoken. Maybe, finally, they had heard our bell.

We had traversed most of the length of this vessel before we saw any life. Then, three heads poked over the gunwale and looked down upon us. Their faces displayed immense surprise at what the fog had churned up for them. We peered back, trying to make out who they were, and what brought them here. Gradually, they recognised something of themselves in us – our clothes, our hair, our skin – and we recognised the same in them. Seemingly, we had travelled all these long days to end up reacquainting ourselves with our own people. We had gone full circle. Exile had brought me home again – though it is fair to say, it was exile of a different kind that had pushed these men here.

One of them spoke.

"Peth in bit a gureuch hui deu in le ma?"

The man who spoke it said it slowly, as if he was expecting me to not understand.

I repeated it for Tigernus, who hadn't quite heard.

"What on earth are you two doing out here?"

The language was our own. These were men of Britain, although by the tone and dialect of their words, I knew in an instant they were not from the horn.

"We've been exploring," I answered.

The three of them discussed what I had said. They were listening carefully to my intonation too.

"In that thing?"

They were pointing at *An Ruen* – and laughing.

"I've been in bigger river boats than that."

"I know. I've seen children toy with smaller vessels on a duck poind."

We used the oars to scull back to the middle portion of their vessel.

"This blasted fog has slowed us down," I explained.

"Us too. We have been stationary for days."

"What brings you here?" I enquired.

"Oh, you know, the usual... fish, women, feasting, beer," he joked. "No, really – mainly the fish. If it weren't for fish, we'd starve. In taking our lands, the Saxons stole our corn, our wheat and our grain."

"You are from Britain?"

"Yes – and no," this man said, somewhat uncertain.

"What do you mean?"

"We are Britons but we live there no more. We are now refugees..."

I knew what this meant. I knew that whoever these people were, they had faced the wrath of the Saxons and had been displaced. This was the way the Saxons created their empire.

"We were forced from our lands to cross the great channel – and to make new lives in Armorica. You know this, yes? We make there *Breten Vyghan* – a new Britain for those forced into exile."

Now I was beginning to understand. These weren't the native Armoricans. No, these were the men and women whom my people had started to label the Bretons.

"You met the Saxons? What are they like?"

"How long have you got? Do you like horror stories?"

The way this man asked this latter question was no joke. I could feel the pain of his words. I could understand now why they were out here, in the fog off Hyperborea.

"Look, I'm sorry we ran into you – and for the oars hitting your masts... Your bell's got quite a soft tone to it hasn't it? Why don't you come aboard for a bit? Looks like you could do with a bit of Breton hospitality."

It seemed too good an opportunity to pass over. Besides, I had many questions for this man, wanting to know how, at the edge of the known world, he had happily brought a whole crew here. I had thought us special, incredible, different – to have made it this far. Now I knew we were not special at all, and that if these men made it across the great ocean, then others would have as well – and would continue to do so in the future. Thus, in tying *An Ruen* to their vast vessel, and then clambering aboard, I felt somewhat deflated. There was, however, a definite feeling of communion with these men, who perhaps were walking the same path as us; who had followed the same stars in the sky, and had suffered perhaps, some similar fates.

Their vessel, named *Azen* (which meant 'Donkey') was a workmanlike beast. As her name suggested, it was hardly the prettiest vessel on the planet but she was strong and stubborn. I could see how she might cut neatly through the ocean and hold her own in any squall. Her construction now showed a familiarity which, in the fog, it had been impossible to discern. She was barge-like in many ways, lacking the grace of the Viking vessels, but she had solidity and stamina. In Lulyn, the boat makers would like her lines. Her three masts gave her strong propulsion too. She probably crossed in a day what it would take us three days to achieve.

Stepping aboard, we learnt the names of the men we had been chatting to. The main converser had been Corentin, the notional captain of this vessel. He was a man who had grown up on the riverbanks of Caresk, and long before the invasions came, he had sworn to take his family to safety in the south. He had two sons, one of whom had stayed behind to fight the Saxons. Word of him had not reached this father for some time. The other two were Rosparzh and Loic. The former was tall and gangly, with a braid of long hair down his back. He looked like he might make a good swordsman, but there was a sadness in him (I later learnt that the family of his lover had been colonised. He suspected she was now forced to make bastard Saxons). Loic was older and rounded, his belly noting a good life of beer and boar.

"My name is Voog," I explained to them, "and this is Tigernus..."

Tigernus bowed, and shook all of their hands,

"A polite boy, your son," offered Loic.

"He's not my son. I picked him up on the way – on Scathynys..."

"I'm an orphan," lied Tigernus, smiling at me, trying to wind me up.

"You've done a good job with him. A fair lad," offered Loic.

"Come," said Corentin. "We have good feasting for you."

"And this is Rat..." said the boy. "He's an orphan too. He's been travelling with us. He'll do you no harm, I promise."

They warily let the rodent board.

Corentin showed us their larder of fish. What was ingenious about it was that they used ice to stow the haul they had already caught.

"It preserves the flesh," he explained. "The meat doesn't rot as fast. Each year we touch upon the icefield enough to haul in some lumps of it. "

"From where the sea curdles?" asked Tigernus.

"Yes – where it clots and groans. Loic doesn't like it much though – do you Loic?"

Loic grumbled an answer.

"Too cold for him."

We learnt much about each other's voyage. They laughed at our progress to Hibernia, and our whale troubles at Hy-Brasil. We explained about the battering we had received, the icefields and 'The Land of Herbs'. They knew nothing of 'The Land of Herbs' (Rosparzh said it sounded like a fairy tale) and they always avoided the ice (Loic hated the cold of the northerly latitudes and wondered about any Viking presence). They did this journey, they said, by electing to take a more southerly route. Perhaps it was longer, but there were fewer obstacles. They always stopped at some small volcanic islands off the coast of Iberia (so they had done this route before?), to cross a stretch of ocean they all referred to as the Sargasso. Only then, did they head northwest towards the ice and then fishing grounds.

"See," went Tigernus. "Told you."

I explained our route in more detail, and was able to show them my maps. Corentin added to my knowledge of the world, suggesting some additions. I was able to contribute to his understanding too. We concluded that these volcanic islands of his were perhaps Ogygia. Ogygia then, lurked somewhere in his memory; Mayda we remained clueless about.

"What do you call this land here then?"

I was pointing to Hyperborea, both on the map, and across the water to the shore.

"We don't have a name for it yet," went Corentin. "It is too big to name. Maybe your word for it – Hyperborea – is good enough."

Some of Corentin's crew brought out salted boar for us. There was also pan-fried cod and herring.

"Have you been ashore?" I asked Corentin between mouthfuls of boar.

"Rosparzh has... But we don't any more. We elect not to go now."

"Why not?"

There were nervous stares between Corentin and Rosparzh. No one looked like they wanted to speak, especially if I was so intent on doing the same.

"My apologies, Voog. Rosparzh does not want to say. Last year, he led a group of eight of us inland. He met... resistance."

This was an odd choice of word for Corentin to use.

"Eight of us went, but only three came back." Rosparzh outlined.

Corentin gestured for Rosparzh to continue. He seemed uncertain whether he should.

"You must tell him, Rosparzh."

"We met native people there. They were fierce – worse than the Saxons. We were attacked. They killed five of us. We could not take their bodies to Annown. We left them there in the forest to rot – or to whatever they wanted to do with them."

Things were now becoming clear. Of course, our actions on these people of Hyperborea might be seen in just the same way as the Saxons' actions on us. There was a bigger picture which I was only now beginning to understand. Certainly then, there were people here, people who needed to be approached in a certain way, people who already had knowledge of the threat from the east. See how what goes around, comes around.

Whilst eating, we caught up on events back home. Because Corentin and his crew had left a little later in the summer than we had done, he had word of incursions of the Saxons past the Great River. Loic informed us that even the Phoenicians had stopped trading; such were their fears over attacks.

"Even the *Ancredhor Mor* stay away," was the considered view of events (Maybe at least one of their vessels had business at the bottom of the sea, we both thought).

The world had changed in our absence, and this of course, led me to worry about the people I cared for back home. What did I mean by people? I only meant one really – Orla. Perhaps I might add Remfra and Kenal's kids.

"Many now cross from the horn," said Rosparzh. "It's been really bad this summer. I don't know where it will end."

"That's why we come over here," Loic said, "To get away from it all. The ocean's the only place you can get a bit of peace these days."

The conversation turned onto holy men and women of this new Christian god.

"Have you seen much of them?" asked Rosparzh.

Before I answered, I explained to him my original profession and commitment to Annown. I didn't want them confusing me as any missionary.

"There won't be any more bleddy Annown, if this lot carry on," argued Loic.

"We get more and more of them," Corentin explained, "from the sea and through the land. We think they are a bit full of themselves if you know what I mean."

"We've met one or two," chipped in Tigernus, wishing to be part of the discussion.

"Oh yes. What were they like then? Pompous fools?"

"They were okay really, weren't they Voog?"

"There is some good in their ways I have found."

I left it at that, though I did describe Warna and Gofan's disappearance.

"That's always the way," noted Loic cynically. "Always some miracle or trick up their sleeves. I put my trust in the druids. You know where you are with a druid."

"Do they still have your people's respect?" I asked.

"Despite everything, they still do," Corentin said.

"Despite what...?"

"Well, you know, the invasions, our need to make a new life – the people have kept faith in them – even though sometimes they have been wrong."

"From what I have seen," said Rosparzh. "The peoples here have similar ways. They have shamans, or druids... We saw them."

"No doubt, one day, more of these holy men and women will arrive here as well," said Loic. "Let's hope they stick to our side of the ocean. Better still if they don't set out at all in their stupid coracles."

I enquired whether they had heard of a druid named Casvellyn – or maybe Eleder. Eleder they had not, but the name of Casvellyn had come to them.

"They say he is powerful – and works the stones at Boscawen Ûn. We have sent ours there in the past for gathering and worship. Do you know him?"

"I know him very well," I said.

It was incredible for me to be talking of him here. I had thought him long out of my memory. Now I was back hiding behind the standing stones of Boscawen Ûn watching his deviancy.

We drank some more wine. Tongues opened. They asked questions.

"Tell me – fogou-builder – how did you come by that wound?"

"What wound?"

I thought Loic meant the scar on my arm where Tigernus had scratched me. But it was not that he was referring to.

"Your wrist."

"It's not a wound," I explained. "I've had it since birth... and the extra finger too."

I showed him.

"Unusual," was his remark.

Suddenly, I realised why he may have asked me. Perhaps Howel's word had spread as far as this *Breten Vyghan*, and this Loic knew of my exile. Maybe even rumour had spread that I had travelled there. That was certainly what Kenal and his men would have thought. You will understand then, why I was wary about saying any more to this Loic. Our paths didn't cross much again, but I knew he found my twisted wrist of interest. Had word come to him about me?

After the isolation on board *An Ruen*, Tigernus was enjoying the company here. I had to remember that Warna and I had pulled him from an already isolated community. The crew of *Azen* were intrigued by his stories about what we had encountered, and loved the tricks he had taught Rat. They also thought him brave for surviving all that distance, and their praise made him smile. He was disguising his frailty.

"Come back with us," said Corentin to me the next morning. "Your passage here must have been no pleasure cruise. We'll drop you back on the horn and then head home – if the Saxons haven't overrun us there too. We're going to leave when the fog bank clears."

"It's a kind offer," I said, "but my place is here."

I might have told him why I couldn't return, but elected not to. Maybe Loic had already made representation. I could not tell.

"What are you going to do?"

"Explore. See what this Hyperborea is made of. Maybe become rich off its mineral wealth..."

"Be careful friend. You have heard of Rosparzh's experiences."

Although what I had heard concerned me, I was not going to let this put me off.

With Corentin's words however, I saw an option. I saw an opportunity.

"The boy," I explained. "You might take him back across for me."

"Really? You want us to do this?"

I explained to Corentin about Tigernus' health. I explained about the curse. The Breton knew of such evil. He noted my concern.

"The bottom line is that he is not well. I have nursed him these long days, but he needs more than I can give him here. He is no orphan. His people still live on the island of Scathynys."

"Yes – I know where he is from but that is a long way from where we plan to sail."

"Drop him in Lulyn then – in the horn – as you said you would do for me. He will be able to make his passage back to Scathynys from there. Such a trip is a mere step compared to going back across this great ocean."

"You wish him no other fate?"

"None," I said. "I sense that if I offer this to him, he will accept."

"And you?"

"What about me?"

"Two's company," said Corentin. "One brings only loneliness and heartache."

I understood Corentin's concern. I had already contemplated the loneliness that might follow.

"He has helped me generously on my voyage, but the time is now right for me to help him. He has a good life ahead of him. Will you take care of him for me?"

"Just as you have done so. I will treat him as my own son."

We shook hands and embraced. Corentin was a good man. I thought our conversation was over, but I sensed the Breton wanted to talk further.

"You know before... when I mentioned the Saxons... as a horror story?"

I nodded and affirmed I was listening.

"I wasn't kidding. I have to tell you this because you are sending this boy back – and I have to be honest, I don't know what you are sending him back to. You may have thought we were not serious about the hordes from the east. We are. We just joke because it is the only way of dealing with it."

We walked towards the bow of *Azen*. The fog still swirled.

"Every man on board here has witnessed the holocaust. Like Loic says, one reason we run out here is for peace – to escape the nightmare. When we return, we don't know what we will face. Voog, there has been such slaughter, such hatred..."

"What are you suggesting?"

"Perhaps that you are right... that remaining here is the best thing to do. Perhaps the boy should stay with you. I don't know just how far they now push into the far west. If you have loved ones there, then perhaps they too should leave, just as we did. It will surely not be long before..."

"Before...?"

"...we are overrun. The death camps, they will come past the Great River assuredly. Maybe already..."

"It's the land isn't it?" I stated.

"How do you mean?"

"We live on a tapering funnel. At the bottom, there is nowhere to go."

As I said this I thought of Howel. I thought of his plans for defences and how all that had turned to dust. I also realised I was talking bollocks. Neither Corentin nor I lived on that tapering funnel of a land any more.

"Are you still sure you want me to take the boy back? Please think about it."

He grasped my right shoulder to force his point.

"I will."

Perhaps, prior to this all had seemed simple. Now another knot had been put in my way which I had to untie. Here the boy had freedom, opportunity and hope. Back home, he might know suffering, enslavement and fear. Would the Saxons reach the far west? Maybe not. Maybe they were content enough to just raid and cause terror. Such a push would sever their supply lines. Besides they wouldn't take too much interest in Scathynys. They could have already raided that rock if they had wished – a long time ago.

Thinking about these matters did not lead to me sleeping well, but by the morning I was resolved. I had thought through the potential conflict here and that across the ocean. Despite the concerns Corentin had put before me, Tigernus would still fare better back home. I told Corentin my decision, which he accepted. I thanked him for his honesty.

"If he has any sense and cunning about him, then he will fare well."

"He has both," I confirmed.

My only difficulty now was in convincing Tigernus himself that his voyage back was a good thing. However, the conversation with him was not as difficult as I had thought. In fact, he raised the issue with me.

"Voog, do you think I should go back now?"

"What do you mean?" I feigned.

"On this ship – the *Azen*."

"That depends..."

"On what?"

"Whether you have had enough adventures... whether you've seen enough of the world now."

Tigernus was looking out into the fog. Hyperborea was in reach of his hand. He didn't answer me.

"Where will you go?"

"You know me, Tigernus. I am always on the move. I don't know... I'll put in somewhere... when I find the right place. Not too far away from here. Somewhere just down the coast I expect."

"Will you be all right? I mean, you heard what Rosparzh said."

"I will have a different way. I won't be looking for a fight."

Tigernus hugged me. He clasped me as tight as Orla once did.

"I think I should go home," he snivelled.

"I know."

"You can always come back," I said, trying to lighten his mood.

"I doubt it," the boy said tearfully, counting off a list with his fingers. "I've had enough of monsters, and ice, and mermaids..."

And then he added. "...for the time being."

Tigernus was never my son, but in that moment he was. I suppose, in some ways, he always would be.

"Corentin will look after you. I have told him what you need. Don't touch the sea too much. Remember that. Eat berries. Check your gums. Promise me you'll keep out of harm's way – if the Saxons come. Hide on the moors. They won't venture up there. Brentigia maybe?"

He nodded.

"Where will they take me? Back to Scathynys?"

"No – not quite. They will drop you at Lulyn. From there, you can easily catch a boat to Scathynys. Some holy man or woman will be travelling no doubt. Corentin says those pilgrims travel back and forth from Santiago – where the children of Breogán are from. Remember them? And in Lulyn, ask for a tanner named Enyon. He'll put you right. Say you know me."

"Enyon?"

"Yeah. That's his name. This is a good chance for you. Another won't come around very soon. You'll be back now before winter sets in properly."

That evening, Tigernus came with me down into *An Ruen* and fetched all of his things. Our vessel now looked rickety and unstable compared to what it was moored next to. We both wondered how we had managed to survive in its small confines for so many days.

"Rosparzh said I'd get a bed – a proper bed."

"Great! You'll sleep like a baby I expect. Now, have you got everything?"

"I think so."

Tigernus had one final look around the boat that had been his entire life. He touched the gunwale. There were many memories for him. He saw Warna I believe, still guiding him, still pushing him in the right direction. I am certain he saw Puffin standing there too – with his mate, and nest of chicks.

"What about Rat?"

"What about him?"

"He should stay with you. He's your companion."

"No. He's been your friend for a while. He should go with you. Let him dine on fine boar on *Azen*. Besides, the crew there need livening up – and he's the man to do it!"

We both laughed.

Rat seemed ignorant of this parting. His whiskers sensed new food supplies rather than a fond farewell to me.

"He doesn't change," I noted. "Now, anything else you need?"

Tigernus looked around the hull.

"Your maps," he said. "May I take them? – to show people where I've been. Otherwise they won't believe me."

I considered his request. They linked me to my father, of course. Initially, I wasn't sure if I could let them go, but as I contemplated his request it became clear they were of no further use to me. I wouldn't be crossing back, and besides what was important to me now was this new world. It was that which I had to map. If need be, I could remember the proportions and angles. It was, after all, how my mind worked.

"Here, have them. Keep them safe. They're probably the best maps now of the ocean we came to cross. See there look – where I have written in the navigational decisions."

I bundled the parchment and skins up into a roll, winding and tying a piece of flax around them to stop them unravelling.

"You'd better go," I said.

In this moment, I was unravelling. I was becoming sentimental. I never contemplated the pain I would feel saying goodbye to him.

"Oh – Tigernus. One thing – don't mention my past to them, especially that Loic... That won't do any good at all."

The boy nodded his compliance. He knew my history and why it needed to be kept secret. I knew I could trust him. I had trusted an ocean to him.

"Goodbye Voog," he said.

"Goodbye my friend."

Those were the last words I had with him. Once up on Azen, he busied himself with the unfurling of the sails like the expert he was. I wished Corentin, Rosparzh, Loic and their crew fair sailing. They wished me luck and providence – and put some salted boar meat my way. For me, the fog's disappearance revealed the coast again; for them it showed an ocean. I watched their stern disappear over the horizon.

So, I had placed Tigernus on a donkey and was letting him wander home.

I, meanwhile, was back to being on my own again.

DEAR LORD, ANNOWN IS YOU and you are Annown. I know that now. I understand it. I understand that the world is sometimes much simpler than I thought. I see that the fogou of my father is a way to both of you. The ocean talked to me and we yipped back and forth like the tides. When the men were below, I talked back. She became my friend. She listened when I needed her. Although I would not wish for more with Tigernus, sometimes I craved her attention. I still read and thought about my life and what might still occur. I must say that within the 'Islands of the Blackmiths' I found it incredible how there could be found both Hell and Paradise. They coexisted only a few miles apart. This was life wasn't it? This was all of us. There was both torture and pleasure. After two days spent in this Paradise, Corentin suggested that we pushed on into the west. You may be wondering where the Hell comes into my tale here. After all, we did not step foot on the volcanic island. You will see, soon enough.

By Corentin's estimate, the 'Islands of the Blackmiths' were around one third of the way across the ocean. We had made good progress. Perhaps our navigation had not been cursed. Maybe I was no anathema to the druid any longer. Certainly, in the lack of storms we encountered, our journey was charmed. The early days of April gave us no showers nor squalls either.

"Luck," said Tigernus.

"Skill," offered Corentin.

There had been much talk of an area of the ocean we were about to enter. Its mystery was enhanced to me by the fact that the mariners on board *Azen* didn't like to talk much about it.

"It's unlucky," said Rozparzh.

"What is it?" I asked.

"*Mor Sargasso*," he said back, lowering his voice.

"And?"

"Not a place you want to stay long in..."

Further enquiries about this area of the ocean revealed that what we were likely to encounter was a portion of the sea where seaweed grew prodigiously. It was also famed for the water's blue colour and clarity. Apparently, mariners could see deep into the depths of the ocean. It was that which worried a lot of them. They did not necessarily want to see what was located beneath them. Giant squids, serpents, vast jellyfish and octopuses were anxiously mentioned to me.

"That's all rubbish," said Corentin. "The only reason we don't like it is because the wind is often calm there. You can spend days drifting. Sailors don't like that see. It makes their imaginations run wild..."

"Is there any way around it?" I asked.

"Not really. it's the most efficient route, even if we get slowed down. Hopefully we'll just touch the northern end of it."

As we approached, I began to notice a change in the condition of the water. It did offer clarity and, floating on the surface, fronds of seaweed started to appear."Just you wait and see," said Rosparzh.

He was right. By the end of the day, the seaweed clogged the vessel, the sargassum weed almost pulling at *Azen*'s form as she skimmed across the surface. Lines of the weed formed around us. I had seen something of this before down by the coast back home, but usually this had not been as concentrated. The redeeming feature of this weed was that playful young sea turtles used the mass to mature in to avoid predation before heading out into the open ocean. We enjoyed observing them.

The wind had dropped. Corentin had suggested using oars but the response from the crew was disparaging. Rowing in seaweed was never easy. The effort required usually resulted in only minimal movement. Besides that, the oars would soon become coated with the weed, and then this would need removal.

It was no easy job.

"That's me told then. Looks like we'll have to sit and wait," said Corentin.

The boredom on board *Azen* caused the mariners to open casks of ale. Someone suggested music, and the next thing, dancing began on the upper deck. To be honest, they deserved it. They had worked hard so far, and such recreation was much needed. Corentin found me reading in the fading light.

"I'm not pulling them out of the drink if one of them goes overboard," he said. "Stay away from it if I was you, Blejan, my lover – or one of them's bound to ask you to dance..."

I laughed at his request. Toward the bow, we heard guffaws of laughter, as someone struck up another crude ballad.

"I'm serious. You might be with Tigernus – but that won't stop one of they trying it on."

Perhaps he was right. I would mind my own business, and steer clear. But I wanted to spend time with Tigernus. It took some time to find him. He had elected not to carouse with the other crewmen. Eventually, I located him at the stern. He had manoeuvred himself over the gunwale, and sat on a piece of wood positioned there for fishing. Initially, that is what I thought he was doing.

"Caught much?" I asked.

My presence made him jump.

"What do you want?" he asked.

"Only to spend a bit of time with you. I thought that while everyone else was singing and dancing, we could be alone..."

"I wanted to be alone."

"Alone?"

"Yes. It's hard to get a bit of peace on this ship. Everyone knows everyone's business."

"Better than on *Warna* surely?"

"I'm not sure."

His tetchiness annoyed me. It was then that I noticed he was trying to hide something in his hand.

"What's that?"

"Nothing."

"Come – show me..."

I reached at his hand but he withdrew it from me. Rage grew in him.

"What's wrong?"

"Leave me alone..."

Then I realised what was happening. I had taken my eye off him for too long. There was enough of what was clutched in his hand for me to recognise it.

"That a comb?" I asked frantically.

"What if it is?"

So, he had had this all this time. The return to Douarnenez had allowed him to find it. I knew how it worked. He couldn't control it. Despite his love for me, the mermaid still gripped him. Aimend had warned me when we had spoken.

"You were the one who said you didn't want to sit too close to the water!" I screamed at him.

"I decide where I sit," was his response.

I knew what was coming. He had already called her. In realising this, I shouted back for Corentin to come and help me, but my voice could not be heard over the din of bawdy shanties. The seaweed too, it was ideal cover for her. I wondered if she had tracked us all this way. Had she been there just off Paradise? Now, she would create a new Hell for me.

"You're too late," said Tigernus, his eyes glazed over. "She's coming for me."

I would not have this. I would not have her take him away from me.

"No. I'm not too late. I lost my father and my mother. I'm not losing you. Not ever."

I scanned the ocean below for her presence. Finally, I would eye this siren. She may have swum long miles, but I had also voyaged. I'd finally take out the bitch.

The moonlight cast its reflection down, and eventually, the weed parted as a wake made its way towards *Azen*. I saw the splash of her tail, the rise and fall of her back; her hair like fine seaweed. When she rose out of the water though, it was not at all what I expected. Instead of seeing the beauty of her – this gorgeous being who had cursed him these long years – I found myself looking down upon me. Her whole face and body were my own.

"I am you, and you are me," she mouthed.

"No," I said. "You are not."

The only object I had in my hand was the holy book given to me by Howel. I threw it hard at her just like when I had smashed the glain upon the downs.

Tigernus remained fixated upon her as the book touched her breasts, then fell, dropping into the ocean depths. Immediately her face changed and she clutched at her heart. Within seconds, her skin became seaweed; her face melted into Dead Man's Fingers and the scales of her tale mutated into brown algae. They fell into the water. In his hands, the coral comb disintegrated into dust. I had permanently lost the word of God, but had found Tigernus again.

27

The Voyage of Bryok, Manuscript, 10th Century CE
This narrative, written originally in either in Old Cornish or Old Breton was
at some point translated into Latin. Marginalia reveal a number of glosses remaining from its original language. The text here is probably a recension of
several earlier versions. There are a number of contradictory and repeated elements in the final section. Graphology has revealed that two different scribal
hands contributed to the version here. Bryok was a legendary traveller and
warrior figure whose adventures draw heavily upon Brittonic mythology. His
chief characteristic was the defeat of sea monsters. Courtesy of the Vatican
Apostolic Library, Vatican City.

EN GWÂV, PERKOU HÂV: IN winter, remember summer. In this, I reverse
my mother's proverb. I suppose initially I thought I was quite alone – but I
was not. Ghosts travelled with me. The swirling fog had cleared at sea, but a
few rolls of it still enveloped the coastline itself. These oozing swirls evoked
remembered conversations, the recollection of forms sat on board *An Ruen* and
snatches of a journey now over. Ghosts usually denote fear and oppression,
but these comforted me. Their forms made me realise that since accepting my
banishment, I had done some good. Their spirits recognised I could be a good
man again. I had thought, at times, that all hope was lost, yet on the other side
of the ocean, I was discovering myself again. When placed in this position,
you must accept every day as an adventure. There is no clock. You do not need
to be anywhere. The sun and moon do not have to dictate your movements. In
essence, you welcome in a freedom – alongside those ghosts.

The long land mass, that I had been following since my encounter with the
Bretons, started to end. Its low cliffs and yellow beaches halted, and they
curved back towards the northwest, leading to a good-sized bay of choppy
waves. I might have selected this route – the land there looked attractive – but
I kept my word to Tigernus and said I would push a little further down the
coast. I had shown him where I felt the run of the coast might go, together with
some landing possibilities. The water I was now in was a kind of basin located
between the longer peninsula back to the northeast and a headland to the south
which, when the fog finally lifted, I could make out on the distant horizon. It
seemed a good location to make for. I kept *An Ruen* fairly close to the coastline
still (I did not know it, but this decision was crucial in my eventual survival).

Sometimes, I anchored her in a bay and took the coracle inland to find water, and anything else that might be of use to me. This included wood, fruit (which needed to be picked carefully, for by now some of it was rotting), and leaves for kindling.

Those beaches and inlets were very still and quiet. It seemed no human had touched them since Annown made them thousands of years before. There, I found great peace, and meditated, sometimes watching the morning rise, as well as the sun set. Because of the time I had now spent observing this new world, lots of features, plants and birds were becoming familiar to me. Although probably not the right terms for them, I gave each a name that I deemed appropriate. They either reminded me of something from my homeland, or had distinguishing features which generated their name. This occupied much of my time.

There comes a moment in each man's life when after a relationship ends, for months and maybe years, he may pine and wish for a return for what he had before. Thus it was, with Orla. But in these days, I can safely say that love finally left me. You may be shocked to hear that – for me to even give it air and breath – but I am being honest. When love is so broken that the shards of it cannot possibly be put back together, eventually one must let it go. I mentioned ghosts being with me. Some remained, that is true; but her face had started to vacate my memory. When I considered this one night, while I was trying to sleep, I realised that my voyage had been purposeful: if nothing else, then it had allowed me to forget. This is what I had intended – that enough distance between us would stretch the cord so tight, that in the end, it would unravel and break. Love had been drowned back there somewhere – in the ocean's depths. Before, when I had been manhandled by Kenal and his men, it was something I would not have believed. It was something I could now accept. An alien shore had induced this in me.

Besides that though, besides love's ebb and flow, was I really any different than I was before? No, I convinced myself. I was an itinerant then, and was still one now. I had no home before, and I still had no home. I had a sack full of tools and they were still beside me. This felt important to understand. It allowed me to snap out of any pretence that I might have, and intimately know myself. So I have seen, many people are unhappy in their lives because they try to be something they are not. This is not a good path to follow, because you constantly hate what you have become. Although the great ocean made me contemplate the world in new ways, all it really did was to give me this understanding. I have to say, I was thankful for it.

Occasionally, along the coast, I had carved my mason's mark – more out of boredom than anything else. The snake and crowbar had been chiselled to last on both pebble and stone. It was no act of imperialism; no wish to stamp my authority on this new world. In some senses, it was just to keep my hand in. I'd been no mariner before, but now I felt like I was one. If I wasn't careful, I'd be a stone-worker no longer. Did I still have the skill? I hoped so. Sometimes, I'd see stones that had such useful angles and surfaces to them that, in front of a builder such as myself, they would need to be brought together. It was almost as if the laws of Annown had intended them to meet and coalesce. Thus, I made sculptures. I corbelled a section of stonework for the sheer glory of it. Perhaps one day, someone would find it, and marvel.

Sometimes, for pure devilment, inland, when I found the right length of stone, I'd erect it in some significant spot. In this way, I echoed my forefathers. There is, as you will know, great satisfaction in lying or crouching low and seeing the stone's length cut into the sky. In time, of course, like everything else, they would topple or be worn away by wind and rain, but I enjoyed these games. For one thing, they got me out of the boat for a few hours; and for another, allowed me to still feel a sense of my trade. For a complete job, I usually add a carving or two – nothing special you will understand – sometimes a repeat of the image of *An Ruen* I had completed in Hibernia. It was usually whatever took my fancy that morning.

These erections had nowhere near the significance of those at Boscawen Ûn – or any others that dotted the horn of Britain – and if a druid asked me what I was up to, I would freely confess I was just having fun. I am sure a man like Casvellyn would have scowled at me for such disrespect. It was the freedom from them, however, that I most revelled in. I realised at home how much control they had over both my father's and my own working practices. How good it was, to not be under their critical eyes.

This was my life then: sailing, naming, carving, erecting. It continued for almost a fortnight after Tigernus had left. With good sail, I contemplated that they might even have crossed the ocean by now, and be in full sight of Silura. Meanwhile, my traverse of the coast was progressing well. This large bay of broken inlets and headlands provided me with good shelter at night, as well as sandy beaches to put into. The grounds here were good for catching crab and shrimp, and these I freely indulged in. Because my diet was improving, my own general health seemed stronger. You see, I was preparing for winter; knowing that I needed to be fit and well to survive it. I sensed that these lands would experience much more snow and ice than the horn of Britain. For this reason, I wanted to put in somewhere soon.

My choice in this matter was not something I had any hand in. Events decided it for me. You would have thought that considering the full ocean I had crossed, *An Ruen* might now be trusted to have survived anything. After all, in 'The Land of Herbs' she had been virtually refitted; her hull relined with wool grease. However, for these past few weeks, I had not been able to re-grease her again, and that is maybe where the problem arose from. Grease acts as a sealant, a barrier between the ocean and hide, pushing the water away. When it fades, the skins become less sturdy and no longer watertight. If I had thought, I might have found some new solution for this lack of grease. Perhaps some native material could have been used, but it was true that I never found anything – and I suppose, had neglected to deal with the problem. Again, because the sea was slight, I felt there was nothing to worry about. I had no great distance to travel now.

One night, I was sleeping soundly, when my body sensed a wetness creeping through the hull. It sloshed in at its lowest point, and so soaked into the sheepskin, and then into my back. I woke when the damp touched my left arm, which was stretched out and held my head. At first, I didn't realise the full significance of the sensation. It merely felt uncomfortable and cold, but when a small wave of water lapped against my arm, I woke with a start. It was pre-dawn and the blackness of the night had lifted. I had eyesight enough to see the situation. The lower end of the stern had a depth of water in it about a hand deep. The bow was less flooded but was starting to lower, as the water shifted its weight, and grew to engulf that end of her as well.

You can imagine that I began to bail instantly, working as fast as I could to tip as much of the sea water overboard as I could. The process was unending though. No matter how hard I bailed, more seemed to be oozing into *An Ruen*'s confines. Abandoning the bailing for a while, I tried to find out where she might be holed. Maybe a repair could be enacted like I had completed before. I checked the new section I had sewn in. That appeared to be in order. No Rat meant there had been no warning system. He'd have spotted the location some time ago – and have given me enough time to effect a repair. This was not the case here.

The problem was that she had utterly lost being watertight. The grease had been essential in securing that, and now I had simply run out. I had to face facts. *An Ruen* was dying upon me. As before, I had reeled in the coracle as my last resort, and had transferred all soaking essentials into her. I was not about to let her go down without a fight though. In the growing light, I could see that I was not far from a creek. If I could make it there, then perhaps eventually she could be repaired. You will understand, the last thing I wanted was for her to sink on the seabed. There, she would be irretrievable. At least if I could get her in somewhere, maybe raise her onto a beach, she could be saved.

"Come on," I was saying. "You can do this."

Raising sail was pointless. There was no wind, and I didn't have the time anyway. Oars were the best option. I locked them in their sockets and powered away. As we pushed forward, you could feel the head water slowly seeping into her. It was rushing past my ankles and lower legs. Towards her rear, it was deeper – perhaps soon up to my stomach while rowing. I tried to ignore it. In essence though, she was actively lowering herself into the water. We were becoming submerged. All I could do now was to try to haul her into the shallows. When in such situations, you always have a belief that you can overcome the odds – that magically her bow will rise, and the water somehow seep out of her like squeezed hide. Tigernus had believed he saw the spirit of Warna before us – guiding us through the storm. If she could return again now, I would be eternally grateful.

"Where are you War-na?" I mouthed, each syllable, a row movement.

Whatever phantasmagorical wish I had, such a spirit did not materialise. Instead of rising, we were rapidly sinking. The creek was ahead of me though. At least I might be able to get her in there now. Such frenetic activity didn't however lead me to consider what I was passing over. It was inevitable that besides sinking we would ground as well. I heard the terrible noise of rocks scraping the hide. Then shortly afterwards, some of the stringers flipped out of place, cracking and buckling. These sounds condemned her fate.

"Fuck," I said. "Now you've done it."

I had.

The whole of *An Ruen*'s hull started to implode. The buckled stringers caused a collapse in the overall rigidity of the hull. Hides started to be pulled apart. Stitching seemed to disintegrate before my eyes. Thongs snapped. The bulwarks wobbled due to pressures elsewhere. I did not realise it, but I had begun crying. I was sobbing, my tears adding to the flood. It was my own Lethowsow. This boat had delivered me like a hand of tenderness over the waves. It was now collapsing into fragmented bone and peeling tendons.

Such was the weight of water in the hull that there was no point in driving her forwards with the oars any longer. I jumped out of her, my feet stretching down to find the mud of the creek. Now she was no longer a vessel but a watery log that I was pushing along. I managed to get her into the shallows, and there, her hull finally grounded and touched the floor. She came to a standstill in the dawn. I felt her exhale in relief. The sea had not quite consumed her. She would not face a future of encroachment by barnacles and crabs – but there was no way that she was ever going to float again.

That was it. The ocean was truly over.

An Ruen was ruined.

DEAR LORD AND DEAR ANNOWN, see how I am back to thinking of both of you again. It seems that I am as inconsistent as the ocean. I know I veer and change just like the currents. But surely, this is life?

I come and go like weed and water. Lord, I know you helped save Tigernus – this time, and long ago, but Annown, you still lurk inside of me. You are the fogou of my mind and soul. Can both of you live together? Can you cohabit inside the complexity of me? Now that I have come this far, I hope so. Maybe in this new world, this new land, things will not need to be one or the other. They can be both.

The next morning, everyone on board *Azen* suffered from hangovers, except Corentin and me. Tigernus' fuddled head had, however, not been brought on by overindulgence in alcohol, but by recovery from the curse which had dominated his existence for so long. Now that the sea siren had been transformed into nothing more than weed, she could do him no further harm. The curse had finally passed. In our quarters, he had apologised to me over and over again, for letting her get to him once more and for not being strong enough to resist her power. I held him tight and comforted him.

"It's over now," I said. "It's over."

I hadn't expected the holy book to have the effect it did on her when I threw it. She must have represented a kind of evil that only the text within it could combat. It proved to me that words could sometimes be used as powerful weapons. Why had the mermaid taken on my appearance? Perhaps she was sensing that she was losing her hold on him. If she could resemble me, then that would have made her all the more attractive and give her greater power to pull him under. I told no-one of the incident. The others assumed that Tigernus, like them, had drunk too much. At that moment, all he needed was sleep and rest.

On the *Mor Sargasso*, the atmosphere was still hot and broiling. We all drank copiously, thankful of the new supplies gained on Ynysow an Oves. The warmth and stillness did not ease up until two days later, when finally Corentin determined there was enough of a wind to unfurl the sails again. Orders were made to head in a more northwesterly direction. This decision pleased most of the crew, for soon the overbearing heat would end. We'd be back in a latitude that naturally suited the Bretons.

While Tigernus recovered, I talked with Rosparzh. I was intrigued because it was well known that years ago he had taken a party into Hyperborea and encountered resistance. I wanted to know what these people were like whom he had met. I needed to prepare myself for my own encounter. On mentioning it to him though, I sensed his reluctance to talk about the incident, so I didn't push him.

"The most terrifying moment of my life," is what he said to me. "Savages they were."

"Worse than the Saxons?"

"By a mile. If you're sensible you'll not go in alone. We were armed to the teeth, but they still ambushed us."

I got to thinking about what Rosparzh had said. Maybe that is where they went wrong. Maybe their look of aggression had caused a counter-response. I wondered if when we reached shore, I should go in alone. A woman would present a different prospect for them. Probably they'd know I meant no harm. I knew however, that Tigernus and Corentin would need some convincing to allow this to happen. I therefore had a job to do with the two of them.

As the dense seaweed of the *Mor Sargasso* started to fade, Tigernus continued to make a good recovery. He was up and eating again – and looked much healthier than I had known him to be.

"Bad one eh?" asked Corentin, giving him a friendly shove. "That ale's rough. It's why I don't touch it."

"Yes," said Tigernus. "A bad one. A very bad one."

He looked over at me.

"Blejan nursed me through it..."

"Ah well. You know what they say: no better use for a woman than helping a man recover from his drinking..."

I gave Corentin a hard stare.

"What?" he said, a broad smile across his face. "I'm joking."

Until this moment on our voyage, we'd had a dearth of sea creatures. Given Tigernus' narration of his voyage with my father, I had expected us to encounter many more species. I had even hoped that in the *Mor Sargasso* I might have seen something interesting – one of the octopuses or serpents that the other mariners feared. Perhaps my monster had been the mermaid. Her fearsomeness had truly been enough to deal with. Why should I wish for anything more? In this, I therefore became thankful that little else had pursued or played with us.

This changed, however, one dawn morning in late April. We were awoken by some intense shouting on the main deck. One of the crew had spotted something out in the ocean.

"What is it?" I asked.

"We call them *Morvyl Ladha*."

I knew what it meant. He was referring to the 'slaying whales'.

"They're fearsome," I noted.

"We never saw any the first time around," said Tigernus, "but I know their power. They eat dolphins and seals... sometimes other whales..."

Most whales of the ocean seemed benign, placid creatures, which might only accidentally cause harm to vessels. These creatures were different altogether. With their black back, white chest and sides, and large dorsal fin, they instantly gave the impression of being hostile killing machines. At the moment, the single *Morvyl Ladha* did not threaten us; we were too big a vessel for it to toy with, but even in its graceful breaching of the surface, I sensed something malevolent about it.

"Do you see its teeth?" asked Tigernus. "They're for ripping prey apart. Most whales don't have mouths like that."

In seeing this slayer of the sea that morning, I had many questions about the ocean, but these questions of mine could also be applied to the rest of the world. If God created all of this, then why did nature cannibalise itself? Why did he create monsters who destroyed what was beautiful? It didn't make sense. At least with you, Annown, I knew what you took but I also knew what you gave. I watched the beast turn and dive. Now I knew the wonder my father had felt (perhaps that is why I had wanted to see such creatures: for this wonder alone). I knew of plesiosaurs, sharks, whales, and walruses. Also, I knew of *Ancredhor Mor* and Saxons. I knew too, of these people of Hyperborea who might also strike at will – and kill. When I thought about it some more, those three were just like these slaying whales – sleek, beautiful, fearsome – and yet all still part of God's creation. This I had learnt. All of them were swimming through the waters, trying to get by the best they could – even if that did mean using the rest of us as prey. In this way, I prepared myself for our imminent arrival at Hyperborea.

28

Cordon-decorated urn, Stone Cist, Bartinney Downs, Cornwall, 1st Century to 8th Century CE
This type of locally-made pottery is named so because it is decorated with raised bands or cordons, beginning in the first century CE but lasting until the eighth century. It may be conveniently described as 'Romano-Cornish' although it continued to be manufactured for a long period after the Roman occupation. Ash and human remains from cremations were stowed in them and placed in stone cists. Such pottery was also for domestic use. It is far from clear how such usage was differentiated.

THE WRECKAGE OF *AN RUEN* had dictated my destiny. At least I was alive and had managed to pull my equipment and the remaining supplies off her. Anything that was not part of the hull, I cannibalised. This included the sheepskins, the remaining oxhides, the oars and the head mast. It was impossible for me alone to have rescued the main mast; given the swampy conditions, the weight of the mast would have pushed me all too deeply into the mud, though I did remove the pebble I had attached to it, onto which I had scratched my mason's mark. So, there in the creek, sat *An Ruen* – broken and plundered; a shadow of her former self. Gradually, over decades, she would decay further. Mosses and lichens would find the wood and cover her stringers and gunwale. Nature would eventually reclaim her and she'd return to the ocean. You know that is the way of all things.

Before, I thought that I alone would decide my final landfall. Now I realised that it was in the hands of someone else. I sat on the bank of the creek surrounded by the debris of the past few months. Each object held a story or carried some greater significance for me. I remembered certain events that had happened at sea, when Tigernus' hand or mine had fallen upon them. The debris also reinforced the fact that my ocean was over. This had to become my land now. But by Annown, how I would have to change and adapt.

Somewhere in the chaos of the wreck, I had lost the clay figurine that I had carried since Silura. Perhaps it was telling me that now I'd passed over the ocean I no longer needed it. A search of the waterlogged hull did not reveal it to me, so I was resigned to letting it go. Something else to go that way, I told myself.

I was now thankful Tigernus was no longer with me. An arrival in this manner would not have been the best of starts for him. I knew he was fond of the vessel too, and to see her wrecked in this way would have truly shocked him. As I have said, there was no plan. I had just been thrown upon the shore myself as a piece of seaweed-coated flotsam. In such situations though, you cannot bemoan your fate for hours on end, nor think of what could have been. I needed to act practically, to start making an existence here. Stopping now was the way to death; to the oblivion I had always feared.

Whatever explorations I would make into the interior, I decided that this creek had to act as my base. Here, I would store my chattels and goods, and here I would construct a temporary dwelling. On the inlet were runs of sheltered rocks, which would keep out the ocean's breeze. With one of these formations, using rocks to weigh down oxhides I made an improvised roof, stretching a man's length of material over me. This I then secured to wooden posts which I had snapped off in the nearby woods, and after sharpening their ends, pushed them hard into the earth. I tied the hides to these posts using the remaining leather thongs, and then set about placing the sheepskins inside this structure. With other stones I constructed a hearth, and further up the creek, where it was more river than ocean, I found fresh water. Wood was plentiful for the fire, and in the creek were a range of good-sized fish (their species was new to me, but they tasted fine). Soon, I suppose, I had transferred the comforts of *An Ruen* to this rocky dwelling, and in so doing, truly became a man of the woods. These were the skills I would need to make my way here.

Each day brought another autumnal rush of leaf fall. I found that when dry, these leaves made good kindling, and improvised their use in every possible way: to wrap food, to wipe arse, to clean. I began to become accustomed to the smell of this land, and started to notice patterns in its wildlife. The weather was generally fair, with that fading half-hearted sunshine that one notes as the wheel of the year turns. Although initially I was tentative in everything that I did, within a week I had come to map and understand the local territory within, say, a couple of miles of the camp. I knew where I might find the best wood, where grew berries and roots, and where deer could be taken. From a hill in the southwest, I could gaze out over this land, making out in the distance other rivers, deep valleys, thick forests, plateaus and lakes. At some point they needed to be explored.

This was the paradise I had sought: the 'Isle of Bliss' then. Here I was free from *Ancredhor Mor*, Saxons and Howel's ambition. I had to keep reminding myself.

Do you remember how I explained that, when I was first sailing in *An Ruen*, that I talked to myself? I came to realise I was doing the same now. A language once spoken distant from this place now reverberated around the trunks of its trees and echoed across its groves. I named the new land with the old words. To hear these words again was joyous and liberating. After Tigernus' leaving, silence had pervaded the boat and it had unnerved me. To speak, to utter, to express one's hopes and one's dreams was essential.

In those days, of course, I contemplated how far Corentin and his crew had progressed. I imagined they were making good speed; maybe enough speed that the iced fish they caught might feed the starving refugees back home. I prayed that Tigernus was following my instructions. I knew eventually he would go back to Scathynys. He would return to the land in which he had been conceived. How long it would take though, I truly did not know.

My thoughts of them, of course, made me remember Rosparzh's words about his encounters with the peoples of this land. That creek I had ended up in seemed uninhabited; his exploration had been further to the northeast, but thoughts of a similar violent event occupied my mind. My time here might be very short. The prospect of being left alone to rot did not thrill me. With awareness that I might be watched or possibly attacked at any point, I set up a cordon around my camp. Using triangles of twigs, low on the ground, I ran threads of fine flax, and connected these to the rescued ship's bell from *An Ruen*. I engineered the string in such a way that if anything stumbled into my camp, then the clapper would ring against the sides of the bell. I thought this an ingenious way of guarding against any hostility.

However, I needn't have worried. I seemed to be located far from any human settlement, and the only thing that made the bell ring was an inquisitive and strange mammal seemingly wearing a black face mask and with a bushy tail of alternating black and grey rings. Although shocking me first of all, I soon came to recognise that he was a friendly creature. I fed him any fish heads I didn't need, and he used his dextrous front paws to shovel the food into his mouth. Most days he visited me to see what I had to offer. Of course, I had a sympathetic response to him, shaped from long days at sea with a rat.

The decision I had to make about my circumstances was whether to spend my winter here at the creek, or to make a move inland. I was already sensing the colder air, and knew that if I were to move, it needed to be soon. I had been keeping a calendar by scratching the days on the nearby rock surface. Three weeks had passed. There was no-one else I could rely on for this information – and it is odd how time drifts if you do not keep a record. We knew this from on board *An Ruen* when famine had hit us. The days were shortening too – the sun a good deal lower in the sky. I elected to move inland away from the coast, but decided that if I found nothing better, I would return within a fortnight and winter here.

Drawing on my experience of dragging Tigernus in Hibernia, I made a framework of wood and strongly tied it together with flax. From it ran two longer lengths of wood which I could grasp in my hands. Just as in Hibernia, I could then pull my possessions along with me on this sledge. You will understand that I did not take everything. It would have been impossible. Some hides had to stay, as did the head mast. But my tools, some food, water and enough materials to build a shelter all came. Across my back I slung the quiver of arrows given to me by Caera as well as his finely-made bow.

That item, I suspect, was my saving.

You will see why.

If one time the ocean had been endless, here, it was the forest. It extended in ways I had never witnessed back on the horn of Britain. I never truly saw its end. The whole world was a place of brightly-coloured canopies and deep leaf litter. Rarely did the forest canopy stop, and sometimes it was difficult to see the North Star by night in order to check my position. I was generally heading west, so chosen because this seemed to be the way this land mass extended, and because it held the most convenient and logical path. I could have elected to march north, but with winter coming, this seemed an unwise move. I must confess: there is an inherent spookiness to such forests. The crunch of one's feet in the fallen leaves and the silence of the solid upwards-stretching trunks made me nervous most days. I felt Annown was with me though. It was not a place Warna's Christian god had ever walked, nor was likely to. This was a landscape I was utterly unfamiliar with. What creatures lurked within, I did not know – nor perhaps wanted to know. At night could be heard the howl of wolves singing to each other out there in the distance. I always kept my bow and quiver close.

In terms of moving through this forest, I had not exactly been quiet, and I dare say my efforts to pull the frame, as well as the songs and conversations I was having with myself, had attracted attention. Silence would have guaranteed me passage perhaps, but clearly I had been as blatant as a pack of yelping wolves wandering through here. Some moments of my journey are hard to remember now, but one moment I can recall as if it happened just a second ago.

Indeed, these moments were about to change everything. They were about to justify my ocean.

It was quite simple really. To rest, I had dropped the frame for a while, and had sat upon the mossy trunk of a fallen tree. I was taking a sip of water, when I sensed the cool presence of others around me. They came from behind tree trunks and bushes, but also from below and above, emerging camouflaged from the ground, and from the rich canopy above. I heard the draw back of several bow strings; wood creaking ready to shoot. Do you remember that deer I told you about that we killed on Fogo Island? I was it. I was that animal. I sensed the proximity of the arrowheads close to my body. They were flint carved, a good deal more basic that the ones Caera had trimmed for me. His heads were of flattened pieces of sharpened iron but these could still rip me to shreds.

All of those surrounding me were of a similar physical shape: muscular, tall and strong. They were dark-haired; some sections of their heads were shaved (some at the sides, and others from brow to back of the neck) but the longest parts of their hair were braided the same as mine. A few had wisps of black hair on their chins but most of their faces were hairless. All had white teeth which shone out of a darker-skinned face. Their clothing was a mixture of fur, hides and leather. I noticed that around their waists was wrapped a belt, into which was suspended a kind of breechcloth. It looked comfortable and well-adapted to the climate here. This was connected to separate leather leggings on each of their legs. These were decorated with beadwork and colourful patterns, and then tied upon their legs and to the belt with thongs. Some held apron panels on the front of this breechcloth; on which were woven symbols I had never seen before. On their tops were leather jerkins not dissimilar to my own, and around these were wraps of what appeared to be either wolf or bearskin. It looked like the land provided all their clothing for them.

I could identify no leader.

The moment was as breathtaking as when I first encountered the plesiosaur. Here was another species of humanity – one which I had imagined, had heard about, and was now encountering. So these were the Hyperboreans.

Amongst the language they spoke, the word "Aquit" kept being mentioned. Amongst the many other phrases and sentences they reeled off, this was the one term I could make out. One of them raised his finger and pointed. I suspected it meant one, but this warning appeared to mean that they needed to be wary. There was perhaps a need to look out for others like me. I might have explained that I was solo, but what good would it have done?

Each one of them was very close now, carefully circling me. Most of all, they peered at my eyes and examined my hair, grabbing fingerfuls of it. My skin too, was of great interest to them. I raised my hands to try to show them I meant no harm. A couple of them gingerly examined my wooden frame, and pulled out various objects. The ship's bell intrigued them, and they jumped at its clamour. When it stopped ringing, they examined its carved metal. Likewise, my tools also proved of interest. There was much discussion about these. They seemed to be noting a similarity to some items they had.

However, it was my bow and quiver full of arrows that aroused most interest.

451

Caera's design for his kind of bow was certainly much more adept than their technology and they noted this instantly, feeling the wood and testing the tension. The iron of Caera's arrows prompted much discussion as well. In a few months' time, I would be showing them how they could be manufactured.

While some kept their weapons pointed at me, others examined my body. They pulled down my trousers to see if I was the same as they were, and laughed. One signalled how small and white my pissle was – wiggling his forefinger like a boar's tail. Another of them though noted my twist of a wrist, and then spied my fifth finger. Again, this caused much debate. Each of them came to look at it and noted its strangeness. My deformity then, coupled with my weapon, may have helped save my life. They seemed to understand that I meant no harm, and started to lower their bows and arrows to the floor, eventually placing them back into their own quivers. There was a long period (maybe an hour or more) of them trying to make sense of me. I suspected my deformity was something unexplained. Then again, here was someone with a weapon like their own. Parts of them were in me. They recognised that. Maybe that is where the Bretons had gone wrong.

I began to speak slowly. I explained who I was and where I had come from. They listened but, of course, did not understand a word. However, just as their language had intrigued me, my language also ignited interest from them. I could tell they were thinking how odd my sounds were, how strange the movements of my tongue were, and what curious shapes I made with my lips.

I repeated who I was and pointed at me, saying my name.

"Voog. I am Voog. Voooog."

The word must have sounded amusing. Sometimes that is the way. Sounds in one tongue echo a rude word or a pun in another. Maybe that was the case here. Maybe the gloop of vowels in my nomenclature amused them. I could not tell.

One of these men, though, understood what I was trying to communicate. He knew that I was offering them my name. A young man, perhaps just seventeen or eighteen years old, he glanced at the others before pointing at his own belly, just as I had done. Then he opened his lips and made a sound.

"Tisquanto."

I hoped that I had heard him correctly. I pointed at him and slowly mouthed, "Tis-quant-o."

He nodded.

I was now using the same techniques that I had learnt with the Corcu Loígde. I knew that with language it was possible to end fear and division; to create a degree of trust and understanding. Of course, I wondered what these people

452

thought of me. Was I some strange figure out of nowhere who had suddenly been plonked down before them? Perhaps I was from a comet; or a being thrown down to earth from the strange lights above 'The Land of Herbs'. They knew my humanity though. They understood that I felt fear and knew pain just as they did.

As I stumbled into their world, I must admit I did feel a sense of guilt though; an idea that had been put into my head from Corentin. Here, I was invader – I was Saxon – intruding upon their world order. I was probably challenging the whole ideology of their being. Maybe they felt their world ended at the creek where I had camped. Maybe they knew of mystical lands to the east, across that vast ocean. Suppose they had bards like Remfra to make up such tales – and mythologise their world? Would my presence bring others – and then others – and then others again? – so that one day, this land would be overrun – just as ours was back home. I knew how greedy humanity could be. I knew how it could be a vulture on the gunwale, watching.

On that day, I was not to find out but, as I am trying to explain, I would come to know them; in the future, I would truly know them as my brothers and sisters.

Tisquanto suggested walking. He gestured with his hand to follow them through the forest. I could not move at their speed. Their curiosity had unfurled my tight packing of the frame, and those items all needed securing again. In the event, a few things got left behind – among them, to my later dismay, the bellshrine. I tried to explain but failed. Did volume make a difference? No. I should have known that from Hibernia. Shouting did no good. I was quite uncertain if I should even go with them. The one saving factor was that they had not yet killed me, nor now seemed likely to. This group were very different from the one Rosparzh had encountered.

I had completed the pulling of the sledge at a walking pace before. This was no longer the case. They were expecting me to jog to keep up. Each of them covered ground quickly, as if they were hares being chased by predators. A second word I kept overhearing was something that sounded like 'Wôpanâak' (I offer it properly here but on that day, I knew not the spelling). I came to understand over the next few days, that not only was this term the name of this group, but also the name of their language. I was therefore in the land of the Wôpanâak and, although then I felt us quite different; the coming days would reinforce many similarities, despite an ocean originally being in the way.

The thick forest finally changed into bushy shrubland, and we had to cross a small, fast-flowing river to reach a plateau. On the plateau, to my surprise, we encountered what appeared to be cultivated fields of a food stuff I came to later understand as being maize. Both delicious and nourishing, this was, over the next few years, to replace fish as a staple part of my diet. Although my first encounter with these people might have suggested that they were primitive, they were far from being so. I had been deceived by their flint arrow heads into thinking they were not as advanced. All that I had learnt about life before needed to be dropped and questioned. I had thought the ocean itself had contributed to that process, but its completion was to be found here.

The fields of maize appeared to have been irrigated and seemed organised into different phases of planting, which no doubt would provide an ongoing crop around much of the year. Was this the world that Hecatæus of Abdera had described? Perhaps so. It being autumn though, perhaps the last of it was being harvested. Women and children worked the fields, some pulling frames whilst larger sledges were towed by oxen. They stopped their labour as the group returned with me. Who was this lone stranger that they had found in the forest? I could see this thought cross their faces. They feared me I could tell, although I smiled back at them to show I was no danger.

Past the maize fields was a village, but it was nothing like what I had known at Carn Euny or even at the fortress of the people of the Calf Goddess. It was a temporary affair, and from what I could see, the people moved between this place – their planting grounds – and their hunting ones. It seemed the hunting grounds were more actively used in the spring and summer, with the fields being in closer proximity in the autumn and winter. Tisquanto gestured to the community of tents and offered its name.

"Noëpe," he said.

I repeated this word and followed him. I came to later understand that this name meant 'the place between the water courses', and its geographical location reflected its name perfectly. The stream in the east that we had crossed before was matched by another wider river to the west. There, I would shortly come to hunt trout with bow and arrow. This was identical to the way we named our land back home (I still say home. Exactly where was that now?).

You may have noted how I was gradually beginning to make sense of this world; although it took a number of months, as my life here unfurled, I started to understand the differences between the *puttackahuan* and the *neesquttow*. The former were smaller roundhouses akin to those back home, but made of a cone of sewn skins, and kept secure by stones at ground level. The latter were the larger dwellings – places of 'two fires' – which held larger families, or were meeting houses. It was an entirely different life to all I had encountered before. These tents were easily transportable, being made of wooden poles and moveable mats. How different this was to the leaden and unmoveable stone of Carn

Euny. I saw for the first time the logic of being transitory; of flowing with the seasons.

In one such *neesquttow* I was, a few days later, placed before elders of the community, who had come to inspect me. Unlike Carn Euny, the leaders here were women; the people followed matrilineal descent and power. They were all ancient, all Warnas, and many of them bent double with rheumatism and aching bones. I was of interest to them though. They were shown my weapons and resources, and on the dry earth of the floor of this tent, I drew a diagram of where I had come from; trying to show them firstly, the forest and the creek where *An Ruen* had wrecked. Then, using a stick I drew in other portions of the coast I knew, some features which they seemed to recognise – among them Fogo Island.

I tracked backwards for them across the ocean to show my origin. This caused great curiosity. What was also incredible was that one of the elderly women was able to further trace the map of the southern Hyperborean coast for me, drawing a long peninsula in the earth. To the east of it, she added a set of islands. After that, she seemed not to know what existed. I drew a picture of *An Ruen* too, in order to demonstrate what I had sailed the ocean in. Likewise, they drew for me pictures of great canoes that their people seemed to carve from trees. These, they appeared to use on the ocean, as well as in the larger rivers. As always in these situations, there was much nodding of heads and much shaking and grunting when they didn't understand. I don't think I ever drew so fast, nor as accurately, as I did that day. They liked watching me.

What I had been received as, I never knew for some time, and since at that point, I only understood a little of their language, I had to accept their generosity in whatever form it came. Sometimes, this was a little maize; other times it was fish, or the flesh of the wild goose. I learnt that *motuckquas* was the name for rabbit, and that *askooke* meant snake. This latter food was a delicacy they sometimes enjoyed. They were surprised when I didn't partake of it. Deer they labelled *ottucke*, and I was able to demonstrate my skills with bow and arrow on some hunting missions. It very much looked like I would not be going back to the creek. I was given a *puttackahuan* of my own, and then garments of their kind – in swap, I believe, for the venison. Initially, I felt self-conscious wearing them, but when the winter wind began to bite, I understood their use, and so wore them more often. I grew to resemble Caera. My own garments, of course, had almost worn out from the crossing, and so skin by skin, and hide by hide, I was absorbed.

It seemed what they wanted most of all, was for me to learn about their culture. Thus, I was always called by Tisquanto and others to watch ceremony and ritual. Rosparzh had been right. It seemed I had merely left one druid order for another. Here, the druids were shamans who were able to connect with the afterlife and the earth spirits. This was their Annown, their Otherworld – and from what I observed, it was not that much different. There were, however, the elderly women and the *ahtaskoaog* (the leading men of the community) who took great measure of what the shaman had to offer. I watched with fascination and through continued involvements came to note that several different deities were worshipped. These, they termed *manito*. Two that I quickly came to know of were *Cautantowwit* and *Hobbomock*.

Cautantowwit was the creator deity who lived in an afterworld inhabited by the souls of the dead. Although placated by sacrifice, prayers and praise, he seemed not always to be benevolent. Dance and ritual taught me that he could cause incurable illness when he was angry. I was intrigued by the fact that, when buried, usually the bodies of the Wôpanâak were placed in graves with a western orientation, the exact direction, apparently, of *Cautantowwit*'s house. This was like my Annown. Although it had other labels here, it was exactly the same. You will believe me then, when I say I wanted to shout this discovery to the stars. This Christian god of Warna's was not even in their consciousness.

The other *manito* was *Hobbomock*. Always associated with the colour black, he was related to their concept for dead, the death and the cold wind that came from the northeast. *Hobbomock* could appear at night in the form of travellers, other tribe members, or animals: bears or wolves. Indeed, initially, it seemed I might be seen as one such *Hobbomock*. I was concerned for my own safety once I understood the shaman's ritual. Hadn't I emerged as a traveller from the northeast? Nothing happened, for which I was thankful, but I saw the power of belief. *Manito*, it seemed were best placated with gift-giving and offerings, just in the same way we worked with Annown. In this, I learnt about their ways of birthing and ways of dying.

Their shaman took some degree of interest in me. It became clear I gave physical manifestation to some prophecy (not this again, I had contemplated). The shaman, who I took to be named Wamsutta, had precisely the same role here as Casvellyn did back at Carn Euny. He was the people's spiritual guide. It was he who declared what offerings should be made, and he who decided how both the living should emerge, and how the dead should be taken. Clad in wolf fur and with the skull of such a creature on his head, he did this at gatherings named *pawwaw*, which all of Noëpe were expected to attend.

Wamsutta was at first not always kindly to me. Perhaps he saw that I had a kind of power beyond his own, and that the people were more intrigued by me than him. This came to alter, though, as he learnt from me, and I from him.

Wamsutta, I discovered, was a man who had seen more than sixty summers. He was agile though and, despite grey hair and a much lined face, could easily keep pace with the younger warriors. He lived alone in a *neesquttow* located just off the rest of the village, similar to the way our druids did with the people of Carn Euny. Like Aimend, he offered medicine when it was needed: his role then concerned both the mental and physical health of his people.

From him too, came the stories. He was their bard, as well as their druid. I sat in on one session where he told a narrative (I believe) about a giant named Maushop. It seemed an origin tale about how the first of their kind had arrived and how in order to allow them to live in peace, he had to rid the land of an enormous eagle that ate men. This he duly did, and then taught people how to hunt and make fire. Although an ocean away from Remfra, both men had the same skills of telling; this delighted the children here. Their contagious smiles were the same as those of the youngsters at Carn Euny.

I had noted he always used the moon to connect with me. He'd gesture to its form in the night sky; after which he would point to his eye and then back to me. After so many times of seeing this, it seemed he had a label for me. I was the 'moon-faced' one. Maybe he felt I could see better at night, or maybe it was a reflection of my complexion – being so fair compared to everyone else. On the earth, he also kept drawing a lone man, and pointing to my left hand. This message, though, I did not work out until a long time later, when we eventually had the power of speech.

Wamsutta falteringly tried to teach me other things. Do you remember that caribou I killed? Although these people hunted, they did not believe in always taking from the land. Sometimes, you had to give back. Hunters sometimes cut themselves to drain blood into the earth – an offering to thank it for what it had given. This was a new way of looking at the world for me, and I have to admit I found it compelling. The Wôpanâak never just took. They gave too. My people could learn much from them. This was how I became part of these people. I thought I understood all of their ways and was beginning to familiarise myself with their language, trying pieces of basic conversation with them – with Tisquanto and Wamsutta acting as my tutors. In clothing, food, lifestyle, hunting, fishing and spirituality, I was becoming more like them every day. Here was where I really left the old Voog behind.

Before, Orla and Carn Euny had shifted from being a memory to become a story. Now, they were shifting into a myth. I even found myself dirtying my skin, to try and fit in. I was gaining community and communion with these people. Perhaps you will judge me for that – consider me flippant, arrogant, and over-hopeful of some reintegration into their society after being exiled from elsewhere. Maybe I was - but maybe too, I did not have a choice. I knew I was not part of them, but despite this I was becoming one of them.

Then, things changed. The stars must have altered their position and shone down upon me. Maybe, somewhere, and in spite of this old faith, Warna was watching, guiding. When an elderly warrior and farmer named Pekwaqhet died, Wamsutta completed the usual ceremonies associated with his passing to the house of *Cautantowwit*. But apparently, it was different from normal. At night, the whole of the community of Noëpe walked for about a mile outside the village, carrying the warrior's body aloft. I followed, and to my great surprise, observed Wamsutta entering a primitive stone-framed souterrain into which the body of Pekwaqhet was placed.

I came to realise that such ritual was associated with the time of year and Pekwaqket's status. He was no ordinary warrior, but a venerated one. He had died just before midwinter, and we all watched the morning sun of the winter solstice poke through the souterrain, lighting up the underground chamber and his body. Perhaps in this way *Cautantowwit* could find Pekwaqhet's spirit.

By sheer accident then, and by immersion into this new land, I had found a fogou. Tisquanto saw me hurry back from the ceremony.

"Fogou," I couldn't help but say to him. "A fogou!"

Gathering dust in my tent was my sack of tools, and I needed to ensure they were ready once more.

LORD AND ANNOWN – AND FATHER, I want to tell you about the frustration of being so near and so far from you. I want to tell you of this, but also speak of all your signs and signals – and miracles. I want to express my thanks for wreckage and passing, for decay and transition. You will come to learn why. You see, another week of voyaging passed after the sighting of the *Morvyl Latha* before we first viewed the coast of Hyperborea. In that time, we had touched upon a part of the sea where the waters 'curdled' (that was Tigernus' word for it) with ice. All of us dressed warmly, and spent more time in the hull away from the gusting northerly winds. Corentin's course had not taken us any further northwards however, so we did not witness the crystal columns which Tigernus had told me about.

It was strange with him. We were clearly moving into a part of the ocean that he somehow recognised. How hard it is to pin down something that is constantly in motion, so constantly fluid, and yet he was attempting to do so. The air, the winds, the clouds, the look of the water, all contributed to this feeling.

Corentin was more down-to-earth in his view of our position. He had calculated our objective by using the stars and by understanding them in relation to their position on the horizon. Tigernus had the skill to be able to do the same, but right now he preferred his senses to locate his past. For me, it was an omen that the fog came down – not only because it had been a part of how Tigernus had described their first encounter with the Bretons, but also because we had left our old world in the same conditions – perhaps witnessing Casvellyn's final renunciation of the past and maybe (if I felt kindly towards him) even his blessing.

"About here, wasn't it?" Corentin suggested, raising his eyebrow and gesturing for a crewman to drop anchor.

Rosparzh and Tigernus looked at each other and laughed. How could Corentin judge such an encounter from all those years ago? How could he pinpoint it?

"It smells how I recall it," said Tigernus.

"Maybe – but you know your position when you were here. Try to think back."

Tigernus peered over the gunwale and looked out towards the shore.

"We were quite tight in," he said, "I remember that. Then you crossed us."

Corentin, Tigernus, Rosparzh and I gathered on the deck to try to pull apart the thick fog of their memories. They were recalling soundings taken but as no-one had written them down, this only added to the haze. I had to be patient here because I was reliant on all of them all to work out where they had been. I couldn't force their recollection even though I may have wanted to.

"Loic would have remembered," said Rosparzh. "He was always good like that. Take him anywhere, and he'd know it."

Loic was not with us though. Tigernus gave me a look at the mention of his name. Before, perhaps, he had been someone complicit in my father's exile. Now, paradoxically, mention of him only brought my father closer.

The fog stayed and this was part of the difficulty because it made certain that landmarks on the coast could not be observed. However, that said, there were huge swathes of woodland and hills which, twenty years ago, one might have been able to distinguish. Now, these blended and became as one. Tigernus remained up on deck thinking over that period. I gave him the space to do it. He needed time to think through where they had come from and where they were making for. I knew he had retraced this moment so many times in anticipation of our arrival. I sensed his fear too – that he should fail me. The crew also grumbled that it had been a wild-goose chase: that distance and time were bound to deceive. How old had he been? Eight? Well, surely he'd have forgotten by now. Corentin persuaded them to have faith in him.

In the evening, I got Tigernus to recall where they had come from. It was not easy. To some extent, the crew were right. Time and distance had altered his perspective on things.

"We came down from the north," Tigernus said, "and stopped at an island filled with caves. Voog and I went ashore. We found grapes there, and there were all these caves. I think he carved something on the beach there, but because of my incompetence, he didn't get to finish it... Then we headed toward the southwest, travelling beside a longer island..."

"I know that," said Corentin. "It's here look."

He pointed to Voog's map.

"Several days then," Tigernus reflected, "with us stopping off occasionally to find water and hunt for food."

"Keep going," encouraged Rosparzh. "Keep thinking it through..."

"Reefs," went Tigernus. "The reason we headed further out to sea was because of them... Shortly afterwards, we bumped into you."

That was it then. If the reefs Tigernus recalled could be located, we'd have the exact position. From there, we could then calculate the direction Voog went in.

"We've no choice but to wait until the fog clears," said Corentin. "My suggestion is you take *Warna* out and track the coast. We'll follow. Once you've ascertained where the reefs are, you'll know where we collided."

The fog did not clear rapidly. Another week passed while we kicked our heels and twiddled our thumbs.

"May weather," said Rosparzh. "It was always like this over here. As bad as at home."

I do not recall the day precisely. In my memory, it was when a colder, drier wind came down from the north and seemed to suck away the blanket. We literally saw it roll out past *Azen*, revealing a complete picture of the landscape. For the past week, we had dropped anchor and hoped this had been the approximate point. Now, our position could be confirmed.

When the fog was gone, the crew lowered *Warna* onto the blue and Tigernus and I climbed down a rope ladder into her. We sailed to the shore first of all, with Tigernus trying to get his bearings. I could see that he needed to come in from the north in order to recall the pattern of the coast. We didn't speak. I let him think. I let his memory of that time expand and dominate. Those hours were endless while he traced the shore, with Corentin paralleling our movement towards the southwest out at sea. To ease the boredom on board, the crew had set to fishing.

How odd for me it was now to sit there with him, and become my father. How strange it was for me to peer upon this land, which twenty years ago his eyes had traced. I drifted into thinking of this. I lulled myself to sleep in the security of Tigernus' skill as a mariner.

"There," he said softly to me. "That's where we turned out to sea."

I opened my eyes and saw a set of reefs upon which foaming white water broke. For me this was one sign, one signal, one miracle of something huge.

"This would be exactly where we bumped into them. All we need to do now is trace every creek to the southwest. That's where he was heading for."

"How long will that take?"

Tigernus didn't answer me. I had hardly needed to ask. I knew it was no five minute job.

Here was where the pin became mislaid in the hayrick.

29

Satellite Image of Tin streaming grounds, Marazion, Cornwall, 9th to 10th Centuries CE
This photograph taken from space in 2012 shows the characteristic pattern of parallel ridges and scarp left by tin streaming, north of Marazion. The ridges are sometimes roughly perpendicular to, sometimes coaxial with the line of the valley, sometimes apparently haphazard, but all are bounded by a scarp which marked the edge of the worked ground and whose height relates to the depth of the deposits. The tin mining industry in Cornwall is thought to have originated in pre-Roman times. Streaming for tin reached its apogee in the 9th to 10th centuries but then declined in the Early Medieval Period, when underground hard rock mining for metals began to develop. Image courtesy of the European Space Agency/Agence Spatiale Européenne.

WHEN THE WINTER SOLSTICE RITUAL was finished, to my surprise, I discovered that Pekwaqhet's body was taken from the souterrain and then placed inside a kind of chamber tomb. I only discovered his eventual destination a few days later, when I found Wamsutta and others completing the finishing touches to the earthworks. They were working hard, using bone tools and manhandling stones into position. Such tombs were constructed in a very similar way to the ones that still dotted the horn of Britain, and in past times had usually been reserved for the burials of great chieftains.

In my Age, we had long since shifted to cremation and cists in which the ashes were placed, but back in the day, this had been the way. Usually, they were composed of four or five large upright slabs, with two marking the entrance. Upon these were placed one large capstone, and then the whole structure was sealed up with earth and a surrounding wall of stone. Because of the great length of time since these had been completed, many had worn away, leaving only the upright slabs and capstone in position. We knew them to be sacred, even though the remains of such chieftains had long since become absorbed into the earth or had been carried away on the wind. No stone-worker ever touched them.

I was, of course, fascinated to find such similar structures here. The same basic processes were being employed. These people were no different from those at home. In the immediate period after Pekwaqhet's immersion into the fogou, I had the frustration of trying to communicate my expertise with stone.

The difficulty was that although I could deliver language in communicating basic concepts, I found myself prevented from being fully involved. I wanted to explain how I could help them, how I could use my skills to further assist their building techniques. When I say that I felt I could offer them advice, I say this purely because there were easier ways of doing certain things. I came to understand that although the lives of the Wôpanâak were as sophisticated as those back home, clearly they were in a moment of transition – moving from the world of wood and skins to a new world of stone and metal.

"What is this fogou 'thing' you speak of so much?" Tisquanto had asked. "Why is it so important to you?"

Through broken conversation, drawings and repetition, I managed to convey some sense of what I meant. I was not sure he fully understood though. Somewhere too, he made a connection between the structure and my name. This is what intrigued him the most.

"You name yourself after what you do. This is our way too."

I came to realise that the construction of such souterrains for all kinds of ritual was something that many of the Wôpanâak spent time doing. The only way I would be able to show them my skills would be to commence building my own exemplar fogou, modelled on my father's design at Carn Euny. Therefore, as the winter progressed, this became my great project. At first, Tisquanto, Wamsutta and other members of the group could not understand what I was doing. I suspect they felt I had become crazy – and wondered why I should concern myself with such a project. After all, the earth was hard and frozen; working outside was cold and laborious. This however, did not bother me.

I was more worried that I was being irreligious or blasphemous. Was it something they would approve of this lone, moon-faced man undertaking? The politics of it were not easy. There was already an established group of men who created such structures, and they too viewed me with incredulity, and perhaps a notion of growing rivalry. Wamsutta mediated between them and me.

However, stone by stone, earth by earth, I was slowly able to show them what I could do. Tisquanto and a few others became intrigued at the techniques I used to move and place stone; they saw me use mathematics to work out load bearing, they watched as I made the souterrains dry and warm – despite the cold weather. This was important. The people of Noëpe had previously not been able to make them as watertight. I noticed that the wider community took an interest in my efforts: women and children came to view the structure, and seemed to comment positively on the quality of the construction. Finally, I seemed to win around Wamsutta and the elders, and was able to show the direct similarities between their constructions and my own. I even took some of their elements into my design here, so that it would be comparable, so that they would fit their culture. My crowbar, chisels, hammers, ropes and pulleys were all used on a daily basis. They became fascinated with these tools and how I used them. From such designs, they constructed their own and gradually began to imitate my methods of working.

Of course, construction projects of this kind are not just about the completed artefact. No. It is the process that is important. It is demonstrating what can be done, but it is also about communication. The more time I spent with Tisquanto, Wamsutta and the other builders, the more we were able to communicate. Daily, I was learning much more of the Wôpanâak language. I did not expect it to be the case, but by their proximity to me, they also learnt my language. Always, there was the building, but at times when we stopped to eat, there was the learning and instruction. Tisquanto and I stripped bark off trees to use as surfaces to write upon. On these lengths of bark, we were able to write our languages and show the symbols for words and sounds. As the structure grew, thus did our abilities to communicate. There were whole periods of time, when I spoke nothing but Wôpanâak, and when we went searching for stone, they would try communicating to me in my British tongue. It was wonderful to hear. The forest, the valleys, the riverbeds and the creatures all talked to me again.

Not only this, though. Fathers taught sons how to speak with me, as did mothers with their daughters. We had amusement swapping from one language to another mid-sentence. I put occasional Wôpanâak words into my tongue, and they occasionally used my words in their own speech. It became a game of communication. There were some days, if you will believe, when I dreamt in Wôpanâak, when the world got re-labelled. Wamsutta said he had visions about my world in which animals were named in my tongue. In such ways, we swapped not only language, but cooking, hunting, singing and understanding.

Even when the snows fell, and we spent much more of the day inside than outside, our worlds became more and more intelligible. Because of the thick drifts outside, the hearth became the place of stories, and there is no better way to learn a tongue than to listen to great narrative orators. The Wôpanâak had as many songs, ballads and epics as we did back home. They had creation and origin tales, stories of how animals came to be, heroic epics that lasted the night, and bawdy and ribald tales for when the men stayed up late. I was asked to speak, and so I did. Somehow, in my own faltering way, I managed to relay some of the tales I knew from my childhood – which my mother and father had taught me – as well as those that I had learnt more recently from Remfra. In time, I found that I was able to give most of the story – and only occasionally stop to offer the explanation of a new or difficult world for them.

You will please understand, though, that it was not my will to impose my tongue upon them; rather more, it was their wish to hear more of it. For them, I was a curiosity, an intriguing and different individual who always had something strange up his sleeve. Still, the questions about my hands and fingers followed. I began to make up stories about them – which all the children believed. The women said that it was my wrist and fingers which made me 'a great maker of stone'. They confirmed what I had always thought. Ir and Ir's words seemed to be ringing true.

Aside from my building skills and stories, the male members of the Wô-panâak were fascinated with my arrowheads and tools. These were of iron, and I knew that if I could show them how these were made, my relationship with them would continue to evolve. I was aiming to give them the gift of a new technology and transform their success as builders, farmers and hunters. Back in the horn of Britain (I could no longer call it home) and in Hibernia, such skills were acquired by specialists – smithies who worked metals. They knew how to manipulate tin and copper, though neither of these metals was a match to the durability of bronze and iron. The concept of metals and alloys was hard for me to explain to the Wôpanâak: the very notion that the rock could offer such resources was completely alien to them. Some days I had to go off and swear to myself, such was my frustration in trying to make them understand. To begin with, from out of my sack, I showed them the lump of bronze I had found on Silura. This had the effect of gaining their interest, and I passed it around the circle of those watching me.

Remember, though, I was no bronze or iron-worker. My whole life had been devoted to stone, and I had to draw on much hazy knowledge about the process – from my time observing the tin streamers and smelters. I was not sure if I could even help them to build a furnace, nor smelt and shape metal in the way that I knew. There was then the additional difficulty of finding metals. In the horn of Britain, I knew precisely where to go for tin and copper, and for iron. A key breakthrough came when we were out hunting and Tisquanto gave back some of his blood to the earth for a foe that he took down. In seeing him self-mutilate, I encouraged them to smell his blood, and in that I was able to explain that iron existed within the red liquid. Did they know this smell elsewhere? Along with Wamsutta's primitive geomancy and my own observations of the local area we were able to locate some layers of iron ore. I think Wamsutta was trying to tell me that the air there was strange. At first, I was clueless as to what he meant but then I realised he had noted the magnetism in the rocks. This formation was about some three miles away from the village of Noëpe, and there we mined it. I laughed at myself. Not so long ago, I had observed those woeful tin streamers on my way from Lys Arth to Carn Euny, and thanked Annown that I was not one of them. Here now, I was one of them, blacked with dirt, as I tried to lever the ore out. You will understand the difficulty we faced. The Wôpanâak had not yet the tools to mine with.

Some limited ore was extracted here by using my crowbar, but the best was found just down the valley in the riverbeds. I kicked myself for not thinking of it before. Alluvial sources were easy to find and did not require the same tools or labour. Once the Wôpanâak recognised the right kind of rock, then the whole community assisted with its collection in the river fans. When we had filled ten baskets, we carried these back to the village. Here, I began the project of constructing a basic furnace. I used my instincts for its construction, trying to draw on remembered knowledge. What I ended up building was a sunken, pit-style one, with a low shaft and a forced draught. We would place the ore on stone cradles and then around them put dense wood. The whole would then be packed with clay caps to allow the temperature to rise sufficiently. A pit beneath would collect ash, while the molten iron would fall down a trough to be collected. Any iron slag remaining would then be pulled out when the furnace cooled sufficiently. This, at least, was my plan.

The first two firings of the furnace failed miserably and I really began to doubt my own ability to create such a device. On examination of its failings though, I felt I understood the problem. In short, not enough air was being drawn into the structure, and the resultant molten iron was impure and worthless. I had the women of Noëpe make two large bellows, sewn from strong caribou leather, which we employed in side ducts. This increased the airflow into the chamber and allowed the ore to melt better, making for a purer molten iron. I demonstrated how clay and sand could be used to form chambers for moulds and how the soft metal might – with great physical force – be beaten into shape. Initially, all of this smithing had to be completed with my own basic tools, as well as adapted pieces of rock and bone. Later though, once the process had been refined, I was able to show them how to make tools to better assist in the process itself. Likewise then, further tools – chisels, hammers and axes – could be forged to assist in our construction of the souterrains. Most of all, the younger boys of the village were fascinated with the process and soon became experts at shaping thin but deadly arrow heads. The flint heads of the old-style arrows were tossed away and we began a new hunting campaign using the deadlier iron. The people of Noëpe saw the difference right away by the quantity of meat brought back. In the coming years, bigger and better furnaces followed, but I was not to know of these yet. Instead, I was happy that, as a stone worker, I had managed to turn my hand to the craft of metalwork.

Wamsutta saw the furnace construction as a kind of new magic, and each day our efforts were blessed and offerings given. The warmth of the furnace returned the ground to its usual colour, melting away the snows.

In such ways then, the long winter passed. When the fogou was completed, I was honoured to see them use it. Ritual and ceremony were performed for new phases of the moon, and for the next part of the year. I found two elderly women inside it one day, making offerings for the saving of a sick child, who had grown weak in the cold weather. A few days later, they greeted me to explain that the child had recovered. The *manito* had been there in the fogou, they explained, to accept their offering and release the child back into this world. Wamsutta took notice of such events; and although he had been cynical first of all, when he saw what I had completed, he understood my capabilities. It had taken me all winter, but I was beginning to have a function in this society. I was beginning to feel like I was no longer a stranger, and certainly no longer an exile.

When spring came, the shaman became more ambitious for both the people of Noëpe and the wider Wôpanâak nation. The people here were just one community of a much larger group. Thus, I was taken to other communities, who explained to me their building needs. Souterrains, which had before been huge community construction projects, thus became much easier under my supervision. My work and abilities were championed by Wamsutta. Our employment started to extend beyond the construction of fogous. The Wôpanâak were able to communicate their needs to me. We had meetings where various elders explained what they wanted me to build. I would talk through what was possible, and draw examples of my work. Sometimes, the souterrains requested were not for ritual use at all, but for the storage of corn and roots. Drawing on my time in Hibernia, I found myself also suggesting that they might also be used as a refuge. The elders saw their potential. How the world had shifted! If only Howel could have seen me now.

Other elders and shamans had ideas about the physical shapes they wanted. The usual pattern was for a rectangular interior that was between four and six times longer than that of the width. They requested others to be more oval-shaped in their construction. Sometimes, as they explained, these were symbolic – representing space for both men (with the former design) and for women (with the latter). Just as at home, others were designed to act as calendars to show solstices and equinoxes; many were built in alignment to the stars, the Pleiades being very popular for the Wôpanâak. In each, of course, I carved my mason's mark: crowbar and snake. When they saw my ability to carve with stone, this gave a new impetus to my work. Each group of the Wôpanâak were usually represented by a symbol or totem. Such real animals, birds or fantastical creatures were requested to be carved in their interiors. I was happy to carve these for those who commissioned my work. As I worked, I taught Tisquanto and others how to do the same. At each location, we built a furnace to supply us with tools, and became adept at working them.

You will see then, how my life here progressed. When spring came, I joined some of the hunting parties. We were able to traverse long tracts of land, and I was able to encounter new landscapes. We walked in each direction of the compass, according to the tracking of animals we were pursuing, as well as with Wamsutta and the other builders and I offering our services to further groups of the Wôpanâak. That summer, news of me spread and much work came to me. They wanted to meet this strange constructor of chambers and furnaces.

After many days travelling, a large community to the east of us commissioned the building of many chambers – here, a complex souterrain was requested, with a number of interlinked rooms. This was a showpiece of construction; perhaps to demonstrate their superiority when compared to other communities. Here, even a chimney was wanted in the complex. The shaman there also requested that as part of its construction we should build drainage ditches to allow water to quickly flow out of the souterrain. Because of the position in which they intended the souterrain to be located, they had a problem with flooding. This had been a problem before when they themselves had attempted a prior project that failed. Once I understood their needs, I was able to design such as system for them. The people here were symbolised by the deer, and this creature I incised on the interior of the souterrain, getting Tisquanto to finish the antlers.

"You see the curves there," he said, " – like branches of a tree. It is a good imitation of this creature."

Such work took us to the end of the summer, but the Deer people were so impressed with what we had done, they asked for further work. A stone altar was commissioned (quite similar to that used by the Corcu Loígde). This was a difficult task, because the only rock we found suitable for such a purpose was located some two miles away. It therefore had to be levered onto rolling logs in order to move it across that distance. The team I worked with had incredible minds. After only some basic tuition, they understood precisely the mathematical implications of what was needed. I showed them how to use frameworks of wood, onto which were suspended pulleys, in order to help lift loads. Thus, with the right leverage and force, massive objects might easily be shifted. Another stone was requested as a marker for the most southerly point of the setting sun. These were similar to the standing stones back home. Such pointers were in my blood so to speak, and their construction was easily accomplished.

Wherever we worked, we set up temporary camps for the duration of the job. Tisquanto had fast realised that I offered a kind of knowledge that he could benefit from. He followed my every move to try and understand how my mind operated. In essence, he became my apprentice. Wamsutta, meanwhile, negotiated with the communities in order to discern precisely the job they wanted, and, of course given approval by virtue of the fact that he was a respected shaman. Whatever community we worked in, all were keen to see the potential for stone. My lessons in Wôpanâak continued, as did Tisquanto's in British. Our talk became longer and more accomplished. Not only did we chat about stone, leverage and carving, we moved onto alcohol, pranks and women. I told them nothing of Orla – or even Aimend.

"There are women in the village who like you," said Tisquanto. "Maybe you should marry one of them?"

"No," I said. "I have had enough of women an ocean away from here."

He seemed to understand my humour, but maybe underneath my bravado he sensed the hurt and pain. I do not know.

I now cannot fully remember the day, but it must have been sometime near the completion of the work for the Deer people, when Tisquanto and I talked on a new level. I can't recall what language we spoke in either. It might have been Wôpanâak or it may well have been British. More likely, it was perhaps an admixture of the two. We were eating a midday meal of corn and venison, close to the roar of a pit furnace.

"Voog, one day I would like to see the land where you are from," said Tisquanto. "I have often wondered what lies east of the ocean. This Britain interests me."

"It's not worth going to," I offered. "It would be a long way to go in order to see structures like these. You're better off staying here. It's full of fog and mist,"

"Nevertheless, your ways fascinate us. We have learnt so much. I see the world very differently now."

I thought about what he said. Guilt flowed through me. My brief intervention had shaped a new direction for his people. I understood this by the piles of iron slag we had created. Where there once had been untouched forest, now sat blackened and fired earth.

"I could say the same about you and the Wôpanâak," I offered between bites of the stringy meat.

Tisquanto continued eating, thinking through what I had said. He put down his bowl.

"Do you intend leaving? One day, will you forget us and go back? You must want to, surely?"

It was a question I had not contemplated. Up until now, all of my energies had been about arriving here, and then surviving in this new world.

"There is nothing for me to go back to."

Tisquanto shook his head.

"There is always something to go back to," he said. "It is the way we think."

His words made me think. For the first time in a year, I had had to confront my past. All the while, I had been pushing it away from me. Now, this young man was questioning me, keen to know about my old world. All that had been before was now lost to me. Of course, I wondered about Tigernus, and hoped that he had safely made it back to Scathynys, and yes, I wondered if the people of the horn were able to resist Saxon invasion, but beyond that, there was little more. Deep in my memory I suppose, I sometimes thought of the Corcu Loígde – and Aimend – but I realised I had become numb. I had detached. My interest, my care, my future, was here amongst these people, who both respected my skills and wanted me to stay. Was there anything for me to go back to? It was the way I had thought in the past, but not anymore. No, I had to conclude. There was nothing. So I told him.

"I used to think that way," I said, "but not any more."

After the meal was finished, Tisquanto took my bowl and cleaned it.

"If you ever do go back, please take me with you," he said.

"It's not going to happen," I said. "Come on. Let's get back to that section we were working on before..."

Tisquanto had many more questions for me about my people. I explained to him how society there operated and functioned. I told him of my journeys too – the strange creatures we'd encountered; the people we'd met; where other parts of this eastern world were positioned – all of which he lapped up. In so many ways, he reminded me of myself: wanting to gain knowledge in order to evolve and progress. This was how this man with a twist in the wrist, and an extra finger, became known in this new world. I became good friends with many of the elders – both men and women; and came to know well the names of the shamans of each community. My coworkers and I had a bond that I would now find hard to break. Wamsutta too, knew my worth.

So, in these ways, chamber followed chamber, and souterrrain followed souterrain – and time passed.

Already the Wôpanâak had a sophisticated society, but I was able to suggest improvements. I drew on much that I had learnt on my voyage. Could there be a central place to care for the elderly and infirm? Could they pool together their expertise in such matters, instead of individual families struggling to cope? Gradually, it seemed, they could. Could there be an equal distribution of food and meat to all? Could even the poorest people have a certain quality of life? I raised these ideas with elders, and although days were spent conferring and talking over these concepts, eventually they agreed. Things became more democratic and fairer. A collective consciousness endured in which 'self' was forgotten. In fairness, it was already ingrained in the Wôpanâak. They just needed someone to tell them so.

When the winters came, we would return to Noëpe, and there regale everyone with tales of our adventures. We would know the ferocity of the brown bears that summer (laughing at our attempts to avoid them), estimate the caribou numbers to the north, reflect on how useless some furnaces were, and have an understanding of what issues faced the peoples we encountered. I came to understand a great deal that before had not entered my mind. Wamsutta taught me about animal spirits and demonstrated how he felt the fogous could work as portals to other kinds of reality (You see how far my stone moving and cutting has taken me?). As portals, Wamsutta tried to show me that his people used the fogous as ways of excavating their past, as methods of understanding who they were. Collective meditation and prayer seemed to be very powerful, although I must confess, despite constructing these souterrains, I could not connect with them in this way. Maybe this was an old problem of mine that never really went away. I was always cynical about the power of the druids – and even this far away, I still was.

That did alter though.

I will explain how.

Something happened that was a kind of miracle. That is how Warna would have put it, I am sure. By now, you have learnt that mentally, I had altered much. I had fundamentally changed my view of the world – forgotten all that I was before – and had transformed into someone new. Maybe I had physically changed too. I mean, in some ways, you would not recognise me as the same itinerant stone worker who walked up and down the horn of Britain, seeking commissions. My dress, my hair, my skin, my walk, had all altered. What had not altered though was my wrist and finger. They were still there – reminding me of where I was from and who I really was.

Looking back, perhaps what happened was a gathering magic – a kind of collective will by one people to alter something – so strong, so powerful that it achieved its aim. I cannot explain it any other way. As you will see, there is no logic or mathematics to what occurred.

When we returned to Noëpe for the second autumn, Wamsutta explained to me that he wanted me to do something. He had been speaking to the *manito* for some time now. Like Ir and Ir, he was full of prophecy, full of a notion of destiny, which I denied and countered, but which he still asserted whenever I saw him. Because of this, I tried to avoid him, and maybe he sensed my lack of enthusiasm for what he was proposing. I went back to Ir and Ir – and wished I had listened further. Would they have known what was going to transpire? Perhaps so.

"Voog, I have a solution for you. I have negotiated it for a long time now. All of the *manito* can make the change for you."

I should have trusted him. If there is anything I have learnt in my journey, it is to put enough trust in others, and not be reliant on yourself alone. Maybe here is where I finally learnt that.

"What change?"

"What you can become, moon-faced one."

Clap trap you see. That's what I thought; and even then, still cynical you will note.

I let Wamsutta do what he wanted though. A few days after our return, he led me deep into the woods. The light gradually changed. We were going to a place where there was little sunshine. We were heading into the dark: an Otherworld, like a fogou. It felt like a place of rats and snakes. As we walked, he asked to see my hand. I gave him my right one to look at. I noted the earth still packed into the nails; the way the swirls of my fingertips were dusted with soil; the calluses that only a stone-worker had. He shook this away, and instead walked behind me to grab my left hand. He peered at it intensely, noting my form.

"The *manito* will now make this better," he announced. "The lone man not alone any more."

We stopped in a clearing and, using his hands, Wamsutta pulled away the covering of leaf litter to find the peaty earth. Taking a bone spade made of a deer scapula he began to dig. He worked with complete focus, not stopping until there was a deep hole.

"The earth will repay you," he announced, his face wet with perspiration.

"What have I got to do?"

"Bury your arm in the ground for one day and one night. I will stay here with you."

I laughed at him and snatched my arm away from him.

"I'm not doing that."

Wamsutta looked surprised.

"Why not, moon face?"

"Because I don't believe... Because it's stupid."

"Please. Do as I ask."

The way Wamsutta said this, I knew he wasn't joking. This was no piece of invented ritual, no placation, or cover up.

"Do this. Your Annown will work for you. I know this place. I understand it."

I wasn't sure if the shaman did. A lot of his type claimed to understand it; the bastard druids back home for one.

Feeling like I could no longer resist his request, I let Wamsutta gently guide the whole of my arm into the hole he had dug. He unravelled a layer of blankets that he had been carrying, and encouraged me to lie upon them. I duly followed his wishes.

"Plant it deep," the Shaman said. "Be as if you are a seed."

I dug into the soil and pushed my fingers into the earth. Small collapses of peaty material fell onto my fingers and then, taking his spade, Wamsutta shovelled the piled earth back in. When it reached my wrist, he packed the material tight to my skin, taking time to make sure all was covered.

"Why are we doing this?" I had to ask.

He did not answer but continued to place more earth around my entire arm. It was now contained within the earth up to my shoulder.

"Get comfortable," he said. "You have a little time here now."

You will realise how absurd I felt. I was face down in a forest somewhere in the lands of the Wôpanâak in a continent I still knew as Hyperborea.

"Try to sleep. Try to forget where you are."

In between phases of sleep, I watched the sky change above me. The sun passed and the same stars I had navigated with came overhead. Wamsutta sometimes rested like me; other times I sensed him walk around me, chanting. The language was Wôpanâak but it was so low and whispered it was hard to make out. Maybe he did not want me to hear it. When I occasionally looked up from my stupor he had placed leaves and crystals in a pattern around the top of my arm. This was just the way the druids used the milpreve stones. I blinked and they were gone again. He lit a fire to warm himself and cooked some food, but he gave none to me. I suffered there, out of respect for him. I had no real idea what he was trying to do. His low chanting worked as a lullaby, and in my sleep I dreamt of many things. Orla's face finally came back to me in such detail that I could see each pore, each eyelash and each undulation of her lips. My pissle became erect at the sensation. I had to move to get comfortable. Waves of wood passed overhead, and in my mind I was shaken by oceans upon oceans: flung about, as if my body were turned inside out.

The next sensation I had was the sunlight peeking through the canopy overhead. Carefully, with his hands, Wamsutta was scraping away the earth from my arm. He got down to my elbow before he swapped to the scapula spade. I felt the sensation of it moving the earth upwards. The bottom of my arm was numb, it having remained in one position for so long. At last, I felt him reach my wrist and fingers. The digits I quickly released from the earthy surround. On my nostrils was the peaty sweat of the earth, warm and full of energy.

"There," said Wamsutta. "The *manito* did their job. It has worked. Your Annown has finally released you."

"Released me from what?"

"Look and see," he said.

I turned over and lifted my arm out of the earth; the same earth I had spent so many years working and nurturing.

Can you sense what had happened? To this day, I cannot believe how it came to be transformed. It was a miracle. When I see him, I still ask about it, and all he does is to smile.

But there and then, I was the one smiling, for I instantly noticed that the twist in my wrist had gone. The skin and bone were no longer deformed. I could move and flex it just the same as anyone else. I was no longer the same Voog. A wondrous ocean of change had fallen over me. But this was not all.

Just as my wrist had been healed, so too, had my fingers. I counted them.

"One, two, three, four."

Then I stopped. There were no longer five of them. The extra one, after all this time, Annown had taken back.

FATHER, YOU ARE SO CLOSE now, that I can sense you. I feel I already know the smell of you, the taste of you, the feel of you. Maybe, as I run, I hear you. You Lord, and you Annown have placed me here. Please, let it happen. Let us meet. That is all I need. Let us smile together. Let us be joined. We need no language for that. We need no ocean now.

Four months it took; longer than our voyage out. Four months of putting into a beach or creek, and then leaving again. Four months of trekking and exploring. Four months of frustration. It took so long that the crew of *Azen* nearly mutinied. It took so long that it drove many of them to madness and despair (not to mention the questioning of my own sanity). It took so long that Corentin suggested I stay off *Azen* for a while – and live solely on *Warna*. It got so bad that the crew started to detest me. Although there was always a fresh supply of meat, game and water, the adventure had become soured. It had begun well, with high hopes of finding my father, but as time went on, all of us grew a little more despondent, a little more afraid that what was sought would never be found. Men who had once relished the voyage began to miss their wives and children. This was ironic as, for many, their nagging wives had been the sole reason they'd left. I was running out of money as well. The wife of a chieftain had a goodly fortune and it was my grandmother's heritage which had helped secure this passage. Time had moved on though. I would soon be forced to pay them on a promise rather than hard cash. There was no point in them fishing for stock to take back. We were far from ice, and had as yet, no return date. We were all in limbo. Any fish not eaten in a few days would simply stink and rot.

Each day, we'd take *Warna* and the other coracles and paddle to the shoreline. We'd step out of the tide and assess whether this was the point where Voog had disembarked. We scanned for clues: remains, bones, hides – anything that might give an indicator that here was where he'd stopped and finally finished his journey. I wasn't entirely sure what we were looking for. I just knew we would have to seek. Whereas before much of the conversation on board had been about how surprised Voog might be if we found him, it no longer touched on this topic. Instead, even Corentin and Rosparzh relished thoughts of home. I understood. They were old men now. I had already dragged them halfway across the world when they should have been sat snoring before their hearths. Winter was coming on. They shouldn't be asleep on the lurch of the ocean. Instead, they should have been at home – in the cradles of their respective roundhouses.

Did I age during this time? It felt like I did. I felt like I had gained lines upon my skin. Early wrinkles of frustration made their way into me. Each day that resulted in another dead end hardened my heart and made me desperate. All we could do was to be systematic in our scanning of the shore. We agreed that we had to turn back time. We had to imagine this place twenty years ago, and what it might have been like then. Thus, the creep of vegetation might need to be negated; lines of fulsome trees had to be imagined as mere spouting trunks. In seeing this, we might be able to see the line of human habitation, and retrace his steps. This is how my mind worked all the time.

What would he have done here?

Where might he have headed for?

What point would he have climbed towards?

In this way I reconstructed him. In this way, I hoped to find him.

There were some limited breakthroughs however. One of Rosparzh's men found a pebble. It had been placed on a stone high above the tidal line. In an instant, we recognised it as his mason's mark. This at least gave us knowledge of his presence, though of course, there was no way of knowing whether it was here that he entered the interior. It was usually Tigernus whom I consulted as to whether he felt this was somewhere my father would choose. He knew him better than any of us. As I pocketed this pebble, he shook his head.

"This is just a marker," he said, "to show us the way. See too, how you can't easily head inland from here. The cliffs are too tall. I know him. Voog would have taken an easier line."

He recalled the time they had landed in Hibernia.

At such finds, we needed prophecy. We needed seeing. We needed oracle, but such phenomena were not forthcoming. We had to guess, and keep on travelling. I had to keep belief. I had come too far to doubt. By now though, it was probably only Tigernus who understood that.

Rosparzh had been tenuous in stepping ashore with us. I understood why, although through all of those months we never encountered any other human life. The isolation of Hyperborea was numbing and disturbing – as if you God, or you Annown, had decided against placing any people here. I realised then how filled with life and energy our communities were back home. It was, however, Rosparzh who made a key find. He whistled at us to gain our attention.

"Up here," he shouted to us one morning. "Look at this."

We did not need to walk far to see what he was talking about. Next to Rosparzh's height was a standing stone.

"A menhir," he shouted.

We scrambled up the bank to observe the structure more closely.

"I don't think the savages built this do you?"

"You're right," said Tigernus. "I know this. He carved something similar to it in Hibernia. See there, it's *An Ruen*. That's him in it."

He pointed to a carving upon the face of the stone. In tracing it, I felt still closer to my father. There, in stone, was his own self-image – more accurate than his mason's mark; a more realistic depiction of who he was. I stared at the stone image of what had made me. My skin turned to gooseflesh.

This menhir kept me going in those hard and lonely days of late August. The stone was too heavy to carry back to *Azen*. In the end, I took a thin piece of hide and with a length of charcoal traced the image he had created. At least I would have something to take back. By night I peered at his picture and prayed. I picked flowers close by, and gave offering to Annown. I gave prayer to God. I recited passages I had remembered and hoped these would help.

Do you understand my desperation?

Do you know how helpless I felt?

I knew that September's arrival guaranteed a long discussion with Corentin. I knew very well the issues he would outline. It was time to go back. He feared the icing up of the northern seas above the *Mor Sargasso*. It was time to return, he said. We had given it our best chance. In my mind, I knew he was right. I always respected him. And yet, in my heart, there was always another day, another estuary that he might have put into.

Tigernus did not let up his search. While other men returned to *Azen* as the darkness fell, Tigernus always went down another estuary, fell upon another beach. Sometimes, he searched by torchlight, hoping that shadows would reveal things hidden by daylight. It was on one such occasion that we pulled into a small creek. The darkness was just settling and this would be the last place we'd look before returning to moor alongside *Azen*. I was tired, barely noticing what we had pulled into. The summer heat had exhausted me. Since my discussion with Corentin, I knew time was running out and it gave my whole body the sensation of fear. My heart shook.

I sensed Tigernus bringing *Warna* alongside something, carefully working the steering oar, but in my mind I thought he was doing this just to jump ashore and quickly scan this location in the twilight before full darkness fell. What he did next I could not have anticipated.

"Blejan, give me your hand."

The way he softly said those five words told me that he had found something.

"Shut your eyes," he said. "Feel with me."

He took my hand and traced a line across an object. The only thing I felt was dry moss and lichen.

"Stone?" I questioned. "It feels like stone settled in one place for a long time. Like in a fogou."

"Feel again."

He then traced my fingers over fragile leather knots and the unmistakable surface of preserved oxhide.

"Open your eyes."

I raised my eyelids. I knew what was there but when I saw it, I swear that my heart missed several beats. In the twilight before us, sunken, muddied, demasted, coated with a thick layer of green moss and grey lichen, and entwined with reeds and bulrushes was the wreck of *An Ruen*. She was more of nature's making than man's now, but her misshapen and collapsed hull were the only portent I needed to make my way inland.

477

30

Stone carving, Halliggye Fogou, The Lizard, Cornwall, unknown date
This carving – apparently of a male figure holding a spear in one hand and a snake in the other – has been viewed as a representation of the god Cernunnos (as found on the more famous Gundestrap Cauldton, thought to date from 200 BCE to 500 CE). Although some observers have viewed this image as a mason's mark, given the complexity of the image, this seems unlikely. The carving is found at the entrance to a *fogou* (an underground souterrain) probably designed for ritual use. By the 5th and 6th Centuries CE, such structures appear to have fallen out of use and were abandoned. Similar structures are found on the eastern seaboard of North America. Image courtesy of Historic Environment, Cornwall Council.

IT IS INCREDIBLE NOW TO document it, but almost twenty years of my life had passed while I worked with the Wôpanâak. I was no longer a Briton. I was one of them. My skin colour and hair were ignored. I was the lone man no more; nor the moon-faced one. My own body had changed much after the miracle (do you know, despite all my scrambling in the earth afterwards, in a kind of 'phantom' archaeology, I never found the fifth finger?). For a while, I continued with the strength and power of my younger days, but when I reached my mid-forties, time started to catch up with me. I noticed that I worked a little slower, drew longer breaths, and peered more closely at what I was doing (my sight seemed sometimes to be as bad as Warna's). I certainly found the winters harder, the nights longer. No man usually likes to face this knowledge. It is a sign he is partway across the ocean of his life. He does not like the second half of the journey as much as the first (though, as I came to discover, it can be just as rewarding). I learnt that I needed help to position the heaviest stones that I had formerly carried in one hand. My hair greyed and my face became lined. Despite my daily cleansing (you have long known this obsession) two of my molar teeth fell out. Distant commissions for refurbishments and building I left to the younger men; with Tisquanto now coordinating the programme of works.

Venerable Wamsutta and I became close – in a way I could never have been with a druid like Casvellyn. With the shaman, wisdom was never enforced or given in expectation of exchange for something else. It came naturally to him. But Wamsutta too, had become immobile, only walking with the aid of a stick in close proximity to the village. For anything further away, a wooden throne was employed, which stronger and younger men carried. He still liked to keep his hand in, directing projects, checking alignments, and ensuring the *manito* were placated. Despite his age, he continued to wake early and begin the supervision.

The people of Noëpe prospered: partially down to our success as constructors; but also by their unending willingness to experiment and learn. Iron production consumed them. They developed alloys, understood the chemistry of different ores and elements, and worked at better refining their furnaces and smelting processes. Always, they wanted my approval for the work completed but, as I explained to them, they were working in ways now which far outgrew my own knowledge. In many respects, they had progressed far and away beyond what was being achieved back in the horn of Britain. Each day, I admired their tenacity and drive. I saw in them, much of me, but something else too – that this Age was changing; that new ideas were going to continue to revolutionise the way humanity progressed.

Although this work drove them, and social equality defined them, the most admirable value of these people was that they kept their old ways. Ceremony was adhered to, as it had always been. Change yes, but only if ancient ritual remained.

My own personal Annown still lurked within me and around me, but it had altered. Sometimes, I forgot a ritual I should have so easily remembered. Certainly, I altered my construction methods, my alignments and calculations to suit what the Wôpanâak wanted; not always me. I had watched Tisquanto transform from being a young man full of enthusiasm to a seasoned professional. I observed him take a wife, have five offspring and then train both his boys and girls with his knowledge. For some years he questioned me about what lay over the ocean, but perhaps when his family came along, he understood there was no longer a need to voyage. He would voyage with them alone: all wonder and joy was here. This was something I never felt I would experience and so I revelled in his pleasure. Likewise, the other men whom I had seen grow up into the profession became my extended family. I loved them all as brothers. Their wives saw me as a benign and reassuring presence; I suppose, a kindly uncle to them all.

I still lived alone. By now, you may think I might have taken a wife. To begin with, there were indeed many offers. It was hard to decline them sometimes: they were pretty, vivacious and filled with spirit. But truly, such companionship was not for me. It would only ever have been for sport and pleasure. You see, although my wrist and fingers were fixed, my heart never really was. How could I live with someone, or even marry them, when I could not fully commit to loving them? This was a story that followed me throughout these years. Often the people of Noëpe felt I was lonely and suggested company; even to the point of developing ambitious arranged marriages for me. But I had seen what they could do – a long time ago, and a world away – so I always steered clear of them. Tisquanto and Wamsutta understood, even if everyone else did not. Gradually, in these past five years, thankfully the offers had lessened. The people realised I was not interested. The shaman never married either, and so I suppose the younger generation, who willed me companionship, came to see me as such. It made me laugh. By forfeit and accident, I had to accept I had become a kind of druid (how oddly sometimes the skimmed stone falls).

We were fortunate not to be involved in inter-tribal wars that I discovered existed in Hyperborea (I never learnt of any other name for the continent, and so I still use that here). I had thought that in such a paradise, on such an 'Isle of Bliss' there would be none of the bitter conflict that existed in the old world. I was wrong there, I have to tell you. On the east coast, we were spared many of the troubles (being too distant and peripheral for any of the larger interior peoples to worry about), but inland, word always came of massacres and great slaughter. They were holocausts of the new world. Such news made women and children shudder, and we thought collectively about greater use of the fogous as refuges (see how Howel continues to haunt me?).

One year, despite knowing of these conflicts, myself and twelve others rode further into the west to discover more of the country. We spent six months uncovering a geography which was not only hidden to me, but formerly closed and cloaked to the Wôpanâak. Such explorations were initiated on my request. With them, we were able to make alliances, share technologies, and learn of others' ways. We brought back new metals, better crops and incredible carvings of ivory (traded down from the north). The plains of this land extended beyond where we could ever travel to. I began to think that discovering it all was as fictitious as humanity ever reaching the stars, or indeed being able to circumnavigate this globe (being able to reach from the horn of Britain to Hyperborea and then on around to return to the lands of the Phoenicians and Africans). Curiosity remained with me then, but I knew I could not learn it all.

Sometimes, I came to realise, it was better that way. Sometimes, hidden knowledge is the best kind. When it comes unexpectedly, it is more joyous.

In the evenings, I often thought back to the great voyage I had undertaken. I now felt a sense of pride in its completion and an understanding that my true destiny had been to work with the people here. That, I came to understand, had been my true purpose. The building I completed back on the horn of Britain –

at Chysauster, at Kynance, at Carn Euny – had only been a small stopping point on my timeline. I had once regarded it as everything. Now, I knew that was not the case.

Recollection continued to come to me at odd times. Out in the forest, small mammals scurried away from our footsteps. I remembered Rat and his ways. I recalled both my hate and love for him in the same breath. In the air, as the rivers met the ocean, were seabirds. I never saw the like of Puffin again though. Both, I supposed, had long since passed into the world of Annown, but perhaps their progeny continued somewhere across the globe: one circling; one scavenging. In the isolated woods of this new world, sometimes I felt I would bump into such incredible creatures as the plesiosaurs – their flippers evolving into feet and crossing huge tracts of country. I knew their survival was in jeopardy. Humanity would hunt them down and cast their line aside. 'Terrible worms' would always be mistakenly feared. Maybe their myth would last though.

The presence of important people in my life remained. Warna, I never ever saw again. Her fate with Gofan always puzzled me to the end of my days. In my mind, I had turned over their disappearance into the rock time and again. However, I was more accepting of it now. This view changed after my own miracle. Perhaps such wonder was possible. Before I had doubted. Now, I did not.

I feared for Caera, Aimend and the Corcu Loígde. What had been their fate? Were they still battling the raiding descendants of the Fir Bolg? So much of their learning I had employed here: from technology to translation. There were times when I wished they might appear before me, so that I could express my gratitude to them.

Ir and Ir, I assumed, continued to live as one on *Sceilig Mór*. Twenty years on, and the climb to the top would be that much tougher, that much harder. Prophecy with the oracle bones and whatever else unfolded in the natural world would help seal their fate. So might Warna's holy book. What would become of them if one of them died and the other didn't? It was hard to contemplate a single Ir.

Memories such as these, therefore, helped me to measure this now familiar world. And over these decades, I tried to stop complacency entering me. I knew it of old. It seemed to have been with me for all of my adult life, and whenever it came back, I fought it hard. Despite my age and lesser strength, if at any point I suspected its arrival, I would do something to stop it: climb a mountain, carve a canoe, fashion a piece of metal, or erect a standing stone. That 'sin' (which was what Warna might have described it as) never came back to me. Other sin, however, was to find me again. It is the original sin that prompted the whole of my tale here. It is the progeny of these annals and this epic. It was the sin that prompted my own Lethowsow: my own flood, my own engulfment, my own ocean.

Yet out of this sin had come wonder.

The wonder came in my nineteenth summer with the Wôpanâak. It was August and the sun was still warm. I was back working on the original fogou I had built for the people of Noëpe all that time ago. Severe rains earlier that year had washed away some of the packed earth on the top surface of it. Now, lilacs and other wild flowers dominated the mound's summit. I was admiring these, and pushing in replacement earth for that which had been lost. Although Tisquanto and his workers had been travelling of late (from the late spring into midsummer), they had arrived back to assist with the maize harvest. They still made the occasional foray into the forest where they had once found me. It had barely changed a bit. There, they could still hunt caribou; perhaps catch the occasional wolf.

I paused in my working because I saw the hunting party returning. They were making great noise, and I watched them push their way through the fields of maize which had not yet been harvested. On the air, I came to realise they were shouting my name.

"They're back early, aren't they?" I said to Wamsutta.

"Mmmm... They told me they'd be away for at least a week."

We decided only two days had passed since they had left.

"What do they want me for?"

Wamsutta shrugged his shoulders.

Now that they were closer, I could now make out what they were saying. They were shouting that they had found something for me. No, when I listened more closely, it was some*one*; not just some*thing*. Was it some*one* for whom I had completed a build – and they had been unhappy with the work? That was always possible. You could never be complacent about it. But I couldn't think who it might be. All the work I had completed of late had gone well in my view. Why should anyone complain?

This was certainly intriguing for me. Who could it be? Who even knew of my existence here? I considered events two decades ago. Perhaps it was Corentin – after all these years. The Bretons were a plucky bunch. If anyone might track me down, it was them. After all, they'd been across the vast ocean before me. But it wasn't Corentin. The form of this person was now emerging out of the tall stalks and golden kernels, surrounded by Noëpe warriors. It was a woman – I could tell that now. No, not a woman – more like a girl: a young woman if you will.

I rubbed my eyes to check. They were not as they were, and I wanted to make sure this was no dream or illusion.

"Look... she is moon-faced," observed Wamsutta. "Like you."

These were words he had not used in two decades.

She was closer now, and as she walked towards me, time instantaneously collapsed. My head went giddy. Had I imbibed watercress or some new drug? I couldn't help but notice the sheer beauty of her face and hair. That was the thing. That was what reminded me. She had skin as flawless as kaolin. By the way she walked, I sensed a headstrong nature. She had a lot of spirit to her. There was an edge of playfulness too. Her features gradually revealed themselves to me as she got closer. I knew those eyes, those cheeks, that mouth, those lips. Something else was there too – something that I knew intimately. If I say I was looking into a reflection, then maybe you will understand.

Tisquanto, still active as ever, had run on before the rest of the group. His face beamed with complete satisfaction.

"This girl is looking for you. She has come a long way to find you. You'll never guess what, Voog? I was able to speak to her. I spoke to her in the language you taught me – and she understood. I told her I knew you well, and that we would bring her to you."

The males of the Wôpanâak had never seen such a girl. To them, she was a goddess. She was the form of that clay figurine I had long since lost. They were unable to take their eyes off her. I was no longer white, but she was. Under her hooded cloak, I saw her peering at me, trying to see if I was what she had been seeking. A moment later, she had pulled back her hood to reveal her face. Her curly black hair, which had formerly been encased in the hood, tumbled down her back. How old was she? Twenty perhaps – but no older.

"Who are you?" I asked, reverting to my old tongue. Speaking it felt odd: rusty as iron left out too long in the rain.

Her eyes lit up. She recognised the words instantly and replied in the same language.

"I am Blejan," she said.

I knew what this meant. It was the word I had once used for 'Flower'. I saw the lilacs bursting from atop the fogou.

"I am Blejan of Chysauster," she repeated, "and I have travelled here from the horn of Britain. I seek a man named Voog. Are you Voog?"

Chysauster: now that was a place I had not heard spoken of for a very long time, and then, the way she said my name; it was as it was meant to have been spoken. All these long years here, and despite their best efforts, the dear Wôpanâak never quite pronounced it correctly; never quite nailing the delicious vowels. For that, I blamed the mess and mishap of a tongue that had named me.

"I am Voog," I offered, nodding.

She was starting to cry.

"My mother was named..." she began.

"Orla," I continued. "And your father was a banished loser with a twisted wrist and a fifth finger?"

She affirmed what I had said.

I showed her my left hand and wrist, wiggling my fingers.

"It's gone," I said. "Annown took it back many years ago. A miracle you might say. This man watched it happen.."

I pointed at Wamsutta, who gave a warm smile to her.

She listened to my words. Slowly her hand reached out for mine.

"And your mother?" I asked.

She shook her head.

I understood. This already confirmed what I somehow knew: that Orla had gone. Annown had taken her long ago.

By now, our hands had reached and I pulled Blejan towards me. I smelt in her the smell of my home, my love, my self.

"Who is she?" asked a puzzled Tisquanto, not in Wôpanâak, but in British. "How does she know you?"

"She does not know me – yet," I answered, "But she will come to do so. I have much to tell her. This is my daughter Blejan; a daughter I have only just found out that I have. And to have arrived here, as I once did, she must have endured much."

I held her tight, as tight as once I held her mother – before all of this; before the entire ocean.

Perhaps in the days before this time, an unseen comet had passed overhead; perhaps, for once, tides stayed stationary and sea creatures of the deep calmed all the waves and tempests. Certainly, by her presence, two broken hearts became whole again.

"Tigernus?" I enquired.

She nodded, acknowledging she knew him. So the boy – I mean the man (he was, after all, now in his twenties) made it. There was so much I needed to know, to find out about – but that would come later. Now, there were more urgent matters.

"Come," I said. "I've something to show you... You *have* to see it. Your mother will have told you all about me – and where we met..."

I crossed the village of Noëpe to where the fogou stood. Its lilacs reached into the afternoon sky: flowers for this flowering of hope. I held her hand and led her down the steps inside. In the fogou's warmth, we learnt of pasts we never knew existed. This was Annown's way. This was the way of the *manito*. From the way her eyes lit up, I could tell she knew the lines of love stretching out from this structure all the way back to our homeland.

"Father," she said. "tell me what happened to you. I want to know everything."

So I did, in that day, and in the days that followed, with the stumbling and struggling words (sometimes coated in hallucinogens and brine) you have now heard.

Yet in all truth, my story, my annals, my epic, no longer mattered. My daughter's odyssey – born too, I suspect, of similar luck and latitude – was sure to outshine my own.

You see, it was not my ocean any more.

It was hers.

DEAR MOTHER, I FOUND HIM. I have achieved what these Christians call atonement. It is for your life and for your death. I have wrong-footed all wrongs. I have turned the past upside down. I spun history on its head. I have made distances contract. For you, I have conquered such hate. For you, I have learned such love. For you and my father, I did this – and yet you know that I also did it for me. I needed to know. I needed to be with him. I think you will understand. We can talk about it one day – you, I and grandmother – in the afterlife, whether that is in Heaven, Hell or Annown. Just name the place. I have no fear of any of them.

I need to tell you what happened after we located the wreckage of *An Ruen*. Do you know that Tigernus and Corentin would not let me go alone? They insisted I was accompanied. But I wouldn't have it. I had already decided. I knew from Rosparzh how these people I might encounter would find me. They'd find me as sole woman, unarmed and unafraid. They would come to know I was no witch or sorceress. That is why I made my own way into the interior. The next morning I left Tigernus sleeping and transferred all that I needed into one of the coracles. Then I made my way to the creek where we had located my father's vessel. There I also discovered what I thought was the remains of an encampment, long since abandoned.

Following all Tigernus and Corentin had taught me about navigation, I walked into the west. I knew that was where he would have gone. I knew that

that was where Annown lay. I knew it was you he sought deep in the fogou. It was your light he constructed. It was you he would have walked towards – knowing, always knowing that one day, you would come.

How many days trek was it? Probably two or three I believe. That was before they found me and started to speak to me. What amazement that after all this distance, they could converse with me in my own British tongue. I knew then – in those tentative questions and answers – that you were only an arm's length away from me. I was the moon-faced one who sought the other moon-faced one upon this vast continent.

Now I am nearing you. To think: all that sailing; all that running. Now it becomes worth the effort. I am brought into the village, and you turn to see me. We speak. They speak in our tongue. What wonder! We hug. Together, we are able to close distance and time. In the fogou's depths, we shared our odysseys. Yes, there is much to recollect, to explain, and to start to understand. There are eruptions of emotion, earthquakes of fear, worry and astonishment. There can be no other way though – not after all that time. I explained much to you: the fates of Melwyn, Cadreth, Howel and Casvellyn. I note your surprise, your astute observations about them, and your understanding. I learn more of Warna, Gofan, Caera, Ir and Ir. We come to know Tisqanto, Wamsutta and the rest of the people of the village of Noëpe. Aimend too, we talk of, until the dawn breaks.

In the days that follow, with you alongside me, I retrace my route back to the coast. You come to know a man who departed from you as a boy. You see how Tigernus has grown and matured. At your meeting, both of you weep with joy. The father gained his son, and the son regained his father.

"You still look the same," you say, tears streaming, "as when I first met you – all those years ago – on Scathynys."

We explain that the mermaid's curse was over. We tell of our union and intention to marry. My father can barely move with happiness. He is paralysed with wonder.

"If only I had known," he says. "If only things had been different. But I am so glad, so thankful... Your marriage puts so much right in the world for me."

He takes deep breaths and constantly smiles.

There, on the ocean, my father Voog meets again noble Corentin and Rosparzh. For the first time, in many years, he enjoys salted boar and ale. The days go quickly. We tell an incredulous Corentin of the British-speaking people here. He declares this should be better known and aims to tell everyone upon his return. When things are settled – and that it is understood we should stay at least for a while – *Azen* departs back to Brittany. *Warna*, along with another coracle, will remain with us, for our eventual return. Tigernus has confidence now in our ability to cross the ocean. You must understand that now that I had found my father, I did not want to let him go again. I knew much about him, but there was so much more to learn. I wanted to know more of his building work here, his fogous and the way he had developed mining and smelting.

The intention was to remain until the next spring and then return. We stayed longer than we thought, principally because my father, in old age, became unwell. I nursed him, but knew that Annown was calling.

When he died, it seemed magic died with him. When we had first met, his arm was straight and strong. But when I later saw Wamsutta lay out his body, the wrist was again at an angle; his extra finger back. Wamsutta explained the miracle he had performed, telling us that death always takes us back to our original state.

"To where we are from," he said. "There, we all face our imperfections."

I grieved, yet my tears were more in celebration than for his passing. The small amount of time I had with him I was thankful for. I had learnt so much from both him and the world he had helped to shape here. We dressed the fogou and placed him inside. They spoke of the *manito* and the moon. I spoke both of Annown and God. Then, we buried him. His funeral was more beautiful than anything I have ever witnessed. People from all the surrounding villages attended. It felt like the whole of Hyperborea mourned his passing.

Before my father died, and before infirmity and illness gripped him, I took down all that he told me in our native tongue. Now I translate it and compile it with my letters. Do you remember my dream for one tongue? Ha – I laugh, for it seems to have come true. Ironically, I translate it into the language of my oppressors: those who sacked my mother and then sacked my mother tongue. Maybe one day, one day far off, it will change – and wrongs will be wrong-footed and voyaged against. Until then, well, until then... read what you may. Tell on what you can – just like my father, just like old Remfra. Stories make a people: they make us who we are. Each is worth navigating; each worth listening to.

When you are in the dark, just listen.

Tigernus and I eventually made the trip back in *Warna*. A slow boat you might say, when compared to *Azen*. Finally, we were able to land on Scathynys, where – away from civilisation and modernity – we agreed to stay and make a life. Much that we had learnt from the Wôpanâak came to be our way. That spring, almost three years on from when I met my father, I gave birth to a baby boy. I named him Voog – and he has the loudest fug-hole of a mouth when he cries, but we love him dearly.

You see now then, that my Paradise, my 'Land of Bliss' was closer than I thought.

Tigernus then, was my Adam.

I was his Eve.

But there was no sin.

In our new Eden, our new Annown, together, we would come to build a fogou. There, deep in the earth and stone, we no longer needed an ocean.